DAUGHTERS

By Consuelo Saah Baehr

Report from the Heart
Best Friends
Nothing to Lose
Daughters

DAUGHTERS

CONSUELO SAAH BAEHR

Delacorte Press

Published by
Delacorte Press
The Bantam Doubleday Dell Publishing Group, Inc.
1 Dag Hammarskjold Plaza
New York, New York 10017

Library of Congress Cataloging in Publication Data
Baehr, Consuelo Saah.
Daughters.

I. Title.
PS3552.A326D38   1988   813'.54   87–30600
ISBN 0-385-29647-9
Manufactured in the United States of America
July 1988
10 9 8 7 6 5 4 3 2 1
BG

In loving memory of my grandparents,
Farida and Musa

Heartfelt thanks to Uncle Issa, whose unfailing response to my greedy requests for information was: "My dear, with me you have carte blanche."

Thanks also to Aunt Mary and Aunt Julia.

PROLOGUE

••••———◆———••••

For four centuries, from 1517 until World War I, the Holy Land was part of Turkey's vast Ottoman Empire and governed—sometimes well, sometimes cruelly—from Constantinople.

Palestine, as the country was then known, hugged the shores of the Jordan River from Galilee to the Dead Sea, a land easily traversed in two days by horse, bordered on two sides by vast desert and on the other by the sea.

Hardly a house stood outside Jerusalem's wall, whose seven gates were closed shortly after sunset by Turkish guards. In winter, rooms were warmed by little sheet-iron stoves, burning olive wood. Cooking was done over charcoal. The food was mostly rice, cracked wheat, vegetables, chicken, and mutton.

The 1860s were watershed years. Jerusalem began to spread out beyond the Old City. Russia purchased ten acres northwest of Jaffa Gate and there arose a cathedral and a vast complex of hostels, offices, and a hospital to care for the Russian pilgrims who came by the thousands. In 1865, the telegraph bureau was installed in the Old City. Foreigners were permitted to own land, and Jews began to build a suburb outside the old walls. By 1869, the road was laid from Jaffa to Jerusalem. The Pasha's wife gave weekly receptions attended by Christian women, and Muslim ladies began wearing French toilettes.

Out of the beautiful Damascus Gate, Suleiman Street led to the Nablus Road, which led to the town of the same name located about thirty miles to the north. At the time, Nablus had the finest bazaar and was known for its fine soap and silverware.

In 1876, Abdul Hamid acceded to the Ottoman throne and, at first, it seemed he would be a progressive and democratic ruler. The Consular postal system was completed and the first steam flour mill was operating in Palestine within the year. By 1892, a railroad line opened from Jaffa to Jerusalem. The locomotives came from America, and the engineers and surveyors from Europe.

Just ten miles north of Jerusalem, on the pilgrim road to Nazareth, lay the Christian village of Tamleh. The vista showed enclosed courtyards approached by narrow, dirt passageways and surrounded by several stone cottages joined together for safety, which was the first concern. Most of the inhabitants carried guns, swords, or daggers.

There were dunghills visible in the village and smoke from the bakery ovens and, often—because there were no civic laws governing the slaughter of animals or the disposal of refuse—there were repulsive odors. Still, Tamleh was ten times more beautiful than the neighboring villages and its progress was swift. By 1900, the village had ten provision shops, four shoemakers, two weaving rooms, four butchers, and a silversmith.

The villagers loved their orchards and wheat fields. They lovingly named each cut and crest in the road—this rise was the 'bosom of pleasure,' that depression was the 'valley of the dog.' As sacred as the land was loyalty to the family. Optimally, they married within the clan and a cousin had first right—a right often exercised—to any girl relative and could take her off the horse on the way to the church to marry another.

Though sophisticated Jerusalem was only ten miles away, the peasants lived simply. They used the fireplace both to cook and keep warm. They used wood for fuel, for they had no charcoal. For light, they laid a wick in a dish of olive oil. They stored their clothes in trunks. Baskets, which they made, were ready containers for food and household items; and clay utensils, which they also made, were used for cooking and to hold food and water. The peasants drank sage and camomile tea, coffee, milk, and wine, but those who drank alcoholic drinks were ill considered. The women embroidered in every spare moment and the village was known for their fine handwork. When the Kaiser visited in 1869, he asked for a sample.

The offspring of the five original settlers cooperated with each other in order to survive. They cleared the land, built terraces on the slopes, and planted grain, groves of grapes, olives, and figs. They raised domestic animals, especially sheep and goats. An acre of land yielded six bushels, and a peasant needed fifty dollars yearly to support his family of six.

There were many denominational schools in the village, but the finest one was the elite Girls' Training Home, run by the Society of Friends. As early as 1889, the beautiful limestone building opened with fifteen privileged boarders. A companion building for the boys' school was completed in 1914, a year when the Ottoman Empire was in turmoil. The lovely, airy structure had to be left to the fortunes of war. The dining room on the first floor was used as a stable for horses of the Turkish soldiers. The upper floors served as a hospital for the armed forces, first of the Central Powers —Germany, Austria, Turkey—and then, as tides changed, of England.

In the 1880s there was a craze of revivalism and waves of foreigners passed through Tamleh. They walked to the shrines on rutted roads, often sick and at the mercy of robbers. The largest number of pilgrims came from Russia, sometimes as many as ten thousand a season traveling overland through the Caucasus or in sailing ships across the Black Sea.

Tamleh wasn't tropical like Jaffa. The higher altitude that dried the Mediterranean air also brought harsh wet winters. In November of 1881, it snowed continuously for two days. The flakes fell so rapidly that they obliterated the familiar night sky with its countless stars. The villagers lay shivering in their beds thinking of the packs of homeless dogs that would be exhumed from beneath the piles of snow. They had no idea they would also find a group of half-frozen Russian pilgrims, foolishly clothed, returning from the shrines of Nazareth. One of those Russians fell ill and remained for a time. Without ever knowing it, he caused a death and a birth and altered three women's lives forever.

BOOK ONE
1882–1920

HEARTS HIDDEN
AND HUMBLE

1

I've never heard her say a word.

From the beginning, Miriam was shy. She had a habit of tilting her head so that it touched her shoulder, believing in her childish way that this made her invisible. She squinted, even indoors, which was too bad because her eyes were her best feature—widely spaced, large, and a dark, disturbing blue—the last visible color of the evening sky. By age five, she hadn't spoken.

Grandmother Nabiha was the first to mention it. "I've never heard her say a word, not even 'mama.' Not even 'papa,'" she added and then wished she hadn't, for her daughter stopped washing her twin sons and gave her a miserable look. "Take her to the doctor," she finished lamely. "Let him at least comment on it."

"What can the doctor do?" answered Jamilla woodenly—she disliked these conversations. "He can't make her talk." She sighed and paused and then, as if making an admission that should have been made long before, she said, "She wants to be deaf and dumb. Like him."

"But it's not right. It's not natural," said Nabiha. And then more softly, "It's not possible." She turned the palms of her hands toward heaven. "It hasn't turned out badly." She was looking for assurance. "You have these golden, perfect boys." She stooped to kiss the matted reddish curls of the babies, who were making nonsense sounds and splashing in the shallow metal tub.

"No," admitted Jamilla. "It hasn't. I thought it was the end of my life."

Nabiha, whose eyes had begun to trouble her, narrowed them against the sun and looked off into the distant hills. The memory of the day she had dragged her beautiful daughter to the hostel to inspect the deaf man who had agreed to marry her was fresh in her mind. They had passed the dispensary on the way, and Jamilla had clung to the doorway and begged her mother to let her see the doctor first. "Hush, hush," Nabiha had hissed. "The doctor can do nothing. Everyone will know. Our shame will be made public."

"But Mama, I can't marry him. I can't."

"You should have thought of that before you let that Russian put his child inside you." Her own words shocked her and she stood rigid. That Russian whom she had nursed so diligently had also infected her husband, who died. So much damage from one act of charity. So much damage from a stranger who entered her life by chance. But she couldn't think of that. She had children to raise. "Come along," she urged her daughter. "Mustafa is a decent man. His face is pleasant. He doesn't look ignorant, as you'd expect. His eyes are lively and a good color. And he's strong, his back and shoulders are developed. His head is well shaped. Come on, come on, if people see us arguing in the street, they'll start to gossip."

But Jamilla didn't give in easily. For several months after the simple, unheralded wedding she refused to look at her husband.

The day her labor pains began, she was out far beyond the cultivated fields gathering brush and had a good hour's trip home. She was a young, untried girl, full of indecision—should she leave the wood and run or simply lay down amid the sweet scented gorse and yellow thistle and take whatever violence was sure to follow? The pain intensified and she crawled to a patch of tall waving reeds, thinking they would protect her from the blazing sun, and scanned the vast fields for a human presence. Then out in the distance, she saw her husband approaching. Mustafa. In that field, as he worked over her, she thawed toward him. She felt his strength and his confidence. He would always take care of her.

"How did you know to come? How did you know?" She kept asking it over and over as if nothing else mattered. He couldn't hear her. He smoothed back her hair, which was a reddish brown, healthy but unruly, and helped bring their daughter into the world. Perhaps it was because he had aided in her birth that he loved Miriam so.

"He's the only man in the village who values his daughter more than his sons," commented Jamilla with exaggerated annoyance when the twins were born. Privately, she couldn't explain it. That thin, withdrawn child was not easy to love.

One morning, when Miriam was little more than three, she came upon her mother rubbing the twins with oil and singing a nonsense song to the plump, naked babies. The words were silly enough to interest a little girl. "There was a little mouse, who built a little house, and in it was a louse . . . here it comes, here it comes, oh, oh, oh!" Jamilla's fingers went running up the babies' chubby sausage arms to catch the louse. She dug between tiny pink toes, routing out that pesky louse. The twins were squealing with delight and Miriam, enticed by the scene, took off all her clothes and climbed up on the bed to receive the same.

Her mother laughed and yanked Miriam off the bed, brought her upright, and swatted her bottom. "You're too old, now. *Yullah,* put on your dress. You want to be a baby again? There are enough babies. You're a big girl."

She went outside, digging her fists into her eyes to hold back the tears. A large hand pried one fist loose. It was her *baba*, Mustafa. She wouldn't look at him, but he placed her hand first against her own heart and then on his. There was the same steady thump in both places, hers a little faster. Reluctantly, she watched as he drew a heart in the dusty ground with a stick and then pointed to his chest. He entwined a smaller heart with the large one and pointed to her chest.

They sat together on the dusty ground and she opened his mouth as she did every so often, put one of her fingers between his lips, and thumped his shoulder. No sound came out. Mustafa pointed again to the dusty hearts and brought one shoulder up to meet his head as if to say, Well, that's how I do it. Then he plucked a fig from a nearby bush, put it behind his back, and brought it out again hidden in his closed hands. She chose three times before she got it right, but he kept smiling and rushing to give her another chance. When she found the fig, he picked her up as if she were a bag of feathers and held her out in front of him and then in his arms.

Baba was calm and patient. His eyes and hands played out what he wanted her to know, and the little drawing stick told her the rest. He was forever silent, but she understood him perfectly. Which was the day she decided to be mute, too? Perhaps it wasn't one moment but many moments.

The spring of Miriam's sixth birthday, her muteness was forgotten for more worrisome things. The ground had a dead, brown look. There had been no downpours to bring back health to the plants and hasten the ripening of the oranges. Wheat was selling at famine prices and all the pains of drought had taken hold. Nabile, Nabiha's oldest son, could no longer drive his wagon to Jaffa, for there was little produce and goods to export. The younger boy, Daud, barely nine, took their small herd farther and farther in the wilderness looking for greenery. Even Nabiha's richer relatives weren't doing well, at least not well enough to help her.

Mustafa, however, was resourceful in finding work. He took Jamilla and Miriam to the lowland village of Philistia to assist the farmers there who had a wheat and barley crop to harvest. He and his wife would receive wages and Miriam was allowed to follow them and pick up any wheat that fell. Miriam was fastidious in recovering every grain, for she saw that when her basket was filled her mother's face had such a look of relief.

April in the plains was like late summer in the mountains and the field flowers were plentiful—crimson iris, variegated lilies, and wild roses. Parts of the ground were black with ants that invaded the wheat stores, making each grain appear as if it had legs. The farmer set fire to the ant cities and rubbed the wheat with quicksilver and egg white to protect it from insects before storing it in cisterns.

The harvesting party was gay and there was much laughing and singing, but the living conditions were harsh. The tent for the women and children was overcrowded. They were huddled together with no privacy and no relief from the constant noise. The donkeys fought and brayed and kept it up all night long. The odors accumulating from unwashed bodies were horrific. When they first arrived, Jamilla had foolishly inquired of a woman where she could bathe. "Hah," the woman had sneered, happy to get the better of a mountain dweller. "There is no water for bathing. We use sand. Perhaps it will ruin your fair skin," she added maliciously.

"What do we drink?" Jamilla persisted.

"Drinking water is for sale. Someone will come twice a day."

Jamilla, who was sensitive to smell, often left the tent and slept outside. Many of the women cried out in their dreams and Miriam would awaken, frightened and disoriented to find her mother gone. She developed a persistent cough from the damp night air that penetrated her bones followed by the day's exhausting heat. Yet nothing deterred her from following her mother and retracing the furrows that had been abandoned as picked clean, hoping to find a few extra grains. She kept her precious sack with her at all times, placing it under her head when she slept.

One night, Miriam was awakened by what felt like ants crawling over her body. Her skin throbbed as if bruised, and scratching brought no relief. By morning, the throbbing abated, but the itching continued. Several times in the next few days, Miriam nudged her mother, pointed to her arms and beat her chest over her dress, but Jamilla was too fatigued or unwilling to understand. She searched for Mustafa, but he was gone.

Some of the men left the fields to work in the brick-burning kilns of neighboring el Mesmiyeh, which paid fifty cents a day instead of thirty, and Mustafa joined them. They put him in a vaulted room to feed the fire with stubble collected from the cornfields of nearby plantations. The room was suffocatingly hot, and only by stripping naked could he endure the heat. In compensation, el Mesmiyeh had an inexhaustible well, and four stout mules raised cool, sweet water.

When the family returned to Tamleh, they were so tanned the twins cried as if they were strangers. Nabiha was shocked at Miriam's condition. "Look at her hair," she said reproachfully.

"The comb won't go through," said Jamilla, kissing and inspecting her babies, who were toddling around. "It would take hours to untangle it and my arms are too weary. It's the tangles that hold the dirt." Seeing how thin her daughter had become and the deep circles around her eyes, Nabiha couldn't scold her.

"Come." She took Miriam's hand. "That body needs scrubbing and that hair . . . *that hair.*"

Miriam slipped her hand out of her grandmother's and began to scratch. *"Ya Allah,"* said Nabiha. "She has a rash, too."

She undressed her granddaughter and found her covered with oozing welts and ran to find Mustafa. He stared at the bony, infested body and his eyes filled with tears. He picked her up and carried her across town to Spiridum Rascallah, who was permitted to dispense pharmaceuticals, and she gave him a soothing salve that he himself spread over the infected bites.

Miriam's muteness affected each family member differently. Her father taught her a few of the hand signs but mostly they communicated by pantomime and drawings. Jamilla, busy with the twins, distanced herself from it and never urged her to talk. Nabiha prayed daily. Nabile asked Miriam privately each day to "just say 'good morning, Uncle'." Daud, the younger uncle, who had been displaced by her birth, detested her muteness and was determined to end it.

One day Miriam hid an abandoned pup at the edge of the yard. Dogs were too numerous to arouse sympathy, but this one had rounded ears and large eyes. Each day she fed him with a rag soaked in milk, but one morning the tangle of vines hiding him was pushed aside and the crate was empty. Her face, still pale from sleep, crinkled into an anxious squint.

She walked back to the house and Daud appeared with a covered basket. He was noticeably short and she had almost caught up to him during the winter. "This what you're looking for?" He lifted the cover briefly and she reached out. "Oh, no. When you say, 'Uncle Daud,' I'll give him back." He poked a knife through the basket weave. "No talking, no dog."

She went to the far edge of the yard to look down the western road where her father appeared on Saturday, coming home filthy with the ash residue of the soap-making in Ramleh. He traveled with his own old dog to warn him of noise and danger, and the dog's collar beat against itself making a familiar sound. But today wasn't Saturday.

Daud moved to the vegetable patch. A slight breeze blew and he lifted his face. Then he sighed, held the dog up by his ears, and put the knife against its throat. "Speak!" he ordered sharply. "You bloody little liar. You can speak as well as anyone." He grazed the throat from ear to ear and a necklace of blood drops appeared. The dog yelped pitifully. The second motion was swift, deep, and sure; and the small round head fell back.

Miriam heard the gurgling before the dog collapsed. She tipped the head back to a normal position, but the rest of him sagged pathetically. "Dead," she said.

"What?" Daud heard it.

"Dead."

"You little fool. Why speak now?"

Her mother found her holding the dog in her lap. "What happened? Are you hurt?" She called to Daud, who was a few yards away pitching stones at the herds. "I killed her mutt. He was digging in the garden."

Miriam was standing by her mother's shoulder. "No," she said firmly. Jamilla was startled as much by the quality of the voice as by the fact that she had spoken. "Lie," said Miriam.

"Take her to see the doctor," said Nabiha after hearing her granddaughter rasp out a few words. "It's a strange voice, but not unpleasant." Miriam's voice was deep but with a lovely, silvery underside.

Dr. Hanser, who had been brought to the village by the Society of Friends, examined Miriam's heart and lungs and looked into her ears and eyes. He took her pulse and recorded her reflexes. Finally, he inspected her throat and had her repeat the vowel sounds. "She speaks low for a female," he said. "Perhaps her vocal chords are withered." He had no idea how to reassure the mother. The patient was in good health. "Send her to the Scotswoman near Sarona. She'll give her lessons in strengthening the voice." He turned to the Quaker woman who helped him. "Perhaps Miss Haefling can write a letter on your behalf."

"Why can she suddenly talk now?" asked Jamilla. She knew the answer but chose to ignore it, fearful of being laughed at, or worse, having people think she was the instigator of the muteness to tie her more closely to Mustafa.

"It isn't anything physical," said the doctor. "She could have talked anytime."

Jamilla, in her confusion, turned pale with anger. "You withheld it on purpose, naughty girl." Her hand came around with force and struck Miriam.

Miss Haefling placed herself between mother and daughter. "No one is naughty, madam," she said softly. "Children have their own reasons and it's difficult for us to understand them. Nevertheless, your daughter needs to be taught to speak properly. There is a fine school at Sarona affiliated with the German Colony where she can receive speech therapy."

"I can't spare her," said Jamilla, already regretting her outburst. "I need her to watch the children during the harvest."

"Then you can send her after the harvest." The doctor spoke firmly. He knew Miriam would speak with or without the therapy, but he saw some value in separating the girl from her mother.

"The expense . . ." Jamilla began. "Perhaps the school's too dear. . . ."

"The German Colony is a religious community," said Miss Haefling. "Most likely, they will take your daughter without payment. Let me write and explain the situation." When Jamilla failed to answer, she added, "The best families send their girls to the school at Sarona."

That night, as Miriam lay in her bed, she heard the monotonous cry of the nighthawk calling to its mate, but she was not frightened. Despite the sadness over the dog, despite the turbulence she had caused, she felt deep relief. Fear had been inside her all this time. Fear of the silence and fear of breaking it. Now it was done.

2

We must have a bath.

Miriam and Mustafa left for the school early one morning down the el-Tirah road, passing the fine orderly vineyards that grew the best grapes in Judea. The road curved down and they could see the cement in the paved roofs had cracked from the summer heat. There would be leaks with the first showers of fall.

Nabiha tucked a bag of sweets into Miriam's pocket. "Eat them on the way, *habibty,*" she said and began to cry. Jamilla embraced Miriam briefly but was distracted by keeping the twins, George and Salim, from straying down the road.

The trip to Sarona took two days. Miriam, looking pale, began to lag toward dusk and Mustafa carried her to a hostel in Ludd, where they spent the night. In the morning, they breakfasted on goats' milk cheese, thyme, oil, bread, and tea and took food for the road. Every so often they would stop, moved by the sights of the pomegranate and mulberry orchards and the palm trees, which Miriam had never seen. They passed the ruins of many soap factories, now in decay.

They were used to walking barefoot and saved their sandals for the villages. The difficulty came with the dust. The pulverized limestone that leeched out of the striated buttes invaded their noses, eyes, and mouths; and Miriam had difficulty swallowing. She stopped frequently and Mustafa looked back to keep her in view.

As they got nearer the sea, the temperature increased but remained dry. They came to the first station of the new railroad from Jaffa to Jerusalem. The locomotive rumbled by, halted, discharged a passenger, and went again. Mustafa, delighted, took a small leap into the air and they waited until it was out of sight before continuing to Sarona.

The school was unmistakable. The area was landscaped with orderly rows of palm trees and formal approaches to the main building, which was made of smooth flush stone with double-height arched windows. A gardener stared at them disdainfully. *"Mughbari?"* he asked, taking them for itinerant Muslims working their way through the villages on the pilgrimage to Mecca. Miriam shook her head. "This is a school for Muslims," he informed them. "Rich Muslim girls." Miriam ignored him and looked at her father, who was filthy with dust. She tucked her hair behind her kerchief and put on a colorful vest from her sack.

The inside of the building was a revelation. The floors were made of polished wood. *Wood!* There were divans against the walls for sitting.

Miss Clay, the headmistress, was taller than her father. *"Ma'salamy,"* she said. Mustafa didn't answer and Miriam pointed to the inside of her mouth. "No speak." Her voice surprised the teacher and, to make matters worse, Mustafa began gesticulating. Miriam reddened but then she saw Miss Clay moving her hands in the same way. Mustafa smiled and seemed satisfied to leave his daughter. When he walked away, Miriam cried into her scarf and ran after him. He made a little maneuver of leaving and then returning to let her know he would be back to visit, and she went inside.

"First," said Miss Clay, ignoring the tears, "we must have a bath."

Leila, the maid, was the first to enter her room in the morning. She took one look at the mattress on the floor and shook her head in disgust. "Stupid," she chided Miriam, who was startled to be attacked by one of her own kind. Leila appeared to be a villager like herself. "If she sees what you've done with the bed, you'll go right back."

Curiosity fought with pride but finally won. "What's wrong?" She had pulled the mattress to the floor as it was at home.

"It belongs on the bedstead. Stupid Christian!"

Instead of cowing her, Leila's attack gave her new determination. She had been selected to be a pupil, while Leila was just the maid.

"Lengthen your neck and throw back your head an inch or so. See?" Miss Clay put her index finger to her Adam's apple. "You can feel what is happening as you make certain sounds." She placed Miriam's finger on the appropriate spot. "We'll begin with *ah . . . aaaaaaaaaaaah.*"

"Agh . . . ahgagh . . . agh." Miriam's sounds caught and scratched. Sometimes no sound came out.

"Very good. Keep your finger on your throat and feel the tension there. We'll try *eeh. Eeeeeeeeeh.*"

"Eh. . . . egheghegh." The room was large, and the wooden floors had a chevron pattern that made her dizzy.

"Uh . . . uuuuuuuuuuh."

"Uughuuuugh."

Each day, beginning at eight, from October until May, Rowena Clay taught two dozen large-eyed Muslim girls to speak and read the King's

English. At the midday meal they learned table manners, and after lunch they embroidered. It had become the "thing to do" among wealthy Muslims, to send their daughters to be "finished" by Europeans. Miss Clay's Academy was sanctioned by the German Colony at a time when the Turkish government was looking to Germany for alliance. When Crown Prince Wilhelm stopped in Jerusalem on his way to open the Suez, he was given half the Muristan, the site of the Hospitallers, the fabulous Knights of St. John. The gift infuriated many Arabs.

Miriam sat with the others in the reading class, but was not expected to participate. Her therapy began at two, when the carriages came to take the others home.

"Keep your neck long and your ribs high. You must speak from here," Miss Clay touched her abdomen. "Stand straight." Miriam straightened by example, for she missed almost everything said in such oddly accented Arabic. As they worked, the sun came through the high arched windows in waves that made the air quiver. She looked longingly outside at barefooted Leila beating carpets in the yard, the closest link to her old life. She didn't want to keep her neck long. She wanted to lie down on the floor and go to sleep.

When the weather cooled and the routine was familiar, she began to follow the words in the primer read by the girls in the morning classes. The book related the life of an English family named Highwood who lived in a white house in Surrey. And, she thought with triumph, proving that she understood, Jamilla and Mustafa Tawal live in a white stone house in Tamleh. "I understand," she cried out with pleasure, but Miss Clay put a finger to her lips.

The ability to read the insipid life of Hugh and Sybil Highwood and their three daughters made her feel powerful. She tolerated the speech sessions but was devoted to the reading. She read along with every girl's halting effort, so engrossed in the story she had to be nudged out of her seat when class was over.

At noon, she ate lunch with Leila but had tea with Miss Clay after the therapy. She envied Miss Clay's (and the girls') adeptness with a knife and fork. Why don't you teach me, too? she wanted to ask.

"Do you wonder why I don't urge you to eat with a knife and fork?" Miss Clay asked one day.

"No."

"Tell me," she said softly, "does your mother eat with a knife and fork?"

This was the last thing she expected to hear. Her mother's face appeared with such clarity it brought a pang of sadness. Her mother rolled the food into balls and put it in her mouth with her fingers. She kept bread on her knee and tore bits to dip into oil. Miriam looked down at her feet, dizzy with shame. Mercifully, the subject was dropped.

She tried to convince herself that her mother was infinitely better off than Miss Clay. Her hands were ever in motion, gathering, cooking, watering, washing. What's more, Miss Clay was just *Miss Clay!* She had no clan to protect her. Whom could she appeal to if someone cheated her or killed a loved one?

There were only a few weeks left to the term, and Miriam attacked her voice sessions with new determination. She held her head erect, her throat arched, her rib cage high, her blue eyes focused directly ahead. "Father . . . bazaar . . . calm. Heifer . . . leopard . . . friend. Toe . . . flow . . . note . . . road. Key . . . field . . . pee-pel . . . pee-pel . . . *people!*"

She was anxious to leave Sarona. "Why is it important for me to speak well?" she asked.

"A beautiful voice delights people of all stations," said Miss Clay, "but being the odd person in the family is a burden."

Three weeks before she was to leave, Miss Clay said something that made Miriam believe she wasn't so bad after all. "Would you like to learn to sign? To use hand language so you can talk with your father?"

All she could imagine were the taunts from Daud if he saw her doing any such thing. "Look." Miss Clay was holding her hand with the thumb up. "What do you suppose that means?"

"I don't know." She looked away.

"It means hello." She put her hand up and did it again. "Hello."

Miriam went to stare out the window at the trees and bushes that still looked so alien. She tried to imagine what her father would do if she came home and waved her hand at him like that. "Hello, *Baba.*" She knew what he would do. He would cry with joy. She turned around. "Show me again, please."

When she returned, Nabiha looked much older. Daud looked smaller. The house looked very small. And crowded. Uncle Nabile had married the Shihada girl, Diana, and she was very fat.

"How could you spend the entire day learning to speak?" Her mother looked mystified.

"Oh, we didn't do that. Part of the day, I sat in class with the other girls." She pulled out a book Miss Clay had allowed her to keep. "I learned to read, Mama," she admitted shyly.

Jamilla looked at the book with suspicion. It wasn't unusual to speak several languages. After all, the Protestant schools taught English, the Orthodox taught Greek, and the Franciscans, who came from the Levant, taught French. The poorest peasant was capable of speaking beautifully accented French. But reading and writing were another matter. Those who could read and write were worlds apart.

3

A young man came to the stand today.

Change comes slowly in most lives, but sometimes there is one decisive moment. One can point and say, "There. My life changed there."

Mustafa's life changed dramatically in the autumn of 1894 when Nabiha's brother, who was childless, gave him two acres on the northeast corner of the village. The bulk of the land was distributed on two sides of a steep hill filled with scrub brush and trees. There was no ready source of water for irrigation. The sole advantage was that the land faced south and west.

Mustafa began clearing as large a portion as possible through the beastly September heat. From dawn to dusk, he uprooted shrubs, chopped down trees, and overturned earth. The peculiar powdery effect of lime rock and the countless stones showing on the surface looked hopeless. To make use of the slopes, Mustafa cut shelves out of the hills and saved the stones to create a ledge that would protect the terraces. He began to sleep at the site, and once each day Miriam arrived with a packet of food. "Well, let's see how far along you are today." She regularly communicated with him in hand language, but still they were partial to the old methods of drawing and pantomime because Mustafa had come to enjoy it. She seldom saw much change in the land from day to day, but she made an effort to show surprise for his accomplishments.

Through the ordeal, Mustafa ignored the lack of water, much as he had ignored Jamilla's anger in the first year of their marriage. Often, especially when she was upset, his wife spoke to him as if he could hear perfectly. "My uncle has given you a gift of nothing," she would say, and to illustrate would point her empty palms upward. It was therapeutic for her to vent her feelings and he always appeared to be listening. She also had adopted some of his physical maneuvers. She would visit the site of his garden and mimic the act of digging and shoveling and wiping sweat off her brow and becoming bent over from the strenuous labor. She would walk around in circles holding her back and looking dazed, as if the sun had scrambled her wits. Then she would shrug and throw her hands upward as if to say, "For what?" At such times, Mustafa would take his hand and erase the creases from her brow. He would point to his head, close his eyes and smile, implying he had a vision of good.

He rented a horse and coaxed Daud, who was a fearless rider, to help him uproot the most stubborn stumps. Remembering the dark, loamy soil he had seen in Sarona, he collected his neighbors' ashes, refuse, and animal droppings and spread the mixture over his future garden. He borrowed a team and plowed with one ox on one level and the other below, for the terraces were narrow. During this maneuver, the stick caught and wouldn't budge. Mustafa dug out, not a rock as expected, but a masonry leader that was connected to a solid masonry pool. These ancient ruined pools, originally built to catch the overflow from the springs, were often used for threshing floors. The largest of them, the Pools of Solomon, south of Bethlehem, when full, could float a battleship. The pool Mustafa found was close to Ayn Fara, a copious perennial spring that didn't diminish in summer. After several rainstorms, the pool began to fill and Mustafa knew he had a source of livelihood for himself and his family.

He put in early crops—cabbage, parsley, peas, onions—and as the weather warmed, added okra, eggplant, cucumbers, squash, and cauliflower. He experimented with tomatoes, which were new to the country but much sought after by the European colonies in Jerusalem. Every two weeks, he added side dressings of the "fertilizer" he concocted from his cache of refuse. By May he was able to bring his early crop to the Jaffa Gate and sell it alongside those of the other village farmers.

The plaza outside Jaffa Gate was the busiest spot in all Jerusalem, for here ended the well-traveled road from the ancient port city of Jaffa. Here, diligences, carriages, bringing imported necessities and luxuries, discharged passengers and goods.

Mustafa fashioned a two-tiered cart with long handles to hold his produce, and he and Miriam pushed it the ten miles from Tamleh every Wednesday. The spot they chose was at the foot of Suleiman Street in front of the French Hospital of St. Louis.

It was the thriving hub of the city. Jaffa Road, though still unpaved, had sidewalks. In just one small stretch, across from the Russian Compound, there was a branch of Barclay's Bank, the Hughes Hotel, a specialty cobbler, and several elegant shops and cafés. The Greek Consulate occupied spacious offices atop one building that housed a branch of the Russian Post Office below.

Inside the walls, the Holy City was vastly improved in health and respectability as the century drew to a close. Mayor Salim Husseini had laid cobblestones over the winding, narrow lanes and instituted regular sweeping, lanterns, and night watchmen. Camels and donkeys were no longer allowed inside the walls. There was a man hired just to cleanse the corners where "people laid their waters." Jaffa Gate was closed at night for safety, and those wishing to leave before dawn had to be lowered over the wall by ropes. The fields behind the New Grand Hotel, which previously had been a casual burial ground for countless animal carcasses that putrified in the sun, were cleared. The mounds of dung and garbage that had threatened health and welfare were diminished. No longer was it necessary to encourage the hyenas to enter at night to eat away at the debris.

Miriam loved the noise, the confusion, and the color. She watched with interest as Turkish strongmen in sashed pantaloons jockeyed huge palettes ladened with bales of cotton and other raw materials through the narrow lanes. Monks and Sisters of every sect—Copts, Muslims, Orthodox, Latins, Jews, and Dervishes—crisscrossed the square in and out of the Holy City in a variety of clerical dress. The ever-present hordes of Russian pilgrims in dark penitential clothes swarmed in and out of the Russian Compound. Villagers, looking to alleviate minor ailments and give themselves a thorough washing, visited the baths.

Overriding everything were the intermittent clouds of dust created by the carriages and animals, for the roads outside the walls were still unpaved. With water collected in a cistern from the roofs of the Citadel buildings, municipal workers dampened the ground several times a day.

Miriam and Mustafa took pleasure in arranging the produce. Crisp okra spikes were laid out like a regiment of sturdy soldiers. Bouquets of parsley were presented in paper cones. Turnips were upended with their rosy points showing over the lip of several large decorated clay bowls. Green beans and peas were kept in the lower tray, out of the wilting sun. Cucumbers, midnight green and shimmering with droplets of dew, were laid out in a row along the back. Scallions and young yellow squash, the blossoms still clinging, filled out the colorful assortment. Eggplants were added as they matured, but the jewels of the collection were the tomatoes. Some, almost two pounds, formed the base of small pyramids, which were quickly grabbed by Europeans who were homesick for this food.

The first few weeks, Mustafa sold out his supply before the morning was over and took the opportunity to inspect the competition, whose puny, ill-formed merchandise sold for the same price as his. He began to have repeat customers, and some offered advice. Sister Charlotte, a Kaiserwerth deaconess and revered head of the German orphanage, told him to double his prices immediately, for the quality of his goods warranted it. Father Alphonse, head of the Ethiopian monastery, put in a weekly order and added a bonus for delivery to the compound on Ethiopia Street. The doctors and nurses of the St. Louis Hospital scooped up pounds of the *haricots vert,* which were long and tender. The Italian Consulate, also on Ethiopia Street, sniffing the glorious basket being delivered to Father Alphonse, demanded the same, with a double order of tomatoes.

By the time the second crop of beans and peas came in, both Mustafa and Miriam were spending as much time delivering orders as selling at their stand. Sister Charlotte urged Mustafa to experiment with a new vegetable, unknown in Palestine, assuring him she would be responsible for the entire crop. "When the Emperor Frederick visited the orphanage and asked what we most wanted him to send us from Germany," said the Sister, "we asked for two barrels of potatoes. All the Europeans feel the same. It's a wonderful staple, very easy to grow." So Mustafa added potatoes to the following year's crop and had an even more successful business the second summer. He enlarged his clientele to include the Counsels of France and England and the Grand Hotel, which had opened on the corner of Latin Patriarchate Road.

Two German hotels, the Hughes and the Feil, asked for his wares, but he refused. The debris being excavated for the ghastly German compound at the Muristan was filling the moat around the Citadel of David, infuriating the locals as well as other Europeans. Mustafa's best customers were still the Ethiopians and he often stopped to sit in the gardens outside their beautiful church. Father Alphonse offered to house and educate his sons, but Mustafa demurred. The twins were barely ten.

At dusk, when deliveries and errands were finished, father and daughter stopped to hear the Turkish Military Band that played twice weekly in the Baladiyya, a lovely public garden which was another of Mayor Husseini's innovations.

Miriam often noticed the young nurses coming out of St. Louis Hospital, their breasts jutting out from crisp bib aprons, their caps firmly anchored on their carefully styled hair. They laughed and chattered together, and often a doctor would join them. The nurses were charmed beings blessed by the universe to live a life of gaiety and satisfaction. The doctors were celestial. She whiled away the hours dreaming, irrationally, of being part of such a life.

It was the end of September of their fifth year at the stand. The potatoes had been harvested, also the cabbage. A few tomatoes were still ripening. Mustafa closed for five months—November through March—while he tilled, repaired, fertilized, and overturned his garden. This year, he planned to build a home for his family. Nabiha's house with Nabile's growing family was too crowded.

Miriam, at sixteen, was almost as tall as her father, with the slim, hard body developed by years of strenuous walking. In contrast, her heavily lashed blue eyes were soft and wistful.

One late afternoon, she was tapping her foot to the music coming from the barracks of the Turkish police where the orchestra practiced. She knew the day was coming to an end when she heard the squeaks and shrieks of the horns (few of the musicians were trained). She had opened the *Palestine Post* and was reading and tapping and wasn't immediately aware of the young man standing there.

"Are you from the Mishwe family? *Dâr Mishwe?*" She felt foolish to be caught tapping her foot, but also he took her by surprise. She didn't think of herself as coming from the Mishwe family, although she was connected through Nabiha. "You're from the Mishwe family," he said more forcefully. "I'm your cousin." He wanted some admission.

"Perhaps." If he were so certain she had no need to confirm it.

"Not perhaps. It's true."

She didn't like his insistent tone and refused to look up.

"You come here every week?"

"No," she lied. He might come back next week. He might come back every week. "Did you want some beans?" she asked quickly. "That's all that's left." Too late she realized there was also a head of cabbage and sat in a state of numb embarrassment.

"How about the cabbage? Is it reserved?"

Ya Allah. "No. But it has worms." Go away.

"Let's see how many worms it has," he said playfully and her shyness turned to stubbornness.

"One worm or ten," she said, looking straight at his chest, "we don't sell bad vegetables."

"Very well, I'll take the beans," he pulled out some coins and dropped them on the cart. "I'll take all of them. And next week, I'll come and tell you how they tasted."

She thought he had turned to leave and looked up, but it was too soon. She caught his profile—short, brown hair ending in curly innocence at the nape of his neck, an ordinary ear and chin, healthy coloring. His teasing voice, however, was threatening. He had spoken to her as if he had a right to expect a friendly response. She didn't want to give a friendly response to him, or to any young man. She liked her life the way it was.

That night she said to her mother, "A boy came to the stand today and said he was my cousin. He asked me if I was from the Mishwe family."

"A boy?" said Jamilla. "How old a boy?"

"I don't know. I didn't get a good look at him. Maybe more than a boy."

"A man?" asked Jamilla, astonished. "How did he look?"

"I don't know."

"You spoke to a man and you don't know how he looked?"

Diana, who was pregnant with her second child, strolled in and picked up a meat-filled hand pie from a tray. "What man?" she asked casually. "A man wants Miriam?"

Jamilla who had not yet dared to form the thought was annoyed that Diana had said it first. "Don't be foolish. Someone just asked if she was from the Mishwe family. He said he was our cousin."

"Ah . . . well. Who is it?"

"I don't know." Miriam wished she hadn't mentioned anything.

"Didn't you ask his name?" asked Diana, overly incredulous. She exaggerated every response to make herself important.

"No," said Miriam. "I sold him string beans."

"I wonder who it is?" said Jamilla. She mentioned several names with brief descriptions, but all were eliminated.

"The next time he comes, I'll find out," said Miriam.

Both Diana and Jamilla turned in astonishment. "He's coming back?" they asked in unison.

"He said he would let me know how the string beans tasted."

4

You must marry someone.

"I hear you can read and write," said one of the visitors. They had come purposefully up the hill, three figures in fine clothes.

Miriam looked at her mother, but Jamilla was twisting her rings. "Very little." The visit was like waiting for honey to drip on a cold day. Slow and stiff.

"Don't be modest," said Jamilla quickly. "Miriam can read or write anything." This was not true. Her mother was sitting on the edge of her chair. The visitors were her aunts, vaguely related through Nabiha. But there was an air about them—they were wealthy. They were dressed in crepe de chine, and their arms jangled with at least a dozen bracelets.

"And you went to the school for rich Muslims? The school for the Darawayis and Faidys?"

"I had little to do with the girls. They went home when my lessons began." Umm Jameel—as was the custom, she was called by her first son's name, mother of Jameel—who seemed to be the important one ironed out her fat fingers. "How is it that rich Muslims go to denominational schools," she asked as if this oversight were Miriam's fault.

"I've no idea," said Miriam. "Perhaps it's for their good. Or for their ill," she added fatalistically.

"Did they teach you sewing?" Umm Jameel persisted. "Do you embroider?"

"They taught the girls the cross-stitch, which my mother had already taught me."

Umm Jameel took a bite of a cookie. "And did you bake these delicious cookies?"

"She helped," offered Nabiha quickly. "Miriam is often away with her father. She interprets for him in his business."

"And from whom do you get those blue eyes?" This came from another aunt, who had been quietly inspecting the room.

Jamilla looked troubled. "No doubt from my husband's family."

After what seemed an interminable pause, the three women rose, exchanged kisses with their hostesses and left.

"It's wonderful," said Nabiha, clapping her hands above her head. Jamilla looked after the departing Umm Jameel and muttered, *"Kalb hamil khurj mal."* A dog carrying a saddlebag of wealth. However, she, too, was smiling.

"Why did they want to know so much about me?" asked Miriam.

"And why not?" said Jamilla with indignation. "That's what they came for. To look us over. They want you for Nadeem."

"Who is Nadeem?"

"Nadeem Mishwe. He's the second son of Umm Jameel. The family's very good." Jamilla's voice became serious. "Her sister, the thin one, is married to a man who owns orange groves in Jaffa. One uncle went to Argentina and sends back gold lira. Nadeem's family has just one vineyard and the grapes are inferior, but he's a first-class mason. He's working on a church in Madaba." Jamilla looked at her daughter appraisingly. She had heard rumors at the *taboon* but had been afraid it was a joke. Even now, her heart fluttered with apprehension that she had misinterpreted. "He wants you for his wife."

For Miriam, it was all too clear. This was the prelude—the visit to make a match. The fat woman was the mother of the eligible boy. She summoned up the weddings and funerals where these three faces had passed and struggled to attach them to a son. Was it the short, pudgy idiot who tied three dogs together so that they tore each other to bits? Was it the tall, thin boy with boils on his cheeks? Was it the balding man who had already lost a wife?

"Baba, do I have to marry? Suppose I don't want to?" Happily no one could interpret what she and her father signed to each other.

Mustafa looked surprised. "Why wouldn't you want to?"

"I like my life as it is. I don't want to leave you and Mama. I like working with you at the stand." The idea of marriage frightened her, but she was too embarrassed to tell him.

"We can delay it," Mustafa signed. "But he's a fine man. It's an advantageous marriage." Having gained respectability late in life, Mustafa, too, was caught up in the idea of a good match.

She went to her mother. "Until now," she reasoned, "I didn't know about them and they didn't know about me."

"That's where you are mistaken, Miss Schoolgirl. They have been thinking of you for Nadeem for a very long time. He's your cousin. He's healthy. Employed. You must marry someone. Who would be better? Tell me, who?"

How quickly it all took place. The men came trudging up the hill as the women had done. "We, the Mishwe family, of the clan of Janin, have come to ask for the hand of your daughter, Miriam, to be the bride of our son, Nadeem."

Please, Nabile, say no. Her uncle was answering for her father. Listening in the back room, she heard Nabile answer, *"Mabrook,"* the traditional word of agreement. It was done.

At the betrothal, Father Ricard placed her in the center of the room and went to get the bridegroom. She felt thin and empty. The new dress was stiff and ballooned awkwardly above the waist every time she moved. What was the priest saying? He had placed someone next to her, but she didn't dare steal a glance. If she looked, she would have to accept what she saw.

The priest was finished. Her father kissed her forehead. Now, she had to turn. She saw an ear, red at the tip. He was nearly shoulder to shoulder with her. There was something vaguely familiar about him. *It was the young man at the vegetable stand!* Then she remembered that several times, in moments of weakness, for lack of anyone else, she had plucked him from that spot near Jaffa Gate and put him in her daydreams. This was her punishment. It had come true.

"You are tall," he said. "Almost to my eyes." He had taken her outside.

She looked at him contemptuously. She was as tall as he. "Is that why you chose me?"

"Perhaps."

"It's a poor reason."

"And what would be a better one?" he asked teasingly.

"Strength," she said. Any answer would do.

"Well, now," he said playfully, "are you strong?" He extended her arm to inspect it, but she didn't feel playful. "You aren't pleased by this match?" he asked kindly.

"My parents have chosen for me, and I will do as they say," she answered quietly.

"That's wise. And honest," he said, making a virtue of her joylessness. "It's better to start a marriage without mistaken ideas. Then there are no disappointments, but, instead, pleasant surprises."

"What sort of pleasant surprises?" she asked suspiciously. She was surprised that she could challenge him so easily. Her peevishness didn't seem to bother him at all.

"Many. The joys of creating a pleasant home and a . . . ." He had been about to add "family" but thought better of it. He blushed.

"You're right," she agreed, reassured by his nervousness. They walked in silence and she looked him over. He was slight, with a long face, like his father's, but with very large, lively eyes, and excellent, even teeth that were visible when he smiled. He had a ruddy complexion, not that awful yellow that men had who smoked the narghilla so much. His hair was thick, a medium brown. He was tanned from the sun, which made his light eyes look lighter. She had seen her cousins married to men who weren't half as acceptable as he. Yet she felt nothing.

"Every girl feels exactly the same way. Ex-act-ly," said Diana, who, since the birth of her son, had an opinion on everything. "But that's no reason to refuse such a decent man." She surveyed Miriam insolently, head to foot. *"Labis el-'ud yajud."* Clothe a stick of wood and it will do well. Miriam had a lovely lithe body, while Diana grew fatter every year.

The evening before the ceremony, the Mishwe women prepared a henna mixture that they daubed on Miriam's hands, arms, and legs, and then wound them with cloth.

Jamilla had never been more maternal than on the morning of Miriam's wedding day. Gently, she removed the cloth from her daughter's legs and arms. She shooed away George and Salim, who were fascinated by their sister's flaming limbs and had begun to wrap each other in the stained muslin. Miriam sat quietly while her mother sponged her face, neck, and back, but then, quite suddenly, tears slipped down her cheeks and she took the rag away from Jamilla. "Mama, I'm frightened. I don't want to go and live with the Mishwes. Umm Jameel doesn't like me." She had a hundred protests, but this seemed the easiest to say.

"Of course she likes you. She chose you for her son. They act high-handed because of the money, but don't worry. Once you have a boy, you'll have some power, too."

"It isn't only Umm Jameel." She was crying harder, despairing that her mother didn't understand. "I don't want to be married. Mama, I can't help it. I know Nadeem is a fine man, but I don't want him. I don't know him at all. What does it matter if I don't marry? Please, Mama, please, don't make me go."

Jamilla looked worriedly toward the door. "The Mishwes will be here any minute." Then, seeing her daughter so desolate, she threw back her shoulders defiantly. She wasn't afraid of the Mishwes. "Let them come. They'll see we're not panting after them." She took Miriam in her arms. "You think marrying doesn't matter because you're young. But in a few years, you'll be the odd one." She picked at the edge of Miriam's under-shirt. "You'll get used to Nadeem. We've all gone through it and nobody went mad. Look at the Ajlouny girl. She hid in the fig huts for a week before marrying Hassan. She was covered with scrapes and thin as a rail at her wedding, but now does she go around weeping? No. Even in the worst cases, things work out."

"What about Mary Salamy? She couldn't marry the boy she loved?"

"Mary Salamy was a fool," said Jamilla decisively. "She made a big commotion. Her brother had to make a trip here from America to convince her. In the end, she married her cousin anyway. Now she has three children and a winter home in Jericho. Don't shed tears for Mary Salamy. Does she even remember the boy she loved? What does a young girl know about choosing a husband? This is a much more reliable method. Nadeem is part of our clan. He'll act honorably."

"Honorably? What does that have to do with me? What does that mean?"

Jamilla thought a moment. "This is the way things have been done for many, many years. We all survived. It will be all right in the end. Come and wash your face."

Would it be right in the end, she wondered? It was so easy to do what they wanted and so hard to resist. Surely her father wouldn't consent to something that would make her miserable. She rose with a sigh, held up her arms, and allowed her mother to slip on the red silk wedding dress.

When she was ready, Miriam stood in the center of the room she knew so well, with all of its familiar smells. The twins looked awed by her beauty. She wore a heavily embroidered vest over her wedding dress. A veil came down over her face and clasped in her hands was a sword, signifying that her family would defend her honor and her chastity.

Daud poked his head in the room. "You're going to ride the horse to the church? Watch out it doesn't run away," he grinned, uncomfortable in the role of well-wisher. Next came her grandmother to bid her a tearful farewell. At the last moment, Jamilla held her daughter in her arms and whispered softly against each cheek. *"Mabrook."* Tears formed again in Miriam's eyes. She took her mother's hand and kissed it.

Mustafa led her outside. Shyly, he touched her veil and pulled out her dress to admire it. That familiar face that had contorted and grimaced to make itself understood looked suddenly unsure. They had walked together all those years pushing the cart. Miles and miles of silence. She stood perfectly still, not trusting herself to speak. She thought he was going to help her mount the horse, but instead he walked a little way toward a copse of oaks and, before she could protest, she saw that he was crying. She had seen him shed tears only one other time, when he was rubbing salve into the insect bites she had received in Philistea.

Baba! Baba! For one thrilling moment, she thought she wouldn't go through with it, but then he came walking back to her, his face composed and smiling. He held her sword until she was safely mounted, then signed his message: "Every day, with all my heart, I will miss you. And each time I think of you, you will feel my blessing." She opened her eyes as wide as possible to stop the flood of tears and bent down to kiss her father one last time. Then, looking straight ahead with her body erect—it was here that she determined to withstand whatever came—holding the sword across her lap with one hand and the reins with the other, she started off toward the church while the rest of the family followed clapping and singing.

5

Come to bed.

The family had retired and left the lower room for the bride and groom. Over the mattress they had set a canvas bower on four sticks with flowers drooping down. Miriam and Nadeem continued to sit like a king and queen. All evening, Miriam had wished she could go to sleep in her familiar bed, but now she was wide awake. Nadeem got up and disappeared into the other room. She thought of how he had removed the paste from her face, the last ritual she had endured. He had anchored his fingers behind her ears and wiped her cheeks with his thumbs. She had been faintly comforted. Now the muscles in her face ached from false smiles. Phase after phase of events, each one nailing her in place.

"Come to bed." She jumped and stood immediately. He handed her the nightshirt his mother had bought as part of her trousseau. There was only the glow of the oil lamp, but she could see he was as tense as she. He left the room and she ran outside, thankful that the heavy door was unbolted. She breathed in, grateful for the sweet scented air, and waited.

"You don't wish to sleep?" He stood a few feet away.

"No." He deserved a kinder tone.

"What is it? The strange house?"

She wished he would stop talking and leave her alone. "Yes."

"You are welcome here. This is your home now," he said anxiously and then, laughing nervously, he added, "it's a nice home, too. Our mattress comes from France." He made a deprecating sound. "My mother succumbs to every promise of European merchandise. This mattress has little springs in it that make it unique. Like . . . well, they say it's like sleeping on a cloud. Perhaps you'll have an opinion in the morning." He waited for her to speak, but she made no sound. "Aren't you anxious to try it?"

"No."

"Were you planning to stand here all night?" His voice had begun to relax.

"Perhaps."

"Then I will have to stand with you."

"Why?" She was mildly surprised.

"In case of wolves. Or hyenas. Or swooping bats."

"Swooping bats?" She turned to him for the first time.

"Yes. Come here closer to me."

She didn't move, so he came closer to her and took her hand. He spoke in a serious tone, and she knew he was talking of their situation. "Don't be upset, Miriam."

"I'm not upset."

"But you're not happy."

"I'm quite happy," she said stubbornly. He put his arm around her shoulder and, for the first time, she didn't stiffen.

"I'm not so brave either, you know. We're new to it together." She felt the accumulated exhaustion of the previous week like an oppressive weight. She had no will left, and pride wasn't enough to withstand the pull of events. It was done. She was a married woman and had to obey her husband. Her shoulders slumped in defeat. He took the opportunity to turn her toward him and hold her in a loose embrace. "Let's go inside."

"Arrange your nightgown." Words made it worse. She made no attempt to move. "Arrange your nightgown." He said it kindly, repentantly. She turned and faced the wall. What worse thing could he do if she disobeyed him? She tried not to think of the whole world doing this. In every house. In every country. The Sultan. Dr. Malouf. She was aware of him pulling down the skirt he had so recently pulled up. One of her arms was out of its sleeve, and he tried gently to put it in its rightful place. When the gown was safely down, he kissed her cheek. "Everything will be all right."

When dawn came, she felt the bed shift and saw that he was sitting up, facing away from her. He felt the mattress move and turned to smooth her hair. Just go, she thought; then I can walk outside.

He brought one of the new dresses he had purchased for her and a new undershirt, which he placed on the bed. "These are for you." He left and she put on the clothes because she had nothing else there except the wedding dress. She had to urinate badly but saw no bedpan. Seeing the passage clear, she walked outdoors toward a copse. First she relieved herself and then sat on a stump, taking huge gulps of air.

"Look," said her mother-in-law, when she returned, "the hem of your new dress is all dirty. Come here, let me brush it for you. What a shame to get it dirty so quickly. Why were you out so early?"

"To get some air."

"Air? Air is everywhere. No need to go so far and dirty your dress."

"Shu ismak? What is your name?" Miriam turned around and saw a very old woman, Nadeem's grandmother, who was tugging at her arm to pull her down beside her.

"My name is Miriam."

"What? What did she say?" She turned to Nadeem and pulled him down beside her, too.

"My name is Miriam," she said again, loudly.

The old lady took a surprised breath. *"Shu?* She speaks like a man."

"All right, *khullus, Yuma.* Stop it." Nadeem's mother interrupted. "Drink your coffee."

Over his grandmother's head, Nadeem was studying Miriam's face. "You have such blue eyes." He laughed delightedly as if this were an unexpected bonus.

"They see as well as brown ones." She realized with shame this was Jamilla talking and tried to make amends by inspecting his eyes. "Yours are *asaleya*—honey-colored." She smiled and the look of gratitude on his face made her feel embarrassed.

A week later, when the last feast had been eaten and the last handkerchief full of coins counted, life settled down to what it would be. One morning, Nadeem said to his mother, "I'm leaving today and I won't return for three weeks."

"Why tell me?" She waved him away. "Tell your wife."

Miriam recoiled at this response. Umm Jameel invited confidences then chided the boys for their dependence on her.

"I will tell my wife," said Nadeem confidently, "but I will tell you, also. After all, I've been telling you where I'm going for twenty years."

"All right. All right." Umm Jameel, approached with such logic, retreated.

"Come," said Nadeem to Miriam, "let's go outside."

They walked in the direction of the Franciscan Monastery. He put his hand across her back for support. "You mustn't let my mother bully you," he said. "It's just a habit with her. She must say the harsh thing. It comes to her automatically. But she listens to reason when it is offered."

"It's all right. My mother does the same. Are you going to finish the church soon?"

"I doubt that it will ever be finished. It's a huge cathedral."

"What does a mason do?"

"He cuts stone and lays it in a course with mortar between the rows to embed it tightly."

"It sounds very difficult."

"It must be set straight, of course. And the mortar must be mixed properly and have an even thickness. Sometimes the design is intricate."

"Do you like this work?" She had just noticed he had a birthmark behind his left ear and that his ears, which had been exposed by his wedding haircut, were large but somehow balanced the shape of his face and gave him an overall pleasing appearance. She had also noted, in their short life together, that he bathed often and ate little for a man.

"I would enjoy my work more if I were in charge. I know more about working with *mizzi hulu* than the *muhandis,* the foreman who comes from France. He uses the wrong proportion of lime. But that's how it is. They bring foreigners to build the important buildings." He spoke as if he had put a distance between himself and the things he couldn't change.

"What sort of church are you building?"

"Greek. In a month, I'll stop and my brother and I will work as guides for the Easter season."

"And after that?"

"After that, I'll look for a business that will make us more wealthy."

"More wealthy?"

"Yes." The sun lit up his face and he looked young and earnest. "I'm a mason for the simple reason that my mother's family owns quarries. This is the easy way, but I'm not the master of my fate."

Not the master of his fate? He had chosen her. "But every man is the master of his fate, unless, of course, God intervenes."

"Well, I will intervene," he smiled.

"Look. Look how the grape leaf is falling apart." Umm Jameel held up the leaf and let the rice and pine nuts dribble out. "You must roll it neatly. Not too much stuffing. Then squeeze it." She stopped to demonstrate. "Like this."

This was part of being married—having your mother-in-law teach you to take care of her son. Zareefa, Jameel's wife and Miriam's new sister-in-law, strolled in and saved her from the row of limp boiled leaves. "What's the difference?" she commented airily, picking up a leaf and then letting it drop. "They'll eat it in five seconds, whether it's tightly wrapped or not." She stretched and yawned. Zareefa was ready to give birth and constantly sleepy. She wasn't beautiful, but her gracefulness and height made her seem so. She had slim hips, a dark, poreless complexion, and a beautiful large mouth.

Umm Jameel ignored Zareefa and redirected Miriam's attention to a squash in her hand. "You didn't hollow this properly. One side is lumpy, the other too thin." Miriam winced as her mother-in-law needlessly threw away the uneven squash.

The quality of life was different at the Mishwes. They were relaxed about money. Umm Jameel overbought food and then threw much away. The mattresses were covered in damask. The walls were smooth. The main room had two divans, although no one used them. She had heard the mattress maker say that no one in Jerusalem sat on the floor anymore, but on chairs. Everyone was wearing frock coats and trousers, so they couldn't sit cross-legged in comfort.

Zareefa rose, pushed her mother-in-law playfully on the shoulder. "Umm Jameel, leave the *kusah* and grape leaves and come with us for some air." She yawned again.

Umm Jameel shook her head but gave them a tolerant wave of her hand and went for the water jars. *"Tayib,* as long as you're strolling, bring back water."

"You certainly know how to handle her," said Miriam when they were out on the road. It was the same town, but the vistas were different. There was a charming glen on the side of the road. Now, in midwinter, with plenty of rain in the ground, the lavender crocus crept around the rocks, and tender shoots of wild anemones crisscrossed the slopes.

"We have a truce," said Zareefa circumspectly. "As long as I might be carrying her grandson, she'll leave me alone. But," she laughed ruefully, "God help me if it's a girl. Anyway," she added airily, "Nadeem will make a lot of money and build you a fine home away from Umm Jameel."

"Do you think it's possible?" In all of her thoughts of escape, Miriam had never considered this.

"With Nadeem, it's possible," she said decisively. "With Jameel, no. Jameel lives to eat and drink. But Nadeem is methodical. He will go, step by step, building something. He's too serious, but you can change that." Miriam didn't respond. "It wasn't a love match?" asked Zareefa delicately.

"He was chosen by my parents. My mother was very joyful."

"But not Miriam."

"In the end, perhaps it doesn't matter. Those that marry for love learn to hate, and those that start out not loving perhaps learn to do so." She was repeating, word for word, something Dr. Ma'luf said to her before the wedding.

"For Nadeem, it was a love match. He looks at you adoringly. You have an unusual voice. It drives men crazy."

Miriam blushed. "His grandmother doesn't think so. She keeps asking if I'm a man."

Zareefa laughed. They continued to the spring, but midway Zareefa began to have pains and they returned without the water. Umm Jameel changed her expression. "Is it true? Is it coming now?"

"Yes. It's coming."

Umm Jameel was quarreling with the midwife who wanted Zareefa to sit in a contraption that resembled a chair with a hole in the middle. "The baby will drop down through this hole," said the midwife.

"*Shu . . . megnuneh, ente.* You're crazy. Get out," said Umm Jameel.

"Please," argued the midwife. "I know what I'm doing. Every lady in Jerusalem is having her baby this way."

"Every *megnuneh,*" said Umm Jameel. She turned to her sister who had arrived. "Please, Halla, get Doctor Ma'luf to recommend someone else. Hurry."

Her aunt, the sheik's wife, arrived and she took Umm Jameel out to the garden. "Zareefa is safe. Don't worry. This is a better position for the baby to come out. Lying down puts the baby in the wrong direction."

"Suppose he falls on the floor?"

"The midwife will catch him. Any one of us can catch him."

"We did it the old way for thousands of years."

"Perhaps not. Perhaps only in our lifetime."

"*Yullah, khullus,*" said Umm Jameel. "Let's go inside."

In the center of the room was the wooden chair with a crescent-shaped hole in the seat and, under it, a large bowl of water. The midwife squatted beside it. Zareefa sat upright. Rivulets of sweat ran down her back and collected momentarily in the dimples above her round pink buttocks, which were framed by the chair in a provocative way. "I feel like pushing," she said. Her voice was childishly excited.

"Not until I say," replied the midwife curtly. Her hand felt Zareefa's belly. "Now it's very hard! Push, push, push! Stop! No more for now!"

There was half an hour more of pushing and stopping, and then the midwife went under the chair and became very busy. "*Tayib,* it's coming. *Ya Allah,* look. Such a beautiful face. Come on, one more big push. *Yullah,* come on." She eased out a shoulder, the body, and finally the legs. But there were no more exultant cries. It was a girl.

Umm Jameel took the baby. "It's only the first," she said with a sigh. "She'll help her mother with the others. She's healthy, *salamu aleiki.* Let God give her happiness."

When the others had gone inside to eat, Miriam took the baby in her arms. The feel of the infant overwhelmed her. This magical being could insure her happiness. She was so perfectly formed. The mouth was like a small double-peaked heart. The skin was softer than the fleece of a newborn lamb. She wanted one just like this. That would make everything right.

When Nadeem came home for his leave, she was eager for night to come. She arranged herself on the bed in what she considered a friendly position.

Eight months after her wedding, Miriam passed her seventeenth birthday and noticed by the hem of her dress that she had grown an inch or two. She noticed also that her breasts were fuller and her waist thicker, but it wasn't until her sister-in-law mentioned the possible cause that she realized she might be pregnant.

"When did you bleed last?" asked Zareefa.

"I don't know. Two months. Perhaps more."

"Perhaps 'more' is the correct answer. Let me see your profile. Pull your dress tight around your stomach. Aha, there you are. You're pregnant and you didn't know it."

Khalil Nadeem Mishwe was born on the third day of the new century. The narcissus were already pushing through patches of snow, promising an early spring. It was a long labor, for he was facing up. "This one will be mama's boy," said the midwife with frustration. "He doesn't want to come out." She tried all her tricks to make him rotate, but in the end, she put her hand in and turned him. "He won't be easy to raise," were her parting words. Afterward, Zareefa told Miriam that her screams could be heard in Nablus.

He was a serious-faced little boy with his father's gray-brown eyes and grandmother Jamilla's palid skin. He looked nothing like Miriam. He could have been anyone's child. Instead of the sweet downy angel she had envisioned, she'd gotten a cranky colicky boy, who spit up the precious few ounces of milk his mother had made and then howled for more. Each day, Miriam guided her short, tender nipple into his mouth and each day he remained unfulfilled. He screamed and gnawed on his fist. After a week of the noise, Miriam gave him to a wetnurse.

Everyone was waiting to make a fuss—the first grandson—but Khalil didn't do well with strangers. Even his father made him cry but that was to be expected, for Nadeem was away for weeks at a time. Miriam washed the baby, swaddled him neatly, rubbed his limbs with olive oil and salt as her mother had taught her. When he slept, she washed his clothes and cooked for the wetnurse.

"Leave him with me," Zareefa urged her. "Go out by yourself." But

Miriam couldn't relax, knowing he was capable of crying himself into a rage for several hours.

One day, she found Khalil smiling broadly and burst into tears. When the baby saw her crying, his chin began to wobble. "I'm sorry," she said. "I frightened you. Don't cry." She rocked him in her arms and kissed his wet cheeks. He hiccuped a few times and then smiled again.

Not long after, Miriam noticed that in the afternoon, when Khalil took his nap, she no longer had the energy to wash and cook. Without intending it, she would curl up beside him and sleep, too. After a week of this seductive fatigue, she realized, with less joy than the first time, that she was pregnant again.

6

It's time for us to move.

In the spring of 1900, the new government road to Nablus reached Tamleh, and Ibrahim Abu Shihady initiated horse-drawn carriage service to the Jaffa Gate for a fare of thirty cents. If a traveler brought his chickens and other belongings, the smells together with the motion unsettled some of the occupants, and it was common to see ashen faces hanging out of windows. The service was a great convenience to everyone, especially the sick who needed to make the journey to a hospital.

Some workers from Bethlehem who built the government road where it passed Tamleh told of a far-away country called America, where men from their village had gone to make their fortunes and were sending large sums back to their relatives. A few men from Tamleh emigrated to the States, and stories of their success caused a painful awakening in some of the young men who were left behind, including Nadeem. He finished the church at Madaba and joined his brother as a guide for the Easter pilgrims, but he was preoccupied. The stories had kindled his ambition.

Miriam was busy with Khalil, and the new pregnancy kept her feeling unsettled. The Sisters of Mar Yusef had received four sewing machines from America and invited the neighborhood women to learn to sew. Miriam and Zareefa made European-style trousers, but the pair intended for Nadeem had one leg slightly shorter than the other. "Nadeem loves you," Zareefa teased. "He's wearing those terrible trousers." He wore the trousers every day and Miriam knew she wasn't the cause of his restlessness.

One night, Nadeem announced at dinner that he was going to build a house for his family. He would put it up himself, he said. His mother stopped eating. "And where do you propose to get the money to pay for this new home?"

"I have enough money to start," answered Nadeem, deliberately filling his mouth with food. It was the custom for young men to build their homes one room at a time, as finances allowed.

"A start? Why start what you can't finish. And what is a start? A wall? Two walls? What good will that do? You can't live inside two walls. You must have four. Plus a roof." She let him digest this information so he could better appreciate her conclusion. "And if there are four walls and a roof, that's an entire room. Not a start."

"What's wrong?" asked his father. "There's plenty of room here."

"There isn't plenty of room," said Nadeem. "It's crowded and will become more so with the new baby. Besides, Miriam is anxious to have her own home."

Miriam looked up, startled. They had never discussed a home. Umm Jameel threw her a look. "It isn't crowded," she said flatly. "Zareefa and Jameel have moved out."

"Will you be happy with a home of your own?" he asked Miriam when they were alone.

"It's what every woman would wish." She had no way of knowing if he was being foolish or not. Could she depend on him? "But what about the expense? Do we have the money?" It occurred to her that she had no idea if they had money or how much.

"It will only be one room at first, but we can add to it," said Nadeem.

"Of course. That's all I would expect." As the idea grew, she became excited. It would be wonderful to have a home of her own! To decide how it would look and to furnish it. "Do you really believe we can do it?"

He was delighted to see her happy. "Yes, I do. In fact, I'm certain of it."

Nadeem ordered a load of *mizzi hulu,* the hard white limestone that held well with lime cement and was the best for home-building. He had the advantage of experience with masonry, but building a house was a haphazard affair. There were no village regulations, no engineers, and no architects. The first task was to dig a hole and make a rainwater cistern, but since this would take precious time away from the main structure, he started with the room.

The wheat harvest was only five weeks away and the fruit harvests would follow, but the haste worked in his favor. He had helped many cousins to build, and now they were willing to return the favor.

Miriam was interested in every bit of progress and visited the site daily. Mentally, she divided the space . . . we'll sleep here . . . Khalil there. The table will be here, the *khabbiya* there.

Nadeem could work on his house only two days at a time, the other days, he took the dusty walk to Jerusalem to act as a guide. Unlike Jameel, who welcomed the carriage ride, he preferred to walk and think. Chagrined that his ambitions had no ready opportunity, he had rebellious thoughts. His parents hadn't prepared him to be competitive or ambitious.

Nadeem's own father was content to farm a second-rate vineyard, which produced inferior grapes. He walked with a small broom with which he swept the dung or snow—depending on the season—from the approach to the Franciscan chapel where he sat and prayed daily. Nadeem wondered what his father prayed for, since his life didn't change. He and Jameel had been educated without foresight. Father Kuta had come to start the Latin Church and scoured the households to fill his school, hoping to attract the parents away from the Greeks. He and Jameel had learned to read and write, to add and subtract, to decipher the Psalter in French, and they had acquired a crude knowledge of European history. They knew nothing of the culture of the ruling Ottomans.

When Nadeem became old enough to serve in the Turkish army, his father had paid a head tax through their sheik to have someone else serve in his place. Perhaps Nadeem would have been better off going into the army and seeing something of the world. Perhaps he wouldn't feel so naive.

Opportunity came in the person of M. Freneau, a vivacious businessman from Paris who wanted to visit Jesus' childhood home in Nazareth. It was a lengthy trip that required an overnight stay. When they camped for the night, M. Freneau asked to share Nadeem's sweet-smelling olive oil soap and was so appreciative of its aroma and benefits that he asked to keep the bar. "I'd like to take some back to France," he said.

"I'll bring all I have to your hotel," Nadeem offered graciously.

Two weeks after M. Freneau returned to France, Nadeem received a cable at the Hotel St. Anslem, which was his base. SEND SOON STOP TEN GROSS MT. CARMEL SOAP STOP EXCELLENT MARKET HERE STOP. GOOD PROFIT FOR YOU STOP LETTER OF CREDIT TO COME STOP.

Nadeem went to the Crédit Lyonnaise and the Deutsche Palestina Bank, but no letter of credit had come through in his name. There was nothing from France at the Austrian post office, either. He had spent his funds on his house. Ten gross of soap, together with the shipping charges, would come to at least one hundred dollars. He would have to believe that, having sent the soap and expended the money, M. Freneau would honor the debt and add a profit. He stopped in the Church of the Holy Sepulcher to think, sitting by himself in one of the side chapels. He remembered that M. Freneau prayed like a child with his hands together, pointing up. He slept on his back, his arms and legs spread out, as if inviting only kindness from the world. He had told Nadeem that he sold lingerie and fine linens in a shop on a wide boulevard in the heart of Paris.

That night, he asked Miriam for the money she had received for their wedding. "It's temporary. I'll return it to you." She went to the chest where she kept her belongings—her special clothes and jewelry—and pulled out a small kerchief knotted tightly to hold twenty gold lira. To spend money for pleasure was considered foolish, so what else was there to do with the money? She gave it to her husband.

The roofing bee for their new house took place just twenty-three days after they had begun, and ten days later they were able to sleep under it.

How different were her feelings in this pleasant room where everything was hers. She knew each slight indentation in the flat stones that Nadeem had fit so expertly to make a charming floor. The room was large and airy with the daring addition of a mezzanine that allowed extra space for sleeping. The walls were smooth and whitewashed, and there were four windows for a cross breeze. The nooks and shelves he built ingeniously into the walls held bedding and cooking pots, and she kept busy rearranging her belongings. She picked flowers, swept the floors, polished, and puffed. Put the chairs first against one wall and, later, against another. She washed and scoured and then viewed the results with an interest that never jaded.

When Nadeem arrived in the evenings, she could hardly wait to show him new curtains or a new arrangement in a corner of the room. As she waited to see him approaching up the old pilgrim road, she thought, I'm eager for him to arrive. It was very confusing. If she didn't love him, why did she feel so satisfied when he ate the food she cooked? And if she did love him, why did she still have moments of intense longing and restlessness? These feelings seemed unnatural. Nothing more was waiting for her. How could her heart play such tricks on her?

One day Miriam walked to her mother-in-law's at dawn to help prepare for a Sunday dinner. The families were constantly visiting and it was unthinkable not to remain for the midday meal. On this morning, she and Umm Jameel had rolled out triangles of dough and filled them with diced lamb or wilted spinach and onions. Miriam took the filled dough to the *taboon,* together with open round loaves spread with *zatar* spice and oil, and waited for them to bake.

Jameel and Zareefa came, and so did Umm Jameel's sister, her sons, and their families.

Zareefa took Khalil on her lap and clapped his dimpled hands together. "Let's see this big boy," she said. To Miriam's surprise, he allowed himself to be kissed. "You've been cooking since dawn," said Zareefa to Miriam.

Miriam inclined her head toward her mother-in-law. She had become more tolerant of Umm Jameel, who in turn was not so quick to criticize the mother of one son, with another possibly on the way. "First the wheat for the tabuleh was too soggy and had to be replaced. Then the dough for the pies didn't rise enough." Miriam yawned unexpectedly and felt lightheaded.

"You're pregnant again, I almost forgot. Me, too. Perhaps we'll have them together. You another boy and I another girl." Zareefa's voice was high with anxiety. She cared deeply about her standing in the clan.

Umm Jameel, looking flushed and weary, finally sat down. It was a crowded table and everyone became engrossed in eating, with the children scampering in between. For a moment, it was quiet.

"I've begun a new enterprise," said Nadeem suddenly.

"Oh . . . what is that?" His mother stopped eating.

"I had a Frenchman to Nazareth, and he was enchanted with the Mt. Carmel soap. He cabled to send ten gross, which I did yesterday."

"He sent you money for them?" asked his father.

"Not yet. Just the cable requesting the soap."

"You sent the soap before he sent the money?" asked Umm Jameel.

"Yes," said Nadeem. "A letter of credit is coming."

There was an uncomfortable silence. "How could you be so foolish?" said Umm Jameel, pushing away her plate.

"I don't believe it was foolish," said Nadeem calmly. "He will pay."

"Why should he pay? He has no need to pay. He has the soap, which he will sell." Umm Jameel answered her own pointed questions and became more agitated as her monologue progressed.

"He will pay because he will want more soap," Nadeem answered logically.

"More soap? Why does he have to get more soap from you? He can get more soap from anybody. There are many who will send him more soap. But I can tell you that none of them will send it without getting payment first. He'll get more soap, but not from you. He'll find another . . ."— Nadeem's father sent her a warning look, but she continued— "fool to send it to him."

The silence resumed. Miriam's face burned with indignation, but to speak in her husband's defense would be more disruptive. Besides, she, too, thought Nadeem had acted unwisely, though she would never say so. The children, alerted to the tension, chewed slowly and stared. Nadeem left the table and walked out into the afternoon sunlight. Umm Jameel rose and followed. "Yes, fool," she reiterated, in case he had forgotten. "How could you do such a thing? Why didn't you ask for advice?"

Nadeem reentered the room with his mother behind him. "It wasn't foolish," he said calmly. "I know the man will pay. I didn't act in a stupid way and you can't speak about something that you know nothing about."

"We shall see, Mr. Businessman," said Umm Jameel, but all the rancor was gone from her voice. "All right, come and eat. It's done."

"It's done and we shall see," said Nadeem and resumed his place at the table and began to eat.

Miriam was glad to return to her uncluttered house with the bundle of extra food that Umm Jameel had packed for her. Three times she opened her mouth to ask about the soap venture, but she closed it again. Nothing good could come from discussing it. She couldn't clarify her feelings about it. It was exciting to think he would succeed, but she had qualms.

"Aren't you going to see if there's mail?" She had waited two weeks to ask the question. The mail came from Jerusalem to Tamleh every other Thursday and was distributed in the village square near the tomb of el-Khalil. Those in a hurry went to Jerusalem, either to the Turkish postal building or to the several foreign post offices maintained by the Europeans.

"I won't wait anxiously, only to come home empty-handed," he explained calmly. "If a letter comes, it will find me." The days lengthened into weeks, and no letter found him.

A month after the Easter season was over, the yellow heads appeared on the grains of wheat. Everyone left home and went to the fields—men, women, children, and babies in their cradles. Farmers reaped simultaneously by law and all willing hands were hired. Nadeem gladly took part, for his funds were depleted.

Miriam's pregnancy made her feel queasy and sapped her energy, but nearly half the women in the village were pregnant and all of them helped in the harvest. They had to leave their lovely clean homes and stay in the *kasr,* which was no more than a crude stone hut filled with flies and the stench of dead animals who had crawled in during the winter. After one night fighting the odors, Miriam and Nadeem chose to sleep out-of-doors, as did many of the reapers, holding Khalil between them. After several hours of stooping in the fields, much of the time with Khalil in a sling on her hip, Miriam's lower back sent out angry protests. She awoke to pain and felt it worsen as the day wore on. Some days the sun was so intense that it made the air buzz and sizzle, but the nights were always blessedly cool. The night mist made the ground damp and cold, but they prayed for it so the grains wouldn't become brittle and fall to the ground. Twice a day, the women started a little fire and held some of the wheat heads over it, rubbing off the husks between their hands and then feasting on the new wheat.

There was some benefit in being busy all day and in new surroundings. Khalil seemed content to be out of their routine and adjusted well to the bustle around him.

There was a respite before the grapes and figs were ready and the Mishwes returned home to the comfort of a bed. Two days before they were to start out again, Nadeem brought a package for Miriam. When she failed to open it, he undid it himself and she saw that it contained a heavily embroidered vest. She left it lying where he put it and said nothing. Something about that gaudy item made her despair. The house still had no proper kitchen or cistern. He had used all of her money for the soap, and now he had wasted some of their meager funds on a useless vest. "Where would I wear such a thing?" she asked at the last possible moment before they went to sleep. Even as she said it, she remembered her own mother excoriating her father in the same bitter tone, but she was too anxious for the future to feel immediate remorse. Her pregnancy made the vest even more ludicrous.

Nadeem began to bounce the vest in his large hand as if it were growing heavier. "Wear it to visit your mother. Or for the feast of Nebi Musa."

"My mother would have more to say about it than I." She lay down and turned her body away from him.

"Well," he said, still good-humored, "I could try to sell it. Give it to Sahadi to put in his shop."

"Do that then, for I've no use for it." She had not meant to sound so harsh, but his dogged good humor made her anxious. She had put her faith and future in the hands of a man who was not realistic. As she lay there, battling her own thoughts, his breathing became rhythmic. A jackal filching grapes from a nearby orchard sounded his stupid, mournful cry. The baby gave a solid kick against her back, sending a ping of pain through her legs. She began to cry softly into her pillow. In the morning, the vest was gone.

The grape harvest was the happiest of the season beginning in late summer. The *kasr* in the orchards where Nadeem and Miriam slept was slightly cleaner and more comfortable than the one in the wheat fields. There was a tiny sunken pit for a cooking fire and another to hide the drying crop. All the Mishwes came, even Umm Jameel; and Miriam felt more carefree than she had the entire summer. Zareefa made light of everything. "Don't worry if he lost the money," she said to Miriam, mentioning the unmentionable. "He'll make it again." She poked all around Miriam's stomach. "What? Are you having twins? You're so big, and still four months to go."

The best grapes in Palestine came from Tamleh and Hebron. Even through the fiercest heat, the clusters grew succulent and abundant. They hired a dozen girls from the countryside to help with sorting and preparing the raisins, first softening them in lye water to tenderize the skin and then coating them with olive oil to keep the insects away. The Mishwes dried almost their entire crop and sold it to the Germans, who provided the crates for shipment and paid three cents a pound. The rest of the crop, sold as table grapes, were transported to Jaffa in panniers, by donkey.

Nadeem and Miriam worked continuously through August and into September. All three were browned from the sun, and Khalil's fine baby hair was bleached at the ends. It was an adjustment to go back to their house. There was still no word from France and Nadeem's spirits were less buoyant. He had to make a decision whether to take another mason's job working on a new Franciscan building in Bethel, where he would earn a dollar a day, or to stick with his plan to find a more open-ended way to earn a living.

One evening, Nadeem asked his father-in-law for the use of the wagon. He spent a day or two amassing merchandise from village farmers and artisans. Before dawn on the third day, he packed the wagon carefully with a dozen crates of figs and raisins, some of the clay *makilas* that Jirius sold in his shop, packing them with straw so they wouldn't knock together, some shoes in various sizes from the shoemaker, some mats and rugs from the weavers on El Megnuneh Street and several jars of freshly pressed olive oil. Without asking questions, Miriam rose and made him coffee. When she realized he wouldn't volunteer where he was going, she packed some food for him—olives, cheese and bread, and a few sweets and fruit. He left without a word and she watched him clatter down the path that led to the carriage road until he was out of sight.

He returned three days later and the wagon was empty. His face was ashen with fatigue and his eyes red and vacant.

"Are you ill?" She wanted to ask a dozen questions, but his manner kept her silent.

"I'm not ill," he answered with unnatural curtness. "I'm just tremendously tired. If you could just make me a cup of tea . . ." When she brought the tea, he was already asleep.

He had fallen into bed as he was and he slept for fourteen hours. The next day, he repeated the process of gathering goods, packing the wagon, leaving with them before dawn, only to return several days later with an empty wagon. Miriam had no idea where he went, where he slept. From the look of him—he always returned filthy and pale—she surmised that he walked, pulling the donkey along, and slept out-of-doors, if at all, guarding his merchandise. When Umm Jameel found out her son was peddling from village to village, she was very agitated.

"A *mugahbeen,*" she wailed. *Mugahbeen,* for the word "danger," was the name given to those who traveled through the dangerous defiles between mountains. His mother had a right to be frightened. The next time he left with his wagon, he was robbed.

When Miriam saw him approaching, still several yards away, she was certain it was a stranger bent on harming her. He was caked with mud, and it had obliterated any color or design in the fabric of his clothes. His hair, too, was matted with mud, and his face crisscrossed with perspiration streaks made him look sinister. *"Ya Allah!"* Miriam put her hand to her mouth to keep from screaming and, then, when she realized it was Nadeem, she froze in place. "Don't touch me." He held out a hand to stop her from approaching. "I have to bathe."

"I'll heat some water," she whispered and turned away, but not before she saw a look in his eyes that made her heart lurch and her eyes fill. It was a look she had never seen on his face before. He looked frightened as a child and also . . . defeated.

When he was bathed and had drunk three cups of hot tea, he told her to throw away the clothes he had taken off. "I don't want them," he said vehemently. "Burn them. I struggled in those clothes against . . . against fate. Against injustice!" His face reddened with emotion.

"Against fate?" she asked mystified.

"The ones who took my money and the goods, they weren't stealing from Nadeem Mishwe. They had no grudge against me. I was just an opportunity to them. A faceless source of easy wealth. Gratuitous, random evil. That makes it worse."

"You weren't the master of your fate?" she asked in a soft, sympathetic voice. She remembered that conversation in the beginning of their marriage when he told her laughingly that he would intervene with fate to bring wealth into their lives. As she considered her husband's once trusting face now twisted with disappointment, she felt a battle within herself as well. She wanted to believe in him, but it was difficult. Perhaps he was wrong not to go back to his trade.

She was against his going again, but his dark determination kept her from speaking her mind. A few days later, when she saw him gathering more merchandise, she handed him a gun. "My father brought this for you. He says you shouldn't go again without it."

"I don't want a gun. The idea of killing someone . . . I don't know. Perhaps, it's better not to have a weapon."

"Please, Nadeem, take it." And when he still hesitated, "Do it because I ask it of you."

"All right." He brought her against him and buried his face in her hair. She became aware of his unique smell and the way he felt against her when they were upright . . . his shoulder blades, the strength of his arms. It was so seldom that they touched each other outside of the bedroom. Even to say good-bye. He took the gun and slipped it inside his wide belt. "I'll take it because you want me to."

In the late fall of 1900, the sirocco lasted three weeks. Each morning, the clouds collected in dark groups above the mountain tops. On the worst day, the wind formed into columns and coated every surface with grit. Miriam, alone and seven months pregnant, couldn't shake the feeling that evil was in store and tried to dispel her anxiety by giving her precious room a thorough cleaning. She removed the furniture to do a better job. She placed the brine pots and store jars out last, covering the mouths with linen and intending to bring them in quickly. She dry washed the smooth walls from ceiling to floor and did the same to the floors, feeling gratified to see the beautifully fitted stones free of dust. She rolled up the straw mats and beat them over a line that Nadeem had strung between two trees in the back.

In the midst of replacing the rugs, she heard a shrill scream from the courtyard. Khalil, who had learned to pull himself upright and take a few steps, had fallen and skinned his knee. It wasn't a serious scrape, but a pebble had become embedded in the softness of his flesh and removing it caused bleeding and heightened her apprehension. She washed the wound and spent the next half hour restraining him from going outside to dirty it again. She felt less anxious indoors, away from the angry weather, and they lay down together on her bed and both fell asleep.

As the sun was setting, Nadeem returned from one of his trips. He was more exhausted than usual, dragging one foot after the other as if the next step would be his last. He neared the house and was greeted by a rancid stench so powerful, he walked around to find the source. It was the cheese that was causing the worst odor, but the coverings had blown off all the food jars and the contents were covered with a scum of brownish-gray dust.

"Miriam!" He began calling while still outside. He had never raised his voice to her, but the sight of so much waste appalled him. "Miriam!"

She awoke disoriented and felt for Khalil, who had drifted to the end of the bed. The bandage was blood soaked and had stained the bed covering.

"Miriam!" What now? Another accident. She didn't remember ever hearing that urgent quality in her husband's voice. The room was still in disarray, rugs half rolled, the bins in the middle of the room. "Look at this!" Nadeem was holding one of the cheese pots. "Have you lost your senses? Why would you put food outdoors in this weather? What were you thinking of?"

She couldn't answer him. A wave of humiliation began at the front of her head and spread like a wash of shameful paint over her body. "I was cleaning," she offered softly. He looked so dirty and bedraggled, she barely recognized him. His eyes looked haunted and the pupils were unnaturally large.

"Cleaning what?" All the cheese for the winter is ruined. All the work for nothing. He went out of the house and began dumping the contents of each pot, repeating the words "a waste of money, a waste of time." Miriam tried to embrace the pots to stop him. "Wait! Perhaps it can be saved." She held his arm but he shrugged her off so violently, she had to grab his shirt not to fall. "Please, wait!" But he wasn't listening. With unusual strength, he was able to lift the largest jars and fling their contents to the winds. Within minutes, all of their winter's stores—the lentils and wheat, the olives and cheese, the olive oil, the pickled vegetables, the beans, the dried fruit—everything was strewn over the parched earth.

At that time of year, the flocks had been driven far inland, looking for ever-vanishing greenery and water. A little later, the milk would be needed for the newborn in the flock. Goats' milk would remain virtually unavailable until early December. Almost in mockery, the wind changed direction, and a velvety warmth caressed their skin. Nadeem's spent anger and fatigue were palpable. It was more than the loss of the food. Miriam wanted to help him. But instead—oh, God, against her will—she also wanted to make it worse.

"You're one to talk of waste," she began in a breathless voice. "I made a mistake. Khalil was hurt and I became distracted, but I didn't willfully send merchandise to a stranger with no hope of being paid for it. I didn't do anything that foolish." As she was uttering the words, her heart was sinking in sorrow. It was exactly this recrimination that had seemed so cruel coming from Umm Jameel.

Instead of angering him, the accusation made him calm. "I should not have been so harsh," he said thoughtfully. "I wouldn't have scolded you except that I'm unusually tired, and the walk home in these dust storms is almost unbearable. But as for your opinion that I acted like a fool, you're mistaken. M. Freneau will pay for the merchandise and generously, too. Where I have been a fool is in expecting a wife to have understanding and loyalty. That's where I was cheated." With this, he walked toward the house. It was only after they were both back inside and she had begun the fire for tea that she saw the gash on his cheek and another on his arm, which was bulging at an odd angle. "You're hurt." She sucked in her breath, at a loss as to what to do first.

"I was attacked at Abu Ghush," he said dully. "Three of them against me, but they didn't kill me, which is a blessing. However," he added in a quivering voice, "I killed one of them." She put his face next to her breasts and inspected the wound as if he were a child. "It needs cleaning." She went in search of a clean rag and water and dabbed at the wound repeatedly until he cried out in pain.

"Gently," he admonished. "No need to scrub it."

"Ya Allah," she said tearfully. "I'm sorry."

He fell asleep as she worked on him, and she had to drag him to the bed and arrange him. He slept almost twenty hours, during which she ran in frequently to watch over him. When he had slept himself out, he prepared to walk to Bethel to see if they could still use a mason for the Franciscan building. "I have to go back to masonry, after all," he said. "I want to live to see our new child." His voice had the leaden evenness of defeat.

"You'll think of something else," she said reassuringly, but it sounded hollow. "Perhaps at another time of year, it won't be so dangerous."

"I have no heart to risk the road," he said with as much dignity as he could muster. "It isn't a good idea for a man who wants to remain alive."

Miriam baked fresh bread for his food pack at dawn. She stood on the dusty road and looked after him until he was a small dot of color in the distance. Twice she called out to him on the pretense that she had forgotten some inconsequential news, but she really wanted to see his face once more and reassure him that he had not failed in her eyes.

No blows could have hurt her as much as his calm forgiveness for her outburst. He was a decent man who worked hard to make their life as secure as possible, and she had paid him by insulting him.

The carriage was jostling her so, she held her stomach protectively, fearful it might bring the baby prematurely. Khalil had fallen asleep against her, but when they reached Jaffa Gate she put him in a sling, carried him on her hip, and walked inside the walls to St. James Road. As she passed the ancient cathedral of the same name, she shuddered. It was said that the martyred Apostle James's head was entombed there.

Past the old Crusaders' Church of St. Thomas was a screened window with metal bars, behind which was located a branch of the Austrian post office. Once or twice a week, mail from Europe arrived in Jaffa by boat. At daybreak, a three-horse carriage brought it to the line of hopeful persons waiting for letters or packages. Consulates and patriarchates would send their *jawasses*, the armed protectors assigned to foreign delegates by the Turkish government, to receive their mail. The heads of Jewish institutions, dependent on outside financial aid, were always in line. After these came the private citizens who waited for the clerk to call out their name. "A letter for Hanna the weaver" or "A packet for Yusef the barber," he would shout. Addresses were imprecise: "the third house behind Christ Church" or "in back of the Pool of Hezekiah."

During the day, while Nadeem was in Bethel, Miriam had begun her secret trips, telling Zareefa that she was going for the heated tiles in the bathhouse to ease a painful back. Some days, she left Khalil—screaming—with Zareefa, so she could walk the distance and save the carriage fare. On her third visit, she had waited patiently through the distribution. As always, she was fascinated by the personal dramas that took place. There was a letter for David the blacksmith from his cousin in Brazil. Nabile the carpenter had received some tools from Germany. Farida Saah received a letter from her daughter living in America, and she began to cry so loud and hard, none of the others could hear the mail caller. Finally, someone realized she was crying because she couldn't read the letter, and a young man offered to do it for her.

When all the mail had been distributed, the postal official returned to his warren of mail slots behind the counter and began to shuffle and reshuffle several soiled and tattered envelopes. Miriam approached the counter but was too embarrassed by her obvious pregnancy to speak.

"Madam?"

"We are expecting mail from France." As with anyone who had never heard her speak, the man immediately took a closer look, intrigued by that haunting sound. "In whose name, madam?"

"In the name of Mishwe. Nadeem Mishwe. Perhaps the address is the Hotel St. Anslem, outside the walls, on Louis Botta Road. It would come from France. Paris, France."

He took the envelopes he had been shuffling and inspected each one closely. Suddenly, he grunted triumphantly. "That is the name. You see," he directed Miriam's gaze to the spot with his finger. "Right here. Mishwe. The *M* and the *i* are almost gone, the ink has been washed out. The hotel returned it to us. This mail has been on two trips, madam. Why didn't you inquire before?"

"We don't live nearby," she said distractedly, not daring to take her eyes off the envelope.

"Well, here you are, then. One mystery completed. I wish all the rest would be united to their owners. I don't like to have mail left uncollected."

"Thank you," said Miriam. The envelope was so undistinguished, she felt none of the exhilaration she assumed would result from the letter. She tucked it in her sack and began the trek home. When she had fed Khalil and put him to sleep, she looked closely at the envelope. On the back was printed *M. Freneau et Frères, La Maison de Trousseau, 22 Avenue Victor Hugo, Paris, France.*

She went down the road to meet Nadeem and began calling to him, waving the letter in the air. "From France," she called. "Europe."

He examined the envelope and looked quizzically at Miriam. "How did it come?"

"I went to Jerusalem for it."

"What prompted you to go today?"

"It wasn't just today. I've been going for several weeks."

"I see." He stared at her face, which appeared almost detached in the pink light of dusk.

"Today I got the idea to ask the postal clerk. As it turned out, the envelope had gotten wet and part of the name was obscured. Since it was addressed to the hotel, they had no idea whom it was for and sent it back to the post office. It's been lying there, unclaimed."

"You believed that Freneau would respond?"

"Yes." Not always. "It didn't seem likely after all this time, but I was compelled to go. I wanted to be the one to get it for you."

He put his arms around her and embraced her as best he could, for her belly kept him at a distance. "Let's eat dinner," he said, "and then we'll open it."

"You're going to wait to open it?" she asked, incredulous.

"If it's bad news, it will spoil my appetite. If it's good news, it will be just as good on a full stomach."

"Bad news? How could it be bad news?"

"Perhaps he was wrong. Perhaps he couldn't sell the soap."

When he opened the envelope, a bank note fell out and, with it, a letter:

My dear Mishwe,

Your prompt shipment was gratefully received. As I expected, the soap was an immediate success. Each customer who bought it brought in five more who wished it as well. We were able to charge thirty cents per bar and even this was conservative, given the demand. It would have gone for twice the price. In any case, the receipts for ten gross came to roughly four hundred fifty dollars. I am sending you half this amount, plus thirty dollars to cover your shipping costs.

If you are agreeable, I could dispose of ten gross three times a year.

Yours most sincerely,
Pierre Freneau

Nadeem stared at the bank note a long time. "I can repay the money you loaned me," he said finally.

"It isn't necessary," she said. As he had been reading, she had remembered all the moments when he had reiterated his faith in the Frenchman and had received only skepticism.

"I will repay it," he repeated. "And we will build a proper kitchen and our own cistern, so you won't have to go to the spring so often."

"I would like a divan," she said unexpectedly.

"A divan?"

"Yes. I would like to put it over against the wall with a lamp next to it. When Khalil is ready, he can read there. I feel sad that I never kept up with my reading and numbers. I want Khalil to be at ease with reading. Not to always struggle as I do."

Nadeem looked at his wife a long time. Her face had a different look each day. Some days pale and distant, with the blue eyes so dark they resembled the sky just before the stars became visible. Now, however, she appeared tenderly young and trusting. "Very well," he said, his heart aching with love, "a divan, too."

She didn't miss the catch in his voice and she, too, felt a new emotion—a letting go—a desire to give herself to him.

When the building at Bethel was completed, Nadeem abandoned masonry once and for all and worked to expand his exporting business. Through a friend in the offices of Messrs. Singer, expediters of packages that couldn't be trusted to the Turkish postal system, he connected with a Greek who wanted to be supplied with crèche figures, rosaries, and other sacred items. He commissioned the best olive wood carver and the best rosary maker and, within a month, sent shipments to both Freneau and K. Theodopolous. Still restless, he visited the new Suq—a sumptuous space with a flowing fountain and scheduled musicales—and spoke to the merchants who sold expensive goods to the Europeans and the elite class who were building mansions outside the Old City walls. Why not ask M. Freneau to reciprocate with merchandise from France? In all the specialty shops that lined Jaffa Road, there was none that sold luxury linens and undergarments from the Continent.

That afternoon, he slipped into the Hotel Petra and wrote to Freneau suggesting this arrangement. Next he looked at several empty shops elegant enough to receive the families who might buy such expensive merchandise. The Grand Hotel had empty space, but the rent was astronomical. However, the proprietor of the apothecary shop that sold perfumes and toiletries was interested in subletting a corner of his shop, with the warning that the public was fickle, ill mannered, and slow to pay.

Nadeem thanked him and accepted the offer. Within a few months he was able to place a modest sign outside. Fine Imported Linens and Trousseau Apparel. N. Mishwe. Prop.

7

I will have to close the shop.

The first years of the new century brought change to the village. The Friends, whose fine girls' school was attracting pupils from as far away as Nablus, opened a fledgling school for boys in more humble quarters. Tamleh became a district seat for the surrounding villages, and the new *mudeer* widened the roads and made people paint their houses and not throw their dirt into the streets.

"Come," said Zareefa to Miriam one morning, "Nicola Khoury has installed his mechanical mill. Let's go have a look."

Miriam was reluctant. "The baby could come at any moment. My shape is indecent."

"Never mind," insisted Zareefa. "You're so thin normally, it hardly looks like anything. Drape your shawl over it. Here," she arranged the fabric over Miriam's jutting belly. "And bring some wheat. As long as we're going, let him grind the flour for tomorrow's bread."

They walked slowly to the market street, each with a child in a sling, but when they arrived there was a long line of women and they decided not to wait. On the way home there was an ominous rumbling and they felt the earth tremble. A woman ran out of the house screaming. "The whole room is shaking. Everything is crashing to the floor."

"It's an earthquake," said Zareefa soberly. "We're better off outside." The sensation lasted no more than thirty seconds but when they reached the house, the floors were sprinkled with fallen whitewash that had broken off from the plaster. Later, Miriam learned that the roof of Nabiha's house had caved in, and she was killed instantly. Daud, who still lived with her, was not at home.

The day her beloved grandmother was laid to rest, Miriam gave birth to Hanna, a placid, chubby boy with the features and coloring of the Mishwe clan. "He has my mother's eyes exactly," said Nadeem, with mixed feelings.

"This one isn't going to give you trouble," said Zareefa. "He looks so peaceful and content."

It was a blessing that Hanna was good-natured, for Miriam was filled with a deep brooding melancholy over Nabiha's death. Calamity could come at any moment and human beings had no protection against it. Earthquakes, famine, illness—random evil, as Nadeem had portrayed it—directed at no one in particular, with no apparent cause and without any warning or defense. While still in the fragile emotional limbo of a new birth, Miriam resolved to have more children, for they were the only solidity, the only protection against fear. As it turned out, she had reason to be apprehensive, for within two years, she experienced a deeper sorrow.

When she became pregnant the third time, Miriam prayed for a daughter, but her prayers were answered cruelly. A girl was born with the cord wrapped around her neck and the face that emerged was ghoulish, wizened, and a deep purple in color. Miriam named the creature Mary and held her until she died. She was barely twenty-two years old, but she felt as if she had lived a much longer time. She developed unnatural fears about Khalil and Hanna's safety, and awakened several times during the night to check on them. Whereas before they had seldom embraced, now she often wept in Nadeem's arms and it seemed that the tears came without rhyme or reason. It was almost a year before she was herself again, before she could wake up in the morning and not immediately experience the feeling that her heart was sinking . . . down, down, down.

"The next time you give birth," said Zareefa with her usual cheerful confidence, "God will reward you. You'll receive an angel from heaven."

In 1906, the Sultan Abdul Hamid had his thirtieth anniversary and the Turks celebrated by building a clock tower, forty feet tall, over the gate house at Jaffa Gate. The clock had four faces, two showing Eastern time and two showing European time. Nadeem brought Miriam to see it, but she was pregnant again and went into labor during the carriage ride and had to return home immediately. Esa was born an hour later, an adorable child who had received the best combination of genes from that vast pool. His skin was the color of new ivory, a dense, creamy white. From Nadeem's honey-colored eyes and Miriam's deep blue ones, Esa came out with round hazel pools of clearest light, with long lashes tipped dark at the end. It seemed this baby was born smiling.

Miriam, who had never fully recuperated from Mary's birth and quick death, not to mention Esa's birth, felt permanently tired. Heavy limbs and grainy eyes were daily companions. She walked—always carrying a child or a bundle—from fields to house to ovens to garden to kitchen to bed. The days passed unnoticed, yet there was a pleasant security in the changelessness of her life. Daud rebuilt Nabiha's house and married a very pretty girl, who was as short as he. Diana, Nabile's obese wife, who could no longer raise herself from a seat without help, still embroidered every day, and made cheese from dried *leben* and appeared daily at the *taboon* to make bread she could have easily bought.

Little Esa grew more beautiful in looks and disposition. At two and a half, he followed his mother for long distances without complaining. Hanna, at seven, could read Arabic and French. True to Zareefa's prediction, he was a quiet boy who felt deeply. He wanted to make his parents happy and always looked for ways to help. Khalil didn't do as well in school as his brother. He had difficulty reading and also a tendency to write his numbers and letters backward. He often balked at going to school, and Miriam had to coax him with sweets and promise to walk with him and meet him halfway on his return. With all his shyness, he had a reckless streak and loved to chase the carriages that now traveled regularly on the new road to Nablus, hitching a ride on their back bumper and jumping off at the last moment.

Now that Nadeem was part of the business community and circulated in Jerusalem daily, he was full of news and opinions of the world and society and especially the government at Constantinople, which the shopkeepers chewed over constantly. Even before Faidy Alami, the tax collector who came to assess the crops, predicted a revolution, Nadeem had already heard rumors. At one of the Sunday gatherings, Nadeem told the family— whispering as if it were censored information—that the Sultan was considered insane. "They say he wanders from room to room during the night, calling up his astrologers and attendants to get consolation from some new terror."

"Perhaps his conscience has the better of him," said Jameel bitterly. Although Abdul Hamid had little interest in Palestine, he had bankrupted the country and ruled with an army of spies.

"In any case, it's of little importance to us," said Nadeem's father.

"You advocate that a madman head the country?" asked Jameel.

"I prefer a known evil to an unknown one. Besides, the Sultan has never bothered with Judea. There's never been a threat of revolt from us, which is all that interests him. We are free to educate ourselves as we like. And to punish our wrongdoers. The police are greedy but not unnecessarily cruel."

"What will happen to us if there is a revolution?" asked Nadeem.

"Who knows? The same thing that would happen to you if there isn't one."

Even with all this speculation and discussion, the events that came late in that year of 1908 were a surprise to everyone. A week after the conversation at the Mishwes' Sunday dinner, a group of young liberal Turks, many of whom had been exiled in Paris, successfully overthrew the Sultan and pledged to put the Empire on the road to modernization and reform. The peasants were certain something good would come of it, even though they had never before felt connected to the far-off government that didn't even speak their language.

The regime of the Young Turks and their Committee of Union and Progress was received with riotous joy. There were celebrations in Jerusalem with fireworks, music, and long speeches. "Long live Liberty, Justice, and Equality," wrote Gad Frumkin in his newspaper *Habazeleth*. Jameel and Nadeem took their families—as did everyone—to Manera Square to celebrate.

For the next year, life did improve. Tamleh was incorporated into a city and Elias Hanna was chosen its first mayor. A representative from each clan formed a city council that began to clean and modernize the town. The shop and inn owners were paid to sweep the streets and install kerosene lamps. Trees were planted in the public places and gardens created. The livestock market was limited to Thursday, and scales were inspected for irregularities. Two new roads were built—one that led to the orchards and one to Birah.

Zareefa and Jameel, who now had three daughters, built a larger home near Miriam and Nadeem, and the two women were daily companions, cooking together and sewing and discussing their motherly concerns. Miriam's pleasure was to sit in the evenings and read for twenty minutes with Khalil, struggling against sleep. Her children were everything to her. Nightly she prayed for their welfare, naming each individually and expressing her hopes for their future. Hanna's legs turned inward, and each night she would rub them with oil so hot he cried out loudly, but that didn't stop her. Hanna had such a peculiar gait that Khalil, deeply embarrassed, insisted on carrying him on his back when they went in public. Miriam prayed that Hanna's legs would straighten, that Khalil would lose his streak of recklessness, and that Esa, her beloved golden boy, would always stay with her. It was better that she didn't know so soon that none of her prayers would be answered.

The populace had wanted so much for the Young Turks to be their salvation that it took a while to see the dark clouds forming. They were already deep into 1910 before the signs of despotism affected daily life and people began to awaken to a new mood, a new frustration.

"Father Ricard says he can't teach us Arabic history anymore," Hanna told Nadeem. "A soldier came and talked to him. He said we must learn to speak Turkish."

"Hanna," said his father circumspectly, "when you have the story correct, tell it to me again. You're talking nonsense." But then, noticing Hanna's hurt expression, he questioned him more closely.

"It wasn't a soldier," said Hanna, trying to be precise. "It was an official. He took Father Ricard for most of the morning to show him the list of new laws."

"Why would he give a priest laws? That's for the police."

"These are new laws for teaching children. They are laws for all the denominational schools. Father Ricard read them all to us and then . . ." —Hanna looked at his shoes in embarrassment—"he cried."

"Who cried?"

"Father Ricard. He said it was the end. No. He said it was the beginning of the end."

Hanna's story and Father Ricard's prediction were substantiated many times in the months following. The Turks decided, rather belatedly, that they wanted an all-Turkish Empire and all non-Turkish subjects would become second-class citizens. Gad Frumkin's *Habazeleth* now openly criticized the regime it had so recently praised, for censorship had become stricter and taxes, which in the old regime had sometimes been collected twice or reduced at the whim of the collector, now became ruinous.

One day, Miriam was walking with Esa to meet the boys coming from school, and two Turkish soldiers on horseback were waiting at her door. In former days, a squad of soldiers was sent out to do police duty, but for the most part, they had dealt with the sheiks who negotiated for clan members accused of wrongdoing. The villagers were always suspicious of any government representatives, refusing to believe they came with good intentions because every entanglement with the government ended with a demand for money.

"Madam?" A stout Turk sat on a restless horse, wearing the sashed uniform and saber of the local Jerusalem police. She had seen them many times around the barracks near the Citadel. But now, in front of her house, peering at her through narrowed eyes, they became a symbol of tyranny and her mind hardened. "We must find Nadeem Mishwe," he said.

"For what purpose?" Miriam asked, looking to see that all the boys were safely inside the house.

"Conscription. We are rounding up the able men for conscription."

"But we've paid the head tax," she countered indignantly.

"It's no longer possible to escape. The Committee for Union and Progress desires that every able man shall serve in the military."

"For what purpose? We're not at war."

"War?" he smiled indulgently at her naiveté and puffed out his chest. "It's not for war. You peasants think only the obvious. It's for the double purpose of strengthening the defense of the Empire and also to aid in the exchange of the populations. We will transplant some Anatolians here, and some Arabs will go to Anatolia."

Miriam looked at the soldier with contempt. She had heard that some families in Jerusalem had been transported, under great protest, to far-flung parts of the Empire. It was an outrage. "You're going to exchange my family?" her voice quivered with anger.

"*Your* family?" he sneered. "They exchange only the best families. It's your husband they want, and it will do no good to hide him," said the soldier, suddenly bored.

"Hide him?" Miriam scowled. "If you are so clever, you would know that he's already in Jerusalem and not come and disturb my children with threatening noises."

The soldiers whispered together. Then, "You say he's in Jerusalem?" one of them asked her.

"Yes. Not in hiding. In the open. He runs a shop at the Grand Hotel."

"If this is a lie, we will return in the morning and he will not benefit from lies."

"The lies are with your government," she answered wearily. "They promised reform but breed only greater hardship and discord."

They had never heard a woman so outspoken, and Miriam was surprised by her own bravado but she was too tired and outraged to be concerned. It was an outrage to serve a government not of one's choosing.

"I will have to close the shop," said Nadeem as they lay together, ready for sleep. She reached over and placed a hand on his forehead as if to erase the worry lines with her touch. "Don't say that. Not yet." There was resignation in his voice, which she felt like a thud in her heart. The shop was his claim to independence. He had conceived and created something that had not been in existence, and now his source of pride would be taken away. The following morning, after breakfast, she broached him with an offer that she felt compelled to make. "Perhaps I can maintain the shop until you return. I used to help my father with his business. Of course, it was simple enough, not in any way like your business." She offered the solution, feeling certain he would refuse. No woman they knew had ever worked, except in the house or in the fields. A few poor women hired out their young girls as servants to wealthy families, but they were protected just like the daughters of the household. Nadeem peered into his wife's face and said nothing, but the following day he asked her to come to the shop with him and she did so, leaving the boys with Zareefa.

He showed her his stock and ledgers. When a purchase was made, he wrote down the item, the price paid, and the name and address of the customer. He showed her his books of money spent and money earned, all in a neat hand. Miriam stared at the columns of numbers and tried to make sense of them, but they blurred and danced before her eyes. Nadeem ran his fingers down the page, talking as he went, but Miriam couldn't concentrate. She was anxious over taxes and soldiers and the threat of change in her life. "It's beyond me," she said sorrowfully. "I'd like to do it for you, but I can't."

"Perhaps I can get someone to do the paperwork." There was anxiety in his voice. "You would have to do only the selling and ordering."

"I could try it, I suppose." The idea of it frightened her. She had been bundled in her small world for eleven years, treading the circular path to her chores, minding children and digging in the garden. Her mind didn't work as it had before.

As they stood speaking, a woman entered. She was wearing a tight-bodiced woolen dress with a white dimity bib that was lightly ruffled at the top and stopped just above the breasts, coquettishly revealing a delicious expanse of pinkish skin. "Excuse me." The woman turned her full gaze on Miriam and with disarming innocence locked on to her eyes. "I'm in need of linens," she said, as if her need might be thought bizarre. "We've just moved here and the trunks with the bed linen were lost. My husband and I are staying temporarily in this hotel. Perhaps you could make up a list for me—sheets, comforters, some summer quilts and blanket covers, some pillow slips and linen towels. We'll be needing all of it. Do you have them with hand-embroidered hems? I'm partial to yellow for a trim. The initials will be LSJ. Linda Searle Johnson. Mrs. Jonathan Johnson." Here she giggled involuntarily. "I'm newly married. We're from Great Britain, but we'll be living here for at least a year. Jonathan's the assistant to the Consul."

The bell-like, utterly feminine voice coming from that rosy face was mesmerizing. Her blond hair was swept up into a high pompadour, creating an extravagant frame for her face. Miriam retreated to a corner of the room while Nadeem brought out some samples. She took an inventory of her own hair and clothes, which now appeared wretched. She tried to stand straight and throw her shoulders back, but they seemed weighed down by her scarf and her ungainly dress. Mostly, she was weighed down by her conviction that no dress or set of clothes would ever allow her to glide across a room on that wave of grace and delicacy that carried Mrs. Jonathan Johnson.

When they were alone again, Miriam asked Nadeem, "You wait on such women every day?"

"Yes, of course. Not as young, perhaps. More matronly. The housekeepers show up these days, not the lady herself."

All the way home in the carriage, a vague unhappiness gnawed at Miriam. She had fulfilled her destiny, as her mother had done, as her sister-in-law was doing, as did every woman she knew. She had three healthy boys and an industrious husband. Why had that porcelain doll in the shop thrown her heart into such chaos? It wasn't envy. It was the uninvited discovery that she could have lived a different life. When they were still several miles from home, she turned to Nadeem, her eyes full of purpose, "I will run the shop in your absence as well as I can." She looked at the ledgers and inventory sheets on his lap. "Tonight, show these to me again and I will try to concentrate. Perhaps my father can help, too. We will need the income when you're gone. I will do it. I must do it."

Nadeem put his arm around her shoulders. "How will you make the trip each morning and night?"

"Perhaps it won't be necessary. My father and I had many friends in Jerusalem in the old days." She was thinking of Father Alphonse at the Ethiopian monastery who had offered to take her brothers into his school. Perhaps he would give her lodging in return for some token work.

The next morning, lying in bed, she realized her back was buttressed by Nadeem's side. She would no longer have the firm, sure line of his body to sustain her during the night. She turned to inspect his profile. "Nadeem," she said quietly, her eyes full of tears, "are you frightened to go?"

"Not frightened but apprehensive. And suspicious of this government. The Committee is thicker than ever with Germany. Enver Bey, the Minister of War, is dazzled by the German military machine and now the Germans are being given free rein. They have whatever railroad concessions they want. This intimacy makes me uncomfortable. If it were simply conscription, it would almost be an adventure. There's an old man who sweeps the street in front of the hotel. He served with the colours and he tells us stories of his time there with great affection. He was a happy man, he says. They made him fit and gave him discipline and taught him customs of hygiene and social grace he wouldn't have learned in his own poor village. Perhaps it will be the same for me."

Even though she knew Zareefa would treat them with affection, Miriam was desolate at the thought of being separated from the children, especially the youngest. "Esa, Esa, how can I leave you?" She was bathing him and as she scrubbed his still plump arms, she blinked away tears.

"Esa, Esa," he mimicked, smiling, and then swooped down into the tub as far as its size would allow.

Nadeem was told to report to the central depot in Jerusalem for processing. The Turks were so desperate for men that those who appeared in decent health were inducted without a physical examination. The chief recruiting officer instructed his minions not to waste time on the hefty ones who could probably "knock down a bull." Nadeem appeared slim, so he received a rude poking and appraisal, which ended in a pronouncement that, while slight, he seemed to be in excellent health. The army was short of NCOs and since Nadeem could read and write, he applied to become one and was accepted for a special school at Damascus. Only too late did he find out that the barracks were squalid and the cadets were herded for work units that lasted from early morning until late at night. He dug trenches until his arms felt like two wretched masses of tortured flesh. Not once did they ask him to read or write.

Back home, conscription was even more strictly enforced. Army service became compulsory for all Christians as well as Muslims. The old oppressions returned in new forms and in increased feelings of suspicion. Nadeem left in the winter of 1911. George and Salim were taken a few weeks later when the age was lowered. Daud went, too, but they soon got word that he had deserted and Miriam wasn't surprised. Daud wasn't made to take orders and live by routine. If he hadn't deserted, he would have killed his superiors or himself.

The young men were transported to their posts on the new Hejaz Railroad that had opened to run from Medina to Damascus and at once put an end to the great army who used to perform the pilgrimage on foot. The annual pageant of the camel caravan was dead. When Nadeem asked a fellow recruit if he knew who had engineered and surveyed the railroad, the man looked at him wearily. "Have you been asleep, man? It's the Germans. German engineers. German surveyors. But"—he brightened and waved a finger in the air—"the locomotives came from America."

Khalil was moody and set up his bed out-of-doors in protest when he found out the details of the new arrangement.

"I'll see you on Saturday evenings," Miriam told him, holding out her hand to him, "and I'll bring a treat from Jerusalem."

"What sort of treat?"

"It'll be a surprise. When I see something that will please you, I'll buy it."

"What would please me is to go with you."

"But you can't. I've no place to put you, and you must stay in school. You must do it all on your own. Zareefa is too busy to listen to your lessons."

"I won't do it. I'll forget everything and it will be your fault."

"Now you've hurt me deeply and your father would be saddened by those words. He's making the biggest sacrifice. All you are being asked to do is to be faithful to your studies and help your Aunt Zareefa."

Khalil apparently had a core of conscience and these last words reached it. He capitulated and took his mother's hand. "When will you bring the surprise?"

"On Saturday. And if you're asleep when I return, you'll find it on your pillow."

"What about Hanna? Will you bring one for Hanna?"

"Something. But not as big as yours." She hoped that Hanna was not around to hear this betrayal, for she had no heart left for arguments. Khalil had yet to find out that Esa would depart with his mother. Miriam hoped by the time the week was gone, he would have adjusted to this news. The thought of leaving baby Esa had broken her heart and she had refused to think of it. One day, as she was walking from the vegetable market, eager to cross into the shady relief of the beautiful Damascus Gate, she saw a woman crying loudly and bearing a small boy in her arms. They went inside the building, which she knew to be run by a colony of Americans. When the woman emerged, her child was no longer in her arms. "Why have you left your baby there?" asked Miriam.

"I can no longer support him," said the woman, an agony of suffering in her eyes. "My husband must go into the army. If I keep the baby with me, he will die of hunger and neglect. Here, they will take care of him and I can visit from time to time."

Miriam bounded up the steps of the American colony building, determined to do whatever she could to convince them to take Esa into their shelter. If Esa were here, she could visit him every day. She could hold his sweet body against her and make certain he ate properly and wasn't frightened or sick.

A month after Nadeem had left for Damascus, she was almost comfortable in her routine. Although deeply worried about Nadeem and the future, she felt a certain pleasurable freedom walking to the shop on those golden mornings, carrying nothing in her hands, no child tugging at her skirts. She was doing without the elaborate headpiece with its row of coins and constricting understructure in exchange for the simple linen shawl draped becomingly over her head. Father Alphonse had readily given her board and, in return, she cooked breakfast and lunch for the few monks at the monastery on Ethiopia Street. Affiliation with a church or a foreign consulate was a life belt in the treacherous limbo of the new government.

Jerusalem was sobered by the oppressive climate but still busy. The square outside Jaffa Gate held many more Europeans. The "new" city had expanded wildly, stretching not only on Jaffa Road, but to the east and north. There were new hotels, cafés, banks, libraries, and post offices. Steamship lines and railway and tourist offices were interspersed among specialty shops within the arcades of hotels. Peddlers shouted hoarsely in the streets, hawking mulberries, dates, old clothing, and sesame cakes. All of the nationalities—Copts, Greeks, Armenians, Muslim and Christian Arabs—traded, worked, and lived side by side with the Europeans. The square-faced houses of the Old City, all built of mellow golden limestone, huddled against the churches. When she saw the men and women farmers still sitting outside the walls, selling produce, she felt nothing to bind them to her. She was a different woman now.

Her chores fit together like a mosaic. She rose at five-thirty, downed a small cup of coffee, swept the yard in front of the church, shopped early at the various suqs for the necessary provisions for lunch, and prepared everything but the finishing touches. From nine to twelve, she was in the shop, arranging merchandise, selling items that were in stock, and writing orders from samples, which always gave her trouble. She tried to be efficient, counted all the linen sheets in different sizes, so many in narrow, so many in wide; so many pillowcases; so many summer spreads, three with such and such initials, four more with a different border. She was never confident she had it right, and she delayed mailing orders to M. Freneau.

She had imagined that the hotel employees and guests would stare disapprovingly at a woman proprietress, but the political climate had softened social attitudes. Sometimes, however, the customers acted haughty, especially servants who were sent by their mistress. They delighted in denigrating the quality of the goods, even though they had no idea of the quality at all.

At noon, she hurried to cook lunch for the monks and to visit for an hour with Esa at the orphanage, bringing him a plum or an anise cake. He was always jubilant, but she doubted it was her appearance. His disposition was as bright as his beautiful face.

At night, she dreamt of piles of sheets in a tangle and also of Khalil. Though she saw him only on Saturday and Sunday, Khalil was often in her thoughts like a burden. Still, each morning the stylish clothes of the Europeans and general bustle of the city took her mind off herself.

One day, a middle-aged Italian man with a goatee entered the shop as she was battling with her orders, close to tears of frustration. *"Bonjour Monsieur,"* she greeted him. French was still the most prevalent second language.

"Madam," he inclined his head toward her. "I am in need of a trousseau for my daughter."

A trousseau! A trousseau was complicated. It involved garments for the bride as well as linens. "I'll show you our samples," she said demurely and then retreated while he inspected the peignoirs and silken nightgowns.

When he had made his selections and Miriam had laboriously written each item in the column, she tried to total the order repeatedly, but without success. She would write down a number and cross it out; and the more often she changed it, the more uncertain she became. As he stared, her clumsiness grew until she couldn't put down anything at all. The man, Mr. Pavotti, shifted uneasily, but his expression was compassionate. "Can I be of help to you, madam?"

"I beg your pardon," apologized Miriam. "I'm not well schooled in mathematics, but there's little I can do about it. There's no one else to run my husband's shop."

"Excuse me, madam, but why can't your husband run the shop himself?"

"The Turkish army has taken him. I've had to put one of my children into an orphanage and the other two are with relatives, but I don't think I can keep this up." She was embarrassed to blurt out her troubles to a stranger, but it was also a relief. "I'm so confused by numbers. Perhaps I'm cheating someone. Or someone has cheated me."

Mr. Pavotti was a man who greatly enjoyed sounds, and although he was listening casually to Miriam's litany of problems, he was also enjoying the unusual but beautiful sound of her voice. "You are another victim of the Committee of Union and Progress," he offered sarcastically. "The Committee of Chaos and Regression is more apt." He took the order pad from her. "Please, let me help you. As a young man, I taught mathematics in Turin. You see"—he began to draw vertical lines on a piece of paper— "the entire numerical system—and your clever countrymen had something to do with it—is based on units of ten. Like so." He brought her attention to the columns on the paper. "We'll put one number in each of these columns. You can add one to the other, or you can deduct a lesser from a greater. But first, you must calm yourself and not resist. What's your little boy's name? The one in the orphanage?"

"Esa." She was ashamed to have revealed so much.

"And how old is little Esa?"

"Four. Soon, he'll be five."

"And how old are you, madam?"

She had to stop and think, then counted back to her wedding day. "Twenty-nine."

"Aha. You're twenty-nine and little Esa's four. So how old were you when the boy was born?" She looked blank and then reddened. "No need to be embarrassed," he said kindly. "Momentarily, you'll know how to find the answer."

He went out to a stall and purchased a bunch of grapes, took them from the stems and proceeded to teach Miriam addition and subtraction with the grapes, placing them in a row, taking some away and then replacing them. "This is an emergency lesson to help you through until you learn how to do the real thing." He wrote out ten problems for her to solve and promised to return on the following day. Even though she was heartened by Mr. Pavotti's interest, she had to face the fact that the bright promise she had shown at Miss Clay's school had been buried over the years. She went to Father Alphonse with her problem.

"Would you be embarrassed to sit with the children across the street?" He was referring to the orphanage run by the Ethiopians for older boys, which conducted classes in reading and mathematics.

"Father, I'm more embarrassed to make so many errors in my business."

She found another ninety minutes in the day and spent it in the classroom with a teacher, who had a face full of boils but taught her how to add, subtract, multiply, and divide and how to read haltingly. Mr. Pavotti reinforced what she learned when he dropped in, but later that year Italy descended on coastal Tripoli and demanded the Young Turks' government to surrender it. With his homeland now considered an aggressor, Mr. Pavotti was recalled back to Italy.

Each day, hurrying from activity to activity, Miriam gained confidence and began to feel a certain happiness. She took pleasure in her surroundings. Ethiopia Street, the most charming block in the "new" city, began at the Street of the Prophets and meandered northward. Its sidewalks were a mere foot in width and were bordered by tall stone walls, a necessary precaution during the time when any building outside the walls was considered a target for marauders. Many of the fine houses had been built in the 1890s, when Miriam and Mustafa had sold their vegetables outside Jaffa Gate, and housed wealthy Muslim families, some prominent Jews, government officials—the Husseinis and the Nashashibis—as well as com-

munity leaders, teachers, and the intelligentsia. At Number 5 was the
German Evangelical Institute. At Number 6, the American School for
Oriental Research. Dov & Gad Frumkin published *The Habazeleth* at
Number 8. Just two short years ago, he had urged young Jews to study
Arabic and Turkish so they could be involved in the new political life of
the Ottoman Empire. But he was now the victim of that government's
oppressive censorship.

On one of those fine mornings, Miriam remembered what Nadeem had
said about the army. It was an opportunity to learn more of the world and
have new experiences. This was precisely what was happening to her.

8

It's mystifying to see you jabbing that needle into that infernal cloth, hour after hour.

The first time she saw Khalil's leg, it didn't look infected at all. It was swollen and distended and the wound appeared as a jagged marking, but by morning the area around the opening was discolored, a frightening yellowish green, and the slightest pressure brought an ooze of pus that made Zareefa cry out: "I should have done something. This is terrible. I didn't realize he was taking rides on the back of the carriages. And then he didn't tell me he was hurt. He said nothing, and I've been so busy with the little ones I didn't look at him so closely. I didn't realize he was limping. I'm so sorry, Miriam."

"Shhh, Zareefa. Don't blame yourself. We'll go to Spiridum and get a salve to draw it out."

Spiridum lanced the wound and gave them a poultice of dried figs, urging Miriam to keep the wound open and moist. "If it closes, the infection will go inward and the bone will be affected."

Miriam applied hot cloths all night, watching Khalil's face. He seemed delighted with the attention and feverish enough to welcome the bed rest. "I want to go back with you to Jerusalem," he said. "Leave Hanna here and take me with you. It's better with you." Miriam smoothed the hair off his face but made light of his request. She couldn't imagine coping with Khalil in the shop or the monastery. "Oh, you're deciding Hanna's fate? Leave him here but take you with me? Very nice. And what about Esa? Shall I stop seeing him, too? Just you and I will steal away. That's your dream, is it?"

"Mama," he said, ignoring her comments. "My leg is moving inside. It's jumping around under the skin. It doesn't feel good."

"What do you mean, 'jumping around'?" Concern now became a nagging worry. When she awoke from an hour's nap at dawn, the leg was back to its bloated condition and even more gravely discolored. When it was light, they hobbled together to the clinic of the Sisters of Mar Yusef, who told her that he required a hospital immediately. "Take him to the French Hospital. St. Louis. At the foot of Suleiman Street," said Sister Ernesta. "Don't wait until tomorrow. This must be treated today."

Throughout the carriage ride, Miriam held the leg on her lap while Khalil slumped against the corner of the seat. The leg seemed to worsen with each mile. The bumps on the road brought moans from Khalil and the other passengers winced. "Madam, why have you neglected this boy?" asked a well-dressed man from Nablus. Miriam shot him an angry look but felt the pang of conscience. Perhaps she should have had Khalil with her. Father Alphonse might have allowed him to stay with her. Or she could have put him at the Spafford Home with Esa. Had she not wanted him with her? "It's not for you to decide who's been neglected," she said to the man, and they continued the ride in silence. The stranger's rebuke was mild compared to what was awaiting her at the hospital.

She sat on one of the wooden benches arranged around an entry corridor that separated two wings and faced a heavy door with a window insert that gave a minuscule view of the Dome of the Rock. She tried to arrange Khalil in a comfortable position and summon help, but he wailed so loudly she stayed with him and waited for a medical person to come by. A woman in dusty black clothing crouched in the corner, muttering in distress and weeping softly.

The room held a mixture of unhealthy odors and her empty stomach rebelled, but in a moment all that was forgotten. A tall, vigorous man in a doctor's coat strode into the room with such authority she unconsciously sat at attention. He looked around, staring momentarily at the weeping figure in the corner before turning to a small girl sitting with her father. He lifted the girl in his arms and she immediately put both fists over her eyes.

"I want you to take your hands away from your eyes," he said calmly. "You may do one at a time, if you like." The girl took both hands away at once revealing a row of small pustules along the rims of her eyes. "Those hands can't go to your face anymore. Will you promise me that?" The girl nodded and the doctor turned to the father. "Why haven't you brought her in before this?"

"I've been working in another village." The man looked down at his hands, too shy to look up.

"And your wife? Your brother? Your cousin? Your ten brothers? Your hundred cousins? Your whole bloody clan? Couldn't they bring her? Couldn't they notice that there isn't one healthy millimeter around her eyes?" His words bounced around the room, reverberating against each wall. "Silence," he mused. "Whenever I ask a question, I'm answered with silence." Again his eyes rested on the figure in the corner. He went to her and pulled her gently to her feet. "Come, Yasmine, no more tears. It isn't as bad as you think and it must be done." Yasmine, for whatever reason, continued weeping and refused to look up. "I'm not going to hurt you. I want to fix your eyes so you can see the world more clearly." If he had been sarcastic with the father of the girl, now his voice was all gentleness. Everyone was thinking the same thing: Why is he speaking so reasonably to an ignorant peasant?

He made such an impression in the room, it was difficult to consider anything else. He didn't look like a doctor, neither bald nor bearded. His hair was a sandy brown, parted to the side and spilling over his broad forehead as if he tugged at it often. His jaw was prominent, but his mouth was so innocent and soft it reminded Miriam of Esa when he was about to cry.

"Is it the operating room that frightens you?" he asked with genuine concern. Yasmine shrugged her shoulders. "Then I will look at your eyes right here." He pulled her by the hand to the light coming in through the small casement window. He took an instrument out of the pocket of his long white coat and held it to her eye. "Look straight at me, Yasmine." He held her face tenderly in his massive hand, tilted the chin as if he were about to kiss her and bent over her with only the width of the instrument separating them.

Miriam was overcome by the intimacy of the pose and, in a stab of emotion that she didn't understand, wished that she were the afflicted woman so that he might be holding her chin in his hand. Immediately, she recovered and turned her thoughts to Khalil's leg and wouldn't look at the doctor again.

The examination over, he looked around the room to see who else needed assistance. When his eyes fell on Khalil's leg, his reaction was swift and violent. *"Why are you just sitting here!"* he shouted at Miriam. *"Don't you see this leg is an emergency?"* He lifted Khalil and walked out of the room. Miriam trailed after him, too shocked to speak.

He put Khalil on a narrow table covered with a blood-streaked sheet and immediately cut a one-inch cross in the center of the wound. Foul material streamed out in a quantity that made them both cry out. At the sight of it, the doctor took Miriam by the shoulders and shook her until she lost her scarf and almost fled in horror. *"Stupid!"* he shouted. *"Stupid, willful neglect.* Are you the mother? *Are you the mother?"*

She tried to speak, but the first attempt brought no sound. She managed a nod, but that enraged him further. "This boy will lose his leg today. He won't walk unaided again. Why did you wait?"

Khalil began to cry and reach for Miriam and this stopped the harangue. The doctor called for a nurse. *"Isabel."* A plump brown-haired woman, barely five feet tall, clad in a spotless white bib apron and starched cap appeared. "We have to prepare for amputation."

Nurse Isabel looked from Khalil to Miriam with compassion in her brown eyes. "Him?" she asked softly, nodding to Khalil.

"Yes."

The word struck terror in Miriam, and with the terror came an overwhelming desire to protect her son. How dare this madman even think of cutting off his leg? "Your head will come off first," she managed to shout. "Your head will come off before his leg." He was surprised by her vehemance, but no less surprised by the quality of her voice. That deep, silvery resonance was so unexpected. He stopped and stared at the woman who had created it.

"You don't wish to save your son?"

"You'll save him without cutting off his leg. You won't cut off anything."

"That might be the only way at this stage."

"You're a doctor. You must know another way."

He exhaled deeply, exasperated and fatigued. "Isabel," he called again and the nurse returned. "The mother forbids amputation. We'll hold off for a day and let her see the damage. For the time being, create a poultice and a drain line."

She didn't know where she got the courage to dispute a doctor. A doctor had been like a god to her and to every villager. In the complicated matchmaking rites of the clans, a doctor was even preferred over a cousin and could ask for any girl he wanted, even if he were an old man and wanted a very young girl.

"There, you see," he said, as if vindicated, "even in these few minutes, the leg has stopped draining and continues to swell. We must apply a new hot poultice every half hour without fail." He turned to Miriam. "Are you prepared to stay up all night?"

"Yes," said Miriam. She had begun to cry.

Throughout her long vigil, the day's events played in her head, especially that moment when Dr. Max Broder—that was his name—had placed his large hands on her shoulders and shook her so violently. She felt two welts where his thumbs had dug in. When he appeared at her side at four-thirty in the morning, his manner was much subdued. He poked at the leg, thumped and pressed all around, oblivious to Khalil's moans. "Good. Good. Don't stop the poultices. Isabel comes at seven. She'll relieve you or assign an aide, if you wish to nap for an hour or two." Miriam nodded dumbly. Her fatigue was so sodden, it was impossible to think beyond the next boiling cloth.

For a day and a half, with constant attention, the leg improved in appearance and size. But Khalil developed a high fever and, in a matter of hours, the leg darkened and became dangerously swollen. Nurse Isabel bathed it repeatedly with carbolic acid, but it didn't improve. When Miriam saw the worried look on Max Broder's face, she steeled herself for bad news. He pressed gently on her shoulders to sit her down. "The infection is spreading inward to the bone. We now have osteomyelitis. We're draining plenty, but we can't see the devastation beneath. It's keeping ahead of us," he ended bitterly, as if the infection was a human, willfully bedeviling him.

"I'm against amputation," she said stubbornly.

"We're taking a chance of infecting his entire system."

"Let me have one more day." She had no idea what she would be able to accomplish in one day, but she couldn't condemn her boy to a life as a cripple.

"Twenty-four hours," he said succinctly and walked away.

In midmorning, Mustafa, who had heard of Khalil's wound, came to the hospital. After hearing the news he signed to Miriam that before any thought of amputation, the doctor should introduce maggots to the wound.

"Maggots?"

"Yes. They will eat all of the putrified material more quickly than any medicine."

"This doctor won't listen to any such thing," she said bitterly. "He thinks we are ignorant peasants. Please, Baba, you get them for me."

Mustafa returned several hours later with a small tin filled with the legless larvae, which he placed inside the wound. Incredibly, they swarmed through the tissue and disappeared. Miriam stopped using the poultice and slumped on the bench, to wait.

About eleven o'clock, Max found her fast asleep. He shook her gently. "Come," he said. "You sleep in my room for the night. Help yourself to the bathing facilities and sleep in a real bed. You'll need all of your strength tomorrow, and Khalil will need you, too."

"I couldn't do that. Where would you sleep?"

"There are plenty of cots in the men's ward. I'll find something. Please. Do as I say. I want you to get a good night's sleep."

His apartment consisted of two rooms and private bath with a sizable tub, which Miriam filled with scalding water and soaked in for twenty minutes. She slipped into a surgical gown that he had insisted she take and padded about the rooms, shyly inspecting several photos—a middle-aged couple in heavy winter clothes, their faces almost obscured by their hats; a young woman with the same upswept curls as the customer who had so unnerved her in the shop that first day.

In normal times, she would have run through the streets naked before sleeping in a strange man's apartment, but life had become bizarre and frightening. She was exhausted. When she swallowed, she tasted lead. What did it matter where she slept? Her first-born son was gravely ill. Her husband was hundreds of miles away. Her life had been turned upside down. She had not once thought of Hanna, for which she was deeply ashamed. She often imagined his little figure as it looked walking away from her down the road, the feet turned in, the gait slow and labored. Yet his shoulders were high. Self-sufficient Hanna was paid with neglect. She had no hope of opening the shop soon. Where was the money to come from? Fatigue saved her. Within seconds of touching her head to Dr. Max's pillow, she was asleep.

She slept for twelve hours and awoke disoriented to find herself in this strange bed. Rest had partially dissolved the tension and dread of the last few days and, as she lay there for the last few luxurious minutes, she couldn't help but fix her mind on the man whose room it was. Why did the sight of him always change her mood? He caused her spirits to rise in a complicated way. He made her feel peculiar, uneasy.

When she investigated, she was relieved to find Khalil still had his leg, which was much improved. The swelling had receded, the skin around the wound was shrinking, and the color was no longer yellow. Doctor Max was not around to comment on it and she was too proud to ask for him.

"He's gone to inspect a horse." Nurse Isabel was collecting bedpans in the children's ward, where Khalil had been moved, when Miriam entered.

"Who's gone to inspect a horse?" Of course, she already knew and was more relieved than she cared to admit. She had thought perhaps he had left forever.

"Dr. Max. He removed the appendix of the Adwan Sheik, whose main line of business is breeding horses. Now the Sheik wants him to have one of his wild stallions so Dr. Max can break his neck." Her mouth twitched in disapproval, but her eyes were filled with affection. "He's as excited as a boy. He rides for an hour at dawn, as if he didn't have enough here to sap his energy. He does all the surgery, you know." Isabel sighed, looked at the pan in her hand and shrugged. "Anyway, he won't be back for a while."

"What has that to do with me?" asked Miriam curtly. "I will be spared a few insults."

"Why, Mrs. Mishwe," said the nurse stressing her Scottish accent, "it seems to me Doctor hasn't cuffed or damned you in quite a while." She winked. "But in the end, you proved him wrong. Lord help me for disloyalty, but the look on his face when he saw the maggots!" She began to laugh helplessly. "To see that manly, intelligent face so at a loss. Totally confused." Isabel wiped her eyes with a corner of her apron and hurried away, leaving Miriam with a great deal to think over. That manly, intelligent face . . . oh, how she yearned to see it.

Worry over Khalil had kept Max Broder safely at the edge of awareness but now he overran her mind chaotically, as the Tenth Roman Legion had overrun Jerusalem. She was restless, tossing and turning in her bed as if sleeping were a waste of time when she could be thinking of him. At first her thoughts were idolatrous. She imagined his movement when she wasn't there: touching a wrist, lifting a listless hand with concern, hoping to transfer his own vigor into it, peering tirelessly into the cloudy eyes of all who came to his eye clinic, conferring with other doctors with perfect concentration that excluded everything—excluded any thought of her. When had she transferred those hands from a fevered forehead to her own body?

"Madam, I asked for the silk spreads, not linen. And I wanted the plain sateen border, not the scalloped."

Miriam jumped, startled and embarrassed. As the overly perfumed matron before her had been talking of tailored hems, she had been struck by the most desolate thought. Before Max Broder, she had never been drowned in feeling—she had missed the main purpose of life! "Of course. Forgive me. I will bring the tailored hems with the sateen border."

She closed the shop half an hour early, not to visit with Esa at the American Colony, but to visit the baths, needing the scalding cascade of water to calm her overstimulated nerves. She inspected her body with dismay. Her breasts did not slope gently into the provocative swelling that she noted on many of the ladies who came into the shop. She was too bony. Her neck was long, however, and her eyes, in the dewy aftermath of bathing, dominated her face like two deep blue pools of refracted light. She washed her hair vigorously and combed it until it dried in silken folds that she coiled hastily—for she had stayed longer than intended.

As she crossed Christian Quarter Road on her way to the hospital, she caught sight of the parched, fading yellow thistle, the last of the summer blooms, and realized it was fall. In the courtyard of the White Fathers' rectory, the arbors were heavy with grapes, each little cluster encased in a small bag. *Ya Allah,* the harvest had come and gone. She couldn't remember a year in her life when she hadn't participated in harvesting. Though she was late, she stopped in the charming garden around St. Anne's Crusader Church to pray. This was where Jesus had healed a man who had been infirm for many years, and she prayed that He would also help Khalil.

Although Khalil's leg was healing rapidly, there was a sizable depression where the infection had done the most damage. He needed laborious physical therapy to keep his leg flexible. He spent two hours in traction, and in the afternoon and evening Miriam helped him through exercises in a large tub of water. Movement was so painful she had to wait an hour between sessions for the boy to recover.

Khalil was tense when she arrived. "I've already done the exercises," he said quickly.

"You've done half of them, according to Isabel. Now we're going to do the other half."

"What good are they? I don't want to do them anymore. They hurt. I want to go home." He was using that whiny monotone that fatigued her as no amount of hard work did, but she fought it off. "Home? And where do you think home is? You need care and I've closed the shop to give it to you. This is home for now." Her voice rose with frustration. "If you're going to waste this time, all the money I could have made in the shop will be gone for nothing." Unblinking will was the key to Khalil. "Come, I'll help you into the tub." She pushed him to rotate the knee inward and out, a millimeter more each time. Once he was loose, she massaged the limb to relax it further and fill it with blood. Finally she helped him navigate a barred corridor so that he could simulate walking without putting too much weight on the leg. After an hour's rest, they repeated the exhausting procedure.

Every time he passed the corridor that connected the two wings she was there, bent over her black cloth, her fingers pushing the needle in and out. It seemed to him that each time she pushed it in, she did so with a dutiful, self-righteous jab that annoyed him. In and out. In and out. And when she pulled it out, her mouth, normally wide and curved, pursed into a stingy oval. She was stubborn as a mule. Courageous. Proud. But she lost all of it hunched over that stupid, useless cloth. "Surely by now," he said, "the embroidered linen of Judea could cover every woman in the Ottoman Empire silly enough to crave it."

She looked up, startled by the attack and not entirely sure it was directed at her. He stood before her, breathing deeply. "Is something wrong?" she asked.

"Nothing's wrong, it's just mystifying to me to see you jabbing that needle into that infernal cloth hour after hour, day after day."

"That's what we do," she said stiffly. "In our village, we embroider. In Nablus and Ramleh, they make Mt. Carmel soap. In Bethlehem, they make beautiful silk wedding dresses. In Bireh, the women are lazy . . ."

"Then Bireh is for me," he said defiantly. She continued jabbing the needle into the cloth with alarming thrust and accuracy until he strode away, his long coat flapping angrily behind him.

The next day, when he saw her there again, she didn't have her embroidery but sat looking ahead with indifference, her hands crossed neatly in her lap. His footsteps stopped before her, but she refused to look up. His shirt and belt showed between his lapels. "I'm sorry," he said. "I had no right to speak to you that way."

"You are free to say anything," she said primly. She wanted to bury her head against him. "It is your right. It is for that very reason there was a revolution in Constantinople." The moment she said it, she felt she had made a fool of herself. The revolution had only brought more censorship. And how could she hope to analyze the motives of the Turkish government. His hand was dangling inches away from her. Each finger had a fine tuft of reddish hair; the fingers were lightly curved, conveying strength. She focused on those fingers as if they were a lifeline and she was drowning. Oh, to touch those hands . . . to feel them on her face!

"No, it isn't. I have no right to impose my values on you. And certainly I had no right to ridicule. The Committee of Union and Progress didn't have that in mind." He smiled. "It is our European conceit, that we know best. Forgive me." He tilted her chin so she would be forced to face him, but she kept her eyes lowered. "Accept my apology."

"As you like," she whispered.

"Would you like some good news?"

Anything that would end this moment would not be good news. "What sort of good news?"

"How suspicious you are. Good news about Khalil."

My God, she had forgotten the exercises and now it was too late. Someone else would need the tub. "I'm late for the therapy. What could I have been thinking of?"

"Shhh." He held her arm. "It's all right. I did them with him. I wanted to see what progress he had made. He was able to put weight on the leg without having it cramp up. It's remarkable. Now does that make up for my rudeness? Here's an admission that hurts. It was your stubborness that did it. Remember . . ."—he sat down next to her companionably—"you said my head would come off before his leg." He was trying to coax her into a forgiving mood, but there was nothing to forgive.

The afternoon had turned to dusk, and the room filled with the characteristic light that set Jerusalem's native building stone on fire twice each day. Out of the small window in the door, she could see the golden rotunda of the Dome of the Rock. The faint strains of the municipal band sounded in the distance. The air was heavy, as if they were in water. Her breathing sounded loud.

"Those words were spoken in fear and bewilderment. I'm ashamed each time I think of them."

He looked down at her hands. "No embroidery today?"

"It's useless work." She exhaled deeply.

"You have the patience and firmness to make a first-rate nurse."

"I'm not trained. What would I do?" she said dully.

"There are many things." His head was bent close to hers, his hands hung between his legs. His eyes—were they gray? green? yellow? It was impossible to tell in this light. They caught and held her own. To her surprise, she stared back, hungering for his attention, welcoming the deep wellspring of emotion he touched in her. "You could do physical therapy. Talk to some of the mothers and persuade them to bring the children in on a regular basis. Khalil will be here for a while."

"I could do that," she said in a tense whisper that made her voice breathy and haunting. He tensed, too, and moved toward her. Her heart was beating out of her chest, thundering like a herd of wild gazelles. Couldn't he hear it?

"Isabel tells me you live in a monastery and work for your keep. We could find room for you here and free you of that responsibility. Then you could give the extra time to us."

Why did that harmless statement frighten her? No . . . "frighten" wasn't the right word. It made her fearful in a thrilling way.

As they were speaking, two women came in helping a third who was in distress. "She swallowed a leech," one of the women said in Arabic. "She took water from a fountain and it had leeches." The lack of hygiene around the cisterns often resulted in leeches entering the mouth and attaching themselves at the opening of the throat. The woman in question kept her mouth opened awkwardly, afraid to swallow.

"You can close your mouth," said Dr. Max. "That little fellow isn't going anywhere. I'll get my tweezers." He returned and took the woman out in the sun to look down her throat. "It's too far down," he said to Miriam who had followed them out. "I can't get a hold of it."

"Let her sit a while in the sun with her mouth open," said Miriam. "The warmth will coax the leech out where you can get him."

Max gave her a look of tolerant amusement. "That's your advice, is it? Well, since I don't have a simple solution, I'll give yours a try. I'll leave it to you to arrange the patient." He raised his eyebrows in a look that implied she was on her own.

"Very well," said Miriam, "but leave me the tweezers."

He shrugged and disappeared into the inner part of the hospital.

An hour later when he returned, Miriam was holding the leech between the pincers. "I bow to your expertise," he said extravagantly. "The fee will go to you." Though she still felt shy with him, she couldn't repress a triumphant smile. "We'll ask Isabel to find a bed for you. And . . . a uniform. The scarf will have to go, you know." He did a quick inventory of her attire. "And the sandals."

"I've got to think about it," she stammered. "Perhaps in between Khalil's therapy . . . I don't know." Fortunately, at that moment he was called away and she was safely alone again.

A shiver of apprehension went through her. Did he think she was more than she was? Would she end up disappointing him? Could she manage all the shop's business in the morning hours? And what would her family think about her association with the hospital? The images of Khalil, Nadeem, and Mustafa appeared in her mind. Khalil's look was mutinous, Nadeem's was sad. But Mustafa understood.

"I cannot give you this package. Any shipment from abroad must be cleared by special permit."

"But I've picked up packages here a dozen times. There must be some mistake. I have no permit."

"Now you must get a permit." The postal official seemed to be enjoying his new power. "How do I know this isn't contraband?"

Miriam didn't know what contraband was. "It's linens from France. We have a shop at the Grand Hotel. Feel free to open it." She looked anxiously out the door where two men she had hired to transport the shipment were holding their palette and waiting.

"I can't open every package that passes through. We aren't equipped to do so. But even if I saw the merchandise with my own eyes, I couldn't let you have it without a permit."

She sighed and went to dismiss the men with the palette and give them a few coins for their trouble. She walked back to the hotel frustrated and dejected. The government had new restrictions every few days and as soon as she had satisfied one, another was added. Each paper and permit had a fee, but worse than the fee were the suspicions visited on every citizen. The merchandise in the shipment would have brought in money that she needed to pay the rent on the shop and to give Zareefa for housing Hanna.

She was deep into the misery of having lost two hours of her precious time and didn't see Max Broder approaching in the crowded street. "Why so glum, Mrs. Mishwe? Is something wrong?" Through the concern, there was a teasing quality in his voice. Was it because he was so certain she misapprehended life and worried over nothing? She wasn't in the mood to be treated lightly.

"I can't get my merchandise out of the postal service." She thrust her chin out as she spoke, as if she dared him to find the situation trivial.

"Perhaps I can help. If I tell them the linens are for hospital use, how can they refuse?"

"They might release this shipment, but there will be others and more complicated regulations will spring up." She was bouncing her fist against her chin in nervous frustration and he took her hand away from her face, uncurling the fingers, and placed it at her side. "Let's worry about one thing at a time," he soothed. "I might have a connection that can help."

The following day he had a more promising plan. "I set the broken leg of a little Turkish boy today and, as luck would have it, his father is one of four in the Ministry of Justice. You'll have no more difficulties with your shipments."

"Thank you," she said, but her voice was questioning. How easy it was for him to deal with the government. He had the power of his profession and, she was certain, of his nationality, yet the native population was regarded with suspicion and treated without respect. This was her country, not his. The idea made her deeply resentful and her face showed it.

"You're not pleased?" asked Max quizzically.

"I'm grateful to you," she said, her face glum.

"If you were any happier, you'd be in tears. What is it? You did want your merchandise, didn't you?"

"Of course, but it's troubling to me that I am a citizen without power while . . . while—"

"While a foreigner is granted favors."

"Dr. Broder, my husband is fighting their war, and I am not granted the basic right of receiving mail without harassment." She was repeating, word for word, what she had heard a man say to the postal clerk, only it had been his son who was in the army. Although she herself could never have expressed her thoughts so succinctly, the words had touched home with her. "It doesn't seem fair."

"Which makes you angry with me?"

His lips were parted and formed such a childlike configuration, she smiled to see them. "No," she said wearily, "I am worse than the government. I would do whatever you asked, too." She had not meant to say that. What a statement to make! What must he think!

"I see." The tone of his voice changed and there was a silence so intimate she felt blood rush to her face. "I shall keep that in mind," he exhaled as he spoke so that the words were almost lost. Her hands trembled and she locked them together behind her. "I've been thinking . . ." he continued.

"Yes?"

"Dr. Ticho and I have been in touch with the local Ministry of Health and we've offered to canvass the surrounding villages to look for signs of infectious diseases. Trachoma is first on our list, of course. But there've been several cases of malaria reported and even more of influenza. We need to encourage these people to visit the clinic. Especially the children. If we send you and Isabel—she to identify the disease, you to interpret and convince patients to arrive here—perhaps we can have a healthier winter. We want to concentrate on the smaller villages, for now, not more than two or three miles on the outskirts. Make a systematic visit of the houses to check the hygiene. We'll know in two or three weeks if it proves worthwhile."

"I could do it only in the afternoons." If Dr. Max had his way, the line for the biweekly clinic would have extended all around Suleiman Street, around the Municipality, all the way to the Russian Compound. He would have liked every family to pass through at least once. "Why don't they come?" he would ask, mystified. "Is it apathy? Distrust? How can you ignore a sick child?"

Immediately, she had a fantasy of bringing half the population of Judea to his doorstep and becoming so valuable to him that he could not do without her. Every encounter with him aroused these childish fantasies. How to impress him. How to become important in his life. But for what purpose? What did she suppose would occur between them? She would have preferred to take up the nursing full time and be done with the shop forever, having no taste for dealing with the customers, many of whom took the opportunity to display their feelings of superiority. But losing the

shop would crush Nadeem. His two letters had mentioned it with longing.
How he loved the routine of managing his stock and keeping his neat
ledgers and satisfying his customers. It was his identity, and she must
struggle to keep it going for him at all costs.

9

If you want me to go, just say so.

So this was how it felt to wear a dress that outlined bones and flesh, that curved around her breasts and dipped at her waist. She touched her curves with interest a dozen times a day, deeply aware of her own body. And the cap on her head, why did it make her feel so capable? She marched through the corridors with purpose, lifting those dainty shoes as if her legs were weightless. Even so, she had been disappointed in Max Broder's reaction to her new look.

"My God," he had barked, as if she had intentionally set out to deceive him, "look at this! There's so much less of you. And your hair . . . it wasn't there before." He never intimated that he liked her new look. In fact he implied, almost with annoyance, that she had somehow betrayed her heritage. Didn't he remember? The clothes had been his idea. For her first week at the hospital she stayed away from him, taking her instructions from Isabel, who was delighted to have her help. Her room was a cubicle, not much more than a closet in back of the children's ward. Yet each night, during those languid moments before sleep came, she transported herself to another bed in a buried wing beyond the surgery room. It never occurred to her that it was right or wrong. She knew only that she had never before had such depth of feeling. It made something completely different of her life.

After four years in Palestine with fully half his patients from the bedouin population, Max Broder could repair a knife wound with such fine stitches the scar was barely noticeable. Many of his patients were oblivious to his skill. Many others were only casually thankful that he had saved their lives, since their religion looked upon death as more enticing than earthly existence. They revered him because he was a doctor, a profession that in their eyes was next to being God, but they would have revered a bad doctor just as much.

It was frustrating because Max was a very good doctor and a dedicated one. He had come to Palestine four years before, filled with high-minded and—he now saw—egomaniacal expectations of bringing the modern techniques of surgery to a backward land that would then be forever grateful. It didn't take him long to discover that a native-born doctor was as rare as rain in July. And native doctors tended to gravitate to Beirut, not Jaffa and Jerusalem. What's more, Jerusalem was glutted with European doctors because every nationality that was represented had brought its own medics and erected its own hospitals and schools. What's more, the specialties that had made him feel so accomplished in Germany were not appropriate here. An eye specialist—for eye diseases were rampant—would have been more welcome.

Instead of teaching, he had learned. He had learned the most from Dr. Ticho, who had his eye clinic outside the walls on the corner of Ethiopia Street. This dedicated man had saved the sight of hundreds of peasants. When Miriam Mishwe met Max Broder in late summer of 1911, he was in the process of retrenching. His ego was bruised, but he wasn't ready to return to the comfortable upper-class life he had left behind. He had come to love the land and developed a passion for Arabian horses. His one indulgence in a crushing work schedule was his ride through the hills of Judea at dawn. Now, suddenly, there was another indulgence.

It's funny, he mused one day, as he bent over a bedouin's punctured intestine, what the human mind absorbs—thousands of details are being assimilated without our consent. Her mouth, for instance. I wasn't aware I had memorized its exact configuration. And those eyes, at once so frank yet so mysterious.

One afternoon, he found her in a small room rolling and stacking bandages on a scarred table. Her back was to him. The set of her shoulders— defiant yet accepting—and the childish slant of the apron's bow at the small of her back touched him. As he watched, she reached above her head and one foot left the ground. He had an overwhelming desire to place his hands where the bow crossed so impudently and have those arms raised to embrace him. He moved silently to her side and turned her to face him. The look of desire on her face dissolved what was left of his will.

He pressed her against him, waiting helplessly for each part of her to find a corresponding groove in him. The moment he touched her lips, a hunger arose in him that was all the more upsetting because he had not known it was there. It stopped him from doing what he urgently wanted to do, which was to bruise those lips with his own, to pry them open. He was surprised at how fragile she felt in his arms, yet her firm breasts resisted the pressure from his chest, arousing him further.

She broke away first and took a step back. The look on her face was one of awe. "I'm sorry—" he began, but she put a hand to his lips. "No."

"Unfair of me to take advantage . . ." he mumbled, sinking his hands deep into his pockets. "Won't happen again." Before she could speak, he was almost running down the corridor.

Her heart was pounding so violently she felt she might have a medical emergency. He wanted her! She touched her lips tentatively. His desire had made them precious. She rushed to her room to stare at her face in the mirror, certain she would look different. How many times did she relive that moment when she first felt those skillful hands around her. She could feel them right now on her back. She had memorized the precise pressure they exerted. And his lips! And his legs and hips!

She didn't see him again for four days and finally worked up to asking Isabel as to his whereabouts. "He's on his first holiday in three years," replied the nurse, "and not a day too soon. He was crabby and too critical before he left. Almost bit my head off because a bandage hadn't been changed."

"But he is coming back?" Miriam felt stricken. Suppose he decided to stay away for good? Suppose she never saw him again?

"Don't look so frightened, my dear. Someone else will look after Khalil. But, yes, he'll be back. Just needs a breathing spell."

She had no hope that he would ever touch her again. No hope that he felt anything at all. But the memory of his touch was so alive to Miriam that it didn't matter. She was in a new body filled with feeling. She felt supremely alive. When she thought of Nadeem, it was as if he had happened in another lifetime. Instead of going home to Tamleh for the weekend, Hanna took the carriage and she took him and baby Esa to a show of trained animals that was passing through. The boys felt shy with their mother. "You look so pretty," said Hanna. "Will Baba mind?"

"What a question!" said Miriam. "Will Baba mind *what?* How I look?"

"Your hair is different." She had put on her traditional dress to see the boys but left off the head cloth.

"Well, I'm so used to putting it up for the nurse's cap, I just did it without thinking."

"Baba won't recognize you," said Hanna, and Miriam could see that he was deeply troubled by the difference in her. Had she changed so much?

"Perhaps I won't recognize Baba," she said impatiently.

When she had kissed the boys good-bye and returned to the hospital late Sunday night, she felt dejected. All the energy of her passion for Max had been dissipated, and she felt that he was ashamed of what had happened and that's why he had left. Perhaps he expected her to go away before he returned. She agonized late into the night, first deciding to leave immediately and return to Father Alphonse and then, feeling fiercely in need of seeing Max once more, deciding to brave the humiliation of having him tell her to leave. She was finally drifting off in a tortured sleep when she heard her door creak open. She half sat up, expecting to see one of the nurses in need of assistance. It was Max. "Shhh." He put his hand to her lips. "If you want me to go, say so."

"Go? Oh, no. I was thinking that you must want *me* to go away. That you were ashamed of what had happened between us." She spoke rapidly, afraid he might disappear before she had bared her heart.

"Wait," he whispered. He stood and removed all his clothes. She could see the outline of his body in the moonlight, and for a breathless moment felt all of the weight of tradition bearing down on her. This was forbidden. This was unthinkable. Right now she should run away. But she couldn't. Her need to touch him bordered on panic. Suppose he went away now without touching her? She went and stood before him and he took her in his arms and parted her lips with his. This didn't satisfy him, and he turned her face several times, placing his mouth over hers again and again, as if each new attempt would afford him the closeness he was seeking.

She couldn't rid herself of the notion that she had lured him there with the intensity of her desire. It was sorcery. This encounter would have to last her forever. She wanted to remember how it felt to be engulfed by his body, a sensation so thrilling it blotted out conscience and duty. He was in need of her, and yet another part of him fought against it. She could sense his turmoil in the small cries that accompanied his kisses.

That didn't keep him from removing her nightdress and carrying her to the bed. With a desperate, weary groan, he signaled that the battle was lost. He became subdued and gentle, smoothing and massaging and exploring her with grave patience. Her nervousness dissolved. "Don't be frightened," he said. She wasn't frightened. She felt beautiful. She could feel her own pulse jumping out of her skin. Tension. That's what it was. A thrilling tension that stopped all reason. Max!

"I want you," he whispered. This admission brought such a thrill to her heart that she began to cry. When he felt her tears, he stopped. "What have I done to you!"

"Shhh. They're tears of happiness." She held his face and kissed it. She kissed his chest and rubbed her cheeks and lips in the soft mat of hair. She was possessed surely, but there was no way to stop. Her body began a devilish rhythm that made him groan. "I can't wait." He parted her legs and trailed a thumb along each thigh from groin to knee. Oh! An agonizing sweet sensation. Please!

He got up and went to rummage through his clothes. Had she done something shameful? Was he leaving? "What's wrong?"

"I've got to protect you from pregnancy." She had no idea what he was talking about but was relieved to have him back and parted her legs willingly. He embraced her so tightly she could feel his pulse inside her. Her head, her heart, her entire body was throbbing in time with his. Her last thoughts were: I've given him something. I've made him happy.

She awoke alone with a momentous shaft of sunlight streaking her comforter at the spot where her thighs lay beneath. Had it happened or was it a dream? There was a pleasant soreness between her legs. But if it had happened, where was the remorse? She had betrayed everything—her husband, her children. There was no forgiveness in her tradition for this. None at all. Still, her heart was bursting with happiness. Without saying it, Max had admitted a need that she was chosen to fill. And she wanted to fill it with all her heart. But what if someone had walked in and found them? It didn't matter. No risk or humiliation could force her to choose against him.

That afternoon, as dusk was creeping through the corridors with that special light, he came quietly to stand next to her. "I've made arrangements to rent a small house so we can be together without embarrassment. I don't want to jeopardize your standing here." He spoke in a regretful way. As if he were an unwilling prisoner of his emotions.

"I've thought of you every moment," she admitted with resignation.

"And I of you." He had lost control of his life.

"It doesn't please you?" she asked anxiously.

"All day," he began gruffly, "while I should have concentrated on the needs of my patients, the feel of you was under my hands. I had to sew a man up twice because the first time, I was mentally caressing you. Come," he said and led her away.

The light coming in the window of his apartment was almost purple. He closed the door and took her in his arms more gently than before. Slowly he undid the buttons at the back of her uniform, untied the apron, slipped his hand inside and moved it across her bare skin. "If you don't wish it, say so," he urged her.

"I wish it," she answered simply and he continued to undress her, sitting her on the bed, like a child, to undo her shoes. He undressed himself and they moved across his bed silently, their skin glowing in the unreal light. Her hair, long and abundant, spread extravagantly around her. "You look like a beautiful painting." His voice was full of emotion.

"The first day I saw you," she said softly, "you examined a woman in the waiting room because she was frightened to go inside the hospital. You bent over her and touched her face and I wished myself in her place. Since that moment there is nothing I've wanted more than you."

"And if there are reprisals? I will get off free, but you will suffer." Without his severe collar and tie he looked boyish, especially with his hair spilling over his forehead. But she had only to place her cheek against his chest to feel his strength.

"I will suffer if you turn away from me. That would be the only unbearable thing." She couldn't remember another moment when she had examined her life and come to such drastic conclusions, yet the words rushed out. She felt possessed, but it was thrilling.

Lovemaking was all the more poignant in the waning light. She could see his eyes, the beautiful texture of his skin, rosy and glistening with desire, the gently muscled forearms. She exhaled deeply, letting go of a life that was no more than a pale, constricted dream. She was a woman now. She was suffused with her sense of femaleness. She had a need to open herself and give and nurture. There was no shock, no holding back feeling. She emitted cries of pleasure without thinking, without remorse. At that moment he moved up on her and thrust himself in with such strength that she felt a surprising stab of pain. "I can't wait," he groaned. "It's too much. It's . . . Oh, God . . . hold me."

She held him until there was no more light in the room and the first few stars became visible through the window. He was sleeping with his face buried in her breasts. She could feel his breath exploding against her skin. Nothing in life had prepared her to hold such joy. To think of life as happening from moment to moment with no past or future.

She had been reared to expect hardship and when it came, to accept it gracefully. The women of the clan sang through their chores; they danced and clapped their hands and chattered on the way to the grueling work of the harvest. Affection was no more of a sensation than her father's huge hand draped companionably across her shoulders. Indulgent love was reserved for the children. Physical love was a duty to be performed willingly because it satisfied the husband and brought sons. She had never heard any woman speak of bodily pleasure. Even those who were thrilled with the match their parents had made for them did not hint that it brought them physical happiness. At the age of twenty-nine, with her body still firm and vibrant, she had assumed that there were no more sensations to be had. And now . . . this! She felt they were conspirators in this thrilling physical novelty.

Max stirred against her. "We have to wait until the first of the month," he said into her shoulder.

"To meet again?" She was surprised.

"For the house I've rented. According to the clerk, I may not legally move until the first of the month. But it's according to the Muslim calendar, so I'm not sure which day."

"Oh." She was preoccupied. "I must go home and see Hanna, in any case."

"Bring him here. I'll book a hotel room for you both. You can bring the baby, too. You can be together in a pleasant suite with your children. Will that please you?"

"I'd like it very much." They exchanged a look of understanding and delight. All shyness was gone.

"I'll arrange it tomorrow."

10

I wish very much to eat.

"Ah . . . the poverty of progress." As he made this pronouncement, the tall, angular man brought the pickax down with unexpected force, catching a full half foot of the dusty pulverized ground.

Nadeem brought down his pickax a moment later, but hardly disturbed the surface. "All right," he said with good humor, "I'll play the dolt for you. What are you saying, George?"

"The advent of the railroad has allowed the War Office to pick the mountains clean of young men. Our once healthy peasantry is now polluted. They've lost their optimism and their innocence. Except you, my friend." The grimy sunburned face was made fiercer by oversized features, but there was affection in the sunken eyes. "You still trust the devil himself."

"You're saying I'm a fool, then." Nadeem smiled at the Kurd, who knew him better than his own brother. They had dug trenches side by side for two months on their march to the Dardanelles. Following Italy's lead, insurrections had begun to break out throughout the Empire as the European provinces demanded their political independence. The marching had continued day and night, and George's feet had become badly swollen. Nadeem had cut open his boots to relieve him and for many miles they had hobbled together, the short, slight Arab supporting the tall Kurd.

"Aha, you see," George gave the ax another healthy swing, "you're infected with my cynicism. May God forgive me. You've saved my sanity and I've repaid you by corrupting your spirit."

"Not you," said Nadeem seriously. "Those strutting Germans. Look, he's coming now, to reprimand us." A barrel-chested man with coarse straight hair bleached white by the sun approached. The government had become so thick with Berlin that it had requested a German general to be responsible for the army's uniform and reformation.

"Never mind, what worse thing can they do to us? Let him come." George resented what he called the Teutonic varnish that had been imposed on the gusty peasantry—a stiff, ridiculous walk and a staccato manner of speaking.

"It's one hour to the midday meal," said the foreman jeeringly. "But only for those who advance the work, not retard it."

"Perhaps you would like to terminate us," offered George. For the last four weeks, they had been creating a proper bed to receive the tracks that would advance the railroad, which was being extended from Konia to Aleppo and would soon cross the Euphrates. The German dream was to link Berlin to Baghdad.

"What better thing would you do with your life? Don't you believe in progress? The railroad now links three major areas and advances your country out of the dark ages. You should be proud to have a hand in it."

"This is not my country," George spat on the ground and Nadeem became apprehensive. "I was abducted illegally. I have no wish to further the Ottoman cause."

"Perhaps you have no wish to eat, either," said the German, ruffled to find an articulate opponent.

"No," said George abandoning his bitter tone, "I wish very much to eat." Nadeem gave the ground several blows with the ax. It unnerved him to see George humiliated. They never had enough to eat.

The German grunted knowingly. "Uh-huh. The stomach is more loyal than the head." He continued to hover.

George did not speak again and Nadeem knew that he was embarrassed to have capitulated in front of the German. He knew, too, that George's mighty swings of the ax were ninety percent will. Having lost the Tripoli campaign, the army unit had been marched back to Konia. The pathetic camouflaged tents in the camp were ragged. "From whom are we camouflaged?" George would ask, his voice full of irony. The uniforms were tattered, too, making the pompous, stiff-legged marching style all the more ridiculous.

Nadeem was plagued by dizziness and nausea, which George assured him bitterly were the signs of slow starvation. Many days he couldn't remember what Miriam looked like. His mind played tricks on him and he felt detached from any life. He was a mass of bones and thought, and some days only George's voice gave him reality.

Even more ludicrous was the fact that not far from their camp, a group of Oxford-educated dandies were excavating an archeological find, the ancient city of Carchemish. The head of the expedition was the prominent archeologist David Hogarth and there was some animosity between him and the railroad men, who wanted his excavated earth for fill.

As Nadeem and George were being confronted by the German foreman, an apparition approached that stopped the conversation. The young man, slight but wiry, wore a blazer of French gray trimmed with pink, white shorts held up by a gaudy Arab belt with swinging tassels (denoting his bachelor status), gray stockings, red Arab slippers, and no hat.

"What seems to be the problem?" Nadeem was surprised to hear him speak fluent Arabic in a cultured voice.

"The German believes we aren't earning our lunch," answered George bitterly. "He resents the fact that we talk to each other. I have difficulty knowing who my enemy is in this army. I had no stomach for killing Italians. I feel the enemy is close at hand."

Nadeem was relieved that the German couldn't understand Arabic.

"And who is his superior?" asked the Englishman as if he had a right to know. "Another German?"

"Who knows? If not another German, a Turk who is mesmerized by Germans."

"They cannot starve you and expect hard manual labor. Have you no grievance committee? You look ill, both of you. I can bring it to the attention of the Red Cross. This is inhuman."

George, for once, remained silent, using the time to look the Englishman over. "What is your position here?" he asked, none too politely.

The agile young man ignored the question. "I like the Arabs," he said simply. "That's why I've taken the trouble to learn your language. I think your government was foolish to break with Great Britain in favor of Germany. They don't understand your temperament." He rubbed his smooth chin and paced a few steps. He seemed to find it difficult to stand still. "Why do they put an army unit to work on the German railroad?"

"This is our reward for the Tripoli campaign," Nadeem answered. "Those who survived were promised safety."

"You won't be here long," said the young man soberly. "The Balkans are following Italy's example. Greece has declared war over Salonica."

"How do you know such things?" persisted George. "Who are you?"

"I'm with the archeological expedition half a mile from here. My name is Thomas Edward Lawrence."

Two weeks later, a representative of the International Red Cross came to inspect the camp and there was an influx of food, which was said to come from America. The quantity of the rations increased, although the food was not always recognizable. They saw a lot of the dashing young man in weeks to come. He often rode by with a companion wearing pith helmet and boots. The two seemed full of spirit, rough and ready to take on anything. About a month after the conversation with George and Nadeem, the Englishman's prediction came to pass. The Balkans decided to fight for their independence, and Nadeem's unit was once again prepared to march toward the coast.

On the night before they left, Nadeem wrote his wife a letter, not knowing when or if he would have the opportunity to write again:

My dearest Miriam,

It is difficult for me to remember, at times, what you look like, or more precisely, your entire face, for I can always summon up the depth and clarity of your beautiful eyes. I see them and hear your voice and picture Esa's charming, alert face and the innocent goodness always evident in Hanna and, yes, the perplexed frown on Khalil —I would give a lot even to see his frown—although perhaps he's grown out of that by now.

We march tomorrow and it may be some time before I write again. My wish is to keep you from worrying over my welfare. We are fed and clothed and treated fairly. I dream of my orderly days running the shop, which, next to you and the children, brings me great happiness. Your courage and resolve to keep the business open sustain me in moments of doubt over the future. Can you imagine my gratitude? My love and thoughts are with you, my dearest. Keep well.

Your devoted husband

11

You look different.

Early Saturday morning, she brought baby Esa to wait under the vaulted arch of the Damascus Gate, where the carriage passengers from Tamleh disembarked. She had sent a note with a man from the village and was expecting to see only Hanna, but Zareefa was first to step out. "You?" Miriam blurted out excitedly. "How did you get away?"

Zareefa smiled. "I brought Meena," she nodded to her oldest daughter, who hung back with Hanna, "and sent the other two to Umm Jameel." The women embraced and Miriam reached for Hanna. The look of uncertainty on his small pale face touched her. He was short for his age and his unruly hair hung across his forehead in innocent spikes.

Zareefa was cuddling little Esa but stopped to scrutinize her sister-in-law. "You look different."

"It's my hair," said Miriam offhandedly. "It has to fit under the nurse's cap."

"It's more than your hair. You look all . . . aglow . . . I don't know how to say it . . . beautiful. Yes, beautiful."

"It's the life here . . . so busy. And the cold weather." Miriam took Hanna's hand, closing off any more discussion of her looks. "Come, let's go put your things in the hotel."

"Hotel?"

"Yes. One of the doctors thinks I deserve to be with my children in a pleasant setting . . . away from the hospital. He booked a room for us."

"They must think a great deal of you at that hospital," said Zareefa thoughtfully. "A hotel . . . I've never slept in a hotel."

"Neither have I," said Miriam. "And we must have dinner out, too. That was the other instruction."

"Oh." Zareefa suddenly relaxed. "Isn't it wonderful? Can we look at the shops on Jaffa Road and Suq Aftimos? And the baths? Can we go to the baths first?"

"Of course. We'll all have a nice hot bath."

"Il hammam, il hammam." Little Esa began to clap his hands excitedly. "I like to take a bath," he said, clipping each word. "I like it!" They

weren't used to hearing him speak in full sentences and everyone began to laugh.

"Do you hear from Nadeem?" Zareefa whispered the question—fearful that the subject would dampen the gaiety of the day, but it still surprised Miriam. They could have been discussing someone she barely knew. "Two letters," she managed to answer, struggling to remember what news they had contained. Fortunately, Zareefa's attention was caught by the passersby. The children, exhausted from the long bath and several hours of walking, had been satisfied to make their dinner out of the abundant snacks from the street peddlers and were in bed. Esa had been returned to the orphanage.

For a few moments before going into the hotel dining room for dinner, the two women had stood side by side in the growing dusk, watching as the wealthy families of Jerusalem threaded their way through the narrow streets, a convoy spearheaded by several manservants holding lanterns to light their way.

"Look," Zareefa pointed to several well-dressed matrons following in the wake of their husbands. "We would be ready to sleep, and they are just starting the evening. There are so many ways to live," she said with longing, "but perhaps they have problems we don't see."

"Perhaps it's just that we're afraid of progress," Miriam said harshly and then softened her tone. "They have servants to do the work. You and I have responsibilities."

Zareefa nodded. "What do you do in the evenings? Do you have friends at the hospital? Perhaps you're too exhausted to care about anything except sleep."

"I have to study arithmetic at night," said Miriam quickly. What if I were to tell you that I lie in bed with a man who is not my husband. He kisses me everywhere and makes me forget who I am. Zareefa, I'm not the person you think. I'm no longer anyone you would recognize. "Father Alphonse put me in the orphanage school; otherwise I would have ruined the business and Nadeem would have to come back to nothing." Her voice sounded hollow and insincere, but Zareefa was too interested in her surroundings to notice. "What do you hear from Jameel?"

"You know Jameel," Zareefa spoke with mock weariness. "He has managed to find himself the most comfortable situation possible. He's in Damascus. In the purveyor's office. You can be sure he'll return with more weight than before."

"Perhaps," said Miriam seriously. "But he might want to paint a rosier picture than exists so he won't worry you. I think Nadeem is not telling me the whole story." Now she remembered that Nadeem had written about the men he had met and very little about himself. He had written a full page about a Kurd who was his work companion. "Zareefa," her voice grew serious, "the talk everywhere is fearful. No one knows what to expect next."

"If something happened to Jameel, I don't know what would become of me," said Zareefa. Her normally relaxed features were scrunched in anxiety. "I would have to marry someone else. And who would want a widow with three girls? Perhaps they would think I can bear only girls."

"You would have to get used to another man in your bed, too," said Miriam, vehemently. "That would be the hardest part." She surprised herself. With all their intimacy, she and Zareefa had never mentioned this subject. "I guess the same possibilities are waiting for me."

"Not you. You have a certain confidence that I lack. Whatever happens, you will find a way to deal with it. Look what you've done already. And I see how you've changed. You can take your part in all of this"—she threw her arms wide to encompass Jerusalem and all its urbane sophistication—"without fear. I could never have managed it."

"We'll see how it turns out," said Miriam, avoiding Zareefa's eyes. Her sister-in-law had brought back her immediate past, and it had the effect of making Max seem unreal. She felt as if she were in a no-man's-land, between both worlds, poised, waiting for the stronger pull to take her.

The first two months of 1912 were bitterly cold. There was a shortage of coal in Jerusalem, and any young man whom the army had not taken could make a good living bringing up fuel from the port of Jaffa.

There were many cases of influenza and pneumonia, and all the hospitals seemed full and were cooperating with each other to prevent an epidemic.

In March, as the weather improved, it was the political climate that became bitter. There were three public executions of well-born Arabs accused of treason against the government, accusations that were probably true, since an infant nationalist movement had begun to take hold.

Khalil, much improved, had been attending morning classes in the old Schnellers Orphanage and helping to cane chairs in the afternoon, after his leg therapy. His mother's new job and uniform—the fact that she was capable in a way he hadn't expected—had a sobering effect on him. He was more self-sufficient and eager to help himself improve his walk.

Max had found a small, narrow house on St. James Road, barely fourteen feet wide, squeezed between a bakery and the convent that housed an order of English nuns. A high buff-colored wall, pierced by an ornate gate so small one had to duck to enter, shielded it from the street. The house was built high and from the top floor, which contained the bedrooms, one could see beyond the surrounding roofs and the wall of the city to the somber hills of Moab.

The neighboring bakery closed at five and the good sisters were usually at vespers when Miriam came to the house after finishing at the hospital. Some days they had one or two hours together, which seemed luxurious. Other days, an emergency would keep Max past the time when it was safe for Miriam to stay, and she would lock up and leave again feeling bereft. Yet it was unthinkable not to come, even if she saw him only for ten minutes. Max defined her life . . . defined the woman she had become. He made her heart beat and her blood flow. Inevitably, their first embrace would end in the wide brass bed with its eiderdown pillows and quilts. The street noises would drift up from below, making her feel protected and, at the same time, a vital part of life.

In the past, her face had always appeared either stern or distracted—not unusual for a mother of three, who might have to meet a crisis at any time. Now, her features were relaxed, her eyes overly bright. Her lips, bruised by tempestuous lovemaking, were a healthy pink. She felt voluptuous—plumped and filled with love fluids. In the waning light of dusk Max often patted her rump and pulled her down on his lap, saying, "You have the most beautiful backside—and I see many, you know. How have you managed it with all those pregnancies?"

How had she managed it? This was the reward of a strenuous life. All those years of walking.

While she waited for Max in the tiny wood-paneled parlor, she often did her school work—for she was still learning—but always stuffed it in her satchel before he could see it. She felt ignorant and unschooled and was especially sensitive to her obtuseness in mathematics. One day, Max came in quietly and was standing behind her before she heard him.

"What have we here?" He had become interested only because of her efforts to shove the papers out of sight.

"Please, don't look," she pleaded, imagining how her ill-formed numbers would appear to him. Her writing was childish-looking, and she was deeply embarrassed by it.

"Miriam . . ." he held her hand and patted it reassuringly. "You mustn't be ashamed of any effort to improve."

"You say that because you're not aware of how little I know. I sit in a class with twelve-year-old boys who learn things so quickly. I do fine at the reading, but the mathematics comes very hard."

He pulled her up and took her in his arms. "You are very wise . . . and courageous. One of the things that draws me to you is your determination. These shoulders . . ."—he put a hand on each of them—"how often have I seen them square back with spirit and . . . and acceptance. Miriam, you have the gift of acceptance, but also the will to take the difficult road. How many women in your village can read and write?" She shrugged. She didn't feel wise at all. And as for determination—she had betrayed her husband, her family, everything, without even a struggle. "No, no," he persisted. "Tell me, how many?"

"None that I know. Only those who teach at the Friends Girls' School, and they are not from the village. Boys are taught, but women learn other things."

"There, you see? Yet despite that attitude, you've made something of yourself. If you had been born in a less repressive culture, you would probably have become a teacher or . . . more."

"Max . . ."—just as he spoke, it occurred to her that he was thinking of another woman. Someone who had meant a great deal to him. She rose and went to the window so she would have the courage to ask the question —"why do I have the feeling right now that you are thinking of someone who became a teacher or . . . more? There is a photograph in your room at the hospital of a beautiful woman. Is she someone you loved?"

When she turned around, he looked suddenly exhausted. He sank into an easy chair and beckoned her to him. They sat together, her head on his chest, his fingers idly massaging her neck, tracing her chin and jaw. "There was someone that I admired a great deal. My parents would have been very happy if I married her. She was the daughter of my father's best friend and colleague. I wanted to make them happy—they had been wonderful parents to me . . ." He stopped talking in midsentence, as if the information were pointless.

Miriam raised her head and arched back to look at him. "Was she beautiful?"

"Women always want to know that—as if it's the most important thing. I don't know. Are you beautiful?"

"Oh, Max . . . you certainly know if she was beautiful or not."

"Well . . . she probably was. She was one of the nicest human beings. Loyal and sensitive . . . giving."

"But why didn't you marry her?"

"I'm not sure I have to answer." He was mildly exasperated. "It's a poor assumption . . . if the woman is beautiful, it doesn't always follow that one has to marry her."

"No, of course not." She felt ashamed. "I'm sorry for prying."

"Never mind. The problem was, I didn't love her. It was as simple as that. I admired her. I liked her. I felt extremely affectionate toward her . . . but there was no . . . no passion."

She wanted to ask, Do you admire me? Do you like me? "Did she marry someone else?" she asked instead.

"No." He looked troubled, almost annoyed. "I think she didn't want to admit failure. She thought I had to get this—coming here, halfway across the world—out of my system and then I'd go home to her."

"Perhaps you will." Miriam felt the power of the other woman. She herself had drawn Max to her with fierce wanting. She began to fidget with her hands, as she always did when she was nervous. "Perhaps she's wiser than you think."

"You're both wrong." He got up and went to the bed to take his shoes off. His movements were so slow and weary that Miriam went to help him. He sighed deeply. "I'm not here to get *anything* out of my system." He emphasized certain words with each tug at the boots. "I became a *doctor* because my father was a doctor. I came here to help the poor because my *mother,* unable to bear more than one child, devoted herself to the poor. Isn't that understandable?"

"No." Her mouth pursed in disdain. "Your work saves lives and brings people out of misery and pain. You shouldn't dismiss it by saying you're simply imitating your mother and father."

"That's not such a bad rationale for one's choices in life. That's what your tradition is all about."

"It's a totally different situation. To go against the clan's traditions would have caused my parents and myself a great deal of anguish, and what would I have gained?"

"What about here, now? With me? Is it causing you a great deal of anguish?"

"With you I have no choice." She had been walking around the room but went to kneel before him, returning his gaze with such an open look of love that the blue of her eyes became liquid velvet. "Nothing is worse than the pain of not seeing you." The last few words were a whisper and had a great effect on him. It was a simple statement of her feelings and asked nothing in return. He took her upturned face in his hands and kissed her forehead, her eyes, and then her mouth. "Now,"—she disengaged herself with a righteous sigh, stood, placed his shoes neatly by the side of the bed, and straightened her skirts—". . . I must leave."

"Leave?" He wasn't expecting that. "You can't leave yet."

"I must." She smoothed her hair, put a shawl around her shoulders, and picked up her satchel. "I have paper work to do for the shop, and Khalil is waiting to have dinner with me. See you tomorrow, Dr. Broder."

She usually felt let down and dejected when she returned to the hospital after an hour of lovemaking, but tonight there was an odd satisfaction. How complicated love was. She was pleased that they had spent the time in discussion and not in bed. She was comforted by the idea that she had left him wanting her. Much later, she remembered what he had said about her wisdom and determination and how they had drawn him to her. Perhaps, but it was much deeper than that. With all his education, Max Broder didn't know himself very well at all.

When the influenza flurry diminished, there was an uncommon lull at the hospital and Max made arrangements for a trip to the beckoning warmth of Jericho. At twelve hundred feet below sea level one could leave the wintery blasts of the Judean plateau and, within a matter of hours, be in a tropical climate, breathing the fragrant air amid orange groves and bathing in the briny waters of the Dead Sea. All the wealthy families rented homes there for the season and avoided the discomforts of the rainy winters. He planned to make the trip on horseback and was excited by the prospect of riding uninterruptedly for two days.

One afternoon, when Miriam arrived at the house on St. James Road, he told her to close her eyes and led her up the stairs. "I have a surprise."

"I'm not good with surprises." She remembered the vest Nadeem had brought home when she was pregnant with Hanna. How uncomfortable that surprise had made her.

They reached the bedroom at the top of the landing and he led her in, turned her toward the bed, and gave the signal to open her eyes with a mock trumpet flourish. There on the bed, amid large boxes and many sheets of tissue paper were—she didn't know what. Clothes? But what kind of clothes? A strange rounded hat was the most obvious. And dainty boots of the smoothest leather. And a navy skirt of wool challis with a short boned jacket to match and a coordinated tattersall vest. A high-collared blouse and stock tie completed the outfit.

She didn't know what to say. "These are for you," said Max, obviously excited with his present.

"They're very unusual," offered Miriam, trying to sound enthusiastic. "They must have cost a great deal of money. But, Max," she looked at him uncomfortably, "where would I wear such clothes?"

"On a horse, of course, my silly darling. It's a riding habit. The latest thing, I'm told. The woman said . . . well, she called this little flounce on the jacket a 'peplum.' Very stylish. Come on, try it on. I chose a woman in the shop who was about your size, and she assured me this would fit you."

"A riding habit? Max . . . it was generous of you to get it, but I don't own a horse." She was about to add that she had a long-standing fear of horses and would not willingly mount one, but he interrupted.

"Never mind. I have two and we're going on a holiday . . . by horse. Cook's has arranged it for me. We'll ride down to Jericho and spend the night out under the stars with a guide to set up our tent and cook our food."

"By horse?"

"Yes. Don't worry, I'll be right beside you. After an hour, you'll be an expert rider."

"How can I leave Khalil . . . the shop . . . my nursing . . . ? Surely you don't want me to abandon Isabel."

"Isabel insists that you do abandon her. I want to investigate illnesses in the lowlands and I need a competent nurse with me." He winked. "I haven't had a real vacation in a year. Would you deny me one now? Isabel will care for Khalil, who needs a little neglect—if you're up to a little honest appraisal. We'll leave this wretched wetness for five days. I've made the arrangements. We'll meet our guides on Thursday right outside St. Stephen's Gate."

Ironically, on the day of their departure, the weather turned mild, and there was the tumid smell of spring in the air. The sun rose, hidden at first by the high ridge of the Mount of Olives, turning the clouds pink and gold. Hundreds of swifts suddenly fled the mountains and flew screaming in the air. From a minaret high above, a muezzin sounded the first call to prayer.

Miriam had never felt so self-conscious, although Max had been enchanted by her appearance. "You look beautiful. If we were in Europe, you would be the most ravishing lady in the party and the most envied."

"And what am I here in Palestine? A village woman trying to pass as something I'm not."

"Forgive me. I didn't mean to sound patronizing. It's just that Europe, for me, is the standard. It's my culture."

"And,"—she tugged at the edges of the fawn-colored gloves and thrust the tip of the crop into the ground—"this is mine."

They waited for the guides to load the tents and provisions on two donkeys before their little party started off down the road that wound around The Mount of Olives toward Bethany. Miriam was petrified of the horse, which seemed too high off the ground for safety, yet she was determined not to show her fear. When the beast began to move in that precarious undulating way, she was certain disaster would strike before the day was over. Still, she said nothing. She would ride the dreaded horse without complaint to the ends of the earth lest he think the women of Judea were inferior to those he had left at home.

The men from Cook's galloped ahead to prepare for a rest stop near the Inn of the Good Samaritan. Jericho was only twenty-three miles away, but the winding, tortuous route, with its high cliffs on one side and steep drop-offs on the other, made the trip twice as long. Robberies and holdups were a common occurrence and two guides, well-armed, followed discreetly behind Max and Miriam.

At a glance, the panorama that greeted them as they began what appeared to be an endless descent made them solemn and thoughtful. The drop-offs were awesome. Barren cliffs and depressions alternated with patches of luxuriant growth. The heavy rains of the previous weeks had sunk the earth in those spots that harbored graves, and you could see the rectangular depressions that would soon alert robbers that there was a tomb to be pillaged.

After an hour of riding, they arrived at the first populated spot and tethered their horses in the ragged village of Bethany. Max stopped to buy snacks—which he never ate—from street vendors carrying trays. The children immediately surrounded him, begging for coins, which he readily gave, but Miriam could see he was inspecting them for illness. The tour guide, eager to earn his fee, wanted to show them the sights. "Very near, doctor, is the church dedicated to the miracle of raising Lazarus from the dead."

Max demurred. Though he was avidly interested in the archeological finds, he was skeptical of the supposed biblical sites.

"Oh, please, Max," Miriam said, surprising herself, "I'd like to go."

"Why?" He looked puzzled.

"To pray there."

"Pray? You're religious?"

She shrugged. "Please, come with me."

"Well . . . it's not my style, but . . . Oh, all right, we'll go to see where the man was raised from the dead. But if you must know, that's a hell of a thing to ask of a medical man."

She smiled and put her arm through his, anxious to fix the details of the moment in her mind: the unfamiliar restraint of the boned jacket, the pleasant support of the riding boots outlining her legs, the soft cotton stock tie against her throat. Her momentary mastery of the dreaded horse made her feel cocky and accomplished, ready to strike out in daring directions. The last restraints of convention slid away like the deluge that washed the jutting mountain rocks clean, and she felt free in a new way. I'm here alone with him, she thought. I can touch him at will. I can look at him without hurry or interruption. For the moment, he's totally mine and I am his.

When they reached the church, they were surprised to find it was no more than a cave, dusty and dark. They descended about twenty steps, each with a candle, and found themselves in a little vestibule, facing a Christian altar. Max knelt beside her without protest. The coolness inside was seductive, as was the subdued light after the blinding sun. Their ears buzzed as their systems adjusted to the change, but after a few minutes they were enveloped by a calm so healing that both were content to be silent and still, drinking in that special peace. Votive candles flickered in rows, as if struggling to survive. Their shoulders touched, exchanging a warmth more intimate than any kiss. His face loomed over hers, inches away, filled with a desire so pure it made his eyes look helpless. It was a moment of forced reflection, and she thought, This is my life. This moment is all of my life. However long it lasts.

After Bethany, the ground rose temporarily and they had to concentrate on their footing, for part of the road was pure bedrock. Miriam became apprehensive about staying on the horse and, with each lurch, she was certain that any moment she would bounce off and be tossed like a rag doll into the chasm.

By the time they reached the Inn of the Good Samaritan, which was adjacent to a Turkish police post, their ears told them they had descended several hundred feet. The temperature had risen, and they were grateful to sink into the pillows of the temporary shelter set up by the guides for lunch. Both were drenched, and Miriam removed her jacket and vest. Lunch was a mélange of cold meats and vegetables doused with vinaigrette sauce, with a fruit compote and lady fingers for dessert. Miriam sat stiffly upright on the cushions, ill at ease. She was unused to being served, and the steward was an extraordinarily handsome young man whose manner was haughty. You're not fooling anyone, madam, was the cold message she received from his sly glances. She picked at her food, too stimulated to eat, making the steward sniff disdainfully, "Madam isn't hungry after such a long ride?"

Max refused any wine or sherry. "The change in altitude will play havoc with us if we have alcohol in our system," he warned.

They were expecting to reach the monastery by dusk, hoping to camp outside of the compound, which was about a two-hour drive from the Dead Sea. They followed the dry channel of a brook for several miles, as if descending to the very bowels of the earth. Not a house or even a tree was to be seen. The winter's heavy rains had washed down the hills to this low spot, and the horses became stuck in choking slime. When they looked up, the hills were barren, studded with outcroppings of rock. At times, through a crevice, they could see the deep blue of the Dead Sea.

The ravines were frightful and, far off, they could spot the pilgrims who had preceeded them that morning led by the guards bearing flaming torches on long poles made of turpentine and old rags. Every so often, they would charge through the surrounding bushes to drive out any bedouin who might be lurking. After a while, the zigzag line of pilgrims disappeared around a curve, and they were alone once more. It was so quiet they could hear the crickets chirping in the herbage and watched bustards and pintail grouse hunt for wooly red caterpillars.

They had miscalculated the time, and dusk came while they were still far from their destination. The moon rising over the brown hills of Moab was eery as it trembled over the waters of the Dead Sea.

Max came up alongside her as she hunched over her horse, her knuckles white with effort. "This is more difficult than I had imagined," he said with guarded sympathy. "Just grip your horse and let him do the rest. He's picked his way over these wadis a hundred times. Your job is simply to stay on."

She nodded and made a valiant attempt to sit tall in the saddle, but one lurch sent her back down over the animal, gripping him with every muscle. Max rode ahead with the guide to survey what they had in front of them. As dusk became dark, almost in unison, the dismal cries of owls and jackals began to bounce back and forth across the ravines.

They made slow progress with only the moon to light their way, but there was nothing to do but continue, or else sleep in the wilderness without supper. The moon gave enough light to outline the chasms and present an eerier backdrop, although no such enhancement was necessary. Miriam would never forget that evening ride or the grim relief over the sudden appearance of the gay-peaked shelters dotting the campgrounds where they were to spend the night.

She dismounted and wobbled briefly on the ground, giving her horse over to the guide to be cared for. Max took a lantern from one of the stewards who came to greet them and led the way to unexpected luxury, courtesy of Thos. Cook & Son. They had outfitted the striped green and white tent as if creating a permanent home. A beautiful Oriental carpet covered every part of the floor, except for the coffee hearth with its heap of white ashes. A large, well-stuffed mattress took up fully half the area, and the other half was a profusion of cushions propped against camel saddles. The cooking was being done outside, and the serving of dinner awaited only the signal that the guests had completed a refreshing wash provided by an ingenious portable shower, which allowed one bountiful cascade of water for each of them to rinse with after soaping up. Miriam replaced the riding outfit with a caftan and sank down into the welcome softness of a large cushion.

She began to fuss with the caftan, pulling it out and then pushing it against her body. "It's lovely," said Max.

"Is it appropriate?"

"Perfectly. You look no different from any other matron on a Cook's tour with her husband. Except, of course, for one small detail."

"And what's that?" she asked anxiously.

"I don't think every matron's husband is eager to do this." He gave her a long, slow kiss, letting his hands stray inside the loose armholes of the caftan to caress her skin beneath.

"Oh, Max, no. They'll come in and see us."

"Shhh," he murmured against her temple. "You musn't worry about anything. No one is paying any attention to us." A throat was cleared on the other side of the tent, and Miriam jumped. The haughty steward brought in a pitcher of water, glasses, and a bottle of wine.

"Set that here," Max directed the man. "And bring the hors d'oeuvres."

"Right away, *Herr Doktor.*"

Max poured two glasses of the wine and handed one to Miriam. "Drink it down. It will help you relax."

Miriam eyed the glass as if it were a loaded pistol. "I've never had spirits."

"Spirits?" he said innocently. "This is wine. Not the same at all. This will calm the nerves and help you enjoy dinner and a good night's sleep. Here, come on, sip it." He put the goblet to her lips and she took a large gulp.

The wine did make her feel better. As if a central inner string that had made everything taut was suddenly relaxed. She felt the tightness around her mouth, where her nervousness showed most, give way. She put her hand over his and smiled, uncaring that two new stewards were now setting up a table in front of them and covering it with many small bowls, each holding a different appetizer. There were dark ripe olives glistening with oil, roasted eggplant, redolent and smooth in a garlicky sesame butter dressing, hot rounds of bread, cheese, and cucumber.

The steward told them in passing that on the grounds there was a large party of Italians and Germans, who were there to shoot game.

"What sort of game?" asked Max.

The steward smirked. "Quail." Then he snorted contemptuously. "You don't need a gun for quail. The birds do the Mediterranean in one stretch and arrive exhausted. When we want quail, we simply put up a net barrier and they fall into it gratefully."

At first, Miriam merely nibbled at the food, more interested in being safely on the ground than in eating. But after the wine relaxed her, she felt the pangs of hunger and dug into the tidbits of fire-roasted meat, which were brought in on skewers and deftly transferred onto the hot rounds of bread.

They smiled awkwardly, their mouths stuffed with the lightly crusted tender chunks that moistened the bread and created an irresistible mouthful.

"There," said Max dabbing at the corner of her mouth, "do you forgive me?" He began laughing uproariously. "I can't forget the sight of you grasping that poor horse by the hair."

"It's nothing to laugh at." She began to punch his arm and pushed him over onto the pillows, the better to pummel him.

"All right," he smiled at her. "You have me here helpless." He had the same look of desire that he had given her in Lazarus' Tomb. "Let me dismiss the stewards." He clapped loudly and the men removed the table and remaining food. Their movements created a breeze that carried in the faint scent of ripe fruit. "What's that smell?" asked Max.

"Jericho," said the steward. "You can smell Jericho's orchards from quite far. Tomorrow, you'll see why," he said archly and left.

Max stood and offered her his hand. "I've waited all day to make love to you. Even the ride couldn't take my mind off it. Why?" he said helplessly, "why is the thought of you so seductive?" He dropped her hand and went to stand at the door of the tent. "I don't take it lightly that you're another man's wife."

"I know." She went to stand near him and was met by a waft of perfumed air.

"I don't think you do. There are many women . . . I could dine at the home of an anxious mother with a marriageable daughter every night of the week."

The remark about her marriage had ruined the moment for her, but this admission made her heart sink because she knew it was true. She had seen the mothers chirping around him at the hospital. She had witnessed the chance encounters on the street with lovely, well-dressed young women who were cultured and educated and whose soft, white hands had never felt the soil. At such times, she asked herself, Why me?

"Why me?" she asked now.

"You're everything I need. You're real and strong and without artifice.

You've liberated me in a way I hadn't thought was possible." He took her in his arms. "There's no one like you for me. No one."

"Oh, Max," she put her arms around his neck. "And there's no one like you for me."

He picked her up and carried her to the sumptuous mattress. "This will be our first entire night together. We won't let it go to waste." After he laid her down he went and got the lantern. "I want to see you." He removed her caftan and his own clothes and lay beside her. "I don't think you realize how beautiful you are."

He traced her chin and mouth—"Here . . . so beautiful . . ."—and began to kiss all around her mouth until his lips came to rest on hers. "Here . . . so beautiful . . ."—he traced the bones at the base of her throat, first with his fingers and then his lips. He continued down attending avidly to little portions of her . . . the fleshy rise where her arms began, working his way around the opalescent mounds until he reached their pink wounded heart. He kissed and nipped and rubbed his cheeks on her with appreciative sighs that made her blood pound. She tried to rise, but he pushed her back gently with a soothing "Shhh . . ."

In this fashion, this man, whose day-to-day life was spent exploring the human body, set each separate part of her on fire. She could no longer think coherently. Her body melded and melted into his. Her skin under his lips became his skin. "Max . . . Max . . ." she couldn't keep from crying out. He traveled down her body, feathering her with his kisses, murmuring love words against her until she felt a crescendo of arousal. For a breathless moment, he was poised above her perfectly still. The mournful cry of a jackal echoed in the cliffs. Max put his head down against her. He opened her legs, smoothing the inner thighs until she felt a fierce desire to force him inside her. She tried unsuccessfully to rise again, but he continued caressing her thighs with his lips and inching ever closer to the throbbing center. The anticipation was so great she dug her hands into his shoulders and then, unwillingly, found herself pushing down, eager for that final thrilling touch. She responded with a sound so profound it destroyed his patience. He climbed up swiftly and put himself inside her and they clung to each other, gasping with ecstasy and desperation. Lost to earth. Floating among the reachable stars.

12

Would you like to go home, mate?

"What is it?" asked Nadeem solicitously. He was worried. George was not walking straight. He was stumbling along as if drunk, sometimes walking on the outer part of his feet, sometimes shuffling and grunting as if it were a chore to breathe.

They had been stationed at Yesilkoy, at the military camp, preparing for the final leg of the march to the Dardanelles. The camouflaged tents had been nestled in the valley, easily visible from any of the surrounding hills. All around was the peculiar stillness of the countryside, with only the cawing of the crows. Inside the camp there was unusual silence, too. These normally garrulous men had run out of talk. They had voiced their fears and resentments, stated and restated their position and thoughts on everything that mattered to them in the world. Now they conserved their energy and tried to keep warm. Winter made everything gray, although it was milder than usual, with a very cold day often followed by several unseasonably warm ones.

The day after they had arrived at the camp, there commenced a week of intense training and maneuvers beginning early in the morning and continuing until dusk. The formations did not have the bite of disciplined movement because of the ragged uniforms. It was difficult to distinguish the officers from the soldiers. On the eighth day they packed the tents and began the march. They marched night and day.

George's feet began to swell again. This time when Nadeem cut off his boots, fresh blood dribbled out onto the road, creating coins of coagulated dust.

"Can you walk?" the officer asked.

George said nothing.

The officer, disgruntled to have a problem, took George by the shoulders. "Come on, man, you can make it. Only a few more days and we have a day of rest." George began to crumple from under the officer's grip. "Leave him for the wagon," he told Nadeem. Word of a wounded man was passed down the long marching line until it reached the end, where a lumbering horse-drawn wagon picked up the sick and wounded.

The day they left George, however, the wagon was overflowing with all the other sick soldiers. When Nadeem inquired that evening of the medic, he assured him George would be picked up by the next wagon.

The battalion moved on to Salonica, where the Greeks were fighting for possession of the city. The Turks had more officers than men and a puny, ineffectual navy. Within weeks, the battle was decided and forever drove the Ottoman flag from all but a tiny enclave in Europe. The retreating army had weakened and was near starvation. Nadeem sustained himself by praying and meditating. God would help him and get him through this ordeal. He stumbled along, in and out of a trancelike state and visions of supreme comfort—torrents of warm water, cascading over his body, a soothing salve over his painfully cracked hands, Miriam's slim, strong hand in his.

The stone that was kicked up by a horse's hoof hit him squarely in his left eye before it bounced to the ground. The intense pain was a rude shock. He fell slowly in a graceful arc . . . this was the only thing left to do: to lie down on the road and be still.

By some miracle, the wagon picked him up and he was taken to a military hospital in Constantinople. He slept for many days, and by the time they got around to offering medical treatment his eye was beyond repair. An English doctor shook him awake. "You won't see anything with that eye again," he said soberly. "It's your choice if we take it out or leave it in."

"What?" He asked the question three times, willing his brain to function but unable to comprehend what was being said to him. Only his sense of smell told him he was in a hospital.

"It's your choice, mate. Take it out or leave it in?"

"In," he answered finally. He had no idea what they were talking about, only that his answer would make them cease trying to rouse him.

"I've recommended that you be mustered out," said the doctor. "At least the wound will take you home, eh? How does that sound?"

"How will I get home?" In his weakened state, the idea of being all on his own frightened Nadeem. He felt as helpless as a child. His partial vision disoriented him as much as his weakened condition.

"By train. The army will put you on a train to Damascus."

"Train . . . Damascus . . ." He was hard put to understand and unable to make a decision.

The doctor placed his hands on Nadeem's shoulders and forced him to focus on what he was saying. "Would you like to go home? Would you like to take a train home, mate?"

"Yes . . . home . . ." Nadeem whispered and then went back to sleep.

* * *

The train was an open car carrying food supplies. For ten days, he sat with sacks of grain and finally carved a niche for himself out of a wheel of cheese to keep from freezing on the passage through the Taurus mountains. When he arrived in Damascus, instead of seeking transport to Jerusalem, he went to the War Office to get word of George. The place was a madhouse. It was crowded with anxious black-clad women demanding news of their husbands and sons. Harassed officials bleated that no information could be given. There was an angry, smelly queue of humanity and Nadeem waited for hours, only to learn that George had been dead for many weeks. "But have you notified his family? Are you certain?"

"Who are you to demand such answers," said the official harshly.

"A friend."

"A friend! How dare you take our time! Isn't it enough that you know he's dead. Do you know his widow? Tell her to come and sign for herself and she will receive a pension of ninety-nine kurus." Nadeem shook his head. Ninety-nine kurus would not even buy bread for two days. "Tell her her husband died for his country and has a place in heaven."

"Perhaps you have the wrong fellow. This one was a Kurd," said Nadeem pleadingly. "A Kurd from the southern province of Aleppo."

The official slammed the wooden window in Nadeem's face, forestalling any more questions. His manner implied that perhaps Nadeem was even responsible for his friend's death, thereby causing the War Office great trouble and an unnecessary pension.

Nadeem was able to catch a ride in the direction of Jerusalem in an open wagon pulled by horses so thin and underfed that, at one point, he and two other passengers had to push the wagon. The ordeal almost killed him, and his worthless eye throbbed so painfully that he considered jumping off to his death. The second day it was very mild, and the warmth of the sun on his face was the most welcome sensation he had ever felt. For the first time in weeks, he felt deeply and comfortably warm, and he fell into a sound and healing sleep during which he dreamt of Miriam and his mother.

She was folding silk summer coverlets that morning, being careful not to let her nails catch the delicate fabric. She counted a half dozen in a pale shade of peach bordered in satin and another half dozen in pale pink. The man standing in the doorway surprised and frightened her. She dropped the stack of silks and screamed. He looked as if he had been brought from the dead. Gaunt, filthy, bearded, his hair matted and dusty. His feet unnaturally swollen, covered with scraps of rags tied haphazardly and, poking out, one terrible purple toe.

"Miriam?"

The voice brought her up through waves of remembering. No . . . it couldn't be . . . She hadn't the strength to acknowledge it. Then came that voice again. "Miriam."

She studied his face, the blank, clouded eye staring fixedly at nothing. . . . Oh, no—dear Mary, Mother of God, help me now and at the hour of my death—*it was Nadeem.*

"What have I done to you?" Had she spoken aloud? She felt unable to move. The demon of guilt flooded her heart full force.

"You've done nothing," he whispered. "Not you. Not you."

How could Mother Mary help her when her first thought—oh, God, it was beyond her control. While her conscious mind processed the ragged, mutilated man before her, some more primitive instinct sent out an alarm. Max! Max was retreating further and further away from her, and her heart lurched with a pain so searing she held the counter for support.

Nadeem walked the length of the room, staring as if afraid she would disappear. "Miriam? . . . Miriam." Before she could answer, he had thrust himself into her arms and was clinging to her like a child. His grip on her was frightening; his fingers dug into her back. She stared past him, her arms at her side, in a state of shock. Slowly, her arms went under his and, as she felt that familiar body against her, she began to weep, holding him tightly and rocking him like a child.

It was almost dusk before she found the time to walk to the little narrow house. Nadeem had gone to the baths for the first thorough washing since his arduous trip. From Father Alphonse, Miriam secured a set of men's clothes to replace the filthy rags he was wearing and took him to the clinic for medical assistance for his feet. She was grateful that Max was away from the hospital, for to face them both was unendurable. Dr. Ticho had come and looked at Nadeem's eye, confirming the destruction, although he held hope that with the return of health and vigor, he might regain some peripheral vision. When her battered husband was clean and fed, she bedded him down in her own room and then rushed to her lover.

She unlocked the heavy wooden door, noticing for the first time the wrought-iron design hammered in with massive nails. Her legs felt leaden climbing the stairs. Everything became precious—the smooth oak bannister, the faint creak of the third tread. She could hear him above. Each movement was like a stab in her heart. Not to see him again. Not to hold him in her arms. Not to feel his closeness and anticipate his warmth each night. She sat down on the final step, unable to continue. After a few moments, he came out of the room to investigate.

"I thought I heard you." When he realized she wasn't going to get up, he sat next to her. "What is it? You look so upset. Has something happened to the children?"

She stared at his face just inches from hers, unable to speak. "I . . . Max . . . oh, Max." He moved to hold her, but she pulled away. "No . . . I can't bear it."

"Can't bear to touch me? Did I do something?" He forced one hand open and placed the palm to his lips. "What is it? Don't look so frightened. Whatever is wrong, I'll help you." The last narrow shaft of rosy light slipped through a panel in the front door, warmed the wooden dado wall that ran along the stairs. It also tinged Miriam's face, turning her skin to gold. She had never appeared so beautiful to him.

"It's over." Her voice was cold as death.

"What's over?"

"You and I." She said it breathlessly, as if time would run out before she could tell it all. "My husband has returned. He's been wounded, Max. Oh, it's terrible . . . one of his eyes is completely useless, and he stares out of it like someone who has seen unimaginable horrors. Max . . ." Her eyes darted to every corner of the vestibule and she kept wiping her palms on her skirt. "While he's been enduring the horrors of hell, I've been with you. My heart and mind have been filled with you." Tears, one from each eye, began to travel down her golden cheek. Her voice was just a whisper. "And still, right now, having seen him, all I can think about is losing you."

Max was silent, digesting what she had said. "It's not your fault your husband has been hurt," he said softly. "It's beyond your control. You've done everything humanly possible to keep his business together and your children with food in their mouths. You didn't ask to have him inducted into the army. You've nursed Khalil through a terrible ordeal, and it's due to your determination and ingenuity that he has both his legs today. You've done all of this and schooled yourself to better handle the business. When I think of the hours poring over books, the emotional pull of three children living in different places . . . All by yourself being pulled and dragged in every direction."

"It isn't his fault either," said Miriam vehemently. At the very least she could argue Nadeem's case. "He didn't ask to be sent away, and now . . ."—she stopped, as if the reality of what was to come had hit her anew—"he's come home to his wife and family. Max, he needs me! Oh, how he needs me! He clings like a child. As if he's afraid I'll vanish."

"But, my dear," his voice was that of parent to child, "he was going to return someday. You knew that."

"But not now." She burst into tears. "Not maimed and sick while I . . ." She leaned against him and cried.

When he felt her sobs subsiding, he took the opportunity to speak. "Miriam, it's natural for you to react like this. You feel responsible. My darling, you've brought me the greatest happiness. Please, don't diminish it by feeling guilt." He placed his hand under her hair and caressed her neck. "We've brought each other too much happiness to turn it into something sordid."

"Don't. If you tell me I've made you happy, it becomes unbearable." She put her arms around him and pressed closer.

"I see so much misery . . . death, loss of hope, strange attacks to the body without rhyme or reason . . . I don't feel guilty for taking whatever happiness came my way." He handed her his handkerchief to wipe her nose. "Come." He led her to the bedroom and sat her down, removed her shoes, her stockings, her dress, and undergarments. He pulled down the quilt and laid her on the bed. She was glad to have him see her. She wanted her body imprinted on his memory. He undressed and placed himself over her completely—hands over hands, chest over chest, mouth over mouth. They moved slowly, legs intertwined, with none of the frenzy of previous lovemaking. Max touched her with utmost tenderness, as if she were wounded, his fingers trailing her skin as if it might tear open.

The poignancy of these last moments was devastating. "My darling. My precious darling," he murmured against her hair. "How I love the feel of you. Your voice haunts my every dream. The dark storms in your eyes, the movement of your body under mine. Don't leave me. Don't ever leave me. We'll find a way."

Through the open window she could hear the hum of pilgrims' prayers, walking the Via Dolorosa. The chanting filled the room and bounced from wall to wall, drowning out all her thoughts. The weight of her lover's body became the sum and substance of her life. This moment would sustain her now and forever.

When the time came, he entered her with a force that was unlike him. Was it fear or anger? She couldn't be sure. Much later, it occurred to her that for the first time since they had begun their intimacy he had not stopped to put on the protective sheath.

The linen shop at the Grand was shut tight and the Mishwes returned to their little house—Nadeem to recuperate and Miriam to nurse him. Their village had a look of prosperity and progress, but for the moment it made them feel alienated. The weather had warmed considerably, and the year's fresh crop of flowers pushed through the soaked ground. Delicate ferns wrapped themselves around the stones, especially near the cisterns and winter streams.

Their own yard looked remarkably tidy, and Nadeem thought of his father and his ever-present broom. "My father has been here. Look, nothing is neglected." He sat on a stump and put his face into his hands. "I'm afraid to face them. My mother will be inconsolable. It will hurt them to see me like this." Miriam placed a hand on his shoulder and said nothing. She felt awkward. As if she had forgotten how to comfort anyone. Then she caught sight of Hanna, who was pitching stones and looking lonely and unsure.

"Come," she said, rushing to embrace him. "Come say hello to *Baba.*"

Zareefa had dusted the furniture and left food on the table to welcome them. The irresistible aroma of wilted onions, refried lentils, and fresh bread soothed them. Miriam immediately brewed coffee, for they had been too harried to have a proper breakfast, and that earthy aroma now added to the coziness.

When Nadeem saw his house, he stood perfectly still and looked at every corner. The children scattered, searching for forgotten belongings and treasures. "Mama, will we stay here now?" asked Esa in his direct way.

"Yes, Esa," answered Nadeem, placing a hand around the little boy's shoulders, "we'll stay here now, all together." His voice lacked conviction and Miriam knew it would be a while before he could have confidence in the future. His anguish tore at her heart.

"What about Mrs. Spafford at the American School? She'll wonder where I've gone."

"She knows where you are, don't worry," Miriam soothed him, burying her face in his silky, loose curls. He was the only one she could touch without equating it with the pain of not having Max to touch. She felt tender and bruised, although there was no mark on her body. His words echoed in her head during every quiet moment. "Don't ever leave me." If she had believed that he would feel that way forever, she might have gone with him. *And leave Nadeem?* Leave her maimed and needy husband, whose faith in her had never wavered?

It was heartbreak either way, but right now the pull toward Max was stronger. She was not foolish enough to believe she could hold on to Max in his homeland, where he would eventually return. In this way station, the Orient, his involvement with her was one more sign of freedom. But to bring home an uneducated foreign woman with three foreign children, one of whom limped, how long would that stern matriarch in the photograph tolerate that? What's more, she, too, would find the price too high. It was delirium to believe she could leave with the children. She was a product of the clan: its traditions had shaped her; its customs had nurtured her; its vengeance for her dishonor would destroy her. Her love for Max would not survive. Still, right now, the pain of losing him was so fresh, so poignant. She felt it repeatedly as a wave of sadness washing over her, isolating her from all other feeling.

Khalil ran in from the outside, moving faster than she had ever hoped on his disfigured leg. "Will I have to go to school now? Mama, please say I don't."

"Not go to school? How could you ask such a foolish thing? You see how I struggled to make sense of the business because I had not been taught as a young girl? I don't want to hear any more. You will go to school next week. Baba will make arrangements with the Franciscans right away."

"But, Mama, my leg. The boys will laugh at me."

"Then stop limping," said Miriam coldly. Max had suggested that there was no medical reason for Khalil's pronounced limp. It might be a bid for sympathy, he had warned Miriam. She tried to recall his exact words, as she often did. As if recalling his voice would keep him near her. Several times, she walked resolutely toward the carriage road, determined to board the carriage and not stop until she was once more in his arms, but the thought of a new parting and all the anguish it would bring, sent her back home again.

"You don't look well." Nadeem's voice broke into a deep reverie as they sat together one morning. Usually she was hovering over him, placing food on the table, fetching, carrying, smoothing some child's hair so that he would start out for school looking presentable. But today she had sat down in the middle of breakfast, unaware that she had done so, and was staring out at a room that was revolving. The shelves showed double, and she felt as if she might be sick to her stomach. "What is it?" asked Nadeem. And when there was no response, "Miriam? Are you ill?"

"I'm fine," she tried to shrug it off. "Just tired. I didn't sleep well last night." Why had she lied? She didn't feel fine and she had slept as she always slept. A realization was fluttering on the edge of consciousness, like a weary moth. This was a special kind of illness. *Mary, Mother of God!* She made herself busy packing food for everyone, delaying any thought until she was alone.

The older children left for school and Nadeem walked to the market street to buy nails. She went to a small hanging mirror. "You're with child," she whispered to her image and became giddy with happiness. She and Nadeem had not been together since his return. *The child had to be*

Max's. She put her hands over her stomach protectively. "Now he will be with me forever."

That night Nadeem held her, stretching himself along the length of her body but made no move to be intimate. He wanted to talk more than usual, and he told her of George and some of the other soldiers. He spoke of the men he had seen die two or three feet away from him. "I wouldn't have thought death was so ordinary," he said. "It just happens, like breathing or eating. One minute you're standing and the next you're slumped in an odd position. Miriam," he tightened his grip on her, "there were so many moments when I was afraid. I was afraid like a child, like Esa."

"Of course," said Miriam, vindicating his feelings. "Who wouldn't be afraid of death? Death is the end of what we know." As she said it, she realized that Max was no longer dead to her. He was alive in her womb. She wanted to express her gladness. Instead she began to move her hands along her husband's body, pausing to caress him deftly. For a long time, he lay still without responding, but as her hand slid down, she felt a tremor through him, although he still remained passive. She continued her fondling, reawakening each part of his body. He let sound escape his lips, a sweet, gentle groan of relief and rebirth. He took over then and began to kiss her shoulders and her breasts and stroked her thighs with patience and tenderness. She urged him on top of her, aware at each moment that this act was her salvation. There was no mistaking his climax—a deep release of tension, fear, all of the demons that had haunted him. "Nadeem, Nadeem," she whispered when it was over. He mistook her relief for ardor and fell asleep somewhat surprised that his previously shy wife had become an active sexual partner. The following day, Nadeem rose early and proclaimed that he wanted to visit the shop with Miriam so she could explain the state of affairs.

"Are you well enough?" she asked, alarmed at his sudden energetic mood.

"Yes. I feel hopeful of the future, my dear, and you are responsible." He took hold of her hand and looked into her face with total love. Miriam's heart stirred.

"Perhaps you should rest a few more days. Your feet are not healed yet. It's no good to walk too much." She feared going to Jerusalem. What would keep her from rushing to the hospital and blurting out to Max that she was carrying their child. "You don't want to have a relapse."

"If we just go through the inventory together, then I can look over the books at home. Please. I want to return to work. There's so much I want to do."

She didn't feel well enough to take the carriage ride, but she didn't want to admit to illness either. She would just have to hope the ride didn't upset her stomach. Each time she thought of the child inside her, nothing seemed too difficult. It was as if she had been given a second chance with Max, without hurting anyone. "I'll go with you, but you must promise not to stay on your feet more than a few minutes at a time. And we'll have to leave Esa with your mother so we'd best allow an extra half hour, for she will become emotional when she sees you again." Each time Umm Jameel saw her son's clouded eye, she wept and wrung her hands with grief and would not be comforted until she was near collapse.

The ride to Jerusalem was more difficult than she had imagined. With each passing mile, she felt a longing for Max that was frightening. She kept her face toward the countryside in an effort to discourage conversation, for she found it difficult to concentrate on anything that was said. A man was smoking a cigar and it gave her an excuse to seek air. Nadeem, too, seemed to prefer silence. His face had lost some of its paleness and he looked remarkably healed.

When they reached the shop, he had an anxious moment. "At times, I feel that I'm still in some army tent dreaming of this."

"When you see how poorly I've maintained the books, you'll realize this is not a dream at all."

"Don't belittle your efforts. It's because of you that I have something to come back to." He looked over at the untended counters of the apothecary shop. The merchandise in the cases was dusty and faded. "That poor fellow has lost his business. Perhaps he's been killed. Have you heard?"

"He lost an arm," said Miriam, suddenly remembering that she had meant to visit the druggist's wife and had forgotten to do so.

"I will not complain again." Nadeem's voice was resolute. "Now, let's see what we have."

He began by inspecting the stacks of regular merchandise, riffling through the soft materials with pleasure. "It's good that we have some inventory. I feel things will become scarce now that Turkey is losing its hold in Europe." They spent the next two hours itemizing what they had in stock and making an order for items that needed replenishing. "Freneau will give me time to pay," said Nadeem. "I'll tell him of our situation."

He would have been happy to work until dusk, but he saw that Miriam looked fatigued and they walked out into the bustle of Latin Patriarchate Road to buy food from the street vendors. As they strolled, unintentionally they passed Max's house and Miriam's heart began to race. The idea of seeing Max became so seductive she sent Nadeem back to the shop and stopped to pray in the Church of the Holy Sepulcher. She knelt in the first pew of one of the small side chapels facing a replica of the Madonna. How kind and loving was the expression on the Holy Mother's face. If only she could pour out her feelings to her and gain forgiveness. "Mother Mary," she murmured softly, "teach me to understand my own nature. Why are we made to feel so strongly? If it is sinful, why did I feel desire so overwhelmingly? I betrayed my marriage vows. I betrayed every social law of my clan, but I feel no remorse. I am overjoyed to bear this child inside me. If it is born healthy and whole, I will devote myself to my family and do what I can to drive the thought of Max out of my mind. Hold me to this vow, but grant me this request."

When she left the church, the sun had shifted, lighting up the faces of the smooth-stoned houses on the street. Was this beautiful scene an omen that her request had been heard? She felt at peace. Her heart was quiet, her body had lost its expectations. When she entered the shop, Nadeem looked puzzled. His face was pale and strained. "Nadeem, we must return. You've done too much."

"In a moment. Look here,"—he pointed to the intricate monogram on a stack of face towels—"the initials are all wrong. The order says ASB but the towels are ASR. We can't ask for payment."

She took the order form and looked closely. "The order is right. Look," she pointed to the letters with her finger. "It's an *R* here."

Nadeem looked at the paper and then let it drop to the floor. He was quiet for a moment. "My eyes play tricks on me. Perhaps they will get worse. If you hadn't been here to verify it, I would have believed we had made a mistake."

"Don't be harsh with yourself, Nadeem. Dr. Ticho said you had to expect some difficulty. But he also said your sight would improve. You mustn't tire yourself out."

"I'll have to depend on you a little longer."

"For what?" she said lightly. "To verify a number? That's nothing. I have depended on you all these years." She saw his face soften with gratitude and relief. "Come, let's go home. The children will be wondering if we're coming back at all."

There comes a point when—no matter how grievous the loss—the inate will of the body and mind to flourish takes over. The ache for Max dulled.

There was a morning when the routine of life swept her along. She went through the day without regrets, and she didn't think longingly of the tartan blanket on the chaise in that cramped parlor where she had sat and done her schoolwork. Her dreams shifted away from Jerusalem.

13

A big healthy girl.

"Ah, finally," said Zareefa, with a satisfied sigh, "you have your daughter."

"Is it true?" Miriam felt such a flutter of excitement in her stomach. It was real. The time had come to face the consequences. The midwife placed the bundle down beside her, but she couldn't think clearly. The clucking women were milling around eager to evaluate the baby. She had nice coloring. A broad forehead. Sandy hair . . . but birth hair was unreliable in its color. Too bad she didn't have her mother's eyes. She wasn't beautiful . . . but what baby was beautiful? She was long . . . nearly twenty-two inches. *Salamu aleiki.* A big healthy girl. For the fourth child in a family of boys, a girl was welcome.

"Mabrook, Miriam," said Jamilla, bending over to kiss her cheek. For a moment their eyes met and Jamilla looked meaningfully at her daughter.

"It looks as if she has your coloring," said Miriam with a weak smile.

"It seems so," Jamilla answered. "But whose mouth?" The question hung in the air and it took effort not to fill the void with nervous chatter.

Nadeem's mother appropriated her new granddaughter, the better to defend her against any but the most complimentary remarks. She, too, was unsettled by the look of the baby. When her sister approached, she set her jaw.

"Such a broad forehead, *habibty,"* Halla said innocently, stroking a wisp of reddish hair that strayed downward.

"And how should it be," rejoined Umm Jameel, "narrow like a monkey's? Her broad forehead is full of brains. Like her father's . . . and her mother's," she added, casting a circumspect look at Miriam.

"But look what a mouth, like an angel."

Miriam looked up anxiously. She had caught a glimpse of the baby, but her mouth had been stretched in a yawn. "Umm Jameel, let me have a look at her."

It was unmistakeable. The mouth was a miniature replica of Max's and it was more seductive in this feminine face. She also had Max's strong jawline. This was going to be a determined child. The eyes were already knowing. How could a baby, several hours old look defiant? Miriam stroked the downy cheeks and made a cooing noise. Did the intensity of desire at conception mold the child? If so, this one came with strength and passion.

"What will you call her?" asked Jamilla.

"Julia, I think."

That evening she saw Nadeem with the infant in his arms, enraptured. For the first time since she had betrayed him, she felt a deep and terrible fear—not of being punished, but of hurting Nadeem. That steadfast, loving face would crumple in pain at the truth. Her heart pounded. She felt the blood draining from her upper body. Her hands were cold. Worse, she knew that she would do it all again because her desire for Max had been beyond control.

"Miriam, you look so pale. What is it? Are you ill? Do you need something?"

"No, no. I'm fine." How could he not know? Please, God!

Nadeem came and sat beside her, still with the baby in his arms. "Why does this one touch me so?" he asked, staring adoringly at the face peeking out of the blanket. "I want to shield her from everything unpleasant. I want to make her life beautiful. My daughter, my precious Julia . . ."

"Let's change her name," said Miriam. Her emotions made her voice tremble. This little girl would bring him so much happiness that, spiritually, she belonged only to him. "Let her be called Nadia. She will be her father's daughter."

For Nadeem, in the months that followed, it was as if he had never had a child. He held the tight bundle for long periods, talking in a soothing voice and predicting all the marvels of existence that awaited Nadia.

Each day he discovered some new spiritual benefit brought about by the baby. "This one has cleansed the army out of me," he said to Miriam more than once. "She has given me back my optimism." As the baby grew and began to babble and toddle behind him, he felt a surge of new ambition and eagerness to surpass old triumphs. Nadia's independence and boldness in everything she did tugged at his heart and made her seem more vulnerable, for he knew that boldness alone wasn't enough. It was up to him to protect her from danger. He would be her security. But in order to do this, he had to have a more dependable income.

The shop could fall victim to the unstable political times, and the income from it was not likely to grow. Goods from Europe were no longer easily transported. There might come a day when he could no longer bring in merchandise. The uninterrupted succession of Ottoman crises had created havoc with shipments from Europe. The war with Italy was barely over when the four Christian Balkan states tried to gain Macedonia and Albania. Turkey was drained of its resources and completely exhausted, and her armies were scattered over too broad a front to be effective. Conversely, southern Palestine flourished for these few years, unable to imagine the devastation that was to come.

The village prospered, giving everyone new hope and opportunity. The lawless outlying enclaves were attracted by Tamleh's stability and it became the county seat, drawing merchants from the surrounding areas, who came to sell or trade their goods and buy supplies. The municipal council was eager to establish standards of morality. Drunkards who violated public decency were fined, as were shopowners who fixed their scales. Criminals were prosecuted according to the Imperial Turkish Penalty Law.

The Friends Girls' School, an imposing modern building set amid lush planned gardens and orchards, was acknowledged to be the most progressive in the area. By 1914, it had attracted forty-eight girls from monied Arab families and a few Europeans living in Jerusalem. And as their parents visited the village and discovered its healthy mountain air, they began to choose it as a summer resort. A large well-appointed hotel was built to accommodate these vacationers.

Enterprising men were building commercial property to house the shops necessary to accommodate all the trade that poured into the village. Traffic had to be directed in the business district. Any fool could make money, and an ambitious man could become wealthy.

Daily, Nadeem, who still preferred to walk to Jerusalem rather than take the carriage, saw structures begun or finished where before there had only been empty land or dusty rubble. At first, he looked upon these new structures with the interested eye of a mason. This one hadn't used a proper mortar . . . this stone wasn't cut properly . . . that house had a badly rolled roof.

Then, for the second time in their marriage, Miriam saw her husband turn moody and silent. "What's wrong?"

"Butruss Hanoos is putting up a building next to the printing shop."

"Butruss? I wouldn't have thought he'd have the courage or the brains."

"Exactly. The foundation is too shallow. He hasn't gone below the frost line. The first harsh winter will bring him problems."

"And this is why you've turned so quiet in the last week? Because you don't approve of Butruss's foundation?"

"No." Nadeem folded his hands in front of him, his face morose. "I wish I were in his shoes. I feel I should be doing the same. I want to get in on this expansion and have a building, too."

"But do it, then."

"It's not so simple. In order to buy land, you need cash. Even if you do the work yourself, you need money for the materials."

Miriam thought a moment. She had no fears for Nadeem's plan, for over the years she had seen that his determination worked in his favor. "I can give you a hundred lira," she offered innocently. "The same that you repaid when your soap venture turned around. I still have it."

"This will require a great deal more money, Miriam. I will have to go to a bank and borrow. And the payment will be more regimented."

"Suppose they give you the money but once you've built the building, no one rents it?"

"Then I won't be able to repay the loan and they will take my building."

"Oh!" She began to frown, but then, having made up her mind to support him, decided to look on the bright side. "But if you do find someone to rent it?"

"Then I will repay the bank and, in time, I will also own the building. It will be a source of income for us."

"Oh!" she made a little cry of surprise. "If the rewards are so great, why aren't more people interested in building and renting?"

"Why aren't more people interested in trade or shipping or emigrating to America? There is risk involved; but the greater the risk, the greater the possibility for reward."

"You've taken risks before without ill effects."

"That's not to say that all my risk-taking will enjoy a good fate."

"I will support you in whatever you do, Nadeem." She took his hand in hers. It was a rare gesture. She considered it a failing that she couldn't be more demonstrative with him. There were many things she felt, but to say them—to find the words and the courage to utter them—was beyond her. "You have always done everything for us."

"I care for you so deeply," he said simply. "You're mine and that's all that matters." For several days, that strange, bold statement invaded her quiet moments and made her reflective.

The next morning, wearing his most austere clothes, Nadeem walked through the embossed brass doors of the Deutsche Palestina Bank.

He had never been inside a bank as a borrower. In the village, the priests often acted as moneylenders and it was a joke that they were less scrupulous than the most avaricious banker.

He was stopped just inside the door by a young man wearing a winged-collar shirt and morning coat.

"Sir?"

The very sound of the word "money" would sound ill-bred in these surroundings. Yet that was his mission. "I'm here to see about a loan of money." What else? A loan of bread? Nervousness made his bad eye throb and his palms itch.

"And who referred you here?"

"Must one be referred? Are you not a public bank?"

"Yes. We are a public bank," said the man wearily. "Please have a seat."

It was a shallow room with a long marble counter protected by a curtain of thin brass rods that reached the ceiling. Nadeem fought the impulse to leave, and soon he was ushered into the presence of a sallow-faced man with a carefully coiffed goatee.

The banker made a steeple of his fingers and tapped them nervously as Nadeem outlined his plan. Then he handed down an opinion on what he had heard. "You want me to give you the money to build a commercial building which you *hope* to rent, and Deutsche Palestina would *hope* to receive repayment—both principal and interest—from the *supposed* proceeds of such a rental."

"That is correct." It was not correct. The way the banker characterized it, the request sounded foolhardy. But he wasn't foolhardy.

"Have you other buildings which you have financed in this manner, Mr. Mishwe?"

"No, sir."

"Do you own any property that you can present as collateral?"

"Just my own home that shelters my family."

"And it's a large family, I would venture."

"Not excessively so. Four children and my wife."

"Still, they are in need of their home. And you have no experience in commercial buildings."

"I worked for many years as a mason."

"I am speaking of the building and management of commercial rental property. Have you any experience along those lines?"

"No, sir."

"Then, I don't see how I can help you. We are not in the business of funding shaky ventures. My job is to protect the assests of this bank and not expose them to undue risks. Your project, I'm afraid, would come under the category of undue risk. If you show some success with this first building, perhaps we would have some interest in the second."

"If I show success with this building, I would have no need of your interest," said Nadeem brusquely. "But thank you very much for your time."

When he stepped outside, Nadeem took a deep breath and walked in the direction of the Crédit Lyonnaise. As long as he was dressed so somberly, he might as well try again.

The garrulous manager of the Crédit Lyonnaise was less disdainful, but his response was the same. No experience, no loan. No collateral, no loan. The Banco di Roma offered advice on square footage and location but still refused a loan. As Nadeem was leaving, the Italian banker called out. "There's a new establishment over the jewelry shop on Jaffa Road. If you have no prejudice in dealing with a Russian Jew, perhaps he'll lend you the money. The name is Slivowitz."

"Thank you," said Nadeem and set out rapidly along Christian Quarter Road to Jaffa Gate.

The sign said Slivowitz Trust, a simple engraved brass square set discreetly at the side of the building next to a steep staircase.

"Slivowitz Trust?" asked Nadeem of the bespectacled man dwarfed by a large mahogany desk heaped with ledgers.

"Slivowitz Trust. Trust Slivowitz. I'm Slivowitz." He said this without lifting pen or eyes from paper and Nadeem, having no alternative, delivered his proposal to the top of Slivowitz's head. "What have *I* to do with such a plan?" said the bent head when Nadeem stopped speaking.

"You might lend me some money for the land and building materials."

Finally, M. Slivowitz set down his pen and inspected his visitor. "I might also join the traveling circus that's here from Egypt. Who sent you here?"

"M. Carbonara from Banco di Roma."

"Why should he wish me ill?" mused Slivowitz.

"My plan is not preposterous," said Nadeem, exasperated. "I have enough experience in the building trade to put up a superior structure. I have conducted an import business for several years without a blemish on my reputation. There's no need to chastise me for trying to do business with you. It isn't as if I were trying to steal your money."

"Stealing, nobody accused you of." M. Slivowitz turned paternal. "If you have a business, why don't you leave well enough alone? Stay satisfied in your business. Let me stay satisfied in mine without worrying over a bad debt."

Despite his frustration, Nadeem liked Slivowitz, and found himself eager to confide in him. "I would do as you say, but I'm afraid that the squabbles in Europe will soon ignite into war. My imports come from

France and she's aligning with Russia, perhaps against Turkey. My family has been through great strife and I want to be certain of their future."

"Do you believe Turkey will be involved in the war? My God, she's been at war continuously. She has nothing left with which to fight."

"Germany will drag us in. Turkey is mesmerized by the German military machine. They believe Germany's strength will be their strength."

"But you don't?"

"No. The Arab soldier will never be aroused to patriotism by the Teutonic method. I have first-hand knowledge of their disdain for our race. At Jerablus, where they are building their railway bridge, they painted numbers on the laborers so they would not have to learn their names. They believe we're savages, and we believe they're pompous fools."

"You were in the Turkish army?"

"Yes. This eye is a souvenir."

Slivowitz mulled this over and his tone became subdued. "But if you don't believe in the stability of Europe or Turkey, what makes you think rental property will be in great demand?"

"Palestine has always prospered, despite Turkey's fortunes. Distance makes us immune. My village is growing daily. I don't know from morning to morning what new structure I will find. We will soon extend our borders closer to Jerusalem. It can only grow bigger." As he spoke, he felt a great optimism for the future, but the man before him seemed unmoved and Nadeem rose to leave. "Thank you."

"For nothing."

"At least you listened."

"Listening is cheap."

"You didn't insult me by telling me my plan was immature."

"I didn't praise you either."

"Good day, Mr. Slivowitz."

"A good day for me, it isn't. I'm going to become your partner, Mr. Mishwe. I'm going to lend you the money."

"How's that?"

"Sit down. We have some details to work out."

When they had settled on the terms of inspection, approval, payments, and repayments, Nadeem said, "I feel ill at ease. As if I were already having difficulty repaying the loan. As if I were burdened with a debt that was doomed."

"That's good," said Slivowitz. "I have faith in a natural worrier. If you felt happy and optimistic, I would worry."

* * *

He bought a patch of land on the Street of the Dyers and Weavers because it was off the main path and not so costly. He put up a two-story building of about fifteen hundred square feet, with the upper floor set back to create a balcony. He made the loan money go far and put in a foundation for an additional structure and covered it over for the future.

His hands cracked and bled from the second week. He had to sleep in a crude shelter at the site to protect his materials from theft, yet he had never been so happy in his life. He worked every possible moment he could spare from the shop. The men from the clan came to help at the roofing bee.

Khalil, now a teenager and tall for his age, showed a great aptitude for selling and, after a few weeks apprenticing with his father, was able to look after the linen business for short periods. Hanna helped him as a stock boy and delivering orders.

A perfumer had rented the space in the shop vacated by the pharmacist and, with the idiosyncracies of their customers to bond them, he and Khalil became friends despite the difference in age. Khalil's new responsibilities had matured him and he enjoyed the role of proprietor, playing it out with relish. He had a feel for merchandise and the sincere interest in human nature that makes for a natural salesman.

"He can make a more convincing presentation than I," Nadeem told his wife. "He speaks knowledgeably of the benefits of percale over combed cotton. Of chintz over muslin. Of dimity over linen. He knows how many threads per inch are in the lisle spreads and why they are cool. He likes to spout these facts. I suppose it gives him a feeling of authority. He tells the customers that the construction allows the fabric to breathe. You should hear him. He behaves as if he has two days to spend with them over the purchase of hand towels, and the ladies feel comforted. Wouldn't you like to see him?"

"No," said Miriam. "I would be far too nervous and I'd interrupt him a dozen times." She had no wish to be in Jerusalem at all.

Nadeem closed his eyes to the possibilities for error in allowing his son to run the business and spent as much time as he could on construction. The face of the building was stone covered over with a golden stucco troweled to a smoothness that took patience and expertise. The windows and doorway were gracefully arched and accented with contrasting burgundy brick in a herringbone pattern. The foundation walls went far below the frost line. He had lived through enough snowstorms to know that the winter weather could be severe, but still there were comments that he was being foolishly cautious.

"It's a handsome building," said Slivowitz when he saw it. "But will it bring in any more rent for its beauty?"

"And sturdy," said Nadeem.

"And sturdy," echoed Slivowitz, uselessly thumping a wall. "Well," he added as an afterthought, "I have a tenant for you."

"Oh." Nadeem wasn't ready to part with his creation. "Who is that?"

"Another man to whom I've loaned money. At least I'll know the health of his business. If he pays you the rent, I'll sleep at night."

"What is his business?" asked Nadeem morosely.

"Cutlery. And cooking utensils from the Continent."

"You think there's a market for such things?"

"I don't know," said Slivowitz, frowning.

While the southern tip of their empire prospered, the Turks had been locked in battle with the vigorous Albanian mountaineers who scored a succession of startling victories, causing the Turks to lose all of their Balkan territory except Constantinople.

The protracted Ottoman and Balkan crisis was attended by almost convulsive efforts on the part of every European state to increase its military and naval forces. The instruments of war had become revolutionized. The giant gun, the scouting and bombing plane, the trench bomb, the tank, poison gas, and the submarine were the new tools of destruction. The French led in the development and manufacture of the war plane, including the Farman, the Caudron, and Breguet. Their world-famous Spad and Nieuport were to become the standard pursuit planes of the U.S. Services in a war where supremacy was settled by one fighter plane battling with another. It was France's great flying aces, too—René Fonck and Nungesser—who would keep the skies cleared of the deadly Taubes and Fokkers of the enemy until Great Britain was ready with her Sopwiths, Bristols, and Hadley-Pages.

There was no hint that war would touch Palestine. Miriam's days were ordered. Life was easier than in the old days. Nadeem had put in a pump and at five each morning, Jirius came to pump water from the garden well into the storage tank. He executed one hundred strokes before going to the next house.

The milk woman arrived next, balancing two heavy jugs, one with milk, the other with yogurt. There followed the egg man calling out, *"Beyyd, beyyd."* At Zareefa's urging, Miriam used these services, conserving her strength for dealing with the younger children, who still needed help. For diversion, she ordered cloth and made garments for Esa and Nadia and, very seldom, for herself, for she had completely retreated to her old life and found few occasions to leave her familiar surroundings.

With Mustafa's help she planted a vegetable and flower garden that was as beautiful as it was fruitful. The property around the house became an appealing maze of paths bordered by purple gorse, vetches, poppies, cyclamen, and the dainty lavender crocus, which the villagers called *seráj-el ghúleh,* lamp of the ghoul, because it is the first brave color bearer after the long, dry summer.

She engaged Baruch, a cotton fluffler from Jerusalem to come and restore all the mattresses. He stayed two days, working far into the night, refusing any food but tomatoes and eggs and frightening Miriam with his habit of putting the lantern too close to his materials.

"He'll burn the house down in our sleep," she whispered to Nadeem. "I feel I should stay up and watch him."

"He's been doing this for many years. You would insult him watching him like a child."

"I'd rather insult him than find my house gone by morning. I wish he'd just sleep at night like the rest of us."

"Consider it a blessing. He'll be finished sooner and you can stop worrying."

"I suppose."

"All right, sleep now," said Nadeem, but then after a moment of silence, he added, "you'd better bring Nadia in here to sleep, just to be safe."

She scrambled out of bed, not needing a second urging. "I'll bring Esa, too."

When they were settled and she had adjusted herself in bed, he spoke again. "I saw a poster today warning against rabid dogs. You mustn't let Nadia near any strange animals."

"Nadia is always the one you worry about. What of Esa?"

"Well, of course, Esa, too. All of them, but Nadia doesn't understand and she is too fond of animals. You know what she has named the dog? La-la. She points to him and shrieks, '*La-la, Baba. La-la.*' This is all her own thinking." Miriam smiled into her pillow, pleased that Nadia brought him so much happiness, but she also enjoyed kidding him about his preoccupation with the baby's safety. "Don't worry. They came yesterday from the Public Health. A man in a horse-drawn van. He lassoed ten strays with his rope. But the poor dogs kept hurtling themselves against the barred window, trying to escape."

"Never mind. Better to have the dogs unhappy than children dead." He raised his head, listening to his daughter breathing noisily in the corner. "Her breathing is always heavy. Do you hear it?"

"It's nothing, Nadeem. She has a little something. Maybe it's the cotton dust from the mattresses."

"Maybe you should take her to Dr. Ma'luf."

"It's nothing. You worry too much about her."

Nadia grew and her preference for animals became more ingrained. She adored the dog until the day Uncle Daud hoisted her in front of him on a gentle gray gelding and took her for a twenty-minute ride into the hills. From that day the request most frequently on her lips was "Hordee. Nadia ride hordee." Miriam, remembering Max's passion for riding, tried to dissuade her, for she still had her old fears, but Nadeem gave in, and whenever they had a horse available he patiently led her around until she drooped from exhaustion and had to be carried to bed.

So many events—so much change crammed into those few years—had shifted everyone's awareness. At thirty-two Miriam was a graceful woman with many elements of beauty and an unassuming confidence. Umm Jameel deferred to her with a childlike reliance that was touching. Her own mother reverted to the age-old custom of calling her *"Yuma,"* mother. Zareefa came daily to chew over some aspect of her life. Nabile's wife, Diana, her weight now over three hundred pounds, struggled up the hill, always with one of her children and, although she complained and criticized, Miriam could see she was the neediest of all.

Two less familiar visitors came from Umm Jameel's wealthiest relatives. The Sheik's oldest son, George, had married Sara, an exquisitely beautiful girl from Nablus, and their firstborn son, Samir, was two years older than Nadia. Twice, the breathtaking Sara, outfitted in her fashionable European clothes, brought her striking little boy to play with Esa and Nadia. He wore linen shorts that buttoned to a linen shirt and white high-top shoes with reddish soles. He seemed unduly serious and very advanced. His mother said they already had a tutor for him and he was learning to read, although he was barely four. "He sits in with the council members when they meet," she smiled as if it were a joke. "He'll be admitted to the Friends' school next fall." Nadia liked him because he had placed himself at her disposal on all fours, and she had climbed on his back and ridden him like a horse. Watching them, Miriam had an odd feeling. These two youngsters seemed to be set apart, even at this young age.

* * *

With no large event to mark its passing, time had less meaning. Nadeem worked harder than ever and the strain showed in the deepened creases around his mouth and the gray in his hair. The loan weighed heavily on his mind and his constant wish was to repay it in full. He returned to take charge of the shop, but Khalil could not be persuaded to continue in school and went to work in the printing plant run by the Catholic Church. Hanna, in his submissive way, returned to the Franciscans for an additional year of reading and mathematics. Of all the children, Esa remained most constant. He didn't outgrow his sweetness or his joyful nature. His face didn't lose its innocence, his curls remained silky, his eyes brightly blue. If Nadia was Nadeem's source of sustenance and joy, then Esa belonged to Miriam. Besides their children, there was the clan to absorb them and enclose them.

Life seemed to have settled into what it would be forever.

14

They beat the drums for war.

In July of 1914, Nadeem, in an uncharacteristic moment of relaxation, opened the newspaper on the glass-topped counter of his shop and was startled to see a photograph, occupying almost half the page, of the French war biplane, the Spad, with René Fonck, the flying ace, at the controls.

At midday, he tucked the paper under his arm, and went to see Slivowitz. He told himself it was for a companionable chat, but it was for reassurance. "Why do they show a war plane on the front page? What has this to do with us? This is between Austria and Serbia." He was referring to the shocking assasination of the Austrian archduke by a Bosnian youth.

"Do you really believe the rest of Europe will stay out?" asked Slivowitz. "And miss the opportunity to reshuffle the territory?" he added ruefully.

"I can't believe they'll come to blows over the antics of the small peninsula states."

"Russia, Germany, and France have been mobilizing for war for the last three years. The only mystery is who will side with whom."

"Surely England won't go against Germany."

"Don't be too certain." Slivowitz sighed the sigh of a man in a world he didn't understand. "Or too logical. Each of them has an exaggerated fear for its safety, and they've been jockeying for alliances long before this. England's mad at Germany because she had the audacity to build up her navy. Germany's furious with France over Morocco. And France and Russia are thick as thieves."

As it turned out, Slivowitz was right. Germany, threatened by England's new *Entente Cordiale* with France and Russia, created "incidents" and found support only from Austria. In August of 1914, Turkey signed an alliance with Germany, from which they expected security against Russia, the power they feared and hated.

One night, the family was at dinner together with Jameel and Zareefa. They heard the monotonous sounds of drums coming steadily nearer. Everyone became silent. "Why are they beating the drums?" Esa was the only one who dared to ask the question.

"They beat the drums for Ramadan," said Khalil. "But this isn't Ramadan."

"They don't beat the drums for Ramadan in a Christian village," said Nadeem softly.

"They beat the drums for war," said Jameel and everyone looked at him as if he knew something more. Then he peeled an orange carefully, scoring the skin neatly into quarters and removing a section at a time. Everyone concentrated on the orange as the drums came closer. What a dreadful, mournful sound!

They went and stood in front of the door, waiting for the drums to reach them and were surprised to see their familiar crier, Jirius. "It's Jirius," said Zareefa in an annoyed voice. Jirius pumped their water in winter and carried water to them during the summer—he was a safe, familiar figure. "What's he up to?"

At the intersection, a few hundred feet from them, Jirius stopped and read loudly from a piece of paper. "Men born between 1876 and 1895 must report to the recruiting center within the next forty-eight hours. Who fails to do so will be prosecuted."

"What does it mean, Jirius?" asked Jameel.

"It means war, *Ami,*" Jirius answered sadly, calling to him like an affectionate uncle. "The war is now real. We have to fight for the Turks." He spat on the ground. "We are at war against France, against England! *Ya Allah!*" He continued down the road. *Dum-de-de-dum, dum-de-de-dum.*

Nadeem was exempted because of his eye, and Jameel was above the age limit. The twins, George and Salim, went again and Jamilla was unconsolable. Daud was deferred because he had pneumonia at the time of the induction and hadn't the stamina to march. Many young men hid in the stone huts in the fig orchards to avoid the army and ventured home only at night. They were called the "army of fugitives."

The first deprivation was the scarcity of flour. In a good year with adequate rainfall, two full sacks of wheat could be had for about eighty cents. But the local wheat supply was meager, for the needs of the larger villages and the cities and had to be supplemented. The great wheat field of the country was the Hauran, east of the Sea of Galilee. Caravans of camels brought sacked wheat to the western coast and as far south as Jerusalem.

One day Nadeem came home and found Zareefa in the kitchen crying. "It's Jameel," Miriam explained. "He's been called up again."

"Jameel is forty. It must be a mistake."

"It's not a mistake. They've extended the age limit. They need men. Will you come later and persuade him to hide?" she asked Nadeem. "He'll listen to you."

"I will."

When Zareefa left, Miriam looked fiercely at her husband. "I'm glad that your eye will keep you out. I have no patriotism for this hateful war. The Turks have ordered my father to grow food for them. For no payment, of course."

"Yes?" Nadeem was distracted. On the carriage ride home, he'd heard tales that frightened him. Turkey was planning to use Palestine as the base for the assault on Egypt and the Suez. The Fourth Turkish Corps was marching through the villages, commandeering supplies. Property was being confiscated, wheat stores taken. The family he had met in the carriage was fleeing from Nablus. "If we stay, we'll starve," the man had said. "Maybe not this week or this month, but soon. It's already difficult to buy oil or wheat, even barley. Medicine is scarce. If there's an epidemic, my children and wife will die. In Madeba, the Turks will leave us alone." His eyes had a tinge of yellow and Nadeem wondered if he were already sick. The man had had a quiet conviction and now, looking at Miriam's anxious face, Nadeem wondered if he, too, should be taking steps to leave.

"Are you worried about the shop?" Miriam tried to read his face. "Will you have to close it? And what about your building? How can the tenant pay rent? People won't be able to buy cutlery—they'll need their money to eat. If there's anything to eat. If the Turks don't take it all." Her normally husky voice was shrill. She was almost whining—something he had never heard her do and he knew it was fear working in her.

"Hush, hush." He smoothed her hair. "Don't worry. We'll manage. I can always do masonry. I'll do what I can until the war is over, and then we can salvage something and begin again. Don't worry."

"Poor Diana," she said, out of the blue. "She's so heavy. Suppose we have to move quickly to hide . . . or . . . to flee. Nadeem, we mustn't leave her. We'd have to help her hide, too."

"Don't worry." Nadeem looked at his wife with pity. He wanted to dispel such thoughts, but in all honesty he couldn't. "If we have to move quickly, we won't leave Diana. I promise. Now, where is Nadia? I want to see her before we visit my mother. Perhaps you'd rather stay here and not go. My mother is sure to be agitated over Jameel. I can save you all of that. I'll say you're not feeling well."

"Oh, no." She seemed alarmed. "I want to go. I feel so sorry for Umm Jameel. She needs me now."

* * *

The perfumer who shared the shop with Nadeem closed down in the next week. "You'd best sell what stock you have quickly," he told Nadeem. "They'll use your sheets for bandages."

Nadeem took his merchandise to the Suq and rented a table in the open air to dispose of what he could. He closed the shop leaving a small sign: Due to extraordinary circumstances, business is halted until further notice.

People greeted each other with narrowed eyes, rubbing their hands other in silent agitation. Those who had their own press had oil a few weeks longer. Those who had stored wheat in their cisterns to capacity had bread but didn't lose the anxiety of looking into the future with fear. The streets of the village were deserted. Merchants no longer put their sacks and bins out of doors to entice customers. The supplies dwindled daily and replenishments, if they were available, were hoarded, to be doled out at exorbitant prices.

By the summer of 1915, when the harvest came the Turks were waiting to take it. The bitterness engendered by this confiscation overflowed into every aspect of life, but there was nothing the villagers could do but make bread out of barley flour until that, too, was scarce.

Miriam's house was a dead house. The children tried to play, but they were uneasy and it made them quarrelsome. Visitors still came, but the greetings were somber and there was a great deal of crying.

Nadia would approach each of the crying women and poke them until she had their attention. *"Wa wa?"* she would inquire solemnly, which was the name for children's aches and hurts.

The milk woman and the egg man didn't come anymore and Miriam usually went into the village early each morning to shop, stopping at the bakery on the way home to avoid using up her supply of wheat. There came the day, however, when she found a queue of about a hundred women outside the bakery, and the bread was sold out long before it was her turn. Still, no one left and the breadless women began to chant and shout as if it were the baker's fault. Miriam returned home with the glassy stare of shock.

"What's wrong?" asked Nadeem when he saw her.

"There's no bread to be had in the village. Not a loaf. Hassam closed the shop but the women stayed there, refusing to go home."

Nadeem didn't respond. He had had his own shock. The Friends Boys' School, a brand new building that had been built as a companion to the Girls' School and was a source of pride and joy to so many, had been taken over by the Turkish army. The beautiful dining hall on the main floor was being used to quarter the horses. He kept the news to himself and ate little of the simmering vegetable stew Miriam placed before him.

"My father sent the cauliflower and squash for us," she said peevishly. "He wants us to have a healthy meal and now you're not eating." There was resentment in her voice, but Nadeem knew it was brought on by fear and he placed another unwanted helping on his plate.

News of the war was sketchy, except for the battle of Jarrab, which proved a decisive victory for the Turks against the English. No one could guess it would be the last important Turkish victory.

There are some moments which are etched on the mind so clearly that no amount of time dulls their effect. Such a moment came for Miriam on a suffocatingly close day at the end of September in 1915.

Jamilla sat at the table very silent. She was an unemotional woman, but that day her eyes were wild. She had unintentionally clawed two bleeding crescents on the back of her hands. Miriam stooped down in front of her and looked up into the tortured face. "What's wrong?"

"Salim is dead."

"You've heard from the War Office?" she asked, shocked.

"No. But Jebra's son was with him at Bersheeba and he's written that many are dead, some from here."

"You're not certain, then." Miriam expelled a breath of relief and rose. "I'll ask Nadeem to check with the War Office in Jerusalem. They'll have to tell us."

"He's dead," said Jamilla and sat stonily until the characteristic instant blackness of autumn snuffed out the day.

Nadeem went to the War Office and—as when he had gone for news of George the Kurd—it was a madhouse. Women, anxious for news, stood in an untidy double line with toddling children weaving through it. The heat and close quarters created unhealthy smells. When Nadeem questioned the officer, he confirmed too quickly that Salim was dead and made Nadeem suspicious. "Let me see proof. Let me see a list of casualties."

"Who are you?" said the official harshly.

"Brother-in-law."

"Tell the widow to come here." Nadeem shook his head in frustration, which annoyed the Turk. "Why aren't you serving your country?" he challenged. "You should wish yourself in the dead fellow's place."

That winter was exceedingly mild and in mid-November, a mother who had lost a child and wished to keep its garments took them to wash in the fountain that served two villages near Hebron. Very soon there were a dozen cases of cholera. By the end of the month, word got around that the disease was in the country and Hebron was immediately cut off from Jerusalem. The government issued orders to the villages to clean the streets and burn any refuse. Whitewash was freely used on the buildings, especially in the poorer quarters, but in the days following, rumors came that one after another village was attacked by the scourge called the *yellow air* in the belief that it was a pestilential breath carried by air. The villagers resisted learning the real cause of the disease—that the bacillus had its greatest opportunity in the running water of the drinking places. It was a somber Christmas and the trees, usually decorated with fat Jaffa oranges, were bare.

January ended with hotly contested reports that the illness was not cholera at all, but people were dying swiftly. "They're having a very bad time of it here," reported the local doctor. The bodies—almost fifty a day —were carried out two to a donkey and four to a camel. The railroad on the Jaffa-Jerusalem line was forbidden to stop anywhere between Bittur and Jaffa, and a few weeks later service was discontinued altogether. People rushed to the shops and bought up what little food there was at exorbitant prices. Some of the inhabitants of Gaza, which was hit hard, moved out to the seashore and lived in tents. Camphor was virtually unattainable, for the natives bought it to make little bags that they smelled frequently.

On the second day of March a man appeared at Miriam's door and handed her a creamy white envelope sealed impressively with red wax. It appeared too expensive to be from the government and, in any case, she had no one in the army. Something about the writing on the front made her heart behave erratically. She tried to pay the messenger but he waved her away, saying he had already been well compensated, and she went indoors.

There was a single sheet of paper and the first thing she saw was the signature, a large *M* and an almost illegible *ax*. The message was brief but urgent: "You must leave tonight. Your village will be quarantined by morning and no goods will get through. The food situation being what it is, you will starve to death if you don't die of cholera first. Take your family and go before morning!" The signature was well separated from the message, as if there were many thoughts he had wanted to place in between.

She went to Mustafa and Jamilla, to Diana and Nabile, to Daud, and finally to Nadeem's parents. None of them would leave the village. Diana cried bitterly, but the tears seemed to relieve her and she dried her eyes and refused to let the "Turkish pigs drive her out of her home."

"No, no," said Miriam, despairing that she had given the wrong impression. "It's the quarantine. No food will come through."

"Miriam, that's foolish," she said, recovering from her cry. "They wouldn't starve us to death."

Miriam told her husband the message was from the doctor who had treated Khalil and taken an interest in him. Nadeem had heard similar warnings in Jerusalem and needed no persuasion. They gathered what they could load on a donkey donated by Mustafa, but after they were packed the longing to remain in their home was so strong that Miriam begged to abort their journey. She took out the message from Max and read it for the twentieth time. "We must leave," said Nadeem. "There's no other way." They set out on foot, with only Nadia on the donkey, heading east to the village of Es Salt where Umm Jameel's aunt was a nun and might take them in.

The immediate fear of quarantine and disease had supplanted fear of the war, and by the time Nadeem and Miriam were an hour out of the village they saw the signs of the impending cordon. The officials asked their destination, but did not detain them. "Watch the fountains and wells," called out one guard. "Many are condemned."

It was so hot. The dust on the road attacked their throats and gagged them, and they stopped speaking to conserve their saliva. Only Esa had energy and he skipped ahead, sometimes running back to appraise them of some horny-headed lizard or chameleon he spotted on a rock. Toward afternoon of the next day, after stopping to rest at dawn, they reached the great depression of the Ghor, which provided a bed for the Jordan. They passed many gorges into which the debris from the hillsides had tumbled, creating a desolate wasteland. Most frightening of all were the narrow defiles with perpendicular sheets of striated cliffs on each side, allowing no place to turn should they be attacked. Nadia crooned softly to herself and stuck her thumb in her mouth, lethargic from the heat and dehydration. The older boys and Nadeem took turns leading the donkey. Miriam kept her eye on Esa, but her mind wandered and from time to time she became disoriented.

On first view, the Jordan appeared as a meandering ribbon of grass. There were muleteers who warned them of the muddy bottom, but when their donkey began to slip and flounder and was in danger of drowning, the men made no move to help. Nadeem cut the animal loose from the packages and Miriam saw all their belongings sink to the bottom. He saved only the food and although he submerged himself several times searching for the water skin, the men called out that it was useless. The strong current had already taken their cargo several miles. Nadeem led the donkey back and forth with each of them atop the animal. When they were all safely on the other side, he sat by himself, his wet clothes plastered around his thin body, and wept into his hands.

They had walked for miles without sight of another human. The only sound was the clip-clop of the donkey and Nadia's sucking and crooning. The glare of the sun added to the air of unreality. Their senses were numbed by fatigue and thirst. Esa was still bouncing ahead although to Miriam, in her weakened state, he appeared to be floating away from her, a small spot of color in the monotone of beige. "Esa, stay near!" Had she spoken or only thought it?

"Esa! Stay near." Her voice seemed to be coming from far away. Was he skipping along the ground or floating above the air? Finally the images settled and he was very clear. Standing near a well. "Don't drink from there. Wait for me." No one is at the well. Why is it so deserted?

"Mama. Here's water and a cup."

"No, Esa. No!"

There are classic signs of cholera and the swiftness of the disease is startling. Esa stopped skipping and began to droop by morning, when they were still several miles out of Es Salt. Within a few hours, his lethargy was so complete that Miriam knew. He lay across the donkey like an inert sack. Nadia walked without complaint but she couldn't go fast. It was almost dark when they reached a small village with a clinic.

The doctor moved swiftly, pulling the rubber tubing from his stethoscope and snaking it down Esa's throat, making him jerk forward and gag. "This will do more good as a conduit," he muttered, attaching a funnel to the end and pouring water into the strangely altered little body.

"He has practically no pulse," said the nurse, alarmed.

"Most likely, he's already in acidosis." The doctor appeared distraught. "Be careful," he yelled to the nurse. "Look! He's so dehydrated, his skin will crack if you touch him." Miriam watched dumbstruck, unable to do more than stare at her son's altered face. He appeared so tranquil and, while he didn't have the strength to speak, his eyes were alert.

As he waited in between pourings, the doctor talked rapidly. "Normally," he said, avoiding Miriam's eyes, "the skin has remarkable elasticity. When you pinch it, it returns to its shape. The natural fluids keep it plump. They also keep the eyes moist. The lips, the inside of the mouth—all the mucous membranes are moist. Madam,"—the doctor had taken her arm—"if we could rehydrate him and his body could absorb it, he would

be himself in a matter of hours. But,"—he threw his arms down helplessly
—"his tissues can't reassimilate water. His eyelids are as dry and brittle as
last year's leaves. He can no longer blink or swallow without pain."

Miriam shook her head. Even as they watched, the small chest rose
more feebly. Was it all preordained? Had God planned this special torture
for her all along? Given her this precious perfect child only long enough to
love him completely?

Esa lingered for two days and took his last breath as his mother stood
by, aching to cradle him against her but fearful of bruising him. The
doctor pulled Nadeem aside. "You must burn everything he touched," he
said brusquely, on the verge of tears, and left the room.

When he recovered, he returned and again spoke to Nadeem. "Are you
Muslim?" Nadeem shook his head, knowing the doctor feared the Muslim
custom of washing the bodies of the dead and spreading the disease further
through the discarded water. "Bury him with all his clothing," he whispered tersely, "and cover him with six baskets of dry lime."

They had him in a grave that evening, as was the custom, with a stone
slab over the small wooden box to keep the hyenas from exhuming the
body. Miriam displaced her deeper grief by fixating on that weight. "No!"
she screamed over and over in her sleep, leaping wildly from the mattress
in the quarantine tent where they had placed the family. "He can't push
the stone away. He's only a small boy. Please, Nadeem, help me take it
away."

"Hush!" He held her forcibly. "You can't remove the stone. He's dead!
He's dead."

Years later, she would understand that he had submerged his own agony
to minister to her. Despite his great love for Esa, he loved her more. For
many days, he forcibly kept her from digging up the frail, wasted body.

They remained in the village two weeks before the officials allowed them
to continue the five miles to Es Salt, where they were taken into the church
building and allowed to sleep. In the months that followed, they all
showed the lethargy of weakened constitutions and signs of malnutrition—
dry, cracked lips, limp hair. Hanna developed night blindness and couldn't
see from dusk until dawn. Khalil began to limp. Nadia, unable to engage
her mother, consoled herself with her thumb and rocked to and fro for
hours. She asked in vain for "horsee," and finally consoled herself with
Jilly, a mangy dog that belonged to the rectory. She and the dog became
inseparable.

Hanna alone ministered to his parents, gathering chestnuts and boiling
them to make a satisfying stew when there was nothing else to eat. He
gleaned the wheat fields after the reapers and seemed to find kernels by

willing them to appear. Many days, he walked the ten miles to the larger city of Amman to trade chestnuts for eggs, which he brought home triumphantly to his father. One day, after making the four-hour trip, he tripped on a stone and broke one of the precious cargo. He knelt beside it, stunned, and hot tears spilled on the ground, making dark spots on the dust. "Poor Mama. Poor *Baba.*"

Nadeem scooped up the soiled, dripping shell and put it in a cup. "Hush, Hanna. Never mind. The other three will nourish us more. You're a good son. More precious to me than any food. Come." He dusted Hanna's scraped knee tenderly with the hem of his aba and used it also to dry his son's tears. Miriam looked out at just that moment and, for the first time, submerged her grief and felt deeply for her husband and son.

Each of them had radically different memories of the year they spent in Es Salt. Nadeem, totally absorbed in getting enough food for the family, did odd masonry and carpentry jobs in exchange for anything that could be eaten. He often walked several hours to surrounding villages, looking for work, using up more energy than could be replaced by what was gained. Food was the first thing they thought of upon awakening. It was a yearning to fill that terrible hollowness that never left. The need to find food replaced every other concern and, in the case of Miriam, it finally even eclipsed the wretchedness of losing Esa.

Their lethargy and preoccupation could be counted a blessing because it kept them from comprehending fully the tragic news that came from home. The disease had indeed visited the village with vengeance. One third of the population perished. Nadeem's father was dead. So was Zareefa's middle girl and Daud's wife and child. Then came the news that was kept from Miriam until almost four months later. Mustafa, her beloved father was gone.

15

My poor, poor darling . . .

One night Miriam awoke to find Nadeem thumping Nadia's back furiously. "She can't breathe. Listen. . . ." A strained, wheezing sound like the creaking of a tree in strong wind came from Nadia's chest. "She's straining for a little air." There was panic in his voice and when the dog, who now regularly slept next to Nadia's mattress, began to mewl at his leg, Nadeem kicked it away, something Miriam had never seen him do.

"It's what she had before," said Miriam, dressing to go into the labyrinth of the rectory, "I'll boil some water and make steam for her to inhale. In the morning, I'll take her to the clinic."

"She was fine all day," said Nadeem, mystified. "It's an attack. She's always had something of this sort. Always coughing or sniffling." He sounded as if he were blaming Miriam for it.

"I was taking her to a doctor that Spiridum suggested the day war broke out."

"You never told me that. What did he say?"

"Who?"

"The doctor."

"We didn't go in. Nadia wouldn't go in because there was blood on the step leading to his office. I was about to carry her, when the news was shouted down the street that we were at war. After that, everyone came out. It was impossible."

"You see," said Nadeem irritably to Nadia, but Miriam knew it was directed at her, "you didn't go to see the doctor and now you're having big difficulties, and there is no doctor here." Nadia took this opportunity to make a strangling sound that sent both parents scurrying to the hearth to boil the water. Nadeem held his daughter over the kettle on and off for the rest of the night, and in the morning he urged Miriam to take her to Jerusalem and try to find the reason for her difficulties.

"Jerusalem? How can I go?" When she thought of Jerusalem she thought of Max, and it was this thought that threw her into chaos.

"Why not? The boys and I will manage."

"But we are at war," she protested weakly, for now the idea of having news of Max was beginning to dazzle her. "It's dangerous."

"It's more dangerous to risk many more nights like the last. Suppose we don't hear her? She could choke to death."

"Yes," said Miriam wearily, "that's possible."

Mother and daughter left three days later. Nadeem and the boys had sacrificed all their stores of food to give to them and packed them compactly so that Miriam could also carry Nadia if it became necessary. The priest at the church gave them a letter for a priest in Jericho, who would give them a night's lodging and perhaps dinner and breakfast to break up the trip.

She had expected to feel frightened; the walking should have been arduous, but to her surprise, she welcomed it. After months of focusing on hunger and uncertainty and grief, it was liberating to leave it all behind. Es Salt fell from view and she was suffused with an unexpected lightness, as if she had laid down a burden.

Nadia, remembering what had happened to Esa on the road, was not so eager to make the journey. "Mama, Mama," she urged, "I feel good now. Why are we leaving *baba?*"

"We have to find out what's wrong with you." Miriam had no inclination to reason with her. Her only wish now was to be away from all the memories of Es Salt.

"But it's nothing. See," Nadia took several quick deep breaths and thumped her chest. "See. Come," she grabbed her mother's hand. "Let's go back."

"No," said Miriam sharply and Nadia began to trail after her, sucking on her thumb and crooning softly to herself. After they had gone a mile, Miriam looked back at her daughter with a feeling of tenderness. Nadia was walking as fast as she could, running to catch up when she fell too far behind. Her childish legs were made more vulnerable by high-topped scuffed shoes that had been sent by some relief agency from the other side of the world. She put Nadia in the sling and carried her for a few yards, allowing her to snuggle against her for comfort and brushing her cheeks with kisses.

As they descended into the lowlands to the south, a more luxuriant green began to appear, stray flowers, and, unexpectedly—for it was late in the season—large patches of anemones in a shade of lavender which she had never seen. They blinked in the sharp brightness, stopped to eat, and slept curled together in the shade of a wild jasmine bush before starting off again. The open road welcomed them and the rhythm of their legs moving one before the other made them peaceful. A farmer, seeing them, ran forward and offered milk and dates.

They smelled Jericho long before they saw it. It's the pomegranates, she thought, and apricots and bananas ripening on the trees. So many memories are entwined with that sweetly perfumed air. There's no harm in remembering how it was, is there? I can summon up his face so quickly, that face whose presence blocks out all other life. Oh, no . . . it's just occurred to me, he could be dead like all the others. Perhaps, he contracted cholera. He treated people every day and it would be difficult to escape the germs. Oh, my God, if I could see him one more time! Just to assure myself that he's well. She pulled Nadia into the first church they saw and prayed fervently that Max was alive.

It was a shock to see the effects of the war in Jerusalem. The streets were strewn with wounded. Men of every description—Turks and English and Germans—lying in filth, begging for medical attention, with no one to give it to them. Miriam wanted to put her sack down immediately and place at least a cloth under a wounded head. It was impossible not to feel compassion. The smells were intolerable. Besides the men lying about, there were many more on foot—ragged, weary men with frightened eyes, wearing the tattered uniform of Turkey, mumbling advice, urging those that could hear them to flee for their lives. There were long lines outside several large buildings and when Miriam inquired as to what they were for, she learned they were soup kitchens being run by the American Colony, the same charitable people who had housed Esa when she was running the shop. She realized how hungry she was and decided to stand there, too, pulling Nadia to her when fights would break out, which they frequently did, as the hunger-crazed populace waited for food.

After they had eaten, they started to walk to the office of the doctor that had been recommended by Spiridum such a long time ago. The location was in the Old City, back in the Muslim quarter, near Herod's Gate. She decided to walk outside of the wall, where it was less congested. But, really, there was no spot in Jerusalem that wasn't congested and, short of walking in the middle of the road, it was impossible to move more than a few feet without some poor soul tugging on her skirts. A wounded man was begging for water and the pleading in his eyes stopped her. She bent down to place her own waterskin to his lips, holding the back of his head. Then something, a premonition, a flutter in her heart, made her look up and there standing before her—as if it were inevitable—was Max.

She laid the man down gently and stood. Her instinct was to reach for him . . . but no! . . . *oh, Max* . . . for a moment, in her dazed and weakened state, she wasn't certain . . . her heart was beating unnaturally. *Max, Max!* She was trembling and nothing would stop it. Trembling with joy but also . . . I must tell him everything. I've been waiting to tell him. He will console me now. The possibility of being consoled by this man who had known her every intimate need opened all the ghastly hurts of the past year; grief and pain washed over her anew and tears began to roll down her cheeks.

"Esa's dead," she whispered to break the awful silence. She wanted so much to embrace him that she distracted herself with images of loss and pain.

"Oh, no . . ."

"And my father . . ."

"My poor, poor darling . . ."

"And so many others. Max, so many."

"I know. I know." She saw that he was exhausted. His eyes, once so confident, were bewildered. The whites were streaked with tiny red lines and the circles around them a dusky purple color. He must hardly eat or sleep.

"Where is the rest of your family?"

"They're in Transjordan." She remembered that it was his note that had sent them away. "We left as you told us to do. I'm sure you saved our lives."

"You're here alone?"

"With my daughter." They both looked down to Nadia, who had placed her face against her mother's skirt and was holding it with one hand and sucking her thumb with the other. For one thrilling moment, Miriam considered telling him. You're looking at your daughter. Our daughter. See she has your mouth, your brow, your coloring. But that's not so important. You should know her, Max, her temperament is so much like you. She bit her lips and looked away. Telling him would hurt so many people and it would only serve her own selfish purposes. No. It would be a terrible mistake.

Right away, he couldn't take his eyes off the little girl. He bent down and took her sweaty palm in his. She let go of her mother's skirt and put her hands to her sides, not shrinking from his stare. "So you've come to Jerusalem with your mother, is that it?"

"We're here to visit the doctor," piped up Nadia in her high but definite voice. "Sometimes I make a lot of noise when I breathe and it scares my *baba*. He says it's because I don't eat what I must. But I do . . . I do," she said fiercely. "Sometimes, I don't cough for many days, but *baba* doesn't remember those times. He remembers only when I cough a great deal."

Max took a deep breath, straightened, and turned away. The sight of that pathetically thin child, her shoes so scuffed it was impossible to determine their original color, talking so rapidly touched him beyond words. He had to blink to hold back tears.

He picked Nadia up and, using her as a buffer between them, placed his free arm around Miriam and pressed himself toward both of them. He was making small hurt sounds, weeping as if he didn't know how. Miriam's tears were silent.

To her credit, Nadia did not move or cry out or ask any questions.

Max pulled apart and set Nadia on the ground. "Do you have a place to stay?"

"I was going to see Father Alphonse after we saw the doctor."

"The doctor? What doctor?"

She was embarrassed to admit she didn't even remember his name, just the spot where his office was located. "He's a specialist in allergies. I had received his name before the war but now I've forgotten it. His office is on Ararat Road."

"Allergies." He bent down again, took Nadia's chin between his fingers to steady her, and pulled down her eyelids. "What is your name?" he asked her.

"My name is Nadia."

"Tell me," he said, putting his hand around her waist, "do you have a pet? A dog?"

"Why do you want to know?" Nadia was obviously delighted by the attention of the handsome stranger. For the last year, no one had really been eager to have a conversation with her.

"Because that might be the cause of your coughing. Perhaps the nights that he sleeps near you, his dander—the dust and hair that he shakes off—might make you cough. Does he sleep near you?"

"Sometimes." She looked unconvinced. "You think Jilly makes me cough? That's silly."

"Nadia!"

"It's all right. Bring her to the hospital. I'll examine her." He looked meaningfully into Miriam's eyes. "She's so poised and talkative for her age. She couldn't be more than four."

"How did you know? I am four."

"Really? Only four?" He feigned surprise. "But you speak so well."

"We really must be going," said Miriam, avoiding his eyes. "We'll go to the clinic." She pulled Nadia's hand forcefully.

"Please stay there." His eyes were saying that he wouldn't do anything to cause her anguish. "Don't put her through any more stress. I'll find a place for both of you to sleep."

"Max, I couldn't. You must be working day and night. You look so fatigued. I don't want to add to your burdens. I . . . I . . . oh, Max . . . I've longed . . ." There was so much she wanted to tell him but how? And for what purpose? She could not betray Nadeem all over again. Her will was so fragile in his presence. But she must stay strong. She must. She began to wring her hands and bounce the knuckles against her chin in agitation.

"Shhh . . . I know. You won't be adding to my burdens. You'll be helping me. Miriam, I need nurses desperately. Please, stay and help. For every man I treat, there are five others who go unattended. Please, I need you."

"I can't stay long. My family is waiting. . . ." She was like a captured bird, anxious beyond words. "They need me . . . we just came to see about Nadia because her father worried that she might choke in her sleep . . . that we might not always hear her in the night."

"Stay as long as you can. Come." He picked up the dusty sack she had been carrying, flung it over his shoulder, and then noticing that Nadia was sagging with fatigue against her mother's skirt, picked her up, too. The little girl's head fell immediately onto his shoulder. Her forehead, still wrinkled with anxiety, nestled in the curve of his neck. Within seconds, she was fast asleep against him.

Miriam felt a constricting fear all the way to the hospital. What would happen when Nadia was left to sleep and they were free to touch? The idea of being alone with him terrified her. When they reached the hospital, however, it was so congested with people, all pleading for help, that he had time only to show them to a small cubicle with a single cot before rushing off. "Use my apartment to wash and then come to the wards. There are uniforms in the supply closet. I don't know how clean they are. Even the laundress can't be spared from helping the wounded."

After two days on the dusty road, she welcomed the soak in a tub of water. How long had it been since she had such luxury? She stayed submerged until the water cooled and she felt chilled and then dried herself slowly, looking at the body that she hadn't been aware of for months. How thin she was . . . bones . . . just bones. Her eyes looked double their size in that emaciated face. How could he possibly find her attractive? Perhaps it was to the good. In any case, there was no time for thinking now. The cries of pain and human anguish coming from the vestibule were constant and threatening. There was an air of desperation and the possibility of violence was palpable. She dressed quickly in the familiar striped dress and bib apron, tiptoed to check on the sleeping Nadia, and went to do what she could.

For the next five days, there was no thought of anything but saving lives and alleviating the suffering of the wounded. Blood was everywhere. It was surprising the way it fell—yes, fell—insidiously out of the body, soaking everything quickly in that heartsickening stain. Every hour there were more men with ragged, angry stumps where their legs and hands had been, with the filthy shreds of their clothing plastered to gaping wounds. And the screams. *The screams.*

She held an enamel bucket and heard the unearthly padded thud of dropping fingers and toes, a hand and, once, a sight that changed forever her memory of horror—a baby boy's shelled leg, the knee still round and dimpled, sawn off. *Sawn off vigorously as a piece of lifeless, stubborn meat.* There was no room for lust in this context. And yet, it was always on her mind. She yearned for him at every instant and the knowledge of it made her desolate and despairing. Twice, at the edge of exhaustion, he wept tears of frustration in her arms. More often, they did no more than hold each other briefly in silent sorrow.

As for Nadia, her life improved. As Max had surmised, her difficulty had to do with animal dander, which he quickly concluded after exposing her. As long as she kept away from the dog, she had no further breathing problems and Max entrusted her with small errands, advising her with solemnity that she was to report directly to him. She quickly established herself in the long corridors, thrilled with the activity and with the importance of being needed. She lived for that moment in the day when Dr. Max would pick her up in his arms and say very seriously, "You are doing a wonderful job. We couldn't get along without you."

On those infrequent days when the stream of wounded slowed, the hospital staff would canvass the overflowing halls for those who were ill but had not required surgery. Miriam was given a corner of the largest ward and had been sponging an old Arab man who outwardly showed no signs of trouble but was running a persistent fever.

"Sister, sister," he beckoned her near his face so he could whisper. "Please . . . shhh, listen," he was whispering unnecessarily because no one was eager to overhear. "I need something. Can you get it for me?"

"What is it? Are you in pain? What is it I can get for you?"

"*Zeit u zatar.* And hot bread. I know where you can find it . . . shhh, listen carefully and I will tell you."

He must be delirious, she thought. He wanted bread with oil and spice. "Are you in pain?" she asked again, not knowing what else to say.

"Sister, sister . . ." he continued in that same conspiratorial manner, *"zeit u zatar* and bread. I know where you can get it for me. Please. Make an old man happy."

She saw that he was serious. "I can bring you food if you're hungry."

"No, no. I don't want food. Please, just listen. I know where you can get it."

There was no sensible way to justify filling the old man's whim when there was so much to do, but his manner touched her. He was old and frail and he wanted a favor.

"Tell me where to get it," she said.

"It's underground." He made her bring her face very close to his. "In back of David Street near the old suq . . . the *old* suq," he emphasized. "You know it? Where they used to sell the meat?"

"Yes. I know it."

"The last building to the right. There are steps down. Knock three times and tell her to give you something for Nassam. You do that for me?"

"Yes. I will."

She hated going out into the streets, to shake herself loose from begging hands, knowing that she was powerless to help. She had tried on several occassions to walk to Tamleh to see her mother, but the road was cordoned off and she was turned back. Yet she slipped out and did as the old man had instructed and, sure enough, after hearing a guarded response from behind the closed door, a well padded arm with at least a dozen gold bracelets jangling delicately passed out a packet of warm food, which Miriam delivered immediately to her patient. She didn't have time to watch him open the package, but he smiled at her with such gratefulness— it was a deeply satisfying moment.

Within the next few days, she repeated this errand three times and the third time she delivered the warm, fragrant packet, the old man held up his hand, asking her to wait. He reached under the bed and brought up a small cotton bag that had seen better days. "I am going to die soon," he said simply, as if the event were inevitable and he had accepted it, "and you have been very kind to me. Please, sister. Take this bag. It's all I have . . . there's a little money in it . . . Turkish money . . . perhaps the value is no good now, but also there's a deed, a lawful deed. Shhh . . . it's all right, don't say anything, just listen. I made a little paper, and one of the doctors witnessed it and signed it. The deed is for you. It's yours. Thank you, sister. You're a good woman. God bless you."

Several times while he was speaking she had tried to dissuade him from giving her his earthly possessions, but seeing he had made up his mind and assuming that there was little there of value, she took the bag and placed it inside her sack without even inspecting its contents. He died in his sleep two nights later.

She had been there ten days and it was no longer possible to justify remaining. It was strange, the fears she had felt initially—that she would not withstand her own desires—had never been realized. The crushing priorities of human suffering had displaced everything else. Max, bone-tired, almost incoherent with fatigue, his tongue thick, his eyes an unhealthy map of blood vessels, could focus only on surgery. Several times, he had urged her into his apartment, but couldn't do more than sink onto the bed, unable to summon the energy for words or an embrace. Before she had finished removing his shoes and hoisting his legs onto the bed, he was asleep.

One evening, while the ward was unnaturally quiet, she was changing a dressing and deep in thought. Without warning, the need to be away from all the sick, despairing bodies took hold and, after checking to see that Nadia was asleep, she ran out the front door and hurried around the corner toward the Russian compound. In the old days, one of her special pleasures was to listen to the evening prayers sung by the nuns. Some of them were old and bent women, but their voices were exquisite. If she hurried she might still be in time for vespers and be lulled by that glorious harmony.

She entered the compound which the Arabs dubbed *el-Moscoobiyya.* Once it had been the first building outside the walls and the busiest area in all of Jerusalem, processing the thousands of pilgrims who arrived each year. But now, with Russia at war with Turkey and Germany, the funds from the motherland stopped and some of the nuns were so poor that they had to work as gravel-crushers for the government. She saw them scurrying through the streets in their dust-soiled habits, heads bent as if they were ashamed.

As she entered the cathedral, she heard the mesmerizing sound. A unified mellifluous sweetness pulled her in, promising to soothe and heal.

She knelt perfectly still, allowing the music to work on her. There came a moment of such lucidity, she stopped hearing the music altogether and focused on her feelings. Something was different. She felt an exquisite peacefulness—a letting go that was exhilarating. She had been living with the threat of her own desire—any moment he chose, Max could have had her. But what she had refused to see was that it would have been her choice, too. *She would have chosen against Nadeem.* Willfully, she would have chosen against her husband for a second time but without the excuse of surprise and discovery. She was horrified by the thought of her own easy faithlessness.

Nadeem was the one, true bulwark of her life. The war and circumstances had taken away his business but not his worth. Not his inner goodness and strength, which never wavered. Which were as much a part of him as the perfect crystal pitch was a part of these bowed nuns. This time there would have been no salvation. Nadeem, forgive me. Forgive me. In that instant, she knew herself more completely than she had thought possible and her first thought was, Why couldn't I see it? Oh, I'm so thankful that there is nothing physical between Max and me. I'm no longer afraid. It's time to return to my family. It's time to leave you, Max Broder.

Her face must have shown that renewed inviolable strength of purpose because Max didn't try to persuade her to stay. He stole away from the operating room for half an hour, and Miriam thought afterward that it was more a need to spend the time with Nadia than with her. Did he suspect? It touched her deeply to see them together. He had several glossy picture books about horses, and Nadia was devouring them with cries of interest and delight.

"She likes horses?" His tone was almost accusatory. As if Miriam had cheated him by withholding this information.

Miriam nodded. "She lives for horses." She had no will anymore to deny him this small pleasure. She felt such affection for him. Such a willingness to comfort him in his aloneness. For that's how she saw him. Alone. If he suspected his relationship to Nadia, it was a small enough gift to let him know he had passed on so much to her.

"How I wish I had the time to take her riding," he looked wistfully at the little girl sprawled on the floor with a book almost as large as herself. "In any case, it wouldn't be safe. Snipers are everywhere and even if you have a travel pass, some of the soldiers shoot without asking questions."

"Why do you stay here, Max?" He wasn't expecting such a probing question and she could see it crushed his moment of relaxation. "It's so difficult and you have another life back home."

The look of bewilderment on his face brought tears to her eyes. "I was going home before the war broke out," he sounded almost ashamed, as if he had botched up a simple task. "But then I got caught up in . . ."—he waved his arms to encompass all of Jerusalem—"all this. I'm going to have a holiday when it's over." His childish mouth hung open, looking so vulnerable, and she thought of Esa.

"Max, Nadia and I must go back. My husband . . . my boys are waiting for me. We must start out tomorrow."

"Start out . . ." he raised his eyebrows in surprise. "You mean on foot? You're going to walk back?"

"But that's how we came."

"It's a miracle you didn't get killed. You can't walk back. *We're at war!*" He rose decisively. "I'll make arrangements for someone to drive you. My patients are always promising me the moon for saving their lives. Let's see if I can call in some of those promises."

She looked stricken. "I can't. Max. I've never been in a car. Is it safe?"

It was the first broad smile she had seen on his face since they arrived. "Of course." He picked up Nadia and swung her up in his arms. "Your mother's frightened of riding in a car. It's up to you to convince her that it's safe. Go ahead, my little horsewoman, tell your mom she's got to join the twentieth century."

"Mama, it's all right," said Nadia softly. Then she looked quizzically at Max to see if she had done what he wanted. "You want us to take the car?"

"I want you to be safe," he embraced her and his voice was filled with emotion. "I want you to always be safe." Nadia put her small thin arms around his neck and Miriam saw the first glimmer of womanhood in her satisfied eyes. She was comforting someone she loved. Her little soul comprehended something that was still hidden. Max put her down and walked quickly out of the room.

They left two days later in a scarred black cabriolet touring coach, whose once extravagant soft napped top had been torn away and replaced by two corrugated steel sheets. Mother and daughter sat scrunched in the back, holding another piece of metal in front of them which was supposed to protect them from stray bullets. Max had wangled a pass for them so that they could travel as "subjects friendly to the realm of the Sultan"—a ridiculous statement since Turkey was being ruled by a triumvirate. Miriam had no faith that any piece of paper could protect them from her main source of fear, which was the car itself.

She would not have guessed that she would be happy to return to Es Salt, but now that they were on their way, she yearned to see Nadeem and the boys. She had always kept some details of her emotional life at a distance in order to cope with circumstances that were not of her choosing. She had coped with the hurts of childhood by not speaking. She had taken the sting out of Miss Clay's impersonal assessments by surpassing her expectations and then scoffing at them. She had steeled herself against marriage—outwardly accepting but inwardly reserving the deepest core of feeling until Max. And now—ravaged by the pain of losing those she had loved most—she had no more will to set herself apart. Khalil, Hanna, Nadeem and, yes, Nadia—they were her life. She was thirty-four years old and she had only now opened her arms to the life that was hers.

16

···—●◯●—···

Miriam, what are these papers? There's a deed here.

Miriam left Jerusalem the second week of March. During April, Bertha Spafford, who ran the American Colony, went to Jemal Pasha, the Turkish commander, who was a dread figure known chiefly for his association with the Armenian massacres in Anatolia a few years before. The Germans had closed her soup kitchens, saying they were American propaganda because the U.S. had declared war on Germany. To his credit, Jemal Pasha acquiesced to Mrs. Spafford's request to reopen the kitchens as long as she did it in the name of Turkey.

The war, however, was not going well for the Ottoman Empire. By late fall, the Turkish army had been in ragged retreat through Jerusalem. As Max stepped outside one morning to get a breath of nonchloroformed air, a soldier warned him that within days, perhaps hours, they should expect heavy cannon fire and street fighting. "The British are in the suburbs," he said. But the cannons never came. On the 8th of December, in order to protect the holy places from destruction by the British, the Turkish high command reluctantly decided to surrender the city. Two thousand Turkish and German wounded lay in the hospitals, with rations for only about twelve hours.

When the British did arrive, Max went out to meet the convoy waving a torn hospital sheet on a pole, ready to beg for medicine and supplies. When the lead car stopped, he thrust out his hand and a pale British face looked out. It was Major General John Shea, commanding the division that had captured Jerusalem.

"I have worked at this hospital for nine years," said Max, with full awareness of his German origin. "I have saved lives of every nationality, including those from Mother England. We are in desperate need of supplies."

"You shall have what you need," replied the British officer, and the next morning lorries came rolling up to the hospital with rations and bandages and medical supplies. Two days later, General Sir Edmund Henry Hynman Allenby, commanding British forces in Egypt and Palestine, entered Jerusalem. As a conqueror, he was entitled to enter the holy city on horseback, a sword in his hand, but as a gesture of humility and respect he walked through Jaffa Gate unarmed, on foot, head uncovered. That dramatic picture of Allenby entering within the walls built by Suleiman the Magnificent circulated around the world and thrilled a war-weary populace eager for a "noble" incident to distract it from the years of carnage. Many of the long-standing residents remembering the pompous arrival, twenty years earlier, of Kaiser Wilhelm II seated on a white charger, welcomed the British with a sigh of relief.

With the arrival of trained medical personnel, Max, on the verge of nervous collapse, left for an extended holiday in Egypt and remained for six months, attaching himself after one brief week of rest to an army hospital there.

Refugees poured back into Jerusalem by the hundreds, the Mishwe family among them. Though it was only ten miles away, it was still impossible to return to the village. Soldiers and their horses were billeted in many homes, and the villagers were scattered.

The churches were taking as many refugees as they could house, and Father Alphonse took Nadeem and his family when they arrived in late December. It was an odd Christmas without the influx of pilgrims, but it was also a time of renewed hope and on Christmas Eve, they went to sing carols at Shepherds' Field near Bethlehem.

After the new year, the monks found the family two rooms in a boarding house in the Musrara section, which was predominantly Jewish, and Nadeem set about deciding how he was going to earn a living. It was a time of change and excitement in Jerusalem, with the signs of British occupation evident everywhere. By spring, the American Red Cross opened their headquarters and began the gargantuan task of repatriation and relief work.

One evening, as they strolled down Jaffa Road for a breath of air, Nadeem pointed out a man to Miriam in Arab dress coming down the steps from a hotel. "See that man?" said Nadeem. "He's not a bedouin at all."

She was amazed, for she had never seen a European wear the Arab robe and headdress with such convincing comfort. "His name is Lawrence. He's an Englishman. I met him by chance when I was in the army. They say the bedouin do his bidding as if he were God."

By the fall of that year, this same Lawrence had entered Damascus with Faisal ibn Hussein, who was to become King of Iraq, and captured it for the British. The Turks had been defeated. The war was over.

* * *

For Nadeem, all his success in life had evolved by virtue of his precocious and active mind, followed by the necessary work to bring his ideas to fruition. Nothing had come easily and, in fact, he was highly suspicious of luck or windfalls. Therefore, he was not prepared for the discovery that he and Miriam made one extraordinary morning in late summer of 1918.

They were still living with assistance from the relief agencies, including food and clothing from the U.S., augmented by odd jobs. Several times, Khalil and Hanna had spoken dreamily of leaving for America, where they would create fortunes, but each time they mentioned the idea, Miriam would become so agitated and morose that the subject was dropped. There was such an influx of foreigners in the city that it was virtually impossible to secure work, and they were able to remain in the two cramped rooms only because Nadeem made repairs on the house and kept the grounds in exchange for his rent. Still, the dwelling was so dingy that Miriam had refused to accept it as a permanent home and had never fully unpacked their belongings.

Nadeem was more practical, and he was constantly undoing a bundle and taking the contents out so they could use them. It was in this fashion that he came upon a soiled cotton bag that was buried among some clothing of Nadia's. It held papers that were mystifying to him and he went in search of his wife.

"Miriam, what are these papers? There's a deed here."

She had to think a while before remembering where she had acquired the bag. "When I was here with Nadia, I helped in the hospital a few days and this old man was so grateful he gave me all his papers before he died. I thought it was little more than rubbish. Oh, yes, he said there was some money in there." Her eyes lit up with expectation. "Did you look? Perhaps we'll find some money."

"There's something much more valuable than money, if it's legal," said Nadeem seriously. "Look!" he pulled out an official paper, which named a specific address deeded to a man by the name of Esa Nassam. Attached to it was a witnessed transfer of the deed to Miriam Mishwe, stamped and sealed. "It's transferred to you. If this is legal, you're the owner of this property, a large piece, too. See here, the dimensions are seventy-five feet wide by one hundred fifty deep located on Abba Siqra Street, running perpendicular to King David." They stared at each other in amazement.

"Nadeem, do you think it's true?"

"No. It seems too extraordinary. I would say it's not true."

Now that he was so adamant, she became defensive. "But here's the deed," she said irrefutably, "and it's transferred to me."

"But how could it be?" Nadeem pushed all the papers away from him, to think more clearly. "Things don't happen like this. It's too much like a magical event."

Miriam rose decisively and began to smooth her skirt. "We will have to go to the registry and see for ourselves. It is true," she added stubbornly, "now I remember that the old man did say he was giving his property to me. Or something like that. I don't remember the exact words. But he also said one of the doctors had witnessed the will. Nadeem, come. Perhaps a miracle has happened."

The bored English clerk at the government office attested to the legality of their deed, and, seeing nothing unusual—after all, he evaluated deeds daily and didn't consider any spot in this infernal desert worth a fig—was disgruntled to see these two dance about like enthusiastic dervishes when he confirmed ownership of the property on Abba Siqra Street.

"Let's go right now to see it," said Miriam and saw her husband hesitate. "Now please, Nadeem, don't find anything more to worry about. Let's enjoy it for the moment."

"Very well. I suppose you're right. If the truth is not as pleasant later, at least we can enjoy it for the moment," he said and they started off, out the Zion Gate to view whatever was waiting for them.

They had not known what to expect. Therefore, the sight of the two dilapidated houses—faintly Georgian, although of the humblest design—connected by a covered walkway sent them dancing again. "I don't quite know why," laughed Nadeem, "but I imagined it was only bare land. And look, two structures. Two solid structures."

Now it was Miriam's turn to become cautious. "I wouldn't call them solid," she said, eyeing the overgrowth and broken windows circumspectly.

"The damage is only superficial," explained Nadeem, who was already pushing back an oleander bush to have a look at the foundation. "The understructure is good. And look here, here's the mouth of a water cistern and the remains of a hand pump. Miriam, I could put this in shape and we could rent it. I could."

She recognized the hopefulness in his eyes and the excitement in his voice and thought of the other ventures that had begun this way. "Nadeem,"—she swallowed hard determined not to cry—"It makes me so happy to see you excited again. You've never complained through all these months and I know how difficult it's been for you. But now there's an opportunity again."

They stood in a tiny, barren courtyard that sloped drunkenly where the bricks had shifted, surrounded by rust and tangle, shattered glass and crumbling wood, in the shadow of two modest buildings, both, they would discover in the next moment, suffering from gaping holes in their roofs—as united and happy as they had ever been in their lives.

Nadeem went the next morning to see his friend Slivowitz and, after divulging the various tragedies that had befallen them—Slivowitz had lost his only son to typhus—Nadeem showed him the deeds and related the circumstances surrounding them.

"I never believed in miracles," said Slivowitz, "and I'm not going to change my mind now. The buildings must be ready to collapse."

"But they haven't collapsed yet," said Nadeem. Now that he had convinced himself of the project, nothing could dampen his spirits. "I will repair them before they do. They won't be extraordinary buildings, but they are fine for boarding establishments. We're living in one now that isn't half so pleasant, and you know the housing shortage is horrendous. I need fifteen hundred dollars for the bare necessities—to get people into them. Afterward, when there's an income, I'll do the rest."

"Of course," said Slivowitz, with none of his old feistiness. "I don't have fifteen hundred, but I'll give you a thousand." Nadeem didn't argue. He surmised that Slivowitz probably couldn't quite spare the thousand. It troubled him to see his old friend so subdued.

"Wouldn't you like to see the property?" he asked brightly.

"I'll come around and have a look when it's done," answered the banker. "Why look now and be frightened out of a night's sleep?" he added, and Nadeem saw a glimmer of his old friend.

It was like the old days. Working from dawn to dusk with the excitement of a child. But this time, there was the added bonus of serendipity— finding little refinements to delight a man who had spent a good portion of his life in the building trade. For instance, he discovered—after pulling away a wisteria vine several inches thick—that the door lintel was beautifully ornamented and the thick front doors, which needed no more than a careful varnishing, each had a carved panel that created a distinguished entrance.

When the houses were habitable, he moved his family into the bottom floor of one building and rented the rest of the space, in which he had created three apartments.

They lived there happily for six months, by which time Allenby and Lawrence had defeated the Turks in both Syria and Lebanon. The war was really over and they were allowed to travel home to pick up the pieces of a remembered life that had no more substance than a dream.

The clan was reunited—those who were left. Jamilla . . . oh, such a look of grief and torment still on her face. George . . . still bewildered without his twin, Salim. Daud . . . without his wife and child. Zareefa . . . without her beautiful middle daughter. And I, thought Miriam, without Esa.

Umm Jameel had changed the least although she had lost her elegant sister, Halla, who died along with the sheik. Their son was now head of the clan, and his son, Samir, was next in line, as it went in their tradition. But life was quite different from the old days. Cars zoomed up from Jerusalem in fifteen minutes. You could travel from the port of Jaffa in less than two hours. The English had brought in the marvels of the twentieth century.

The Friends' schools for both boys and girls reopened and soon gained a nationwide reputation. The elite of the occupying forces sent their children there to rub shoulders with the elite of Palestine. The students replanted the beautiful trees, which the Turks had hacked down to feed their locomotives. Samir, the sheik's son, was enrolled but no other boy or girl from the village. It was too extravagant and, also, the parents feared the seductive Western ideas would rob them of their children. The elegant Friends' compound, beyond the isolating ornate fence, was another world. The parents were right to be afraid. It *could* rob them of their children.

"Nadia, come here."

"No. I don't want to."

"Come here, Nadia."

"I don't want to. You're going to comb my hair."

"And . . . is that a crime?"

"My hair is fine like this. You don't have to comb it."

"Your hair is not fine." Nadia's reddish birth hair had not darkened, however, it was thick and curly and difficult to comb. "If we don't comb it today, tomorrow it will be twice as tangled."

"It's my hair and I want it messy. It doesn't bother me that it's tangled. It doesn't bother *baba*. Why should it bother you?"

"I don't know," Miriam answered honestly. "But it bothers me a great deal."

"Well, it's my hair and it *doesn't* bother me."

Miriam stared at the small prominent chin set in a combative thrust and the thin arms crossed resolutely across the narrow chest, defying coercion. On Nadia's face was Max Broder's mouth—a unique configuration that was so vulnerable it inspired a need to protect. Through her frustration— for this scene was repeated almost every morning—she admired her daughter's bravado and her adult vocabulary. She had never spoken in a babyish way. "I'll do it gently and try not to hurt you."

"You always say that."

"I don't have time to argue anymore. Just let me comb your hair." She tried to keep her voice from rising.

"I don't want it combed. I don't. I don't."

Miriam moved toward her daughter, grabbed the slim wrist—the hand was in a defiant fist—and pulled her between her legs so she couldn't escape. A seven-year-old girl, yet she was more exhausting than the boys at any age. She had prayed for a girl, had fantasized about a sensitive tender girl who would be a calming influence on a household full of males, but Nadia was anything but a calming influence. She had a nervous energy that made her fidgety when indoors. She was a poor guest wherever they visited, unwilling to submit to any graceful act of affection. "Why do I have to kiss everybody? Why can't I just say hello?" What was worse, she had the determination and poise to assert herself. It didn't help matters that Nadeem was her willing slave.

Now, in her mother's grasp, Nadia became stonily silent. Even when the comb caught and pulled painfully, she didn't cry out. When Miriam was finished and the long, copper braids were laid side by side against that straight back, there was no acknowledgement that, yes, she looked better.

"There now, that's better." Miriam tried for a reconciliation, annoyed with herself for feeling guilty. The hair fights were a daily fact of life. If she allowed such a young child to rule, soon there would be chaos. The hair had to be combed, if only for health reasons. So why did she feel ill at ease? "Don't you feel better?"

"I felt fine before," came the stony answer. "Can Hanna help me with the horse now?"

"The horse? You plan to ride the horse now?" She needed brush for the fire and had planned to send Nadia, but Miriam didn't have the energy for another fight. Nadia knew it and looked for the familiar signs: first, her mother would sigh, a quick far-away look to hide her eyes, then a reluctant . . . yes. "All right," said Miriam, "but only for half an hour. I need kindling."

She would ride for an hour because her mother would lose track of time. As she was leaving, however, she caught a glimpse of her mother's profile. A few strands of hair had escaped from under her scarf and in trying to tuck them in, she had made the scarf sit at an odd angle. It made her mother look helpless and sad and Nadia felt a sudden rush of love. "Mama," she rushed to Miriam's side and hugged her so fiercely they almost fell over.

Miriam was still feeling all the ambivalences that Nadia created. Why should it be like this? She had been prepared to love this child beyond reason. The night of her conception was still a vivid memory. But Nadia was as complicated as the love that had created her. Still Nadia clung, pumping her arms as if to remind Miriam that she was not responding to this expression of love. On the third pump, Miriam gave in, tilting her daughter's face, smoothing the pale cheeks, touching a finger to her lips and then to each of Nadia's eyes. Well, Max, this is all I have of you. The mouth, the forehead, the coloring—a shadow, but enough to keep you safely in a corner of my heart.

Hearing Hanna come in, Nadia let go abruptly. "Please help me with Gala. Just help me mount her and then you can leave me alone."

"You know I won't leave you alone on that horse," said Hanna. "I have to stay and lead you around."

"But you don't. You don't."

"I do, I do," he answered softly, following her outdoors.

The horse had come in a cart with a note two months after they had returned to the village after the war: "Please, could you board this horse for me? I find it difficult to keep him here and, lately, there is little time to ride. I will arrange for food to be sent and, if there are additional expenses, please let me know." A postscript told the real story. "If your little girl wishes to exercise the horse for me, I would be in her debt."

Miriam knew the horse would never leave, but what still puzzled her was Nadia's passion for riding. Had he passed that down? She longed to tell him how much Nadia loved the horse, but it would have been an expensive fulfillment of desire. From time to time, the old longing returned —as if his touch were hovering inches away and all she had to do to relieve her need was to reach up, but such moments always passed. No. Her resolve was still intact. No matter what. She would not contact Max.

When Nadia had her eighth birthday, Miss Emily Bailey, the headmistress of the Friends Girls' School came to the house and asked to see Miriam. "Could we take a little walk down the road, Mrs. Mishwe?"

"Of course, but wouldn't you rather come in and have some coffee?"

"Thank you, but I think our discussion is better served by the open air."

Miriam put a shawl around her shoulders and they started down the road in the crisp January air. When they were well past the house, Miss Bailey began: "Every year, the Friends schools have a few scholarships to dispense to worthy students who could not otherwise afford to attend. The money for these scholarships usually comes from grateful alumni—some of whom have emigrated to America and made their fortunes. Less often, the money comes from local personages, out of the blue, for a variety of reasons. We received such a fund recently from the estate of Dr. Max Broder, a German physician who worked at the French Hospital in Jerusalem.

Miriam stopped walking abruptly. Her legs trembled and her heart was pounding furiously. "Estate? You said 'estate.' Was Dr. Max . . . Broder . . . is he . . . did he . . ." She couldn't say the word. "Is he dead?" she asked finally in a voice so strained that Miss Bailey held her arm for support.

"He died three weeks ago, according to his lawyer. He fell from a horse and broke his neck."

Oh, no! No! No! Had she cried the words aloud or merely thought them? "I must return . . . My children . . . The baby . . . Nadia will be coming home from school."

"Mrs. Mishwe, please. There's something else. Obviously, this news has shocked you, but what I have to tell you is very important. One of the stipulations of the bequest is that a scholarship be made available to your daughter."

"Nadia? For Nadia to go to the school?"

"Yes. To board there. It will cost you nothing. She will be brought in on an academic scholarship. She's a very precocious little girl, according to the lawyer. It seems Doctor Broder was impressed with her intelligence when she was his patient and made a notation to do something for her. I suppose his death speeded up the process. He instructed his lawyer to see to it that she is educated. He specified two other children besides your daughter and left the rest of the bequest to our discretion, with the stipulation that Nadia stay at the school as long as she desires." Miriam kept her eyes straight ahead, hearing bits and pieces but not trusting herself to respond. She felt such an overwhelming sense of sadness for Max and underneath a black wave of grief. He had included two other children in the bequest to put Nadia's scholarship above suspicion because he loved her. He had loved his little girl. A broken neck! Oh, Max! My poor, poor darling.

There are times when life is kind in a peculiar way and it was kind to Miriam that winter of 1921. She caught a cold that developed into pneumonia and was feverish for so many weeks, no one suspected that all the wetness on her pillow were tears of sorrow, of regret for the unfathomable wellsprings of attraction that made one human being desirable above all others.

BOOK TWO
1924–1935

HEARTS BURNING
AND BRAVE

17

I was different, too, and it was my mother who made fun of me.

Miriam waited three years before accepting the scholarship offer to the girls' boarding school. She knew Nadeem wasn't crazy about the idea and that held her back. "She's already a handful," he said with rue but also underlying pride. "She wants to disassociate herself from all the things her parents do. Our relatives annoy her. She thinks we cook too much and eat too much and sing too much and talk too much. A fancy school isn't going to make her more tolerant of the life she has and . . ."—again his tone was rueful—"it's the life she has to live."

"It's true," said Miriam, "but when I think of denying her that wonderful opportunity . . . even though I know she'll use it against us. . . ."

"Precisely."

"On the other hand, she'll be cultured and educated. That will give her confidence. Sometimes I feel she's not confident at all and that's why she's stubborn."

"Yes, she lacks confidence."

"She needs the advantages the school will give her."

"Do you have your heart set on sending her?"

"I thought it didn't matter to me, but it does. I want her to have it." Max wanted her to have it. She couldn't face the guilt of denying his last wish for his daughter.

"Then send her," said Nadeem quietly. "We'll make the best of it."

On her daughter's last night at home, Miriam made a steamy bath and over Nadia's protests—she was embarrassed to sit naked in front of her mother—scrubbed her. "They're going to put a lot of ideas in your head." She dug the sponge into Nadia's back.

"Isn't that why I'm going? They're supposed to put ideas in my head."

"Just remember where you come from." Round and round went her hand.

"Mama, you're hurting me."

* * *

When Nadia's belongings were folded in the brand-new suitcase, Miriam took a napkin full of cookies and laid it on top. "Don't put food in. They have food there."

"It's only sweets. Give them out and perhaps you can make some friends."

When Nadia arrived at the red-roofed palace and got a look at the confident, well-groomed princesses who would be her classmates, she slipped out and left the cookies under a mock orange bush and prayed no one would trace them to her.

There were thirty boarders (including eight from England and Europe). For a tuition of fifteen French gold lira yearly, they were taught to think, recite the classics, and "sit quietly each morning and wait upon the Lord."

The school was oriented toward excellence through discipline. In 1889, the founding faculty had read like a directory of straight-spined Yankee conservativism. Henrietta Strong taught English. Adora Leighton was the general matron. Belva Farquhar, a lady physician from Iowa, offered herself for medical work. That stalwart group reached land by jumping off rope ladders into the erratic waters of Jaffa harbor.

Fifteen affluent Christian fathers had to be persuaded to give their daughters to a handful of pale foreigners in upswept pompadour hairdos and dimity blouses, so they could be radicalized by Western ideas. No traffic jam materialized at the Mission Gate, but finally, one "cuckoohead" came forth and asked, "Please accept my daughter into thou's school."

The Friends had come to educate girls (and boys), not make snobs of them, but the values they encouraged (the very idea of cataloging one's values was egregious) resembled the prep schools of England and America. They played soccer on a superb, even field and learned *tennis!* (who even knew what it was) on private courts. Students were required to do chores but that was considered charming. Something to excite the *bourgeoisie:* "*What?* Paying all that money so Camilla can sweep floors?"

In the Quaker schools, there was a unique way of taking attendance. Each girl announced her presence by responding to a line of Scripture.

Miss Amelia Smythe, in a starched, tucked shirtwaist, still unbruised by a day of teaching, pulled open her Bible with the colored string markers. "Violet Abdo—" she began, " 'A soft answer turns away wrath.' "

" 'But a harsh word stirs up anger.' "

"Rose David—'God is my refuge and my strength.' "

" 'A very present help in trouble.' "

"Elisabeth Eden—'For behold I create new heavens and a new earth.'"

There was no response. Elisabeth sank into a somber silence that made the blood coagulate.

"'And the former things sh . . . sh . . . shall not be remembered or come into mind,'" Elisabeth stuttered and the class slumped in relief.

Miss Smythe went to Proverbs for the *G*'s and *H*'s which were numerous, to Isaiah for two *L*'s and to the Psalms for Nadia Mishwe. "The earth is the Lord's and the fullness thereof."

The room was cold and the short hairs crackled on Nadia's neck, like wires. The school had no central heating and she was never warm enough. The fullness thereof. It could mean anything. Dear Jesus, please help me. "The earth is the Lord's and the sky and the sea is His, too," she said hastily. "And us, the people."

The laughter was hideous. Miss Smythe held up a grayish palm. "Your thought is accurate, Nadia, although the Bible's phrasing is different: 'the earth and those who dwell therein.'"

"Jasmeen N'am—the Lord is my light and my salvation; whom shall I fear . . ."

At FGS, as in any school, there was a tough, bright core of girls, secure but fresh out of charity, and they feasted on Nadia's answer for a week. "This spoon is the Lord's and my shoes and the table."

"That dog is the Lord's. And that stick. And us, too, the people."

"You are so stupid," someone whispered in her ear. The words cut deep, but she wasn't brought to tears as they'd hoped. She was twelve years old, but she was no fool. She wasn't like the other girls. They made fun of the way she ate. The way she walked. Even her thinness was a disadvantage. She felt rage toward her parents.

She knew two things. She knew she wasn't stupid. And she wasn't a crybaby. There were two other girls who were worse off. Maha, the only Muslim, was petrified of the dark. Her religion forbade photographs, so she clung to handkerchiefs saturated with her mother's perfume for comfort. The smell gave Nadia a headache. Then there was Willie, an overweight American girl with a cleft palate, who slept next to her in an identical white metal bed. Her speech was so muffled and phlegmy you had to guess at the words. *"Whyahyhha ga humm,"* Willie would suggest when the girls picked at Nadia like crows over a dead mole. *"Ga humm. Ga humm,"* she repeated agitatedly, as if Nadia were in the path of an oncoming bus. Willie, whose folded, malformed lips couldn't utter a single untortured word, was urging *her* to go home.

"Shut up, Willie. Just shut up. I'm not going home," she said, cutting the air with the side of her hand. "I belong here. It's all paid for. I can stay as long as I want."

Willie, who always looked hopefully at her neighbor's plate because she was never quite full and who was spooked by the swarthy bedouin sheiks who occasionally visited, was flabbergasted by Nadia's love for the school. *"Ghu lock et, hgea?"*

"Of course, I like it. This is the best school in the world."

When Willie urged her to go home, alarms went off. She would never consider leaving. Through the morass of pain and uncertainty, there was something here that made her feel as if she belonged. The Anglo-Saxon reserve suited her just fine. There was none of the loud laughter and constant singing and kissing and general fuss that was always going on at home. She didn't feel suffocated here. From the six o'clock morning bell, the day was planned. There was, in everything, a seriousness of purpose. Best of all—opportunity for personal success. There was a piece of embroidery in her mother's kitchen drawer that was soiled and frayed from being undone and restitched many times because Nadia couldn't learn to embroider. That rag told the whole story of what went on between her mother and herself. By some miracle, she had been taken into this school. They would have to hack her up and mail her out piece by piece to get her to leave.

At Christmas there was a short vacation and she went home. Her mother tore a piece of bread and innocently dipped it into gravy and popped it in her mouth. Nadia wanted to slap her. Aunt Diana bit into a piece of fruit and allowed the juice to dribble down her arm, and she felt a gagging loathing. Khalil was too fat and his pants bunched around his buttocks. Hanna chewed with his mouth partly open. Her feelings were chaotic.

"Perhaps you don't want to return?" her father said, hopefully.

She almost screamed. "Of course I want to return."

In the spring of her thirteenth year, Mr. Kimble lined seven girls up on the tennis court. No one had an advantage here. The game was a mystery to one and all.

"I want you to take this ball," said Mr. Kimble. "Throw it a few feet above your head with the left hand, then hit it with the racket while it's in the air so that it lands in that right corner."

He might as well have told them to hold the racket between their teeth while drinking a bowl of soup. Three girls didn't hit the ball at all. The other three dribbled it on the wrong side of the net. Then came Nadia's turn. Her hands were large and strong from years of gripping horses' reins. She threw the ball in the air and slapped it securely, hooking the racket to direct the shot to the right corner. Mr. Kimble wiped his glasses and asked her to do it again. She did it so accurately that he made her repeat it eight times. Everybody stared with the interest reserved for the bizarre. Nadia Mishwe, the girl who had barely mastered the correct use of a fork, was good at tennis. She was great at tennis.

"You have the makings of a good serve," said Mr. Kimble. She had no idea what he was talking about, but she felt supremely happy.

By spring, her table manners were exemplary. Her mother caught on. Aunt Diana caught on too and didn't like what she saw and what it implied. "He fasted and fasted and had breakfast on an onion" was her bored response, implying that Nadia's fancy education would get her nowhere. "When you marry, you won't need to know how to play tennis," she said. "That won't help."

"It makes Aunt Diana angry that I go to FGS," Nadia said to Miriam.

"Angry? I don't think she's angry. She's not used to a girl like you. We used our hands to dig rocks out of the soil, to gather wheat and beat the olives off the trees with sticks. Your life is too different from what we're used to and perhaps not realistic."

"But you know how to read, Mama." She had always cherished that curious difference in her mother.

"Yes. I was different, too, as a child. And it was my mother who made fun of me. But still, I didn't achieve enough to make people envious. And they excused me because I was a mute man's daughter. They thought I had calamity enough."

Whenever her mother spoke of the past, it brought back a dim but tantalizing memory of their visit to Jerusalem during the war. When they had met *him*. "Oh, Max," her mother had sighed. Two simple words but it sounded as if she had been waiting, holding in all her feelings for him.

Nadia had liked Dr. Max, too. He was handsome, tall and strong, and he helped the sick. People were always kissing his hands and thanking him for saving their lives. He had been thrilled that Nadia liked horseback riding as much as he.

"Don't you remember that doctor who told me the dog was making me cough and sneeze?" she would ask Miriam, hoping her expression would reveal something.

"You told him he was being silly."

"No. Did I?"

"You were just a little girl."

"He gave me a bag of honey drops and told me I had two choices: to live without the dog and stop the dripping and wheezing or to live with the dog and get used to the dripping."

"You remember all of that?"

"Yes." You remember, too, Mama. You don't want to forget, either.

18

There's nothing we can do. We can't make her stop growing.

When she was fourteen, Nadia grew five inches in seven months. Her clothes suddenly shrunk and her features, especially her nose, grew out of proportion.

If she smiled, her nose splayed out and she became grotesque. When she sat, she twisted her legs and arms toward her. Everything made her perspire. She saw pity in the eyes of her relatives. Pity and relief. At least my daughter has a sweet, round face, some meat on her bones. "Miss Bailey says I'm the athletic sort." She tried to make light of it, but she was frightened. Her breasts were growing. Little plump cones jutted out and took shape. They looked like the budding horn stumps that appeared on the baby goats.

"Athletic," muttered Miriam, swallowing her criticism. The image people had of Nadia was not that she was quiet or shy or *athletic* but that she was *difficult.*

"She's tall," said Nadeem to Miriam when Nadia had turned sixteen. Miriam knew he was concerned, not over his daughter's lack of beauty—he loved her blindly—but for what it did to her personality.

"Her face is long and too strong." Miriam felt disloyal, but she, too, wanted to unburden herself.

"Does she ever tell you anything? Does she say, 'Mama, I like the school. I'm doing well. The girls like me.' Does she have friends? Do you think she feels comfortable there? What's the sense of making her go to a place where she doesn't feel comfortable?"

"She feels comfortable there," said Miriam tersely. "It's here that she feels ill at ease."

"Why do you suppose that is?"

"Probably it's her age. She doesn't want to think she needs us. She's out of step with her cousins. They're intimidated by her schooling and she feels they band together against her."

"She seems to be suffering deep inside, Miriam. I don't know what we can do about it."

"There's nothing we can do. We can't make her petite. We can't make her face fill out. We can't make her sociable and gracious."

"Do you think we can get her interested in a boy? Nabile Thomas has a boy and he asked me about Nadia."

Miriam shook her head. "If you mention anything like that to her, she'll refuse. She won't cooperate."

"But we're her parents," said Nadeem and his voice was righteous. "She can't always have things her way."

Miriam looked at her husband with surprise. She had always felt powerless when Nadeem protected Nadia. Now, the idea that he would demand her obedience gave her a childish thrill. "You're right," she said. "We'll do what we think is best."

By night she thought better of it. "Nadeem, she's only sixteen. She loves the school. Would you really make her do something now? I've never talked about this with her."

"It's about time you brought it up then."

"I'm . . . afraid to bring it up."

"Afraid?" He looked surprised. "Afraid to talk to your own daughter about her future? This boy is a good choice for her and there may not be another as good."

"Nadeem, there'll be others. Let's wait."

"There won't be another that has everything right, like this one has, I tell you. We have to do it now. You'll see. The excitement of it will work on her and she'll come around. Her cousins will be envious and she'll be the center of attention."

Nadeem made the arrangements, but Miriam knew Nadia wouldn't come around. She knew what he wasn't saying and it made her feel sad and helpless. He feared Nadia wouldn't receive many offers and perhaps her youth was the best asset she would ever have.

"Why do you want to go to such a rigorous school? My sister goes to Mar Yusef. It's a good enough place."

She looked at the boy as if he had spoken an obscenity. What made him an authority on what was good enough for her? "It's the best school in Palestine," she said firmly. "The American consul says so and the British consul agrees. Every visiting scholar makes it his business to stop by and lecture to us. Anyone who graduates can pass the London University Exam or the National Matriculation Exam. How can you ask such a question? If you had a choice between having something that was just so-so and having the best, which would you choose?"

The boy was frowning. He wasn't expecting such aggression and it confused him. She could see he was deciding whether to be aggressive in return or to be polite. He sighed and shifted so that instead of sitting squarely on the couch, he was angled toward her. "How do you like to pass your free time? Or perhaps you don't have any free time in this fancy school." He said "fancy" in a sarcastic way, so she knew his feelings were hurt.

From out of nowhere, she had this sense of freedom to say anything she pleased. It was wonderful not to care how someone reacted. "I pass my free time playing tennis. I'm mad for tennis." She was trying for an off-hand brittleness precisely because it would annoy him.

"Tennis? Where you hit the ball back and forth?"

"Well . . . that's not all of it." To explain the finer points of the game would be useless. He would scoff. "How do *you* pass *your* free time?"

"I don't have much of it," he said proudly. "My father and I have the franchise for the Singer machines. Do you own a Singer? Do you sew?"

"No. I never learned."

"No? That's strange. It's hard to manage a home and family without knowing how to sew. Without owning a machine."

"Is that what you tell the ladies when you're trying to sell one of your Singers?"

He smiled for the first time. "We don't have to *try* to sell them at all. Orders are waiting before the shipment is unloaded off the boats. We never have enough machines to fill the demand."

She thought for a moment. "Well, then, what's your job? I mean if you don't have to sell them."

"I still take orders," he said, slightly offended. "And I demonstrate and also service the machines."

"Oh."

"Are you interested in a home and a family?" he asked, sounding a little like an exasperated parent and she thought, He's too young to be so . . . serious. But then, something about the way he kept scanning her face quickly and then looking away, helped her catch on that this meeting was no casual encounter. Her mother had taken his mother out in the garden for lemonade and left them purposely alone. *Oh!* This boy was meant as a suitor! Her face colored and she couldn't trust herself to speak. She answered with a shake of her head. "I'm surprised," he said, accusingly. "I thought this was something that was on your mind."

"Well, you're mistaken." Unhappily, her voice shook and diminished the effect. "I'm sorry but you were brought here under false pretenses. I'm not the girl for you. I'm sure there is a girl for you, but it's not me."

He was stunned—like an animal caught by a bright light. He digested the full blow to his ego and gathered his dignity with more presence than seemed possible under the circumstances. "You're right about that," he said scornfully. "You think you're too good for me, is that it? Do you have so many offers that you can be so high and mighty? I don't think so. Whatever else they teach you at that school, they don't teach you to be realistic. Let's see who marries you, Miss!"

While he was there she was furious, but when he left she was scalding with shame, her cheeks flaming, her eyes burning. She could stand anything, her height, her looks, but she couldn't stand the idea that her father wanted to protect her from life by marrying her off. She remembered the boy's haircut that had exposed his ears in a pathetic way. He had groomed himself especially for her. *Ya Allah!* Stood in front of a mirror and thought how he would look to her. Then he must have been so disappointed. She remembered the way his feet had been exactly together, toe to toe. She had probably appeared more pathetic to him than he to her. Otherwise, why would his voice have been so cocky with confidence, as if she would be thrilled with his attention? As if he were her lord and master and she had to obey. That's what her parents had in mind for her future? *They wanted her to go to some small plain house and obey that boy for the rest of her life.*

Uncle Nabile's daughter had been chosen by an old village man who had become rich in Argentina and returned to find a wife. During the ceremony, Nadia had been almost weak with relief that she wasn't the bride. There were dreadful stories of girls who thought they were marrying one man and, when they removed the heavy wedding veil, found themselves married to another. She was appalled that Nabile's daughter went so meekly to her doom, but no one else saw it that way.

She was disappointed with her father but felt rage toward her mother and a need to hurt her.

"Do you think Dr. Max would like what you did?" she confronted her mother when they were alone and was satisfied to see Miriam's face turn a ghastly white. They had never uttered that name between them. "He sent me to FGS for a reason. He wanted me to be well educated and learn something about the outside world and be a part of it. All you wanted was to turn me over to the first man available—some idiot who asks why I have to go to such a fancy school. As if it's too good for me. As if I have to answer to him."

Her mother remained silent. She shook her head and looked frightened and then turned and walked out into the yard.

Instead of feeling triumphant, Nadia felt miserable. For a few days, she considered writing the boy an apology. One horrible night she even considered that he was right, no one would ever marry her. But time passed and she never wrote. She felt worst over what she had done to her mother and fantasized achieving something so impossibly grand it would wipe out all her mother's sorrows. She imagined herself marrying the most desirable boy in the village and elevating Miriam to a place of influence and pride. Oh, how it would thrill her mother if she married Samir Saleh. She wasn't foolish enough to believe it would happen, but it was satisfying to drift off to sleep imagining the triumphant scene.

At the end of her sixteenth year, Nadia had a physical transformation. As sometimes happens after puberty, there was a dramatic shift in the proportions of her face and body. She stopped growing and her features balanced out. Her face appeared to have been carved to expose its understructure. It was a powerful face, the kind that, quite often, can be more compelling than classical beauty. Her hair settled to a rich reddish brown. She wore it long, hitched up on either side by combs that created a smooth demure pompadour around her forehead but left the rest of her mane to spread out in an extravagant dramatic cloud that added width to her face and softened the features.

It was a face full of contradictions. The pale gray eyes, not particularly large but heavily lashed, were private and distant. The nose and chin and jawline were angular and prominent. Then, amid all that Teutonic sternness, there was the most seductive mouth imaginable, with generous, sculpted lips; that peaked twice and whose voluptuous pinkness was framed by a unique ridge. When she opened her mouth, even the slightest bit, it was an invitation to be kissed, and there was no other way to see it. Yet kissing was the last thing on her mind. She was a serious person, dedicated to her studies and the sport of tennis.

As if to rescue her from a grim, humorless life, along came Margaret.

"No, no, no!" The sobs were loud and exasperated.

Nadia raised her head and called over, "Are you ill? Shall I call Miss Bailey?" Dark blonde hair in need of a good washing hung in sections, hiding much of the face.

The weeping stopped. "Don't call anyone unless it's a man who's prepared to elope with me and take me away from this cold, dank room." The new English girl sat up. "I'm going to become ill," she predicted with resentment. "Everything is so . . . so *uncomfortable!* How do you stand it?" She surveyed the room with such distaste that Nadia put her head down not to be included in her line of vision. "Where are you from?" asked the girl. "Italy?"

"No. From here." She was pleased to be thought from such an exotic place.

"Here? You can't mean right here. Where exactly?" Her voice was upper-class British, and the clipped words made her sound impatient.

Nadia bristled. The English could be so insulting. "Yes. From right here. In ten minutes, I could walk to my house and find my mother." Now why had she brought her mother into it?

"What? You're a native?" Her upper lip lifted awkwardly when she spoke and her "What?" came out "Whot?" "Why don't you leave?"

"I want to stay," Nadia answered coolly. "I like it here."

"Awh, Gawd, don't be insulted. In a way,"—she stopped to blow her nose—"it's a back-handed compliment. I watched you play tennis yesterday when they were showing me around and I was certain you'd had dozens of lessons in some fancy European club. And now . . . well, it's quite the opposite. You're from here." She mulled this over then came to sit with Nadia.

"You'd better hurry and make your bed." Nadia threw back the covers and got up. "We're supposed to tidy the chapel and prepare it for the meditation. They won't tolerate lateness for chapel."

"Whot? They'll chuck me out?"

"I'll show you the routine, if you like."

"Mmm. How do you tidy a chapel, anyway? Isn't it just full of pews? Suppose I don't want to tidy it? Will they expel me?"

"Not immediately. I think they'd give you another chance." She had no idea what they would do.

The girl sat on the edge of the bed, face in hands, looking woefully at her long, thin feet. "They'd never chuck me. My father would charm Amelia Smythe out of her shoes. He'd stare at her for about twenty seconds as if she's the most important person on God's earth, and she'd be pudding in his hands."

That speech—the offhandedness, the imagery, the irreverence toward her elders—made Nadia feel that she had been thrust, through sheer luck, into the hot white center of modernity.

Her name was Margaret and for the next two hours she loosely imitated bedmaking, sweeping, furniture arranging, with none of the newcomer's earnestness. When the boys trooped in to chapel, she looked them over as if they were being paraded for her pleasure. And during meditation, while everyone else sat quietly to "wait upon the Lord," she took inventory of which boy had what.

"Which one do you fancy?" she asked matter-of-factly, as they walked to the first class of the day.

"I don't fancy anyone," Nadia answered sharply.

"Hit a nerve, have I?" Margaret grinned.

When it came time for the roll-call responses from Scripture, Nadia snickered. This would repay Margaret for the tactless remark.

Miss Smythe flipped her Bible to Paul's First Letter to the Corinthians. "Margaret Madden—If I give away all I have, and deliver my body to be burned, but have not love . . ."

Margaret straightened and placed her hands together in a reverential pose. ". . . I gain nothing. Love is patient and kind; love is not jealous or boastful; it is not arrogant or rude. Love does not insist on its own way; it is not irritable or resentful; it does not rejoice at wrong, but rejoices in the right. Love bears all things, believes all things, hopes all things, endures all things. Love never ends . . ." she took a deep insinuating breath. As if she had experienced a love that had never ended.

"I see you've been a student of the Bible." Miss Jones smiled briefly and glanced at her roll sheet for the next name. "Nadia Mishwe—Faith is the substance of things hoped for."

"The evidence of things not seen."

There was something about Margaret—and it took only a few days to realize it—a lack of reverence for convention and a forthrightness. Margaret had an incredible knack for, as she put it, "pinpointing the vulgar truth of everything" and then blurting it out. She was also incredibly smart. Nadia began seeing things Margaret's way and it had the cumulative effect of making her feel older and more in control.

Friday evenings Margaret took the jitney to have dinner with her father who was the National Relations Commissioner for the Mandate government. One evening she returned early and in a talkative mood.

"Here," she pulled out a soggy napkin containing anise cakes and dumped them unceremoniously on Nadia's lap.

While Nadia ate, Margaret lay with her arms under her head, one leg propped over the other. She closed her eyes as if reviewing the evening's events. "Victor Madden . . ." she began, stating her father's name as if it were the title of a book she was considering. "My mother left him, you know," she said quickly and sat up.

"The day she left, she said to me, 'I love him. I do.' She wasn't leaving him because she didn't love him. Now, this was difficult to believe because she *did* leave with another man." Here Margaret scrunched up her face to punctuate the discrepancy in her mother's motivation. "She wrote to me afterward—something bizarre. What's more bizarre, I believed her. The letter said: 'I've left your father because I love him too much. He would have destroyed me in the end. Therefore, when a man came along that I liked well enough, I saw my chance to escape the fatal charm of Victor Madden. I won't be left alone when I'm too old to attract anyone. One day, you'll understand. Please forgive.' Can you imagine such planning? But it makes sense, don't you think? I understood right away." She gave a little weary sigh. "I don't know what Victor's up to," she said in a sad tired voice. "He had a woman there tonight."

"I guess he's very handsome," offered Nadia. She could not imagine a father who was that interesting.

"Not only handsome," said Margaret. "Irresistible. Wait'll you meet him. You'll fall for him, too. Speaking of which, there's only one thing in this whole place that interests me, present company excluded, of course. It can be summed up in one word."

"What's the word?" asked Nadia lazily.

"Not 'what' but 'who.' "

"Who?"

"Mmmm. And the who is a he."

"I hope it isn't a teacher," said Nadia, alarmed. "Is it one of the boys at FBS?" She sat up.

"Just one."

"Who?"

"There's only one worth anything and he's worth everything. Think."

"It's not Samir, is it?"

"Precisely."

"Well, you're after the wrong fish. His future's carved in stone, like the Ten Commandments."

"Whot? He can't have a say in his own life?"

"Not in the way you have in mind."

"I want him," Margaret wailed. "He's absolutely gorgeous. I love his hands. They're spectacular. Large and strong . . . why they could proba-bly crush my. . . . oh, never mind." She sighed.

"He's my cousin," said Nadia. She had never thought much about the relationship but now she was glad to impress the unimpressible Margaret. "When we were toddlers, I used to ride on him like a horse."

"My Gawd!" said Margaret, sincerely surprised. "Your cousin?"

"Well, we're not that close. His father's the wealthiest man in our clan. They own extensive vineyards and half interest in a hotel in Jerusalem and who knows what else. He lived with the bedouins for almost a year in the wilderness to be toughened up. They're very strict with him. And, of course, every mother has her eye on him for her daughter." She had a perverse need to make him as attractive as possible to Margaret. It was difficult to think of Samir without also seeing his background—the wealth, the powerful father, the exquisite mother, the stepsister who was as plain as he was handsome—all ingredients for high drama. "He engages the imagination on many levels," she said loftily, "and the most tantalizing speculation centers around which girl he will choose to marry."

"I'll fight for him." Margaret giggled. "He's so attractive . . . those brooding eyes. And that triumphant glow to his skin. He always looks as if he just fought for his life and won."

"His mother was considered to be the most beautiful woman in Nablus." She'd heard that said so often in the family that she mentally stated it each time she saw Samir. "She's very young. It's the sheik's second marriage and he's *twenty-four* years older."

Margaret whistled. "Has Samir . . . uh . . . hinted at the girl of his dreams?"

"Not that I know of. You can be sure if he had, the girl would have shouted it from the rooftops. He is the man of the hour." Nadia's tone was somewhat bitter.

"Too bad you can't make a bid for him yourself," offered Margaret. "But you'd have me to contend with."

"I could make a bid for him," said Nadia seriously. "It would be the most natural thing." She suddenly felt very queer discussing all the clan's deadly little secrets so casually. Nevertheless, she plodded on. "In our tradition, the best bride, the most desirable, is a cousin. I'm his cousin."

"*Très bizarre,*" said Margaret, "but then why not? Don't tell me you don't think he's special. I mean, when he enters a room, it's transformed. His . . . *confidence.* Yes, that's it. Confidence is everything," she added with conviction, as if she'd just discovered this to be true.

"I've never been a fan of Samir's," Nadia's voice was sober, as if she were unwilling to confront her reasons. "He makes you react to him, which puts me off."

Margaret had a devilish look. "Did you ever stop to think that he's trying to make *you* react, precisely because you're not panting over him?

Some men are like that, you know. They must have the odd lamb that's not in the fold."

Nadia shrugged but then offered serious advice. "Don't set your heart on Samir. He's the ultimate product of our tradition. He's been raised to follow his father's plan to the letter. And that plan does not include any marriage outside our nationality."

"Hmmm. Well, lucky you, you've got the inside track now, haven't you?"

"I don't want the inside track," she said hotly. "I don't want any part of Samir Saleh." She was jealous of Margaret's feelings for Samir, yet she found him so threatening that she wanted to run when she saw him.

"Hit a nerve, have I?" smiled Margaret in her infuriating way. "You must be daft. But never mind, leaves the field clear for me."

Nadia felt two ways about Samir. When they were young, she had hated him. He used to smile at her in school whenever their paths crossed. His smile seemed to say, I know where you come from and I know where you must return.

She stopped hating him on January 10, 1929 when he was already nineteen, preparing at FBS for the London Matriculation Exam. That day the Ford Foundation had sent a documentary film on the horses of the Midwest and the school had invited the villagers to view it. When the horses came thundering on the screen, the Arab parents shouted in fright and held each other.

Her father had came out afterward, still excited, and said to the crowd, "It's fantastic. It was so real, I called out in alarm."

She was embarrassed that her father was so naive. Samir, watching Nadia's downcast eyes, came over and stood with Nadeem. "Never mind, *ami,*" he said amiably, "when the sheik saw it the first time, he overturned his chair and called to my mother, '*Yullah,* come on. *Umi.* Move. They're coming!' "

Everyone laughed. If the sheik could be fooled, then it wasn't so embarrassing after all. Her father had laughed more heartily than anyone and Nadia had been so grateful. New emotions had sprung up and she didn't know how to react.

Several days later, she had said to Samir, "I've been compiling facts about you."

"Oh? What have you come up with?" he asked, his fine eyes smiling. He felt no threat from any corner.

"You're kind when you don't have to be," she tried to sound offhand, as if she had dug through many faults to find this sole good attribute.

He shrugged. "What else have you found out?"

"Nothing that I want to talk about," she said, suddenly unnerved by those brilliant eyes focused on hers. For the first time, she was tongue-tied with him and hurried away.

What else have you found out? His voice was a lovely mix of the lilting Judean accent with an overlay of the Continent. Aunt Zareefa said that was because he had been tutored by a Scottish woman when he was quite small and had learned her inflections. Her mother said it was more than that. It was the voice of privilege.

She would have had to be blind and deaf not to speculate on how it would upgrade her life to be married to him. She would have had to be comatose not to daydream over him as a lover. There was an aura about Samir—it wasn't only the wealth. He was friendly but also detached and deeply private. Behind that handsome face was a hint of hidden pain that made any woman, Nadia included, feel duty-bound to distract him. And the most delicious fantasy was to distract such a man by making him lust over you.

Girls paraded in front of him at any family function. Some of them were quite beautiful and a few were both beautiful and smart. One, Jaqueline George, was beautiful, smart, and rich. Nadia kept her distance. It would be mortifying to fall in love with him and know that he simply tolerated her.

If she loved him, she'd want him to be preoccupied with her to the point of madness. Dazed and wounded with desire. Sick at heart with jealousy.

Each of their encounters stood out in her mind with vivid details. When wristwatches were still a rare sight, he had appeared wearing a gold one with a tan leather strap. He twisted his arm casually to look at the time and she had considered him the most sophisticated person on the face of the earth. One of her first grown-up memories was of his profile in chapel —dark lashes making a shadow on his cheek, the curving innocence of his ear, the sincere look of thoughtfulness. Was he praying? And what was he praying for?

Each time they met, she came away with something more and hammered a new detail into place, building her personal portrait of him in her heart.

19

Is there some maiden there that has your heart?

He would remain ambivalent over Fridays for the rest of his life. But they would also serve to remind him that discipline has its own rewards. Wasn't the soccer match more enjoyable after the tedium of the language speaking trials? His father had attended today and, to please him, Samir had put on the long, double-breasted serge *combaz* the waist belt, which doubled as pockets and held his valuables, and topped it off with a *tarbush*.

He looked forward to changing into the maroon and gray soccer uniform and hurried to the locker room. Phillips, an English boy who had become a frequent companion, walked beside him. They were a striking pair. Samir had the healthy color of the desert, a golden complexion accented by fine dark brows and large brilliant eyes. Phillips, on the other hand, had the straight flyaway hair of his race, with a complexion that reacted badly to all but the mildest weather.

"Let me have your hat. That's what I need to give me some panache," Phillips removed his tweed cap, grabbed the tarbush, and set it jauntily on his head. "What do you think? I'll wear this to tea and the girls will swoon. My clothes are so boring compared to yours."

"I was thinking exactly the same," sighed Samir.

"You can have mine any time you say. Can you imagine me going back to Eton with the rope and the cloth around my head?"

Samir placed Phillips' cap on his own head and was so pleased with the effect he smiled broadly and executed several extravagant poses. "Please keep it," said the English boy. "You look positively dashing, while I merely appear to be what I am—a pale boy from the British Isles. What do you say we exchange clothes altogether? I rather fancy your robes."

Samir looked wistful. "My father would feel betrayed."

"Betrayed?" Phillips voice rose almost to a whine in disbelief. "Because of a silly hat? You can't be serious."

"Yes." He was still posing before the mirror. "You see," he said with mock seriousness, "I am the hope of the future and must be beyond reproach. It would embarrass my father if his son chose to dress in Western clothes. It would show disdain for our culture."

Phillips shrugged. "Sounds like a heavy load. What happens when you go abroad to college?"

"I don't know," said Samir thoughtfully.

"I don't see you at Cambridge in the headcloth and *aghal.* That will cause a ruckus and not a pleasant one, either. You see,"—Phillips bared tiny, even teeth and gave an exaggerated false smile—"my countrymen are rather snobbish about the nationalities. And while you are a splendid specimen of manhood, they will tend to treat you like a leper if you flaunt your differences."

Samir's face became stiff. "Will they like me more if I pretend to be one of them?"

"Gawd, no. They'll probably stone you. They'll want you simply to try your best to be unobtrusive and obsequiously fawning and to lend them your last piaster, which more often than not they'll forget to repay."

"This is how you evaluate your countrymen? I'm offended," said Samir teasingly.

"This is how I evaluate my countrymen with regard to forcigners," Phillips answered carefully.

"And yourself?" asked Samir, one eyebrow raised. "You feel the same about me?"

"Absolutely not. If your brilliance on the soccer field weren't enough to impress me, I would have been swayed to your camp by your loyalty and friendship. You have singlehandedly taught me higher mathematics. What's more, you have made me believe that I've learned it myself without your help. You've been generous beyond measure without being a dolt. I have only to admire one of your possessions, whereupon you press it upon me as if I would be doing you a favor to rid you of the item. You are handsome, yet you have no concern for your looks other than to slick your hair down nervously on the playing field. You are strong as a bull and could box any boy into porridge, yet go out of your way to avoid confrontations. At times, I hate you for your goodness, Samir." This last was said with a wide-eyed puzzled look that transformed Phillips' face into what it might have been like when he was a toddler.

Samir removed the cap from his head and placed it on Phillips' straight sparse locks. "I don't blame you. Come, let's get to the field and see if the Botsford boys have grown some more. Will the girls attend today?"

"Yes. Why? Is there some maiden there that has your heart?" Phillips liked to speak in elaborate words, believing he was imitating the flowery speech of the Arabs. It was a habit that had caught his fancy, and Samir was accustomed to and sometimes amused by it.

"And if there were? Wouldn't I be the fool to confide in you? You'd drag the girl to me immediately and say, 'Mademoiselle, you have this poor fool's heart in the palm of your hand.' "

"That might hurry things along."

"You're assuming the girl would return the feelings."

"Of course. What girl would refuse you? Rich. Handsome. Smart. The hope of the future. Just choose the one you fancy."

"I don't fancy anyone in particular. And yourself?"

"I would happily take Meena, if her father weren't Muslim. I believe their custom would demand that he cut off my manhood if he even suspected I thought of Meena."

"Quite true," said Samir. "Forget Meena. Now, let's go. We're late."

They descended a few steps and went out a back door to the soccer field. It was a splendid sunny day and both boys instinctively looked back to survey the scene. The building stood stark on a hill, exposed to the winds that blew from the west and north. "It's strange," said Phillips, "but for the few dressed in the headdress, this could be a school in England. It's out of character with the countryside."

"Feeling homesick?" asked Samir.

"Not quite."

"You never explained why you left Eton. Is it too personal?"

Phillips took a deep breath and reduced his speed. "I fell into a physical enchantment with a young woman who lived in the parish house near school. One evening, unable to control myself, I borrowed the master's car and attempted to drive to see her. But I hadn't the least notion of how to operate a car, not even how to turn on the headlamps. Immediately out the gate, I collided with a tree."

"Did you get thrashed?"

"No. My father said—I'll never forget it—he said, 'son, you are sixteen. These are years of insanity to be endured as best we can. For your protection, as well as mine, I must incarcerate you.' Then he placed me here. He said it would test my soul."

"I was incarcerated to test my soul also," said Samir. "But it happened earlier. And under vastly different circumstances."

When he was twelve his father had come one day and taken him from school without explanation. The following morning they started out before dawn, riding steadily southeast beyond the walnut and olive orchards where the land dissolved into bumpy open space. On the edge of the steppe there was a customs station, but once past that they were in the uncharted desert and Samir could think only of how long it would take them to retrace their steps.

Their shelter for the night was a shallow gully and supper was hard cheese and chewy bread.

The following day, his father said, "Samir, we're going to visit the Lord of the Desert," but they were in total wilderness and the small compound that soon appeared was comprised of about forty simple black goathair tents. The children were ragged, the dogs cadaverously thin, the camels mangy, and the armed men—with braided lovelocks jutting from their *kaffiyahs*—menacing. The women's robust tinted faces were shaded by complicated wound cloth that looked as if it would suffocate them.

"This is the compound of the Lord of the Desert?" said Samir derisively.

"Yes."

"But it's filthy. There's nothing here of value or comfort." He was proud of his assessment.

"Even if it were as you describe, which I assure you it is not," said his father, "you would be amazed at how little man needs to be happy and how carefree one can be without possessions." Samir did not believe he could be happy without possessions, which seemed proof of an insufficient character.

He was certain they had arrived unnoticed, but his father refuted him. "At least ten pair of eyes and that many carbines have been fixed on us for the last ten miles."

"Will they harm us?"

"Never."

"How can you be sure?"

"As strangers, we are inviolable. It's an unwritten law. The blood price of a guest is double that of a man killed in battle."

Were these forbidding-looking men concerned with any law, written or unwritten?

As they spoke, a hook-nosed man approached, preceded by a slave who placed a small rug at Samir's father's feet and then stepped aside as both men stepped on. "God's peace," said the bedouin lord, placing his hand over his heart.

"Returned to you a hundredfold," answered Samir's father.

The shadowy tent they entered was covered with luxurious rugs. The chieftain, leaning against a throne of cushions, motioned Samir and his father to sit at his right.

Slaves and guards with their guns and daggers took appointed places. One man, missing a hand, used the black stump in a violent manner to adjust his rifle. To Samir, everything, including the wretched coffee water boiling noisily on the embers, spelled danger.

The chief slave brought a hunting falcon on a short block, removed its leather hood, and threw a pigeon before it. With a movement too swift to be visible, the falcon pounced on the bird and gashed it to death.

The closeness of the room, the incense, and sweet aroma of coffee made Samir feel ill. He watched, with a sinking heart, as slaves brought in huge platters of food.

His father spoke animatedly to the chief and when he finally rose he ignored Samir, refusing to look at him.

"You are going to sleep now," said his father.

"And in the morning, we'll leave?" asked Samir. His father didn't answer. He placed both hands on Samir's shoulders and kissed his cheeks. "Good night."

When he awoke alone, Samir looked at the tent ropes that held their horses, but only his mare was there and he knew without looking further that his father had left him and returned home. *Why?* His heart throbbed with anger and confusion, and he sat trembling.

The camp came to life with clouds of smoke from several cooking fires and little clumps of children, puppies, and lambs huddled together. Women sat on the dusty ground, shaping rounds for bread. He had the doomed feeling that no one knew him.

He mounted his horse and guided it in the direction from which he had come, riding slowly, remembering the hidden guards with their carbines and half expecting to receive a bullet through the heart. Once free of the camp, he galloped confidently northwestward, elated by the thought of his escape. He would ride home.

After two hours, the landscape was so unchanging he began to doubt his direction and dismounted. He stroked the horse's damp flesh, noting with a slump of will that the animal was tired and thirsty.

There was no sound save his own breathing. A bustard flew down in the distance to peck on the wooly red desert caterpillars, and he was so thrilled to see another living thing that he watched until it flew away.

The sun was not moving in the expected arc to confirm his direction. He was lost and certain to perish from dehydration or starvation, if some wolf didn't attack him first. He covered his face with both hands and cried.

There was a sound. His crying half obscured it, and it was so unexpected that he jumped mightily, which caused laughter. *Laughter!* Stranger than the laughter was the sight of who had laughed. A boy. Smaller than Samir and with no part of him showing—he was swaddled in the most suffocating costume—except a round glowing face and confident eyes. His short legs barely gripped the animal.

"Where did you come from?" asked Samir.

"Same as you. From the camp of the Rualas." His voice was very high. He's just a child, thought Samir.

"You've been following me?" Now we shall both die, he thought ruefully. This baby boy and myself.

"Of course. You're in my keep. I'm responsible for your welfare," he said loftily. "Why are you crying?" he asked with chagrin, as if it were a reflection on him.

Samir ignored him. "Where is my father?"

"Your father left before dawn to return to your home." Samir swallowed hard. Here was proof positive of his sentence. "Why did you ride out this morning?" asked the boy with a quizzical frown.

"I was returning home."

The boy struggled with what he had to say. "You are riding in the wrong direction." There was an embittered silence, during which Samir adjusted the straps of his food pack and refused to look at the boy. "You are meant to remain with us. My name is Marwan and you, I know, are Samir. Come," he coaxed, "let's return." Grudgingly, he followed the little horseman, who took off confidently.

There was still only the beige vastness, but now the sun illuminated one portion of the sky from beneath dark clouds that threatened rain. Imminent moisture imbued the air with incredible freshness and Samir took huge gulps. The knot in his chest loosened. At one point, Marwan stopped and pointed down to some animal tracks, which appeared to have been made by a large paw, and presently they saw the owner, a huge black cat, licking himself in the shade of a stunted bush.

"Panther," said Marwan, his childish face full of concern. He held out a palm to keep Samir from continuing, rummaged in his garments and brought out a Mauser. With little preparation he aimed and shot the animal in the throat. *"Hullus,"* he said softly. It was done.

He brought out a long knife which he plunged into the animal's chest with surprising strength. "Would you care for a paw as a souvenir?" he asked Samir.

Samir shook his head. He was amazed by the marksmanship. The smug indifference he had felt was no longer appropriate. Marwan had saved them from certain danger, for the panther could have easily overtaken them. From time to time he stole a disbelieving look at the courageous little fellow and rode with him obediently to safety.

In the days that followed, Marwan was his tie to life and the only buffer from desperate loneliness and homesickness. He was four months younger and half a head shorter than Samir, with six fine braids that reached his hips. He had to guide his horse with his thighs, for his legs were too short but he was amazingly agile and a fine shot. He ate with his family, but otherwise seemed to live entirely without supervision, even though he was the sheik's son.

Marwan was unbelieving when he learned that Samir had spent the last six years learning to read and write, to handle a knife and fork, and to play soccer. He was shocked that he didn't know how to make a fire, slaughter a lamb, hunt game, fire a rifle, or use the *rhumb,* the knife that was like an eleventh finger to Marwan.

From dawn to dusk, the little wild creature taught Samir the skills of survival. "You must know how to shoot," he would say seriously, as if danger were at hand. They worked with flat pebbles and a crude sling, aiming for the wooden pegs that held down the tent ropes. When they progressed to the Mauser—Marwan's most precious possession—Samir was already a decent marksman. Marwan showed him the likely places for game and how to stalk and kill. There was a precise spot on the neck and a proper angle at which to plunge the knife. One needed strength. One needed a fierce mental attitude. "The idle and cowardly lose their wealth," piped the boy in his high voice, and Samir wanted to smile because the lofty words hardly went with the stature. "The brave and energetic prosper."

"Why do you choose to live like this?" Samir asked. It had occurred to him that Marwan's father was wealthier than many of the villagers, yet this life held relentless hardship. They slept on the stony ground, chilled to the bone by night, and suffocated during the day. Water was precious and rare, for these were the dryest days of the year and it would be two months before the rains began to replenish the water holes. Food was monotonous. The frothy, salty camel milk fresh from the udder was repulsive, but there was nothing else and he reluctantly began to tolerate it. The occasional meat was cooked so rare he couldn't touch it, yet the young men fought for the raw heart of any animal that was slaughtered, guzzling the blood, believing it gave them strength and virility. "Don't you yearn for a different life?"

Marwan looked quizzical. "Where else would I live? I was born here, as was my father and his father before him."

"But it's so difficult. There's a much easier way." As he said this, anxiety rose in him. Would his father come back to claim him? And when?

Marwan laughed. "Easier for whom? We welcome the hardships of the desert. We love them."

"But why?"

He answered with an innocence that made Samir ashamed for questioning. "We love the desert life because it is ours."

But it is not mine, thought Samir with sadness.

One early morning, after the moon had set but while it was still dark, Marwan shook him. "We must ride into the wilderness," he said and handed Samir a waterskin and some dried dates. Each rode a dromedary while two riderless mares cantered at their side, held by lines to the camel girths. A few miles out of the camp, Marwan, rifle in hand, flung himself from the camel onto the back of his mare, unslipped the line, and raced off in a cloud, yelling wildly. Samir made three attempts to do the same but fell twice. He couldn't ride bareback and found himself gripping with his thighs for dear life. He reached Marwan, who was casually pitching stones at a pile of bleached animal bones.

"I thought you were in danger," shouted Samir.

"You were supposed to ride as if danger were near," said Marwan coolly.

"I almost broke my back. Who ever heard of riding a blasted horse without a saddle! And jumping on him at that!"

"It's the way it is done."

"It's a good way to kill yourself."

"It is the way we ride for the *gazu,* the raid," he said stubbornly. "It is the way we move our camps. It is the way we protect our grazing areas and our flocks. In order to survive in the desert you must be ready to move swiftly from the camel to the war mare. It is the only way to be a man. We must try it again until it is as easy as walking."

Samir rubbed his back. He thought, I'm never going to be in a raid. I'm not going to move a camp. One day I will return to my home. Yet Marwan was already retying his line to try again. They worked all day on the maneuver and Samir was enticed by the spectacular look of the transfer when it was accomplished properly. Using the left wrist to launch himself, Marwan lifted both legs up and to the right then swung gracefully between the two animals and landed squarely on the back of the mare, unhitching the line at the same instant he spurred the horse. Then came the wild yell of freedom. The thrill of speed atop the most splendid horses in the world, the "drinkers of the wind."

They rode back to camp at dusk, weary and hungry, but all the way Marwan sang. "We sing on a long ride," he said. "It makes us feel more cheerful. And it comforts the animals."

A few days later, Marwan awoke him again, but this time with more food and water than was necessary for a day. "We're going to hunt the wolves that are attacking our herds," he said. "Will you ride with us?"

"Of course." This was the first real occasion to use all his new experience. They were part of a large party of young men on their horses, several of them armed with a slender lance. All of them chanted or yodeled merrily as they rode. Marwan was fondling the Mauser, which he wore in his belt.

"Will you shoot the wolves with that?" Samir pointed to the gun, all too aware that he lacked such a weapon.

"No." Marwan smiled slowly, as if the question was preposterous. "One doesn't use a Mauser on wolves. We use the *rumh*, the lance. Here," he handed him one of the slender bamboo spears which were about fifteen feet long with a triangular steel head. "You carry it sideways and you spear your wolf like this." He leaned to the side and with a mighty thrust embedded the spear in the ground. "But I carry this gun with me always. There are enemies of my father who would like to have me dead." His face grew somber and, briefly, there was fear in his eyes. "Before I was born, he lost three sons."

Several of the men with rifles had ridden ahead to the foothills to cut off the retreat of the wolves into the mountains. At last, these men flushed out two wolves and Marwan and Samir gave chase. "You must get ahead of him to thrust," warned Marwan. Suddenly, Samir felt the front right leg of his mare give way and he went headlong over its neck, landing face down. Marwan had to return for him, and he felt mortified, "It's not your fault," said Marwan. "Moles have undermined the ground. Look at Jebra!" He pointed gleefully to one of the slaves. "His horse disposed of him as well. He took a toss. And look there, another one." Samir felt a pudgy hand dusting off his chest and his embarrassment diminished.

They mounted again and rode about twelve miles to a spot where, it seemed, everyone was off in a different direction chasing a wolf with a lance. Samir was thrilled when he spotted a wolf and went for his bushy tail. His horse was as eager to follow the bandit and together they galloped madly, finally overtaking the animal. With an exhilarating burst of energy, Samir executed a stab so violent that his spear acted as a vaulting pole and threw him in the air. Fortunately, the ground was soft and he was unharmed. To his amazement, the wolf was impaled through its middle. Marwan was grinning wildly. "You have the brave heart of a lion, Samir," he said soberly. "I wish to make you my blood brother." He caught a few drops of the blood from Samir's scraped arm and rubbed it between his eyes. Then he clasped him in a fierce embrace.

In the weeks that followed, Samir's passion for the bedouin life caught fire and he became an obsessed pupil. He forgot about reading and writing. He had come in October and now it was February. He couldn't recall his father's face, or his mother's, or the half sister's he loved. His old life was no more than a meaningless dream. The desert was everything. His beautiful dark hair fell below his shoulders, and he allowed Marwan's sister to braid it into lovelocks. He grew at least three inches and knew by the coming of spring that he had passed his thirteenth birthday. The muscles in his arms and back and legs were taut, and had he had a mirror he would not have recognized the wiry boy he had become.

He grew to love the feeling of riding fast, his long locks and head cloth fluttering, his camel's hair cloak—a precious gift—flapping, a carbine balanced on his lap. He could vault onto the back of his horse with a single swing over its flank and twist of his body. He learned not to expect his stomach to be full. No future delicacy would ever taste as good as a mix of wild honey, with a dollop of goat butter floating on top, spread on freshly-baked herb cakes. Best of all, he learned to love the sweet stillness of night and the silver sand reflecting that most magical vision—starlight.

Often, he and Marwan sat in on the councils where the tribal heads planned their strategy and settled squabbles and conducted business. The nomadic tribes bartered their camels, wool, cheese, and butter for tent fittings and saddles, cloth and foodstuffs. When the fine days of spring finally arrived, the mood of the camp changed dramatically. There was laughter and singing and playfulness.

"From now on we will be on the move," said Marwan one magnificent morning and, the next day, the women pulled up the tent posts, rolled up the unwieldy cloths and loaded them on the camels, and the entire tribe with their flocks and herds and horses began drifting to their permanent watering holes. The rain had awakened the earth all at once, creating an overnight sensation. A rich green haze tinged with silver was the backdrop for delicately colored blooms. The camels and flocks ate greedily, making up for the barren months.

When they made camp, the young men went about the real business of the bedouin life—the *gazu*, the raid for camels, the true measure of a man's wealth. They were now full of purpose, eager to make the forays in the stealth of night, exhilarated when they unhobbled the camels silently and then drove them home, half triumphant, half fearful. Samir saw a change come over Marwan. He was no longer the gay companion. He was itching to be on a mission. To ride his mare fast and find an enemy, any enemy against which he could prove himself.

"But suppose he kills you?" asked Samir, who could not appreciate the desire for something so dangerous. One moment of glory that could snuff out your life. He was frightened but wouldn't dare admit it.

"They would not shoot me, nor I them," Marwan said. "Raiding is honorable. Only common robbers kill you."

Still, when it came time to join in the raid, Samir rode without euphoria. There were certain things about the bedouin life that would always remain a mystery to him. That certainty of purpose—there was no indecision in their character.

He didn't shrink from danger—that would have been unthinkable—but he didn't take pleasure in riding over rocks and rubble to outwit their pursuers or crawling on his belly to reach the prey unnoticed. At night, when they made camp and lit a fire with *ghada* sticks and that magical stillness settled over the violet-colored dunes, he yearned to go home and resume his life. Homesickness, held at bay for so long, now wrecked his powers of concentration. He dreamed of home and his father. He held imaginary conversations with his sister, speaking aloud when they were riding fast and no one could hear him.

"How long am I meant to stay with you?" he asked Marwan one day.

"You could have left anytime," said Marwan, but he seemed surprised and hurt by the question.

"You mean I could have left right away?" Samir was shocked.

"Yes, if you really had wanted to."

"But you didn't tell me that."

"But you never asked."

It would have been the most natural thing in the world to say right then that he wanted to go home now, but he knew Marwan would take it personally and he couldn't hurt his friend. He would tell him soon, but not right away.

The next night, Marwan awoke him before midnight and coaxed him to ride with him alone on a raid. "We'll bring back a camel each. We can do it."

"Your mother and father would be heartsick to find you gone alone, Marwan," he said, stalling for time. It was a foolhardy idea.

"If you don't wish to go with me, I will go alone," he said.

"Wait and go with the men." Samir tried to sound casual and reasonable, although he didn't feel casual at all.

"If you don't go with me, I will go alone," said Marwan defiantly, and Samir rose wearily from his cozy sheepskin and cursed the lack of supervision for this hotheaded boy.

"I will go," he said, hoping that they would find nothing and return to camp by morning.

They rode for three hours without seeing any campfires or other signs of life. As dawn was approaching Marwan drew rein and came up next to Samir. "Now we must hide or we will be seen and our mission will be obvious."

"Why is it obvious?" said Samir. "We could be just two boys with nothing on our minds."

Marwan was insulted. "That's impossible."

They dismounted and hid out behind a sand dune and had just pulled out a fistful of cheese when Samir saw a shadow cross in front of him. Two savage figures approached and stood just a few feet away.

"How did you arrive?" asked Marwan, stunned.

"We didn't arrive," said one of the men derisively. "We were here all along."

Samir remembered something Marwan had told him. Unmounted wayfarers are usually robbers and murderers.

"What do you want?" asked Marwan and his voice was tremulous.

"You tell us," said one man and laughed.

"Ask God," said the other.

"What tribe do you belong to?" persisted Marwan.

"Beni Nufud," replied the man and this time, both laughed.

This insolent answer seemed to settle it for Marwan. He pulled out his Mauser and shot twice, felling both the startled men. However, one of them, his face full of rage, was able to pull out his own pistol and shoot back. Marwan cried out defiantly, *"La! No!"* and his boyish hand shot out to ward off the bullet that exploded in his face. Before the robber could shoot again, Samir grabbed the Mauser and emptied it in both the men. His heart seemed to be racing up and down his body and found no spot that could accommodate its violent beating.

He felt uncontrollable anger toward Marwan. "You little fool. You little fool. Why did you have to come here? Why? Why?" He shook his blood brother, willing him to respond, but Marwan just lay still his life fluids soaking into his clothes. He rode back to camp with Marwan propped in front of him, cradled in his arms. It was slow going, but he couldn't have left him there alone.

Throughout the ride, he crooned the cheerful songs Marwan had taught him. He must hear me, he thought. He must. He didn't have a clear memory of all that happened next. Only that they wanted to take the body from him and he resisted with all his might. He felt horribly responsible for the tragedy. He should have asked to go home and this would have distracted Marwan from his quest for danger. He shouldn't have given in to Marwan and ridden with him. He should have persuaded him to stay at the camp. He could have saved his friend. How much his heart ached! Over and over, he heard that startled cry, *"La! No!,"* and saw that small palm thrust out, pushing death away.

Within days he was returned to his family. He asked for Marwan's curved knife, his *rhumb,* which he kept close to him day and night. It had the smell of Marwan and the sweat of his hand on the handle. It was the last thing Samir touched at night and the first in the morning. Even in later years, when his months with the bedouin were nothing more than a distant memory, touching the knife gave him comfort.

20

I'm not trying to get him to prefer me at all.

A hulking Botsford guard was running in front of him and Samir stopped to dribble, blocking the tackle with his shoulder. Each time he moved the ball, he looked around quickly but there was no free man, so he speeded up and pretended to charge for the goal. The guard grinned, baring oversized teeth.

"You large boys should be playing rugby," hissed Samir.

The guard continued to smile but his eyes remained on the ball. Samir saw Phillips fifteen feet to his left and did a little quick step, passing with the outside of his foot, then ran upfield. As the ball was returned to him he grinned at his bewildered guard. In that fatal second, a green Botsford shoulder sped by, a foot hooked the rolling ball, steered it away, and kicked it high in the air. It rose sharply, sailed overhead, and landed at the feet of the opposing inside center, who scored.

"Pride goeth before a fall," croaked Phillips at his side.

Samir shrugged. "It's what I deserved. But it's not over yet." He looked up at the clump of FGS girls who always attended home games and served tea afterward to the visiting team. In the second tier, next to Margaret—they were always together—sat his cousin Nadia with an expression . . . was it an ill-concealed smile?

He had the ball and kicked it far, running after it to the action. Stefano, the right wing, killed it with his chest, dribbled toward the Botsford goal and lost it. Samir caught up with the advancing attacker and lunged at him, forcing a change of direction, but the boy tripped the ball up his leg and batted it to a waiting teammate with an inhuman rotation of his knee.

As the receiver prepared to kick, Samir was so close that the ball smashed into his knees and ricocheted to the middle of the field. It was about to bounce again but he dove horizontally, raising his head just enough to give the ball a solid send-off. Stefano took off and scored as Samir hit the ground in a painful slide, scraping the side of his face. From the ground he looked up at the second tier. She had not seen any part of it! She was glancing at a book! Margaret pointed to her cheek to indicate his wound, frowned with concern, and then blew him a kiss. Just then the horn signaled the end of the second quarter, and the teams retired for half time.

The FBS boys had two moral obligations during their stay at the school: the first was to replant the olive trees that the Turks had burned to fuel the railroad. The second duty, optional and more personal, was to purchase, with money earned at menial tasks, the sturdy chairs made by the orphans at Schnellers for the dining room. During sporting events, Samir, wearing a wooden tray suspended from his neck, sold ice cream wafers to the crowd of locals who attended the games.

Margaret waved. "We'll take two please," she called across the aisle. He finished a transaction and climbed to the row below the girls. "That's a nasty scrape," she said, narrowing her eyes, "but for a splendid cause. You're marvelous with the ball," she gushed, then reached down to him. "Here, let me blot your wound. My handkerchief's clean." She dabbed at his cheek, wetting the cloth with her tongue. "Don't mind me, they say saliva has healing powers. Well, it must be true. Animals use it, don't they? They're always licking, licking, licking over any little wound."

He was enjoying himself and Nadia was having a fit. She was bouncing her fist against her chin in agitation and looking away as if the scene were too much to believe. Samir grinned and gave Margaret a wafer. Her hand lingered on his cheek and then on his fingers as she took her ice cream.

"Here's a pound," she said. "Keep the change."

"That's much too much." Nadia spoke for the first time. "The wafers are only thirty piasters."

"It's to buy the orphans' chairs, isn't it?" Margaret waved away the change. "Perhaps this will make his quota." She pronounced it "qwoatah," which made it sound silly.

"It's too much money," Nadia said accusingly, as if he were taking advantage of Margaret.

"Well, it's my money now, isn't it?" said Margaret.

Nadia shrugged.

"I'm doing the tea later," Margaret whispered, dabbing once more at Samir's cheek. "I baked the scones myself. Stop by."

"I will."

"That was a daring save. You know what they say about soccer players, don't you?"

"No. What do they say?"

"My father says it's a sport that requires neither height nor heft so much as valor, perseverence, and daring. Nadia, wasn't it daring, diving into the air like that?"

"I missed it," she said. Her jaw was set and two red spots showed on her cheeks. Samir looked at the book on her lap.

Margaret looked at one and then the other. "He wanted you especially to see it," she chided Nadia, whose mouth became a thin red line of displeasure.

Samir stepped down to another tier. "I thought the girls were here to lift our morales," he said lightly.

"No," insisted Margaret, realizing she had hit on something interesting, "you were watching for Nadia's reaction. You looked at her twice from the field."

"Perhaps he was looking at you," Nadia shot back.

"That would be lovely, but it's *you* who have hurt his feelings."

Samir smiled enigmatically, looking above their heads at the crowd. A slight gust ruffled his hair and he sighed and lifted his chin.

Her peevishness is no longer charming, he thought, stepping back onto the field. She's grown up. Her mouth has grown up, too. If she would relax and forget herself, her lips would . . . part open from the—*sheer bursting weight*. He felt warm. It took no effort at all to imagine the healthy pink glow of her face over the rest of her body. Over her long, strong legs. Her parted lips, glossy with desire, insinuated themselves into his brain. He bit down hard on his own lower lip and looked for the ball.

It was wrong to think of her in that way. It was disloyal. It was second-rate. They lost the game.

"You can go to hell," Nadia said and then slumped down in defeat. "How could you?"

"What are you so huffed up about? If you have no interest in him, what's the difference?"

"That's not the point."

"Yes, it is. Perhaps you're afraid of rejection. If you had some idea of winning him, you'd show your true feelings."

"Oh, Margaret, just stop it."

"As it turns out, your way is a good strategy. The idea is dawning over his brain like the sun rising over the Mount of Olives."

"What idea?"

"The idea of you." Foolishly, she allowed that thought to root in her imagination. The look on her face was enough to encourage Margaret. "The burning issue is, why you? Why should this perfectly splendid boy/ man be smitten by you? You're not a classical beauty."

The words stung. Once. Twice. Margaret had hit on the exact issue that did burn in her heart. Samir did, at times, act friendly. Was it just that she was familiar to him? And, if, by chance, he was deluded into liking her, what would he do when the delusion was over? "Margaret, shut up."

"I won't and you should listen because I *know* what he sees in you."

She was hooked again. "Oh?"

"You have the type of body . . . how can I put it? Long legs never hurt. And at the thighs, where everyone else drifts into wayward masses, you're hard as a boy with a high little ass. Then there's your mouth. It's full and moist. It dips and curves. Coming at the end of your rather solemn face, it's a shocker. There's this irresistible juxtaposition of seriousness hiding a wanton nature. You're a mystery."

"Margaret, you're daft. You really think Samir has figured all this out?"

"Not consciously. It just works on him. Face it, luv, you've got *it.*"

"What is *it?*"

"You know . . . like Clara Bow. It's a quality. You can't quite define *it.*"

It was so tempting to believe it all. And so utterly stupid.

21

Ah, love . . .

"Suzanne Lenglen, the glamorous French tennis star, displayed little brown moons under her eyes, suggesting that she came to the court without sleep after a night of carnival." Margaret drew in her breath with appreciation. She was reading from an outdated issue of *Time* sent by the Society of Friends in Indiana. "Do you think a night of carnival means petting, kissing, or more?"

"Petting and kissing. Not more," answered Nadia, putting out her palm to stop an imaginary love-crazed suitor.

"Give me a little kiss, will ya, huh?" Margaret sang and vamped. That song, together with "There's Yes, Yes In Your Eyes," were *the* popular imports played over the shortwave radio.

"What are you gonna miss, will ya, huh?" answered Nadia. They fell on each other, laughing helplessly.

From old issues of *Colliers* and *Life,* their bibles of sophistication, the girls compiled a little glossary of slang: "the cat's pyjamas" denoted ultimate desirability; "nuts" expressed disgust; "lousy" was something contemptible; "to carry a torch" was to suffer from unrequited love; "for crying out loud" was the ultimate expression of exasperation (Margaret's favorite); and "crush," a word Nadia finally put to use in May, on one of those sweet spring nights when the spirit wells up with the pure joy of the physical universe.

She stood alone in the foyer, half hidden by an urn filled with bushy, flowering red jasmine, gathered in armfuls that morning to delight the parents who had come for the recitation. She sighed, filled with inexplicable longing, and fingered the ragged paper in her hand on which was scribbled Matthew Arnold's "Dover Beach."

The proper recitation of poetry was important at FGS and, once a month, the parents came to listen.

"For crying out loud," said Margaret, "everyone goes fast asleep at these things. The Muslims think we're talking gibberish. They get nothing out of it and English poets say very little about the afterlife, which is more important to them than this vale of tears."

On an evening just like this, after Nadia had recited all seven stanzas of Tennyson's "Sir Galahad," her grandmother kissed her cheek and muttered into the air, "Reap the wind and harvest nothing." Her way of saying Nadia spent time on activities with no lasting benefits.

Miss Smythe said if they hoped to sit for the matriculation exams they must be well read. They must know the great literature of the world. "The great literature of the world," shrieked Margaret, ". . . is either crying over spilled milk or making too much of everything. Life is very simple, really."

"You can make fun of it because you're English," offered Nadia wisely. "For us, it's something to admire."

From her safe nook in the foyer, she could hear that the boys were finishing their recitation, which meant the girls would begin. She would have to take her place in the auditorium. " 'Ah, love . . . Ah, love . . . Ah, love . . .' "—she spoke with exaggerated emotion—" 'let us be true/ To one another! for the world, which seems/To lie before us like a land of dreams, /So . . . various . . . so? . . . beautiful! . . . so new,/Hath really . . . hath really' . . . ooh, what does it bloody have?"

"It 'hath really neither joy, nor love, nor light,' " came an unequivocal deeply masculine answer from the other side of the foliage.

She sucked in her breath, bit down on her offending lips and waited. To be heard using that word! She knew that "bloody," while it sounded harmless to her, was quite coarse to the English. An eternity was perceived, but only several seconds passed during which her mouth felt dry as a gully. " 'Nor certitude, nor peace, nor help for pain . . .' " The voice now had an urgency. He was trying to get her to continue, to answer with the next poetic line.

She unclenched her jaw and let go of her lips. " 'And we are here as on a darkling plain,' " she said timidly without any of the expression the line demanded. " 'Swept with confused alarms of struggle and flight,/ Where . . .' " What came next?

" 'Where ignorant armies clash by night,' " came the resonant answer.

It was no voice she recognized. Was it a parent? Perhaps an intruder! She began to tiptoe away, hoping to reach the door of the auditorium—from which she should not have strayed—without facing . . . *him*. She felt an incriminating awkwardness in every step.

"You stumbled on '. . . so various, so beautiful, so new,' etc. That's where your problem begins." The voice reached out and stopped her in midflight.

"Yes," she acknowledged, still facing away. That's where your problem begins.

"Well? Don't you need to learn it? Come here. It isn't as if you've got a week."

"No." She turned to face a tall, slim man elegantly dressed in a flat woven tweed cut in a smart, shaped style. His brown hair was parted to the side neatly and brushed back, exposing his face in a daring way—like the men who posed in the motor car advertisements whose hair (and their caution, she surmised) was driven back by the wind, making them appear headed toward inevitable danger. It was a confident face, with a strong but appropriate Roman nose, pale eyes, and a wide mouth that was twitching, trying to contain a smile. She tipped her face up to him, crimson and unsure, hoping for the best. "I beg your pardon . . ."

"Not at all. I beg yours. You came to practice your lines in privacy and now I've thrown you off. It's hardly fair." Again, his mouth curved upward. What was the appropriate response? Her fervent wish was not to appear stupid. Right then, his lighthearted expression changed to one of concern. "Why so worried?" he asked. "Haven't got the lines tucked in memory?" He gave her a reassuring smile—a smile that seemed too extravagant for a girl her age. "You're in luck. I happen to be an expert on 'Dover Beach.' Come . . . give it another try . . . 'Hath really neither joy, nor love, nor light.' Come on, repeat after me . . ." He crooked his finger as if to charm the words out of her.

" 'Hath really neither joy, nor love, nor light,' " she repeated, unconvincingly. She looked around the hall, at her hands, at the patterned floor, and then again at his face.

"Think of it as *J L L* . . . or to make it more personal, Jack Loves Linda . . . joy, love, light . . . 'neither joy, nor love, nor light.' Followed by that tragic tale, Charles Pines for Penelope. *C P P* . . . 'Nor certitude, nor peace, nor help for pain.' " His face was serious as a priest.

" 'Nor certitude, nor peace, nor help for pain,' " she repeated and then continued. " 'And we are here as on a darkling plain/Swept with confused alarms of struggle and flight,/Where ignorant armies clash by night.' " She looked away to the side to briefly escape his gaze, for he was hanging on her words, mouthing them with her as if she were a toddler. "I've got to go now." Yet she stood still waiting for his dismissal.

"There you are," he said with kindness. "It was just a stumble. You'll do fine."

She ran down the corridor but then slowed down, aware of the clatter her shoes made. At the door of the hall, she looked back. He stood perfectly still, framed by the burning red bush, his tweed-clad arms comfortably across his chest, the corner of his lip hiked up in a smile. His eyes held fast on her retreating form. She smiled, both thrilled and embarrassed that he was still looking at her.

Samir stepped into the foyer, expecting to find it empty. He had been reprieved from listening to the girls' poetry in order to arrange the seating in the parlor for the tea social that was to follow. The well-dressed man at the end of the hall caught his attention first. Then, in a moment of devilish serendipity, he saw his cousin Nadia turn to bestow on this stranger an irresistible smile of such tenderness that it jarred Samir. Her face in that subdued light seemed as fragile as the mist that rolled in before dawn and hovered magically before it delivered itself to the thirsty foliage. The irony of the moment wasn't lost on Samir. Had Sammy George not omitted four lines from "Annabel Lee," crassly curtailing Poe's lament for his beloved, the scene would have gone unwitnessed. He had stepped into the hall seconds too early, and now that exchange of private smiles took hold of his imagination and made him restless. He had the uneasy feeling that he had apprehended something that was as yet unknown to the participants.

Maha had just begun "Geist's Grave," when Nadia took her seat. " 'That liquid melancholy eye' "—Maha was being embarrassingly melodramatic in her recitation, whining out every word as if she were auditioning to be in films—" 'From whose pathetic, soul-fed springs seemed surging the Virgilian cry. The sense of tears in mortal things . . .' " At this point, Maha, moved by her own words, began to weep. There was a great deal of embarrassed shifting by the audience and Maha's mother cried out emotionally, "It's all right, *habibty,* " a gaffe that sealed Maha's social fate at FGS.

"What's she crying about?" hissed Margaret to Nadia. "Geist was Arnold's dog. That bloody poem is about his dog. That girl's balmy, I swear. She's an idiot. Now, look," she rolled her eyes heavenward in disgust. "Miss Smythe has told her to sit down. She doesn't have to finish, so I guess, I'm up . . ." Margaret passed through the row of knees with resignation and then proceeded to give a flawless rendition of Wordsworth's "The Solitary Reaper," sweetly dedicating it "to the hardy women of Palestine," which forever endeared her to half the audience. Nadia was so surprised she forgot to go next. "Your turn, Madam," said Margaret archly.

She stood and faced the row of parents and noticed her father, dressed in an unfamiliar European suit, tugging and picking at his jacket as if trying to make it as long and comfortable as his familiar aba. Why couldn't he stop arranging it and be still? His neighbors were staring at him. She cleared her throat meaningfully and began her recitation. Midway through, when she had gained some confidence, she dared to search the rows for the man in the foyer and found him standing at the back. Their eyes met. He smiled encouragement, as if she were his special project, and made a little flourish with his hand in salute. Her heart reacted. A handsome man's attention was something so new and unexpected. She returned to her seat feeling elated.

Of all the dainty tasks learned at Friends', pouring tea from the ornate silver urn engaged her imagination most. She had watched Miss Smythe's delicate New England wrist dip and bend, pouring a perfect arc of dark liquid without concern, a confident smile on her lips as if she were eager to give her guests not only tea but all the goodness that was inside her. "Eating should entail spiritual sustenance, too," Miss Smythe told them. "Food should be given gracefully, generously. But certainly our Arabic girls don't have to be told such things. They have made a religion of hospitality." Tonight, Nadia was one of the girls chosen to pour and she sat in the seat of command, surrounded by nested cups, little pincers for sugar and lemon at her fingertips. A deputy paired the cups with saucers and handed them up. She poured and held the cup a moment in the air while inquiring smilingly, "Lemon? Sugar?" This was the ceremony that satisfied her soul.

"Got scullery duty, eh?" Margaret sneered, coming up from behind and digging her fingers into Nadia's shoulders.

"Three sugars, please," demanded a voice from above. The voice was familiar. Before she looked up, she knew it was her poetry coach.

"Two will do." Margaret grabbed the cup from Nadia, plopped two cubes into it with her fingers and handed it to the man. "Too much sugar rots the teeth," she said sternly.

Nadia's first thought was, Oh, Margaret will interest him now with her brashness.

The man smiled indulgently. "Margaret," he said, "you were superb tonight." He looked down at Nadia. "And you pulled yourself out quite handily, too, although I would guess your interests lie in something other than poetry." His candor was a surprise but not deflating. He made her sound vastly more interesting than a scholar of poetry.

Margaret went to stand between them. "Nadia," she said with mischief in her eyes, "this cheeky man is Victor Madden, my father."

"How do you do." He had extended his hand and she had no choice but to let him have hers, but the news fell like a bomb. The room blurred. *Margaret's father!* It was one of those awful awkward moments when one's expectations are so wrongly placed that the spirit falls with a thud. He had been her special encounter, an event to play with in her mind. And now . . . *Margaret's father!* She had wanted him known only to her and now . . . the whole thing was spoiled. As if it were Margaret's fault she had a father, Nadia had an instant desire to put great distance between herself and her friend. The Black Sea would have been about right.

The tea drinkers had dwindled and she excused herself awkwardly, unwilling to look at his face, and went in search of Nadeem, who was standing by himself. His hands, crossed in front of him, turned a black fedora around and around. He walked to a chair but, before sitting, pulled out his trousers like a man accustomed to dealing with the loose skirt of the aba. Nadia felt a stab of tenderness and loyalty. He had worn the suit only to please her.

He rose to greet her and she kissed him. Usually she chastised him for making no attempt to mingle with the other parents, but tonight she said nothing. She noticed with some dismay that she had grown slightly taller than he.

"*Baba,* it's all right if you wear your regular clothes. You looked so uncomfortable in that suit." She tried not to sound critical, unwilling to make him the victim of her sudden black mood.

"Was it so obvious? I tried to sit still but it's extremely itchy."

"No, it wasn't obvious," she lied. "It's just a surprise to see you in a suit. You didn't have to come tonight. You'd have been asleep by now." The programs began at a time when her parents were usually ready for bed. "How's Mama?"

"Mama's fine. She wanted to sleep early tonight." He looked down at his feet with interest, not used to seeing them when wearing his usual long robe. He looked up again and his face was serious. "Mama's not fine. Khalil and Hanna are finally going to America. She cries about it every night."

"They always say they're going, but then they don't. What would they do in America, anyway?"

"Butross's son is doing well there. He travels door-to-door in the better neighborhoods, taking orders for linens. It's quite a business. Now he's going to open a shop in a town where the rich Americans go to escape the cold winters. The town is called Palm Beach and it's directly on the Atlantic Ocean. The sea is right there, so they say. It comes right to the edge of the yards of these large houses. Can you imagine? That vast ocean coming right up to your house?"

"Khalil might go," she said thoughtfully, "but Hanna would never leave you."

"I want him to leave us," said Nadeem. "It's no good for him to stay behind."

"*Baba!* What a thing to say."

"I say it because I love him. It's strange, Hanna seems independent because he doesn't say much, but he is the most attached to us. He needs to make his way in the world. Not to stay with us. Anyway,"—he sighed and smiled lovingly at his daughter—"we still have you. After June, you'll be home for the summer."

"*Baba,* I want to sit for the Matriculation Exams. Perhaps I'll stay here and be tutored so I can take them next year." She knew he wasn't expecting to hear this, but it was a relief to say it.

"Why, *habibty?* You'll be graduating next year. You'll be finished with school."

"Miss Smythe says I could pass them and she wants to enter my name. She says it would give me a feeling of accomplishment for my hard work, even if I don't go to the university."

"The university." He echoed her last word with a melancholy look in his eyes.

"If I passed, I could be accepted to the sophomore class at the University of Beirut. Even though I don't attend, I'll know that I could have gone. Samir Saleh is sitting for the London Exams. He's going to a university abroad. He had to stay here an extra year to be ready but that's because the boys' school had to start anew after the war and didn't have a full staff."

"Is that so? Samir is going abroad?" He raised his eyebrows with mild surprise, but his heart wasn't in the subject. "I think your mother will be happy to have you home again. With the boys gone, the house will seem too quiet."

Nadia remained silent. Her mother was eager to have her home, and she was eager to stay at school. She looked longingly around the room. Miss Smythe poised and confident, floated from group to group. Miss Bailey, comfortably stout, had hold of the girls who had no visitors. The swarthy Muslim parents, straining toward their full height, curious, inspected the English. Two Italians stood in the center, proud and charming. She loved this ordered world—every hour had its own rhythm. She felt at home here because she was accepted.

"What's wrong? You have such a troubled look on your face. What is it?"

"Nothing, *Baba.* How's Gala? Is she getting exercise? I'll be able to ride her myself soon."

"Yes," said her father but he seemed to have shrunk into his jacket. She realized that it sounded as if all she had to look forward to was riding Gala. Then she remembered who had given her Gala and her heart ached for her father. There were times when she felt older and wiser than her parents. As if she knew things they were too innocent to understand. It was such a lonely feeling. "Come," she said putting her arm protectively through his, "I want you to meet Margaret before you leave. She introduced me to her father, and now I want to introduce her to mine."

A quick survey of the room showed no trace of Margaret and her father. She was about to look for them in the hall when Samir approached.

"Ami." He bowed his head slightly toward Nadeem. "Hello, Nadia."

Why is his tone peeved, she wondered idly but was more occupied with finding her friend. "Have you seen Margaret?"

"Yes. She and a man just pulled out now in a loud car."

"That was her father," said Nadia, and her voice showed her disappointment. "I didn't realize she was leaving with him."

"Well, don't look so dejected," he said, and again there was that scornful reproach. "She'll be back."

After a moment of awkward silence, Nadeem spoke. "You're going to the University of London?"

"If I pass the exams."

"To study what?" persisted Nadeem.

"Economics."

"Economics? But you have your father's business. Why not learn about your father's business interests?"

"But I will, *ami.* That's part of economics."

Samir was being overly gracious to her father and . . . *cranky* to her. There was another side to Samir Saleh. He was capable of a certain detachment that could be cowering if it was directed at you. He looked through people more than at them and could wither the fainthearted with a cool disinterest that chilled the heart. She felt it now.

"You have to go to London to learn about your father's business?" asked Nadeem, with a rueful laugh. "Why not just ask your father?"

"It's my father's wish that I go," said Samir.

"I see. It's your father's wish to send you away and it's my wish to bring Nadia home, but she wants to try the exams, too. She doesn't want to come home."

At that moment, her spirits began to collapse. She kissed her father affectionately and embraced him. *"Baba,* it's late. Thank you for coming, but I know you would have been in bed a long time ago. Say hello to the boys. I love you. I love Mama."

"All right, *habibty."* He was about to put the fedora on his head, but reconsidered and kept it in his hand. He walked to the door, turned back again to have one last sight of his daughter, and walked out into the darkness.

"You're going to take the Matriculation Exams?" Samir asked and she couldn't decide whether he was genuinely surprised or making fun of her.

"And what's wrong with that?"

"Nothing. If it will be for some use."

"You feel I won't put it to use?"

"Women in our clan have never worked. And none that I know of has ever attended a university." He stated it as simple fact, yet she felt that she had disappointed him in some way.

"And does that mean none ever should? Perhaps I'll be the first."

"Perhaps," he said softly.

Still feeling wounded from her gaffe over Victor Madden, she let down her guard. "I envy your going to London. Going home is . . . well, it's a letdown. I always seem to disappoint my parents' expectations."

"You don't want to settle down?" he asked gently.

"Not right away. There's so much more I want to experience. Your sister's not married." She challenged him with her eyes. "Julia strikes me as having good sense."

"Sorry to disappoint you, but I'm quite sure Julia will be engaged this summer."

"Oh." She was at a loss.

"You can marry and still have good sense," he said with a little mirthless laugh. "Do your parents agree with your . . . modern view? They don't mind if you don't marry?"

"It hasn't come up."

"I see."

"And yourself?" She couldn't control the sarcasm. "What fortunate girl will have the honor of marrying Samir? Every mother in Tamleh has spent her house money on lamps for El Khalil, for the miracle of having you choose their daughter." She was referring to the old superstitious custom of leaving candles and food at the tomb of the prophet in the hopes of gaining impossible favors.

"Really?" He smiled and traced a pattern on the floor with his shoe. "And is your mother lighting a candle as well?"

"Who knows? Perhaps she is." She couldn't help smiling. "Wouldn't that be ironic?"

"Yes," he said. "That's precisely what it would be."

Nadia stayed at school an extra six weeks studying *Richard III* and *Othello*, two of the works required for the Matriculation Exam. The days had been sunny and the nights cool—the type of weather that enticed an increasing trickle of summer vacationers to the new Grand Hotel. Margaret had left the country to answer a summons from her mother, so it was a surprise when Victor Madden came roaring up the Nablus road in his Singer Coupe.

She was outdoors, reading. As he parked and she realized who it was, she stood, hoping he would turn and notice her. "Ah," he said with pleasure, "just the person I'm looking for." He walked toward her. "Am I interrupting your studies?" Even as he said it, his eyes crinkled mischievously.

"Oh, no." It was obvious he *had* interrupted. She smiled and reconsidered. "It's fine. I can do this another time." No one else wears such splendid suits was her first thought. The straw-colored linen clung to his broad shoulders and chest and molded softly at his waist.

"Good. I want to talk with you." He looked around, then motioned with his arm toward the grounds beyond the building. "Can we stroll down this way a bit? They won't mind, will they?"

"No. Of course not." She was intoxicated by the sound of her own voice, which had acquired a slightly British tinge. He stopped to appreciate the view and the spectacular variety of flowers and she waited. Right about then she felt she should ask about Margaret, but bringing up his daughter didn't fit in with her feelings.

Within seconds he said, "Margaret's spending all of July and August with her mother in Italy. My ex-wife's come into a bit of money and they've rented a villa on the Ligurian Sea." He said this proudly, as if his ex-wife had shown astuteness rather than just had good luck.

"Oh."

"I doubt we'll see Margaret here again. If she tires of her mother, she'll go to her grandmother in London."

"Does that make you sad?"

"Yes, it does. Margaret's wonderful company but that's the least of it. I love her."

Inexplicably, this admission shocked her. That this exciting man should admit to loving her friend was bizarre. It was as if he had claimed to love her, too. A rivulet of perspiration traveled down her long neck and over her breasts. She felt its stinging sensation as it crossed the soft, tender center.

"You're perspiring," he said solicitously and handed her a handkerchief.

Down, down, they walked into a valley of wild daisies as high as their arms. A heat wave rose and he took off his jacket, handed it to her to hold and rolled up his sleeves. The sight of his bare arms gave her a jolt.

"Margaret tells me you live here in the village. I didn't believe her," he said morosely, as if he would have liked to apologize to Margaret right then.

She bristled, attuned to the rancor over the British presence and their presumptions. "I've lived here all my life except during the war. Why is it so hard to believe? It's not Borneo."

"It's a splendid home. But your coloring doesn't seem typical."

"My grandmother is fairer than I. She had bright red hair as a child. My mother's eyes are blue. Half my cousins are too fair to take the sun at all." She stopped talking. He was focusing those gray eyes on her. I'm not that interesting, she thought. Any moment, he will discover it and try to leave. "Down in Jericho," her voice trembled, "the population is darker, but still varied." She shrank inside.

"You've put me in my place," he said. "From now on, I'll mind what I say."

From now on?

"Do you speak Arabic at home?" he asked.

"Mostly. Some English, too, now."

"Can you read and write in Arabic?"

"Of course."

"My questions aren't meant to be boorish. I'm trying to find out more about you."

"I've told you everything," she said. "I speak Arabic, and I can read and write it, too."

He smiled. "That's simply perfect. I was hoping that was the case."

"Why?"

"I need someone just like you to help on a special project."

"A special project?"

"It's a matter of public relations. I need someone who understands the nationals and also understands me. Someone pretty who will smooth the path." He lingered on the last word, as if he were including her in a conspiracy. "Would you be free to begin work in late summer?"

Up to that moment, she hadn't understood what he was leading up to. Someone pretty. "You want me to help you with your project?"

"Yes. For a salary, of course. Does such a job appeal to you?"

"Oh, yes, but I'd have to ask my parents."

"Talk it over with them and let me know." At this point, the field of flowers became dense, making it difficult to walk. They took exaggerated high steps and made sweeping motions with their arms. They looked at each other and laughed, tried to walk forward again, and continued to laugh before finally turning back.

22

I wish you could just relax and be yourself.

She had been home eight days, all spent thinking of Victor Madden. She might have daydreamed that he kissed her, but she wasn't yet crazed enough. She daydreamed long conversations wherein she was brilliant and he was amazed.

When her mother or father stared at her, she'd wince and harden her heart. They wanted her safely at home, then safely married, then safely put away in a small house in the village, without any more queer ideas. She was saving the question of Victor's job offer for a moment when she could barter something to make them happy.

Her mother was making cookies to take to Julia Saleh's bethrothal party. "You've given the linens," Nadia argued. "That's what they're expecting from us. Why do we have to bring food, too? It's excessive."

Miriam took a dollop of dough and worked it deftly in her hand, making a hollow to receive the almond paste, and then pinched it closed. "We've always taken food."

"That was in the old days. Sheik Saleh doesn't need our cookies, Mama. Couldn't we arrive somewhere without all this . . . baggage?"

Khalil, who had heard the last of the conversation, set his jaw. "You won't have to carry anything, madam," he said sarcastically.

Miriam remained unperturbed. She was used to Nadia and also engrossed in her own thoughts. "Have you seen Samir lately?" she asked. "He's going to London next month."

"I saw him at services every morning. And the boys always came over on Friday nights for the British films."

"When you were both small, you used to ride on his back. He was very patient with you. Now, he might be embarrassed to be reminded."

"So am I." She took one of the baked cookies and bit it. "He's determined to be different from everyone. Many times, he's the only one wearing the agal and kaffiyeh. However," she sighed, resigning herself to Samir's better qualities, "he's a good soccer player."

"His father expects it. And,"—Miriam looked meaningfully at Nadia, working the dough more strenuously—"I tend to agree with him. It's important not to lose everything to the British."

"Oh, Mama, we're not going to lose everything. What is there to lose, anyway? Wearing this dress instead of a long one doesn't make me English. You should see the really British girls. They care nothing about their family at all. My friend, Margaret—her parents are divorced—she calls her father by his given name. 'Victor,' she says when he shows up unexpectedly, 'you shouldn't be here.' They speak to each other as if they were equals." She sighed. "If you must take the cookies, that's plenty. You can't expect to feed everyone."

"All your cousins will be there," said Miriam. She wanted some promise of cooperation.

"I'm sure." Nadia knew precisely what that meant. A man you could marry will be there. Be pleasant. At least be as pleasant as the other girls.

"I wish you would just relax and be yourself."

"Mama, if I'm myself, it'll be a total loss. You want me to bat my eyes at the boys. And giggle." This was a good time to bring up Victor's offer.

"I want you to be pleasant," said Miriam earnestly and put down the piece of dough.

"Don't worry about my future. I've already had a good job offer."

"Stop talking nonsense."

"It isn't nonsense. I've been offered a lovely job with the Office of National Relations." It was best not to mention that her superior would be the man she had just described as so liberal. "I have this fancy education, let me earn some money with it."

"Your father will have to decide."

"Perhaps I'd cooperate more if he gave in."

Miriam was interested. She knew Nadeem would say yes. "We'd have to make sure it's proper."

"What could be more proper than the government?"

"Nadia, it wouldn't hurt to be sociable. There might be someone there."

"We're assuming the poor man would also like her," said Khalil, "and that would be a miracle."

"Hush," said Miriam.

"Nadia wants to marry her horse," he said, not intending to be humorous. "She wants to marry her horse and also go to work to support him. Face it, Mama, you have an odd one."

"I've always been the odd one," said Nadia, "so why can't I reap the benefits of it and have some freedom?"

Miriam was still on her own subject. She set her shoulders. "These meetings are important. They give young people a chance to see each other and talk. It's a way of doing things and you shouldn't be so ready to dismiss it. Life isn't so black and white as you like to paint it."

Unexpectedly, Nadia had a twinge and felt sorry for her mother. They had been so close once. She remembered being tucked in a sling and bouncing against her mother as she walked. She wanted to say, Mama, I'll act just as you want me to. I don't want to make you struggle over me. I want to make you happy. Which young man shall I attract? Just point him out. I'll charm King Abdullah himself just to make you smile. Aloud, she said, "You and Aunt Zareefa probably have someone already picked out. Tell me now and save yourselves a lot of trouble."

Julia Saleh, gracious and soft spoken, wealthy and educated, had the sort of plain looks that women could appreciate—they knew the value of the tight-pored unblemished skin and healthy pink coloring—but men found unenticing. At twenty-two, ordinarily a year of despair for an un-married girl, a wealthy entrepreneur from Jerusalem—a man any girl would have welcomed as a husband—had discovered Julia's goodness and asked to marry her. Her father was overjoyed and her betrothal party was the most elaborate social gathering ever attempted in the village.

The event was held at the sheik's summer estate, ten miles north of the village, a beautiful setting amid healthy, productive vineyards and orchards. Thos. Cook & Son was hired to set up three tents. The property had newly erected stables and an elaborate watering system, but the only shelter was a stone cottage, a nostalgic relic of the old days, which Sheik Saleh refused to update.

He'd added a tennis court as a gift for Samir's fifteenth birthday. Se-cretly, he considered tennis the most demented pastime, yet it gave him satisfaction to provide such a gratuitous indulgence. It had cost three hundred pounds sterling, but it was worth it for the look of surprise it received from every European guest.

All the food for the party had been brought in a large truck and laid out in the middle tent. Five whole lambs, stuffed with pine nuts and peppered rice, were being roasted on spits. Tomatoes, cucumbers, and radishes were arranged alongside tubs of roasted mashed eggplant smothered in simsim paste and garlic. Baby summer squash had its pale innards scooped out and replaced with peppered rice studded with spiced bits of lamb. Tender-ized grape leaves rolled like piquant little sausages around a vegetable mixture had been steamed on a bed of meat bones, allowed to cool, and doused with lemon juice. Pickled turnips and beets, glistening green and black olives, plump rounds of cheese and stacks of bread baked throughout the day whetted appetites for the succulent lamb to come.

The entire Mishwe clan made the trip together in one tightly packed jitney with Umm Jameel denouncing the vehicle at every sharp turn. Nadia bolted from the bus, relieved to be away from Miriam's admonitions to "be sociable," and went in search of the bride-to-be.

Julia was four years older than Nadia, but they had always been drawn to each other. "Lovely." Nadia spread out the blue georgette skirt. "You look calm and relaxed. I'd be so nervous."

"I was nervous yesterday." Julia placed her hand on her cousin's bare arm and leaned over to kiss her cheek. "Thank you for the linens. They arrived yesterday. Did you see them?"

"No. *Baba* had them sent to you directly from France. Are they pretty?"

"They're beautiful. Let's sneak away to the cottage and I'll show you."

They walked to the little house, which, although meticulously clean, was in sharp contrast to the posh amenities of the estate. It consisted of one large room with a stone floor and a deep fireplace. Two alcoves were curtained off for sleeping and the beds were the old-fashioned spun cotton mattresses on a roughhewn trestle. The center of the room was dominated by a long oak refectory table, which was piled with gifts.

"You've got to see these." Julia bent down to a linen chest inlaid with mother-of-pearl and olive wood. "Your father had my new initials embroidered on the spreads and towels." She pulled out more pieces. "Look, the coverlets are peach, bordered in white satin, and the sheets are white, bordered in peach satin." She rubbed her hand across the material. The sheets reminded them of what came with marriage and they were silent.

"Julia, didn't you ever want to get away from the village and do *something* that had nothing to do with the family?" Nadia spoke breathlessly. "My parents would weep if they knew the things I wish for."

"It never occurred to me to protest," said Julia.

"Aren't you frightened now, even a little? These are the last few days you'll be free."

"I'm not." Julia's face was frank. "Peter is my miracle. And I don't mean that he saved me from spinsterhood, although I'm sure that's what people think. The miracle is that I've found my perfect situation. He makes me feel . . . *comfortable.*" She looked out one of the small windows, searching for the right words. "That doesn't sound exciting, but I've never felt comfortable within the family since my mother died. Samir is my father's main project, and rightly so. He has extraordinary abilities. Did you know he spent a year with the bedouin? He was almost killed. He's generous and not at all self-centered." A wistfulness came into her voice. "I'm going to miss him terribly."

"I envy his going to London," said Nadia. "That would be my ideal. To go where no one knows me or cares what I do. People have never liked my going to FGS. My own aunts and cousins thought I was trying to be a snob." She shrugged. "I've been offered a job with the government. My roommate's father needs an interpreter." For one wild moment, she considered sharing her fantasies about Victor Madden, but perhaps Julia wouldn't understand. She might appear like a silly girl with an impossible crush. "Where are you and Peter going to live?" she asked instead.

"In the Old City. We've settled on a charming stone house off St. Francis Street, and I'm going to decorate it myself, top to bottom. It has three floors and a little square-walled courtyard to separate it from the street. It's the sweetest house, Nadia, with odd nooks and one spectacular wood-paneled room. I can even choose my own flowers for the garden." She smiled with anticipation and pleasure. "I don't know why, but the thought of furnishing that house makes me dizzy with happiness. Nadia,"—she had a new thought that excited her—"you can come on your lunch break and help me choose things. I'll cook for you in my own kitchen."

"Of course I'll visit." They stood and threw their arms around each other and danced a few steps. Julia dropped her hands. "I'd better get back to the receiving line, but you don't have to. Go have a look at the new stables. Samir says you're crazy about horses."

"Samir talks about me?" she was surprised.

"You intrigue him," said Julia. "We were teasing him about the sort of girl he would marry, and he said perhaps it didn't matter so much. That most of the girls he knew were predictable. Then he said, 'excluding Nadia Mishwe. She's daft for horses and murder on the tennis court.' "

"Thank God my mother didn't hear that," said Nadia. "Can you think of a worse recommendation for a girl?" She was pleased to hear that Samir thought of her. If he found her interesting, maybe Victor would, too. "I *will* go look at the horses," she said gaily.

She walked away in long, bouncy strides, feeling the muscles in her calves. There was power in her lithe, well-exercised body. It belonged to her to do with as she wanted.

On the morning of his sister's party, Samir had awakened with feelings of relief and satisfaction. The previous day he had received news that he had passed the grueling two-day London Matriculation Exam and he could be admitted to the sophomore year at London University. He picked up Phillips, who had also passed the exam and was set to attend the

University of Glasgow, and they drove to the farm in Samir's new Humber coupe.

"Phillips, this is my mother. Mother, Thomas Phillips." Momentarily, he thought Phillips was going to make a tasteless remark, thinking he was the victim of a practical joke, for his mother's beauty often embarrassed people. The English boy recovered and mumbled, "Howdoyewdo."

She offered a smile so dazzling that even Samir, who had seen it countless times, was surprised. She had small, perfect features, with eyes that widened at their outer edge, giving her face a dreamy look. Once in Jerusalem, a tourist claiming to be a film maker infuriated his father by following them and begging her to appear in a moving picture.

"Samir," she reached to kiss his cheek, her face as noncommital as a judge's.

His father, on the other hand, was always darting about, his robes flying, a look of intensity on his face. He listened to this one and that one with sincere interest. He had a full, jowly face of excellent color, a prominent nose, and fine, even teeth. He was shorter than his wife, though they were seldom side by side. If Samir had to sum it up, his father made people feel energized and hopeful, while his mother left them dissatisfied.

"Come," Samir took Phillips by the arm, "I want to show you the stables. The farm is an anomaly. It has the most sophisticated plumbing system in Palestine, but the house is no more than a shack. My father insists that we all cram ourselves into it once a year for the fruit harvest, though none of us does the actual work. It's always open and ready to shelter any passerby because my father has this romantic idea of the purpose it had in the old days. He says many young men hid here during the war and escaped conscription in the Turkish army." Samir punched Phillips playfully, "If you find yourself pursued by an angry father because you've disgraced his daughter, you can always find shelter here."

When they reached the stables, they heard a feminine voice talking seriously to the horses, and they cleared their throats. When Samir saw that it was Nadia, the first thing he thought of was the scene in the foyer of the school, when she had smiled at Margaret's father. She looks lovely, he thought, and an unexpected bittersweet feeling overtook him. He wished that Phillips weren't there.

"*Megnuneh.* I'm daft," she said, continuing to caress the flanks of a sorrel mare. "Hello." She held out her hand to Phillips. "Don't tell my parents I'm here. I promised to be sociable and scout the eligible boys."

"You have two right here," said Phillips and then, patting the horse, he added, "and another here."

They all laughed. "Have you seen the tennis court?" asked Samir. "How about a match? I'll find you a pair of Julia's shoes." They had been urged to dress casually, for it was to be a long day spent out-of-doors.

"I don't think your mother would like us to play on the day of your sister's betrothal."

"She doesn't mind what anyone does," he said. "And my father wants the court used to get a better return on his investment."

She hesitated only a moment. "All right."

"I'll get the shoes and meet you at the court. It's straight across that path." He took Phillips with him and returned alone. "Rheema and Leila are showing Phillips the orchards."

After she put on the shoes, she held the racket as if it were a sword. "I see you're going to take this seriously," he joked. "The look on your face is for combat."

"You're the second person who has used that word to describe me. Miss Bailey once told me I looked combative."

"That could be said about you."

"She said I didn't smile enough. But why must everyone go around with an idiot grin? Isn't it all right just to be yourself?"

"You've never smiled much at me but,"—he shrugged—"it's not necessary."

"Women are always smiling to show some man their good nature. They stop smiling soon enough. You must be sick to death of smiling girls. Has a woman ever frowned at you? Here, let me show you how it looks." She scowled, crossed her eyes, and then smiled; and for the second time he was entranced by the intricate curvature of her mouth. If, at that moment, he had cut through the profusion of his own taboos, he would have known that he wanted to kiss it.

They strolled onto the court and played a set, which he won. Before the second set, she walked to the outer limits of the court in a little circle with her head down. She cast a long, determined look at him as he waited patiently on the other side. "Samir," she said soberly, "this time, I'm going to beat you."

"Really? You've decided, have you?" He took a deep invigorating breath. It was a beautiful day. To the west was the Mediterranean. To the south were the spires and rounded domes of Jerusalem. He could also see his mother standing in the middle of an admiring crowd. Poor Julia. Even though it was her party, her stepmother was the one who received the attention. She was only thirty-seven or -eight. His father had been a widower with an infant daughter, wealthy enough to marry anyone he chose, and he had chosen Sara David, the belle of Nablus.

He looked back at Nadia, who was his mother's emotional opposite. Her face was flushed with effort, her eyes squinting into the sun, her expression intense. She was really going to try to beat him, a foolish strategy for a girl, her mother would tell her. To show herself superior to a man in anything was social death. He smiled to himself. Wouldn't she be furious to hear such a thing. She would attack him like a tiger. Still, the determination on her face made her appear more vulnerable than formidable. He served the ball. It took her thirty-five minutes—she ran like a demon and used every advantage—but she beat him.

"I would give you another chance, but my parents will be looking for me. Oh, look," she pointed to an arriving car, "here's Father Simon. Don't you have to be in the ceremony?"

"Yes. My father wants me to give Julia away. My first act of command." He smiled to show he didn't take himself too seriously.

As they walked toward the tents, they passed the stone cottage. "You're welcome to come here and ride. The cottage is kept up by Mary Thomas at the bottom of the hill. Use it as much as you like. The horses would benefit from a good fast ride."

"I'd like that." She was impressed with his graciousness. He made it sound as if she would be doing him a favor to ride his horses.

He looked down at the crowd. "Julia looks lovely."

"She's very happy to be marrying Peter."

"Yes. And you? What are your plans now?"

"Margaret's father has asked me to take a job as interpreter for his agency."

That bit of news changed his lighthearted mood. "What do your parents say? They won't allow it," he stated flatly.

"Yes," she insisted, and there was defiance in her voice, "they will."

"Oh." He was nonplussed and studied her face for more clues about Victor Madden. Had her voice caught as she said, 'Margaret's father.' She met his gaze fleetingly but then looked away.

"And you?" she continued, sounding offhand, "will you become engaged next summer? Who's the lucky cousin?"

"That's one issue on which my father and I disagree."

"What? On getting married?"

"On marrying relatives. In England, it's against the law, I think. I'm not keen on it, either."

She was surprised by the statement and the seriousness of his tone. "Why not?"

"I don't think it's sound. I don't think it's good genetically for the children. It doesn't give them the best chance."

"Don't do it then," she said quietly and he thought she appeared slightly dejected. "You have the whole lot to choose from." He noticed that when she was trying to sound the most sure, she had a habit of facing away, as if to hide some frailty. She was walking ahead of him and he had a moment to study her. She had swept her hair up carelessly to reveal a slender, sculpted neck with well-defined tendons that became pronounced when she turned her head. He thought, she will never see herself from this vulnerable angle. I feel I should protect her.

At this moment, she turned and caught the unmistakeable look on his face. "Nadia," he reached out and put a finger on her lips and felt their incredible softness. His entire body focused on her mouth. He wanted to cover it with his, to feel it move under his own lips, to taste her, to bruise her. For an instant—it couldn't have been more than three or four seconds —he reveled in the exquisite sensation that ignited his body. There was the maddening pressure of full breasts caught against him. He raised his hand and reached to caress that soft, velvet fullness and then—it was over. She pulled away with a look of fury in her eyes. "Did you have a bet with Phillips?" All that talk of taboos. " 'I'm not keen on marrying relatives,' " she mimicked him cruelly. "Oh, Samir,"—her eyes were filled with angry tears—"how *could* you?"

He knew that nothing he said would make it right and let her run alone toward the group while he turned back to deal with his discovery.

Why her? Why, when he could have chosen from so many girls? "I *did* mean what I said about marrying relatives," he muttered to himself. "I won't do it to myself or to her." He walked quickly toward the crowd and thanked God that he had passed the Matriculation Exams. In two weeks, he'd be safely in London.

23

You're in love with him, aren't you?

"Of course. You must be Nadia." The attractive, well-groomed woman stretched out her hand but only grazed fingers before retrieving it. "Georgia Leeds. Victor's away for two days. A friend of Margaret's, are you?"

There was something wrong. Georgia Leeds was clipping the ends of her words as if she resented speaking at all. "Perhaps I should come back when Mr. Madden returns."

"No." *Click, click, click* went her heels. *Clip, clip, clip* went her words. "He wants you to get accustomed to the place." She took a folder of reports out of a filing cabinet. "I'll show you your office, but don't get settled in. We're moving to the new hotel in the next block just as soon as the suites are painted."

Nadia followed her into a windowless cubicle incongruously furnished with an ornate mahogany desk and a flashy Oriental-looking chair. A fan had coaxed a breeze in the other room, but here the air was heavy and still. She swallowed hard and pushed back her hair from her damp brow. "These are some progress reports on what's been done to improve our relations with the local races." Georgia Leeds put the folder on the desk. "You'll get some idea of what our problems are." Her voice was breathy and insinuating and Nadia decided she, like so many, was unhappy to be away from her country. Yet she wasn't prepared for what took place at lunch, which, at Georgia's insistence, they had together.

"You're in love with him, aren't you?"

Nadia dropped her fork. "In love with whom?"

"You're in love with Victor and you're certain if you stay close to him, he'll fall in love with you, too."

"That's not true." She considered getting up and walking out, but a part of her weighed the idea that this was the way sophisticated people behaved. "I'm happy to have the job." She was feeling pleased that she was handling the situation.

"Oooh, job, job, job! There's no real job." She stabbed at her meat impatiently. "Don't you see? He just wants to have you around."

She was too stunned to answer right away and then, although excited by the idea, she got control of herself. "He wants me as an interpreter. To talk to the bedouin."

"He can get twenty men from the office pool to talk to the bloody bedouin. But they're not nubile popsies." She looked around at the diners with such a look of frustration that Nadia felt sorry for her. "Just be warned."

"Warned of what?"

"Of Victor's predilection for anything in skirts. He can smell it a mile away. Right now, when he's well aware that his new raw recruit was coming in, he's taken the Jolly Boat to Tyre with the woman who does the payroll. If he puts a bag over her head she'll do fine. Big boobs and tight skirts is how she advertises her virtues." Satisfied to see Nadia blanch, she softened her tone. "Just take it from your Auntie Georgia, if you're serious about wanting a job, keep your affections on some nice chap outside the office. Our friend Victor's after only one thing."

His new raw recruit. Taken the Jolly Boat to Tyre with the woman who does the payroll. Our friend Victor's only after one thing. The phrases strung together like freight cars on a locomotive chugging through her brain, each loop bringing a stronger wave of incrimination. How stupid she had been to think he found her special. Anything in skirts. He can smell it a mile away. That awful, crude image had made her almost afraid of Georgia. Her thighs tightened and she pressed them together and rocked slightly in her chair.

When Victor showed up on the third day, she was too resentful to say a civil good morning. When he asked her to have lunch, her suspicions doubled.

"Thank you, no." She said it so quickly and sharply that he blinked.

"Lunch makes you angry, does it? Is it unhappy memories of luncheons past?" He looked around. "Angry over this cramped little office? We're moving soon."

She had to smile. He saw her as so much bolder than she was. His fresh shirt and polka dot tie and lopsided smile were as disarming as ever, but she made up her mind to stick to business. "I really don't see the purpose of my being here. There's a pool of interpreters you can choose from. I've read over all the programs for coaxing the Arabs and Jews and Muslims to feel affection for the British and for each other, and I think they're thoughtful and inventive. I couldn't improve on any of them. You probably thought I was far more knowledgeable and could give you something beyond this, but I can't. I can't. Don't feel you have to stick to your offer. It's perfectly all right. I'm not disappointed."

He looked dazed. "What in God's name are you talking about?"

"I can't see the purpose of my being here. There's no real job for me."

"Ah . . . that's better. Now I get it. Hmmm." He put his hand to his chin. "I can see why you might feel that way. Some aspects of public relations are amorphous. Certain contacts—it can be as simple as a successful luncheon where the food is just right—will soften a man's heart and make him willing to accept you as a comrade, while an elaborate reception with a full band will harden him against you. If you deliver Lord Cavendish's sincere felicitations in your lovely classical Arabic, how can it not make a difference?"

She looked doubtful. "But what about day to day?"

"Oh, there's plenty of translation needed—the local editorials, news items. And many days we'll be in the field. We're going to go where the people are and where the problems can be witnessed firsthand."

"Where? In the streets?"

"Perhaps in the streets, but I have something else in mind. Something in the area of sports. There's no better way to cement relations than with friendly sports competition. Now, have you changed your mind about lunch?"

Nadia looked worriedly in the direction of Georgia's desk and Victor caught the look. "I get it. Georgia's been warning you about me, is that it?" She turned bright red. "Don't worry. Georgia should have gone to work for the Temperance Union around the corner. She feels a passion to save people from themselves. Come on."

There were three wonderful aspects to the luncheon. The King David Hotel was easily the most glamorous building in all of Jerusalem. It had been designed by Swiss architects and belonged to the same Egyptian Jew who owned the famous Shepheard's Hotel in Cairo. The building was made of *mizzi ahmar,* the pale rose stone that turns golden with the sun. The window frames and shutters were a lime green. Sudanese waiters in white pantaloons and red tarbush carried food-laden trays across polished marble floors while piano music played in the background. The second wonderful thing was that several of her remarks made Victor smile. Right before her eyes, he seemed to be growing more interested in her. The third wonderful thing happened at the end. Just as she had tilted her head back to enjoy a healthy laugh, the picture of a carefree woman, living on the very edge of modern life, Samir Saleh was led to a table at just the perfect angle to witness the entire scene. It was all she could have hoped for.

* * *

"Where were you?" Miriam sounded angry. She was angry but trying to control herself.

"I went shopping for a new skirt."

"A new skirt?" Her voice was both ridiculing and accusatory. "Samir was here to say good-bye."

"So?"

"He waited forty-five minutes. He wanted to see you." Where Samir was concerned, her usually serene mama was like everybody else—anxious, hopeful, and obsequious.

"Oh, Mama, what does it matter?"

"What does it matter? Nadia, what's wrong with you? You take delight in dismissing any important thing."

"Important to you perhaps." Her mother's eyes became anxious and Nadia regretted her dismissive tone. "Suppose I had been at home. What do you think that would have accomplished? Absolutely nothing. We would have talked for a few minutes, I would have wished him good luck. He would have wished me good luck and felt that he had done the proper thing. That's what's really important to him. He's a rich, privileged boy, Mama, and he's going to marry a rich, privileged girl."

"That's not true. He helped me with the spinach pies. He actually rolled out the dough and even filled some of them—he was anxious that he wasn't doing a good job, can you imagine? He's not arrogant in the least. Nadia,"—her mother's voice became conciliatory, but Nadia knew it took great effort—"stop over there. Go to his house and tell him you're sorry to have missed him."

"No. I'm not going to do that."

"Nadia, please. He seemed so humble. Almost as if he were afraid you wouldn't see him. I got the feeling, well, I think he cares for you." She looked up from her cooking with such a childishly hopeful expression that Nadia felt embarrassed to see it.

"He doesn't care for me, Mama. He feels at home with me, that's all."

"No, I don't think so." Miriam looked thoughtful. "I'm not just being foolishly romantic. I could tell he was feeling something."

When Nadia thought of Samir, she thought of the kiss and it kept her angry and confused. When she thought of the kiss, she remembered the hungry action of his lips at the moment when they pressed on hers. Even if it had started out to be a casual kiss, it had not ended as one. She hated him for using her like that, but a part of her was thrilled to be so wanted. He had probably come to apologize. "Mama, I can't go. Please, don't ask me. And anyway, what good would it do? He's going to be in England for a long time. We'll both be very different people when he comes back."

Samir sailed from the port of Jaffa with twelve other passengers on a coal-burning cargo ship of the Khedevieh Line, which was under English control. He left on September 11, allowing himself three weeks to make the trip and arrive in time for the fall term at the London School of Economics, which had become recognized as part of London University for the BSc degree in Economics. The ship dropped cargo at Naples and Lisbon, and that was the last comfortable climate he was to know.

The school was located in Aldwych just off The Strand and and about a mile from Bloomsbury, the central University site. He was assigned a cold and drafty room on Fitzroy Street but it might as well have been off the face of the earth as he knew it. He had left his home during the hottest and driest season. Now he was never—and this included the time spent in bed —quite warm enough. The pervasive damp chill took its toll. He developed a miserable head cold that hung on.

He was unsettled and lonely, and his loneliness centered around one person. It was a time in his life when he needed something to dream about and represent all that he loved and missed of home. And the only girl he had to dream about was Nadia. He couldn't really miss his mother or father, and he had become used to having Julia gone. Phillips was at the University of Glasgow. Who else was there to whom he could feel an attachment? He built silly little daydreams about her as he tried to find some warmth in the drafty ancient halls. He doodled her initials and sometimes her name on scraps of paper. On the playing fields at Malden, he imagined looking up at the stands and seeing her there. He couldn't forget the feel of her wide, sensual mouth. She *had* returned his kiss. It was fleeting, but he had felt it.

As Margaret had said, she couldn't have done a more thorough job of bewitching him if she had hired a sorceress.

The first time Nadia had the opportunity to be off with Victor, tucked into the Singer, the flagship of the Mediterranean Fleet put into Jaffa and they went with two local mayors to call on the admiral. There was a temporary platform where the dignitaries sat for a brief ceremony, during which Victor gave a short, humorous speech. A slight breeze ruffled his hair and turned up a corner of his jacket, and this, for some reason, made her feel peculiar and excited. He loomed larger than life—charming and able. A man among men. Before, she had been infatuated, but now she felt weakened and fragile as if her strength had leaked out. That was her last peaceful day.

Her mind was as intractable as a stack of papers left near a window during a gale. Victor's teacup and Victor's chair, Victor's worn, grainy briefcase, Victor's hat flung on a peg or his blue cashmere scarf slipping dangerously toward the floor, Victor's laughter heard through the wall, and Victor's footsteps approaching—any of these made her numb to everything but the anticipation of his presence. Perhaps he would enter her small office . . . could she draw him in by willing it? Some days, she felt so beautiful and was certain if he would only come in and see her, he would realize it, too. It was an exhausting game.

Within two weeks, she had lost four pounds. She was desperate to control her emotions and distance herself. For several days, she became overly prim and officious, as if she had a righteous grudge. When she tried not to love Victor, she wanted him to think she hated him.

"I say, are you put out over something?" he asked solicitously.

"Not at all."

"That's strange. I notice a little pulling in around that remarkable mouth. As if some dolt hasn't considered your feelings. Have *I* upset you?"

Oh, Lord. "Nothing like that."

"I seem to remember you know your way around horses."

The remark was like holding out a lolly to a cranky baby. He was trying to mollify her. "Yes."

"Good. It's going to come in handy. I'd like to join the Ramleh Vale Hounds and infiltrate the local landed gentry."

"You don't need me to do that."

"I do need you," he said, giving her the full treatment.

She lived on that sentence for a week.

"Baba, you wouldn't believe how much squabbling there is over nothing. I feel ashamed sometimes."

"Hmmph. Ashamed? Don't waste your shame. The British duped an entire country. Let them feel ashamed."

"Baba, there's constant complaining. Some of the new Jewish settlers don't even speak Hebrew, yet they insist that Hebrew should be the official language. And the Arabs feel it should be Arabic. And, of course, neither wants to see anything printed in English. Everyone wants only his religious holidays observed. On Fridays, the Christian and Jews can work but not the Muslims. On Saturdays, the Christians and Muslims, but not the Jews. On Sundays, not the Christians. Some of the immigrants from Poland and Galicia are accustomed to swimming nude, but the local people are appalled and want them arrested. They throw stones. One things leads to another, and before you know it a riot breaks out. Everyone is on the verge of madness."

"No one is on the verge of madness. That's propaganda served up by the British. They are bleeding our country. Even the lowest British clerk receives an allotment to send to his family, and they use our money to buy British goods and British property. Instead of feeling ashamed, ask your boss about the vast sums that are leaving the country. My banker sends them out."

After a few weeks, she stopped talking about her job. She wasn't a traitor, but she could not see evil in a man like Victor Madden. He was compassionate, generous, and able. He went through the streets greeting businessmen and peasants alike with friendly good will. It wasn't his fault that the British had won the war and the right to govern. It would pain her father to hear it, but she didn't share his suspicion and resentment toward the Mandate Government.

She bought a new riding outfit, a trim, tailored beige jacket and dark brown jodhpurs, burgundy boots, and a black cap. Margaret had once told her she was born to wear pants. "You fill them admirably without looking vulgar. Pity the man who has to walk behind you and not touch," she added sourly. Her own buttocks were flat. After her purchases, Nadia lived with a constant flutter in her stomach that made her lose interest in food.

The third time they drove to the Ramleh Vale Hound Kennels between Lydda and Ramleh, William drove and Victor joined her in the back. Along the road, they passed several of the enamel post office signs that were printed in Arabic, English, and Hebrew. At each place, Victor asked William to pull over because the signs were vandalized. One or two of the languages were scratched off.

"They deface the signs in hopes that the other nationality will disappear."

"I'm ashamed that my countrymen can be so petty," she said.

"None of us is beyond pettiness," he said amiably. "While I was in college, I had a roommate who never bought soap or tooth cleanser but always helped himself to mine. I was eaten up with resentment and found myself skulking in shadows waiting to catch him in the act. I'd wait up till the wee hours to stop him from washing his face with my soap. I even stopped buying soap and went a week without it myself to force his hand. Well, it didn't force his hand at all. He went without it too, but his life wasn't tainted by bitterness. I learned a great lesson from that boy, Timothy Reems."

"But you were right. He should have bought his own soap." She'd never heard anyone speak as he did. He had an opinion on everything and it was always the exact opinion she would have had, too.

"Perhaps, but that's not why I hated him. I hated him because he showed me that I was crippled by pettiness. I was willing to sacrifice my well-being over the cost of a bar of soap because I felt threatened by his difference. I cordonned myself off from him but had to watch him like a hawk. Precisely what's going on in your country. The nationalities exclude each other, but then they must keep a vigil lest their antagonists get the better of them." He raised one eyebrow and tucked in his chin as if he were going to say something especially provocative. "Sometimes, individuals cordon themselves off. They don't want anyone to intrude. They are afraid to share themselves."

They were approaching the driveway of the kennels and she waited to answer until William had let them out and went to park the car. "You're talking about me," she said accusingly. "You're saying I'm afraid to share myself."

"Of course I am. You keep everything hidden behind that disquieting, sensual face." At that moment, the houndmaster approached and she was left to deal with those words.

Sensual. There must be a different meaning than the one she knew. He wouldn't say anything so intimate to her. He wouldn't say her appearance was carnal.

"You ride to hounds with your employer? That's your job?" Julia put two plates on a small table in the study. "Let's eat here. The sun streams in this window and we can have a look at the garden." She rolled in a cart that held a tureen of lentil soup, cheese, bread, and sliced tomatoes. Marriage had released a new confidence in Julia. Today she was wearing a long peasant skirt with a knit top that made her look like a struggling artist. She was one of only a handful of women who had learned to drive and scooted around in a Humber sedan to the admiration of the community. "I've never heard of a job like that. What sort of man is he? Do I sound too much like your mother?"

"Don't worry about that. Victor has his own ideas of how to do a job. He likes to get out and mix with people instead of getting information from reports. People speak to him candidly and he persuades them that it's to their advantage to get along together. Of course, he's always promoting the Mandate Government. 'We're not callous imperialists twenty-four hours a day,' he says. They are doing *some* good, Julia."

"I see." Julia was skeptical. "And has he convinced you, too, that the English have only our good at heart? I have to admit the post is improved since the days of the Turks. Peter gets his mail from abroad so regularly, he can't catch up. Besides the post, what else have they done? Oh, yes, there are the riots and work stoppages. We never had those before the war."

"Planning. They've planned the neighborhoods around the Old City. Behind the railroad, there's a nice development with a lovely pine wood. No one can put up a house just anywhere. The streets are much cleaner, too."

"Look," said Julia. "The soup's stopped steaming. I've kept you from eating. All right. If you like your job, I won't play devil's advocate. Mr. Madden is a man of the world and you're very dear to me."

"Don't worry about me." She took a sip of her soup and looked around the room, which contained a deep fireplace faced with terra cotta tiles and flanked by two overstuffed loveseats upholstered in flowered chintz. The polished cotton drapes and the tablecloth on the small table they were using were of the same design. "I love this house. This room is comforting. Do you sit here in the evenings?"

"We rarely have an evening free. Peter has to entertain visitors from abroad. We either take them out or I serve dinner here. Afterward we sit in the parlor and hear the gossip from Europe and America. In New York, they have dance marathons that last for weeks. Doctors stand by to help those who collapse. Some die of heart failure. Can you imagine such non-sense?"

"I can imagine wanting to do something that takes you out of the ordinary. Julia,"—she felt shy—"I have those feelings. Sometimes I think that if I don't do something exciting now, I'll find myself shut away forever."

"Something exciting?" Julia repeated. "Are you certain you're not developing a crush on your boss? Now why did I say that?"

Nadia tore her bread into bits. "Perhaps because I'm thinking it."

"Oh, dear. Is it serious?"

"It's always on my mind."

"And on his, too? He hasn't done anything, has he?"

"You mean physical? Oh, no. He doesn't even see me in that way. I'm the one who's nuts with infatuation."

"I'm not the right person to sympathize with you because I'm not on his side. I had always hoped that you and . . ."—she wiped her mouth—"Samir . . ."

"Oh, God! You and my mother. He stopped to say good-bye before he left for England and my mother had us engaged. Samir and I aren't suited. He must be busy with his life in England."

"I've heard from him." Julia went to a desk across the room as if she'd been waiting for an opening. "He's lonely." And, as if one statement were related to the other, she followed with, "He sends regards to you."

"Does he?" She shrugged. Another time she might have been intrigued, but today she was too full of Victor Madden.

"Infatuation," sighed Julia. "That makes me feel really old." She wrapped a piece of soft, hot bread around a piece of cheese and took a bite. "My excitement is reading novels. I've just finished *Back Street* by Fannie Hurst. But there'll be no reading until I redo the upstairs. There are two unfinished bedrooms. I was hoping one could be a nursery, but so far there's been no reason . . . You can stay over any time."

They finished their lunch, blinking contentedly in the sunshine. If you had scoured the borders from Galilee to Gaza you wouldn't have found two happier women. Before she could rush back to Victor, Julia asked Nadia to help her choose among several swatches to cover a settee for her bedroom. Nadia asked to borrow a record of "The Rhapsody In Blue" to play on Khalil's new victrola. When she gave her the record, Julia said, "I wish there was something really important I could do." How could she know that in three short years she would get that wish?

He had definitely liked her in the beginning. He had teased her in a special way. But now he was meticulously polite. What had she done wrong? The raw weather had made the ground too sloshy for treks into the country, and for several weeks she spent her time at a desk translating articles from the local press.

After he had called her sensual, she had imagined a string of thrilling aftermaths. I tried not to love you (uttered in a desperate voice and followed by a troubled kiss). Stand beside me and don't say a word, whatever I do (spoken grimly by a man who had fallen in love against his will). In reality, all he said was "good morning, good night," and "no need to translate the entire editorial; just give me the gist of it."

She became accustomed to living with a dull eagerness. Once, out-of-doors, she was about to step off a curb and he put his hand under her arm protectively. As they walked, she moved too slowly and he "crashed" softly against her. Hadn't he held her deliberately a few extra seconds?

She didn't know why he had liked her before and teased her good humoredly, and was now preoccupied and distant.

* * *

In late February three things happened. Khalil finally left for America. He was a thirty-year-old bachelor going to seek his fortune, but Miriam was filled with anxiety. She snapped at everyone. As if that weren't enough, Grandmother Jamilla caught pneumonia and died so suddenly it left everyone thunderstruck. They hardly noticed the third calamity— Samir's father, the sheik, had a stroke.

When the weather improved, Victor began holding gymkhana race meetings in the open country behind Jaffa. During these equestrian field days, both Jews and Arabs could enjoy the pageantry and place small bets. Many hours were spent traveling back and forth, and to Nadia's regret, Victor passed the time talking obsessively of England.

"This red soil reminds me of Devonshire," he said, looking apologetic. They were driving through the rolling downs around Lydda. "I'm sorry. I miss England, although that scoundrel Ramsey McDonald and his Labor Party are making it intolerable for a thinking person. I must be homesick. This country is beginning to remind me of home." At various times he remarked that he'd seen cricket played near Ramleh. And was noticing many homes with Georgian fanlights over the doors.

Each remark was a hurtful slap. He wouldn't think twice about leaving her.

One day, they stopped at one of the suqs. When they returned to the car, he mused, "They're selling cloth by the yard. Just like in England." That silly remark made her lose her temper. For a moment she loathed him. "Perhaps we sell goods by the yard because it makes sense and *not* because it's done in England. And you might notice that for every house with a fanlight, there are thousands with Mediterranean vaulted ceilings. The new YMCA is designed by an American—he also did the world's tallest building. We have influences from all over. Look at the onion domes of the Russian Compound and the godawful Rhineland castle the Germans built on the site of the old Hospitallers. The British influence is only the most recent and not necessarily the most lasting." She was perspiring. Her throat was dry. Her eyes felt as if they were melting in a solution of steaming wax. Oh, Lord, I'm raving like a lunatic. I'm angry because he's not paying any attention to me.

He pulled over to the side of the road and stopped the car. She got out, thinking he meant to leave her there. Then he got out and began to laugh. "Wonderful. You were absolutely splendid."

"I was rude," she said icily. "Nothing you said deserved that outburst."

"Well," he wiped his eyes, "no hard feelings. Let's have a late lunch.

There's a Trappist monastery near here at Latroun that serves the best wine in the country. Good food, too."

She got back in the car without saying a word.

Once inside the dining hall, his good humor disappeared. His shoulders slumped and she was sorry to see him that way. A monk carried in two heaping trays to serve the few diners. "See that fellow?" Victor indicated the brother. "He's taken the vow of total silence, although they send him in here to keep me company when I'm their only customer. He left the monastery during the war to fight for France and was decorated several times for bravery. Now he's back, content to be silent after all the excitement." The monk brought a bottle of wine and while Victor opened it Nadia looked around. The dining room was small and intimate with spotless starched nappery.

After tasting the wine, Victor poured some in each glass and took another long sip. "Admirable to have so much self-control that you can live without the sound of your own voice."

"Self-control isn't everything. He might admire you. He might envy your qualities."

"What? Riding to hounds? Ridiculous pastime. Grown people led by a pack of overstimulated dogs to chase a fox that seldom gets caught." Again his shoulders slumped. Perhaps he was sorry they had come here.

"Why do it then?"

"I don't know. I love it . . . the riding, the people, the silly excitement. The fact that it's all for naught really appeals to me. Life's so serious and sometimes so sad. Death . . . war . . . missed chances . . ."

"Missed chances? You?" What missed chances?

"Mmmhm. You see, I never had the gift of long-suffering."

"You've the gift of graciousness and affability." She had a quick fear that the word didn't mean what she thought. She took a sip of her wine and when she looked at him over the rim of the glass, she saw a look in his eyes that melded her bones and left her weak.

"It's hard for me to say this." The soft pad of his index finger made a slow circuit of her silky jaw and chin, grazing her lower lip before coming to rest again on the starched tablecloth. "For the last few weeks, I've thought of you in ways that would make your parents despondent."

She looked down. "I don't understand." Oh, yes, I do. I do.

"I've wanted to kiss you and have you kiss me back. Too often, I've imagined what it would feel like to have you in my arms." He glanced across the room to where the monk was slapping the crumbs from a vacated table with the snap of a napkin. She, too, glanced nervously in the monk's direction. "You're not aware of your own effect on men, Nadia."

"Margaret said something like that to me once."

"She did, did she? That girl has the wisdom of a witch." He reached across the table to hold one of her hands. "I wouldn't have predicted this," he said ruefully. "You took up residence in my imagination that first night with Mr. Matthew Arnold's poem."

"When you said I had a sensual face, I looked the word up in the dictionary and found a couplet there by Atterbury. It said: 'No small part of virtue consists in abstaining from that wherein sensual men place their felicity.' " She was surprised that she remembered anything.

He smiled and pressed her hand. "Atterbury was a fool. There's no virtue in abstaining from pleasure. It's cowardly. And since when has the dictionary delivered a sermon with its definitions?"

The monk brought their food and she snatched her hand away, embarrassed. In this case, she decided, Mr. Atterbury's warning was merciful. Aloud, she said, "How did he know what we wanted to eat?"

"They serve only the dish of the day. I think it's veal. Is it all right?"

She stared at her plate and nodded. How could she possibly swallow anything when her throat felt so dry and narrow. It was the shock of having him confess his feelings so candidly. She wasn't prepared for it. "It's fine." She took another sip of wine but refused to look at him.

"Why don't you look at me? Have I made you angry?"

"Oh, no. Not angry."

"Well, what then? Disappointed? Disgusted?"

She ran her fingernail in the soft nap of the tablecloth, aware that her next words would change her life. "Happy," she whispered, staring so intently at her plate her eyes no longer focused. "Very happy."

"Well, now, isn't that marvelous!" He placed his hand over hers and rubbed his thumb against the palm. "Want to leave right now or finish eating?"

"Finish eating. I couldn't bear to have the monk think we didn't like the food."

"Mmmm."

When they got into the car, she was cold as ice, shivering, and filled with anxiety. "There's something wrong here," he said. "One shouldn't plan a kiss. It should be a spontaneous outcome of deep feeling. You're white as a ghost. I feel self-conscious, don't you?"

"Yes." She felt as if she were about to commit a crime. She kept looking at his profile for clues as to his intentions, but he appeared grim and unsettled with a crease of worry marring his forehead.

"We won't kiss then," he said obstinately. "I want this to be right."

They drove for about fifteen minutes in the waning light. Then he pulled off the road and turned to her. "How many times have you been kissed?"

She looked down. "Once."

"That often?" He whistled in mock surprise and she had to laugh. "And was it a kiss you welcomed?"

"No!" she almost shrieked. "Not at all."

"Well, now . . . that puts a new light on things." He appeared worried again.

Her inexperience had made him lose his desire for her. "You don't want to kiss me now?"

His face softened and she saw a totally new emotion in his eyes. Soft and vulnerable and, oh! . . . uncertain. He took her face in both his hands and held it like a captive bird. "You're so young. A brand new heart without any cynicism. A truthful heart without artifice. You see, my dear, quite ingeniously, you've put me on my honor." He rubbed his thumb against her cheek and looked so wistful that she wanted to console him.

"Well, then," she leaned forward, "I'll have to kiss you." An agony of wondering—months of it—were ended. She was enclasped in his arms, muffled into his chest, inhaling the sweet clean smell of warm fabric. Her last clear thought was that his lips were softer than she had expected.

For days after that kiss, she ached to be touched again. But it was also thrillingly fearful. She just assumed there would be more kisses. He would arrange for them to be alone. But where? In the car? In his apartment? She could not imagine being alone with him in his apartment. She appeared in the office, trembling beneath her light wool challis jacket. A piece of paper felt like lead in her hand. She didn't feel the desk or the chair.

"Good morning," he called out exuberantly but he didn't come in. He would come in later. They couldn't be obvious.

She waited and waited for some word, a nod, a wink. He remained aloof. When she finally ventured outside her cubicle, he was all business and she returned to her desk, burning with shame. He avoided her for several days and she thought what any young girl would think. He had been curious about kissing her, and now he was no longer curious. One afternoon, she was standing with Georgia by a window and he was walking away from the building with a woman. Georgia turned to her. "The payroll clerk." Nadia looked distressed. "Well, you knew you had to share him, didn't you?"

She felt such pain and humiliation that she rushed away, unable to hide her feelings. She felt stupid, used. After work, she stopped at Julia's, unwilling to go home and face her mother's probing stares.

Julia was pregnant and too caught up in her impending motherhood to notice much. Just when Nadia was feeling sorry to be there, almost suffocating with discomfort, Julia asked if anything was wrong, but when Nadia said no, she began to ramble on about Samir. He was traveling all through Great Britain. He knew London as well as Jerusalem. He was really getting an education.

She left more dejected than before. Samir was living a life of achievement and fun, while she was squirming inside as if maggots were running loose in her veins because she had made a fool of herself over a man twice her age.

24

Made any friends?

"I came to see *you,* of course, but that doesn't mean we can't have some fun with the opposite sex." Phillips had come from Glasgow for the weekend. He looked around the room, picked up a mandolin, and began to strum it.

"You could have *that* kind of fun in Glasgow."

"London whores are the best. Cleaner than the French but with worse teeth."

Samir blinked. "Aren't there any nice, willing girls in Scotland?"

"It's not the same with nice girls. I want someone who's not frightened by it."

"Going to put up a sign to that effect?"

"I know where to go. Come on, get dressed." Phillips brushed his hair at a small mirror above a stained sink and pulled at his face. "I'm assuming you're experienced," he said cautiously. "I mean, all the way."

Samir was lacing his shoes, bent over. He looked up from this position. "There's a place in Jerusalem where wealthy men enroll their sons on their fifteenth birthday." He was hoping to shock Phillips.

"You're not serious." Phillips stared at Samir through the mirror. "You make an appointment as if you're going to take piano lessons?"

"Almost like that. A woman in a spinster's bun interviews father and son and then assigns a teacher to you."

"And . . . ?"

"And she shows you how."

"You mean what goes where?"

"Everyone knows what goes where. She shows you the finer points."

"My Lord! What a cold-blooded little ritual! She sat there and told you everything?"

Samir grinned. "Not exactly. She made me demonstrate."

"My Lord!"

"Yes."

"Did she show you anything . . . *unusual?*"

"No. Just the usual," lied Samir. As a matter of fact, the woman had had him in a full tub, almost drowning him in the process.

"Let's go," said Phillips, his mouth dry as dust.

In Soho they found the whores looking cold and uncomfortable in their finery. Samir's partner had chipped front teeth. He didn't want anything from her, but she was smitten with him and he went through with it. When Phillips wanted to return the next day, Samir urged him to go alone.

"What's the matter? Are you in love, or something?"

"Not in love. I think about someone from home."

"Really? Anyone I know?"

"We're making too much of it," said Samir, annoyed by his friend's lascivious interest. "It's just my cousin. You met her at my sister's engagement party."

"Uh-oh! Watch out," said Phillips. "Here it's called incest. Or almost incest. The kids come out mentals. At best, they don't win academic prizes."

"I agree. Besides, she's not interested, so it isn't an issue. She's not even that pretty."

"How do you know she's not interested?"

"I kissed her and she flew into a rage."

"Hmmmmm."

"Hmmmmm *what?*"

"If she flew into a rage, she was probably angry with herself for liking it. She probably loved that furtive kiss." Phillips looked pleased with himself.

"For that kind of loyalty, I'll keep you company in Soho. Come on."

As they walked, Phillips had a rare moment of introspection and insight. "You're melancholy, old boy. Do they treat you badly here?"

"Not really."

"Made any friends?"

"I'm friendly with a Jew and a Hungarian."

"What is it, the outcasts' club?"

"Of course, I have my athletic friends. Fair, lanky lads. We've great camraderie on the playing fields or sculling, but afterward we part company."

"Too bad, but you can't say I didn't warn you. What about girls? I should think the girls have much more sense. Aren't they swooning over you?"

"To date, all the swooning over me has been done by boys."

"Uh-oh! The dandies are after you."

"And they don't take no for an answer. One was a duke's son. He took me to his castle for the weekend, crept into my room and, with the eyes and voice of a toddler, asked if he could get in my bed."

"And you screamed and woke the entire castle."

"I said if he came near my bed, I'd knock him out cold. Then, he said, 'What would it take? Money? Social position? My father and mother could launch you.' The next morning, I hitched a ride to the train. And that wasn't the end of it. He accosted me at school and asked if I'd changed my mind."

Catharsis didn't lift his spirits. Late that night, when Phillips' train pulled into the cavernous King's Cross Station, Samir felt melancholy.

"This may be good-bye for good," said his friend, pointing to the locomotive. "This is the famous Flying Scotsman, a *cause célèbre* in Parliament because of reports that it speeds through the nine-hour run in only seven. But the cars careen and give you hair-raising thrills. So if I don't see you again, old man, I want to tell you how much your friendship has meant to me." He was joking, but still Samir was touched.

The term had three months to go and it seemed an eternity. Most of what he learned was unlikely to be of use in his real life, except for one project. They were using one of the new Rothschild vineyards as a case study for profitability. The vineyard, planted several years previously, was about to bottle its first vintage. The project fascinated Samir and he devoted himself to finding out the most minute details of the wine-producing business. He wanted to persuade his father that they begin growing grapes for wine on part of the property. As it happened, he never finished the project. Three days after Phillips' visit, a cable came from Julia. There was an emergency at home and he had to return right away.

He was in the office. She could hear him walking around. She knew what every sound meant. Now he was hanging up his coat, putting down his briefcase on the desk. Now he was walking to the window and staring out at the city. Now he was perched on the corner of his desk, shuffling through papers. Soon he would come out to stir up his troops. Georgia would give him any memos from the High Commissioner's Office, Edwina had his calendar of events. Nadia had the synopsis of opinions in the local press.

He came in, closed the door slowly, and deliberately and sat in a chair next to her desk as if he were being interviewed for a job. He was silent for a long time, looking straight at her. How could he stare so calmly? The desk was only two feet wide, so they were quite close.

"I have your folder," she said. "There aren't any angry denouncements, for a change. There's a nice review of the open-air concerts."

He took the folder, put it aside unopened, and continued to look at her.

"What is it?" she asked.

"I can't stop thinking of you."

"Thinking what about me?"

"Thinking about *you*. As a person. Your integrity. Your generosity. Your willingness. And behind it all—a lovely feminine dignity. I think that could come only from a core of strength. Where did a young girl like yourself aquire so much strength? I can't stop thinking of you. You're not cynical. You don't cling. You don't giggle. You simply wait. Like a beautiful cat that knows it's a rare species and that, eventually, everything it wants will come."

Thank you, Lord, for letting him think that about me. I want to do nothing but cling to him. "Why have you shut me out?"

"I have no right to ask anything of you. You're half my age. My God, you've only been kissed twice, and one of those times it was against your will. I feel I'm taking advantage of you, and I feel I have to make you aware of all the consequences."

"I can't ask you to have an affair with me. I know the standards for women in this country. Whatever I ask of you, I have to think about it seriously. I have to court you properly. I have to think about what we're going to be to each other. What would you like us to be to each other?"

"I want to be with you. Wherever that leads us."

"All right. We'll start from there. Let's go for a drive. We won't ask any questions or make plans. We'll see what happens."

"Nadia, you're working later and later. I never see you at home. When your father gave permission for you to work, he was thinking it would be a different sort of job. He would never have said yes to this."

"Did *Baba* say that? Did he say he would never have said yes?"

"He didn't say that, but we don't like you being away from home so much. We're supposed to guide you, and how can we guide you if you're never here? I feel something is happening to you."

"Nothing is happening, Mama. I have to work, that's all."

"What is it that you do?"

"A lot of things. It's a difficult job to define."

"I don't like it. Rheema teaches at the kindergarten and she's home by three-thirty. I don't even like you going back and forth every day. Especially with all the incidents on the buses. You're still a young girl and we're still your parents."

"Mama, nothing's going to happen to me. Don't worry."

"Don't tell me not to worry. You're too young to see danger even if it's right next to you. You don't know everything about life, even if you think you do."

"Good night, Mama. I'm tired. I'm going to sleep."

"You haven't heard a word I've said. What did I just say?"

"Of course, I heard what you said. You said *Baba* would not have said yes to this job."

"That's not what I just said at all. You see! Something *is* going on!"

After they spoke, she couldn't remember what her mother had said or what she had answered. When she wasn't looking at her mother, she couldn't even remember what she looked like. There were days that were lived at such a high pitch of emotion, she couldn't remember any details. Whole sections of her life were blank. Only his face made an impact. Only his voice reached her ears.

"Nadeem, it's your right. You can go there and find out what she does. You can speak to this man. You can ask him what her duties are. What hours she's required to be there. He'll understand that you're her father and have a right to know. We can't just let her continue to do as she pleases. Something is happening. I can feel it. She's all into herself." There were many fears regarding her daughter that Miriam couldn't even put into words—there was a distance, a smug smile that covered a world of secrets.

"I can't spy on her. She's given me no reason. It's wrong not to trust her. She's always been used to dealing with her own affairs, and now you can't suddenly start treating her like a child. She'll be resentful. She'll turn away from us. I can't."

"You mean you won't. You mean you won't." She said it twice, her voice tight with anger. "You've always been blind where Nadia's concerned. You've always been afraid of her." She wanted to shout. Your daughter is doing something wrong! Do something! But she wasn't his daughter, and the guilt over that kept her silent. Nadia was too much like Max. Obstinate and unwilling to look at anyone else's point of view.

"Baba," Samir said softly. The air in the room was stale and his stomach felt queasy. The sheik was dozing but his head was at an odd angle, like a doll left unnaturally arranged by a careless child. He had never seen that robust face with eyes closed, and it frightened him. Someone had buttoned his white linen nightshirt all the way, but the neck no longer filled the collar.

His father had suffered a stroke that had paralyzed the right side except for minimal use of his hand. He could barely stand. And there was something else so embarrassing, even the gossips didn't want to discuss it. His beautiful young wife had left him.

"Sara's gone to America to visit her brothers, so he's there in the house all alone except for the servants." Julia had driven alone to meet Samir's boat. "You'll find it hard to believe that he can't move. Do you ever remember seeing him sitting still, except for meals?"

"No. Is he terribly depressed?"

"Not at all. His acceptance is so touching. He's not bitter about it. He can be very cheerful, especially when I bring Ambrose."

"Why didn't mother come back? Why is she still in America?"

Julia looked straight ahead and gripped the wheel. "He says she's not going to come back. He says that she's gone for good."

"What?"

Julia's voice broke. "Samir, I can't swear that it's true, but it's not just gossip or I wouldn't mention it. *Baba* speaks about it freely to me. And the heartbreaking part . . . well, he doesn't feel sorry for himself at all. I hated sending you that cable, but there are decisions to be made and I was afraid to make them by myself. Now I'm so glad you're here. Is that too selfish?"

"Of course not. How could you not tell me?"

He had declined Julia's offer to accompany him into the house. He wanted to be alone with his father, and she had to return home to her little son, Ambrose.

"Samir?" The sheik jerked up as if to sit, before remembering he couldn't manage it alone. "Help me into the chair so we can talk, *habiby*. I'm sorry they called you from school. Who told you? Julia? Well, she meant well, but such a long trip and what can you do?" Samir offered his arms and the sheik leaned on them until he was upright. "There." He squinted. "You look tired. What's the matter?"

"I'm not tired. Just the voyage. We landed quite early. *Baba* . . . what happened?" It was a shock to see his father's face. One eye stared crazily, roving to the left while the other looked ahead. Samir had such an intense desire to cry he had to blink rapidly and rub his face.

"What happened is that I can't run around anymore. As for the cause . . . who knows?"

"Does it hurt?"

"Physically, no. It's quite peaceful at times. It forces on me the art of reflection. I've run around, always fidgety, scurrying all my life. I'm even a little stooped, not from age, but from butting my head into the wind to move faster. Now God is saying, 'Take your time.' " He sighed and slapped his good hand down on his lap. "Tell me, how's the great university? How is London?"

"London is very frenzied. The streets are always crowded."

"Do you enjoy it?"

"The British can be very cold and snobbish. They've come around toward me because I have money and help them win their soccer games. Also, I don't care whether they accept me or not, which of course confuses them."

"You only have three months left for the semester, then you have the summer here."

"*Baba,* I can't go back now. I can't leave you."

"Of course you can. And you will. I don't need you yet. I can still make decisions and Peter helps me. Julia brings Ambrose and I forget everything. Take advantage of the time you have left."

"How could mother . . ."

The sheik made a dismissive sound by clicking his tongue against his teeth. "Your mother did what she had to do. Her mother and brothers are in America, and it makes perfect sense for her to be there. We both save face."

"But why aren't you angry?"

He was silent and his jaw became slack. He was thinking carefully about what to say. "She had no experience in coping with bad luck. I knew that when I married her. If I'm honest with myself, I can't expect qualities now in adversity that weren't there to begin with."

"But, *Baba,* how could she leave you when you needed her?"

"You won't believe me, but she was more humane than I gave her credit for. She went across several oceans to be unfaithful so as not to embarrass me. She could never have stayed, Samir. It wasn't in her."

"Why don't I want to flee?" he asked softly.

"Ah, well, you have a different heart. You learned the lesson of duty at an early age. You welcome it." He became thoughtful and looked down absently, as if remembering something. His bad eyebrow was so arched it looked as if he were having an epiphany, some brilliant realization that captured his imagination. "Samir, I want to tell you something. When I left you in the desert, remember? . . . when I rode off, knowing you would wake up alone and feel abandoned—Samir . . ."—a tear formed in his unparalyzed eye and rolled down his cheek—"it broke my heart. But you see that year served you well. It made you into a real man. Now help me get dressed and we'll go outside. I can lean on you and we'll sit in the garden. You can help me with my shoes. You know, one of the things I miss most is being able to tie my shoes. I always felt so satisfied when I tied my shoes. That set the day for me."

Samir slipped a clean aba over his father's head, touching him gingerly at first but then with more confidence. He bent to put on the soft leather shoes and was shocked at how small the sheik's feet were. As he was tying the second lace and straightening the aba around the legs, he felt something warm running down on his hand. He almost cried out but managed to check his reaction in time. He undressed his father with a matter-of-factness that denied pity. He brought out clean clothes and different shoes and began again. When he was through, he put the shiek's bad arm around his own neck, raised him up, and together they hobbled into the surprisingly warm February sun.

Three days later, because his father insisted, he returned to London. He and Julia had hired Muffi, a huge Moroccan who could lift their father easily. Muffi was respectful but jolly, with an impish sense of humor. Satisfied that his father was in good hands, Samir returned to England. He would finish the semester to please his father, but he knew that he would never return for the final year. The business had to be run. The future—it had always seemed so far away—was here.

He had opened the tiny pearl buttons on the back of her blouse, grumbling at each obstinate loop. The soft silk had parted willingly and he ran his hand down the length of her. "Such a beautiful straight back." He kissed three places: the nape of her neck, the middle vertebrae, and the base of the spine. While he did this, she was perfectly still, but she couldn't keep from thinking, He's in command. He's had much experience with the female body. They were on his bed, which was made of a polished burled wood outlined in walnut, with a scrolling back like a sleigh. The entire width was taken up by a square down pillow covered in creamy white linen. He turned her over, pushed up the blouse, and stared at her breasts. They lay relaxed against her body, perfectly centered, the nipples as tender as the secret inside of a newly unfurled rose. His face hovered above one pink center, his mouth opened, his tongue darted out to meet it. His lips enclosed it and slid with a feather-light touch up and down just once, then stopped.

"I can't. I can't do this to you and I can't continue like this any longer."

"Nor can I." She didn't move to cover herself. She was beyond that. She lay there, immobilized, her eyes on the textured ceiling, waiting for life or luck or the devil to make all her choices. "What are we going to do?" she asked, totally detached from any answer. Her voice was noticeably deeper and more adult.

"There's only one thing we can do." His voice was weary, as if they'd been negotiating for days.

"What is that?"

"Well," he said, looking miserable and sounding forlorn, "I could ask you to marry me."

He was joking. No one would speak so casually of marriage. He might as well have said, Oh, this chair's not comfortable. I'll have to move and sit on that one. Slow, stony hatred began to build inside her. "That isn't fair. Or funny. You want me to jump with joy and then you'll double over, laughing at me. I hate you for joking about that."

He looked confused. "Joking? I'm not joking."

She remained solemn and angry, waiting out any preamble to a burst of laughter. "If you're not joking, how can you speak of marriage so lightly?"

"What should I do? Bend down on my knees and weep? Nadia, marriage is not cataclysmic. It's simply a legality. Do you think people feel one whit more in love because of marriage? Quite the opposite. It often puts a dampening effect on ardor."

"Then why are you asking me?"

"Because I want you. Because I need you. Because you're the freshest thing that's come into my life in a long time." Her mouth eased a bit. The crease of suspicion on her forehead spread out. Perhaps he did mean it, after all. Only it would have been nice if he had said he loved her.

"Mama, I'm going to marry Victor."

"And I'm going to be Queen of England." Even so, Miriam dropped her favorite bowl. It was a large and sturdy one and had held her rising dough for twenty years.

Most of their important conversations had taken place like this, while Miriam was handling food, and the smell of whatever she was cooking always accompanied the memory of the event. Today she was making Easter cookies. It was a laborious effort because the dough wasn't easy to work, and it had to be filled and rerolled between the palms and formed into a circle and pinched together. All the plump, pale rings—at least a hundred of them—remarkably alike, were placed evenly on the baking sheet. Hours of work. "No, Mama, I mean it. He's asked me and I've accepted."

She stabbed viciously at the dough—now without a resting place—as if it blanketed all the evils in her life. She hadn't even looked up, and Nadia felt a gagging resentment rise in her throat. "Victor Madden. The man I work for. He's asked me to marry him and I've said yes. I'm going to do it, Mama. I love him." Her voice was thin and high.

The unique, paralyzing anger a parent feels toward the improper arrogance of her child licked through Miriam like a well-fed flame. Twice she let out a chilling laugh. "You foolish girl." She shook her head and laughed again and then put the dough down and slapped her daughter across one cheek and then the other. "Don't you dare speak like that to me. Don't you dare tell me so brazenly what you and some foreigner have decided."

Nadia was trying not to cry. "I've accepted and we're going to be married. I mean it." At that moment, she sounded so childish it was almost laughable.

"You mean what? You mean nothing, you silly girl," Miriam hissed. She picked up the largest shard of the broken bowl and smashed it down to the floor again. "You silly, silly girl."

"Nadeem, don't let her go back there. We don't have to send her back to him. Forbid her to leave the house."

"If I forbid her, she'll leave before I finish speaking, then our worries will begin."

"It'll keep her away from him."

"She'll find other ways of meeting him. We can't lock her up."

"Since when can't a parent control a child? We can forbid her. We can act as parents."

"I was thinking we could meet the man. He's not going to harm her. He's a government official and can't afford a scandal. I would think she's quite safe. If we don't go against her, perhaps the idea will die by itself."

At that moment, she hated Nadeem. She hated his patience and that unquestioning love that made Nadia so able to manipulate him. "She isn't yours," she wanted to scream at him. Instead, she said, "The idea will not die of itself, you fool. She'll never go back on her decision, even if she grows to detest him. This is a man who has already discarded one woman and he'll discard Nadia, too. He's a philanderer. He'll ruin her life, and I'll remember that you let it happen."

His bad eye turned so cloudy that she was afraid he was having a stroke, as Father Leclere had done while giving Communion. She wasn't repentant. "I would like to hurt you," she said viciously. "I would like to gouge out the other eye." Then she walked away, blinded by tears that flooded her eyes but wouldn't fall.

She wouldn't speak to Nadia or look at her except to ask, "Have you come to your senses?" Even as she said it, she knew her tactics would bring the worst results but she was powerless to stop herself. "He's a divorced man. You're throwing away everything. *Everything!* And you know what? He'll throw you away. Yes, he will tire of you and throw you away." Nadia, her back straight and her eyes cold, never answered.

Mindlessly, Miriam even tried to talk to Max. To ask for his intervention in whatever world he existed. "Oh, Max, I can't lose another child. I can't."

25

·········

Miss Nadia marry Englishman.

He returned from London in late May on the *Rothenberg*, a coal-burning cargo ship of the German Lloyd line carrying twenty-eight passengers. They landed at Jaffa on a brilliantly sunny day, which was balm to him after nine months of British weather. Once ashore, he breathed in that special, scented air, happy to be back in his homeland. On the other side of the customs station, Muffi was waiting with the Hispana-Suiza.

"Your father don't want we wait for luggage," he said apologetically. "Bring you right home and get everything tomorrow."

"But you'll have to make the tiresome trip again. I don't mind waiting," said Samir.

"Not tiresome," said Muffi. "Driving is exciting. I love it."

"Very well," Samir smiled. "I won't rob you of the opportunity. Let's leave quickly, the baggage may come down too soon."

They drove out of the city with the delicate fragrance of orange blossoms wafting through the car. "How is everyone?" Samir asked casually. He wanted to hear any news of Nadia, which was silly because Muffi knew little about her. It was just a childish desire to discuss her. The possibility of seeing her brought back his desire with intensity. But then a very strange thing happened.

"Everyone satisfied. The grape crop very good this year." Muffi spoke in the stilted cadence of a country man trying to imitate the British, yet leaving out the occasional verb or article. "Your nephew Ambrose is growing very cute." They left the plain and began the ascent to the hill country, feeling the change to the drier air. Muffi was silent but he kept grunting, as if mulling over any tidbit of news that would entertain Samir. "The whole family is discussing situation that is unexpected and this has to do with Miss Nadia."

"And what situation is that?" Samir was uneasy. As if Muffi had read his mind and were playing to it.

"Miss Nadia soon marry Englishman." With this, Muffi turned to glance at Samir and enjoy the reaction to this special news. "Family very puzzled. Upset."

Samir moved to the edge of the seat and almost made Muffi stop the car. Surely he had the wrong information. How could Nadia marry an Englishman. What Englishman? "You must have the wrong information. That sounds like mischievous gossip." There was a thud in his chest and he felt betrayed.

"It's true," said Muffi with a weary grunt, as if he too was undone by the news.

"But her father will forbid it."

"*La!* No. Her father allow it."

He sat in silence the rest of the ride, his mind filled with chaotic scenarios of Nadia and her unknown Englishman to whom he gave the face of Leslie Howard, having just seen him in a film. After all these months, his heart still churned at the thought of her. And the thought of her with another man destroyed his peace of mind. He composed himself enough to speak. "Who is this Englishman?"

"Divorced," said Muffi in his economical pattern. "Too old," he added. "His daughter friend of Miss Nadia at the school."

Again the information brought Samir to the edge of his seat. "She's marrying Margaret's father?" Even as surprise made his voice rise, the news seemed inevitable. Hadn't he seen it coming from the very beginning, that first night in the school's foyer? Perhaps he could stop her.

"Don't know name," said Muffi. "He tall man. Work for government. Miss Nadia she work there, too."

"It's wrong," Samir said vehemently. "Very wrong!"

Muffi grinned, delighted to be the bearer of such provocative news. "She should marry own kind, you think? Cousin."

"It doesn't have to be a cousin," he said crossly. His aversion to marriage between close relatives was stronger since he had lived in London and realized it was such a taboo. Genetically it was unsound and now, in his mood, Muffi's rote pronouncement annoyed him more.

"Muffi, don't go straight home. Stop in Jerusalem. You can use a coffee, I'm sure, and I have an errand."

When they approached Jaffa Gate, he became impatient with the car and asked to be let out. He walked to the Mandate Government Headquarters. "Miss Nadia Mishwe, please."

The girl at the desk reacted to the handsome young man in the beautifully cut suit by fluttering her eyes. "Who shall I say is calling?"

"Is she here?" He hadn't expected to find her so easily.

"On the second floor, in the back. Shall I call her down?"

"No, thank you." He took the steps methodically, one at a time, as if each step confirmed his good sense. He would have a talk with Nadia and the sooner the better. Once he got home, there would be little time. But right now he could convince her of her folly. After all, he was of her own generation. She would listen to him. In the heat of his determination, it never occurred to him that he was acting presumptuously.

"Samir!" She was shocked to see him. "I thought you were in London."

"I just landed today. I haven't been home yet." She was wearing a mauve voile dress with a white organdy collar. Her hair was loose, spread all around her face—a beautiful, dark copper cloud. She had penciled her brows—it was the fashion—to look older, no doubt, but it had the opposite effect and this evidence of her vulnerability evoked in him an overwhelming tenderness. She looked lovely and a phrase came to mind, "the bloom of a girl in love."

"And you stopped here? Why?"

"Muffi, who helps my father, came to drive me home and he told me your news. Can you come out for a few minutes and have a coffee?" It was a small office and he scoured the walls, imagining scenes of intimacy.

"I suppose." She looked uncertain and searched his face for his true purpose. "Not too long, though. I have to transcribe these four pages for Victor before five."

Did she briefly caress the paper? There was a look about her, a new confidence but also a softness, that totally transformed her. Was it the fact that she loved someone else that made her so desirable? She exuded a womanliness that was palpable. He felt its potency in that close space. It was in her eyes and in the way she held her body and especially in her lovely mouth.

He led her outside, conscious of his hand on her arm, happy to be out of that small room, and they walked together to Jaffa Road to the Hotel Fast.

"Would you like lunch?" he asked when they were seated.

She was trying to read his intentions and she had a wary look. "Just a coffee." When he had given the order and they were alone, he leaned forward with his eyes focused on her. "How was London?" she smiled nervously.

"You can't be serious. You're not going to marry Victor Madden."

"Oh," her eyes turned hostile, "so that's what this is all about. Who sent you?"

"No one sent me. I haven't even been home yet. But I couldn't just stand by and let you do something so foolish."

Her face reddened with indignation. "*You* have decided it's foolish? You don't even know Victor."

"He's a divorced man twice your age."

"Oh." Her lips held the small round *o* shape. "I have never thought of it that way, but I'm not shocked. Those are just words and they don't really portray him." Now she looked at him with uneasy understanding. "You haven't been home for months and you stopped here on the way from the boat to talk to me? You must think I'm a fool if you thought you could change my mind in a few minutes." Her eyes became hard and cold. "And don't pretend to be so shocked over the age difference. I've seen too many girls in our family sold off . . . yes, sold to men twice their age . . . but with a big difference. They were strangers. I know Victor. And . . ."—she lowered her eyes shyly—"he's everything I want."

"Nadia, I'm not judging him because of his age. But he's from a different culture. He knows nothing of what you're made of. What's important to you. What you expect from marriage."

She laughed. A short stingy laugh. "And you know what's important to me?"

"Yes. Probably better than he."

"I have to go now," she said, rising, and momentarily she put aside her anger, "I'm sorry you wasted your time. You must be tired and your father must be eager to see you. How was the university?"

"The university was fine," he said thoughtfully, his mind was not on the university. "I have to wait for the results of a paper on logic. Other than that, I'm finished for the semester."

"Do you feel finished?" Her brow was furrowed, as if she really wanted his answer. "What I mean is, are you getting your fine classical education and are you a man of the world now?" Her tone was sarcastic. "Coming to discipline the country girl?"

"I don't know if I'm a man of the world. I feel quite helpless right now. You're making a terrible mistake, Nadia. I wish I could make you see it."

"I really must leave. I hope you'll come to my wedding." She walked out and left him there. And after a few minutes, he sighed and went to meet Muffi feeling more desolate than before.

For two days, he prowled about the household, fidgety and withdrawn. He had a lot of business papers to look through, but he found it difficult to concentrate. His father had become considerably weaker, but he still struggled every day to participate in his affairs.

Samir was taking a walk through the village and came to the street where Nadia's parents lived. It seemed quite natural to go and speak to them, and he wondered why he hadn't thought of it before.

He found his Aunt Miriam in the garden, patiently cultivating the soil around the vegetables, murmuring to herself. At first he thought she might be praying and felt embarrassed. She had always had an air of mystery and, of all people, made him feel shy. Her beautiful eyes seemed to see right into his heart.

"My father said vegetables grow better if you think well of them as you cultivate. I'm talking to them, but you mustn't think I've lost my mind."

"Your father must have been a wonderful man," he said with feeling. "My father talks about him often."

"Yes, he was." She straightened and started to walk toward the house. "I'm so glad you came to see me. You're a wonderful sight. Would you like a glass of lemonade?"

"No, *amti,* I'd like to talk outside." He was surprised that she could be so calm, considering what her daughter was about to do. "Are you pleased about this marriage?"

Her shoulders slumped. "I could accept anyone she chose if I thought it would bring her happiness."

"And you think Victor Madden can bring her happiness?"

"No." She looked at him shrewdly. "Nadia's always been headstrong. She'll go through with this and it will ruin her life." Her expression changed and she became agitated. "We can't lock her up. She's threatened to leave with him for England." Her eyes were filled with frustration. "Why couldn't it have happened some other way. If you and she . . . You had a great deal in common." She ran her hands down her skirt. "You were the two special children."

He had the queerest feeling, an intense desire to admit to his aunt and to himself. "I do love her," he said quietly. "I love Nadia."

She looked stunned. "Why didn't you say something? This is such a tragedy. Have you told her you love her? Maybe that would make a difference."

"I can't tell her." Now the pain was in his eyes. "I can't in good conscience marry my second cousin. There's too much potential for physical problems and mental ones, too. I know it's done, but I can't do it."

Miriam turned her back on him and walked a few yards to a small copse of trees where it was cooler. He waited a few minutes and followed her. "I'm sorry," he said softly. "I've only just become aware of how much I care for her. It's my misfortune, too, you know."

When Miriam turned around she appeared slightly dazed. "Nadia isn't your blood relative," she said in an echoing whisper. "Your uncle isn't her father. If that's what's holding you back, don't consider it a barrier. Only, please, you musn't tell anyone. It would hurt too many people. I'm telling you now because I don't want Nadia to ruin her life."

He was deeply embarrassed, as if her revelation was too intimate, but then he felt elated.

She looked at the near hills dotted with the yellow heads of the wheat almost ready for harvest. "Her father's dead now. He was a German doctor who practiced in Jerusalem before and after the war. He was a dedicated surgeon, vigorous, the son of a doctor. He loved Nadia, although I never told him outright that she was his. I'm sure he guessed. He sent her the horses."

Samir shook his head. "That's where the obsession with horses comes from. And the coloring. And the stubbornness." He grimaced. "You and Uncle Nadeem seem so devoted."

"That has nothing to do with it," she said tersely. The set of her shoulders and her voice told him that, despite her revelation, she was still his aunt and in no way subject to his judgment. She put her hands on her hips. "What are we going to do?"

The basic facts had not changed. "Nadia loves him, not me. What can we do?"

Her eyes became hard. Her jaw was set with determination and she stared at him, offering a challenge. "I lost a child—a beautiful boy— during the war. It was one of those devastating things. He was well one day and dead a few days later." She blinked rapidly but two tears escaped down her cheeks. "I can't bear losing another child. If Nadia marries this man, I'll lose her. He'll take her away and later—probably quite soon— he'll tire of the responsibility of marriage and make her miserable. However, Nadia will stick by him forever and suffer silently. He's a weak individual without a sense of duty or honor. Samir, you must help me."

"How can I help you?" He looked perplexed.

"There is one way," she said fiercely. "We can still win one way."

Victor Madden had a suite of rooms on the third floor of the large house off the Street of the Chain, behind the Khalidi Library. A pair of French doors allowed him a spectacular view to the east to the Temple Mount.

They were charming quarters and Samir thought, well, the man has taste and finesse. For the first time, he felt trepidation over what he was attempting.

He took a deep breath, climbed the steps that ran along the outside of the house, and raising the heavy brass bit knocker allowed it to fall forcefully against the lion's lips.

Victor Madden was at least three inches taller than himself. He smiled before he spoke and before he knew who Samir might be. "Are you looking for me?" he asked, politely.

"Yes. I'm Nadia's cousin. Samir Saleh." He held out his hand, briefly. "May I come in?"

"Of course." He lifted one eyebrow and smiled ruefully. "I'm sure Nadia will be pulling out new relatives for years to come. But I must say, you don't resemble the rest. Your accent is different. Please sit down. Would you like a brandy or something? You must live abroad."

Samir remained standing. Everything he had been prepared to say sounded pompous and overblown in the presence of this convivial, sophisticated man. Finally, while Madden fiddled with a bottle and glasses, he got it out. "I'm here to persuade you not to marry my cousin." To his surprise, Victor Madden neither turned around nor stopped what he was doing. "Here we are." He set down a crystal decanter and two glasses. "Please, sit down. Over there, that's the most comfortable chair."

"She's not prepared to cope with your way of life. Not that she isn't strong-minded and capable, but Nadia's strength comes from rebellion. She needs to prove something."

Victor took a long sip of his drink. "You think she's marrying me to prove something?"

"Exactly. I don't doubt that she's infatuated, but deep down, it's your total difference that really makes you so attractive to her."

"Well now, that doesn't say much for me, does it? Or for her. It makes us out a couple of misguided fools." His tone was more amused than bitter.

Samir was silent, then he said softly, "I've no doubt that you love her, but I'm not sure you'd love what she'd become if you took her away from here. She'd become dependent and insecure. She's only a young girl. Deep inside she's been shaped by our values. That peculiar English brittleness toward everything sentimental would confuse her. She would make the fatal mistake of loving you too well, while you would love her only superficially."

This time Victor was silent and at a loss. "Touché," he whispered. "Touché."

She had left the Hotel Fast fighting back tears and almost running to her office. He had thought she was a spineless idiot to be easily persuaded. With each step, another more incriminating aspect of his behavior hit her and by the time she reached her office hot angry tears were streaming down her cheek. She regretted having gone with him at all, but—and for this she had only herself to blame—she had been so happy to see him. She had been waiting to share her news with him and seek his special approval.

When he had appeared at her desk, her heart had leapt. He was such a magnificent sight and—this knowledge hurt most of all—she was not immune to the most powerful man of the clan. Now she felt like such a fool.

He hadn't come out of friendship, because he had missed her. He had come out of arrogance and conceit. He was going to single-handedly bring her to her senses. It was so humiliating, implying her needs and desires were of no consequence at all. Only his will mattered. Only *he* had the power to decide her fate. Oh, God! She couldn't stop crying. She would never change her mind. Never! Finally, her tears diminished and she turned back to the pages on her desk that she had to transcribe. In two weeks this would all be over. She would be beyond Samir Saleh and his power to hurt her.

A few days later she told her mother she had changed her mind. She wanted the smallest wedding possible. There had been no proper bethrothal because of the circumstances. Victor had simply asked Nadeem for her hand and, when it was granted, he had opened a bottle of champagne and poured a glass for all present. It was civilized but simple, with none of the excess of feasting and elaborate sword dancing and suggestive songs. No troupe of triumphant relatives carried her trousseau up the Jerusalem Road. She and Victor had together picked out a few pieces of jewelry, including a wide gold band. Nadeem had written to his old friend M. Freneau for a trousseau and it had arrived through the mail. There was no showy red-striped Bethlehem wedding gown and gay jacket. A local seamstress made a dress from a design Nadia picked from a magazine. It was high-necked, silk taffeta, buttoning down the back and ending in a bell skirt that came to her ankles. The headdress was a simple tiara with a short net veil. It was only at the last minute that her mother asked her for some small token of tradition. "Please, Nadia," she pleaded after her daughter was dressed, "wear my veil. The tiara and net are so different from anything we're used to. My face was covered entirely. No one saw me and I saw no one until after the ceremony. I haven't asked much of you, but it won't hurt to have this small bit of tradition."

Nadia felt such a pang of conscience. She had not allowed her mother any of the usual satisfactions connected with a wedding. "Of course, Mama," she said in a soft voice.

She asked Aunt Zareefa's older girl, Rheema, who was happily married to be her matron of honor, and Victor was bringing a colleague from the office. There was a moment that morning when she felt that all the details were getting away from her and she had felt peculiar, as if she didn't quite believe that she and Victor would be together that very night.

At the last moment, her father brought Gala to take her to the church. The horse was so old that he walked slowly. "You don't have to do it," he shrugged and looked sheepish. Her dress was not meant for sitting atop a horse, but he had seen it done this way all his life.

"You'll have to lift me up to him," she said, smiling down at her father, "and lead him very slowly."

So in the end, she began her marriage in the age-old tradition, atop a horse, a sword in her hand. When she entered the Roman Catholic Church of the Holy Family, the oldest church in the village where once the donkeys had roamed at will during the ceremonies, she wore a heavily embroidered veil that covered her face entirely, as a favor to her mother.

At the entrance to the church, she felt her bridegroom take her by the elbow and lead her to the altar. From beneath the veil the smell of jasmine and oleander drifted up and she took a deep breath and relaxed. She felt a thrill of adventure and squeezed the hand that held hers and felt the reassuring pressure returned. She was so glad it would all end now and she could begin her life. She heard the priests entering the church and smelled the contents of the censer, which preceeded them and was swung by the altar boy. The ritual began, Scripture was read, partly in Latin and partly in Arabic. And finally, there came that moment when rings that had been touched to the head and lips of the groom and slipped momentarily beneath Nadia's veil were placed on their hands and then changed about. Flower wreaths were placed on their heads. The Bible was brought down between them, dividing their joined fingers. Then the priests led the bridal party in a march around the church with all the guests following. There was nothing left but for the priest to make the final pronouncement: "You are wedded until death do you part in the eyes of God and this Church and man. Those whom God has joined together, let no man pull asunder. Go, and may God be with you."

A gun was fired outside the church and Nadia, startled at this unexpected report, threw back her veil in alarm. The church was totally still. The first face she saw was that of the man in whose fingers her hand was entwined. It was Samir. She cried out. *"You!* Where's Victor?" She ran toward the door, stopping before her mother and father. "What have you done with Victor? Oh, no. No, no, no!" She finally understood and began to shake. "Mama, you did this to me? Where is Victor? Mama!"

Miriam looked away and spoke in a leaden voice. "He sailed yesterday for England."

"For England? What did you tell him? What did you do? Mama,"—she shrieked and the sound echoed back in the stone church—"it's not true." She was gagging with pent-up sobs. *"Baba,* is it true?" Nadeem nodded, looking so grieved she almost embraced him. Instead, she took the veil which she still had in her hand and threw it to the floor in front of her mother. "Here is your veil!" She stomped on it with her foot. "I don't want to see you. *Any of you!"* She picked up her skirts and ran out, mounted

Gala, and rode toward home. There was a little valise that she had packed to bring with her to the hotel and she picked it up and remounted. It was strange but, through it all, she knew precisely where she would go. There was only one place to go.

She would go to the country cottage at the orchards. No one would be there, for the harvest was still a month away. She would be able to think there. She would be able to ride and think and plan her escape. Not for a moment did she stop to remember that the place of refuge she so eagerly sought belonged to her new husband.

My dear,

The pain of what you see as a callous rejection will blind your understanding of what I'm about to say. But I've really acted in your best interest. My darling girl, I wouldn't have brought you happiness.

By nature I'm a man who walks easiest without attachments. This dashing, cheerful fellow, when held down by another's needs, turns moody, sarcastic, cold, and, ultimately, mean-spirited. I deluded myself into thinking that you were young enough to be independent and resourceful. We would each go our own way, I thought, and come together when it suits us. But in my heart, I know this would prove untrue. I was using you as insurance to outwit the loneliness that hits us dashing fellows of a certain age. *That* was callous.

You deserve a full life, with children and an adoring husband who will be devoted to your happiness. You deserve your family and friends and culture to give you strength and support. In time, after our return to England, you would have felt cheated and displaced. It would have been a lonely household, for, although we never discussed it, I doubt that I could reconcile myself to beginning another family.

You are a woman of depth and passion and dignity. Please find it in your heart to forgive your devoted friend,

Victor

She tore the letter into tiny pieces and rode out beyond the scrub to the barren desert. There, still atop her horse, she picked out each bit of paper out of her pocket until all of the hateful letter was scattered to the wind. She had given herself to a man who had thought of her as no more than a convenience.

Once rid of the letter, she lifted her shoulders. "No more tears for Victor Madden," she said aloud. On her way back to the cottage, she stopped at the small paddock where several foals, no more than six months old, were cavorting. "They're so young," she said to the trainer.

"Yes, madam. Some are still babies but, still, they've got work to do. In this paddock, they develop their shoulder muscles." He smiled. "My name is Farid."

"Hello. What happens when they're no longer babies?"

"The older ones go into the rectangular paddock twice a day to try and outrace the gazelles. They learn what competition is all about. They build up their quarters and hocks."

"Do they all make it?"

"Oh, yes. Out of this stock, yes. Some are stronger than others, but by eighteen months they're ready to be saddled.

"Could I help you? Could I work with them?"

"Of course, madam," he said respectfully. She was puzzled by his deference. No one had ever called her 'madam.' It wasn't until she was tucked in bed that night that it hit her. She *was* the madam. She was Madam Saleh, mistress of everything. All these splendid animals belonged to her.

Farid patiently answered all her questions, frankly surprised and gratified that a woman took an interest in his work. Nadia spent all of the mornings and most of the afternoons grooming and exercising the horses. She stroked them and talked to them and cheered when they outran the gazelles. The rest of the time she rode all around the property, past the orchards and olive groves, eastward. There was a transition area where the cultivated land merged with the land of the bedouin farmers who were the bridge between the town and the desert. The Sheik had not been ashamed of cooperating with his neighbors and was in partnership with them in the horsebreeding business.

The Salehs had large herds that they grazed farther and farther afield as the grass grew scarce. Occasionally, while riding, Nadia came upon a lone shepherd and, once, a shepherdess, who seemed so young that she offered to take her home but the girl smiled with embarrassment. "No madam, I must stay with the herd."

"But where do you sleep? How do you eat?"

"In the tent." She pointed to a piece of canvas draped over four poles. "There are dates in my pack and hard cheese. I have a goat for milk and bake bread here every day." She dragged out a piece of sheet metal and placed it over some rocks sitting in a pile of ashes. She was proud of her resourcefulness; no one had ever been interested in how she managed.

"Suppose a wild animal comes?" Nadia wasn't convinced of the girl's safety. How could she sleep at night knowing this waif was out in the wilderness, at the mercy of wolves and foxes. It was a totally desolate area.

"My dogs warn me."

"Wolves can rip the dogs apart."

"Oh, no. I kill them first."

"You shoot them?" Could this tiny girl handle a gun. Was it safe?

The girl laughed heartily. "No, madam. That would scatter the flock. I kill them with my lance and the knife."

"Oh, no! You don't mean it! Who put you here? It's not safe."

"Please, madam. It's very safe. I'm happy for the job. My brother had it, but he's too old now. Don't worry."

But she did worry. The girl looked so frail. And it was such a lonely spot. She couldn't have been more than thirteen or fourteen. She went back to the spot a week later, but all trace of the girl and her camp was gone and the area was picked clean of any green scrap.

She never returned to the cottage before late afternoon and ate gratefully from whatever simple dish of food was left by Mary Thomas, a part-time caretaker who lived at the bottom of the hill. After the hours of riding and fresh air Nadia sank into her bed at night too exhausted to think. Ultimately, she would have to face up to her life, but not yet. One day she stayed out later than usual and it was almost dusk when she entered the cottage. A violet sky gentled the light coming through the windows, making the room appear more comforting than it was.

Her skin, already rosy from the outdoors, was aglow from the heat of the ride, and her hair, sunbleached and unbound, fell exuberantly around her face and shoulders. Despite the healthy bronzed skin and bountiful mane, her gray eyes appeared vulnerable, as if trapped in an unfamiliar place. A thin cotton shirt was snug against her breasts and riding breeches outlined her hips. She had unbuttoned her shirt so that her long neck was visible and also the hollow below her neck that ended with her breasts. In the cool semi-shadows of the stone room, she looked beautiful.

Samir gripped the mantel against which he stood to keep from taking her in his arms. He hadn't bothered with the lamp.

When she saw him, she instinctively went toward the window. Did she think she could crawl out and escape? The silence was uncomfortable and her skin crawled. There was so much to say, and yet there was nothing to say. The question foremost in her mind . . . why had he done it? He had education, wealth, and good looks. He had been groomed to lead from infancy. Rasa Tabul or Jaqueline George would have gladly married him and they, like him, were prepared for such a marriage.

Her anger had dissipated during these two weeks, and she was left with a leaden resentment. "Why did you do it?" she finally asked.

He sat down, bending over his knees, with his hands dangling before him. The pose indicated the aftermath of an emotional struggle. "Not out of arrogance," he said. "It was nothing like that. One day—it must have been a few years ago—I caught a glimpse of you at a soccer game up in the stands. The sun had caught your hair at just a certain angle so that it seemed you were being singled out by heaven." He gave a short rueful laugh. "Something had your attention—it wasn't my brilliant playing—and you turned. There was a look of defiance on your face. I thought, why should a young girl feel defiant? Defiance means you're struggling against something that threatens your independence. I thought back to your parents, to Miss Smythe or someone else at school who could be trying to subdue you. Then I realized it went beyond that. You were defiant for some deep and personal reason that perhaps you didn't know yourself. That's when I fell in love with you." He hung his head and stared between his feet. "Of course, I didn't know it was love. I was intrigued, as a young man is intrigued, and, yes, mainly because you weren't paying attention to the game in which I was the star. The other girls were cheering each play, but I couldn't get anything out of you."

He went to stand at the mantle and she was grateful for the chance to study him without having to face him. She had expected anything but this. The silence was palpable and held them in place. He was wearing Western riding breeches and boots but on his head the traditional headgear. His face, framed by the kaffiyeh, was flushed, the dark brows prominent, the large eyes soft and earnest. His hands looked strong and capable, yet again made innocent by the leather watch strap of the student punctuating his wrist. She was surprised to find that she wanted to touch him, but then it came back to her that he had tricked her. He had willfully maneuvered her into a marriage without her consent. He was selfish, unfeeling, despotic. "Why have you come here," she asked derisively, "to claim your bride?"

"If you mean physically," he answered—and she was aware that his eyes swept over her body—"the answer is no. I don't want to force myself on you. You're welcome to stay here as long as you like. It's your home now. I've had them bring Rami, a fine gentle horse for you to ride and my mother has sent a girl to cook for you. She'll stay with Mary Thomas. I've rented a house on the old Jerusalem Road. It belonged to Mr. Maloof, remember? I'll be waiting there for you whenever you're ready to come." He took another long, unnerving look at her and then left promptly. She heard the sounds outside as he mounted and galloped away.

It was the talk of the town. Samir and his new bride were not living together. The week of festivities that followed even the most humble wedding never took place. The bride had ridden off on her horse. Poor Miriam.

Poor Nadeem to have to deal with such a girl. As for Samir, there was no explaining his behavior. Why such an exceptional man would have chosen such a troublesome and plain—yes, all in all, she was hardly beautiful— and ungrateful woman, no one knew. Perhaps she was pregnant. *Ya Allah,* that's what the English had done to the morals.

She stayed at the house for another week, riding Rami, the most comfortable mount she had ever had, a magnificent horse that seemed attuned to her in every way. She tried not to think of who had brought her this wonderful horse. She purposefully exhausted herself so as not to have to think of the inevitable.

One night though, she awoke and sat up. Her head was as clear as it had been in weeks. He had said he loved her. He had said, 'that was the day I knew I loved you.'

26

I was afraid of never being loved back.

She felt foolish knocking on the door of his house. She had waited until dark because he was more likely to be there, but she had no idea how he would greet her. Now that she wanted him, the thought that he loved her seemed remote. Maybe she should leave right now before he answered. To arrive at a strange house looking for your husband, with no idea of how it would end . . .

The door opened.

"Hello." Was that her voice?

"Hello." He was in shirtsleeves and the skin around his eyes was dusky. He was tired. His hair was tousled, as if he had run his hands through it a thousand times. He was sorry that he'd married her and was anguished over how, in God's name, he could get out of it. She trembled. "Are you cold?" he asked, but there was no emotion in his voice.

"No. I'm frightened."

"Frightened? Of what? Of me?"

"Not of you."

"Then of what?"

"I'm frightened that you don't want me anymore." Frankness might provoke that little teasing that would tell her he was on her side.

"Aah." He nodded his head up and down. "So that's it. Well, we could discuss it right here—if you still don't want to come in. Or you could come in."

His tone was lighthearted, thank God. "I'll come in. Thank you."

She had tried to look her best. She was wearing a straight navy skirt covered by a long wool sweater with a belt. In a fit of anxiety over how she could glamorize herself, she had cut the front of her hair and it now hung in curly bangs across her forehead. She had smeared every crazy thing around her eyes to make them look larger but had left her mouth naked. If they kissed and he tasted lipstick, he would know that she was trying to be more glamorous than she was.

"This is where you live?" She walked a few steps here and there but retained nothing of what she saw. "Charming . . ." It was a blur of half-timbered stucco. She had passed this house a hundred times without any premonition that it would be important in her life. How odd.

"Yeah." He rubbed his chin and then ran his hand through his hair again. "After being on my own in England, I couldn't seem to settle in at home. It was time I had a place of my own."

There was a deep silence that made her excrutiatingly aware of him in a new way. His blood seemed close to the surface of his skin, making it glow. If he would only put his arms around her and put an end to her anxiety, but that seemed so unlikely.

"Why would you think I don't want you anymore?"

Her mouth felt dry and she swallowed. "You look tired, for one thing."

"I could be tired for any number of reasons. Why would that necessarily mean I'm tired of you?"

"You look emotionally tired." What did that mean? God, stop me from talking nonsense. England had changed him. He seemed much more sophisticated than when he left, and she felt very provincial.

"Ah. If that theory makes sense, would the opposite also be true? You look marvelous. Does that mean you're not tired of me at all?"

The compliment stunned her. She looked to see how serious he was. To answer would be to betray her feelings before he had declared his. Well, hadn't she come to do exactly that? To tell him she'd decided to be his wife, after all.

She needed courage. She felt young and inexperienced. It was so difficult to slough off pretense and commit herself. There was a lifetime of vulnerability and only her obstinacy to protect her. He had always been held up as someone unattainable and she had been the poor relation. She wasn't even pretty. What fool in such a position would say I love you and I hope you love me back.

"It's hard for me to answer you, Samir. I'm not good at baring my heart." That was true enough and the strength of that statement helped her along.

"Who is?" he said somberly.

She was able to get control of her voice. "If I tell you I've decided to come back, you could say, 'it's too late, little lady. You had your chance.' Samir,"—she looked at her hands and fidgeted with a silly friendship ring, a gift from a girl whose name she couldn't remember—"I don't want to be alone anymore. I want to be here with you. I had to get over my resentment of what you did to Victor, but in the end . . ."—she looked up at him with wide, puzzled eyes—"Victor was so easily persuaded to leave me." She paused for the big statement to come. What a curious little house. Ridiculously, at that moment, she noticed that the room had extra angles. "I also have to face the fact that probably"—it was so difficult to say these things—"I loved you long before you considered loving me." The room was so quiet, the words exploded in her ears. "You can understand. I was afraid of never being loved back." Oh! What a thing to say.

He was just staring. What did that mean? A damp breeze made the hairs on her arms move. Why did his eyes look as if pain were just beneath the surface? "Samir?" She went and put her arms around his waist, feeling, with a shiver of surprise, the solid back. A warmth that included the comforting smell of his cotton shirt enveloped her. He brought his hands up and pushed back her new bangs to see more of her face. He gave her a thorough, penetrating look and placed his mouth over hers. Her will snapped in two, pathetically brittle against an onslaught of relief and exhilaration.

They kissed like lovers who have been separated by tragic events. His lips parted and she had her first taste of her new husband. He took a quick, hungry tour of her mouth and then, as if wary of frightening her, stepped back. Her hand caressed his bare, warm neck, and that small proof of her right to him filled her with hope. She pulled away and looked at him. "Is it going to be all right?"

"You're my wife," he said, as if she'd forgotten. He put his hands in his pockets and looked down at his shoe. "I'm deeply sorry for the way we got married. I thought you were making a mistake with Victor. Even so, I was sorry the moment it was done." She shrugged. She wouldn't say it was all right. She wouldn't say anything. "You shouldn't blame your mother," he added. She shrugged again. She had blamed him primarily, but now she was certain it was all her mother, and a remote anger had to be tucked away. He waited, then said, "I was going to bed when you came. But perhaps you're hungry."

"No. Please go to bed. She hadn't even thought. Things were moving too fast. She felt tall and gangly and unable to move or say anything graceful. He was going to have to handle everything, but he looked uncomfortable, too.

"Aren't you tired?" he asked.

"No. Yes. A little."

"The bed is big enough for both of us."

"Is it?"

He pointed to the other room. "I sleep in there." She let him lead her into a small bedroom with the same odd angles. The bed was for two, and she wondered if the size was an accident or had he expected her to come to him all along. She walked as far away from him as the room allowed.

"Are you frightened?"

"Should I be?"

"No."

"Why not?"

He thought a moment. "No one's ever died of it."

She smiled. "That's good."

"I won't rush you."

"I know."

"I'm glad you're here."

"Me, too." She didn't sound convinced and her eyes darted around the room, as if looking for a way to escape.

"I'll put the light out," he said gallantly.

"It's all right." She sat down on the bed facing a wall with a washstand. She heard him undressing in the dark. His shoes. He stood up. His trousers and shirt. Everything. She felt the bed move and heard the springs creak. He was waiting for her. "Don't worry," she said. "I won't disappoint you." She still didn't move. That moment, if she could have received a wish, it would have been to be beautiful. Then she could accept his passion gracefully. She wanted him to be awed by her beauty and to desire her to madness. She wanted to ask him if he loved her, but she said, "Here we are," as if summing up an exhausting journey.

He moved across the bed and she felt his breath on her neck and his hands on the buttons of her sweater. He undressed her with deliberateness —as if now that she was in his care, he would do everything for her—and placed her in the center of his bed. He found her lean, taut body staggeringly sensual. Long legs and hard, smooth thighs, beautiful, broad, sculpted shoulders and such a flat, wide midriff that her breasts rose up as a sumptuous surprise. "Look at you . . . so beautiful . . . ."

"I've never thought of myself as beautiful," she said.

"You are to me." First he lay alongside her and then he raised himself up and kissed her.

"I was just wishing I were more beautiful." She spoke into his lips.

"Shhh."

He traced the outline of her body and then began again more seriously from shoulders to breasts to the center of her belly. She kept absolutely still, until he smoothed back her thighs in an effort to widen the space between her legs. Then she tried to sit up. "Shhh. Don't worry." He held her down with kisses. "It might hurt," he said as he eased himself inside. At this point, a sound escaped his lips that made her totally alert. He said something like "ooh" or "aah," a moan that at first she mistook for disappointment and then realized was an irrepressible sigh of pleasure, which meant he was thrilled to be in this incredibly awkward position. She was embarrassed to be listening, but the sounds had a curious effect on her own nervous system. Little electric currents ran through her body each time he moaned, and she found herself raising her hips to meet him. For the first time she believed that he might really love her.

Then, as if a warning light had gone on in his head, he stopped all sound and movement. Right away she knew what had stopped him. He was wondering if she were a virgin. She held her breath, waiting for him to continue, but the drama of what might have been kept raking through her mind. What if Victor hadn't held back? What if Samir found that another man had been there first? Would he get up and leave her there and never return? Suppose something was wrong that wasn't even her fault? She heard him sigh when he broke through, but this time the sigh made her wary. Was it passion or relief? He went deeper and deeper inside her. Oh! She could feel him and she wanted to squeeze herself around him, holding him inside until . . . "Samir . . . stay still . . . for God's sake. Stay!" Good God. She had been pushed into talking about it.

"It took a lot," he said to the air. He spoke and exhaled at the same time, which made it sound as if he were just out of a crisis. She knew what he meant. It *had* taken a lot to bring them to this bed. It remained to be seen if he would find it worthwhile.

She fell deeply in love—that old knocking behind the ribs and breathless surprise—after she began living with Samir. He was tolerant and thoughtful, traits she hadn't expected from a man who had been the center of attention all of his life.

The miracle was, they were uncannily alike. Both preferred to be out-of-doors, even in bad weather, over anything else. They still read difficult classics, like students preparing for placement exams. He liked to tease her over the way she held the book up to her nose and sat favoring one haunch, as if still sentenced to the cramped prison of the Friends' middle-school desks. "Too vain to get glasses?"

"My eyes are perfect."

She teased him about his wardrobe—actually she was awed by the quality and quantity of his clothes, which far outnumbered hers. She was stunned by the revelation that his mother had had a dressmaker's dummy made to his adult measurements and it was stored at a London haberdashery, where they could make up anything from underwear to three-piece suits and have them fit perfectly.

Her cooking was awful but he considered that amusing and hired Mary Thomas's daughter to prepare the main meal. "You'll be doing her a favor," he told Nadia. "She wants to repay me because her mother lives on one of the farm cottages rent-free."

"What will I do?"

"Mrs. Smythe told me the girls' tennis team needs a coach. And they can always use an extra pair of hands in the science laboratory."

There was a more visceral side to the relationship. Nadia was so tempted by sex that, often, it took over her will. Some days, whatever touched her body—her underpants, her brassiere, the edge of a table innocently meeting her crotch—aroused her. Riding a horse made her so wildly excited she rubbed herself against the animal until she came. During lovemaking, she wasn't above maneuvering her body or grabbing him to satisfy a greedy, throbbing spot. She would have died if Samir commented on her style because when she wasn't aroused, she was chagrined. She would catch him smiling down at her, as if he were amused by a charming weakness. He never said, 'Wow, I didn't expect you to be so *hungry.'* Yet that's what it felt like. Hunger.

After lovemaking, they liked to relive their shared past while sprawled on their bed. "Remember the time . . ." he would begin and then they vied to recall schoolday catastrophes. The day they had gone to Jerusalem with Mr. Knudsen to see *Henry V* and Hanna Taban had dropped his camera from the balcony, hitting a woman below and knocking her out. The spring Margaret mistook a can of potpourri for Darjeeling tea and served it to the British Chief Secretary, who was judging the English speaking contests. The afternoon that Pudgy Watson had slipped on the slick soles of his new shoes, unwillingly skating into the headmaster's wife from St. Luke's School in Haifa, who was visiting. "She went down like a bird," said Samir, laughing so hard it sounded like choking. He seemed so young to her, rolling helplessly on the bed.

"Did you really hate me all that time?" he asked.

"You did everything right and that annoyed me. Everything about you was better than anyone else. You had a wristwatch that I coveted for two years. It had a round gold case and Roman numerals and a tan strap."

"I'll give it to you now," he offered sheepishly. "It's around somewhere."

She ignored him and waved her hand in the air. "It wasn't the watch but what the watch stood for. You were so poised. You had perfected a cold, disinterested stare that absolutely paralyzed me."

"No. It wasn't cold. Cool, maybe. But never toward you."

"Perhaps. But fear that I might provoke that arctic blast kept me from wanting to get anywhere near you. I didn't want to be one of the pack, hoping to get my ration of glances." Those remembered feelings were still very real. "I wanted you to be delirious over me alone."

"I was glancing at you all the time and got scowls in return. I didn't know what to make of you, but it's true what they say about playing hard to get. I was intrigued."

"And now that I'm yours? Are you still intrigued?" She wouldn't have believed that she'd ask such a dumb question. Love had undermined her good sense.

"I think so," he teased and smiled but when he saw concern in her eyes, he amended it. "Don't worry. I'm delirious over you alone."

"Oh, Samir."

Each morning, he met the egg woman and the fruit and milk sellers, squeezed and scrutinized each selection and brought it inside for his wife. He was proud to make the coffee. "I learned how to do it in England over a sterno can. Now I'm an expert," he would say, shaking the pot skillfully at the moment it threatened to boil over.

If he had been practical, Samir would have had his office in Jerusalem along with the exporters who bought his figs, raisins, and olive oil. But his father had conducted business in the heart of the village and he did the same. He liked walking through streets where almost every stone was familiar and greeting people he had known all of his life. When he took his place as the newest member of the village Council, it seemed that all the pieces for the life that was planned for him were in place.

He went dutifully to the office on Hilo Road every morning—he would have preferred to scoot up to the farm in his Singer coupé and poke around the vineyards or watch the new foals race the gazelles to develop their hindquarters. Saturday mornings were reserved for a soccer game with old schoolmates. They called themselves the Lions and wore green and silver uniforms. When he returned home, his face bathed in dampness, his eyes bright, his legs boyishly innocent in the soccer shorts, Nadia's heart would shift and knock furiously. How could she have known she would love him so?

The Children's Care Society was the most popular organization for young matrons with time on their hands. The goal was to fill empty little stomachs with a hot noonday meal and bundle underprivileged bodies in warm clothing before sending them back to the classroom. It was everything that made a woman's heart tremble. It was *edifying!*

Righteously fatigued, their skins glowing from the steam of the dishwater, the women gossiped with earned satisfaction. Nadia Saleh's new living arrangements created all sorts of puzzlements.

Matron Number One: "Why? Why did he marry her? Why did he wait for her? Why is he so happy she's finally deigned to live with him? Why does he treat her as if she's done him a favor?"

Matron Number Two: "Because. It's obvious why he married her and why he's decided to be a devoted husband. Why he coddles her and why she behaves as if she's entitled."

"It's not obvious to me. She's interested not one but two sophisticated men. How? What does she have that's so compelling?"

"I've thought about it a long time and now it makes perfect sense. She and Samir had the same education so they can talk to each other. That's one thing. She's one of the family but not too close, so that's a plus. She knows how to eat with a knife and fork and serve tea and all that, so she won't embarrass him. But the number-one overall prime motive is that he considers Nadia an excellent investment. Like his farm or the hotel or the groves."

"What are you talking about?"

"Samir has invested in Nadia's childbearing potential. He wants a baby factory for strong boys with fair skin, hazel eyes, and the height that the Saleh family lacks. *That's* what makes that marriage make sense. If he wants to continue his line, Samir had to get himself a bonus breeder."

In 1931, while Samir and Nadia adjusted to married life, the village adjusted to being discovered as a summer refuge by tourists seeking to escape the paralyzing heat and humidity of the lowlands. Investors created a Resort Corporation that widened and repaired the remaining dark, narrow streets and opened new roads. Older mud houses were demolished and springs reactivated. Three hotels sprang up, a grand outdoor restaurant, plus a row of boutiques selling such items as suede ankle-strap shoes from Italy and French bathing suits.

As always when he saw building activity, Nadeem became restless. "I'm going to renovate the property in Jerusalem," he told his wife. "I can get two good-sized apartments in each wing, up and down, and while I'm at it, I'll electrify and install indoor plumbing." Miriam shrugged, which he chose to interpret as approval. "I'll repave the courtyard, might as well, so cars can drive in." She gave him a sly look. "You don't think it's a good idea?" he asked.

"I didn't say that."

"Why the look?"

"Because you won't stop at that. You'll find something else to do to those houses. And something else after that."

"No, no," he said. "That's it. But I'm also thinking we could open the linen shop again. Right here in town." Mention of the shop brought back powerful images. It was like a rude punch to her chest to be reminded of those days so suddenly, and her face must have shown it because Nadeem looked stricken. "You're thinking of when I came back from the war," he said softly. "My eye . . ." His hand went up to cover the right side of his face.

She was thinking of Max. She sighed and shook her head. "Who's going to buy such fine things?"

"There are a lot of people walking around with money in their pockets and nothing to do all day but spend it."

"And you think they'll want to spend it on bedsheets? You think Muslims from Jaffa know enough to sleep on French percale?"

"Yes. They're on vacation. They have the time to shop and the inclination to be lavish. Would you be willing to help me? Just during the busy hours, of course."

"What else do I have to do with my time?" she said, and her voice was melancholy. "It isn't as if I have a dozen grandchildren to fuss over." The idea that none of her children had reproduced was a daily reproach. The fear nagged her that it was somehow her fault. "If you want to start again, I'll help you."

While Nadeem renovated his apartments, Khalil wrote to announce that he had married. He had settled in Sarasota, Florida, and made a good living assembling fine trousseaus for the wealthy winter residents. His wife was a relative of the Norths. ". . . they're a prominent circus family. Perhaps you've heard of them? Estelle, my wife, is a year older than I, but it makes little difference and we have a very pleasant life."

Miriam was in shock. To have her son write so calmly that a woman loved him made her feel peculiar. Then she decided her new daughter-in-law was too old to have children. She envisioned a garish woman in tights, who risked her life by walking on thin wires or being shot out of a cannon. Nadeem said that being related to the family didn't mean she was a performer, but Miriam remained cranky and grumbled over all the other foolish things her firstborn had done, including running after carriages, which had almost cost him his leg. Khalil wrote again to say his wife was pregnant, and Miriam was so overjoyed she went and told everyone personally.

"Zareefa, I'm going to be a grandmother. Someone will call me *siti.* Finally."

"*Mabrook. Ya Allah!*" Zareefa considered her five healthy grandchildren the greatest thing God had ever done for her but seldom mentioned them to Miriam because it was like rubbing salt in a wound. The news was an enormous relief. "Nadia's pregnant," she said and clapped her hands together.

"No. It's Khalil." She looked annoyed, as if Zareefa had made an avoidable mistake. "I'm glad he's going to have a family around him. It's important. Look at us. No one around."

"Don't worry," said Zareefa. "Now it's Khalil, soon it'll be Nadia."

"I'm not worried," said Miriam and, unaccountably, Zareefa felt she had said something wrong.

She had been married eight months. Two hundred and forty-two mornings of waking up happy. Even the weather had cooperated. The winter rains had come down in isolated torrents and then were gone, leaving hard blue skies. February had been so mild that all the spring flowers shouldered their way out of the damp earth to feel the benefits of the early sun. There had never been a greener March than this.

On the first day of the ninth month of her marriage, Nadia sat up in bed and stared at her husband's bare back as he looked out the window. She noticed that despite his musculature, there were two vulnerable bones that extruded from each shoulder. He took a deep breath (was it a sigh?) and the delicate protrusions disappeared as his shoulders slumped.

He turned around. "Maybe we should think about building a home now so you won't have to deal with it when you're pregnant."

Like the gossamer flapping of a moth's wing, a thought wafted through, barely reaching consciousness. After so much lovemaking, why aren't I pregnant? "You mean here? Build a house here?"

"At the farm."

"But your father doesn't want anything bigger than the cottage at the farm. He'd be upset, wouldn't he?"

"He's the one that suggested it. He's very forgetful. The other day he asked me, 'Where are you staying?' When I told him we were renting, he was surprised. He said he'd thought I'd want to build a house up at the farm for all my children."

Again the moth's wing nudged her consciousness. "Where would we start. I hadn't thought about it at all."

"You could go and see Reinhold Spier. He's the English architect. Some of his houses are behind the King David Hotel. Why don't you go and look at them?"

"I'll ask Julia to go with me."

She never got around to calling Julia. The tennis team had two important games coming up. Then she caught a head cold and ran a slight fever.

By that time another month passed, her period came and the idea of building a house for a population of children that she had not even begun to conceive made her feel uncomfortable. She liked the little rented house. Samir could walk to work. She could walk to town. And there weren't any extra bedrooms to fill.

The harvest months of 1932 came and went, leaving a fabulous crop that would become the one to boast of in future years. Their first wedding anniversary passed. She gave her husband a beautiful leather briefcase with a gold buckle engraved with his initials. He gave her the most promising horse at the farm, a speckled gelding she had watched being born.

"There is no question that he adores you," whispered Julia after they had drunk a champagne toast to celebrate and the men had stepped away.

Later, as they prepared for bed, she asked, "Are you concerned that I'm not pregnant yet?"

"*Concerned?* Why should I be concerned?" He was a terrible liar.

"You must wonder. Do you ever say to yourself, 'We're doing everything that everybody else does. Why doesn't my wife get pregnant?' "

That was almost exactly what he said to himself. "No."

"Three times in two days you've started a sentence with the words 'when we have children . . .' We've been married a year . . . there's been ample opportunity. I'm healthy. You're healthy. Every month, when I see that I'm not . . . I feel as if I've let you down."

"Let me down? You're not willfully stopping yourself from conceiving. You'll do it. We just have to try harder."

It annoyed her that he was so matter-of-fact. How was he so sure she'd do it? And if he was sure, why did he think they had to try harder?

Approaching the crest of the hill near her daughter's modest house, Miriam stopped and placed one hand above her knee to reassure herself of the strength of her thigh. It was early morning and she watched—as she had done countless times—as the sun cut through the mist, miraculously unveiling the brown hills, the blue sky, and the deceptive ashen gray of the olive orchards. She had intimate knowledge of each bend and cut of the road. She could count on a shady respite under the pines, but there would be no cover from the skimpy cypress. She had stopped at the point where she could see the remains of the terraced gardens that had been her father's triumph. Those had been innocent and satisfying days, requiring only physical effort. But now, today, she felt emotionally *murky*. It was resentment of such long standing she could barely guess at the true origin. She had, at times, felt anger toward the boys. Sometimes despair. But Nadia was the one who could make her weak with resentment.

* * *

"This would really do much better near a window. If you don't give it more light, it'll stop blooming." Miriam was picking dead leaves off a potted white cyclamen, but she was also aware of Nadia tapping nervously on her knee.

"Mama, why are you talking about the cyclamen?" Tap, tap, tap. "There are hundreds more just like it outside. It doesn't matter whether this one gets brown leaves, or blooms, or dies. Anyway, that's not what you really want to know."

Miriam sighed and brought her hands down on her lap, a signal that she surrendered. "I would have thought you'd be living in the big house." This was not how she had envisioned her daughter's life with Samir. Making do with this funny little house. It worried her that perhaps Nadia wasn't taking her position seriously.

"I don't know. We just stayed here. I like it because I can walk to town." She knew it was just this type of vague answer that drove her mother crazy.

"All of your cousins have *some* involvement that keeps them busy. Rheema's with the Women's Aid Society. She serves milk and warm lunches to children who can't afford to eat. *Haram.* Poor things." She paused. "Rheema's sociable and gets around. And it doesn't interfere with her children and her husband. She keeps her house. She sews. When she goes to bed at night, she's lived the day."

"There's no need for me to sew."

"It isn't only the sewing, that's just one—"

"Well, all those things. Why shouldn't I give someone else the business to sew for us and pay them? As for the Women's Aid Society, those women have never liked me. If I do anything, it'll be with our horses."

Horses. Horses. Always those infernal horses. "It's strange, I grew up terrified of horses. My Uncle Daud always liked to scare me by riding up very close to me."

"That's awful."

"No. He was angry because I was taller than he. We were almost the same age." She began to pick at the cyclamen again. "Some people have resentments that they don't understand." It had occurred to her more than once that Nadia was punishing her by not getting pregnant. "It can poison their lives." She folded her hands across her lap and looked to her right, where a window allowed a view of a charming flower garden. The blue of her eyes was fading, but she was still a striking woman with no gray in her hair. "Have you ever forgiven me?" she asked suddenly.

Nadia ignored the question. "You mean do I love Samir?"

Miriam looked surprised that her daughter understood her so quickly. "I've never used that word." She curled her lip and sneered. "Love is a word for your generation. Our word was . . ."—she thought a moment—"duty, I guess. Or obedience. My father told me to marry Nadeem, that was it."

"What good did it do me to be independent?" said Nadia. "You got what you wanted."

"But it *was* the right thing," said Miriam vehemently.

"Then why are you asking me if I've forgiven you?"

Miriam looked down at her hands and massaged one with the other. "You don't seem settled."

"What shall I say, then? That I'm content?"

"I can see you're content." She felt as if she were speaking to her daughter under water. "But—"

"Oh, we're back to that. What I do with my time."

"Nadia, I'm not trying to make you account for yourself. But it's not healthy to have so much time on your hands."

"You want me to give lunch to the orphans with Rheema? The orphans are being suffocated with care." Right after saying that, she finally understood what was disturbing Miriam. "You want me to tell you that I'm sick at heart because I can't do anything as simple as getting pregnant? I am sick at heart." She was silent and tears formed in the corner of her eyes. "I think Samir is horribly disappointed."

"Oh . . ." Miriam moved closer on the couch and put an arm around her daughter so that they were head to head. The pose was stiff, and she realized she hadn't embraced Nadia in many years. "Shush," she said. "He's not disappointed. I had the boys and, look, where did that get me? Esa died. Khalil and Hanna are in America. They don't even see each other. They live thousands of miles apart." She shook her head. "Who knows if I'll ever see them again."

"Mama," her face was serious, as if she were confessing something for the first time, "there's something wrong with me." After saying that, she had a troubling epiphany. She wanted her mother to say it was all right. She wanted to be forgiven for not living up to the grand marriage Miriam had arranged. "I've let you down. And Samir."

"There isn't a girl in this village who doesn't envy you. Of course, you can carry a baby. Has Samir said anything?" For the first time she looked worried.

You mean does he blame you? You don't want to know if I've forgiven you. You want to know if Samir has forgiven you? "No, he hasn't said anything."

"There, you see!" Her relief was unmistakable. "If you want my opinion, you should forget about it. Put pregnancies and babies and all of that out of your mind. Just forget about it. Then it'll happen."

"How does your husband enter you?" She froze with embarrassment. The doctor had just completed a lengthy manual examination, which she perceived as having yielded damaging evidence. "Is it ever from behind?" he asked casually.

She almost fell off the table. She shook her head and then felt guilty. At times, Samir did enter from the back, rotating her until he could get himself in. The contact with her vagina from the lower lips was so pleasurable, she often put herself in a position that invited it. He always turned her over at the last minute.

"That might be something for you to try," offered the doctor matter-of-factly. He was a short, bald man with small, well-padded hands. "If the semen can be directed straight up, it might do the trick."

She found it nearly impossible to relate the conversation to her husband. "But he must have said something," Samir prodded.

"He said . . . Samir, what he said was so intimate, I can't say it. I just can't."

"For God's sake, Nadia, he's a medical doctor. He wasn't flirtatious, was he?"

"Oh, no. Nothing like that."

"Then, what? Did he examine you? Are you all right?"

"He examined me and he didn't say I wasn't all right."

"Then why aren't you conceiving? Didn't he have any suggestions?"

"A position."

"A position? What position?" He finally caught her meaning. "Oh . . ."

"From the back."

"He said that! Oh, my God, I should do it from the back?"

"You should aim straight up. He said that might do the trick."

"Oh, my God! Well, we can try it."

He aimed straight up for twelve days and it did the trick. Her period stayed away.

He was at a Council meeting, idly drumming on the table while reminding himself to bring up the issue of allowing the open produce market to operate on Wednesday, as well as Thursday and Saturday, when he noticed his mother-in-law in the doorway. It was so unlikely for her to be there that his heart moved in warning. "What is it?"

"You must come quickly." This was all she could force herself to say.

"The meeting . . ." he motioned to the men at the table who were watching them. "Can I come a little later? Are you in some difficulty?"

"Your wife is bleeding to death."

Without warning—it was the sixth month, they had both felt the tender kicks—the baby had ripped away. "When the tenth one comes, you won't remember this," said the midwife, but Nadia didn't want to be consoled. She wanted facts.

"How can a baby be healthy one day and dead the next? I didn't do anything strenuous. I didn't fall. How could it just *happen?*"

Helene, the midwife, threw up her hands. "There could be a dozen reasons, but what does it matter? We can't bring the baby back." She was purposely vague because, privately, she wasn't optimistic. The placenta had torn away long before the miscarriage. The cervix was overly dilated. There were certain women whose wombs didn't close properly. Sooner or later, the pressure of the growing baby forced them open. Next time, she would make Nadia stay in bed.

The second time Nadia got pregnant, she went to a specialist and his only warning was to cease intercourse immediately, advice he gave to all his patients. "Don't let your husband put it in here," he said, touching her vulva. "I'm sorry to be crude, but you'd be surprised how many I get who don't know anything."

She carried the second baby four months before a glossy red, sizable mass released from between her legs after a few mild cramps. She was drying herself in the bath at the time and the quantity of blood against the white enamel was so dramatic that she began to scream and was heard by the egg woman.

The packing between her legs soaked up the remains of her conception. "What am I going to do?" she whispered into the fist held against her teeth. If she didn't clench her mouth, she'd have flown apart.

"We'll never have a child," she said to Samir when they were alone. "I can't carry it. I can't do it right."

"You'll conceive again," he soothed. "You've done it twice, and the next time we'll take more precautions."

"Just please don't say one thing."

"What is that?"

"Please don't say the only thing that matters is that I'm all right." The litany of what he might have said ran, without ceasing, through her head:

It scares me to death that you can't have a baby. Or: If you can't bear children, this thing is going to go rotten. Or: Look at all the women I could have had. Why did I marry you? Would it have been better if he had become angry and blamed her? Yes.

She had been wrong about her love for him. It wasn't that flimsy, dreamy longing that played along the surface of her heart. It was this deep pain and despair because she had been the one to disappoint him.

He put his face beside hers on the pillow and lay still with his lips against her cheek.

The doctor had a name for what had happened to her babies, which he threw at her with unintended cruelty during the final visit. "An incompetent cervix," he pronounced. "You can keep on conceiving, but I don't recommend it." She sat perfectly still, her hands clenched, her jaw stiff. She was defenseless. She couldn't imagine ever feeling carefree again.

Cousins who had never liked Nadia were eager to befriend her now. Her bad luck, by some logic, made her more acceptable. But socializing was the last thing on her mind. She needed hard physical activity. Samir eased the way by announcing (almost on cue) that his wife needed to rest and regain her strength. She recuperated at the farm, working as hard as the burliest man. Her shoes were dusty, her hands calloused, her face red and then brown. If the men were embarrassed by it, too bad. She needed to be exhausted to sleep and stop thinking. Spring and summer passed and, with them, her third wedding anniversary. Julia, three months pregnant with her second and reeling with morning sickness, didn't argue when her brother requested that she not make a party.

By year's end, Nadia felt strong and healthy and knew it was time to try again. This time, her body wouldn't let her down. She became obsessive about it, and if Samir sighed or yawned after dinner she would fidget. "Something wrong?" he would ask.

"I was hoping we could try . . ." She had to spell it out which made her cringe.

"Nadia, we've tried three times this week."

There! He knew how many times. That meant it was on his mind, too. "This might be the moment." Her lips squeezed together, losing their exotic dips and curves.

He winced. It was something he couldn't quite admit, but it gave him an extra jolt to have his wife so intent on intercourse. He even liked the fact that she was almost businesslike about it. The combination of her earnest eyes and her voluptuous mouth set him off. He could feel an erection begin and his imagination, in the grip of arousal, translated her directness into sexual forthrightness.

I want you to put it in me right now, he imagined her saying with those wide gray eyes no more troubled than if she had asked for a glass of water. He felt absurd having such adolescent fantasies, and somehow disloyal, but he also knew they never touched his deep respect for her.

No one could know the things he loved about her. He loved her back. She was slim and the bones made a sculpture that felt sumptuous under his hands. He liked the exaggerated bones and muscles and the warmth. When she lay on her stomach, he liked resting his cheek on one of the mounds created by the cleft that swooped down to her buttocks. He liked the feel of the sturdy, grainier skin, so different from the velvety softness of her belly. He liked her height. He liked standing next to her and being able to look into her eyes and to kiss her without bending over. He even liked what appeared to be a scowl but was more a look of inquiry or a habit of protecting her eyes from the sun. She had a private smile—not broad in any sense—just a little folding in of her lips. For him, it was a substitute for feelings not easily expressed. It said, or he imagined it said, I'm yours, and that vulnerability defined and uplifted his manliness. He felt very strongly that he belonged with her.

Only once had he briefly regretted his marriage. He had been sitting outdoors sharing breakfast and a newspaper with his brother-in-law. "I want to hold the bird." Ambrose had tugged repeatedly on his father's arm, dislodging it from the armrest and causing Peter to grunt with annoyance. "They're afraid of you." Peter had answered absently, determined to continue reading.

"Why?"

"Because you're not another bird."

"I'm nice."

"Of course you're nice."

"I want to hold it." Again Ambrose had yanked his father's arm and this time the paper went flying.

"Ambrose," Peter said wearily, "let me finish this paragraph."

"All right." The little boy had taken a shiny green olive off of a plate and begun to scrape the meat from the pit with his tiny front teeth. Samir had watched with fascination. My father chews in exactly that manner, he realized with amazement. It's my father's mouth. The same setting of the teeth, the same jaw. The clear, invincible link of one generation to another. The strength of the past became so precious that his heart ached with disappointment.

Nadia had begun to clear the table, but he took the dishes out of her hands and put them down. "Why are you so desperate to have this baby?" He was thinking that perhaps it would help her to talk in simple terms.

"Why? *You're* asking me why? You *expected* to have a son. It's the most important thing in your life. And not just one son, several. Why are you asking me a question like that?"

"Because I want to tell you that you're putting too much emphasis on what *I* want. I made the choice to marry you, remember? If you've had failed pregnancies, it's not your fault. Did you connive to marry me under false pretenses?" He had started out to say something different. Something kind and reassuring but far less generous. Suppose she thanked him and forgot about having children altogether?

"No."

"Well, then?"

"Oh, Samir." Tears appeared. "It's not that simple. I *want* to give you children. You deserve them."

"Well, I don't know about that." He felt relieved. "I don't know who deserves them." The room had a terrazzo floor, and his voice sounded unexpectedly resonant and poignant. "You know something? You cry like a brave woman. Your voice gets stronger."

"That's because I despise tears."

He cocked his head, thinking things over. "My father had a brother, Jacoub, who never had children. He was a wonderful man with a lovely wife. He always played with everyone's children. Don't you think he deserved them?" Right then, the idea of his wonderful Uncle Jacoub's childless life disturbed him. You could be a decent man and still not get what you wanted.

"I remember him," said Nadia. She wiped her eyes and ran her hand under her nose. "Yes, you're right. He brought me presents at Christmas, and I always felt puzzled and guilty." She blew her nose. "And what about Uncle Nicola, remember him? No wife or children."

"But he had tuberculosis as a child. They were afraid he would infect any woman he slept with. Poor man. It turned out he was really cured. He lived to be ninety."

She picked up the dishes again. "It's not the same." She shook her head in a desolate way. "You expected children."

"Since the children are for me, I'm telling you to relax." He took the dishes out of her hand and put them back on the table. "Let me see you smile. Come on." He poked at her chin and she smiled stiffly. "Does that mean you feel better?"

"I suppose."

"Fine. Now let's go to bed. I'm tired."

"Samir?"

"What?"

"Could we still try?"

He turned around, shook his head, and smiled. He still felt the stirrings of an erection. "Certainly." He began to unbutton her blouse.

Her face became alert and quizzical, and she pulled her blouse together. "What's wrong?"

"I just realized how stupid I've been."

"Stupid? About what?"

"To believe what you just said." She looked astounded at her own naïveté. "How could it be all right? Your entire life has been a preparation to pass on your heritage to your children. Your very upbringing . . . the sheik sent you to the desert to make you fall in love with your heritage. Samir"—she backed away from him to make her point—"children are everything to you. Why would you lie to me about that?"

He wasn't the least bit sheepish. "I feel certain you *will* have children. It's too bad that it's not easy for you. You have to be more careful than most women, but I know that in the end we'll have a child. I can't tell you how I know." He smiled innocently. "I just know."

"And that's it?" She looked disappointed.

"That's it." He tried to unbutton her blouse, but she pushed it together again.

"Sometimes I have the feeling that our marriage was inevitable. My mother never let up about you even when it seemed hopeless."

"She wanted the best for her daughter." He reached for her, but she stepped back.

"It wasn't your high standing that captured her. I think she had made up her mind that our marriage was *fitting.* It wasn't your money. She likes you. She wanted someone constant for me the way my father has been constant with her. Maybe she thinks we're the kind of women who need someone to love us until we understand what's good for us." A wistfulness overtook her face, as if her heart's desire were out of reach, over a ravine that kept growing wider. *But she wouldn't want you stuck with a wife who couldn't bear children.*

He stood in front of her and began to unbutton her blouse for the third time.

"Samir, not here . . ."

"Yes, here." He had already made up his mind.

"Wait till we go inside."

"I can't . . ." he trapped her between the table and the door, dug out her breasts from the unopened brassiere, and brought them out to be framed by the partly opened blouse. "Look at that. They look like a pair of newborn animals." He bent down and rubbed his face between them, letting each nipple rake against his cheek and become hard. He used his lips, above the waist, while his hands undid her skirt and pulled down her panties. "Ah," he sighed when he finally cupped her bare buttocks. "Sit on the table." She stood rigid. "Sit on the table and open your legs."

She was staring at him stonily, not certain he was serious and unwilling to look foolish. "Come on." He prodded her backward until she was against the table and then lifted her up, unable to resist tracing the crease between her buttocks and digging his fingers into the damp opening while his hand was momentarily trapped under her. She squirmed.

"Wait," he whispered. He crouched down, brought her to the edge of the table, smoothed back the silken inner thighs, and pressed them open. She made a funny noise and shrank back.

"Yes," he said. Her pubic hair was springy, a healthy, reddish triangle of fuzz that was dramatic in its neatness. He searched through it with his tongue and she almost leapt off the table. He started to say, See, but kept quiet. He pressed his face against her, fascinated by the blissful feel of soft, bouncy hair against his cheeks. He hadn't expected to find the act of tonguing his wife so wildly pleasurable. Her skin was hot and she was rotating upward to give him better access. The fleshy inside of her upper thighs presented satiny-smooth walls, and he rubbed his face against them, too. Her hands were on the back of his head pushing timidly at first, but then more boldly. "Don't turn back now," she pleaded—words he found remarkably novel. Within seconds, that simple sentence catapulted him into the far reaches of desire. He pushed her down on the uncleared table. A few pieces of china clattered to the floor, but he climbed on top of her and gripped the edge, anxious that one or both might fall. He did a quick careful push-up and entered her again.

The spiked, sharp noise of a glass shattering against the unforgiving polished stone didn't stop him. He kept thrusting. He had a flashing vision of her former haughtiness and his brain called out with the sweet satisfaction of adolescence, I'm all the way in Nadia Mishwe.

When Nadia became pregnant a third time, she returned to the midwife, Helene, who told her that if she had any chance of making it through nine months, she had to stay off her feet, preferably, on her back.

27

Hide the baby. Mary Thomas is coming up the hill.

The twenty-ninth verse of the Gospel according to Matthew depicts a God who is capriciously cruel. "For to everyone who has will more be given," it begins, ". . . but from him who has not, even what he has will be taken away." From the Saleh family who was so unsuccessful in producing children, He took away the one they had. He took Ambrose, who toddled out of his parents' tent during a seaside vacation and drowned.

Julia, dazed with grief, tried to make sense of the tragedy. Why would God want to break her heart? What purpose did it serve to have her beautiful boy lying swollen and lifeless amid a tangle of weeds? Yet she owed it to the new baby to go on with her life as best she could. For Peter, the death of his beloved son changed everything. He stopped expanding his importing business and bought a hundred prime acres of vineyards adjacent to the sheik's land. He urged Samir to begin the fledgling wine business that he had spoken about since returning from London. "I've got enough money. Now I want to do something that will live after me."

When Julia gave birth to a little girl in February, Peter had already planted a thousand cuttings and enjoyed the life of a gentleman farmer. Julia was afraid he would resent the fact that this little stranger was alive and Ambrose was dead. She wasn't prepared for the dedicated slave that hung over their new daughter's crib cooing and babbling to coax a smile out of those pursed, sober lips.

Amelia Sa'd, who ran the counter at the dry goods store put into words what everyone else was thinking. "God scavanged the entire family to make the handsome Ambrose, leaving no decent feature for the rest of Julia's brood."

Ambrose had had his mother's nose and chin, his father's eyes and broad brow, the sheik's robustness, and Julia's dead mother's fine bone structure. He was cheerful and outgoing. Delal was a different story. She had her mother's close-set eyes and Peter's broad nose, her paternal grandmother's weak chin, and no cheekbones of note.

To her parents, she was perfect. Julia doted on her infant daughter, squealing when she smiled (at seven weeks), bragging when she rolled over (at three months).

It wasn't only a mother's pride. Delal was extraordinarily precocious. And willful. "You're a lucky girl," Julia often told her. "You can always know that your father will buy the moon to make you smile." It crossed her mind that Delal, through circumstance, held a place of unique importance. She was the crown princess, with no competition. Julia would look down at the determined look in Delal's watchful eyes and have the uneasy image of her diaper-clad infant standing triumphant amid a field strewn with all of the Saleh family's dead infants—the lone survivor. Woe to any child that came to displace her.

"Imagine how it would be if we couldn't have had another child," Julia said to Peter more than once. "Imagine how desperate Nadia must feel." Having lived through what seemed a senseless tragedy, she empathized all the more with Nadia's predicament. If there had been a way for her to carry her sister-in-law's unborn child, she would have done it.

In the summer of 1935, she had the opportunity to do the next best thing: to act as Nadia's arms and legs while Nadia remained safely horizontal, waiting out the final, crucial eight weeks.

While their sturdy hybrid vines took root and grew, Peter and Samir prepared for a long-planned trip to the San Joaquin Valley in California, an area that closely resembled theirs in climate and soil, to study the techniques of long-established vintners. Their wives moved to the relative coolness of the orchard cottage and set up housekeeping until their husbands returned in late fall.

Nadia wasn't taking any chances. She allowed herself only five or ten minutes of being upright each day and spent most of her time half reclining on a lawn chair with her legs slightly elevated. In desperation for some activity, she learned to knit, though none of the garments she turned out had sleeves of equal length.

The summer—sparkling mountain days with cool, star-filled nights—passed quietly. Miriam came twice—riding the jitney as far as the main road and then traveling the last three miles on foot while carrying a bagful of anise cakes and spinach pies—and spent the night. She was the rare visitor, for everyone else was busy with farming. After bringing in the wheat, the estate workers took their vacation prior to the grueling work of the grape and olive harvest. Farid and a helper came for a few hours at dawn and dusk to place the older foals with the gazelles for racing and then return them to their own paddock. The sheep were much further north, looking for better pasture.

The main distraction during the day was Delal's constant babbling, which was both amusing and disconcerting. When her mother placed her small hand over Nadia's belly to feel a kick, Delal would become very alert and reach to do it again, slapping her hand exuberantly at the place she had felt the movement.

"Not so hard, darling." Julia would rein in her daughter's arm. "She does seem interested," said Julia. "They'll be good friends." But Nadia would wish—guiltily—that Delal wasn't so excitable. Secretly, she didn't think her baby would benefit from Delal's hyperactivity. "It looks as if we're bound together now, with the vineyard. I'm happy it worked out this way. Let me take you inside now to lie down. I'm going to Mary Thomas for some fresh bread. I think this is the day she makes the sweets, too. Shall I bring back a tray or just two pieces?"

"How about four? Two for you and two for me. Do we have to share them with Delal?"

"I don't see why?" Julia giggled, put the baby in a sling, and got her purse. "Come on, you're going with Mama while your aunt rests." She went and stood by Nadia's bed and saw her grimace. "What's the matter?"

"Nothing much. It's my back. It's going *ping, ping, ping.* Did yours do that? It feels dull and tender way down below."

"My back hurt from time to time, especially near the end. Maybe I shouldn't leave you."

"Of course you should. I'm going to nap. Julia, don't look so worried. It's just a little backache."

She awakened just before Julia returned, with the oddest feeling. Usually, the baby's kicks nudged her from sleep, but she hadn't felt any movement all day. She monitored herself all evening but there wasn't even the slightest tremor. She wanted to talk about it, but even generous Julia was sick to death of hearing about this pregnancy. If she didn't feel anything by morning, she'd have Julia drive her back to town.

She had been asleep about two hours when the first serious contraction jolted her awake. It was a sudden vicious pain that rose swiftly to full potential and turned her stomach to rock. What was it? "Oh, my God, Julia. *Julia!*"

The muscles unknotted and she threw back the covers, preparing to get up but another, more devastating, contraction arrived and peaked. *"Juila!"* She felt warmth and stickiness between her legs followed by a third contraction, and then an unmistakable movement of mass. She knew what it was. *"Oh, no! Dear God, no! Julia, please, help me!"*

"What is it?" The bed was a bloodied mess. "Oh, lie down quickly. Just lie down. The baby's come. It's born. *Oh, no . . . I'm so sorry. Look!"*

It was no more than twelve inches long and it was a dusky purplish blue. But there was no movement, no struggle to breath. Nothing at all.

Julia pressed on Nadia's abdomen and urged her to bear down to expel all of the placenta. "I don't want you dying, too. Bear down. Come on, we've got to get everything out. Samir wouldn't forgive me. I wouldn't forgive myself. Bear down now . . . *now!* That's good. That's good. Here it comes . . . Oh, thank God. This looks like the whole thing. Wait. I'll get some towels to pack you. Look at this. *Oh, my God . . . all this blood."*

She returned with soft linen rags and when they soaked through, she went for more. To her relief, the bleeding subsided. It was almost dawn and Nadia, who hadn't spoken, tried to sit up. "Julia, listen to me. I'm all right. I mean I'm not demented. Please don't think I'm demented because of what I'm going to ask you."

"Shhh. Lie down. I don't think you're demented. You're a brave, brave woman. The closest friend I've ever had. You're like my sister. Nadia, I love you. If there were a way I could give you back your baby, I'd do it. I'm so sorry. It's as if it happened to me, too." She talked in quick, short sentences. Tears streaked her cheeks. "It's still there . . . a little boy."

"You mustn't mention him again. Promise. You must help me bury him and not tell anyone what's happened. Not yet. I can't bear any more condolences. I don't want any more pitying looks or advice. Please, Julia. For now, just help me bury him, that's what you can do for me."

"You mean, just you and I? Just dig a hole in the ground? What about . . . what about a . . . casket?"

"I have a wooden jewelry box . . ." Her face was as white as the unused linens in Julia's hands. Her hair appeared too red by comparison and the contrast was unsettling. "He's so tiny. It's my fault, you know. I couldn't keep him in long enough. I couldn't give him the time he needed."

"Don't blame yourself. You did everything you could."

"I want to get up and help you. I can make it. I'm hardly bleeding now. I want to bury him tonight."

"I'm not sure it's right to do this . . . not to let anyone know." Julia felt peculiar. Maybe Nadia had gone temporarily mad. She looked so ghostly with that burning halo.

"It's what I want. Please. It's what I have to do. I'll baptize him myself. I'll just do it." She took water from a glass and anointed the wrinkled blue forehead with her thumb. "I baptize you in the name of the Father and of the Son and of the Holy Ghost. God be with you, little one."

They dug a hole next to a patch of wild flowers in an isolated part of the grounds. Nadia insisted on doing her share of the digging, even though Julia warned her repeatedly that it might make her hemorrhage. There was a lovely wild almond tree that had grown nearby to mark the spot. Julia looked uncertainly at the small wooden box. "The other two miscarriages were lost," said Nadia reassuringly. "The midwife took one away and the other . . . half of it was left in the bathroom at home and the rest . . ."—she shrugged—"I don't know where it went. This one is just a bit further along. No one will even think to ask. It was a miscarriage, that's all."

She stayed in bed for three days and healed quickly. On the fourth day she sat in the garden, and on the fifth day she walked to the near paddock and sat in a canvas chair and watched the horses nuzzling each other and cantering about. On the sixth day she saw a little bird try to fly out of a nest and fall to the ground. When the mother bird looked for her injured baby, Nadia's heart broke open and she began to cry. She sat in the garden, keening and rocking on the dusty ground. She walked home, gathered herself in bed, and cried for the better part of the night. From time to time, Julia came and placed her arms around those heaving shoulders and kissed the tangled hair, but she was relieved that her sister-in-law was finally grieving.

"Don't you think we might tell someone? It's been two weeks, although you wouldn't know it. Nadia, you look wonderful. Look, darling, be optimistic. We can find another doctor in Beirut and perhaps he'll help you. I just feel you should let your mother know. She would want to be with you."

"I'm being unfair putting you through this. I know that." Panic filled Nadia's eyes. "Just give me two more days. Then we can drive back and I'll tell them all. And Julia . . . I'll never forget what you did for me."

Toward evening, they were sitting under the large walnut tree on the side of the cottage, Delal playing at their feet, when they heard a loud humming noise overhead. Both women reared back to search the sky and caught sight of a small plane momentarily set afire by the last few rays of sun. The plane dipped and rose erratically and, in one heart-stopping instant, fell several hundred feet as if it were a puppet on a string. They jumped to their feet. "Is that right?" asked Nadia, still gazing upward. "Shouldn't it fly more smoothly than that?"

"He must be an imbecile trying to show his derring-do. A young imbecile. There it goes now. I shouldn't think he'd try that farther inland. Fool!" Her voice shook with anger but when she saw her sister-in-law staring in surprise, she stopped. "I'm too vehement, is that what you're thinking? Look how careful you were, and still you lost the baby. But that mindless fool up there is tempting death for amusement. Well, anyway, he's gone." No sooner did they sit down than they heard a tremendous roar and another noise. A thud. Did the earth tremble?

"Is that a quake?" Julia jumped up, alarmed, and grabbed her daughter.

"Sounded more like thunder. Wouldn't that be something? To have a thunderstorm in July?" She paused, unwilling to say what both were thinking. "You don't think—?"

"The plane?"

"Maybe we should go and have a look."

"It must be miles away. They travel quite far in the space of minutes. We can't go out now. It's almost dark."

"Whatever it was, it's gone away. Listen. It's so quiet now. I'll ride out tomorrow and have a look. It's a good excuse for me to get some exercise."

That night, she had the first refreshing sleep in weeks. Her dreams were kinder. She dreamt of being in a field thick with flowers and, suddenly, a little path opened up and she was able to walk through. At dawn she was wide awake and the first thing she thought of was that she wanted to take a long ride out to the wilderness where the little shepherd girl had tended her sheep. She crept out silently so as not to wake Julia and Delal, mounted her horse with care—she hadn't bled at all for ten days—and rode off slowly, enjoying the freshness of the air and the first whiff of optimism.

She rode for an hour, amazed at how far the irrigation ditches kept the earth green, even now. Nothing appeared disturbed. But there *had* been a noise. Could it have been a piece of a meteor? She stopped to rest before turning back but then felt an urge to continue farther. Here, the summer drought had taken its toll. The earth was parched and cracked. Bleached animal bones appeared from time to time, and she wondered if she should have brought the gun Samir had given her.

In the near distance she could see softly striated buttes with breathtaking rings of purple and deepest rose separating the myriad shades of tan and beige and brown. She reined in the horse and took in the magnificent scene. There was a stillness that was so healing she almost wept. This is as close to eternity as I'm likely to get in this life, she thought. Images sprang to mind of loved ones who had died. Dr. Max . . . she could still remember his face. Julia's Ambrose. Her own dead baby. "I feel close to the dead here," she said aloud. Then, looking down, she saw something shiny, a sizable piece of metal with numbers on it.

She urged the horse on, unconsciously tightening her muscles for whatever else she might find. Yet nothing—not a lifetime of preparation—could have conditioned her for the scene that caught up with her in the next moment.

Nadia got off the horse and walked right up to the crash. She was horrified but mesmerized. The body of the plane looked as if it had snapped in two with the back jutting up at a peculiar angle. A man's severed arm lay against the top of the seat as if he were sitting there engaged in casual conversation. Strapped to the wrist by a handsome plaid band was a watch whose black, fully readable figures gave the time as 4:47. A woman was draped, half out of the wreckage, upside down like a gifted gymnast. Her dress was bunched around her waist, exposing her buttocks and thighs. Right below the innocent folds of a satin slip was an open, deadly gash that already showed the peckings of desert birds. Bustards circled the air. Nadia thought, I've got to pull her dress down. I've got to do that much. She tugged at the limp voile skirt and draped it modestly over the legs. There was a wrenching look of surprise on the beautiful face. She was so young, barely a woman, and she hadn't expected death. Who would? Briefly, Nadia passed her hand over the broad forehead, feeling the urge to comfort the poor thing, even in death. "Oh, I'm so sorry," she said, exploding into a sob. "So very sorry."

As for the man, there was a crumpled ball of cloth just barely visible beyond the right wing. A shoe dangled crazily from a foreshortened leg. Was that an adult body? Was that all of it, compressed from impact?

She wanted to flee, but her arms and legs felt like lead. Julia would be worried. The horse, as if sensing her distress, turned around and went a few yards, stopping to chew on an unexpected clump of grass. The sight of that miserly and unlikely patch of green made her feel unspeakably sad. She had been staring down, eyes brimming and blurred, but something made her focus. She saw what looked like a yellow package on the ground. *Oh, dear God! Mother Mary! It was a baby!*

It was lying thirty feet from the wreck, cradled in a small depression that had managed to trap enough moisture to sustain a cushion of herbiage. The infant was wrapped tightly in a blanket, militarily neat and taut, the type of paralyzing swaddling that would soon lose favor as too restrictive, even cruel. Unexpectedly—Nadia almost didn't trust her eyes —the neat little package *began to move*. The infant wriggled a tiny arm out of the outer yellow bunting and swiped its wind-blistered lips with a fist. Then it gave a lusty cry into the vast brown waste.

"The tea will help," said Julia, gently swabbing the cotton over the raw skin. "She's so swollen . . . *oh! look at her ear lobe!* It's one big blister." As she continued dabbing the cool tea over the parched, raw skin, tears slid down her cheeks. "The poor little thing. Suppose you hadn't gone? Suppose you hadn't found her? She's so badly windburned!"

"Do you think she's getting enough liquids? I'm more worried that she's still dehydrated." Nadia squeezed the little mouth and once more, dripped water, drop by drop, into the tiny *o*. The lips were cracked and bleeding and she hated touching them, but without water the baby would die.

"I'm going to offer her the breast," said Julia. "She needs some nourishment. Delal will just have to have a little less."

Nadia looked at her sister-in-law with eyes that were suddenly bright as moons. "Of course! Do it now. *Please.*" Julia, who hadn't expected to make good on her promise so quickly, hesitated, shrugged, looked sheepishly over at her own daughter, and began to undo the buttons on her blouse.

The baby gave one sharp cry as she rooted for the breast, but the thrill of getting nourishment overcame the pain of working the cracked lips. Both women unconsciously worked their mouths as if helping to suck. The baby's eyes were swollen shut like two bulbous mounds that completely obscured even the long lashes. The cheeks, too, were twice the normal size. The nose, the lips, the ears—everything was grotesquely swollen. Julia sighed and wiped her teary cheeks. "I guess, we'll have to take her to the police."

"No!" It came out a vehement refusal.

"But Nadia we have to turn her in. This is someone's baby."

"Those were her parents," said Nadia. "And they're dead. She's nobody's baby."

Julia looked at her sister-in-law with alarm. "But they had relatives. Whoever those people were, they've got relatives and the relatives will want to know what happened to the baby."

Nadia looked as if she were in a trance. "If I hadn't come along, she'd be dead right now. *I* found her. *I* want to nurse her back to health. We'll tell them she was too sick to be moved. She *is* too sick to be moved. Don't tell them about her yet." Her eyes were frantic. *"Please."*

"She could use a few more days with us, I guess." Julia didn't like the look on Nadia's face but realized it would be dangerous to disagree with her now. She was still in shock. Two frights so close together. First her own terrible miscarriage and then this. Mangled bodies. Poor Nadia. Let her have a baby to hold a few more days. What harm would it do? They'd play dumb if anyone questioned it. They'd say the baby needed care. They'd say they thought it was a foundling. They didn't even have to admit to seeing the crash. Oh, God, it all sounded false.

* * *

"Hide the baby," said Nadia. "Mary Thomas is coming up the hill."

"Why hide the baby?" said Julia defiantly. "We've had her three days."

"I'm not ready to face anyone. I haven't decided what to say."

"I don't know what that means," said Julia.

"Please, don't argue now. Just don't let her come into the house. Tell her I had a restless night and that I'm sleeping. Tell her anything. I'm supposed to be pregnant. She'll understand."

Julia gave her a look that said, I'll give in this time, but we're going to settle this later. She spoke to Mary for ten minutes and then returned.

For a long time she was silent but when her sister-in-law made no inquiries, she plunged into the news, relaying the details in a stony, warning monotone. "The crash is already being detailed over the radio. The owner of the plane reported the passengers missing, and they sent out a search party. They said all three died. A young couple and their infant daughter. The man was here to scout for Arabian horses—that was his business and he'd been here before. The woman was his wife of two years. The child was barely six weeks old." She sighed and her shoulders slumped. Then, as if it were her closing argument, she added, "They were Americans."

"I know," said Nadia softly.

"How did you know?"

"Before I left, I thought it would be best if I took something from the parents. I took a gold ring from his hand and a locket from around her neck. The ring is inscribed inside—Harvard May 18, 1931. That's a university in America, isn't it? It must have been a graduation present. Her locket is engraved too. It says Leonardstown, Maryland 7-2-30. Something important must have happened to her during the summer of 1930. Maybe that was the day they met. Julia,"—her eyes were unnaturally bright, glowing with some inner certainty. They were focused on the still distended face in her arms. Something miraculous had happened. The baby had opened her eyes—"Julia . . . no one knows the baby's alive. She could be mine. She *is* mine. All I have to do is give *birth* to her. I'm going to give birth to her and you're going to help me."

Samir was returning to his room at the Hacienda Gardens Hotel, which was not a hotel at all but a semicircular grouping of one-room houses with peaked tiled roofs and black rough-hewn doors set into thick adobe walls. There was a piece of paper attached to his door. On it was a cartoon drawing of a little man with a jaunty cap carrying a tray on which was a card that read A Message For You. At the bottom someone had scrawled "Telegram at front office!"

He didn't remember the walk across the gravel driveway. He took the most direct route and brushed against the bushy schefflera plants overhanging the narrow sidewalk. Inside the office, a smiling girl with a flat, too wide face—a face he would never forget—handed him the yellow envelope. YOU HAVE A DAUGHTER STOP BOTH OF US FINE STOP LOVE NADIA.

He stood there, dazed. For a moment he feared that he was going crazy, and he stumbled out of the tiny office and took deep, grateful gulps of rose-scented air. Inhale, he coached himself. Exhale. He began to calm down. Just as suddenly as the muddle had spread, it receded and his head was as clear as a crystal night. Already his chest surged with the bittersweet twinge of parental love. Thanks be to God!

BOOK THREE
1935–1958

HEARTS WOUNDED
AND WISE

28

That kind of perfect beauty breeds unhappiness.

"She's the most beautiful baby in the world. The *most* beautiful." Samir nuzzled his cheek against the downy head of his daughter.

"Mmmm." Every mention of the baby's looks made Nadia's stomach squeeze together. She felt overstimulated both by happiness and fear. The baby was *too beautiful.* It would be a few years before the true miracle of that face came into its full magnetism, but even now, almost bald, she was extraordinary. It wasn't only the singular placement of her features or the dense, satiny quality of her complexion, it was also the intelligent look of inquiry in her eyes and the sweetness of her disposition. Nadia would look at her baby and be thrilled anew. This was so much more than she had expected. "I found you," she would say to the baby when they were alone. "I saved you. You're my little girl."

She was christened Nijmeh—Star—which seemed appropriate for the shining happiness she brought to her parents. Julia was a tense godmother. Over and over, she imagined someone saying, And whose baby is this? Not Nadia's. Why on earth would you think we'd believe it was Nadia's. And wouldn't someone think the baby looked too big for a newborn? Nervous and perspiring and still not convinced she had done the right thing, Julia made a feeble attempt to account for the fine fuzz of pale hair—brown but very close to blond—as ". . . probably from Grandmother Jamilla." Nadia had thrown her a stern look and Miriam countered quietly that her mother's hair had been reddish-brown and very different in texture. The straight delicate nose was seen to come from Samir's mother's face, as were the rounded cheeks. The beautiful hands and long limbs were undoubtedly from Nadia.

Julia kept resolving to put time and distance between herself and the baby to save herself the emotional turmoil—the most hateful thing was lying to Peter—but she couldn't stay away from her goddaughter. She felt a heavy sense of responsibility.

Nadia was too busy to brood. Taking care of an infant took up every hour of the day. She had to mash and puree three meals and spoon minute amounts of food into a mouth that would grin and let it all dribble out. During the bath, she was so afraid of losing her grip that she climbed in the deep tub with Nijmeh. Afterward, she dressed her in batiste balloon rompers or hand-smocked, lace-collared dresses. Unshorn lambs and smiling giraffes were appliquéd on her quilts. Her bed was veiled with silk netting held back with wide ribbons. Outdoors, Nijmeh was wheeled along the streets in an elaborate canopied stroller.

Often, while diapering her daughter and subjected to her naked stare, Nadia's conscience would rasp and prod. Do you wonder who I am? Do you have any memory of the other mother? It seemed not. Nijmeh sucked her thumb and hummed, babbled, and drooled. She slept peacefully, flat on her back with arms curved upward. She banged her head into Nadia's chest with glee when she was picked up. She flexed her knees and was ready to vault with eagerness when Samir came into view.

As she grew, her true hair came in dark, closer to the color of strong tea, thick and straight and smooth as a skein of silk. It was cut blunt below her ears, the style for little girls, and held to the side with a barette. Her eyes, pale at birth, settled into a dark unmistakeable green—the color of wet leaves. A peculiar minute spike on the outer corner doubled their impact. Her skin, while not as light as Nadia's, was dense and poreless and quick to color. Her beauty was disturbing and difficult to absorb. It defined and limited her life. It was the first and, often, the only thing anyone thought about her. Beautiful, beautiful Nijmeh. What else was there left to say that could matter? Nadia and Samir became her refuge from the constant stares and comments. They were her wall of protection.

Because of the political turmoil, the most frequent family diversions were the sumptuous Sunday dinners with Miriam, Nadeem, Umm Jameel, Aunts Zareefa and Diana and their husbands and children, and frequently, Julia, Peter, and Delal. That was the core of the family that remained. Each member—even Diana in her small dark house (Miriam often slipped her money, which she accepted without comment)—took a turn putting out a feast of spiced vegetable stews built on a bed of marrow bones, pignola and meat pies in chewy pale crusts, wilted spinach gleaming with oil and onions, olives and pickles, cucumbers and tomatoes, charred eggplants dressed with sesame paste and garlic, trays of nut-studded sweets, darkened and sodden on the bottom with a residue of rosewater and honey.

All the women took a turn at holding Nijmeh, even Diana who seemed personally affronted. Until then, she had the most beautiful girl in the family.

It was a predictable life, simple and uncluttered, and Nadia settled into her role with a new willingness to befriend and be befriended. She wanted Nijmeh to be accepted. And loved.

In 1937, the agricultural depression that had gripped the world had repercussions that extended to the eastern shore of Maryland. Jason Walker, a prominent land owner, still depressed over his son's untimely death, became despondent over the decline of his cotton and cattle business. He put a gun in his mouth and blew out the back of his head. "I can't understand it," sobbed his wife. "We had all the money we could possibly need, even with the losses." A search of several safety deposit boxes revealed seven hundred thousand in cash.

The Palestine Post picked up the story off the Reuter's wire service because it tied one tragedy to another. The handsome thoroughbred scout had come to a tragic end with his wife and child. Now his father had taken his own life. Apparently God had no mercy and His lack of it sold newspapers. CRASH VICTIM'S FATHER A SUICIDE OVER BUSINESS ILLS ran the headline.

Julia read it. "Oh, my God," she yelped before she could stop herself.

"What is it? What's wrong?" She looked over to Peter with shock in her eyes. "For heaven's sake, Julia, what is it?"

"This poor man . . ." she stammered, "the father of the young pilot who crashed here last year . . . he's committed suicide over business problems. This terrible depression has taken so many lives . . ."

Peter shrugged. "If you want to be shocked, I'll tell you ten terrible stories right here in Jerusalem. You don't have to take your pity all the way to . . . where is it? Where did this man live?"

"Maryland. They call it the Tidewater region." She looked as if she'd seen a ghost.

The next day, she took the clipping to Nadia. "Look. You should know about this. Nijmeh comes from a large distinguished family. It says the father . . ."—she gulped—"Nijmeh's grandfather is to be buried at Laurel Hill, the family estate. He's survived by his wife, two daughters, one son, and five grandchildren. Nadia, they're her cousins."

Without hesitation, Nadia tore the clipping into fine little pieces. "Samir has never been happier. He adores Nijmeh, can't you see that? I would do the same thing again and again," she said vehemently. "The only cousin she has is Delal," she added firmly. "We have two fine girls, Julia. They'll grow up together just as you always wanted. Look at them." The girls played at their feet. "They'll be the best of friends."

The two most privileged toddlers in the village stared as if the other were the ultimate irresistible toy. Within the next ten minutes both would grind crackers into the irreplaceable hand-knotted silk carpet and their mothers, blinded by adoration, would ignore it.

Nijmeh offered her duck, her bear, and her musical bird in quick succession, scanning her cousin's face for signs of happiness. Delal flung each gift to the side. She looked at her mother. "A baby," she said.

"Yes," Julia answered, "another baby."

Delal put her pudgy fingers on Nijmeh's rosy cheek and patted it. "Nice," she said, biting off the end of the word and giggling deliriously. "Nice baby." She slapped the cheek again, grinned and then struck once more, so hard that the startled Nijmeh let out a baffled howl.

"Oooh." Julia rushed to hold her daughter's hand captive. "That hurts the baby. You love Nijmeh," she explained in a coaxing tone. "You don't want to hurt her."

As it happened, although Nijmeh adored her cousin, Delal never learned to like Nijmeh. At some visceral level, she understood everything. Nijmeh had begun by stealing some of the breast milk that was rightfully hers. And that was just the beginning.

It was always in the back of her mind and she had learned to live with it. But this was different. This had made her dream of death.

They started out early to avoid the worst heat but before they crossed the square to reach the road to Miriam's house, the hot east wind was nipping at their heels. Julia's news about the Walkers had let out demons and being out was better than staying in. She couldn't afford to have her strength eroded. She was drawn to her mother's house for a good reason that had not yet occurred to her although she'd climbed that road more than once that week.

The sirocco, at best, was suffocating. At its worst, it had a chemical effect on the nerves, killed cattle, and stunned the hardiest of men. Nijmeh stopped and held up a dust-covered sandaled foot to her mother. "Off."

"Oooh. I can't take your shoes off." Nadia looked around for a place to sit. "Let's stop in the post office and see what the trouble is."

"Pebbles out."

Nadia knew that Rose Muffrige, the postal clerk, would have something to say about her taking Nijmeh out on a day like this. "Let's take the pebbles out right here. Sit down."

Nijmeh sat immediately. She patted the sidewalk and then put her hand to her face leaving a black smudge. She turned over her palm. "It's dirty."

"Everything's dirty." Nadia emptied the shoes, rebuckled them, and rose to leave. They crossed Main Street, past the Roman Catholic church and school, past the old Friends Meeting House, veering left to the dirt road that led to her mother's cottage, which was shaded and set high up to receive any available breeze. They walked a few yards in silence. She could hear Nijmeh panting, each breath punctuated by a grunt. *"Heh, heh, heh."* Heat waves danced above the road. Nadia stopped and looked back. "Are you hot? Oooh. Look at your face. It's so red. Are you all right?"

"Too hot," said Nijmeh.

"I know you are, sweetheart. I didn't think it would get this hot so early. Can you walk?"

"Walk."

"I could carry you."

"I'm too heavy. I walk."

"We'll be there soon."

By the time they reached Miriam's house, Nadia was agitated and remorseful. "We shouldn't have come." She took Nijmeh to the sink and began to sponge off her arms and face. "Her feet are all swollen."

Miriam, who had been silent during Nadia's ministrations, crossed her arms in front of her. "You're making too much of a fuss."

Her words were unexpected and made them silent. Nijmeh looked from one to the other.

"Her face is terribly red," said Nadia.

Miriam turned to Nijmeh. "Does anything hurt you?"

"No."

"Do you feel sick?"

"No." She answered timidly and glanced at her mother.

Nadia, feeling fragile, had decided to deal gracefully with her mother's words, but just then she realized why she had sought out this tidy kitchen so eagerly. "There, you see," her mother was saying, "she's sturdier than you think. This is the weather we have and everyone walks in it if they need to. We've learned to live with all sorts of discomfort. Don't make her feel she has it so bad. She's a beautiful girl, but it's better if you let her take life in her stride."

Mama, didn't you have a secret, too? Dr. Max. Help me deal with mine.

"The important thing is that she's caught your interest," her mother continued. "I never had my mother's interest and that's the worst thing. It makes you feel lost." This unexpected confession made Nadia's eyes fill, but she held back. Her mother was not asking for pity.

"Can we have something to drink?" she asked to show she wasn't annoyed. She felt better.

"Of course. I have lemonade and cookies, unless you're ready for lunch."

"Lemonade and cookies," Nijmeh said, speaking with such unusual clarity that the women laughed.

When they finished eating, Miriam took them outside. "I want to show you something," she said to Nijmeh. They followed a neat straight path bordered by miniature ivy. "Look, the ants got into the wheat and each one is taking out a grain. It's like a caravan of ants." What Nijmeh saw—it made her stoop down so that her bottom scraped the ground—was a ribbon of moving wheat, as if each grain had legs, in a precise, undulating line. "Can you imagine how much work it is for them, carrying twice their weight? It makes me respect them for their courage, even though they're stealing my wheat. I respect you, too," she said, knowing she was speaking too grandly for a girl not yet three. "You're a good girl who does many hard things without complaining." It was her way of telling Nadia she was proud of her. It was her way of saying she loved her.

All the way home, Nadia felt the comfort of her mother's kitchen. She thought about the cool, amazingly fitted stone floor and the wooden open shelves holding well-worn utensils and beautiful old clay bowls. There was always an abundance of tasty food ready to fill anyone who wandered in. Sustenance and power were in that kitchen. More potent than hugs and kisses, which are easily given. Her mother had never coddled her. Even during the war when they had walked from one town to the other without relief, without enough to eat, she never expressed pity. Thinking back, she was in awe of her mother's gift of acceptance. She had never transmitted fear to her children, even though life had been fearful. She wanted to pass the same things on to Nijmeh but didn't feel capable.

That wasn't the worst of it. Many times she wanted to cling to Nijmeh. To bury her face in that soft neck and confide everything and then have Nijmeh respond, "You're the only mother I want."

29

The only really good thing that's happened is that baby. He loves her more than life itself.

Unrest. That was the press's catchword for the late thirties. You had the picture of people thrashing about in their beds and then collecting in the streets to writhe and share their agitation. No one was happy with the Mandate Government—not the Muslims and Christians, who suspected the British intended to step up immigration of Jews due to the troubles in Germany, and not the Jews themselves. It became usual for bombs to go off at the gates to the Old City. Snipers peppered buses with gunfire. Violence incited more violence and, when the frustration became unbearable, there were work strikes that lasted for months. During the late 1930s, the crisis in the Jewish world increased immigration tenfold. The Palestinians became alarmed and revolted against British policies. A royal commission of inquiry admitted that the promises to the Jews and to the Arabs were irreconcilable and that the Mandate in its existing form was unworkable.

While they were sympathetic to a Partition Plan to create a Jewish state, the commission realistically pointed out that "Muslims would resent most deeply the setting up of a Jewish state in close proximity to the Old City . . . ." and that ". . . Jerusalem is sacred to the Christian faith, not only the Old City, within which stands the Church of the Holy Sepulchre . . . and the Way of the Cross, but also the surrounding area, the Garden of Gethsemane, Bethlehem and the Church of the Nativity, the village of Bethany, and the road to Emmaus." The sympathies of Britain continued to seesaw, and whichever group was out of favor took out its rage in violent acts.

The fatalistic view that sudden death could come at any time led people to take their pleasures as they came. One of the great pleasures of the villagers, especially the women, was to watch Samir with Nijmeh. It wasn't only the sentimental kick of seeing a man enchanted with his little girl. It was this particular man with this particular girl. If Samir pulled down

Nijmeh's dress or tightened the ribbon around her braids or helped her climb on a bench to wait for him, it became an irresistible tableau. "Isn't that something! Look at that face! Isn't she so cute?" Rose Muffrige, who worked in the post office, summed it up. "Nothing's ever been easy for that family," she said. "The only really good thing that's happened is that baby. And now he loves her more than life itself."

For Nijmeh, her father was easily the most important part of her life. She didn't know any games (nor was she interested in them) because she had no companions to teach them to her. She was familiar with the things that interested Samir and they satisfied her. Often, when she was very young, her chubby legs were draped over his shoulders and her hands held his head as she accompanied him on short early morning walks.

Other times she was hiked up on his arm. Or she fell asleep with her face against his chest. The smell of his wool tweeds in winter and his spongy cotton abas in summer were as comforting as her blanket and her thumb. She was capable of giving him exactly what he needed: loyalty and unquestioning devotion.

As she grew, they had long, rambling conversations during which he gently hammered facts into place. The stems of the young fig trees were braided two together for strength. The grape clusters were lifted off the ground onto smooth stones to ripen blemish-free. The vines were pruned and the cuttings mulched the fruit so it wouldn't be scorched by the sun. "See here," he would say, "what's under this pile of dry leaves? Anything worthwhile?"

"Nudding wuthwhile," she would lisp, knowing she was in for a surprise.

"And what's this?" He'd pick off the dead leaves and reveal a cluster of firm, white grapes, which they ate.

He showed her a knot that could be slipped out in an instant but could also hold anything tight.

"An elephant?" she asked.

He laughed. "When I was a boy, I had to tie my horse to a camel and then—in one fast move—untie it and leap from the camel to the horse." It sounded as if he were trying to impress her with his daring, but he enjoyed telling her about himself. "This knot was the one I used and it never let me down. A boy taught it to me."

"Oh?" She was instantly jealous. "A little boy?"

"Yes, but I was little, too, at the time."

"Was he a nice boy?"

"Why? Do you know a boy who isn't nice?"

"*Siti* Miriam told me about a boy who was very mean to her. She says he killed her dog, but she still loved him."

"This was a brave boy. He's dead now. He died in my arms." He hadn't expected to say that.

"*Oh!*" Quick hot tears of sympathy spilled over her cheeks.

"Hey, hey, hey." He bent down and wiped her face. "It's all right. It happened a long time ago."

"But you didn't forget the knot he taught you?"

"No. And a lot of other things, which I'm going to teach you."

Just as Marwan had done for him, he set up a small tent so they could practice marksmanship by shooting pebbles at the pegs with a slingshot.

At least once a week, they passed the spot where the old Jerusalem Road crossed the Friends' school had stood. The Mediterranean lay to the west, a straight, unindented coastline that dissolved into a wide, fertile strip. In the late months, the orange groves were pure gold. Next came the secondary ridge of hills. "We're at the top," Samir would say. "We live on the primary ridge, the most beautiful, the most civilized." He would turn her to face the east. "There's the Ghor. That's the bed for the Jordan River. It begins here and goes all the way up, up to Galilee." They could see the Dead Sea, the lowest spot on earth. "See how quickly the land falls away, one cliff after another."

"Like stairs."

"Exactly. Like a beautiful but dangerous staircase. The mountain we live on is safely hidden unless you're coming from the west. That's why the first family settled here. When Tamleh began, the entire town was related."

"Everyone here is related to me? Even Jo-Jo, the *meguneh.*"

"Not exactly. Jo-Jo wandered here and decided to settle down. There are some others. Joseph Lam came from Rafidia. His father was a shoemaker and his mother was a midwife who delivered many children, including me. The Razals came here from Nazareth, but the boys married local girls. The older boy left and settled in another country. He went to England."

"Is that good?"

"I wouldn't do it. I wouldn't live anywhere else."

"I wouldn't do it either. Never."

"We even have a Muslim living here. Let's see if you know who it is?"

"Father Breen?"

He laughed. "No. It's Mr. Saleem, the plumber. Let's say you're probably related to seventy percent of the people. When you marry, it will be to someone you've known most of your life. I knew your mother when we were babies."

"I'll marry Delal."

He laughed again. "No. You have to marry a boy. There are lots of them around to choose from. But that won't happen for a long, long time."

"Can I marry you?"

"No. I'm your father. Suppose I had a lot of children—I couldn't marry all of them."

"Do you want more children? More than just me?"

"No. That's not to say they might not come, but I'm happy just with you." He meant it. He loved her beyond words.

And she, the product of two thoroughly Yankee Episcopalians, who had not bred out of their English-Scots roots for four generations, felt her heart squeeze together with pride and satisfaction to be Samir's child.

As it happened, no child came to displace Nijmeh. Nadia had one more failed conception. "No more pregnancies for you, young woman." The doctor had his mouth clamped in angry disapproval. "One of these times, the womb will tear in a way we can't repair. You'll die. Think about that in case you decide to disobey me." He looked at her as if she had already disobeyed and his predictions had come true. "Nijmeh will lose her mother and be raised by a stranger."

He gave her a rubber circle with a rigid edge and made her squat like a frog and insert it inside herself while he felt to see if it was seated properly. He didn't have to paint any more pictures. She used the pessary every night.

Christmas, 1939. The war clouds had formed, but America had no intention of participating in what she considered someone else's confrontation. The Jerusalem newspapers were quoting Charles A. Lindbergh (whose influence was second only to that of President Roosevelt): "We must not be misguided by this foreign propaganda that our frontiers lie in Europe," he pronounced. Senator Vandenberg swore never to send American boys to war under any circumstances. Others thought the war was just so much manufactured hysteria.

They were wrong. World War II began on September 1 at 5:20 A.M., Polish time, when a German warplane bombed Puck, a fishing village on the Gulf of Danzig. Although Congress was set against involvement, Roosevelt helped the Allies by closing U.S. waters to "belligerent submarines."

The conquest of Poland took less than two weeks and then Hitler played a waiting game with the Western Front. Americans refused to get excited, although expatriots sailed home. As with everything the people were polled, and two thirds of the country wanted no part of the war but took a sudden interest in geography. Rand McNally sold out their large-scale European maps.

The war was so quiet and (for the moment) uneventful that those who had hoarded hundred-pound sacks of sugar and cases of chicken noodle soup and canned peas felt they had acted impetuously. They had not. Early in 1940, the Wehrmacht invaded Denmark and Norway. France and Greece fell by midsummer, and it was a blood-chilling jolt to wake up and find that Mother England was vulnerable. Shakespeare had said, "This England never did, nor ever shall!/Lie at the proud feet of a conqueror." Would this still hold true?

Britain had nothing to gain by alienating the Middle East, and she had begun a plan to limit Jewish immigration. If this was expediency on Britain's part, it worked. Jews and Arabs alike fell over themselves, helping England's war effort. There was a general anxiety over the threat of a German invasion, but none came. Schools didn't close, as in World War I. Soldiers from the battle zones in the Mediterranean came to Jerusalem on leave. Refugees from Poland and Europe came to stay and lived in camps. Inflation was rampant and rationing imposed, but the war that devastated most of the world brought a period of peace to Palestine and a sort of do-or-die adolescent gaiety to Jerusalem. Various Royals waited out the war ensconced in the luxurious King David Hotel.

Giddy. She always felt giddy—impulsive and lighthearted—when they were headed for the King David Hotel. Something about the feel of her legs in nylons. And the smell of *Jean Patou* behind her ears. Even tonight, when Samir had dropped a disturbing remark, she was upset on the surface but feeling—what was it Margaret used to call it—a divine frenzy, underneath.

"What do you mean you're not sending her to Friends?" The car swerved dangerously. *"Samir!"* She always complained about his driving, although he was far from reckless. The truth was, she didn't trust cars. Or other drivers.

"Sorry. There was something on the road. What were you saying?" They were driving to meet Julia and Peter for dinner. Jerusalem's nightlife was vastly improved since the sniping and bombing had stopped. People were thrilled to go to concerts and dine out without feeling it might be their last supper. Most Thursdays, they left Nijmeh with Miriam, had an evening out, and frequently stayed overnight. It was one of the few ways they spent their money, having cooled on the idea of building a house. The sheik's health had deteriorated and the obvious sequence would be for them to move eventually into his big house. If they built it would be at the farm, but Samir refused to do it while his father was alive.

"Was there really something on the road, or do you just want to distract me?"

"Why would I want to distract you?" He zigzagged again and then grinned. These evenings out made him lighthearted, too.

"It's not funny," she said good-naturedly, then became serious. "She'll get a wonderful education there. No other school is close to it. Friends is the best place for Nijmeh."

"That's not true."

"How can you say that? It was so much a part of our lives. It shaped our thinking."

"It didn't shape my thinking as much as it did yours. My year in the desert was more indelible."

She wanted to challenge him, but they had reached their destination and he was distracted parking the car. When they entered the dining room, the maître d' gave them a message from Julia. Delal had a slight fever, so they would not be joining them. (The truth was Peter had gout but was ashamed to admit it.) "We'll have a table for two, then," said Samir and they were led away. Every few feet, he nodded to someone he knew. The women's eyes lingered on Samir, and then Nadia received—the *look*. Oh, well. She was used to that. She felt that old sense of disbelief at having bagged the best prize, though by no means was she through with their discussion.

"Sorry to miss Julia?" he asked. A trio—the card on a stand identified them as Yugoslavs—played a medly of Cole Porter tunes, and one of them was singing in English, ". . . you're the nimble tread on the feet of Fred Astaire . . ." Samir tapped his fingers on the table.

"No." Her tone let him know there was something serious to come. "It's the one school that has everything."

"What? Oh, we're back to that." He pulled his chair in and hunched over the table. "Nijmeh is too trusting. I don't want her exposed to every new fad and radical idea. Those precocious European children have been shuttled around to accommodate their parents. Their morals are nonexistent. I know because it was like that in my day. It's much worse now."

She was about to say they had survived it, but he would be reminded of how much she had been influenced by Margaret and of how she had almost married Victor Madden. "Your niece goes to school with Europeans, and Peter's no fool."

"Delal has the will and cunning of a twenty-five-year-old woman. No

one will influence her. I don't envy Peter bringing up that bundle of will."
He stopped speaking while the waiter put down their drinks. "Nijmeh is
different. She's all loving heart and trust. She would put herself in anyone's
hands."

"You make her sound like a piece of fluff. She's tough, Samir." Actually
she was touched by his description of his daughter. It thrilled her that he
loved her so completely.

"Strong of spirit, yes. But too trusting. If she had one finger's worth of
Delal's natural cunning, I would feel more relaxed."

Well, she thought, am I going to give in now and stop hammering on the
subject?

Nadia looked around at the grand old dining room and felt a wave of
nostalgia. She couldn't see those turbaned waiters without remembering
how berserk she had been when Victor used to bring her here for lunch.
Adrenaline-crazed. As if some fantastic adventure were about to involve
her. Well? It had. She shuddered and gulped her drink. She had been
singled out for adventure, all right.

The waiter brought their soup and hesitated before leaving. "See that
couple?" He was proud to offer titillation with their double consommé.
"Prince Peter of Greece and Princess Irene. They're waiting out the war in
the Greek Orthodox Patriarch's palace. Over there,"—he pointed to an
impeccably dressed handsome man—"Aly Khan. One of the richest men
in the world. His father, anyway. He's a little short, but who cares, hah?"
He flashed his teeth. "Enjoy the soup."

Did Samir have a point? Nijmeh *was* good-natured. So eager to please.
But she felt too strongly to give in. "You want to put a wall around
Nijmeh, and my loyalty is split," she said softly and this clearheaded
statement made him stop eating and look up.

"Not a wall. Just limits."

"I'm a product of Friends and you couldn't find a more docile, provincial woman."

"You're not provincial."

"Of course I am. I'm the Madonna of the Outdoors." She laughed. "You
know who called me that—she didn't think I heard her, of course—Diana.
I thought it was funny. I use the farm and walk and ride over the property
more than anyone, and isn't that what you love and want to preserve? I'm
satisfied with the country life. I don't even yearn to go to Beirut to shop
and gamble, like Julia does. I've worn this dress far too often. I'm a country girl. Wait—I just thought of something. My mother says she spent two
thirds of her waking life out in these hills. She claims to know every major

stone in the road from here to her house. Am I just repeating what my mother did?"

"There's nothing wrong with that."

She pursed her mouth and finished her soup. "I haven't budged you in the least. I haven't gotten anywhere."

"Where did you want to go?" He reached out for her hand and smiled. "I don't want you to be angry."

"Then, will you reconsider?" The fact that he was holding her hand in full view of the other diners gave her an emotional jolt.

"I can't."

"Oh, Samir. I had my heart set on Nijmeh going to Friends. It's perfect for her. I want her to have all those wonderful experiences. These are modern times. Nothing's going to happen to her."

"I don't want to take the chance," he said. "I don't want her to be modern." The look on his face put an end to her pleading. His fears were visceral and went beyond Nijmeh. He feared losing control. He feared life without a family. Had he ever suspected anything? If she had given him five children, he wouldn't feel so protective of the one. He was too much of a gentleman to remind her that Nijmeh was his only chance to pass on what had been entrusted to him.

She stopped arguing but allowed herself the luxury of a small snit for a reason that made her feel flushed and edgy. She was always too eager to make love and, sometimes, she wished she could hold back and have him coax her. Suppose she stayed in a snit and didn't turn to him when he touched her? What would he do?

"Do you feel like dancing?" he asked. The Yugoslavs were playing "Bei Mir Bist Du Schön."

She laughed. "We don't know how to dance to this."

"That's true," he said. "But I feel like holding you in my arms."

The few times he had thought about his deathbed, he had envisioned crowds of people lining the room, brothers and sisters, in-laws, nieces and nephews, countless first and second cousins, and, above all, children and grandchildren. So it was a shock—even more than the fact that he was going to die—that there were only two solitary figures.

Samir stood by the window, alternately looking out and glancing at his father. Julia sat holding his hand.

"Where are the girls?"

"Delal's too boisterous. I was afraid she'd tire you."

"Delal's like me, you know." He was whispering in a voice so frail the words vanished before they escaped his lips. "I see a lot of . . ." he couldn't continue.

Julia nodded. "I know. She can't sit still. And she's very smart. I don't envy her teachers. They're weary. I can see it in their eyes when they talk about her." The sheik tried to smile. "Oh, *Baba,* I'm sorry. I won't talk anymore."

The sheik's eyes moved to Samir and he came to his father's side. "Nijmeh?"

"Nijmeh has a cold and I was afraid to bring her."

He raised an eyebrow and grunted as if to say, What does it matter? What is a cold to a dying man? He beckoned for Samir to bend down. "Be careful with Nijmeh." That was not precisely what he wanted to say, but he had to be economical. His second grandchild touched him in the most provocative way. She was beautiful, but not with the empty, fragile looks of his wife. Nijmeh had knowledge and substance and strength of character that made her beauty almost heartbreaking. His every instinct twitched when he thought of her. He didn't know how or why she had happened into his son's life, only that she had appeared when she was desperately needed. Never for a moment had he believed that Samir had anything to do with her conception. Still, he loved her and regretted not being able to protect her. Ten thousand dollars in French gold Napoleon coins were stored in her name in Barclay's Bank to be presented on her twenty-fifth birthday. That was one way to help her.

If he hadn't been so wretchedly tired, he would have liked to have warned his son. He wanted to say, Don't think you can change too many things in life. Look at me. I ran around trying to control everything and, in the end, few things turned out the way I envisioned them. Enjoy your daughter and let her be.

Yet hadn't he done the same with Samir? Sent him down a precise, narrow road? Samir had been a splendid, open boy but with a will of stone. Nijmeh wasn't as strong. Samir could spend a lifetime creating her and, in the end, she would belong to the man she loved. The idea of expressing all those complicated thoughts made his head swim. No. The time for advice was over. Samir was on his own. How strange life was. Julia had been ignored and allowed to make of her life what she would, while Samir had been tended like a hothouse flower. So why was Julia's life so effortlessly pleasant, while Samir's was persistently dogged by shadows?

He felt certain that if he had a few more months to think it over, logical answers to his questions would emerge. He had done what he thought was best and he would do the same again. Perhaps this was only a temporary wrinkle in the fabric of time, and the plan would work itself out after he was gone.

He waited for solace to come. He waited for his heart to relax, for his chest to expand and broaden, for his mouth to curve upward with relief. He waited for one puny sign from God that what he hoped for was a possibility, but there was not enough time.

"Are you going to take the cookies to Slivowitz?" asked Miriam, "or forget them again?" She opened the package, pulled out a sugar-coated ring of dough and offered it to Nijmeh, who was going with her grandfather to the King's birthday parade.

"I didn't forget them," said Nadeem. "He can't eat the cookies. They're not kosher."

"Of course they are. I didn't mix animal and dairy."

"You didn't cook them in a kosher pan."

"Oh, Nadeem, for heaven's sake. Take him the cookies. Tell him we cooked them in a special pan. Tell him anything. What difference does it make? He lives alone and eats in restaurants. He'll be glad to have something homemade."

"Miriam, if we don't leave right now, Nijmeh and I will miss the one o'clock bus. I'm not going to take the cookies and I'm not going to lie to Slivowitz."

"Ya Allah." She stomped back inside the house but despite her annoyance was secretly thrilled at Nadeem's obstinacy. He always stood firm when he was right and never lost his dignity. She opened the package and looked ruefully at the perfect little rings of confection in her hand. Then suddenly her face brightened and she ran down the road after her husband.

"Nadeem . . . *Nadeem* . . ." He looked back and stopped. "It's all right. I made them in a kosher pan. I mean, I made them in a new pan. Zareefa brought me a new pan and this was the first time I used it. Now you can take them."

Nijmeh looked soberly from one to the other to see who would win. Nadeem sighed and took the package in his hands. "All right. I'll take them but I'm not promising anything. It could be that there'll be some other obstacle we can't forsee."

Miriam, her mood transformed, bent down and kissed Nijmeh. "Have a good time," she said. "Take care of *sidi.*" Then she stood in the road and waved to them until they disapeared.

"Your grandmother is a determined woman," said Nadeem.

Nijmeh nodded and offered her hand to be held which, inexplicably, made his throat thicken. He loved his granddaughter for many reasons.

But the most compelling—he wouldn't admit this to anyone—was that she was Nadia's daughter. Beyond that, there were the special delights of a child of six or seven. The portion of touchingly innocent legs left exposed between her hem and the cuffs of her socks made her seem so vulnerable. He gladly accepted her company whenever it was available, and for the last two years he had taken her to the King's birthday parade, importuning the banker Slivowitz to let them watch from the balcony of his office on Jaffa Road.

He took her to Slivowitz not to show her off but because the old banker loved to see her. "I'm a Jew," he would tell her gruffly, as if it were something exotic.

"A Jew?" she would say questioningly. She was never afraid to speak up.

"That's right. A *yahudi* is what your grandfather would call me. *Yahudi.*"

"What does that mean?"

"It means nothing. Your grandfather and I have been friends for thirty years. Twice I've lent him money and he always paid me back. Even when he lost it, he paid it back. He goes to church and I go to the synagogue because, by me, Christ isn't God. He was an interesting man. Poetic. Obsessive. But not necessarily God. Unless we're all God. In that case, all right."

"What kind of a thing is that to tell a child?" asked Nadeem, but he knew Nijmeh could take it. "You call Christ an obsessive but interesting man?"

"It's true. Figure it out yourself."

Today, when they arrived at the suite above the jewelry store, Nadeem was shocked at how old his friend appeared. He had seen him just six months ago. Slivowitz looked confused to find them there.

"We came to watch the King's birthday parade," said Nadeem.

"Ah, the King's birthday. Tell me again why we should celebrate the birthday of a foreign head of state who doesn't know his . . ."—he looked at Nijmeh—"where it comes out from where it goes in? Those bastards have lied to us both and we look forward to waving flags for George VI. Is he thinking about *us* at all? Does he care one whit if we're flourishing or dying? We're idiots!"

"Can we sit on the balcony?" asked Nadeem.

"Of course. Make yourself at home."

"Thank you. Will you join us?"

"Call me when the camel corps comes. I want to see them move their bowels and have the British regiment step in it."

"Come watch now," said Nijmeh, peering back into the dark office. "You can sit next to me." She patted the space on a bench and squeezed to the right to make room for him. "I can hear the music. They're coming. Quick, come out or you'll miss it."

"You care if I come out?" asked Slivowitz.

"I want you to."

"Then I will."

When he sat down, she took his arm because they were squeezed onto the bench. "Hold on to me so you don't fall off."

All the branches of the army paraded past them, even the women's regiment (which made Nadeem mutter). Then came the camel corps from Transjordan, which was a colorful relief from all the display of guns and weapons. Nijmeh left her seat to get a closer look.

"You're a lucky man, Nadeem Mishwe," said Slivowitz. "You have a treasure beyond words. A sweet heart. A caring soul. A face of such beauty it makes me want to cry. Don't let her see me cry. She'll think I'm crazy and I don't want that. I want her to want to come back."

Nadeem nodded. Looking at Nijmeh's straight back, he felt an old intrusive twinge that willfully invaded his mind. There were so many mixed images that could torment him—even now—if he let them. They crisscrossed in his mind, interrupting his peace at odd moments. Interupting his sleep in the old days.

Nadia may or may not have been his child. Bits and pieces of information would trail along, one bit attaching to another and adding up to proof that certain events might have had a different origin. How many times had he counted back the days and months to try and pinpoint her conception and then felt miserable for being disloyal. The woman that he wanted by his side *was by his side*. He had longed for her during the war, as an angel must long for heaven, and God had kept him alive to return to her.

He had nothing to gain by knowing. And there was everything to lose. That afternoon, staring at the back of his precious granddaughter he met the idea without flinching and put it to rest, once and for all. He was, as Slivowitz said, a lucky man. He wouldn't change a thing about his life. He had read somewhere that we are all—even those who would deny it—blindly adoring of our own lives exactly as they are. He knew this was true for him.

If Nijmeh had been a boy, Samir would have sent her to the *École des Fréres* to be toughened up. But for his daughter, Samir wanted no outside influence and hired Mr. Setapani from the School for Oriental Research to tutor her in French, mathematics, philosophy, literature, and history. They worked outside his office where he could keep an eye on them. When lessons were over, her outdoor education began.

At eight, she learned to shoot. The man hired to instruct her had mixed feelings. He considered it bizarre for a girl—who should have been playing with dolls and jumping ropes—to spend so many hours with her still dimpled knuckles curled around a six-pound gun that could, with no trouble, blow a man's brains to kingdom come.

When she was nine, Samir decided that she must learn to use a knife. They isolated a small lamb, who, sensing separation from its mother, rooted itself to the ground. Muffi finally carried it to the back of the house, and Samir showed Nijmeh how to hold it. One hand went between the front legs, the other, with the knife in position, arched the neck. "You have one opportunity. One," said Samir. "It must be deep. It must be quick and clean." She had practiced repeatedly on an old stuffed sack, but now her legs trembled dangerously.

The first stroke wasn't deep enough, and the animal danced around bleeding until Muffi finished it off. She was going to ask not to do it again, but her father's eyes were determined. With the second victim, her stroke was swifter and deeper but too arched and ragged. She had to do it once more to get it right.

Afterward, Samir walked away without a word and dinner that night held no conversation.

During those years, Nadia and Samir had two lives. One was centered on their precious child, but there was a core where Nijmeh was excluded and all that existed was their mutual dependence. Over the years, Samir fell in love with Nadia anew. He had never known another face that so clearly revealed its understructure. It represented very nearly what she was. Thoroughly open. Her honesty was part and parcel of her sensuality. It was the reason she opened herself to him without setting limits to her sexuality. She didn't know how to hide behind coyness, and this was the quality that had always aroused him with staggering intensity. When he wanted her and she was wearing that expression of utmost earnestness, unaware of his thoughts, his heart swelled with something close to adoration. Here was the nourishing center of his life. The one true thing that mattered. His wife.

Delal had a different upbringing from Nijmeh's. At three, she was enrolled in the progressive Montessori School. By five, she spoke passable French and could plunk out "Sur le pont d'Avignon" on the piano. She could read and print simple words in legible block letters and sat with

Peter many nights deciphering the important stories in the newspaper. At seven, she began tap-dancing lessons and transferred to the small but prestigious *École Française*.

She had distaste for the outdoors and was bored by the business pursuits her mother would inherit. While Nijmeh was visiting the bedouin tents of her father's business partners, Delal was visiting Beirut with Peter and buying faddish clothes brought in by the French. She was the first girl in Jerusalem to own a pair of American dungarees (which even she hadn't the nerve to wear outdoors.)

Nijmeh knew the lineage of every horse on the farm. Delal knew the words to every song on the Hit Parade, an American program she received over the Armed Forces Radio. Her favorite song was "Hubba, Hubba, Hubba, Hello Jack" sung by Perry Como. She had no clue to its meaning, only that it was *modern!* The swingy tune and antic words made her feel as if she had her fingers on the pulse of the world.

"Julia!" Samir rose from his desk and came around to kiss his sister's cheek. "What a surprise. You haven't been here since we redecorated."

"No." She wasn't interested in looking around. She had a mission. "I wanted to see you alone and this seemed the best way."

"What's wrong? Is Peter all right?"

"Peter's fine. Delal's fine. I'm fine. I came to talk about something that's none of my business. Technically, it's none of my business, but in my heart . . ."—she massaged her upper chest—". . . Someone should speak to you about Nijmeh."

"What about Nijmeh?" He looked surprised. "She's here, no? Outside. There's nothing wrong with Nijmeh," he said emphatically, and Julia shifted her weight and looked for a place to sit down.

"There's nothing wrong with Nijmeh yet, but, Samir—how can I say this without making you angry?—you're not allowing her to be a child. Oh! I've put it badly." She pushed herself to the edge of the chair. "That sounds awful because I know you love her, but she can't shoot and ride and slaughter animals and go around in braids and long dresses all her life. Who is going to befriend her? She should be surrounded by girls her age. She should be allowed to dress up and go to dancing parties. I love and respect you. You're my ideal of what a brother should be, but it needs to be said. Even if it just makes you stop and think. I know why you're doing it. *Baba* sent you to the bedouins to be made self-reliant, but you were a twelve-year-old boy. And strong. Nijmeh isn't even ten—a girl." She was rushing to get through it.

"Calm down." He took her hand. "I'm not going to hit you. You think I'm too restrictive with Nijmeh, is that it?"

She nodded. He let go of her hand and went to stand by the window. "Julia, for the first time in my life, I'm fearful."

She inhaled deeply, undone by this revelation. "Of what?"

"That I have no control of my life. That because of some devilish caprice, one morning I'll wake up and there'll be no family left at all. *Baba*'s dead. We have no brothers." He ran his hand through his hair. "For the first time, I'm furious with my mother for not having had more children. She was unforgivably selfish. It wouldn't have meant that much to her and it would have made such a difference if we had a brother." He turned around.

"But, Samir, you can't put the burden of all this on your daughter's shoulders. She can't single-handedly carry our entire family into the future."

"I want her to feel deeply rooted. I want her to feel that her roots are above everything else."

"Perhaps they shouldn't be. Perhaps her happiness should be first."

"If I do the job right, her loyalty and her love of her culture *will* be her happiness."

Julia sighed. "I haven't helped at all."

"You have. I've been thinking of putting Nijmeh in a boarding school during the week. I think it would be safer, with all the bombings and sniping going on. Did you know Joseph Lam was injured coming through Damascus Gate? I've thought of *L'École Française*. It's a small school and well supervised. The girls wear a simple jumper uniform, so she'll look like everyone else."

"Oh, that's wonderful." Julia laughed. "Have you told Nadia? Oh, Samir. She'll be happy in school with all the girls her own age. Delal will look out for her. Ooh, wait until I tell Delal."

"The worst day of my life," wrote Delal in her diary, "was the day Nijmeh came to my school. It'll be all right, though, because I can take care of her. She's dumb in many ways. I gave her my test, just to see if there was any hope for her. There isn't. I asked her, 'If you had a cracked glass and a good glass and a guest came, which one would you drink from?' She immediately said, 'the cracked one.' She's one of those idiotically 'good' people who are either murderously boring or murderously dumb. There's no hope for her, which suits me fine. She'll never understand that she has to pay attention to what's going on. Ha, ha, ha."

* * *

When her mother came into her room on Saturday mornings, it was for one reason. "Would you like to go with me to the farm this morning? You could have a riding lesson and we could help Farid with the horses."

"All right."

"Are you sure you want to go?"

"Yes, I do."

Nijmeh would rather have done ten difficult things than ride those horses. Her mother expected her to love it and to say she didn't would have crushed that look of expectation.

She had been given a complete riding outfit—boots, breeches, coat, vest, shirt, and hat—and felt ridiculous in it. As quickly and efficiently as she learned from her father, that is how clumsy she was at learning to ride from Nadia.

On Saturdays, her mother appeared at the side of Nijmeh's bed already dressed in jodhpurs and a linen shirt. In the fall and winter she wore a thick black sweater over the shirt and her pale face stood out like a cameo against the black. Her long hair was loose and plentiful, overflowing her shoulders like a cloud of sunlit copper. Her mother was perfect.

She spoke in a low, husky voice that Nijmeh tried to match but couldn't. It wasn't as low and silvery as *siti*'s voice, which she also loved, but it was the voice she would have wished to have. That voice made any word, any name—it made Nijmeh—sound extraordinary.

The ceiling of Nijmeh's bedroom was high and the floor was made of polished stone. Her mother had done everything to make it cozy—drapes and canopies and heavy rugs—but it still wasn't cozy and Nadia always stopped and looked around the room as if she were disappointed by the way it had turned out. Nijmeh thought the room was like her life—large, open, and cool.

Once her mother had said, "Darling, you do like riding, don't you?"

"Yes."

"I hope you would tell me if you didn't; otherwise, I would feel very bad."

"Why?"

"Because then I would feel that you didn't trust me enough to tell me the truth." Nijmeh didn't respond. "Part of the reason I love you so much is that I know you. I loved you when you were a baby but much, much more now that I know you."

Nijmeh looked alarmed. "What do you mean? You know what I'm thinking?"

"Sometimes. The expressions on your face give you away. I know what they mean from years of watching you. I know when you have good news to tell me. I know how you eat and how you sleep."

"Do I snore?" asked Nijmeh. She felt relieved. Her mother didn't know much.

"No."

"That's good."

Nadia had two feelings about riding with her daughter. There was the pleasure of passing along her expertise but also an ever present fear. Suppose they were to ride too far and reach the spot where the plane had crashed. They might come upon some forgotten bit of debris and Nijmeh would want to know what it was.

30

"In the morning, in the evening, ain't we got fun?"

Very early—she couldn't have been more than three or four—she learned to tap dance and sing like Shirley Temple. "On the good ship *Lollipop* . . ."—tap, tap, slide, tap, tap, slide—"It's a good trip . . ."—tappety-tap, tappety-tap . . . "—to a candy shop . . ."—hop, hop, knee up, turn, turn . . .

She did it well and looked very cute, but it wasn't enough. They had always been examined as a pair. She was the funny-looking one. If Nijmeh had walked in, eyes and minds, including those of her parents, would have flown to that astounding face.

Nijmeh's face was never boring and Delal knew, with a grudging respect, that this was because she wasn't empty-headed. Her father put her through hell. She had to play soccer (ugh!) and go on idiotic hiking marathons to chart all the desolate desert spots where no human had trod for hundreds of years. On Saturdays, she had to swim at the YWCA. Her mother's demands were crazy, too. She made Nijmeh train in the art of dressage—got up like a man with a bowler hat and sitting on a stupid horse to coax it to show off. Two crazy parents who made her wear clothes from the year one, who never allowed her to have a decent haircut, who hadn't bought her even one chemise or a pleated skirt or buckle loafers. What galled Delal more than anything was *the waste*. Nijmeh wasted everything about herself. She was fundamentally without any awareness of the effect she had on people or *could* have on people. She was fundamentally *stupid*. Squandering her looks. Squandering her brain. Delal could look around a room and know what was *going on* in the room. She always knew where there was opportunity and took advantage of it. That's what made her life exciting.

There was something else she felt about Nijmeh that she couldn't even stand to think about because it brought such a wave of confusion and discomfort. It had to do with the queer feelings she had for Uncle Samir. She had concocted a fantasy that she played out before she fell asleep. She was seated on his lap and then his hand would circle her shoulder, at which point he would bend to kiss her cheek, but she would have turned her face so that he met her lips instead. He couldn't help but stay there. On her lips, that is. Then, of course, he would pull away but ever afterward she would imagine that he looked at her in a special way and tried to find ways of being alone with her. The humiliating part of this fantasy was that when she wasn't wanting to play it out, she loathed Samir for making her feel so queer. He had never even asked her to sit on his lap, whereas her own father was always picking up Nijmeh around the waist so that her rump was in the air and plunking her down on his lap and stroking her hair and hugging her without ever thinking twice about it.

Delal was blessed with the genes for academic brilliance and was easily the smartest girl at *L'École Française,* but nobody envied her. It didn't take her long to discover that brains were okay, but the teachers were more responsive to the pretty girls. They listened to them more carefully, called on them more often, and made more of their accomplishments.

One day, she was sitting in the locker room after a game of lacrosse that Helene Haddad had caused them to lose. Helene, riddled with guilt, kept rehashing the highlights of play, hoping to be reassured. Delal wanted only to scream at Helene, but instead she said, "Your voice is clear as a bell. It's really beautiful."

The rapt look of appreciation on Helene's face was so profound that Delal was embarrassed to see it.

On another occasion she approached Maria, a popular girl from the inner circle. "Gee, you have great hair," she said. "It bounces when you walk and it hangs just right."

Maria, who had never considered her hair any big asset, hesitated only a moment, and then her mouth stretched out a mile in a grin. Delal sought out Sonia and zeroed in on an unlikely attribute, her long, graceful neck. People devoured praise. They seemed starved for it. She wasn't sloppy with her words. She found the very best thing to say and then said it sincerely. Many of the girls had never had such a heartfelt and imaginative compliment. They decided Delal was fun to have around. She never complained. If anyone asked how she was, she answered, "Splendid." To admit to unhappiness would remind them that life wasn't rosy for unpopular girls. She played the French horn in the school band because it was big and shiny and made her stand out.

Her daily litany in front of the mirror was, "You're a master of illusion," a line culled from a billboard for Binky Bonaventure, a local magician. She always gave the impression of being in a hurry, with many things to do. She kept away from Nijmeh. She wasn't rude but she was distracted or busy—whatever it took to discourage chumminess.

The spring she turned eleven, the school presented *Peter Pan,* and the coveted role of Peter—with a costume of green tights, a glamorous spiked green tunic, and a jaunty cap—went to her cousin. Delal was distraught. In her mind, the pinnacle of achievement would be to appear on that stage wearing that fabulous costume and uttering those humorous lines that made the audience respond with helpless laughter and adoration. She wanted to be Peter and nothing else would do. She memorized all of Nijmeh's lines and mouthed them with her during rehearsals. At night, unable to check her imagination, she slapped that perfect face until it was red and swollen.

A few days before the play, there was a half-day holiday. Emir Abdullah (with Britain's blessing) was being crowned King of the Hashemite Kingdom of Jordan. Delal invited Nijmeh to visit for the afternoon. "My father got me some new records," she said. "We'll play them on the victrola."

Nijmeh went gladly. To her, Delal was smart and sophisticated. Delal was daring and original. Delal was witty and outrageous. Delal was *family.*

Delal put on a record of Eddie Cantor singing, "ain't we got fun?" "Isn't that fantastic?" She did a little pirouette and began singing along. " 'In the morning, in the evening, Ain't we got fun?' Do you like it?"

"Yes," said Nijmeh.

The record stopped and Delal said, "Let's go outside and I'll show you a magic flower that will bring you any wish you want." Nijmeh laughed, a reaction that annoyed Delal.

"I wouldn't have thought you'd believe in magic."

"Why is that?" asked Delal curtly.

"You're too smart."

"What wish would you want?" asked Delal.

"I'd have to think," said Nijmeh. "I don't have any particular wish."

Delal frowned. "See, that's where we're miles apart. I have at least ten—fifty—wishes at my fingertips."

They walked to a small patch of brush behind the courtyard. She took a leaf in her hand, held it near her forehead, closed her eyes, and chanted: "Shiny, shiny flower all aglow. Bring my wish before I go." Delal opened her eyes. "Now you. Take the leaf," Delal urged Nijmeh to break off the largest leaf, "rub it hard so that the juice comes out on your fingers and rub it on each cheek. When you're done, close your eyes and make a wish."

It never occurred to Nijmeh not to do it. She wanted to please Delal and show her that she liked having fun, too. By the following evening, Nijmeh was in an agony of itching. Her face had swollen dangerously, and her hands and arms were covered with patches of blistered skin. She couldn't open her eyes wide enough to see her way across the stage, much less play the role of Peter. "Oh, dear," Mrs. Boulanger looked around helplessly. "Does anyone know some of Nijmeh's lines?"

"I know them," said Delal. "May I try?"

The teacher looked pitiful, her shoulders slumped in defeat. Visions of a cherubic Peter were dashed. "All right, dear. Let's hear what you remember."

Delal was very good on the stage. She was impish and relaxed. From the audience's distant vantage point, she was better in the part than Nijmeh would have been.

Mrs. Boulanger rushed to congratulate her. "Delal, you saved the play," she said. "I can't believe it. The part couldn't be in better hands. I thank you and the cast thanks you and the school thanks you. You *are* Peter Pan."

Delal smiled and said nothing. Being a star was exhilarating, but something far more important had been accomplished. She had been pitted against Nijmeh and had found a way to win.

February 4, 1947. The radio reported that the London talks had ended in failure. Britain might impose a solution but also might want the Palestine problem placed before the United Nations, which some predicted would result in Russia backing the Arabs and the U.S. backing the Zionists in the Security Council.

The Arabs said: They're going to give our country to the Zionists. Just like that? Who will do that? The U.N. at Lake Success. What a foolish name. The Zionists said: They'll never partition. World opinion is against us. The resolution to provide a Jewish homeland went round and round. The Jews, fearful the plan would be defeated, went on a terrorist rampage. Arabs retaliated. Railroad lines from Haifa to Cairo were regularly blown up. The buses from Tamleh to Jerusalem stopped running, and the mood was grim.

Christmas Eve, 1947. Tense and strange. No carols could be sung in Shepherds' Field because of the curfew. Most of the holiday mail had been lost because of a robbery at the main post office, and the Mishwes received no holiday greetings from their sons in America.

Miriam crocheted a large red stocking for Nijmeh to hang on the field-stone fireplace in the sheik's house. She stood vigil each dawn at the green-grocer's, hoping for one last shipment of Jaffa oranges to place in the toe for luck.

Her relationship with her granddaughter was disappointingly formal.

She worried that the deepness of her voice made her sound stern. She wanted to tell Nijmeh a joke, but all the jokes Zareefa told her were risqué —they had to do with British soldiers having sex with simple country girls. Sometimes she would sit next to Nijmeh with a protective arm over her shoulders as if to soften the stiffness of their conversation. "Tell me, how is the school? Do you like it?"

"Yes, of course, *siti.*"

She always said the same thing and worried that Nijmeh might assume she was senile. At times, she had to squelch a desire to say exactly what was on her mind: How do you feel about your overprotective father and your horse-crazy mother? Are you disappointed? And what if Nijmeh said yes? What could Miriam do about it? Wasn't she the one who had put the marriage together?

She wouldn't have done anything in her life differently, except perhaps kept up her schooling. She didn't regret Max, although now his memory was pale and cold. Her comfort and satisfaction came from an unexpected reliance on Nadeem. He took care of her more than was necessary. She was strong and fit, yet he always took her arm when they walked, as if he needed to feel her reality. He liked to bring her food at family picnics, fussing over her plate until it was filled with her favorite things. "Here it is," he would say, placing a napkin on her lap. "What else? Is there anything else?"

He retrieved her shoes from wherever she kicked them off and placed them side by side, ready for her. He cultivated her garden, painstakingly picking off the weeds. He never went down the road away from her without turning back to wave. Their marriage had appeared so arbitrary—a girl from this household and a boy from that one. They hadn't chosen each other out of love or necessity. Yet despite that, he had decided to adore her.

The only way she acknowledged his devotion was to accept it. She didn't have the gift of graceful thanks and her attitude toward him—it appeared to be indifference but was really fear of closeness—had hardened into habit. She was on the verge of discovering how much he meant to her but, as it happened, it was soon too late. The Christmas orange didn't bring luck.

In that indelible year of 1948, the rain came very late. It was January 4th before the precious water descended in torrents and, despite the regular noise of bombs and the frequent funerals, everyone was overjoyed to see the springs fill up. Three days later Nadeem, at Miriam's urging, went to Jerusalem to look for mail from the boys.

It had been a while since he had walked on the Nablus Road, and he anticipated each landmark with a peculiar psychic comfort. Even as a boy, this walk had always lifted his spirit. Around the first hill that rose from the valley, there were still traces of the ancient Roman road. To the east was Tel el-Ful, where Saul had lived. He stopped on Mount Scopus to experience the same awesome view of Jerusalem's domes and minarets that Alexander had seen. Down the slope he could see the British war cemetery with its rows of crosses. So many lives had been taken during the first tragic war. So many promises had been made and they had come to nothing.

Nadeem was shocked to find that already he needed a zone pass to go from one part of the Old City to another. The streets were deserted and some of the shops were bricked up, others iron-shuttered. The Semiramis Hotel had been blown up the previous day and everyone was still in shock. Bulos Meo's Oriental Shop on David Street had its shutters closed, but a small side door opened and he stopped to wish Bulos a happy new year before continuing.

As he walked, head bent against the raw wind, it never occurred to Nadeem to return home. He knew these winding streets as he knew his own house. He had his favored spots in the Old City that reminded him of the days when he was a part of the merchant community and arrived with the throng of workers each morning. Customarily, he entered from Damascus Gate, as it was the most convenient, but he hadn't been in the city for many months and had the urge to go around to Jaffa Gate and see what was new. Just as he approached, he heard a roar and saw an armored car barreling toward the gate, and then one of the occupants threw a bomb into the throng of people. The driver then turned, drove back to the corner of Princess Mary Avenue, threw another bomb, then accidentally crashed into a wall.

The screams of pain and horror were intolerable, yet he felt compelled to go and help the wounded. He picked his way through the debris and was surprised to find himself weaving and his legs unsteady. Then he felt a wetness in his midsection. Blood was seeping through his jacket. "I'm hit myself," he said aloud. *"Ya Allah."* He grabbed a man standing nearby. "Please, I'm Nadeem Mishwe from Tamleh. Please, go and tell my wife how it happened. Miriam," he called out. "Miriam . . ." He slumped to the ground and slipped in and out of consciousness. In the distance, he could hear the ambulance siren and, momentarily, he felt secure. But it wasn't to be. By the time they found him, he had already become the seventeenth casualty of that day's violence.

* * *

She didn't say a word for a week. Zareefa wouldn't leave her side, but when she went home to get a new supply of clothes Miriam ran to the cemetery and began digging up the grave with her hands. By the time Zareefa and Nadia found her, she had made a sizable hole and was sitting dazed inside it, keening and rocking back and forth. "Mama," said Nadia, putting her arms around her mother. "I want to take you home with me. You can come to my house and stay." She was oblivious to their presence and continued to rock and cry without tears. When dusk rolled in, she became quiet and both women lifted her between them and took her away. "It was just that day," she said in a haunted voice, "just *that* particular day that I realized he was everything in the world to me."

"I know," said Nadia. "I know."

"No, you don't," she said crossly. "You don't understand. Not *after* the bombing. *Before!* As he went down the road—he had to walk because the buses weren't running—I looked at his back and I realized what he meant to me. I wanted to run after him—one of those impulses that you stop and weigh. I let him go." The last sentence came out dark and husky as if her throat were coated with pain. "It was too late."

The year didn't improve. Reports that a partition plan was gaining favor came from U.N. Headquarters in New York. Preparations were made for war and the large dining room of Friends became a hospital. In Jaffa, civilians were evacuated by the truckloads. The price of petrol went to four dollars a gallon, and four times that much in the crucial cities. Food became scarce overnight.

On the night of May thirteenth, Samir and Nadia, Peter and Julia, Umm Jameel and Miriam crowded around the crystal set as the High Commissioner, Sir Alan Cunningham, made a very sad farewell speech. There had been such faith and bright hope in the British when they took over in 1922. And now the Mandate, pledged to insure the rights of the Palestinians, was stealing away in the dark of night. There were no ceremonies, no flags waving. It was a dark hour in British colonial history.

After the speech, there was news that the American freighter *John H. Quick* had left Galveston harbor for Bordeaux with enough wheat to feed all of France. This was America's outstretched hand to war-crippled Europe. The announcer quoted Mr. Churchill, who hailed it as "the most unsordid act in history."

"Hmmmph," muttered Peter. "And how does he characterize Britain's duplicity toward us? The most sordid?"

Miriam, who was still in the grip of the farewell speech, was weeping. "I remember when the British troops reached Jerusalem during the First World War. I was working in the French Hospital, and we all ran out in the streets begging them for medical supplies. They gave us everything we wanted. When the Mandate began, we danced in the streets. And now . . ."

That night Nadia and Samir fell into fitful sleep with the sounds of British convoys on the road to Haifa's harbor, from which they would set sail on the stroke of midnight. "Tomorrow," said Samir, lying with his head under crossed arms, "we will awaken to a country without a government."

The fall that Nijmeh turned fifteen, *L'École Française* initiated a dance for eighth- and ninth-formers and invited the boys from St. George's School.

The dance came as *too* much of a surprise to Nadia. All day she had to stop what she was doing to absorb the rude fact that Nijmeh was on the verge of womanhood. It took her by surprise and made her moody.

The occasion demanded a special outfit, and mother and daughter went to several shops along Jaffa Road and tried on dresses. They were exhilarated to be doing something so promising. Nadia made faces behind the saleswoman and vetoed dress after dress. Too fussy, too bare, too green.

At least two silk taffetas (one dazzling red with a sweetheart neckline) would have done the job. In fact they transformed Nijmeh from a beautiful adolescent into a sensual woman of at least twenty. Nadia stared at her stupidly and a buzzing began in her head. The word "sultry" kept popping to mind, an adjective she didn't want applied to her daughter. "It would be awful to be overdressed," Nadia said and Nijmeh agreed. "You don't want to look as if you're wearing a dress that's too grown-up."

"No."

Late in the day, with little time left, they settled on a navy batiste with a white voile Peter Pan collar. It tied in back and was not appreciably different from the dresses Nijmeh had worn at age six. With it, she wore patent-leather strap shoes and lace-trimmed socks. At five-foot five and with a healthy pair of breasts, the flat bodice made her look malformed and ridiculous.

The other girls—they had discussed their outfits *ad infinitum*—were wearing their first grown-up clothes. Delal was in a black satin sheath (worn with two-inch heels) with cap sleeves and a cowl neckline filled with a red silk scarf.

To start the evening off, Madame Boulanger wisely lined up boys and girls on opposing sides and had them meet in the center of the auditorium and dance with their opposite number. Through this democratic method, Nijmeh was twice moved around the floor by a short, red-faced Greek boy named Socrates. Many boys (most were sons of military families more at home on the soccer field) were determined not to dance but didn't mind standing around talking with the girls. Some played with the punch, slopping it around to amuse their audience. A few paired off and continued dancing.

There was a moment, after the music stopped, when Nijmeh was alone in the middle of the dance floor, singled out for public viewing. To those overstimulated pubescent eyes, she looked bizarre. The girls were titillated by the prospect of disaster. It was *unbelievable!* "She's wearing Mary Janes and socks! Socks!" A deadly flush crept up Nijmeh's neck. The mistake was so obvious now. For one awful moment, she couldn't decide which way to turn. In her confusion, she let out a sharp cry. Delal let the remarks go on for a while and then told Nijmeh to go with her to the ladies' room.

"Who dressed you like this? Your father?"

"No. My mother and I chose it together."

"I don't believe it. Why would you want to do this to yourself?"

"We didn't do it on purpose," said Nijmeh.

"Oh, no?" said Delal archly. "It looks to me that someone wants to keep you in the cradle. Well . . ."—she untied the sashes and retied them in front and to one side—"push the collar inside and take off your socks. It'll look as if you've got stockings on. That's about all you can do."

"Go back out," said Nijmeh. "You don't have to stay here with me."

Delal, who had no intention of staying with her, reapplied her lipstick, gave her one more exasperated look, and left.

Nijmeh leaned against a sink. She could feel her underarms and back becoming wet from perspiration. What was she supposed to do? She sat on the tile floor and put her head in her arms but then, worried someone would think she was ill, stood again. Her mother, who was in the second contingent of chaperones, was due any moment and Nijmeh cringed. She'd have to deal with that, too. Her mother was so *innocent* and sometimes that made her angry. Was it innocence or just not wanting to be bothered with things that didn't interest her?

She went out and took a seat in the farthest corner of the auditorium. Two other girls danced together a dozen feet away. The rest were crowded on the opposite side of the room. In time, her mother arrived and began to walk toward her.

"Why are you all by yourself?"

Nijmeh shrugged. Her hair was disheveled and her dress was rumpled from too much handling.

"Why not join the others?" Nadia's voice was high-pitched and anxious. "They're all paired off."

"I don't think so. Not at all."

"Well, they're sort of all together."

"And why not you, too?"

"Everyone's with the person they want to be with," she said reasonably, "and I didn't want to butt in." Then, seeing that her mother in no way understood, blurted out, "This dress is all wrong. It's too babyish. Everyone thinks I look like a freak. The girls had a good laugh over it."

Nadia swallowed several times. Moment by moment, she was assessing the situation and adding it up. She wanted to put her arms around Nijmeh and ask her if anything more terrible had happened, but that would have made things worse. This was all her fault. "I have to chaperone over there," she said apologetically. "Want to sit with me?"

Nijmeh shook her head. "I'll wait here."

They drove home in silence, with Nadia glancing sideways every few minutes. When she had parked the car and turned off the key, she said, "It was my fault. I'm sorry. I was so intent on doing the right thing and I did everything wrong."

"It wasn't your fault."

"Yes, it was. I'm not up on those things the way Julia is. We should have had some advice. You must be very angry with me."

"I'm not angry with you, but you have to promise something."

"What's that?"

"You musn't say anything about this to *Baba.*"

"Why not?" It was her intention to confess the whole thing to Samir.

"I don't want him to know. It's over now and I'll forget about it soon, but he'd be terribly hurt."

Nadia was so moved by this statement, she readily agreed but afterward, in bed, she became deeply disturbed and went to Nijmeh's room. "Are you afraid of your father?" she asked.

"No. I'm not afraid of him."

"Then why do you want to protect him? You're assuming he can't handle the truth, which isn't so. Many things have hurt him, but he's come out of it just fine. You have to be yourself with him and tell the truth."

"I'm myself."

"Always? And what have you kept from me? Do you do the same thing to me?"

"I haven't kept anything from you."

"What about the horses? Would you have told me if you hated that?"

"Yes," she said and looked away. She had kept so many things from her mother it made her head swim. Her mother was so insulated in her own world. But instead of feeling resentful, she felt protective.

"I don't want to make any mistakes with you. I want to be a mother who does the right thing. And one who understands. Nijmeh, I do understand. I do."

"I know."

"Was it awful tonight?"

"I've been avoided before." It wasn't only the dress that had put them off. She wasn't able to attract the loyalty and interest of other girls. They *did* avoid her. She couldn't trade wisecracks with them or commiserate, as they did, about their small eyes or long noses or wide hips. Even the girls who fainted and gagged in science classes became heroines of sorts. But she loved math and science and excelled in both.

"*Oh, Nijmeh.* The girls are resentful maybe."

"Perhaps. But *siti*'s right. I shouldn't whine about every little thing."

"Her life was *really* difficult," said Nadia, as if apologizing for her mother. "During the first war, she almost starved to death. Plus, of course, my brother died."

"I know. My life isn't bad at all."

"We seem to be outside of some things. We don't fit in easily, but your *siti*'s right. It's not that bad."

"No."

"Goodnight, darling. I love you."

"Me, too."

She returned to bed no more relieved than when she left. It had never occurred to her that she couldn't give Nijmeh everything in life that she needed. It was precisely that certainty that had given her the courage to take her in the first place. Love wasn't enough. There was another life that Nijmeh might have lived. Perhaps more rightfully hers than this one.

"Am I supposed to entertain the jungle princess?" Delal hissed to her mother in the kitchen. When the families visited, Delal usually found an excuse to be busy. She thought the entire Saleh family weird. "Why don't you talk to your brother about that girl?" She refused to call Samir "uncle" because he wasn't her full uncle. "Why don't you break the news to him that we're living in the twentieth century?" Julia continued setting out dishes of snacks but kept her mouth pursed. "Everyone laughs at her. She's never allowed to do anything with the rest of us. The seniors went to Cairo for the Christmas trip, all except Nijmeh and Nadine Risik, who had her appendix out. *Why?* We were chaperoned. What is your brother afraid of?"

Julia did a quick scan of her daughter's face to see if they were going to have a sincere conversation or simply argue. "Well, she's such a—"

Delal's small eyes narrowed. "Go ahead. Finish it. She's such a beayoo-tiful girl." She grunted twice. Was it to prevent her mother from actually saying it? "Do you expect me to be alone with her?"

"Yes, m'am." This was Julia's no-nonsense tone. "She's your cousin. You're practically sisters."

"Are you kidding? We're from opposite continents. We don't look alike. We don't think alike. If you and *half* uncle Samir weren't *half* related, I'd never talk to her. She's not my type."

"Please, Delal, don't start that now. Just take her to your room and visit. Remember, you want to learn to drive, and I have the car *and* the key to the car."

"Mmmm. If you're going to put it that way . . . I'll give her some fashion tips." She rolled her eyes. "Haven't they heard of underwear? She still doesn't wear a bra. Why can't she get a haircut? She might as well stick a knife in her belt. The jungle girl."

She sighed and went to her room. Her refuge. She liked to say that unlike Nijmeh, she was an indoor girl. She was very good at indoor things. She organized parties, trips. She also enjoyed giving advice for unsolvable problems relating to boys. She had several advice manuals—all from France and the United States—on how to have a successful conversation with boys. "Talk about animals," she advised. "Men love animals. Say, 'Oh, my dog has fleas. What should I do?' Never ask questions that he can answer with a yes or no."

The Armed Forces Radio had a lot to do with the Americanization of Palestine during the war and the effects remained after it was over. Young men about town listened to Frank Sinatra, Glen Miller, and the Andrew Sisters over the radio at the Christian Men's Club, where they played French billiards, but Delal, with her own radio and a phonograph, was as familiar with the Hit Parade tunes as any American teenager. American movies were plentiful, too—*Casablanca, How Green Was My Valley, Wuthering Heights,* and *Flash Gordon.* While the warlike conditions raged all around her, she was learning the words to "Chattanooga Choo Choo" and "Rum and Coca-Cola" and also how to jitterbug. Her favorite song was "Slow Boat to China" for the simple reason that it had to do with adventure and sex. Delal was itching to have sex. She had grown taller than her mother, to the decent height of five foot four. She had a good figure and nice skin, whose sallowness could be obscured with light Pan-

Cake makeup. Her hips were a bit wide, but unless she was wearing a sheath skirt it wasn't noticeable. She had excellent posture and, when everything was in place, appeared almost attractive.

Nijmeh at eighteen was approaching five foot seven, which would be within an inch of her final height. Her face had broadened and lost some of its compactness, and the cleft in her chin had deepened. Her eyes had become darker, a velvety green with flecks of brown and were deeply set, giving her a startlingly clean and dramatic look. Nijmeh was gentle, cheerful, quick to smile. She had no cohesive wardrobe and never looked put together. It hardly mattered.

When the families were together and talked of the girls' future, they discussed a career for Delal and marriage for Nijmeh. Peter wanted Delal to go to law school, but she just shook her head with chagrin. "You know what the men would do to me if I became a lawyer?" She gave a short, rueful laugh. "Let's just say I'd spend all my time proving a woman could be a good lawyer. I'd rather go into a profession that no one considers *important.* Journalism, maybe, or broadcasting." She looked to see how Peter was reacting. "News announcers have a lot of influence, but no one thinks much about it. They have the power of the airwaves . . . *ta tah,*" she gave a trumpet flourish. "Yes. I could do something very interesting being a news announcer."

"Read the news? You can't be serious. You should study law. With your mouth and gift for persuasion, you'd make a brilliant lawyer."

"If you send me to England or America to study law, I might like it there and not come back. You stand the chance of losing me to some faraway place." She winked at her father. "If Nijmeh said that, her father would go into shock, but you don't seem to mind at all."

"I mind," said Peter. He did mind but not for the same reasons as Samir. He loved Delal as an only child but more so for the person she was. He liked her forcefulness and her impatience. Her daring and her independence. It would have been a terrible blow if she moved away from him.

"So . . ." It was a "so" meant to sum up the past quickly. Delal, who was never at a loss, was at a loss.

Her room was festooned—around the dressing table and on the walls—with memorabilia. Framing the mirror was a picture of Elizabeth Taylor getting out of a limousine in her sweetheart-necked wedding dress on the day she married Nicky Hilton. Another photo was of Vivien Leigh in the cloak she wore to meet Lord Nelson in *That Hamilton Woman.* The third picture was of Charlie Chaplain as *Monsier Verdoux.*

"Isn't she great?" Delal indicated the radiant Liz. "She has violet eyes."

"Who is she?" asked Nijmeh.

"You don't know who Elizabeth Taylor is? Didn't you see *Ivanhoe?* Didn't you see *A Place In The Sun?*" Then, as if looking forward to being shocked again, she pointed to the picture of Vivien Leigh. "Do you know who this is?"

"Of course. It's Vivien Leigh."

"And *who* is Vivien Leigh?"

"She's an English actress."

"Very good." She grunted, mollified, then sprawled on the bed, propped her head on a bent arm, and stared at her cousin. Her small, bright eyes darted around the room then returned to Nijmeh. "You know, it bothers me . . . you don't do anything with yourself. I can't figure it out. I mean, I have to *really* try to look good, but you take fantastic raw material and *squander* it. You could be like them." She pointed to the photographs. She turned onto her stomach and looked away. "God, if I had your face, I'd be . . . Queen of England! Well no. I guess you have to be born into that."

Nijmeh looked uncomfortable. She walked around the room. "That's what most people talk about with me. It's as if I don't exist as a person. Just a face. If I go into a store in town, no one just says, 'Hello, Nijmeh.' They talk about me as if I'm not there. 'Look at that face,' they say. Then they either make a peculiar noise like '*ay, ay, ay,*' as if I'm adding a burden to their lives, or they make some terrible prediction. 'Samir has his work cut out for him.' " This speech, together with the awkward imitation of the village women, surprised Delal and made her laugh.

"Hey, I like that. But don't lump me in with them. I think *you* have *your* work cut out for you with your father. Does he make you dress like that?"

"What do you mean?" Nijmeh smoothed her skirt.

"You don't mind my saying this, do you? According to my mother, we're practically sisters and that gives me the right to tell the truth, no?"

"I don't think you're trying to be cruel, if that's what you mean." Nijmeh shrugged but her face remained guarded.

"Of course, I'm not trying to be cruel. It's time to stop wearing an undershirt. You should definitely be wearing a brassiere."

Nijmeh's face turned so red that Delal jumped up from the bed. "Hey, don't be upset. I'm going to show you something." She opened a dresser drawer. "Try on one of mine and see what difference it makes. Instead of looking flat and squashed, they'll stand out." Nijmeh fondled the small lace garment. "Take off your blouse and try it on. Come on, I've seen boobs before."

Nijmeh undid the buttons of her blouse and slipped the knit camisole over her head. "Oh!" Delal was dumbfounded. "Your nipples are pale pink! Mine are brown. All the ones I've seen are brown." Nijmeh put on the bra and inspected her profile in the mirror. "See," said Delal, "no more embarrassing jiggles."

"Let's see how it looks with the blouse," said Nijmeh, obviously pleased.

"Don't let your mother buy the heavy cotton ones. These are silk. Want to try on my dungarees?"

"Your *what?*"

"They're pants. All the girls our age wear them in America. We ordered them from a catalogue, but I can't wear them in the street. I'd be stoned. You know what else I have that's contraband? *Tropic of Cancer,* the Henry Miller book. He describes *everything.* Every other page someone is fornicating. If a woman is giving a music lesson, you can bet the student will put a hand up her skirt. And the woman is *always* grateful. It would have to be someone very special for me to be grateful. His books are so filthy, they're banned in America. Speaking of which, this summer my father might take me to New York. I know for sure we're going to Paris and London, with a stop in Scotland to visit the University of Edinburgh. And the University of London, too, not that they're likely to take me. I'm not sure they're ready for Delal George." She took a breath. "And what are you going to do?"

Nijmeh, who had been transfixed by this deluge of information, looked down at her hands. "I'm ashamed to tell you. You'll think it's queer."

"I can take it." Delal was enjoying herself. "What are you going to do? Wait . . ." she held up a palm, "I know. You're going to wrestle a lion in the desert, bring him to his senses. No? No. You're going to ride a gazelle bareback and then cut out his heart and eat it raw. No? Okay, tell me. What are you going to do?"

"I'm going to spend three weeks alone in the wilderness. I'll be tending a flock of sheep and taking care of myself. My father did it when he was a boy. It made him strong." She spoke matter-of-factly but also with a certain resignation.

"I have news for you," said Delal bitterly, "you can be strong for life doing a hundred other things. You don't have to go out in the desert and be mauled by wild animals and get heat stroke. Or raped."

"Raped?"

"That's right. Raped." She waited for this to sink in. "You want my advice? Have a tantrum. Just say to your father, 'I don't want to go to the desert and you can't make me.'" She squeezed her eyes shut as if preparing for a blow. "'You can lock me in my room or beat me or not let me eat, but you can't *make* me tend sheep. You can't! You can't!' You should rebel. I don't want to insult your father, but he hasn't heard about the twentieth century. Nobody has clued him in." She sighed and relaxed after her performance. "God, you've got great boobs. You can keep the bra—a present from Cousin Delal. I'd like to be a fly on the wall when the first guy gets a load of your pink nipples."

"You've figured out a lot of things." Nijmeh spoke softly. Delal couldn't tell if she was upset or not. She herself felt mixed emotions. How could you hate a girl who was so removed from opportunity? It was pathetic. She got up and straddled a chair.

"You know what's weird?" she said thoughtfully. "You don't look like your mother or your father. You have that cleft chin. There's an actor with a chin like yours. His name's Kirk Douglas. Maybe, by some trick of fate, you're related."

Delal's words were unexpectedly threatening. Countless times the thought had come: I don't have one feature of either parent. Rheema had her father's eyes and his heavy eyebrows, Aunt Zareefa's nose and mouth. Delal was unmistakeably her parents' daughter. Aunt Diana's children were a testimony to the prettiness buried under mounds of fat. As a child, Nijmeh often closed her eyes and moved a hand across her parents' faces. She had had plenty of time to memorize their features by look and feel, and she knew that no part of her matched any part of them in the same undeniable way.

31

I've never slept with a strange woman before.

"Mama, it's not so bad. It makes me feel as if I've accomplished something."

"But aren't you frightened?"

"No. Nothing's going to happen. And I have the gun . . ."

Nadia sighed and rubbed her temples. "But suppose someone *does* come?"

Nijmeh shifted around so she could put her arm around Nadia. They were sitting side by side on her bed and the springs dipped to bring them close. Nijmeh was aware of the beautiful smell that always surrounded her mother. She could see close up how her mother's face was made. Every feature seemed laboriously chiseled. Her mother was the most unfrivolous person she knew. And the most private. She was like a tantalizing mystery that her father wanted to solve. Her mother could appear so wistful. She wanted to say, What is it that you don't have but wish you did?

Now Nadia's lovely mouth was pursed with worry. This was the second summer of her "field trip," but her mother was as nervous as before. "I have the dogs to warn me; then I can prepare to defend myself. No one's going to kill me."

"This is the way your father plans to build up your self-confidence, but who knows what could really happen. Tell him you don't want to go. You've gone once."

"I can't. He's planned it very carefully. How could I tell him I won't go?"

"I wonder why he isn't afraid for you."

"Part of it is my doing. I like the challenge and he knows it. He's right. If I had nothing on my mind except clothes and parties, I wouldn't feel like a strong person."

Nijmeh never let on that she was desperately afraid. No amount of rehearsal would take away the ghastly fear of being out alone on that vast plain. Even in the heat of noon, fear kept her cold. After the third day without human contact, she would become so dispirited that anything would make her weep.

She imagined a hundred different deaths—all of them violent. She imagined the sheep stampeding over her. The dogs tearing her apart from hunger or anger or madness. A few times in her life, she had seen dogs go mad from rabies. At night, she would lie rigid next to the campfire and try not to listen to the animals' grunts, which sounded so alarmingly human that she was certain a man was within inches of her, poised with a dagger, ready to cut out her heart. Some desert maurauder who had no value for human life would kill her over a piece of cheese. She would lie rigid, eyes closed, feeling that to open them would be to confront a thief and die.

Fear, she had been told often enough, was part and parcel of life. Fear, her father had said—and she had not understood—is an old friend. She had rehearsed so many scenes of confrontation with an unexpected visitor that on the evening one came, it seemed inevitable. Except that it wasn't danger that approached. It was James.

The dogs started barking before anything was visible. Still, she got out her gun, checked to see that it was loaded, and cocked it. She didn't want to be unprepared. On the other hand, a prime rule was not to fire unless your life was in danger because the sheep would scatter.

She saw the rider and her heart began to pound. He came all the way up to her fire and she got a good look. He was a young, stylish man, seated expertly, wearing good leather boots that some servant had polished and—on the hand gripping the reins—a ring that testified graduation from a secondary school. His hair was windblown. It was brown with lighter streaks made by the summer sun.

He looked at her and at the gun and said calmly, "You don't have to shoot me, you know. I'm not dangerous. I'm just lost. I could have sworn I was going south, but evidently I was going east. Where am I, anyway?"

"I'm not required to answer." She was relieved but not ready to trust him. "I have to protect myself and my flock. I don't *have* to shoot you, but don't think I'm not capable of it." Having said this, she immediately wished she hadn't put it so harshly.

"May I get down?" he said reasonably. "I want you to look at me. Look at my hands. A desperado's hands would be calloused and cut. The fingernails would be broken and caked with dirt. These are a student's hands." He seemed pleased with the logic and clamped his lips smugly. She wasn't moving. "See my belt? It's from Harrods in England. My mother bought it for me. Where would a robber get clothes like these?" She remained silent and the gun stayed where it was. "Well, yes, he could have robbed some poor student, but then still his hands wouldn't be well kept."

She gave a contemptuous grunt. "My hands are calloused, my finger-nails are chipped and dirty, and I'm not a thief. I go to a fine private school." She sounded silly.

"Oh? That's odd. Maybe I should be afraid of you." The gun went down to her side. "That's better." He dismounted. "I feel a lot more cheerful without that gun pointed at my face." He tied the horse to one of the poles holding the tent. Then he went to the fire and rubbed his hands briskly. "It was warm when I started out, but I'm chilled through." This confession of vulnerability surprised her. She moved closer and he got the first good look at her. "Oh, my." She tried to remain stern-faced but had to smile. "I don't know what to say." He looked to his right and at the sky, perplexed. "I get lost, I find myself in the middle of the desert with night coming. Miraculously, I reach a campfire. A woman greets me and threatens my life, and then when I see her face in the firelight . . . I'm not going to pretend I'm not surprised." He looked around and smiled sheepishly, as if he yearned for a third party to share this event.

"Excuse me," she said, "I've got to leave you on your honor. I hope you won't try anything."

"Don't leave! Where are you going?"

"I'm going to choose one of the lambs and slaughter it."

His expression changed to one of alarm. "*Slaughter?* Are you serious? Why? You're expecting someone?"

"In my culture, when you shelter a stranger, you're responsible for his welfare. It's a duty to get the best that you have and prepare it for him. I'll roast a nice baby lamb."

He held up his hand and shook his head. "I can tell you with every assurance, that isn't necessary."

"It may not be necessary, but I must do it. That's part of the reason I'm here. To do what has to be done."

"No, no, no. Wait a minute. Suppose you got that lamb. And suppose I could bear watching you hack up the poor animal. How on earth are you going to cook it."

"I would truss it and build a spit and roast it over this fire."

"Wouldn't that take hours?"

"Possibly. I've never done it before. I mean the roasting part. I've done the killing many times."

He stepped back and shook his head, deciding how to handle a woman who had killed many times. "I won't be here long enough to wait for such an ambitious meal. I'd like—if you allow it—to have a few hours of sleep and then be off at dawn. And there's another thing—"

"What's that?"

"How would the two of us consume an entire lamb? It would be so wasteful. Just offer me something warm—a cup of coffee—and I'll feel well taken care of."

She had lost the advantage. What he said was absolutely true. "Well, if you're certain you can't wait . . . It *would* be wasteful."

"I can't wait. And it *would* be wasteful. You have my word."

He sounded relieved and she thought about how she must appear to him. Impractical and silly. He was probably an Englishman who privately considered them all savages. She began to feel a dull resentment. "Are you English?"

"Half and half. My mother's English, my father's Arab. We live in Jerusalem half the year. I've been at Cambridge for several years, so I sound English. I try not to pick up the accent, but it creeps up on you. I probably resemble my mother. And you . . . ?"

"Oh . . . I've been told I resemble my great-grandmother, but I can't be sure. She's dead." She wanted to ask more questions, but saw the fatigue on his face and remembered that he wanted to sleep. "I'll make the coffee."

She sat, legs crossed, near the fire and waited for the little pot to bubble over several times, handed him the filled cup, and watched until he took the first sip. Then she arranged the long skirt around her legs and became very busy tracing on the ground with a stick. There was no wind at all and the light had turned an opulent purple. Breathing became pleasurable as humidity seeped into the air.

He sat on the ground, his long legs bent—he was quite tall—gripping the tin cup and looking out at the scene with narrowed eyes. He had a large head, even though his hair lay flat, and a broad forehead that shadowed his eyes. There was a noticeable bump right below the bridge of his nose. He might have been described as "rugged" except for his long eyelashes and remarkable silky hair.

"I don't suppose you'd tell me anything about yourself."

"There's not much to tell."

He threw his head back and grunted. She saw that when he moved his head quickly, his hair moved back all in one piece. "Well, without knowing anything, I can tell you you're wrong. You could start by revealing why you're here doing something so . . ."—he was choosing his words carefully so as not to insult her—*"different."*

Her stick was busy making tic-tac-toe grids in the ground. "I'm building character," she said sarcastically. "I don't want to be just another spoiled rich girl."

"There no chance of that happening."

"Why not?"

"A spoiled rich girl wouldn't have jumped at the chance to kill and truss a lamb. A spoiled girl would have let me starve."

He was laughing at her and, momentarily, she hated him. "I'm going to sleep now," she said. "There's an extra cover," she pointed to a corner of the shelter. "But you have to promise me that you won't do anything to . . . I'm offering to share this tent, but you're honor bound to respect my hospitality."

"I will, of course. I wouldn't harm you. I'll sleep over here." He indicated a space at the foot of the fire, perpendicular to her space. Before she got up she undid her hair, which was held in a ponytail by a wide rubber-band. It fell over her shoulders, and she was aware that he was staring at her.

He finished his coffee quickly, dragged the sheepskin over, and stretched out. When he was settled, she lay down, too.

The night had turned quite cold, so they both inched closer to the fire. When everything was still, she became excruciatingly aware of him. It was the kind of intimacy that was so extraordinary she felt keyed up. She was lying on her stomach, arms folded under her cheek. He was stretched flat on his back, which seemed too trusting a position, even in sleep. One arm was arched over his head with the fist grazing his forehead. His hair fell back straight and soft like a child's, but otherwise he looked big and substantial.

She could have reached out and held his hand, which was tempting. Suppose that entire arm were around her and she could sleep in the crook of it, her face nestled against his chest? The idea of being held—it had never occurred to her—was so enticing that she had to clench her hands into tight fists under her to keep from reaching for him. Finally, exhausted and overwrought, she drifted into a half sleep.

A little while later, the dogs barked. He was up in an instant and she heard the click of a gun and that made her jump, too. She hadn't known that *he* had a gun. She went behind him and grabbed his wrist, holding his arm from the back. "No. You musn't shoot. Please. The flock will scatter." For an instant she allowed herself to lean against his broad back. It couldn't have been more than a second, but there was a feeling of giddiness and relief, as if she had accidentally stumbled on a beneficial secret. She let go of him.

"The dogs were barking."

"Yes."

"What's out there?"

"I don't know, but we can't shoot yet." There was another loud bark and a howl. She took hold of his arm again. He looked down at it and she let go.

"You're trembling." He put an arm around her shoulders, but she shrugged him off. "Are you afraid?"

"What if I am? Who knows what's out there. It could be a panther or a wolf. I've heard of panthers being in the desert."

"I'm not saying you *shouldn't* be scared. I'm glad to hear you admit that it's dangerous." The barking stopped and the dogs came back and arranged themselves around the fire. He put his gun on the ground. "I couldn't sleep very well," he said softly. "I've never slept with a strange woman before."

"I haven't slept with a man."

"I don't dare bring up the question of why you're really here. You're an educated young woman. If you need a job, I can persuade my father to give you one. He has the Weber Electrics franchise. Do you know the building on Jaffa Road? There's no reason for you to be out here in the wilderness. Suppose a real criminal found you?" He spoke quickly, as if he had been saving his objections.

"I'm here because I want to be. No one *put* me here." His assumptions were irritating.

He rubbed a hand across his face, trying to understand. "Why do you want to be?"

"To prove that I can take care of myself."

"I see." He didn't see.

His tone was so patronizing she went back to her spot and sat down, preparing to sleep again. He might as well have called her a liar. Or a fool. "Good night."

He sighed. "Good night to you."

Wasn't he going to say anything else?

"Whose idea was it for you to do this?"

"I told you."

"I know what you told me, but somebody has brainwashed you and given you gospel law, and you're petrified of deviating from it. If it were your own idea, you'd be more practical. The first thing on your mind wouldn't be the finer points of hospitality. You'd be thinking more of your safety." He sat up. "You've got to be a little more practical."

"I didn't hear myself ask for advice *or* sympathy. I'm doing fine."

"Nobody said you weren't doing fine. But I'm worried about you."

"It was *you* who was lost. It was *I* who rescued you. You were going the wrong way, remember? You'd have been chilled into pneumonia or died of thirst or been mauled by an animal. Oh, I forgot . . . you did have a gun. Do you know how to use it?"

"I've shot game," he answered, not at all offended, "but I'm sure you could shoot rings around me."

"I've been shooting since I was seven."

"Terrific. What'd you shoot, your teddy bears?"

"Very funny. Targets."

"And when did you become the big killer of lambs?"

"Nine."

"And you loved every bloodthirsty minute?"

"Oh, no. I hated it. I had nightmares over it."

"That's a relief," he said, vindicated. He lay down again, and she could hear him arranging his skimpy cover.

Again there was silence.

"Why didn't you tell me you had a gun?" she said accusingly. "You pretended to be afraid of mine, when all along you could have brought out yours."

"That's right!" He sat up as if she had just proved a crucial point. "You never ordered me to put my hands up, and you never asked if I had a gun. Two mistakes. *That's* what should have been on your mind, not fixing me the meal of a lifetime. Suppose it hadn't been me? Suppose it had been a real thief?"

"Who said you were in charge of my welfare?" Her voice was unexpectedly loud, and the dog cocked his head and looked from one to the other and growled mildly.

"Huh? That's the pot calling the kettle black. You were determined to be responsible for mine. Remember?"

He had her. *"C'est bien,"* she said crossly.

"She speaks French, too!" He lay down again with a sigh.

She knew she wasn't going to go to sleep, but what was the use of arguing with him. He was right. She *had* been careless but only because it was obvious he wasn't a thief, and she wasn't about to admit that. "What does it matter? You didn't kill me, and in the morning you'll be on your way."

She waited for him to keep arguing over her safety, but he was silent. *Please say something more.* He was breathing steadily. She would have liked to talk to him all night.

She awoke first and stopped to study his pale sleeping face. The brows and jaw and mouth were those of a man, yet his early-morning pallor made him look innocent. There was a deep, sculpted niche right above his mouth that she hadn't noticed. Ultimately, it wasn't his looks that intrigued her as much as his openness. He was free to do or think anything he liked.

The thought that in a few minutes he would go on his way and leave her alone made her feel desolate. The fact that he had been concerned about her safety and indignant over her carelessness made her peculiarly happy. But that wasn't the whole of it. She felt the stirrings of sexual longing. In the night, she had put her arms around herself, idly caressing her own shoulders, but she had wished it were his hands on her.

He moved, and she jumped and went to revive the fire to make breakfast. If he were going, let him go quickly.

"Good morning. What are you making that smells so good?" She was moody out of self-defense and kept her head down, stirring the little pan of batter. He turned slowly and took a deep, appreciative breath, then pointed to the tent. *"That* was our shelter? Without the fire, we would be stiff by now." He sat down and she handed him a filled cup and a bread cake smeared with honey. "Thank you." He squinted and took a good look at her. "Are you angry with me? Did I say something to offend you."

"No. I'm trying to feed you quickly. You wanted to be on your way early, didn't you?"

"I don't *want* to be, but my parents will be worried."

"I'm sure." She pursed her lips, determined not to say anything she'd regret. What she wanted to say was Please don't leave me. She made herself busy well away from the tent, but he came looking for her.

"You're a remarkable girl." She shrugged. "Can I do anything for you before I leave?"

"What did you have in mind?"

"I don't know. I thought you might need help rounding up the sheep." He looked out over the flock and shook his head. "You really know how to keep them together?"

"The dogs do most of it." She went and took a canteen out of an elaborate fitted backpack that straddled a donkey.

"That holds all your possessions?"

"Yes. My father had it sent for me from Switzerland. Everything fits in. They do a lot of camping in the Alps, I guess."

"Yes, they do, but it's recreational. Nothing like this." Her eyes veiled over. "I'd better be on my way." He put out his hand. "Thank you for everything."

"Here. Take this canteen. You'll need it. I have plenty of water."

"Thanks again."

"It was nothing," she said coolly.

"Oh, yes, it was." He took one of her hands in both of his. "I don't suppose I could persuade you to leave, too. This is no place . . ." She shook her head to stop him.

"You don't *have* to stay here."

"Yes, I do."

"You don't. You may choose to . . ."—she didn't answer—"but there are other ways to gain self-reliance." Seeing she was very sober, he smiled. "We could run away to London. Jump on my horse." She gave him a fierce look. "Well, you wouldn't dissolve, you know." She remained silent. "Sorry. It sounds as if I have no faith in you, but that's not true." He let go of her hand, and she watched him mount his horse and start off.

When he was well out of sight, she sat down with the extra bread cakes and fed the crumbs to one of the dogs. Tears came into her eyes and spilled over the animal's mangy fur. Two other dogs tried to nudge their way onto her lap. She still had six days before another shepherd would come and relieve her. There would be many hours to figure it all out—why she felt so horribly disappointed to see him leave. She looked around at the overwhelming *monotone*. Brown everywhere. *You don't have to stay here.* It was a silly thing, but until he said it she had never considered that she had a choice.

The *Directrice* of *L'École Française* was little over five feet tall, but no one would have believed it. Two attributes gave the illusion of height. She wore only white or black dresses or suits, simple high-heeled pumps, one important piece of jewelry, and a disarming loose chignon on top of her head.

More effective than her fashion sense was her insight into human character. She knew when to go with the moment and when to stick to the letter of the law. This afternoon, she had decided—rather impetuously—to go with the moment.

"Yes, *monsieur*." She stared appreciatively at the handsome young man. He was freshly shaved and his shirt was crisply ironed and his tie knotted just right. "How may I help you?"

Before he spoke, he gave her a generous smile. "*Madame*," he lingered over the word, "I would like your permission to have a visit with my cousin. I'm here only for two days and I'd be sorry to miss seeing her."

All her sensory antennae went up. "It doesn't seem too much to ask." She returned the smile. "Who is your cousin?"

The young man curled in his broad shoulders and took a significant breath. "The most beautiful girl in your school. The girl with the green eyes," he smiled and looked wistful, as if he were being poetic when she knew damn well he was being devious.

Eh bien, she'd help him out. "Ah, you could only mean one girl . . . Nijmeh." I should have known. He looks delirious.

"Yes, but please, if you could just not say anything to Nijmeh just yet. I'd like to surprise her."

"Aha . . . yes." This whole thing smelled higher than a week-old fish, but it was *audacious.* And *inventive.*

"If I wanted to take her for a cup of tea, would that be against school policy, *madame?*"

The *Directrice* pursed her lips and made a little noise to indicate that it was a foolish question. "Why would anything as civilized as a tea between two caring cousins be against school policy? Our senior girls must only sign out properly and return before six when we have our own supper. Of course, I'm assuming that you will be discreet and not expose her to anything deletirious." Her look warned him of unspoken horrors should he renege on this promise.

"Of course. And I'll see that she's back at the proper time. Please, not a word about who is here to see her."

"Not a word."

On her way to find the "most beautiful girl in her school," she peeked out the window and noted the license plate on the sports car parked in front. Ah . . . Saad. She even knew the family. So much the better. She hurried down the corridor in search of Nijmeh.

"*You! Oh!*" She put a hand to her lips and he was afraid she might scream, so he put his hand over her mouth and wrapped his arms around her in a warm hug. "Don't say anything just now," he whispered in her ear. "I told the *Directrice* I am your cousin from abroad. I'm sure you have many questions, which I'll answer in due time. I've had great difficulty finding you. My God, wait'll you hear! I didn't know your name—that was stupid!—so I had to bluff my way through every private school in the area. This country's *crawling* with private schools. The *Directrice* says I may take you out to tea, so let's get out of here before she changes her mind. I have so much to say to you. I'm going to remove my hand now, but you must promise not to scream. Promise?" She nodded and he removed his hand. "Let's get out of here."

He guided her out with his hand under her arm and opened the door to the car. "Act friendly—she may be watching out the window. If I had been in her position, I wouldn't have done what she did. I would have called the police."

"How do I act friendly?"

"Just keep smiling and look happy to see me. That would be the normal thing."

"I am happy to see you."

He put the car in gear and roared out the driveway, scattering pebbles. She kept her eyes fixed on his profile while he drove out on the road that led north.

"No," she squealed, grabbing his arm. "Don't go this way. It's the way to my house."

He nodded, executed a sloppy U-turn, and drove in the opposite direction, picked up the Street of the Prophets, and sped past the developed neighborhoods until he reached a lonely stretch of road. "Did you say you were happy to see me?"

She hadn't taken her eyes off his face. "Oh, yes."

He grinned in private appreciation of his success. "That's a relief . . ." —his voice wound down and he spoke slowly, tracing the line of her jaw with his finger. "Since I left you . . .—God, it seems like such a long time —I've thought mostly of you. I thought I probably wouldn't see you again because the chances you would survive that *adventure* seemed minimal. But, you did." He waited for a look of contempt, but her eyes were wide— a green so unusual he stopped talking a moment to appreciate them. "I didn't know your name or what school you attended. I figured out that it had to be a secondary school and one that taught French, so I didn't try the German or Italian schools. That only left about fifty others."

"But how did you know who to ask for?"

He put the car in gear. "That was my least favorite part of the charade, I can tell you. I had to assume an oily, man-of-the world look and ask for— now, don't be disgusted . . . remember, I had everything against me— 'the most beautiful girl in the school. The one with the green eyes.' Two of the principals became very agitated and thought they had an imbecile, or worse, on their hands. One chased me out of her office with a broom and ran after me all the way to the car." Nijmeh began to laugh and he joined her. They were laughing so hard he stopped the car again.

"But what about *Madame?* She knew it was me?"

"Right away. I had to control myself and keep from picking her up and throwing her in the air out of sheer gratitude. She said, 'Ah . . . you could only mean one girl, Nijmeh.' Your name is Nijmeh . . . star." His eyes sparkled with satisfaction. "Remarkable. I'm going to call you Star."

"And you? I still don't know your name."

"I'm James." He turned in his seat and put his arms around her. He kissed her gently, pulled away, and then kissed her again, a deeper, hungry kiss, which she returned with such intensity that he became uneasy. She wasn't some English popsie, eager to be felt up. Her open response to him was innocent. What girl in her right mind would wind herself around his arm without any coyness? "We don't have much time. It's already five, and I need twenty minutes to get you back. I wouldn't let *Madame* down by being late. I owe her a lot."

She tightened the stranglehold on his arm, as if it were keeping her from spilling out on the road. "I wanted to run after you when you left me that morning. It's all such a mystery. But I had never felt so happy in someone else's company. I wanted to sleep in the crook of your arm. Is this too bold? I don't care. Remember, you sat up in the middle of the night and yelled at me for not making you put your hands up?" She rubbed her cheek against his arm. "You were so matter-of-fact. As if we'd known each other for years."

"And I was right, too," he said indignantly. "How could your father have let you do such a thing?"

"Hasn't your father wanted you to carry on the family tradition?"

"Not my father. He went to school in Massachusetts. In the United States. He's not a nationalist."

She scrunched up her brow. "Mine's the opposite. He wouldn't approve of my seeing you, so we've got to be very careful."

"I'm not so bad," he smiled, "I'm about to enter law school. He'd like that, wouldn't he?"

"I don't know."

"I told *Madame* I would be here only for two days, so I can't show my face again. How will I see you?"

"You can call. We receive calls between five and six in the evening. And I'll find a way to meet you. Don't you have to go back to school?"

"Not until late January. We have three months . . ." He kissed her again and then started the car. "We'd better start back."

They were returning with the sun in front of them, and it cast the famous golden glow over the bare, reddish mountains and buildings. "I'll find some way to see you." The windows of the car were closed to keep out the dust and, in that space, his deep voice droned soothingly and then it rose in righteousness. "After all, we're not criminals. We can see each other. We're grown people."

Their meetings were necessarily short—an hour or two robbed from her ordinary activities. On Friday nights, she usually took the three o'clock jitney home, but now she waited until five. "I stayed to use the library," she'd tell her mother, and her father didn't get home until six so he didn't know at all. She took a new interest in her clothes and once or twice asked

Delal to go shopping with her. Delal was immediately suspicious. She sniffed out a difference in Nijmeh's attitude. Her usual wide-eyed stare was gone. For once, she looked like she had something up her sleeve. What could it be?

James and Nijmeh had become bolder, and instead of skulking off in the car to some deserted vacant lot they sometimes went to a museum or to a movie. Once he took her to his home while his parents were out—she was shocked at how wealthy he was—and up to his room. She had lain on his bed with him on top of her, humming with happiness, kissing her mouth and her throat and—after she willingly opened her blouse—her breasts. When she realized how frenzied he was and how hard he had become, she moved her hand down. "Don't touch me now," he warned. "I'm . . . too excited . . ."

"James," she whispered, "please. Do whatever you want to . . ."

"Are you crazy? Your father would kill us both. Look . . . just hearing you say that has cooled me off. Nijmeh," he looked at her sternly. "You can't be so trusting and willing."

"Why not? I love you."

"Is that it? Is it your wild love for me?"

He said it in a joking way, but she nodded and made no attempt to cover herself. She was lying on her back, her pupils were so dilated that the green was just a slim halo for the black center. Her breasts were jutting out enticingly and he closed his lips around them gently and allowed them to pop out before he enclosed them again. His hands went under her and he eased the fingers of both hands between her thighs while he still held onto her buttocks. She stirred and tried to pull her legs apart, but he kept them closed. She struggled to open her legs wider and started moving with him, butting herself against him rhythmically until he allowed her to open herself to him. "Oh, God . . . I'm going to come. Wait!" He pressed himself against her and buried his face in her breasts. Her legs went around him, and she made so much noise he put his hand over her mouth just before he came all over his bedspread.

"I love you," he said tenderly, buttoning up her blouse. "I was sure I wouldn't fall in love like this, but I was wrong. I love you," he said again and kissed each of her palms. "We're going to go to your father."

She jumped off the bed so fast the springs shuddered. "James, don't say that. We're not going to my father. You can't even say that in jest. It's not funny."

"I'm not trying to be funny. I want to marry you. What's wrong with that? I'm twenty-four years old. I'm not a criminal or destitute. This may come as a surprise to you but I've been called . . . well,"—he looked sheepish—". . . eligible."

"It has nothing to do with you. It's me. He'd never approve of anyone that he didn't choose himself."

"How do you know? Has he said so?"

"No, but I know."

"We'll have to tell him sometime."

She slumped down on the bed again. "Why? You'll be leaving in a few weeks. I'll prepare him while you're away."

"Nijmeh, I think I could convince him. I don't like you taking the brunt of it. Let's tell him together."

"James, no. You don't know my father. I'll prepare him during the spring, and we can go to him when you come home in July."

He dropped the subject but the very next time they met, it was on his mind. "I'm going to telephone your father and go to see him: Hello, Mr. Saleh, you don't know me, but I'm in love with your daughter. Now wait, before you shoot that gun, hear me out . . ."

"No," she screeched and he saw that she was terrified.

"Hey, I'm sorry. Relax. If you're that upset, I take it back." Her face was still tense. "Here," he said, "have an apple." She shook her head. "All right, I'll eat it myself." He took an enormous bite and made such a loud crack that she turned to look at him and then screamed.

"James, no! *Wait!* You've eaten part of a worm."

He looked at his apple. "So I have," he grinned. "Oh, well. I'll just take the other half. Maybe the poor thing will connect inside. I seem to remember they regenerate."

"*James, no!*" She grabbed the apple. "Don't eat it." She screamed again as the worm fell into her lap. "I'll have to find it."

"Hey, here it is." He held it up and she screamed again and put a hand over her eyes. "It's all right. See, it's not real. It was a joke."

She didn't hear him. "You ate it! Oh, my God."

"No, no. It was a joke. See? It's rubber. It's painted rubber. I put it in the apple."

"*You* . . ." she pressed her lips with her hand, as if letting go would make her hysterical. "It's painted! Oh!" She began to laugh. "I thought you ate it!" She laughed so hard that tears formed in her eyes.

"You're laughing," he beamed. "That's wonderful."

She fell in love like an unsophisticated girl. With her mind, her heart, and her body. He made her laugh and held her hand and kissed her. He was so handsome. "I am desperately in love," she would whisper to herself in the early morning. Desperation was the accurate word for what she felt. An overwhelming physical greediness. An insistent desire to be touched. She would twirl her long hair around her fingers and dream of his kisses and caresses. She would begin to perspire and become soaked, lying in her bed and recreating his arousal, her own response—legs wide, skin flushed and burning, lips bruised, the feathery feel of fingertips, a breathless anxiety. My beloved wants only me! This is what I was made for. To be a woman for him! Finally, life made sense. How could she have lived before? How could she have been satisfied?

Her openness made James shake his head, as if something that would have been very dangerous with anyone else was safe with him. Still, it overwhelmed him and he would wince and look around for someone to share the novelty of finding a girl who was so breathtakingly, *foolishly,* honest.

"You're lucky it's me you're offering your body to," he'd admonish. "At least I have the sense to save you from your wanton behavior. You're supposed to play hard to get."

"I love you. Why should I play hard to get?" she'd ask logically.

"There, you see! What sane girl would make such an incriminating statement! It sends a man running for cover."

"Will you run?"

"That's the other thing," he looked perplexed, "I find it not threatening at all. I'm honor bound to protect you from some other lout who would take advantage of your . . . I'll call it generosity."

She didn't care what he called it. For her, it was the unexpected familiarity that made life exciting. She liked his proprietary arm thrown around her shoulders. He pushed back her hair and adjusted her sweater or yanked her across a street of traffic. She was his. "You want to make me happy," she reminded him.

"That shouldn't be such a novelty. Didn't Mama and Papa want you to be happy?"

"My father wants me to be happy as long as I'm doing something he approves of. 'Loyalty' is the word I hear most often." She had never spoken or thought of her father in such harsh terms. The freedom of it made her overstate the case. "If I do exactly as he says, he smiles. If I don't, he becomes distant. And when my father's distant, the people around him might as well be in Siberia. My mother . . . well, she's another case altogether. She's never recovered from having me, I guess. There were several miscarriages before and after me. She looks at me sometimes as if I'm going to disappear. She's not a very relaxed person unless she's out-of-doors or on a horse. Then she looks magnificent. I love to see her ride."

James sighed. "That sounds about par for the course for mothers and fathers. Don't feel you did any worse than the rest of us. My mum's whole existence is playing bridge and making crepe-paper roses for all her charity balls."

Perhaps James was right. Perhaps her parents were no more strict or idiosyncratic than anyone else's, but she felt differently about them. It was no longer her father's smile and her mother's eyes that danced before her prior to sleep. They were fuzzy figures compared to the clear visceral reaction to closeness with a man. She was drenched in the sweetness of it. Love swept her clean and broke the old connections. Her connection to her father snapped like a dry, brittle twig.

32

How do you know you can trust me?

Something was up. Nijmeh wasn't Nijmeh. She was twitchy. Her mouth was drooping and she played distractedly with a ring on her finger while she spoke. Where was that old placid goody-girl? "You look as if your dog died." It was titilating to watch that face all crumpled. "What's wrong?"

"Why do you think there's something wrong?"

"Are you kidding? You look glum. I've never seen this dark side of you," she said sarcastically. "This may sound rotten, but I'm surprised that you can be *emotional.*"

"I wanted to go to the films," said Nijmeh. *"King Lear* is showing with Laurence Olivier."

"That's why you're upset? Incredible! I didn't know you were interested in films. You could probably *be* in films." Delal enjoyed pointing out the larger picture in people's lives.

"Don't say that in front of my father. He'd have a heart attack."

"Yeah, I know. So why can't you go to the films?"

"There's a meet and I'm supposed to participate. My mother's counting on it."

"You mean a horse thing?" She had never understood all the passion over horses. She knew it was chic for girls to love horses. It was supposedly a sign of good breeding to go gaga over the beasts, but she didn't like them at all. She didn't like the smell, and she was frightened of falling off. She was more than a little respectful of Nijmeh's ability.

Nijmeh smiled briefly. "That 'horse thing,' as you call it, is the King's Meet for the Art of Dressage."

"Ugh. You go in for that sort of thing? Do you actually crave it?"

"No. I like the horses, but I hate the silly posturing. My mother has this thing about it. It's the only demand she makes on me, so it's hard to tell her it doesn't appeal to me."

It's the only demand she makes on you because your father makes all the others, dummy. "Why don't you go to the flick anyway?"

"The what?"

"The flick, the film. So you'll miss one lousy meet. Your mother will forget about it. Two hours later, she'll be her old self. Take it from me, mine is never as heated up as I predict she'll be over anything. My father's even worse. He hits the roof over something and then is so contrite he goes out and buys me a present. Parents are crazy. You just have to know how to manage them."

"You make everything sound so simple, Delal. Your mind is very clear-cut, and you don't agonize over every move."

"Well, some of us are like that. What do you say? Are you going to defy Mama and emancipate yourself? Take my advice. Don't tell her in person. If you leave a message, she can't argue with a piece of paper. You really like Shakespeare?"

Her eyes lowered until just the lashes were visible, splayed out—two near tears still clinging—like little stalactites against those pale contoured cheeks. "It isn't only the film. I want to meet someone."

"The plot thickens! Holy Moses, who is it? Wait. Don't tell me. It's a male, right?" This was unexpected and it made Delal uncomfortable. Nijmeh was holding out on her. This explained the sudden interest in clothes. Good God, if her father found out! She wished he would find out.

"His name's James."

"Oh, boy! He's a foreigner. *That* will definitely give your father that heart attack. Is he crazy about you, this James?" Her tone was cold, but Nijmeh was too upset to notice.

"I don't know," said Nijmeh "I only know I'm crazy about him. Delal, you musn't mention this to your mother or anyone. If my father found out, it would be awful."

"I'll say! That would be the end of James!"

"Don't say that," Nijmeh hissed. "That would not be the end of James. It might be the end of me, but it wouldn't be the end of James."

"Why are you confiding in me?" asked Delal. "How do you know you can trust me?"

"I don't." She stopped smiling.

"Well, what's it going to be? The horses?"—Delal's voice deepened dra-matically—"or danger?"

"Danger," whispered Nijmeh. "I guess you've convinced me."

"Good. Remember, you only live once."

Once she knew what Nijmeh was up to, Delal could think of little else. Her skin changed temperature and she could feel her blood running along. There was a sense of outrage at being *left behind*. In her imagination she found the man of her dreams over and over. Someone handsome and distant and involved in important work. Perhaps she would work alongside him. Her body was all ready for love. She had read in a book about a heroine who "ached" to be kissed and had thought Yes! That's it, exactly! She ached to be kissed, too.

That Nijmeh already had a man drove her crazy. The words went round and round. It isn't only the film. I want to meet *someone*. Then she got the idea of spying (only for a moment did it make her squirm) on them and getting a look at the man who loved Nijmeh. It was important to see exactly what Nijmeh had found for herself; otherwise the idea was horribly threatening. People went to museums to see intimate paintings, and that wasn't considered voyeuristic. So why was it wrong to sneak into the Bijou to see her cousin with James?

They were in the last row. His arm was around her back and they were looking at each other, not the screen. He was tall, and in the dimness it seemed he was older, too, a real man. Accidentally, the light from the screen lit them and she saw his hand around Nijmeh's upper arm. He was stroking her skin, gently at first and then—oh, my—much more insistently. She could feel that masculine finger on her own skin, and it made her feel hot and then cold, as if all the hair on her body were standing on end while a breeze blew through it. Did others evaluate her the way she was evaluating James? Did they secretly laugh at her for being cheerful? Did they think she was trying too hard? Did they feel sorry for her?

When they walked out, Delal watched James's face and knew instantly what kind of a man he was. Good at sports. Good at most things. She recognized that unworried look of someone who made eyes light up when he appeared. Confident and full of vitality, he made his way through the crowd as if he deserved to go first. He was dressed in just the kind of clothes that appealed to Delal—rough, tweedy, expensive clothes. He was what she would have dreamed of for herself and that realization made her bitter. She couldn't take her eyes off him, but he was oblivious to her. Resentment left her limp. She felt that Nijmeh, by having someone, was ruining her own chances of finding someone as nice.

"Mother,"—it was after dinner and Julia was reading in the study— "what would you say if I told you Nijmeh is sneaking around meeting a man? A foreign man."

Julia closed the book around her finger. "Delal, what are you talking about?"

"I asked my question first. What would you say if she was?"

"I'd say it would break her father's heart." Julia's voice was circumspect.

"Why would it break his heart? I mean, as opposed to making him angry?"

"Samir has raised Nijmeh to take over his role in the community. She's his spiritual heir, his personal production. If she were to be taken away by a man who wasn't right—especially a foreigner—I don't want to think about what would happen."

"Well, she is."

"She is what?"

"Sneaking around and meeting a foreign man."

"Delal, are you sure?"

"Of course I'm sure. I've seen them. They go to the movies and neck."

"Oh, no!" Julia rose.

"Oh, yes! Not that I blame her. He's very cute. But if your brother wants Nijmeh to stay a virgin, you'd better tell him she's on the way to crossing over the bridge." Delal sighed and then grinned. "Poor Samir. All that work for nothing."

"The father is Charles Saad," said Nadia. She looked pale and stunned. The news that her daughter was deeply involved with a man made her panic. She couldn't shake the idea Nijmeh had inherited weakness of character from those *other* parents. Some sexual mania. If she were compelled by forces beyond her, she couldn't obey. She hadn't wanted to think of the *other* parents, but, now, making life decisions for Nijmeh frightened her. Perhaps they should let her alone to do as she wanted. That was the least they could do. Oh, God, why was remorse coming now, at this late date? It was different for Samir. For him, it was the simple need to protect his flesh and blood. "They have the Weber Electrics—"

"I know what they have," he said impatiently. "Every time a phonograph is sold or a record or a radio or a toaster or any appliance, he gets a cut."

Within a few days of his sister's call, Samir found out what he had to about James Sheridan Saad and his parents. He had no strong feelings about the mother. *But the father!* The father was a dandy who had lost his own father during the cholera epidemic at the onset of the war. He wore cravats, or whatever you call those things that Englishmen stuff into their shirt fronts to herald the idea that they are *at their leisure.* He smoked little dark-brown cigarettes inserted into a long holder, which he used to punctuate his sentences. He had adopted the worst traits of British aristocracy and leached out his own nationality. An opportunist without roots. The sort of man Samir detested.

The mother was the daughter of an upper-class Whig who had left his seat in Parliament to become Managing Director of Weber Electrics, a large, diversified appliance company. Lavinia Saad was elegant, well-intentioned, and superficial. Her one daring act had been to marry the dashing *Méditerrané* she had met during a summer visit to Cape Cod. He had appeared in perfect white suits and wore his thick hair slicked back. The sun had turned his skin to gold. He had a new business degree, flashing dark eyes, and a devastating accent.

"You're not mad because he has a successful business?" Nadia knew it had nothing to do with business. It was the English blood. Was he still bothered by her involvement with Victor?

"Of course not, but I hate the fact that he stays here simply *to make money*. If he could make a better living elsewhere, he'd leave forever."

"Are you sure that's the way it is?"

"Yes, I'm sure. He's the kind of man who loves to be loved by other nationalities. They spend half the year in Europe with her family. They have no ties to Jerusalem other than his lucrative business."

"The young man is going away soon," she said lamely. "Julia said that Delal told her he's going to law school in Edinburgh. Perhaps it'll die a natural death."

"No," he said. "This is serious. Nijmeh's not a glib, superficial girl. If she's involved with this man, she's given him her whole heart."

That Friday afternoon, he went to bring his daughter home for the weekend. He waited for her in the parlor, and when she saw his eyes she knew he had found out. Oh, God! Her mouth went dry, her eyes burned, and her heart doubled its speed. Her body was preparing for defense.

"What's wrong?" The stiff, formal room made her whisper.

"I came to give you a ride home."

"Oh?" She had been so eager to see James that her father's presence while it made her fearful also made her resentful. "I can't go home with you. I was planning to stay until the last minute to do some work. You should have given me some warning. What a shame, you've wasted a trip." Her manner was strained and formal, and she could see his surprise and hurt.

"I'll wait for you."

"Wait?" He continued to stare at her. "Why are you looking at me? What's wrong?"

"Nothing at all," he said. "You're a beautiful young woman, and I'm startled at how quickly you grew up."

"Quickly?" she squealed. "Not quickly at all. Delal grew up quickly. I took forever."

"But now it's done." He couldn't keep the sadness out of his voice. "You're a woman."

"*Baba,* don't wait. Please."

"Of course I'll wait." He became diabolically calm. "I want to take you home myself."

"There's something wrong. I know it." Her voice was shrill.

"What could be wrong?" he said stiffly, and she saw his mouth tighten. "You tell me."

She couldn't tell him anything. "I'll get my things."

They had dinner without mentioning James. She felt as if she could reach out and grab the air and it would crackle from the tension, but her father carried on a conversation. He spoke about Charles De Gaulle as the only hope of France, and he said that Eisenhower was exactly what America needed. He said that a friend of his had ordered a television set for them and it would come in a day or two. Before bed, they sat like three stones, listening to the radio. The parlor of the sheik's house had a vaulted ceiling and terrazzo floors that made the broadcast sound ominous. The announcer said John Foster Dulles had visited Jerusalem on his way to Amman. He had stopped at the Mandelbaum Gate for barely twenty minutes, distracted and unapproachable. The Arabs, who had expected a sincere and fruitful diplomatic exchange, were bitterly disappointed, said the announcer.

The next morning, Samir asked Nijmeh to accompany him to the farm. He had two horses saddled and they rode together around all of the acreage and out into the wilderness. He was silent. The desert had a curious effect on him, especially at this time of year when the first showers were bringing the cracked earth to life. He couldn't help but compare his predictable routine with the precarious days he had known as a youth with Marwan, and it made him introspective. Fledgling bustards chirped in the low grass. Soon the entire area would glow with green and the scent of the flowers would perfume the air. He saw that Nijmeh, too, was moved. As they reached the crest of a hill, a pack of wild gazelles came toward them at full speed, then dashed to their left without breaking rank, and then zigzagged wildly to the right. Their pacemaker was a white buck, so dazzling that momentarily father and daughter were transfixed.

"He's so beautiful," she said. "It makes me sad to see him."

"Why sad?"

"A hunter will pick him off in the next day or two."

"Undoubtedly."

"His life is at its peak. He's so perfect. His legs, his head, his eyes are perfectly made. It's such a waste. I don't understand that part of it at all. Why does he have to die?" Her eyes were full.

"If he dies now, with one swift crack to the heart, it's better than being mauled to death by a wild animal when he's too old to run."

"Baba . . ." the beauty of the scene made her feel bereft, as if James were already a memory. But that was frightening. Everything she saw made her think of him. She wanted him to see the buck and experience this perfect morning. The urgency to see him clouded reason and made her reckless. Her father must already know all there was to know. No doubt he had already traced James's family back a few years. There was no need to pretend. "I love him," she said. At that moment she was sure her father would give in. "You're not going to take me away from him, are you?"

"You were never his."

"But I am! *I am!* He makes me happy. And free."

Samir moved closer. She was the treasure of his heart. Nothing suited her beautiful face more than the wide-brimmed hat. The shadow it made emphasized all the strong planes of her face, the peaks above her mouth, the deep cleft. He shifted position on the horse and flexed one hand, suddenly tired and frightened. Her face appeared *sensual.* Those wide eyes that had looked at him with faith for so many years were wary. His imagination went in wild directions, presenting a vivid picture of a failed life. His own failed life if he lost her.

"You'll marry the right man and it won't be the son of an opportunist." His voice became hard and dull. Other fathers had panicked at the idea of turning their daughters over to another man, but Nijmeh was his only link to the future. "All this belongs to you; all of it is in your hands," he warned. "Your place is here with someone who has the same roots and the same commitment."

"If you only knew him, you'd feel differently. He's so sure of himself, and he has the power to make you feel sure, too."

"I don't doubt it. If you love him, he must have great charm, but charm isn't enough."

"You make him sound shallow," she said bitterly and then, echoing precisely what James had said, she added, "you don't have to slaughter lambs and fight off wolves to be a substantial person. Your definition of goodness is so narrow."

Samir looked stung. Even though he knew that wasn't what he'd taught her, the accusation had the power to hurt. She seemed possessed. If she thought she was in love, it was an idea foisted on an unknowing, vulnerable girl. He struggled to keep anger out of his voice. "I have no definition of goodness," he said simply. "I only have a job to do. And that is to instill in any child of mine a powerful love of the land. If I don't do that and other men like me don't do it, who will care for our past? Who will bring all our traditions into the future? It would be tragic if there were nothing left."

She saw a look of sadness and vulnerability in her father's face, and she was torn between the strong desire to console him and the equally strong pull to not capitulate. Her tenderness toward him made her angry and frightened, as if it were proof that she was too weak-spirited. "I wouldn't turn my back on those things. If James thought they were important to me, he wouldn't interfere. He wants me to be happy." Her voice was too high and thin. Her happiness sounded like a frivolous goal. "Please let him come and meet you," she added in desperation.

"I would feel dishonest giving you false hope." It was strange. If he closed his eyes, he could forget what had happened and see her future as it should have been.

"Then how can you say you love me?" she shouted. "You're no better than a dictator. It has to be all on your terms." The words flew out. She felt such uncontrollable rage that she thought her heart would stop or explode.

"Not a dictator," he said gently. "Just a father who has lived long enough to see the pitfalls of short-term delirium. This is your first crush. There'll be others. You'll see."

His smugness made her gag. "You think I'm an idiot who's being swept off her feet by the first man who pays attention to her? That's not true. I could have encouraged a lot of boys who were interested. But I chose him. You don't want to think that I have any sense because that would ruin your neat theories. But I have. *I have! I have good sense and I've chosen the best possible man to love. This time, Baba, you're wrong!*"

The possibility that there was a kernel of truth in what she said made something burst in Samir. "Don't you dare raise your voice to me. You're not wise enough to make the best choice, no matter what you think."

If she had had something to smash, she would have smashed it. Her heart was pounding so hard it made her tremble. Horrible despot! She hated him. All she could do was hurl words at him. "You can't make me marry anyone. You can tie me up or lock me in a room, *but you can't make me do anything!*" She gave him one more hard look. "Even if I wanted to obey you, I can't," she said with spite. "I love him too much. I can't give him up." She was looking forward to making him angrier, but he remained silent. She turned the horse around and rode away, imagining he would gallop after her and hold her back physically, but when she turned to look, he hadn't moved at all.

* * *

"I've spoken to my parents," James said quietly. He had come by the school, shown himself to Mme. Boulanger and, miraculously, she had allowed them to leave together.

"Really?" It had not occurred to her that his parents had anything to do with it. "And . . . ?"

"They were surprised. They didn't know quite what to say. I guess they'd always assumed I'd marry someone"—his voice became sarcastic—"from the vast pool of international beauties."

"Oh?" There was hurt in her voice.

"Hey . . ." He put his hand under her chin. "I didn't say that I *had* planned to do that. I merely said that's what they thought would happen. If you want to know the truth, I don't think they thought much about it at all. And anyway, I don't see what you're so put off about. You're not going to get rid of me, Nijmeh." He grinned, put his hands behind his head, and sat back as if preparing for a long, embattled stay.

"Oh, James." She was all over him with kisses. Then she curled up against his chest and put her arms around him and cried softly against his shirt.

"Why so sad?"

"Nothing's going to be easy."

"Certainly it is. It might be hard here, but has it ever occurred to you that this isn't the whole world?"

"It's been my whole world." She was thinking that he should have been a little less carefree.

"Maybe it can stop being your whole world. There are other ways to live." He said this with a tone of slight superiority which made her think he had wanted to say it before.

"I love it here."

"You've been told you love it."

"That's not true." She knew it was true, but she also loved it. "Can you say this isn't beautiful?" They were facing east to the dark hills of Moab.

"You should see the light in Paris just at dusk. That's beautiful, too."

His reasonableness irked her, but she had no answer. Paris. She had never pictured a life away from here. She had never thought of Paris at all and now, with just those few words, he had set up a longing to see it.

Samir did nothing to prevent her seeing James, which left her with a feeling of dread. She was too proud to ask. Samir's calm was disturbing to Nadia, too. After the first few agitated days, he seemed emotionally free again as if the problem had evaporated. It was the same unnatural calm he had displayed when she kept miscarrying. "I know you *will* have a child," he had insisted, as if his will were all that was needed. She had never rid herself of the notion that finding Nijmeh was somehow tied to Samir's perfect faith. How many times had she seen him wait out a difficult situation with that unshakeable *knowing* that the outcome would be right. He was doing it now, and it broke her heart to think of unsuspecting Nijmeh thinking she had won out. But it was for Nijmeh's own good, wasn't it? Her head went round and round.

Finally she said something. "You didn't forbid her to see him?"

"No. What can I do, lock her up?"

"Aren't you going to do anything?" Nadia, too, was fearful.

"I have to think about what to do," he said. "It was my own fault, after all. I didn't realize she was a woman and would begin concocting ideas of love. We'll have to see what young men are available. Do you have anyone in mind?"

They were in bed and Nadia sat up. "Let me see . . . When it's your own daughter, no one seems right."

"The best thing would be to lure her away, but I have to have something to lure her with."

"Let's see if I understand this correctly," said Delal. "You want me to receive your boyfriend's letters when he goes abroad and pass them over to you secretly?" She was purposely using language that would embarrass Nijmeh. "I would be the go-between?" She put a finger to her brow. "Do I want to do that? Do I want to take the risk of offending your father? To say nothing of my mother, who would probably never forgive me for aiding the man who caused her brother misery? I would be taking a big chance." She pretended to be mulling it over. Delal was surprised that Nijmeh hadn't caved in to her parents' demands. "Why don't you just go with him? Keep it simple."

"Well," Nijmeh looked straight ahead. "For one thing, he didn't ask me."

"Oh. Too bad." She looked mildly apologetic. "I guess you really love him." Nijmeh nodded. "He'll probably ask you to marry him when he has a profession. He wants to offer you a decent life. It's not such a long time, you know, and in the meantime, he'll keep in touch—through me."

"I'll find a way to make it up to you."

"Well, let's see if he writes, first," she said breezily. Nijmeh was a very different person now. The face definitely showed that something had happened. Around the mouth—she chewed nervously on her lips. Maybe she did that to deflect her sexual needs. She had been reading about nymphomaniacs. Nijmeh's eyes looked as if they'd seen a thing or two. Maybe she'd done it with James a lot of times.

"The letters will be addressed to you. Will that be a problem?"

"Not at all. Have them sent to the paper." Delal—approaching twenty and with more than enough credits to graduate—worked three days a week reviewing films (and reporting on minor crimes) for *The Palestine Post.* "No one will be the wiser. I'll keep them safe. By the way, have you slept with James?"

Nijmeh looked surprised but not shocked. "No. I wanted to."

"So?"

"He wouldn't. He thought it would be too damaging."

"Damaging? How?"

"Because a girl in my situation . . . sheltered . . . and my father . . . . well, the whole thing. He felt it would be disastrous."

"It would be disastrous only if he weren't planning to marry you. If he only wanted to use you for a quick thrill. You know, get into your pants and then say, 'ta ta' and be off. Then you'd be soiled goods—as they say—for the husband who got you." She waited for some response, but Nijmeh had none. "Well? Is he or isn't he planning to be your guy forever and ever?"

Nijmeh blinked. It was a relief to talk frankly. "I love him desperately. That seems an odd word to use with love, but when I can't see him I become desperate."

"How can you be satisfied to give him a few kisses and be madly in love? You've got to give him a good reason to think that this is it. That he's obligated to you and, for all intent and purpose, you're already 'married.' "

"Obligated? I don't want him to feel obligated."

"Committed, then. You like that word better?" She brought her hands together on her lap and sat up straight. "Look, you're probably thinking I haven't had so much experience with men, so what do I know. But I *do* know. Men like James . . . they're never *desperately* in love or ever *really* unhappy. Oh, they like the odd little challenge. Winning at sports, drinking beer faster, or doing the daring deed. They're hardly ever crazy for love. They're usually crazy for war or money, but not your James probably. He's had too easy a life."

"You make him sound weak and he's not."

"Not weak. Just not tried and tested in the same way as a poor man or one who's plain. When it comes to love, you have to make up their mind for them. It takes work and a little psychology. You've got to paint a little picture for James of the two of you as really bound together, and that usually means sex. It's not such a big deal, you know. I mean in any other country. Only here, they make it seem as if it's the difference between life and death. But it isn't. If you want to keep James and make him feel committed, I would make it my business to go to bed with him."

This little speech left Nijmeh with an odd expression on her face. A look of discovery. "I think you're probably right."

"Of course I'm right." They were both silent. Nijmeh was looking down and Delal took the opportunity to stare. When she spoke, it was with unaccustomed sincerity. "I keep thinking if I stare long enough, I'll finally get inside your face and see how it's made. See how you're made. The difficulty is, I can't seem to get a good enough look at you. It's just skin and bones, but it's so much more than that."

"Skin and bones is *all* it is. What you've got up here,"—Nijmeh touched her head and her heart—"and here, is what draws people to you."

"That sounds sweet, but it's not true," said Delal calmly. "If a man decides to marry me, it will be because of my money. Maybe afterward he'll find out what's in my head and in my heart, but not soon enough to make a difference." Nijmeh started to protest, but Delal held up her hand. "Please, this isn't a bid for sympathy. Believe me."

"The things that attract people are hidden and mysterious. My mother was no beauty and my father—he could have had anyone—chose her. Besides, no man that you decide on will have a chance to escape. You're a determined girl, with astonishing confidence and a generous heart."

33

There is a man who is both cultured and accomplished . . . a doctor.

When he thought about it, Samir felt unprepared to negotiate a bethrothal for his daughter. He had always felt *above* all that social jockeying. It was so artificial. He had assumed that the man for Nijmeh would materialize when he was needed. This stupid assumption now placed him in a peculiar position.

If his father hadn't died. If his mother hadn't left. If he had had more brothers and sisters. If the wars hadn't killed so many people. If so many young men hadn't emigrated to America. If the Partition hadn't wreaked havoc on so many lives. Then there would have been a network of family to handle the matter of Nijmeh's betrothal. As it was, any one of his office girls knew more about the eligible men on the marriage market than he. The girls had discussions that sounded sensible (when they weren't giggling). In his vulnerable state, he was tempted to seek their help. They had practical information that he lacked. They also had the instinct needed for matchmaking. But what could he say—I need a prince for my daughter . . . and fast?

A more discreet source of information was Rose Muffrige who worked at the post office. People said Rose knew everything that went on, that was about to go on, or that had already ended. It was a bitter joke. He would have argued mightily that gossip had no good end and he didn't support it as a pastime, but he needed information.

Rose was surprised to see him and particularly so early in the morning. "The boss comes for stamps? Why?"

"To find out what's going on. Isn't this the place?" No use beating around the bush.

Rose, a large-bosomed woman with an elaborate upswept hairdo, was precisely framed by the shiny grill. She looked artificial and theatrical. "I'd be embarrassed to waste your time with silly gossip." She lowered her eyes shyly.

"What gossip?" he asked eagerly.

"Comings, goings, budding romances. Who's adding to his house.

Who's changing jobs." Rose, in her nervousness, was too eager to rattle off her credentials.

He stared at Rose as if he expected a performance. "If you had a daughter, which young man would be your first choice for her?" He tried to sound casual. "Someone cultured . . ." his voice trailed off. This was awkward.

Rose looked dumbfounded. Samir was making her his confidante. She waved her hand in the air, trying not to appear flustered, and took up his sentence. "Someone accomplished. Humble yet strong. Someone a wife could respect." Samir nodded. "Oof . . ." The task was too much for her. "There are boys and there are *boys.* Let me see." She was quiet for a long time as if riffling through a mental file. She also looked worried. Someone she considered eligible might make Samir laugh. Nijmeh was a precious only child.

After a few moments, her eyes brightened and a smile of triumph spread over her face. "There is a man who is both cultured and accomplished, *a doctor,*" she whispered and looked around. "He's on his way home here for a visit. Paul Halaby. You remember his grandfather owned the first car. He drove it even if he only had to go one block. The family was always modern. They sent Paul to Johns Hopkins, the finest medical school in America. He was the only boy, after all, and they wanted his life to be important. He's tall," she emphasized, as if this statistic would clinch her choice. "After a few years in practice, he'll be back here for good and take care of all of us. He's my first, second, and third choice. He would be perfect for Nijmeh."

He didn't know what to say. This seemed to be the end of Rose's monologue. He cocked his head, nodded, and mumbled good-bye. Outside, he rotated his shoulders, first forward and then backward to release tension. It was the first time in many days that his mind wasn't buzzing with too many thoughts. Could he trust this suggestion? At least he had taken some action instead of just brooding. Any girl would be excited over a doctor. Paul Halaby. Of course. Now he remembered the name. The parents had gone with their son to the States.

Paul Halaby. Paul Halaby. His mind latched on to the name, and it went clickety-click with each step. He turned it this way and that. He pictured a tall, dignified man in doctor's clothes with a mask across his face. A doctor was important. He dealt with life and death. My God, could this be the answer?

He was the textbook case of the hometown boy who goes away and makes good. His father's brother had gone to Johns Hopkins in Baltimore,

Maryland, and become a doctor, and when Paul Halaby reached college age, he followed his uncle to Maryland and medicine with admirable dedication. He was the only son in a family of five girls. Early on, his parents had made him believe that he was the earth, the sun, and the moon, and he grew up with the expectation that life would treat him well and give him every opportunity. After graduation, he was offered a residency in his specialty, which was obstetrics and gynecology, at a medium-sized hospital in Washington, D.C.

He had been a resident for two months and was examining a young woman complaining of persistent cramps and also an irregular menses. His fingers were well inside the patient's vagina while the other hand pressed down on her pubis to better palpate the uterus, which felt engorged and spongy, two reliable signs of pregnancy. He stopped probing and was formulating the words to deliver this news.

"Don't take your hand away. *Please.*" Her voice was intentionally sensual, and he was so startled that he yanked his hand away.

"Nuts. I should have kept my mouth shut. A few more pokes and I would have been there. Now what do I do?" She was annoyed. She lifted her knees, took her legs out of the stirrups, and rocked herself from side to side. He was stunned and uncertain, but also deeply aroused. The more she rocked, the harder he became. She stopped rocking and flapped her legs, bringing her knees together and then letting them fall apart. That didn't exactly cool him off. "Come on, lover," she said smoothly, "don't leave me like this."

He barely had the patience to unzip his pants, and climb on top of her. "Hey, not so fast." On one of his upward strokes, she let him slide out and closed her legs to tease him. "Take it easy." He was too far gone to accommodate her. His hand parted her legs and he put himself inside her quickly, which made her *ooh* and *ahh.* She grabbed his backside, digging her fingers between his buttocks. "Put your hands under me," she commanded. "You're not touching where I need it, damn it. Come on, lift me up. You're a doctor, don't you know what I need?" He was so close to coming that he was beyond being insulted. He pressed her to him, and she arched and wound her legs around him. With his body shuddering and his conscience shattered, they climaxed together, which seemed idiotically romantic, seeing as they had attacked each other like animals.

"Oh, God, I'm late," she said immediately, jumping off the table and disappearing behind the little screen. "By the way, did you find the problem?"

"The problem?" he was still in the throes of deep regret.

"The cramps. Remember?"

"Oh, yes. It looks like you're pregnant."
There was a long silence. Then a sigh. Then, "Damn."

When he had the courage to tell one of the other residents what had happened—not the whole story, just that a patient had requested that he not remove his hand during a vaginal examination—the young doctor had grunted ruefully, "You lucky sonofabitch. I'm in gastro-enterology. I get the middle-aged men with cranky bowels who haven't passed a nice rounded turd in years. Of course the nurses are ready to hump any time, but they want dinner first and who has the money for that?"

In the fifties, any doctor over five feet tall—height was so important that Alan Ladd was placed on a hidden box so he would photograph taller than his leading ladies—could have anything he wanted from almost anyone. Not only sex but good tables at restaurants, good service from car mechanics, smiles from the dry cleaner, choice produce from the grocery clerk. "Doctor" in front of a name acted as a beguiling ether that softened people, made them munificent, respectful, eager to please.

For the masochistic women of the fifties, the doctor was the ideal lover. Doctors were busy with important things. Too busy to think about sex, except, of course, if you caught them unaware and, against their better judgment, coaxed an erection out of them. The idea of this important, dedicated, tousled-haired man *innocently* finding succor right under his nose—in a woman's body—was romantic manna. Doctors could have it any time they wanted it, with anyone they wanted, wherever they said. They didn't have to sweet talk or cajole. They didn't even have to say Thank you. Only You're welcome.

Paul Halaby had two additional enhancements, not that he needed them. He was fairly good-looking and had the European patina that was dynamite for women of that generation, who had been sold a bill of goods by Hollywood about dark and handsome lovers. Just before he left the American capital to find a wife, he had bedded eighteen women on the staff of Bedford Hospital and five patients, all but two of whom had initiated intimacy. This was in addition to casual dates outside his profession. He had a partially subsidized three-room apartment in one of the large rental buildings on upper Connecticut Avenue, which also housed three other doctors from Bedford whose wives were delighted to feed Paul hot, tasty meals.

Though he was amoral when it came to American women, Paul still clung to his background and it was this nagging fear of losing it all—of being set adrift in this new country without any of the comforting traditions of his childhood—that sent him back to the village to look for a bride. He was thirty-three, a doctor with a promising career and undeniably attractive. They might as well have said Jesus Christ was back in town, for every mother's head was dancing with possibilities.

Peter George's head was dancing a little ahead of all the others, but he kept his plans a secret. Casually, he asked his sister to give a small party before the whole village descended on the visitor. Perhaps the doctor would take the time to see his beloved Delal for what she was, a charming, educated young woman with exceptional abilities. Perhaps he also needed a little financing to enhance his own practice.

January's weather was always quixotic. It could be delightfully warm and dry. Or miserably cold and wet. The old-time farmers insisted there was a pattern to it, but they couldn't agree on what it was. On the day Nijmeh went to say good-bye to James the air was damp, the visibility poor, and before the bus got halfway to Jaffa Gate, it began to snow heavily. The big flakes accumulated and, within minutes, only the rotundas of the mosques and the Russian Compound were visible. The bus plodded along into no-man's-land, which seemed appropriate for her mood.

The other passengers looked around as if to ask, Will we make it? When they saw Nijmeh, they stared. She was wearing a mouton fur coat—her parents' Christmas gift—which was very becoming.

One of the women looked down at Nijmeh's feet with dismay at her thin-soled shoes. "*Shu,*" she cried, "*habibty,* you'll catch cold." In her tender state, that simple bit of friendliness made her eyes fill. What am I going to do without him? she asked herself. Now that he was finally going, she felt inadequate to hold him. She was trying to invent the woman that James would leave behind.

She tried to think about her future in a hopeful way so she wouldn't appear sad to him. He would be in new and stimulating surroundings, while she faced the same routine. A few of the girls at school had found places in American colleges—Swarthmore, Davidson, and Vassar—and they were very excited. She was already overeducated and should have been at a junior college. She could probably even be admitted with advanced standing to a university. Maybe she should tell James she had plans for college, too. She didn't want his last memory of her to be of someone whose life was aimless.

"I don't want you to think of me as someone weak and dependent," she said when they had settled at a table in a small coffee shop near the Via Dolorosa. "I'd hate that."

"No chance of that," he smiled.

"I don't want you to think of me as a person who can't think for herself, either."

"Now why would I think that?" He was still amused.

"You've accused me of being brainwashed often enough." Her lips clamped together and grew thin. She inspected his profile and, while it was unsmiling, it wasn't grim. He wasn't despondent. "If you recall, it was I who constantly nagged to consumate this relationship." She couldn't keep the edge out of her voice although she knew it was damaging. Their lack of physical involvement loomed as a fatal mistake on her part. Delal was right. How could he feel bound to her and keep her close to his heart when they had never made love? James looked around to see if anyone had overheard. He reached for her hand across the table and pressed it between both of his. "I regret one thing," she said softly.

"What's that?"

"That we haven't been lovers all along. I'd feel so much better if that were the case."

He put on what she thought of as his "fatherly face." He was moved but also perplexed. "We went all over that. I didn't want to put that kind of pressure on you."

"I didn't feel pressured. The only reason not to do it was so you wouldn't spoil me for someone else, isn't that so?"

It appeared to him that the waiter smirked. He leaned a little closer and whispered. "That's putting it very succinctly."

"But you're the one I care about, so what's the difference?"

"There's logic in there somewhere," he smiled. "You won't believe me, but I understand everything you're saying. Nevertheless I feel protective." He doesn't want to do it, she thought. Now it became imperative.

He was dressed for business with a tie and a heavy flannel suit. The seriousness of his clothing made him appear unapproachable. Again, there was that awful sense of panic. He had appeared in her life at a time when she wasn't expecting anything. It was that innocence that had brought him. Now she was expecting too much. He didn't need her as much as she needed him. This was her last chance. She had to do something bold. "James, let's go somewhere. A hotel."

He looked surprised and then concerned and then unusually serious. "Are you sure that's what you want?"

"Yes." She didn't have the nerve to ask if he wanted it, too.

"All right." He blotted the melted flakes off her face. "If that will make you happy, we'll do it."

Make her happy? She was just mindlessly patching up all the loose ends that plagued her. What was it about him that made her breath catch with anxiety? He was too much to hold in her mind. He could stop loving her and go on his way at any moment. Only love would hold him there. She couldn't pin him down and contain him. In a very real sense, she was at his mercy.

They rented a room at a small hotel on the Street of the Chains. The bed was so high that her feet dangled when she sat on it but it also allowed her and James a beautiful view of the flakes coming down. It was a garret room, with half the ceiling sloped and the walls papered with cabbage roses.

He looked so handsome. Wearing a shirt and tie made his head look larger and softened his features but also made him seem powerful. "This is how you dress when you're at work?"

"Yes. Are you impressed?"

"You look . . . *in command.*" His frame of reference was vastly different from hers. She could see the way his family lived. They had an English maid who laid out their pajamas flat on the bed, with the arms and legs outstretched as if all they had to do was lie on top of them and button up. She considered that so bizarre it made her laugh, but the little niceties also intimidated her as if she weren't polished enough for him. Of course, at school, anyone without exquisite manners soon got the picture, but this was something beyond manners and it made him more valuable. At times, she would stare at the back of his neck or his profile or the way he sat with his long legs stretched out and crossed carelessly at the ankles.

"It's the same old me," he said, smiling, and put his hand on her face.

"I can't shake the feeling that once you go I won't see you again."

"Why wouldn't you see me again?"

"I can't explain."

"It's not going to happen. When I return, I'll be half a lawyer. You want to marry me this summer? You can come with me to Edinburgh in the fall."

"Oh, James." The idea seemed so remote it had little impact on her confidence.

"Does that mean you'll consider it?"

"Of course I'll consider it."

"I'll live on that for six months."

"Do you need something to live on, too?"

"Oh, Nijmeh, do you have to ask?"

She undressed without nervousness but with a sense of fatalism. He breathed deeply, and sighed, and stared. "Can you even guess how beautiful you are?" She smiled and put out her hand. He shut off all but one small lamp, stretched out beside her, and brought his face very close to hers. "You're my beautiful desert girl. I'll never forget that night when I saw you for the first time."

"Tell me again how you felt," she whispered. "Tell me how surprised you were." She loved hearing that story.

"Surprised? That isn't the word for it. Electrified," he teased. They were turned toward each other, their faces inches apart. His leg was over her, pinning her down. "Within five minutes you had threatened to kill me and then to slaughter a pathetic lamb for my dinner. I thought, Wow, this woman's *different.*"

"That's all? Just different?"

"A few other things. You were brave and competent. So matter-of-fact. It wrenched me. I remember riding away with such a heavy feeling. It hurt me that I had to leave you to fend for yourself. I felt responsible for you already."

"Was that how you felt?"

"Yes. I was determined to find you. All those days looking and with so little to go on. But I was determined."

"And now?"

"Now I'm anxious to leave so I can return for you. Does that make sense? I feel as if I've known you for ages." He closed his eyes. "I can imagine how we'll look when we're old. You'll be toothless but still beautiful. I'll still be wildly in love with you."

"*Oh . . .*"

She had been right to make him bring her here. Wasn't this what love was? Opening yourself completely to another? He'd never forget this. He was bound and melded, swooning with feeling and desire. Closer than breath and heartbeat. This is what she wanted for her life.

Why then, in the midst of feeling, was there a hollowness with a deep, engulfing core? This would surely break Samir's heart. He would not understand. Or forgive.

Outside the window, it had stopped snowing and the light had turned purple. Soon she would have to leave. James was up on his elbows, his hands on her cheeks. "Hush," he said, brushing away tears she was not aware having shed. "It's all right. It's going to be all right."

34

My sister is making a party for one of the Halabys who's come from America.

"Papa, please don't make me go."

"Of course, you're going. My sister is making a party for one of the Halabys who's come for a visit from America. She wants all of us there. Since when don't you join us for a visit?"

"Your sister would be relieved if I didn't show up. She thinks I talk too much. They all think you've spoiled me."

"You make her Sara look dull, maybe."

"I don't make Sara look dull. She *is* dull. She has one reaction to everything. If I said the King was wearing earrings in public, or if I said too much rain had ruined the lilies, she'd have the same reaction—a dumb, round-eyed look. Do I have to waste a perfectly good afternoon talking nonsense, Papa? Papa!" He had stopped listening.

"Delal, if you're so clever at deducing motivation you should know that all your whining won't move me an inch. You're going to your aunt's and you'll talk to your cousins."

"What sort of unnatural satisfaction do you get from bullying me into going? And you can't dictate how pleasant or unpleasant I'll be or how many words I'll utter."

Her father sighed. "I'll never worry over how many words you utter." He couldn't back down. He had planned this for his daughter's good. He had to look to her future.

Delal was indefatigable when it came to beating a discussion into the ground. She tried to wheedle out of the visit for another fifteen minutes and was still going strong. She really didn't want to go. In fact, she was considering calling a young man at the office to go and see the new Jacques Tati film, which she was reviewing for the paper. I could call him, she reasoned with herself. One *pal* calling another. But, as it turned out, her father wouldn't budge and she was forced to do what he said. She went to her aunt's house, and the man of her dreams was waiting there.

Her first glimpse of him, he was sitting on her Aunt Mary's too-low damask couch. His long legs had to bend to the side, and she saw the outline of his calf through the trousers. His hand, resting causally on his knee, was so large and beautifully formed that she had an unprecedented urge to trace each rosy knuckle. She was a fastidious girl and saved his face for last. He was wearing a white-collared shirt and a polka-dot bow tie.

His hair was very straight. And he must have used some sort of cream on it because it was neat, with a precise side part that looked like a short, straight road in a forest. If he hadn't been a doctor, his looks wouldn't have been extraordinary. She knew that much. *But* given his status, nice eyes became flashing orbs of darkest light. His hair was *dashing*. His paleness was *interesting*. A tall, slim man with decently broad shoulders and chest became a heart throb when he was also a doctor. To help along the legend, he seemed remote and gave the impression that he was thinking of something vastly more important than what was going on.

The girls were fidgety, circling him like anxious, thirsty bees. Seated at his right and unwilling to give up her spot, Rheema's eldest, obviously smitten, kept heaving the large breasts that had been the bane of her existence since puberty. On the other side, Leila's daughter was attempting to talk knowledgeably about Frank Sinatra and Harry Truman, the two American names she knew. Sara was giggling nonstop at whatever was said, whether serious or banal. As Delal traversed the room, he looked above all the bobbing heads, caught her eye, and held her glance for a moment. As sometimes happens between a man and a woman, there was energy, a spark, and a challenge in the look. Without stopping to think, she gave him an exaggerated, flirty wink and didn't look back for his reaction. Thank God Nijmeh wasn't here.

She sized up the situation: The only interesting thing that could happen between herself and this man that afternoon had already happened. She wouldn't dilute it by grappling for his attention. She was smarter, more wordly, more sophisticated than all the girls there, but they were prettier. Whatever she said would sound stiff and out of place. Her Aunt Mary's living room was not the spot where she shone best. Fortuitously, a tire on her father's prized Humber blew on the way and he spent much of the afternoon trying to have it replaced. He had no idea that his daughter had passed the visit, which he had arranged so carefully, hiding in her aunt's bedroom, reading a book on flower arranging from cover to cover.

She never expected to see Paul Halaby again, yet she found herself daydreaming about him the next morning. She dressed him in the appealing white doctor's garb while they had an animated conversation on all the subjects she knew best. Of course, he was stunned by her expertise in government, the economy, musical comedy, architecture, every song in *South Pacific.* "Some enchanted evening . . . !"

The house was empty and when she tired of being scintillating, she turned the phonograph up high and sang along with Johnny Ray, modulating her voice to a tremolo to croon, "If your sweetheart sends a letter of good-byeyiyi." The song was being played repeatedly over the Armed Forces Radio, and she couldn't get enough of it . . . the delivery more than the words, which didn't apply to her. The thought flashed through her mind that they could apply to Nijmeh. Well, she'd have a swell song to console her. Her voice was husky and quite good. Her hips were dipping and turning to left and right. From time to time she shook her upper torso and undulated her body downward. She had forty-five minutes before she was due at the paper, and she wanted to wrench every sweet note out of the record. If she had thought anyone was watching her dance and wiggle and scrunch up her face with abandon over those sappy words, she would have died.

He stood at the entrance to the room, his sleeves rolled up to just above the elbow. "I knocked repeatedly, but . . . You must be Delal." It was a warm day for February and his open face was flushed and amused. How sleek he was. All smooth skin and shiny hair. His shirt bloused out over his trousers. Did Americans come calling in their shirtsleeves, or was he too confident to care what anyone thought of him?

"Why must I be Delal?" She sounded intentionally cranky—as if he had interrupted her fun instead of causing mortification. As she hoped, he lifted an eyebrow, surprised and interested. If he dared mention the wink, she'd deny it.

"Aren't you?"

"Maybe. What do you know about Delal?" She focused on his hands. First he had draped them above his hips, with his jacket tucked through one arm. Now they were crossed over his chest and hugging his upper arms, his lovely, tapered fingers on display.

"Not enough." This flustered her and he smiled.

"You have beautiful hands."

"Thank you."

"You don't do manual labor."

"Perhaps my work has made them beautiful. They deliver babies. I'm Paul Halaby." He caught her eyes and held them, but this time she looked down and he had control of the situation. "Your father invited me here. We share a mutual interest in tennis, and we were supposed to play."

"Tennis? My father has no interest in tennis."

"He said he did. That's why I'm here." He smiled again. "Do you suppose he wanted us to meet? Is this a trick to bring us together?"

"Oh, for heaven's sake. I don't believe it." She was mortified. "My mother and father would never do anything like that. There must be some mistake. Anyway my father's not here. So you see, it *is* a mistake."

"It isn't necessarily a mistake. What if I wanted to see you? Are you already taken."

"You mean taken like a squash at the market?" Her tone was too sharp.

"No. I mean taken, as in spoken for, married, engaged."

She narrowed her eyes as if the subject distressed her. "I've been close to it twice, but it wasn't meant to be." She was gambling that her candor would engage him. If you admitted things freely, people rushed to your defense. "I think I frighten young men because I'm too . . . well, as you can see, I don't censor my thoughts. I gather news for *The Palestine Post*, and it makes me forward. Aggressiveness isn't so hot in a woman. Does it put you off?" She held her breath. Suppose he said yes and walked out.

"No," he said softly. "It doesn't put me off. However, I was only going to ask you for a simple date. It isn't necessary to tell me every lurid detail of your life."

She knew he was joking but, even so, she was just uncertain enough to look so quizzical and vulnerable that he moved toward her. What happened next was so extraordinary that each of them saw it as an omen. He took her in his arms and placed his mouth over hers. It began as a simple brush of lips, but as the current traveled downward from the contact with her mouth, he increased the pressure and she returned it. Nothing stopped them from continuing. He parted her lips and she allowed them to be parted. He investigated slowly with his tongue, allowing the tip of it to dart in and out of her mouth, and her body trembled. He left it in and for the briefest moment, unable to stop herself, she sucked it deeper before quickly breaking away.

"Are you sure you were invited for today?" Her back was to him. She wasn't so brave, after all. "My father wouldn't invite someone and then leave him stranded."

"I probably have the wrong date. But still, I'm glad I came." His voice was gently teasing. "Would you like to meet again?"

Would I like to breathe? "Yes." She hesitated. "We did meet before, you know. I was at the party on Sunday."

"I thought so, but then you were gone."

"I don't like groups."

"That shouldn't be a problem." She took her time removing the record, which was spinning aimlessly. "I'm having dinner with relatives tonight, but we could go out afterward. Is there a film house here?"

"Of course. The last showing is at eight-fifteen. Can you be here by eight?"

"I'll do my best."

She watched him leave in a small brown convertible, which was so low that she couldn't believe his legs would fit in. Later, she had difficulty believing he had been there at all. It seemed more likely that he was a vivid daydream brought on by the irresistible music. But no, her heart was pounding and her mouth still felt the invasion of that tongue.

When her father rushed in, she ran to him, too excited to hold back. "Papa, Papa, Paul Halaby was here."

"I know, I know. What a shame. My watch stopped. Was he annoyed?" Her father's anxious look made her sober.

"No. It was all right. He wasn't annoyed."

She went into the bathroom and looked at herself in the mirror. The elated smile was replaced with a frown of despair. If only her eyes weren't so small and so close together, she might be able to *do* something to make herself stand out. She examined her face, running her hand down to her throat . . . a nice neck, nicely textured hair. Her features were all crowded in the center of her face, giving her the pinched appearance of someone who was afraid, or worse, suspicious, or still worse, emotionally miserly. Oh, no! She had grand passions.

She sighed and forced a gleeful smile at her image. Tonight, I have Paul. Then she scowled. He likes me. I know he does. I could feel it.

"I want to wait for him outside, *please!*"

"For heaven's sake, Delal, let us just greet him," said her mother.

"We'll say hello, shake hands, and that's it," said her father.

"You don't have to shake his hand or say hello. Don't make anything of it. Just let me slip out the door and go to the films with him. You're making too much of it. He really just wants to be distracted. It's not as if he's really interested in me. It's not as if he's a serious suitor. Papa, please. Don't make anything of it. I don't want you to be disappointed if it doesn't work out."

"Disappointed? What nonsense! How could I be disappointed when I have the cleverest girl in Jerusalem? We won't shake his hand. If you feel anxious about it, slip out the door, and we'll be quiet as church mice."

Tangled dreams wrenched themselves from tangled webs and burst forth into bright fields of flowers. The world was no longer a hostile place.

She had learned to be clever, to gauge each man's capacity, and play to his vulnerability. Sometimes, she beguiled them enough to have a glorious day or week, or even a month. They were comfortable with Delal and had fun. She could discuss anything—the government, political gossip, the new films, music, art. She dragged them along to her interesting assignments and they had a good time. She knew the best restaurants, the best barber, the best tailor, the best place to buy almost anything. She made them forget that she wasn't a beauty. A young man would call repeatedly and she enjoyed long, lazy conversations, curled up on her bed. Over the phone, there was no one more scintillating. She would hang up feeling exhilarated, certain that they loved her. But in the end, all of them, even the ones who were fools, stopped calling.

But now, she felt as she imagined a beautiful woman might feel—shiny and clean.

For the next few weeks, she and Paul spent many days together. He picked her up at the paper and sometimes accompanied her to cover a cultural story. When they walked side by side in the streets she flaunted their handholding, which was still considered unladylike. But with him, it was a show of ownership. She was his girl. And he was hers, too. Someone who *deserved* her. Accomplished and handsome. Intelligent and mannerly. Suave and sexual. A man of the world.

Her mind was so taken up that when the first letter arrived from Edinburgh, she had no idea whom it was from. The masculine script was straight up and down with high, peaked capitals. This wasn't the tissue-thin paper that usually came from overseas, but a creamy, thick envelope. Mlle Delal George, it said, with the *D* so large and extravagant that it caught her interest. Inside was another sealed envelope and a single sheet addressed to her. "Delal: I'll show up on your doorstep one day with a bouquet to express my thanks."

The note had a queer effect on her. Already overstimulated from the success with Paul, she felt the conqueror's greed to triumph again. She fantasized enticing James and juggling both men in torrid love affairs. Images of her own power jostled one another, mixed and intertwined in that complicated personality.

The letter was in her pocket to give to Nijmeh during a gathering of the clan at Miriam's. She wanted a chance to get Nijmeh alone and was searching for her around the back of the house. She passed a pretty trellised porch when she heard—through the crisscross of wood and wisteria —the compelling sound of her own name.

"Money isn't *everything*," said a feminine voice (Diana's?). "If it was, Peter would have had an offer for Delal."

An embarrassed giggle followed. "Oh, that's cruel."

"The cruel thing is to put her next to Nijmeh. God might strike me, but I'd say He's the cruel one."

It was a stunning blow. She felt cheap and pathetic. People must see through her. Repeating waves of heat lapped at her until she was burning with shame. She touched the forgotten letter in her pocket and sucked in her breath with surprise. Here was her weapon to fight this war. She'd never give Nijmeh the letter. Let her know how it felt to suffer rejection.

The next day, the envelope was put far back in her office desk drawer, under a ceramic dish for moistening stamps, where it was soon joined by two more letters from Edinburgh. When Nijmeh finally asked if mail had arrived, Delal looked wistful and shook her head. Nijmeh, looking forlorn, invited an opinion.

"Well, let's see," said Delal with exaggerated concern. "What could have happened?" She stretched her mouth to signify her opinion of men's promises. "His plane could have crashed. His hand could be broken. He could have amnesia. Or he could be a faithless skunk. Take your pick."

Nijmeh smiled weakly and shook her head. "No. It's nothing like that." A dull, protective anxiety insulated her from daily life and the need to plan a future. James was her future if she could hold on to his reality. Approaching twenty, she was overeducated and biding her time to receive her baccalaureate. Please, James, she whispered into her pillow, don't slip away.

Peter George waited two weeks before interfering in his daughter's love life. He called Paul Halaby into his study. Delal, who had been detained at work, would have screamed with horror over what he was about to do.

The room was pleasant, with a leather sofa and bookshelves, a soft-colored Persian rug, and richly paneled walls. Peter had turned off all the lamps and allowed the irresistible golden light of dusk to transform the pleasant room into an entrancing sensual delight, where leather and wood and colored wool were bathed in a flattering glow.

Paul was impressed. "What a fabulous room. This is what I would like my office to look like."

Peter grunted. He was in a hurry. "Your purpose on this visit was to find a wife, no?"

Paul looked at him quickly, then recovered. "If it happened, yes. I wasn't going to force it."

"I understand. In these modern times, I'm sure a man like yourself wants to feel he is marrying because he wants to, not because his parents have arranged a match. I know this is the modern way." He left no doubt that he didn't think much of the modern way. "The young ones want to choose for themselves, although we didn't do so badly with the old ways. Divorce is not uncommon in America, and perhaps that comes from marrying for passion." He spat the word out. "That's what the current generation mistakes for love—lust. I happen to believe one chooses a wife for other reasons, and love follows. It happened so in my life and in many lives I know."

Paul listened. He wasn't there to agree or disagree, but he liked and admired Peter George. "Those thoughts were on my mind when I made this trip . . . but also I was anxious to see the country again, if a wife didn't materialize."

"Has Delal convinced you differently?"

He laughed. "She's a very interesting woman. I enjoy her company."

"No more than that? I can see that you have some feelings for Delal," he said tentatively. "Am I wrong?"

"No." Paul looked ill at ease, "You're not wrong."

Peter didn't like what he was about to do. He knew his wife would disapprove and his daughter would be wild, but he did it anyway. What was the harm in sweetening a deal that was already eighty percent accomplished? He sat back in his cushioned, oversized chair and twirled to face the windows. "Paul, I'm an indecently wealthy man,"—he sounded almost morose—"and because I no longer care much about making money, everything I touch returns a healthy profit." He twirled back to face his desk. "There's a bittersweet side however . . . you see, I'm a generous man. It would be my pleasure to have ten daughters and give each one a dowry and a wedding fit for the Queen of England. But—what am I to do?—I have one child. One." He held up one finger. "Delal is a wealthy woman. She is almost wealthier than I because I've invested her holdings more conservatively. She has land, a trust fund. She knows nothing about it. Nothing. At age twenty-five she'll come into half a million dollars."

"But, Peter, I . . ."

"No, no." He held up a hand, "I know this is the farthest thing from your mind. It is *I* who wish to bring it up because it's been weighing on me. Delal could do well for herself without me. She's capable of earning a living at any number of professions. But,"—he threw up his hands in a gesture of helplessness—"I love her with all my heart, and it's my pleasure to make her rich."

Paul laughed nervously. "That makes it nice for Delal."

"In the old days, you know, the suitor and the father struck a bargain before a bethrothal." Peter George, who could negotiate six-figure deals with a London banker while perusing a luncheon menu and eyeing the waitress's derriere, had his heart in his mouth, awaiting the next words from the young man before him. He paused and fondled a gold paperweight. "Have you any inclination to do such a thing?"

Paul laughed again. Peter didn't like that. Laughter at this point was a sign of indecision. "I feel it's between Delal and myself for now. But I can tell you that she's a delightful girl. Delightful."

Peter George sighed and stood. He hadn't accomplished anything. Delightful? Delightful meant nothing. After being offered a healthy sum of money, all he could come up with was *delightful*. It didn't look good, damn it. "I understand. And, Paul, as far as Delal is concerned, this little talk never took place. She would feel humiliated if she suspected I spoke to you with such frankness."

"It never took place," said Paul gallantly. Both men walked innocently out into the living room at the precise moment Delal walked in.

"Have you two been talking about me?" She looked at her father accusingly.

"Of course not." He winked broadly.

She knew what that wink meant. Paul must have said something to him. Perhaps he had asked for her hand. She felt such a thrill of happiness it was difficult to make sense.

That night, after a concert of baroque music at the YMCA, they climbed into her MG, which Paul was driving, but he didn't start it right away. The air was velvety, with just enough warmth to comfort the skin and a gentle breeze. They had begun the evening with dinner outdoors on the terrace of the King David Hotel. Delal was wearing a black silk crepe dress she had purchased that afternoon. It was cut on the bias and flowed over her body in one provocative line. She felt beautiful. She had her hand on the side of her seat and because the car was small, it was very close to his thigh. He looked down and placed his hand over hers and then removed it and rested it casually on his lap. Unconsciously or not, he seemed to be directing her to touch him. She knew enough about that. Men needed physical release and maybe he was trying to tell her. But suppose he wasn't saying that at all and he found her actions repulsive? She searched his face for a reading and saw that he had a strange smile.

"I don't want to be a tease," she said, trying to forestall any misunderstanding. "Tell me what you'd like me to do. Does this do anything?"

"Of course." There was an embarrassed pause. "Something is happening right now."

"Oh." She jumped and lifted her hand.

"Don't be frightened. I won't do anything you don't want." His voice was serious and breathy. "Give me your hand back."

She didn't want to do it, but there was no graceful way to refuse. He placed it back over his crotch and, this time, she didn't need him to tell her what was happening. She felt as if she were suffocating in that small space, as if her head were swelling, too. She looked straight ahead. His arm had gone around her waist and his hand was on her outer leg. "I love your backside," he said huskily. "I've been wanting to do this for so long." He moved his hand over her buttocks and under her seat and at the same time he kept eating at her skirt with his fingers so that he could get to some part of her skin. His questing fingers pulled at her outer buttock, gathering the skin the same way he had gathered her skirt. It forced her vagina apart and when his persistent fingers reached their destination, she was very wet. She was also terrified that she was ruining her chances with him. "Paul, please. No."

"Shhh, it's all right." His voice was impersonal and she was already sorry that it had progressed this far. She began to take her hand away, but something told her she couldn't stop now. That would really anger him. Somewhere she had read that once a man was aroused, he had to complete the act. Almost as if affirming her thought, he clamped her hand down on him and moved it up and down. "Like that," he urged, and again there was that impersonal tone. "A little faster." With each instruction, she became more upset. She didn't want to do it. She wanted it to be over. She wanted the evening to end and the carefree, promising relationship they had before to come back. She was also afraid to make him angry so she moved her hand up and down, and finally he grabbed at her buttock in a painful squeeze and held down her hand hard against him, making a noise like a long, low whistle.

"Now I've done it," he said, regaining his composure. "Ruined a perfectly good pair of pants."

"Was it all right?"

"Well, I would have preferred it to be more intimate, but that's not possible right now. Your father would skin me alive, wouldn't he?" His voice was teasing again. "Anyway, I wouldn't do that to you. This was the best we could manage. But you have to let me do the same for you."

"It's not necessary. I don't expect . . ."

"I don't want you to feel ashamed. I can do to you what you did to me without violating your virginity."

She wanted to die. As bold and sophisticated as she felt, she had no frame of reference for discussing such intimate things. "It isn't necessary. Really, it isn't."

"Of course it is. Don't you desire me? Don't you have physical longing?"

"Yes." Pause. "I do." Right now she didn't. Nothing.

"That's good. Because if you didn't, I'd think we were wasting our time. You've got a terrific body, Delal, don't shut it away."

A terrific body? Oh, maybe it was going to be all right. She felt her hopefulness return. "I promise. I won't."

As she prepared for bed, she rehashed it all again. He didn't seem any different afterward. He had even been eager to help her do the same. Maybe her anxiety was for nothing. Still, she lay awake for a long time. She couldn't shake off the sound of his voice while he was being stroked. He was so cold and impersonal. Like this. Up and Down. A little harder. It didn't sound as if he were talking to someone he cared about. Maybe he was just using her while he looked elsewhere for someone to marry.

Why did that thought lead to thoughts of Nijmeh? No one had ever forced her to do what Delal had done. No one would ever tell her she had a terrific body, as if she were just a piece of meat without a soul or feelings. Maybe he had no intention of marrying at all. He hadn't taken her in his arms and called her darling or told her he loved her.

The next afternoon, she called him. They hadn't made plans, and she wanted to find out if he would come by.

"Tonight I've got to be a good boy and visit my mother's family—cousins of cousins—the Mishwes. Do you know them?"

"Of course. One of them married my mother's brother." Right there she had a premonition that made her feel a thud in her stomach. She wanted to get off the phone. "If you get away early, call," she said quickly.

"Let's hope."

Miriam reminded them that Umm Jameel was a distant cousin of the Halabys through her mother and, therefore, the logical person to invite Paul to dinner.

Nadia asked for a sit-down dinner, but Samir convinced her that the guests should help themselves from a buffet table and sit where it was comfortable. The day before, they came to look around Umm Jameel's house, and each privately despaired that it was small and dowdy. What could they do? It was too late to change the locale. Everyone had his special idea of the irredeemable feature that would offend the guest. Nadia thought the furnishings were too old-fashioned. "The house needs painting," said Miriam, as if reading her mind. "Your father used to come and putty around the windows and shore up the cement, but now it's neglected."

This prompted Samir to let his hair down. "It's so dark. And small." He thought the lack of books and art would make the family look uneducated and shallow.

"The house is very dark because of the tiny windows. It's not so small," said Miriam. "Three families lived there when I first got married."

"Do you think he'll get a bad impression?" asked Nadia.

"I think if you intended to impress him, it won't be here," said her mother, who had fixated on the shabbiness of the curtains.

"We should have had it at home." Nadia pushed back her hair off her temples as if it were too heavy. "We're expecting a lot to happen. Suppose Paul simply has something else in mind?"

"That could very well be, but you have to go through with it."

Their nervousness was for nothing. When Paul saw Nijmeh, he could have been sitting in the Black Hole of Calcutta and it wouldn't have bothered him.

He couldn't help staring. He couldn't take his eyes away from her without wanting to immediately look again. No one was saying anything and—with the room so small—it could have been excruciatingly tense, but he felt relaxed. He had a drink in one hand and a small plate of appetizers on his lap, restricting his movement, and he got rid of them both. He had never seen such a perfect face, but even more riveting was the absolute openness and vulnerability behind it.

Suppose he hadn't met her? When he considered all the teas and giggling women, and then trying to convince himself that Delal, with her pinched little face, could make him an ideal wife because she would be forever grateful . . . At least he hadn't caved in when the father offered money. He wouldn't have that on his conscience, though it had been tempting. He convinced himself that he had acted well, and this angel was his reward.

He inched his way along the sofa until they were no more than a foot apart. "I don't remember you from my childhood."

"I don't remember you, either."

Adrenaline shot through his body. "I'm mad at myself," he whispered, leaning over.

She looked puzzled. "Is something wrong?"

"I can't believe I wasted so much of my visit without having met you. Now I only have a month left. That's a darn shame." He was still whispering, and the others in the room busied themselves in the kitchen and around the table.

"Was there something you wanted to do?"

"I wanted to persuade you to marry me." It was a hard line to deliver seriously and, at the last minute, he laughed. Just in case she thought he was crazy.

She was looking at him with those remarkable green eyes but not really seeing. She had mastered a deceptive attentiveness, but her mind was totally caught up in something else. "I've heard a lot about you," she said, and he knew she couldn't remember what she had heard. Instead of making him anxious or disappointed, her distractedness made him resentful. He'd put her on the spot. "Oh? Tell me three things you've heard." She flushed and looked blank. "Just to show you I'm a nice guy, I'll help you out. I'm thirty-three years old, unmarried, in good health, and with good prospects of earning a living."

"That's very modest," she said, "because I know you're also a doctor. A very good one," she added to assuage any hurt feelings.

"That remains to be seen. But the issue here is you. I don't know anything about you."

"I'll be twenty this summer."

"That's it?"

She smiled. "Unmarried."

"Now that's what I was waiting to hear."

Nadia placed a bowl of rice on the table and glanced discreetly in their direction. "I couldn't hear what he was saying," she said to Samir in the kitchen, "but he was smiling and she was smiling."

The following day, he called her late in the afternoon. "Is this too soon to call?"

"Too soon for what?" She knew who it was.

"You'll think I'm too eager."

"Are you too eager?" Her voice was flat. He was being flirtatious, and she didn't want to respond to it. Don't be eager at all, she wanted to tell him.

"Absolutely. Can I come and see you?"

"I don't want to give you the wrong impression." She didn't know what to say. "I wish I could say it gracefully."

"Say what gracefully?"

"That I'm not free."

"What do you mean you're not free? Not free physically, or emotionally?"

"Emotionally." She was talking more than she wanted to talk. Why didn't he just get off the phone?

To his credit, he didn't miss a beat. "You don't have to be free. I'll just stop by for a chat. You can stay as un-free as you like. See you in half an hour." He was unstoppable.

When he arrived, he beeped the horn. She came out and he walked around and held the door. "Hop in. Hop in."

"Are we going somewhere?"

"Driving. Or dancing. Would you like to go dancing?"

"I don't think so . . ."

"How about it, we could go dancing in the dark? Come on, let's go." Before she could resist, he had her in the car.

"I have to get a jacket or something."

"I'll get the jacket. You stay here. I'll be back in a minute." He went a few steps and then returned. "Where can I find the jacket?"

"There's one on a clothes tree right in the front hall. It's black and white. A houndstooth check."

"Right-o."

He got the jacket, tossed it onto her lap, and then they were barreling down the road, with the radio blaring.

He *did* distract her, even if it was just thinking how to turn him down. Now it was a relief not to think of James. Time was chipping away at her confidence. At night things got worse and in the morning a little better. She needed to talk to someone and get an outsider's view of things. Maybe she would call Delal.

He was driving along and whistling. She was grateful that he wasn't so talkative. "I don't know how to dance," she said and folded her hands demurely in her lap.

"There's nothing to it. I'll show you."

"Do you go to dances?" She was surprised. The men she knew might dance at weddings, but they didn't *go* to dances. "Are you good at it?"

"I went to dances in college and I'm pretty good. Not bad."

He took her to a small club about five miles out of Jerusalem on the road to Jaffa. There was a floor show consisting of eight girls wearing military hats that tied under the chin. They were clad in shorts and halters with bare midriffs and they danced in unison. Afterward, the band played some Latin tunes, and Paul took Nijmeh's hand and made her dance. He held her in his arms, but she remained stiff with her back arched so she wouldn't have to lean against him. She didn't want his hand across her back and his chest brushing her breasts. He understood, but he didn't let that daunt his good humor and tried to teach her a dance called the mambo. "Look," he said, "this is a dance you'll like. You don't have to touch your partner, and he doesn't have to touch you." She shrugged off the sarcasm. Whatever he thought was his business.

The next morning he came to the house without calling and Nadia answered the door. "I'd like to see Nijmeh," he said. "Is she around?"

"Yes, of course," said Nadia. "Why don't you sit down and I'll make some coffee."

"Thank you, but I've already had coffee. I'll just wait here." He waited a long time and it became embarrassing because he could hear voices arguing somewhere in the back of the house. He knew without hearing the actual words that the mother was urging her to come out and she was resisting. He refused to think about it. If he had taken everything at face value, he wouldn't have gone this far. She would come out eventually.

When she finally appeared, her face was determined. "I've given you the wrong impression," she said.

"That's not true. Don't worry about it. I'd like to drive down to Jericho to have a swim and look around. It'll be nice to get some sun. What do you say? Come along, okay? We'll have a swim, some lunch, and come back before night."

She shrugged. "What can I say?"

"Don't say anything. Just get your bathing suit."

When they were well underway and the silence threatened to become difficult, she said, "How is it in America?"

"Like night and day."

"Very different from here?"

"Totally. There's total freedom from social pressure. Well, almost total. There's a stigma for women who have children out of wedlock. I know firsthand that's still a taboo. I see real anguish when I deliver the babies."

"Are they just nice girls who made a mistake?"

"Sometimes. Some are girls who haven't the vaguest idea how babies are made. Just ignorant. They refuse to believe me when I tell them how it happened. They laugh."

She noticed that when he talked about his work, he was very different. Very serious. "You like delivering babies?"

"Very much. I never fail to get excited. It's quite a thrill each time."

"Are you lonely in America, or do you have friends?" She was just being polite, although she would have much preferred to be quiet and think her own thoughts.

"I used to work almost all the time. But now I've finished my residency, and I'll be on a different footing at the hospital. When I go back, I'll be more on my own. My friends are other doctors and their wives. A patient might become a friend, but that doesn't happen often. It's a nice life. Very pleasant, but eventually—maybe five, six years—I'll come back here to practice. This is home."

They spent the afternoon swimming in the Dead Sea. The water was so briny they bobbed around like corks and it was impossible not to giggle. He made her wear his shirt in the water so her shoulders wouldn't get sunburned. "With that skin, you've got to be very careful. The shirt will dry before we go home." There was a little pavilion near the water and he ordered a lunch of chicken smeared with lemon and garlic, which they cooked over a fire. They ate in their bathing suits with the sun warming them. Afterward, they swam again, showered, got dressed, and drove home.

"What shall we do tomorrow?" he asked when he dropped her off.

"I can't see you tomorrow."

"Why not?"

"No specific reason. It just isn't right."

"I don't see why not. We can go up to Nablus. I want to buy that special soap they have there and take it back. It's so much more fun when you're along."

"I don't see what good this is doing you. If you're trying to find a girl to marry, why are you wasting your time with me?"

"Wasting my time?" he looked astonished. "I enjoy your company tremendously. I'll pick you up at ten, okay?" She nodded. "Okay." And he was off.

On the drive home from Nablus, they stopped at a restaurant on the road and Paul ordered a bottle of wine, which they finished with lunch and which left them both more mellow than usual. Nijmeh, especially, felt her guard was down and she began to analyze her behavior. She had started out feeling nothing at all. Now, she felt some respect and liking. When they were leaving the restaurant he had put his hand under her elbow and guided her into the car. She had to admit that she had liked having his hand on her elbow. Maybe that was the wine. May it was just that any man was a stand-in for James. She did feel fuzzy-headed. When they arrived at her house, he shut off the motor, brought her face around, and kissed her cheek. Then he held on to her chin to keep her steady and kissed her lips. His tongue went zipping along from one corner of her mouth to the other and then he brought it back. She hadn't exactly returned his kiss, but she hadn't pulled away. She was able to tolerate it, which seemed an important discovery. It was just a pleasant awareness that an attractive, interesting man was available. She felt very confused.

He kept showing up—one day at a time. If she wasn't home during the day, he'd come back in the evening. Her parents encouraged him, so it wasn't hard to keep returning. It was Paul's good luck to be courting her during the most poignant season of the year. The days were sunny with just enough humidity to be refreshing. In almost any direction, just over the next ridge, they'd come upon a field crowded with wild flowers as far as the eye could see. He took her to the Easter rituals as if they were tourists. The crowds pushed them together, and she got used to having his arm around her waist or shoulders.

By mid-April, eleven of James's letters made a neat, crisp stack. Delal held them in her hand and riffled the edges. She had read each one and sometimes she read them in sequence. It was an interesting study in human nature to see the rise and fall of emotions. Gaiety and anticipation were followed by bewilderment and anxiety. Finally, a sense of despair crept in. Despair was a relative word. It wasn't the sort of despair she felt —the eroding self-esteem, the devastating sense of powerlessness.

Odd passages from the letters reverberated in her mind. He used Nijmeh's name frequently. I love you, Nijmeh. I followed a girl several blocks because she squared off her shoulders with your same brave shrug. There are three types of weather patterns here: Damp and rainy. Rainy. And Damp. The countryside here is mostly desolate. It makes you review your life as if you've been told you're going to die. When I review my life, I keep coming back to you, to your beautiful face. To your eyes which haunt me. It's been two months and I haven't any news of you. I've taken up golf. The first thing a Scotsman tells you when you're on the golf course is that the Scots invented golf. They want you to be surprised and unbelieving and, since it means so much to them, I oblige. Are my letters reaching you? I haven't heard a word and the term is half over. Not one single word from you. It's . . . *mystifying!* Are you there? Are you all right? About my studies . . . I couldn't have imagined how compelling they would be. The laws of a nation are so . . . *organic.* You can read the history of the race in its laws. Are you embarrassed to tell me that your feelings have changed? You're much too courageous to evade the truth. I'm sure of that. I love you.

It was the most satisfying thing she had done in her life. Keeping those letters from Nijmeh was equivalent to covering her wounds with a soothing salve. In that small community, it didn't take long for word to get around that the Halaby boy was head over heels for Nijmeh Saleh. Wasn't that a match made in heaven?

It took her three days to get the letter just right. It had to be a crusher and irrefutable. She couldn't take the chance that James would come winging back and invade the Saleh household. The letter had to make him cynical and vengeful. It had to provoke him to get drunk and buy himself a sleazy prostitute.

Dear James,

It was my fervent wish that I wouldn't have to write this letter, and if my own inexperience hadn't made me so impetuous this whole mess wouldn't have taken place. But there you have it. The first man who came along brought out all my emotions, and I couldn't distinguish love from infatuation. Now that I'm truly in love, it's all so painfully obvious.

I've met someone. A doctor whose specialty is delivering babies. I tell you this so you can see that this is not the choice of a fickle, silly girl, but something well thought out (our relationship, you must admit, was not). Paul is gentle and good and right for me in every way.

Your sweet letters are stacked next to my bed, and I read them and feel sad. Paul has a practice waiting for him in the States, and by the time you read this we will probably be married. When you meet the right girl, I'm sure you'll forgive me.

My affection always,
Nijmeh

When she wrote those things about Paul, she knew they were untrue. He had not been gentle or good. He had been a lazy listener and mildly petulant, self-indulgent, and lacking in imagination. Even knowing all this, she would have gladly had him back.

"Delal, I have to talk to you." She had tried to reach her cousin the previous evening and all morning but she hadn't been successful until late afternoon.

"Why don't you come by?"

"I'll take the bus. Can you meet me? It's better if we meet outside your house."

"Why not? We'll have a coffee."

"So? What's up?" Delal tried to keep her voice light. One thing she didn't want was to give any inkling of what she was going through. How many hours had she sat waiting for Paul to call? Especially in those first few days before all hope had faded. She hadn't played it right. She had let him touch her in such an unattractive way. How many times had she lifted the receiver and dialed his number and then disconnected before it had a chance to ring. If it rang, he would answer. If he answered he would be apologetic and ill at ease. Sickeningly insincere. What did she want him to say—I don't like you enough? Leave me alone? She felt ashamed for herself and her father. She had warned him not to get so excited, but he had been excited anyway. And now, here was the cause of it all, wanting to be consoled and reassured.

They had chosen a restaurant with dim private booths. Nijmeh had ordered a lemon Coke and Delal an iced coffee.

She stirred the Coke round and round. "Do you think I was just dumb with James?"

"Dumb?" That's exactly what she was. Dumb. She thought of the neat stack of letters in her desk drawer. You were dumb not to see how much I hate you.

"Dumb to think it meant more than it did."

"You and a zillion other women." She spoke in a flat, dispirited voice. "Men are faithless. You know that song, ' "If I'm not near the girl I love, I love the girl I'm near." ' Everybody thinks, Oh, that's so cute. Men are like little boys. It's not cute. It stinks."

"You're probably right, but I can't believe it. When he comes home, I'm going to confront him. He has to come home. I keep thinking that when he comes home, everything will be all right."

"Then you're a fool, Nijmeh," she said with unconcealed bitterness. "You have the idiotic notion that you're eternally lovable and this is just a little lapse. As a matter of fact, he probably won't come home. He knows what's waiting for him here. It's a sad fact but true that now you're James's little burden."

This brought a real look of grief to Nijmeh's face. Her mind opened up to accept this appraisal as if it had the seal of a judge. Delal was so wise to see it. All along, she had hung on to the idea that eventually James would come home and he would have an explanation. If he didn't come home, nothing would ever be resolved. She'd just be left in this limbo. Her face drained of color. "How can he not come home?"

"You know Mary Bevins? She writes that column, 'Mary's Parlor.' She calls around sometimes and asks people their plans so she can fill up space. I suggested she call James's parents. I thought maybe I could find out something."

"And . . . . ?"

"And they've rented a villa in Italy from the first of May through the summer. They're going to Livorno. It's a little resort town on the Ligurian Sea. James is supposed to join them there when he's finished for the term. Very wise of him, I'd say. And cowardly."

Nijmeh's eyes filled with tears. She looked down and rearranged the condiment tray with shaking hands. "I can't believe he just dumped me like this," she said. "He never even sent his address. He didn't think that much of me."

"That's right." She was silent a moment. "By the way, did you ever sleep with him?" Nijmeh nodded. "Too bad. Now you'll never know if easy virtue is what turned him off."

There were many things to recommend Paul. Her father looked so hopeful. Her mother walked around as if she had eggs in her shoes. They didn't want to ask her any questions for fear of interfering. Paul was more than any girl could hope for and too good to dismiss. Maybe it was for the best. She would please so many people. Her head went round and round. Oh, James, why did you dump me? Why did you make me love you and then dump me? There seemed no hope.

As if sensing that she was weakening, Paul made his opening plea. He was tactically brilliant. To avoid any dramatics, he brought it up casually while they were driving. The more matter-of-fact he acted, the less threatened she'd feel. "Nijmeh," he said, keeping his eyes on the road. "More than anything, I'd like you to marry me. I know you don't feel as strongly as I, but I want you to think about it. Just think about it, okay?"

"I'm not going to think about it. It isn't possible."

"How do you know that unless you think about it? Just give it a little space in your head. I just want to beg a tiny bit of space from whatever else is taking up your thoughts. Now, that's not asking too much, is it?"

"No."

She wrestled with it for several days, then one morning she stopped her father before he went to work, and they went out for a walk along the path. It was the first time they'd had an intimate talk since their fight over James. "Paul has asked me to marry him."

"I'm not surprised," said Samir. "He's been around quite a bit. How do you feel about it?"

"I respect him. It's difficult to do what he does. And he's very matter-of-fact about it, too. That's appealing."

"I think he's a good man," said Samir. "What do you think?"

"I think he's a good man, too . . ."

"But?"

"No buts. He's smart. Very concerned. Very serious about his profession."

"What was your answer to him?"

"He told me to think about it, and that's what I'm doing."

Samir took her in his arms and kissed the top of her head. "I have only one thing to say to you. Don't take the offer lightly just because it seems to have come easily. Paul is unique, do you understand? There's not going to be another like him very soon."

"I know."

In the end, that's what did it. How could she refuse such an eligible man? Paul played it just right and Samir played it right, too. They had brought her around to see that it was unthinkable to refuse. Part of it also was recovering her pride. It was a rebound reaction. Part of it was the unexpected comfort and relief of pleasing her father again. She had missed being close to him. He had two new creases originating at the inner corner of his eyes. Her mother's eyes, lips, and skin had been one pale color, as if someone had leached the exuberance out of her, but now her healthy flush had returned. Even her grandmother, who was still despondent over *sidi*'s death, managed a smile. She felt numb but grateful that she had stopped causing pain to those she loved. Still, at the very core, she knew she didn't love Paul at all. Her heart was now and would always be elsewhere. She had been foolish to think that happiness came so easily. Happiness didn't come at all.

"You look so morose, Star. Those lovely eyes are shadowed. The lower lip . . . droops. No joy." He spoke slowly and deliberately, and she couldn't tell if he was being sarcastic or sympathetic.

"I'm sorry." While Delal had felt light and bouncy as a thistle on the wind with Paul at her side, Nijmeh felt sodden, as if she'd drunk too much water or her periods had accumulated and wouldn't release.

"Why should you be sorry? You feel what you feel. Perhaps you could tell me what it is you *do* feel."

He *was* being sarcastic and this disturbed her. "I feel grateful, of course."

"Grateful?" This surprised him.

"I expressed it poorly."

"You expressed it honestly."

"But, Paul, I . . . ."

He broke out in a smile. "I love to hear you say my name."

There. Now his tone seemed nicer. She looked down and saw that she was wearing a dress she'd worn on a day James packed a picnic lunch and driven south. They'd sat on a plaid blanket in a field of wild flowers, thousands of them as high as their arms. Walls of daisies hid them and the yellow centers cast a golden shadow over his skin. It had been a moment of perfect happiness. "Lie down," he'd commanded, pretending gruffness.

"No," she had giggled. "Someone might come."

"Lie down. No one will see us."

She'd lain down and he'd stretched out on top of her, but each time the wind blew the flowers would sway and she'd begin giggling again, certain they were visible to passing cars. This dress was tied up with love, with James, and laughter. It made her sad to be wearing it with Paul. It was unfair to blame him for her misery, but she had a lifetime to make it up to him.

"Nijmeh,"—Paul bent to be closer to her and spoke seriously—"This stage . . . well, right now, we're in a very unsettled atmosphere. We're neither here nor there. But once we get to the States, our life together will be more predictable. We'll have a chance to get to know each other and . . . you'll see. I'll make you happy." He cupped her face in one of his hands as if to capture it. She stayed perfectly still, lowering her eyes until he forced her to look at him by pressing on her jaw. "Is it so difficult to imagine being happy with me?" She remained silent. "Answer this, then. Why are you marrying me? Why have you compromised yourself?"

"It's not a compromise. I want to marry you. I won't insult you by telling you I love you now. But I respect you and I'm honored that you want me for your wife. I won't disappoint you, Paul. Just be patient with me."

He stood and raised her up, pressing himself against her briefly in a loose embrace. "I won't rush you. It's enough that I have you."

She cried herself to sleep that night and all the nights before the wedding. Paul was aware of the daily puffiness around her eyes, for he was obsessively aware of everything about her. A woman cries herself to sleep only over love gone awry, he thought with bitterness. She loves someone else. He experienced the first wrenching pangs of jealousy. Whoever he was, the joke was on him, poor bastard. She was his now and forever.

On her wedding day (they were taking a flight to Beirut that afternoon) she awakes at dawn thoroughly alarmed and unprepared. Time has just been swallowed up and now there are only a few hours left. She had wanted to take photographs of the farm, of their house, of Aunt Julia and Uncle Peter. Maybe she should go out right now and take pictures of the orchards and the vineyards. Most precious would be a picture of the land beyond the cultivated fields. She wants to have nearby a replica of the bare brown hills with worn ledges and edges, banded round and round with the sediment of centuries, some looking like clam shells set down, others made long and sloping by the deluging rains, still others with vaulted halls harboring unreachable, chilling secrets. These somber tones—more poignant than the most beautiful field of flowers—are the colors that pierce and pick apart her heart. Today, this morning, she would do anything, *anything,* not to leave.

Unexpectedly, her mother is also up and they meet on the path that leads to the old tennis court, which is now overgrown. Nadia was remembering that this was the place where Samir had first kissed her and also the route taken with Nijmeh the first day she found her. "I didn't think I'd have to part with you so soon," she says in a husky, trembling voice. "Perhaps it was inevitable." She wants to say, Perhaps it's my punishment for stealing you, but of course such a catharsis is unthinkable.

"I'm afraid," says Nijmeh unexpectedly. "I don't know what's waiting for me there."

Her mother agrees and her heart feels as if it is flying apart, but she composes her face and takes a deep breath. "It'll all turn out well because you're strong. And generous. Things might be hard in the beginning, but they'll soon work out. Remember that your father and I will be thinking of you every day. You will never leave our hearts."

35

You rotten bastard! Where have you been?

"You rotten bastard! Where have you been? Somebody says you're married. Is it true?" She was an olive-skinned brunette with coarse features and a voluptuous body. She worked in the Pathology Department, and he had been sleeping with her for months. She was the best technician the hospital had and, as she often reminded him, knew more about medicine than half the doctors, which was possibly true. She had grown up in New York and had a certain brashness that excited him physically but made him cringe socially. Although he had told himself many times that she meant nothing to him—she was simply "lay" insurance—it upset him when she was busy and couldn't see him.

Two months before he left to find his bride, he had asked Rita to stop seeing other men. "It upsets me," he said honestly. "I know it's unfair to ask it, but I'm asking anyway."

"Well, in my book, if you don't want me to see other men, you have to tell me I'm your one and only. After that usually comes more serious stuff." She was trying to be offhand but her eyes were hopeful, and he knew that if he told her he was serious, she would have been pathetically happy. Tough, streetwise Rita would have cried. He had no more serious stuff in mind, and now she knew for sure.

"I didn't plan it this way," he said.

"Plan it what way, you rotten pig? To use me as a goddam hole to stick it in until you found someone good enough to marry? Of course, you planned it this way, but you're too much of a prick to admit it." She picked up a folder holding patients' records and threw it at him. She did the same with a delicate shell ashtray and a cup holding pencils.

"Hey, cut it out! What are you doing?"

"I'll cut it out when I'm damn good and ready." She was crying and shouting. "What I really hate is the hypocrisy. If you had said all along, 'Rita, I love fucking you but you're not the girl I'll marry—be warned,' I would still have done exactly what I did. You wouldn't have come out such a pig and I wouldn't feel so filthy. I feel like shit on the street."

He was massaging the back of her neck to quiet her down. "Hey, Rita, sweetheart, don't cry. I'm sorry. You were a big part of my life." His hand went around her back and he brought her close to him. He felt her large breasts against his chest. He kissed her forehead. She lifted her face and found his mouth. "Oh, God, I've missed you," she said. "No one does it like you, Paul. We were so good together." Her hand was on his crotch. "Open it right now. I want to take it in my mouth."

He didn't waste time accepting the invitation, and she began to work on him. He stood there with a sheepish grin and then he felt as if the top of his head would open up. "Ah . . . ah . . ." he had to suck the breath in through his teeth to keep from yelling out.

He pushed the back of her head, but she struggled free and looked up at him. How ridiculous he looked with his green knit Ivy League tie, his button-down shirt, his slicked "good boy" side-parted hair. All that for the establishment and his big, stiff prick for her. "Are you really hard, lover?" she asked.

"Are you kidding?"

"Good. Now go shove it into your wife." She got up, cleared the rest of his desk with a sweep of her arm, and marched out.

"Hello, darling." He found Nijmeh in the kitchen wearing capri pants and a ribbed black turtleneck sweater that made her coloring more astounding. She was meticulously pouring oil into a measuring spoon. Several bowls containing the ingredients for her dish waited in a row to be combined. He lifted her hair and kissed the back of her neck.

"Paul, wait. I'll spill the oil."

"Forget the oil. Let's go inside."

"But what about dinner? You'll be hungry."

"I'm hungry for you."

He thought she would follow immediately, but she stopped to close the bottle of oil and to find a dish on which to place the oily spoon. He decided that if he had not been there waiting, she would have completed her measuring and maybe even washed out the spoon. It annoyed him.

It wasn't the love story of the century. Paul, beneath the superficial thrill of bagging such a breathtaking girl, expected her to be dispassionate and punished her in advance. He was chronically tardy, often silent, and sloppy at lovemaking. Statistically, he was among the majority of middle-class husbands, according to the Kinsey Report which had recently come out, fifty-five percent of whom had affairs and never brought their wives to orgasm.

He made no provisions for the crushing changes in her life. There was no more country acreage or sports. No stepping out into the welcoming arms of quiet lanes and trees. No extended family. No horses to ride. But worse, for a girl whose life had always had structure and precise goals, there was no central focus to guide her.

They lived on upper Connecticut Avenue in eight hundred square feet painted a muddy beige with too much pink. When Paul left for work, sometimes as early as six, Nijmeh got up, took a shower, vacuumed, and washed the two breakfast cups and saucers. Sunlight streamed into the apartment at midmorning, and seeing the dust swirling in the air made her realize how pointless it was to think anything was clean. The Sun-Brite Laundry came once a week to take his shirts and the sheets and towels. The other stuff, she washed in the basement of the building with coins from his dresser.

On Sundays, they had a late breakfast of bacon and eggs, which Paul cooked. While they ate, he read the real estate section, circled several ads, and then let it drop to the floor. "I'm going to make a lot of money," he would tell her with grave conviction. "My practice is growing and if I manage it right, it can be very lucrative." Every weekend, he would condense their future into the simplest terms. "We're going to buy a nice house and furnish it to the teeth. This is what men work hard for. To have a really nice house and invite successful people. This may sound too simple, but if you strip aside all the froufrou, that's the American Dream in a nutshell."

He persuaded her to stop calling herself Nijmeh because ". . . you'll save yourself a lot of explanations. No one is going to pronounce it properly and, besides, people are suspicious of foreign names. Nijmeh means Star . . . from now on I'll introduce you as Star."

"It's so theatrical. Won't people laugh?"

"Believe me, no one's going to laugh."

She went along with it because it was harmless and there were things that disturbed her more. He was always either exhausted from work or a night delivery or groggy from sleep, which made him unapproachable. She wanted to be companionable, but how could she engage a person who was desperately in need of sleep? Often, he was too tired for sex.

Most troubling was his drinking. When he ordered a "double Scotch," it sounded reckless, as if he couldn't get drunk fast enough. Yet he never did anything silly, so she had to assume the liquor didn't affect him.

"Fix me a drink, honey," he would ask with the weariness of someone who needed oblivion. Once she'd suggested a cup of tea instead. He had looked up from his slumped position and told her, "My afternoon delivery today gave birth to a blue-eyed little girl, seven pounds, three ounces. She had ten fingers, ten toes, a turned-up nose, and a hole the size of my fist at the base of her spine. Within a week, fluid will build up in her head and swell it to twice its size. We'll have to drill a hole in her skull to drain it. I had to face the mother, the father, the grandmother, and the parish priest. I don't want tea. I want a double Scotch." After his first gulp, he had added philosophically, "All doctors drink."

He *was* a doctor and the importance of his work overshadowed her needs and her feelings. She saw very quickly that whatever would fill her life, she had to seek out on her own. The nurses and patients treated him as if he were precious, and on the days she met him for lunch he did look glamorous in his baggy, sterile uniform, the operating room mask dangling from his neck. It helped her to see him in that setting. He'd take her on the cafeteria line and explain the food with good humor. "Here's meatloaf . . . it's like *kibbeh,* but not as tasty. And potatoes. They mash them up here, I don't know why. Carrots, you already know. String beans, you know. But not this, I bet. Not Jell-O. The texture is repulsive, but a lot of people must buy it. It's out every day." As they ate, he'd watch her reaction to the food, as if he were anxious to please her. He was one of those people whose energy level shot up in public but not at home.

Walking became her salvation. Out of the apartment and up Connecticut Avenue, she passed a drycleaner, florist, beauty salon, and three restaurants. Farther north, there was the zoo where she would sometimes stop to watch the seals swoop and rocket through the water. When the sun became fierce, she went into the monkey house to visit the gray gibbons who swung recklessly across the cage with increasing speed, as if recent good news had made them crazy with joy.

When the weather cooled, she walked south on Connecticut, past the Shoreham Hotel and the Calvert Street Bridge, eating up the miles with a long stride until she reached Lafayette Park and the White House. If she turned west onto K and walked along the letter streets F, G, H—lined with narrow, frame houses painted in sweet colors and collared with patches of lawn and flowers—she reached George Washington University. The look of the carefree students made her feel . . . *unfinished.* She had been trained all her life to take charge of a complicated enterprise, but she didn't have the training for the most menial job in America.

A man on television had said that beautiful women live in an unreal world where all their wishes are granted and they can't face reality. What a thing to say! But might it be true? No one had ever wondered if she would turn out well or have a successful life, or even if she would be happy. It was taken for granted. She was not only beautiful but Samir Saleh's only child. She had learned how to cope with physical hardship and how to conquer fear but not how to face reality and get what she wanted out of life. It was sad to be beautiful, though no one would believe it. It was an edge that everyone begrudged her yet were eager to have themselves. It was like having an unbelievable skill and being told it was criminal to use it.

Walking through the outer reaches of Dupont Circle, she came upon more humble territory that turned her mind in a different direction. There were two blocks of identical attached yellow-brick houses that were grimy with years of soot but sat high up to take advantage of breezes and views. They were nicely proportioned, with large front porches and gracefully pitched roofs. Her grandfather Nadeem had seldon passed a structure without mentally "purchasing" it and making a "fix-it" list that would bring the building to optimal health. That roof needs rolling or it will leak by spring, he would say. That door isn't hung properly. Look how it rubs the sill. That whitewash was applied with the wrong tool. As she passed the blocks, with the yellow houses, she, too, began to refurbish them mentally. The brick would look better painted white. Replace the concrete walks with brick. Put in planters along the narrow stoops. Install more graceful front doors.

It kept her absorbed, but when she returned home her will sagged and she saw herself as dangerously foolish. As if her mind were off the track.

The events of the last four months collapsed in time like a long, vivid dream. Surely she would wake up to see her familiar room and hear their old dog barking and her parents' soft voices echoing against the tiled walls of the sheik's cavernous kitchen. Her life had become alien, as if a malevolent eye had searched and—gratuitously—settled on her. But who would listen with sympathy? She was considered a very lucky woman. She was married, but she didn't feel married. She already had a future, and it was her own immaturity that kept her searching for a different one.

Dear Mama,

I've made a terrible mistake and perhaps Paul, too, would be relieved if this marriage could be dissolved by some magic wand. Or better yet, had never taken place. I want to work and do something worthwhile. Not this emptiness.

She never sent such a letter to her mother. She never even wrote down such words, knowing she would tear them up. She never even willingly allowed such a condemning string of sentences to find a place in her thoughts. They were just bizarre, random words that popped up out of nowhere. Human nature was unpredictable. Outwardly, life was orderly, but people's thoughts weren't orderly. At times, they were destructive.

Dear Mama,

Paul sent me to buy things for the house, but truthfully I had no idea what to buy. They had quilted covers to put over the toaster and the breadbox. What a waste. I bought dishtowels and a soap dish and a metal utensil for mashing potatoes. Paul likes them mashed and I've learned to make them with butter and milk.

That sounded much better. That's what they wanted to hear.

She wrote regularly to her parents and grandmother and occasionally to Aunt Julia, describing what was unique about Washington. Certain sights lingered—the throngs of laughing young girls in summer dresses pouring out of government buildings, stepping daintily onto buses and trolleys. They seemed so innocent and eager. The wives, on the other hand were, cold and efficient. They took command of their houses and their maids and their children.

Department stores—one was named Woodward and Lothrop—contained every item one would need in a lifetime. You could buy a nightgown or a bed or a lawnmower—oh, did her mother know what a lawnmower was? Then there was television. It was against her nature to sit in the house during the day and be entertained. She wrote a three-page letter to her grandmother trying to describe *Beat The Clock:*

It's so silly. Imagine two adults crossing a room, each twirling a pie plate at the end of a stick while their ankles are tied together. Oh, and they only have thirty seconds to do it. This is a serious country, but this show is on every night. People love it.

She could imagine Miriam trying to make sense of such a complicated letter, but she would be pleased that Nijmeh thought she read that well.

Letters were written back. The rain was plentiful or it was scarce. The crops were lush or skimpy. Horses foaled. Cousins had babies. Diana's granddaughter married Mr. Saleem's son and—after the ceremony—Mr.

Saleem (remember, he was the plumber) dropped dead. They finally were drawing up plans for a large modern house at the farm. It would be two stories with a mezzanine overlooking the living room. We'll break ground next year, after the rains. They never mentioned the political troubles, but they didn't need to. She could read about them in the local papers.

She wasn't surprised when he came to her house in late July. He had been home two weeks and she had been expecting him, but she hadn't counted on the emotional punch of seeing him "in person" with his rugged face enhanced by the exuberant healthy look of exercise and summer sun. Momentarily, she was as tongue-tied as any uncertain girl facing an attractive, self-assured man.

This was the moment that made her stomach tighten and her blood run too fast. "Are you looking for me?" She said it so pointedly that he had to smile. She sounded unabashedly hopeful.

"I don't know. Are you the famous Delal?"

"I am. The one and only. Come in." He seemed larger in the room, and she looked for a place they could sit down. "Let's go out in the garden. There's a bench. You're so tall . . . I'll strain my neck looking up at you." She laughed nervously and led the way out and they both sat down. "Now. What can I do for you? Is it about the newspaper?" She knew it wasn't about the newspaper. "You didn't like something I wrote?"

"Oh, no."

"Well, if not the paper,"—she lifted her shoulders and threw him a puzzled smile—"what?"

He looked around. "I'm James," he said slowly and then eased into a smile so enchanting, she could do nothing but stare. He flexed his fingers then chose a point fifteen degrees to his left—it happened to be an oleander bush—and stared with unfocused, rueful eyes. "Nijmeh never answered my letters. Not once. Not a word until she wrote to tell me she was getting married. I read the letter several times but"—he brought his eyes back to her—"I can't accept it. I don't quite believe it. Am I being dense? I want you to spell it out for me."

There was such poignancy in his voice that she swallowed hard and looked grave, as if she were trying to explain a death caused by carelessness. "James . . ." she breathed out, "no word from her? I gave her your letters." She looked away, plucked a leaf off the bush, and smoothed it against her palm. "Nijmeh's had an unusual upbringing, so you musn't judge her too harshly. Emotionally, she's like a child. She was always told what to do and what to think. She might not have *known* what she felt."

"Is she gone?"

"Oh, yes. Married and gone." She lifted her arms to simulate swift flight and watched his face. He was sitting bent over, his arms propped on his thighs. Each time she spoke he lifted his head and gave her a penetrating look. The open collar of his shirt grazed a tendon on his neck and she wanted to run a finger over it. When he looked down again, his hair slid over his forehead.

"I'm sorry. That's not what you were hoping to hear." She waited a decent interval, then slapped her hands down on her knees as if to signal that they needed to clear their minds. "You're all through with law school?"

"No. I have a while to go."

"Is it your own choice? Or Papa's?" The tone of her voice invited confessions.

"Half and half. It's a good profession." She knew he liked it. Hadn't he said so in his letters?

"My father wanted me to study law, but I told him I didn't want to be a trailblazer. A woman lawyer—it's like waving a red flag at the establishment. I'd rather choose communications, which is definitely the coming thing and I'll be right in there. Anyone who stops to figure it out can see that you can influence the ordinary man when he's relaxed and susceptible. When he's listening to his radio or television. In England and America, television's already a big thing and it's going to be big here, too." He was recomputing her worth and coming up with a different total every minute she kept talking. Oh, this is a different sort of woman. She's *avant garde*. She's intelligent. Incisive. Fun.

She had to leave for work, but she was thinking of ways to keep things going. He probably would be happy to keep on discussing Nijmeh. After all, that's what had brought him here . . . But she'd give him more time to dwell on Delal before reminding him of his lost love. "I was just about to go to the paper. Care to come along? I have to hand in some copy and then cover a speech at Government House. Come along, if you like."

He thought it over. "All right."

"I'll drive."

"You drive?"

"I've been driving since I was seventeen. You know, driving is a funny thing. If you're too smart, you tend to be a bad driver. But I'm smart *and* a good driver."

"I'll be the judge of that," he said good-naturedly and slid into the bright red MG with an appreciative whistle.

"You'll see," she said, putting the key in the ignition. "You'll apologize before the day is over." When they were seated, she was so overstimulated that she put the car in reverse by mistake and they went backward. "Oops! See, you've got me on the defensive, but just wait. I'll surprise you yet."

Later that evening she went into her father's study and sat on the arm of his chair. "Papa, I've decided to continue with school. I want to study international law and perhaps combine it with communications."

"Delal, you know that's my heart's desire for you. I'll call the dean at the American University in Beirut. You could start in the fall."

"I don't want to go to the American University. I've thought about it carefully, and the best place for me is Edinburgh. The university there is exactly right for what I want."

"But it's so far, and what if it's too late to apply? Are you sure? Edinburgh? Why not England? I'll take you myself to look around."

"Edinburgh will take me. It's not too late. I've asked for advice from several men at the paper. If you want to make me happy, Papa, send me to Edinburgh."

"Of course, *habibty.* I want to make you happy. Anyway, it's not so far away. In a plane, you can be home in a matter of hours. Will you be able to take care of yourself? Have you thought it out?"

She slid onto his lap and put her arms around his neck. "You know very well I can take care of myself and, yes, I've thought it out. You'll see I'm right. Edinburgh is the best place for me."

36

Has anyone helped you get
your beahrens?
My what?
Your beahrens, your beahrens. Has
anyone shown you around?
Oh. No.

She met Larraine on the floor of Ginny Hargrove's kitchen. Larraine was
down on her knees picking up miniature hot dogs wrapped in dough,
which were scattered over the polished linoleum. "Help me pick these up,"
she drawled. She didn't bother to look up. "They just all sailed off this
damn tray."

"Sure," said Star, kneeling down.

"Ginny's floor is so clean . . ." she strung out the word, 'cuh-leen'
". . . you could lap up soup off it." She curled her tongue down and then
up, as if she were slurping up liquid. "So what's the difference, right?" She
wasn't asking for reassurance. She was merely sharing information.

"They look fine," said Star. Ginny's house (and yard) were perfect.
Scrubbed as an operating room, she kept thinking and could not get herself
to lounge back and deflate the cushions. Paul, to her surprise, was very
much at home. He sank right into the Hargroves' damask Lawson sofa,
punched down a throw pillow to stick behind his back, and asked for a
Scotch on the rocks.

"You drink and joke around. It's just fun. They're nice people," he had
explained when the invitation came. "I've played golf with Sterling and the
guys and enjoyed myself, but three other doctors would be just as nice.
Friendship is superficial here. The bonds don't last forever. They're nice
people, though. It makes life at the hospital more pleasant."

She couldn't think of Ginny Hargrove as "nice." Efficient, well-
groomed, capable, and remote were more like it. The house, however, was
charming. Nasturtiums at the mailbox in a wooden tub. A gravel driveway
cushioned with small white stones. To the right, a swing set, slide, sand-

box, and wading pool. To the left, a tool shed with a mansard roof and a rooster. Straight ahead, a lovely gray clapboard house with white shutters and a slate-blue door. Ginny greeted them wearing a long gingham skirt, a sleeveless shell that buttoned up the back, and white ballerina slippers. Her hair was bobbed, with spikes coming down the forehead. Hands long and slim, nails polished. "Hello. Welcome." Then came a shift in expression, but Star was used to that. Women reacted to her looks so she wasn't surprised when Ginny Hargrove gushed that she was really happy to have them, while at the same time her mouth turned down with disappointment.

"What a lovely home you have," said Star. The mouth stayed down. "The flowers, the shutters—everything."

"Well, aren't you nice."

"I think that does it," said Larraine and stood up. She was a woman in her late twenties, only five foot two but with a wiry frame and thick curly hair that boosted her height. Owlish tortoise-shell glasses covered half of her face but she still squinted. She squinted down at the tray. "We shouldn't stuff ourselves with these and then sit down to dinner. Doesn't make sense." Star smiled but said nothing. "Want a pig in a blanket?" Larraine offered the tray. (She pronounced it "peeugh.")

"What?"

"That's what they call these things."

"Oh. No, thanks."

"Good girl."

Larraine giggled and then Star giggled. When they went back into the living room, Star accepted a drink and it made her giddy. Little slick remarks were passed that would make her glance at Larraine, who would wink back.

Paul brought over a very tall man with such a boyish freckled face she thought he might be someone's son, but it was another doctor. "Tom Heywood, my wife, Star."

Tom sat down next to her. He was grinning (at nothing) and immediately propped a leg on the ebony coffee table. "When Paul said he was going home to get a bride, I hadn't expected him to come back with *you.*"

"Why not?" She was concerned about the leg on the table and wanted to urge him to take it off. She glanced at Larraine, who in turn raised her eyebrows and her shoulders.

"You know, a girl from the old country. The image is of a plain little thing with a babushka on her head and then that son of a gun—he pulls you out of the hat."

Across the room, she heard Larraine mutter, "Oh, brother."

"Jerusalem is one of the most sophisticated cities in the world," Star said. "It's crawling with private schools for its girls . . ." Crawling. That was the word James had used the day he was trying to find her. Any thought of him still hurt. She lost interest in educating Tom Heywood. "What I'm trying to say is that babushkas aren't so popular these days."

Paul returned with two fresh drinks and handed one to her. "Tom, why isn't your wife here?"

"She's in the ninth month and wants to stick close to home. This is our fourth. My wife's been pregnant for four years, but she loves it. Happy as a pig in mud." Larraine's drink went down the wrong pipe and she began to choke.

Ginny rang a little bell to alert everyone that dinner was about to be served. When they gathered at the table, there was an incident that catapulted Star deep into Larraine's camp. She took the chair next to Paul, but Larraine's husband, Chuck (orthopedics), edged Paul out and said, "No fair. I'm sitting next to this ravishing creature."

Paul laughed. "Guess I'll have to go after Larraine."

"Tough luck," Chuck answered. There had been a lot of casual ribbing in the group, especially after the second round of drinks. When Jim Brent had patted his midsection and claimed not to need the fifth handful of mixed nuts, his wife had answered, "You sure don't, Porky." But afterward, she had kissed him and assured him that she loved every chubby ounce.

Chuck's voice had a special hardness and no consoling reprieve. Star had assumed Larraine was tough and resilient, but her small, angled face looked confused and embarrassed. She blinked behind her glasses. Star wanted to show support but thought it might make matters worse. Paul looked at her gravely, as if reading her mind, and shook his head.

The party had begun in early afternoon, and it wasn't quite dark when they reached their house. Paul called his service, took off his shoes, and went to sit in a chair by the window. He asked her to get him a drink, finished it quickly, and asked for a second. When she brought it, he pulled her down on his lap and began to play with her nipples. "Tom Heywood thinks you're quite a dish," he said and his hand went under her dress and searched for the elastic on her panties. "He whistled at the memory of your shapely form and asked when I was going to bring you around to the hospital." He waited for her to respond and, impatient with the tightness of her underpants, grabbed a portion of her buttock. She said nothing. "Were you flirting with him?"

"No."

He brought his hand from under her dress, circled her upper arm, and squeezed. "Perhaps you didn't realize it."

"I realized everything. I was polite."

His hand tightened. Her arm hurt, but she wouldn't say so. "You have to be careful here. Men interpret friendliness differently. There aren't many social restraints and there's a lot of sleeping around." He released her. "When Tom was talking about his wife being pregnant, I thought about us. I want to see you pregnant for four years, too. I want to see you with a string of babies waiting for me when I come home." His hand returned to her buttocks, but she knew he was done in by the liquor. His eyes were almost closed. She waited for a while and then took the glass out of his hand and went into the kitchen.

He couldn't admit it, but her beauty frightened him. In his mind, every male in the District of Columbia was waiting for him to turn his back. Their first day in the States, in the dining car of the train from New York, the black waiter had hung around the table, swiping at imaginary crumbs —"Yah, suh . . . yah suh . . ." and moving around to get a better look. "The table is clean enough," Paul had said sarcastically. Inside, he was enraged.

Both men and women stared at her, some brazenly, some shyly. She took it in her stride, but it was unnerving to him. It made him proud in a nervous way, but it also made him unreasonably angry not to be able to control the way people stared at his wife.

She was happy to hear Larraine's drawl over the telephone a few days later. "Ginny Hargrove says you're brand new to this country. Has anyone helped you get your beahrens?"

"My *what?*"

"Your beahrens . . . your beahrens. Has anyone shown you around?"

"Oh. Paul does when he can."

"Want some company today?"

"Yes, I'd like that."

When she arrived, Larraine inspected every inch of the apartment as if a desperado were hiding in it and she were the law. She eyed the dishes in the sink. "I keep my sink full of suds," she said, "and just pop the used dishes into it through the day. That way I'm not left with a lot of dirty dishes when I'm tired at night."

"I'm not tired at night," said Star. "I don't have enough to do."

"You don't?" She drew out the words as if stalling for time to find a solution. "What do you want to do?"

"If I knew, I'd do it. I'm not trained to do anything. What do *you* do all day?"

"Well, I'm newly arrived in the leisure class." She sat down and crossed her legs, which were smooth and shapely. "The first six years of my marriage, I worked for the government while Chuck finished medical school. I was tired all the time and so was he. So then he started making some money and I figured, well, if I want to stop working, I'd better get pregnant, which I did."

"Oh," said Star, "you have children?"

"No," she said and her voice became thin. "Not exactly." She sighed and shook her head. "I don't want to turn this visit into a somber occasion, but I lost my little girl just a year ago. Oh, God," she lifted her eyebrows to forestall tears, "I didn't *lose* her. That sounds so awful. Like I was an absent-minded idiot and left her somewhere. She died."

"Oh, no. I'm so sorry."

"Me, too," said Larraine, "but what can you do? It was a virus that attacks the heart. One day they're perfect and the next they're dead. When you're a doctor, it's really hard. You go through all the training and you can't even save your own child. I don't think Chuck's over it yet. He's really bitter."

"I can understand why," said Star. She felt mildly guilty for judging him so harshly.

"Well, look, I told you about it so we can get it out of the way. If you heard it from someone else, you'd feel funny around me, but now we can just put it aside. Okay?"

"Okay."

"Let's see what else you've got here," she got up, walked across the room, and opened a door to the linen closet. "Where do you do your laundry, in the basement?"

"Yes."

"Don't go down there by yourself. You don't know what kind of creeps are walking around. Do you have laundry to do today? I'll go with you."

"No, thanks. Not today."

"Where do you buy your food? Do you have a Safeway near by? It's okay for vegetables and dry goods, but you should buy your meat at Magruders. Ask to see it before they cut it; otherwise, they'll give you steaks that are fatty." She looked around to see what she was leaving out. "Spic 'n Span is good for the kitchen floor. Put a little in a bucket with some warm water and use a sponge mop." She sighed and sank down again on the sofa. "So . . . you want to find something to do while Paul's out wacking babies' bottoms?"

It went through her mind, This woman is crazy. I've got to be careful. Maybe losing a child had unhinged her. But once she got used to the delivery—it was a very specialized verbal shorthand—and the thick southern accent, she found she didn't mind the outrageous intrusions.

That evening, she told Paul, "I think I could be good friends with Larraine."

He was eating at the time and didn't respond until he had cut a piece of meat, put it in his mouth, chewed, and swallowed. "Not a good choice."

"Why not?" Quick anger rose in her throat.

"Larraine is *dissatisfied.* I mean, it's understandable, losing the kid, but to tell you the truth, she was probably like that before."

"She's not dissatisfied at all."

"Maybe that's not the right word. She's sort of a wiseguy, except she makes fun of things that aren't funny. What I think is that she's insecure and that's her defense. She doesn't fit in, but Chuck is okay. Everyone likes Chuck."

"I don't like Chuck."

"You don't? Why not?" He was really surprised.

"I don't like the way he treats Larraine. He doesn't mind embarrassing her."

"He's a very good doctor," said Paul victoriously, as if that point collapsed her theory. "What you don't know is that he's carrying her."

She didn't understand. "Carrying her?"

"She's no asset to him. She's too opinionated and it's embarrassing. She's a liability. I wouldn't be surprised if he got rid of her."

When he said that, she changed the subject to stop him from going any further. That was a terrible thing to say.

Still, Paul didn't mind at all when Larraine showed her "the ropes," as he called them. "By all means, go ahead. It'll do you good." He probably felt it was safe to admit she needed some coaching from a person like Larraine. He kept reminding her that they would have to take their turn at entertaining. "Watch how they do it and do the same thing. It'll make you feel more secure. If you want any sort of life—a life that's interesting—then you go along with it and do things that way, too."

Larraine saw it another way. "You're looking at twenty-three dollars worth of meat," she said one day when Star was helping her prepare for the crowd. "That was my weekly salary at the Department of Engraving just seven years ago. At least the butcher trimmed it before he weighed it." She began to separate the steaks. "One for each and two extras in case someone wants seconds. You know what I hate? I hate when someone just takes a bite or two and leaves the rest. It isn't the money. It's the idea of taking something you don't want without thinking. I usually stare at the plate in the kitchen and try to figure out who did it." She stopped re-arranging the meat and looked contrite. "I'm sorry, sugar. I know I sound cranky but it's these 'pay-back' dinners. They're so *orchestrated*. You *must* have *filet mignon*. Or medallions of beef, as Ginny Hargrove calls them. You *must* have asparagus or some other exotic vegetable."

"What's an exotic vegetable?"

"Carrots aren't. Too homey. It's got to be string beans with slivered almonds or poached endive. Ugh. And the potatoes—mashed is my favorite, but forget it. And you must have a gal serving, although I'm going to be the gal tonight."

"I'll help."

"Better not. Chuck wouldn't like it. The whole thing would be solved if we had a buffet. I prefer a nice ham or turkey myself and everyone helping themselves."

"What would happen if you served turkey?"

"Gee." Larraine looked puzzled. "They'd eat it, I guess."

If Larraine had been born twenty years later, she'd have been involved in the Women's Movement. She had the heart and questioning mind of an independent woman, the kind who would come into full flower in the seventies and eighties. In 1955, she was often bewildered by her own frustrations. The gift of humor and a high metabolism saved her, but she could smell something phony a mile away. And she saw a lot of phoniness in their social life.

Star wasn't as cynical. For one thing, Paul loved the dinners and became very animated. He needed the order of that life and those clearly defined goals. Being around death and disease made him crave structure and control. The other men respected him, and she saw that he often held the floor in a discussion. Even Sterling Hargrove, the senior man among them, took Paul aside for private consultations. She knew—he had told her countless times—that they also admired him for having landed her. Paul's present status was the result of foresight and skill. He was exactly where he wanted to be.

Around the end of November, she noticed they were both more relaxed. He had begun to attend auctions with one of the other doctors and it was a good diversion for him. The odd piece of furniture or accessory made his face light up and it was something he liked to talk about.

Star accepted the status quo—she no longer winced when she heard her new name. It didn't occur to her that there wasn't that unity of purpose that would have made them a team. During the best of times, she and Paul were chugging along parallel lines, but it was always for a short run. She seldom mentioned Larraine because it brought forth unwanted information about Chuck. He had a girlfriend with whom he was seriously in love. It was just a matter of time.

On a dismal morning in early December, Larraine came by with puffy eyes and a cheerless face. "I think Chuck and I will probably get a divorce," she said hopelessly.

Star said nothing, hoping she had misunderstood and in the next breath Larraine would make a joke. They both sat silently, eyes cast down, playing with their hands, and she realized Larraine was serious. "Oh, no. I'm so sorry."

Larraine, who looked ready to cry, struggled to get control of herself. "I'm sick of crying. What I've got to do is find a way of earning a living."

Surely there must be a good, sincere phrase of consolation, but she couldn't find it. Everything she said sounded so unconvincing. "Could you go back to college?"

"I can't afford to go to school just to enlighten myself and make good conversation. I've got to find a way to make a living. I was thinking of nursing, but that would take too long."

"*Nursing?*" Star was shocked. "I'd think you'd want nothing more to do with medicine."

"Yeah . . . Maybe that's my torn psyche trying to hang on. It's a relief, in a way—the divorce. If you're expecting an avalanche every day, it's a relief when it comes, as long as it doesn't bury you. I hope it doesn't bury me."

"Do you still love him?" She couldn't imagine loving Chuck, but then she hadn't known him as a young lover or borne his child.

Larraine bit her lower lip to keep from crying. "I guess. He was very passionate. We had sex all the time and I'm going to miss it."

Star had no response. The idea of sex was a distant secret that she couldn't inspect or try to understand. The maneuvers she went through with Paul were best kept out of mind. "How can I help? You know I would do anything."

"Moral support. That's about it. What I'll do, I think, is take a real-estate course. That's something women can do that's a little interesting. It appeals to me probably because my Irish grandmother was almost religious about owning property. Owning a piece of the earth was very important to her. She kept her money in a handkerchief until she had enough to buy the next plot."

"Where will you live?"

"Chuck's taken an apartment and I'm staying in the house until we sell it. Eventually I'll have to look for something smaller. And cheaper."

Star touched Larraine's hand with her own. "I'd be very sad if we stopped being friends. That won't happen, will it?"

"Of course not. I was even thinking you could take the course with me, for something to do. You're always saying you'd like to fix up every dilapidated house you see on the street. Well, here's your chance to get into the business."

"I'll talk to Paul."

"Sure. Ask him."

At first Paul was against her taking the course, but the very next day he brought it up again and said he had had a talk with Chuck, who thought it would be a good idea if Larraine had a friend to bolster her up. "He's relieved that she wants to do something constructive," said Paul. "Go with her, if it'll make you happy."

"I'm not doing it to relieve Chuck," she said, "but it will make me happy."

The course began during the third week in January. On Mondays, Wednesdays, and Fridays at five o'clock, she and Larraine squeezed into the Number Seven rush-hour bus that cut off to Rhode Island Avenue, where the class met in the basement auditorium of a bank. Together with fifteen other fledgling realtors, they sat alert and willing in front of Fred McKay, whose family had been in the business for three generations and managed a large realty office in the District and two branches in Montgomery County.

"Property," he told them that first day, "any property—even a vacant lot—is more interesting to me than anything else in the world. Property is more tangible and more interesting than mere money. It's a spot on this earth and you know there are only so many spots. So . . . whoever passes up the opportunity to acquire his portion of the earth is just plain stupid." He was hoping to entice some of them to work for him as agents. He wanted to teach them how to excite the buyers, but he also wanted to spark the hope that one day they'd be buyers, too.

"Now," he continued, "this is something you're not going to believe. The United States government will pay for anything you buy, in the way of property. That's right. Every year, they reduce your taxes because you own that property. They feel sorry for you. They say, 'Oh, you poor thing, that property is becoming older and more decrepit every day. Pay us less taxes and keep the money for yourself.' Of course, everybody but Uncle Sam knows that the exact opposite is true. The property is *appreciating* in value. And we can use it as collateral to buy another piece of property that the government will pay for again. Now, are *you* going to go up to Mr. Eisenhower and whisper what's happening in his ear?" He shook his head. "Neither am I. Isn't it foolish not to take advantage of this astounding money-making situation? You bet it is!"

By the time they walked out of the room into the crisp winter air, Star and Larraine were trying to push away the wild fantasies. They couldn't even speak during the first few minutes. "It's hard to believe what he says about the government being so stupidly generous. I wonder if he's telling the truth."

"He must be. He teaches this course every year. If he weren't telling the truth, some student would have come back and shoved him around a little."

Each week, Fred McKay tackled a different aspect of buying and selling property, and he had a truckload of "success" anecdotes that made his students drip saliva onto their shirts and blouses. They learned about financing, land values, zoning laws, tax credits and shelters. One of the most provocative evenings was on the subject of "cheap bait," which amounted to hints on tapping into the buyer's subliminal awareness. "You can add a couple of thousand to the offers you'll get for a one-family house by boiling a cinnamon stick in water just before the buyer arrives. He'll start to think of his mother's apple pie and his boyhood, and he'll feel totally at home."

Fred McKay encouraged his students to answer ads in the paper and go through at least twenty-five properties and give them a rating as investments and for value. During that week, Star and Larraine looked at ten one-family houses, two multiple dwellings, and two business properties. When they returned home, bone weary, their notebooks crammed with particulars—cash flow, city taxes, heating systems, sewer systems, schools, and the quality of the drinking water—they were both on the verge of confessing something to the other, which they feared was immature and irresponsible.

"Most of the people in that class are learning to sell real estate. I don't want to sell real estate," said Star.

"You don't? You don't like it?"

"There's something I think I'd like better."

"What's that?"

"I'd rather own something of my own. I'd like to take one of the properties we saw—maybe that row house on Seventeenth and M—and redo it. What appeals to me is fixing something up with a fresh coat of paint and new shutters."

"Yeah," said Larraine, "then what?"

"Well . . . you could either rent it or"—she shrugged—". . . sell it, but it would be tough selling something you just saved from ruin." Larraine was silent, which was unusual. "What's wrong? You think I'm unrealistic?"

"No. I feel pretty much the same way. We're both unrealistic, but I'm even more so because I can't afford to fool around. I'm going to be supporting myself." She took a deep, meaningful breath. "How much money do you have? I don't mean Paul's money, I mean cash you can get your hands on."

"Two thousand dollars."

"Really? Does Paul know about it?"

"No. It's in my drawer. My grandmother gave it to me and told me not to tell Paul I had it."

"I have three thousand that I saved when I was working. Chuck knew about it, but when he started earning big money he must have forgotten." She chewed on her cuticles and thought. "Even if we could make a down payment with five thousand, how could we get a mortgage? We don't have any collateral."

"My father would give me money if I asked him, but I'm sure Paul would feel insulted if I did that."

"You're right," she said glumly. "He'd have a fit."

"There's a trust fund from my grandfather, but it isn't due for a couple of years." She was chagrined to admit that she had never asked the amount of the trust. (She wasn't even certain it was money.) If it were a dazzling figure, it would boost Larraine's morale. Many times she had the urge to do something nice for Larraine—surprise her with a baked pie or iron her clothes—although it wouldn't make a lasting difference. It wouldn't make Chuck love her again. Once she had thought, I'll tell her about James. *Larraine, I had a lost love, too.* But the words—she couldn't formulate a satisfactory opening sentence—stuck in her throat. The hurt and disappointment were still with her. "We could ask McKay," she said brightly. "He just *loves* to make it look like child's play, so let's see what he has to say."

The aimlessness of the previous year—and the loneliness, too—were replaced by purpose. She felt useful and on the verge of something. Paul sniffed out her new mood and was suspicious that she wanted to take her energy and interest out of their life together and place it elsewhere. He would flatten his mouth and shift both eyes sideways, as if he were exasperated. "There's something I have to say to you." She came to dread those words. The "something" was always a warning: Don't be naive.

Don't get carried away. Don't get too chummy with Larraine. She thought some of the junk he brought home from the auctions made him seem naive but she would never have said so. She still respected him deeply for saving people's lives. Next to that, any small fault was inconsequential.

37

⚬⚬⚬ ❦ ⚬⚬⚬

Oh James . . .

It was the simple desire for revenge that gave Delal the furious energy to chase James. She was near him and Nijmeh was not. That was extracting retribution. But James was a man who had been presorted at birth to invade women's fantasies and Delal wasn't immune. She kept imagining a moment when he would be driven to kiss her.

A bonus of coming to Edinburgh was her appreciation of university life. Graying, clear-eyed men served up knowledge as if it were the key to a worthwhile life. She became smug and pious over her intellect. She also wanted to get rid of her virginity and learn to smoke.

She needed a place to live, which she envisoned as a garret with sloping ceilings. After a street-by-street search—Edinburgh was a canyon of heavily ornamented gray structures—she found two tiny rooms (with toilet and sink inside but the bath—she paid extra to use it—in the hall). The flat faced a barren courtyard but had a domed skylight—she could see Orion's Belt from her bed—and a tiled, working fireplace. It was an ordeal to drag logs up four flights of stairs, but struggle was now an enobling part of life.

Oriental rugs and pink bulbs in fringed lamps made the room (and Delal) look softer and prettier. She was satisfied that she had seen a room like it in a Charles Boyer film.

When the semester was underway, she began a social life of sorts by inviting aquaintances to her place on Friday evenings and urging them to bring friends. Her rooms were underheated, like everyone else's, but she had a phonograph and the latest long-playing records. The landlady was supplied with schnapps to forestall any resentment over the traffic.

It took her a long time to find James. During the first few empty weeks, she was convinced he wasn't there. It was with relief and stomach-jolting joy that she spotted him late one afternoon lounging back on the steps of the quadrangle, with his face upturned to the sun. Too unnerved to attempt conversation, she waited and followed him to see where he lived. She monitored the quadrangle each afternoon and discovered that one of his classes let out there on Tuesdays and Thursdays. What's more, he often stopped to browse in a second-hand bookstore halfway between the university and his rooms and she chose that cozy, unhurried setting as the ideal place for them to "meet."

They were standing between shelves, their privacy assured by thick walls of books. *"You . . ."*—he was more than a little surprised to see her —*". . . here!"*

"Hello. It's Delal," she said stupidly. There were new lines on his face, but the overall effect was so much more enchanting than any vision of him she could have dreamed up. The flesh-and-blood James sent her heart racing with anxiety. Self-assurance fled. Next to him, she felt frumpy. The red muffler around his neck was just one sign of his confidence and dashing nature. His hair fell in a silken clump over his brow. How wonderful it must be never to plan the effect that put you in the best light.

"Well, hello," he said finally. "How are you?" Good, civilized James. Asking how she was, as if they were having tea. As if she hadn't changed his life and come thousands of miles to ensnare him.

"Fine. Just fine. I wasn't sure if you were here."

"I'm here," he said.

"So am I." Just then, her toughness ran out. She was afraid of ruining it and decided not to linger. "I'm in kind of a hurry now, but why don't you drop by on Friday night? Twenty-two Thierry . . . can you remember that? Top floor. It's sort of a standing open house." She stalked off briskly, her heart pounding like a jackhammer.

When she saw his large head filling her doorway that Friday night, she had a moment of pure happiness. He had come to her. The thing to do was not to make a fuss. Act as if it didn't matter. She hardly spoke to him the entire evening, other than to catch his eye across the room and ask him to stoke the fire. When the evening ended, she felt emotionally exhausted, as if she'd taken a grueling exam. The next time, she would allow herself more conversation.

She bought a black jersey dress and had her hair cut but then blamed these calculated "lures" when he didn't appear that Friday or the next. It had to do with trying too hard, which mostly resulted in failure. She felt dull, as if her bright hopes were ill-placed, and it took until Thursday to recuperate and shrug off that deadly feeling of rejection.

On the third Friday he was back. She met his eyes over the heads of the crowd and began to tremble so uncontrollably she had to hug herself and bury her hands inside her arms. Part of the trembling was the thrill of being saved yet one more time. The other part was fear. She had begun to understand how seriously she had interfered in his life.

He had come alone and while he wasn't officially her date, at least he wasn't entrenching himself in another woman's life. He found a spot on the floor and did his share of talking. She caught a word here and there: Hegel . . . synthesis . . . Vittorio De Sica . . . Two girls circled him all evening, but he left alone while there was still a crowd. All Delal could do was drape herself against the doorway and urge him to come again.

Of course seeing James made her think of Nijmeh. Sometimes she would imagine that Nijmeh was at her house on a Friday night and James would walk in. She could see them turning to each other wordlessly but with tears of happiness. He would take her in his arms and smother her face against him. Then they would leave without even a good-bye and never return to 22 Thierry.

Nijmeh deserved what had happened to her. She should have followed James to the end of the earth, but she had no imagination. She didn't know who she was and then was grateful when someone decided for her. Her father had decided she was his alter ego meant to fulfill his fantasies. Now Paul, no doubt, was turning her into his handmaiden. Did Paul ever make her really hot? Probably not. Well, they deserved each other. Delal knew what was best for Delal and went after it. The trick was not *ever* to admit defeat.

Nat King Cole's perfect smoky voice was coming from the phonograph. "Dance, ballerina, dance, and just ignore the seat that's empty in the second row . . ."

"What a callous jerk." Delal blew a puff of smoke at the ceiling. "It's her big night and he didn't show up." She had her head thrown back on the hard horsehair sofa, her legs were stretched in front. It was a pose meant for philosophical reflection after an evening of wine and music.

"Who didn't show up?"

"The man in the second row. Her lover, I suppose. Why couldn't he have been happy for her success? Why did it have to be love *or* success? If it had been the other way around, she would have been there cheering him on."

He was sprawled next to her, groggy from having consumed at least three quarters of a bottle of Beaujolais. But her statement made him sit up and look at her. "Delal, you're the oddest girl. You're analyzing the song?"

"Why not? Millions of people are listening to those lyrics and all of them are critical of this poor girl who simply wanted to use her talent."

He shook his head and sank back, but she could see he was amused. "I can always count on you for the unexpected."

Good. That means I've got your attention. She was conscious that the wine stupor had loosened his body and made him sink closer against her. His head was almost on her shoulder. "I like to think things out."

"Yes, that's it. And you've got a very logical mind. One and one . . ." —he reached over, took her hand, and isolated two fingers—"had better add up to two, or you'll have Inspector Delal beating the bushes." He had the two fingers squeezed inside one of his hands, and it made her heart jump around like a rabbit. Was he going to take her fingers to his lips and kiss them? Was he going to use them to pull her against him? A look of surprise came across his face. At that moment, all her expertise in human relations was for naught. She was helpless. Unendurable desire pulled her to him, but she couldn't kiss *him*. Suppose he didn't want to? *Please . . . you've got to kiss me or I will die . . .* His other hand went around her neck as an anchor. A sweet agony overtook her. *Now!* She parted her lips in anticipation as he brought his face close and placed his mouth against hers. *Oh, James . . .*

"I want to take your temperature. Open your mouth." She was still half asleep and had only opened her eyes to see the time.

"I'm not sick."

"This is not because you're sick. It's to be sure you conceive. I want you to get pregnant."

"Is it necessary to do it that way?"

"Well, we're not doing it the other way," he said sarcastically. "Open your mouth."

She had been wondering herself why she wasn't pregnant. Many nights he didn't touch her and she thought, Maybe I'm for show and he has someone else for sex. He came in at all hours, sometimes two or three in the morning.

She tried to care and feel outrage, but instead she felt guilt and humiliation that she had failed on every level. She hadn't kept her part of the bargain. She hadn't learned to love him. But he didn't love her, either. The truth was that Paul, while he might be proud to have her for his wife, didn't really trust or like her. He was suspicious that she wanted to take something out of their lives and place it elsewhere. Her energy or her interest. To herself she reasoned, Why are we having a baby? But the consequences of saying such a thing out loud were too serious.

Her involvement with McKay was a pocket of security. It was something safe and engrossing to give her purpose and faith in her own identity. What had started out as a playful speculation was becoming more real as McKay showed them the mechanics of the trade. She and Larraine had hopes of going into business, but she couldn't tell that to Paul. At least not yet. They had divided the city into quarters, systematically following leads and answering ads. There were many possibilities. They had pinpointed an area north of the Capitol Building as a realistic starting point. It was run down but showed signs of reviving. If they could afford anything, it would be in a neighborhood that hadn't yet been "found." "Never say die," said Larraine. "If we want it badly enough, something will break. You could offer yourself to the loan officer, sugar. Just kidding." It was seductive to daydream.

That past week, they had traipsed—with trepidation—through the new "beatnik" turf lined with coffee houses on the edge of Chinatown. "See those men?" whispered Larraine. "They don't work. They think we're all crazy and our values are crazy. They think we're emotionally dead. They write the filthiest books. Every other word is 'fuck.' Fuck this and fuck that, and this fucking thing and that fucking thing. They use it as a noun, an adjective, and a verb. They call women 'chicks' and money is 'bread.' They lack drive and that's putting it mildly. But sometimes, when I'm a little drunk, I think they might have something. Maybe we *are* emotionally dead."

Every day for two weeks, he stuck the thermometer in her mouth before she got out of bed and, three minutes later, recorded the reading on a chart he had posted on the wall. "You'll see," he volunteered after a week, "it'll shoot up when the egg drops. It's a very reliable system. This is what I advise for my patients who have trouble conceiving."

She wasn't having trouble conceiving. They didn't have sex frequently enough. This seemed such a cold-blooded way to go about it.

On the fifteenth morning, he read the thermometer but instead of getting up to record the figure, he began whistling and put it down beside him on the floor. "This is it! We're gonna make a baby!" He seemed more light-hearted than she'd ever seen him. He pushed the blanket away and pushed up her nightgown and rolled on top of her. The sun was streaming in the window and she felt horribly self-conscious. "Hey, don't look so happy," he quipped.

"It's so bright."

"Yeah . . . well, we've got to make hay while the sun shines." He grinned and she could feel the beginnings of his erection. He bent over her as if he had a job to do. "It would help if you put your hand down there."

They had a routine. He would feel a breast, which she took as a signal to let her hand travel down and trace the outline of his penis. He would bend over her and suck on each breast for several minutes, throwing his outer leg over both of hers so that he could press against her. With one of his hands, he'd smooth out the fleshy insides of her thighs, a preamble to trailing his finger between her labia and, depending on the wetness he found there, climbing on top of her, pushing her legs out and up, and putting himself inside. If he were particularly tired, he'd whisper, "Lift your fanny so I can get in deeper." Once astride, he braced himself on his elbows and executed an agile series of thrusts, which, while they benefited him, never allowed contact with her clitoris. Occasionally, he'd whisper his progress, "Wait . . . don't move. I don't want to come too fast." She'd lay still as a clam, afraid to breathe.

Most of the time they said nothing. Star became mildly aroused about the time he climaxed. She didn't feel resentful or deprived. She felt relieved that he was through.

When James had kissed and touched her, she had responded with love and arousal. Her body had been extravagant, gathering liquids and pouring them out, radiating heat, pushing for an unfathomable closeness. Afterward, she felt opulent and languorous and sated. When Paul's hands traveled under her nightgown, she let it happen because he was supposed to have access to her body. Sometimes she stayed in the bathroom until he was asleep, but her conscience didn't allow her to do that too often.

"You do want a baby, don't you?"

"Of course I do."

It was their second year together. She hadn't seen James during the summer which he had spent in Italy with his parents. A postcard arrived with a picture of the "Pieta." "I'm getting reacquainted with the sun," he had written. "Italy is colorful, warm, and picturesque. Hope things go well for you at home. J."

Her immediate response was to hate him. He had climaxed over some part of her outer body many, many times. Should he have thanked her for sex on a postcard? No. He should have written something personal in a letter. She had a worse thought. Was this a duty postcard to assure himself more hand jobs for next semester?

Her defense was to be unavailable but the reality of James—broad-chested, tanned, teasing, and smiling—made her desperate to be with him. She was relieved to be wanted and eagerly escalated their intimacy to real sex. He hesitated. She spread her legs and brazenly fingered herself until he complied. What triumph she felt that first time. She squeezed and pulled to make him go deeper. The first searing stream of liquid caught her by surprise. She felt giddy, then triumphant.

On the same day that Star felt her baby's first really solid kick, Delal took James in her mouth. It was an oppressively gray afternoon, but the weather was obliterated by the performance on the wide, freshly made bed.

Oral sex wasn't her act of desperation to keep a restless lover from straying because James, if not in love, seemed content. His gentleness and physical loyalty was endearing as well as puzzling. There was no mention of love, but she kept thinking he might love her and not know it.

Delal *wanted* him in her mouth and her eagerness made it easy to accept. She loved kissing his chest and back and the feel of his skin repeatedly drew her fingers and lips to it for tactile pleasure. "James,"—she was inching down his body on her hands as her breasts bobbed seductively—"just lie there. No matter what, don't move."

"What if there's a fire?" He was stretched out on his back, enjoying the rain outside from the warmth of her bed.

"Shhh . . ." Her face was between his legs, kissing the inside of his thighs, her tongue darting out to test the firmness of his skin, her lips and cheeks nuzzling and rooting into him.

He couldn't lie still. A statue couldn't lie still under that assault. "Delal . . . how can I keep still? If you knew how that feels . . . I won't last long at this rate. Come back here."

"No," she said firmly, as if she knew better what was good for him, "This is what I want . . . to kiss you here . . . and here . . . James, don't get up. It's all right." She took his penis in her hand and placed her lips around it creating a snug collar.

The delicate pressure together with the friction created by the grainy surface of her tongue, made him hold his breath and recede into a private world of selfish pleasure. Ecstasy was no mere word. "Suck . . ." he urged, too aroused to leave that part to chance. "Could you," he pleaded, ". . . suck it now? I can't tell you . . . how *wonderful* that feels! Delal . . . I can't hold out too much longer . . . turn over . . ." She ignored him and began to flog the shaft with sweet sadism. Back and forth and all around and, at the same time, the snug collar of her lips rode up and down in long, deliberate strokes.

He groaned and called out to her like a man at the edge of the world. She felt triumphant. When he started to come, she clamped her lips around him more tightly—she couldn't abandon him now. It sounded as if he were whimpering, as if nothing on earth had ever moved him this way. He tried to rise and reached for her. How could he leave this? she kept thinking. How could he possibly leave this? She released him very tenderly, raised herself off the bed, and walked tall (and naked) to the basin, where she spit out the semen and rinsed her mouth.

Afterward, she gulped down a glass of wine and got into bed beside him. Neither said a word. He lay on his stomach, his partly open lips tasting her shoulder, one arm around her waist. She considered it a job well done and felt more peaceful. The crisp bed linens caressed her bare skin and sent out the reassuring smell of scrubbed cotton dried in the fresh air. She closed her eyes. God bless the laundress. God bless the landlady for finding the laundress.

Love and sex and the anticipation of sex had made her thin and her hips, stubbornly wide all her adult life, were taut and bony. In the newly narrowed ribcage, her breasts appeared large and seductively round. She was proud of her body and she enjoyed being naked. She liked the look of her skin in the pinkish light. She liked drinking wine in bed and feeling it go down into her empty stomach. She liked putting the cool glass to her forehead and cheek and then setting it down so she could free herself to be kissed.

"Delal?"

"What?"

"Will you ever do it again?"

"Do what again?"

"What you just did."

"I haven't the vaguest idea what you're talking about."

"You don't? What a pity."

"I guess you'll have to show me."

"Clever. Very clever. You're a wild creature. The boldest girl I've ever known. And smart, too."

"Really? You think I'm smart?" She was murmuring, too relaxed and groggy to fully form the words.

"Of course."

"Am I too bold for you?"

"Not yet."

He had not said she was beautiful, but it was almost as satisfying to hear him call her smart because he was very smart. "If you weren't here, I'd have gone raving mad in this town." Her hands were moving across his chest. "Everything is so solidly *gray*. You know what Samuel Johnson said about Edinburgh."

"What who said?" he asked. Her words were muffled.

"Samuel Johnson. He said the whole country was a wide extent of hopeless sterility."

He took exception to such a harsh assessment. "This is a land of abbeys and castles and they're built to last for centuries." He raised her up beside him and put an arm across her shoulders. "Besides, I sort of like the look of the place. Don't you like the loggias and the arcades around the quadrangle? It looks medieval, like a true place of learning. The figure in the quadrangle, the one on the dome? What do you think it represents?"

"Don't know."

"It represents youth holding aloft the torch of knowledge."

"Ah, yes. The torch of knowledge. I hope they'll let me make use of it back home."

"Having doubts about coming here?"

"Certainly not." She sat up straighter. "You?"

"Me? I'm satisfied. But I would have probably contracted pneumonia in this constant drizzle if it hadn't been for your warm, willing body. I can always raise a little heat by thinking of you."

"I would say the same. Thank God for your warm,"—she placed a grateful kiss on the center of his chest—"willing,"—another kiss on his stomach, where the hair grew symmetrically—"body."

When they were snug in bed like this, she was tempted to say something emotional. Look how content and happy he was. The words—strung together just right and delivered with feeling—rattled around in her head. James, I love you. James, have you any idea how much I love you? Fear and good sense kept her silent. He wasn't expecting words of love. He was expecting wisecracks and independence. "We really should make it our business to do some sightseeing. There are only five fine things in Scotland that should be seen."

"Five? How'd you come up with five?"

"Trust me, I've researched it. First is Edinburgh, which we already know. Second is the antechamber of the Fall of Foyers. Third is the view of Loch Lomond from Inch Tavannach, the highest island. Four is the Trossachs. And five is the view of the Hebrides from . . . from I forget where. These are not my choices. They are Samuel Taylor Coleridge's. He said the intervals between these five grand things are very dreary. Don't you think we can trust Samuel Coleridge?"

"I'll trust you,"—his hand slid down her thigh and his leg nestled between hers and wedged them open—"and you trust Samuel Taylor Coleridge."

38

***

I'd like to see you excited, too, honey.

When Paul and Star Halaby began the second year of wedded life in 1956, America had reached a peculiar plateau. There were no burning issues. People were dedicated to personal security and *getting ahead.* Women read the *Ladies' Home Journal* to learn how to cook and decorate. They wanted to be liked by other women and to *keep up.* The house of choice was multi-leveled. You stepped up to the bedroom and stepped down to the living room and stepped out a sliding back door to a patio with a barbecue for carefree entertaining. It was unthinkable to express doubt over marriage or find fault with government. Pogo, the satirical cartoon strip, encapsulated the stubborn optimism. "Bug [Eisenhower] Sez 'Jes Fine' " was the head-line in Pogo's newspaper.

Paul was no more venal than the next man. Perhaps, set adrift from the anchor of his culture, he was morally reckless regarding his marriage vows, but in any assessment he would have been tagged upstanding, hu-mane, the salt of the earth, and social dynamite. Like the men around him, he craved wealth, a fine home, the latest model car, and at least four sons to send to Harvard or Yale. However, when his wife became pregnant his need for wealth took a quantum leap and became an obsession.

He no longer was content to live in a three-room apartment on upper Connecticut Avenue. Neither did he want a townhouse on Massachusetts Avenue or around DuPont Circle. After a Sunday afternoon spent follow-ing a sales agent through a development house in Silver Spring, he came home glum and thoughtful. He didn't want to live in a house where the rooms were ill-defined or L-shaped, where there were no full floors, or where his neighbor's lawn cojoined his. He wanted to settle in or around Chevy Chase or Bethesda, or Potomac on half to one acre of land, upon which was set a *true* center hall Colonial or a brick Georgian with propor-tioned pediments over the windows and a fanlight over the front door, or a *true* English Tudor constructed of half-timbered walls with stucco infill. He wanted a living room and a real dining room, a library and a foyer, a kitchen with a pantry, and the bedrooms had to be off a landing up a graceful full flight of stairs. Outside should be a rolling lawn and tall, full evergreens that had had the time to mature.

These were the terms used by the successful men he knew to describe the things they considered desirable and necessary to their happiness and self-esteem.

Armed with this knowledge and dressed as if attending an afternoon wedding, he took his beautiful wife, dizzy from morning sickness, and presented himself to the most prestigious realtor in Bethesda. She flipped and mused over her listings, until she arrived at a card that revealed the proper information. "Come with me," she said. "I think I have a house that will fulfill your requirements."

The house, situated on Bradley Boulevard, which sounded like a busy highway but was just a winding country road, was white clapboard with two symmetrical wings adjoining a wide center portion. There was a detached garage, with an apartment on top for the help.

Two towering and impressively symmetrical evergreens hogged most of the front lawn, but this was more than compensated for in back, where a brick path led to a guest cottage covered with rambling roses. To the left of the cottage was a concrete lily pool, next to which was a tennis court, and a covered free-standing loggia with—the real estate agent seemed very pleased to point this out—an outdoor jack into which you could plug a phone, so as not to have to rush inside to answer a call. "Very handy for a doctor," she purred.

The house proper more than met his requirements. It had *two* living rooms. One could conceivably be called a drawing room, which was better than a library. A short walkway between the two rooms was ornately paneled, and to Paul and Star's complete amazement, the agent pressed one of the panels and it slipped open to reveal a *secret compartment.* "For your jewels," smiled the woman, knowing full well these two had not had a chance to accumulate any jewels.

"This place is too much," said Paul. "I'm not going to pretend I don't love it. I love it. Isn't it great, honey?"

"It's lovely."

"How much?" asked Paul.

"It's priced high," she said slowly, "but you have to remember that there are two peripheral dwellings. The guest cottage is essentially a complete residence with its own kitchen and bath. And there's the garage apartment, again, a complete dwelling. This is in addition to the main house, which is almost four thousand square feet. We won't even discuss the built-ins and extraordinary detailing that would cost a great deal to duplicate. Sooo, considering the uniqueness of it, a full acre, and only thirty-five minutes to midtown, seventy-five thousand is really not exorbitant."

He groaned and bent forward as if the figure were a punch to the gut. *"What!"*

"Doctor Halaby, you've only been looking at developer housing. You're going to find that in the custom-built or in the older homes—this is actually in the mini-estate category—that figure isn't really out of line. Remember, you have the Montgomery County school system, the best in the area. Your next-door neighbor is the senator from Texas. He has small children who will, no doubt, play with your children. You have to think of the peripheral values and not look upon this as just a place to live. It's brimming with opportunity on many, many levels."

He was so quiet on the drive home, Star assumed he was crushed with disappointment. "Paul, I could write to my father and ask him for the money."

"No." He didn't appreciate that. "That's the last thing I'd do. It would look as if I couldn't support you."

"I'd be just as happy in a lesser house. Don't feel you have to buy such a grand place to please me." She said that, but another part of her was way off somewhere else. She couldn't really think about the house. There were things that were happening between them that she couldn't talk about. She hardly had the courage to admit that sometimes—really, all the time lately —Paul was using sex as an occasion to be physically rough. He had strong hands—long, graceful fingers—and they could press until her flesh throbbed. He liked to hold her down, one hand around each arm, pinning her to the bed. There were awful welts she could have shown him. But she was ashamed to admit that he could hurt her or wanted to hurt her. She was ashamed to admit it because there was so little she could do about it. Whom was she going to tell? Sometimes he raked through her hair, grabbed it directly from the scalp, and pulled at the moment of climax. "Sorry," he would mumble when she protested. It used to happen when he had been drinking but now—in the last month—it happened every time.

He leaned over and kissed her cheek. "That's sweet, but I'd like you to be excited, too. Part of the fun is seeing you excited. The men at work make jokes about how grabby their wives are. They say, 'My wife wants a whole new kitchen. We just got a new car, but she's not satisfied, she's got to have the latest thing.' They complain about their wives, but they're really bragging that they can satisfy them. It makes them feel like big spenders. Penny Haywood keeps Tom hopping. She ridicules him about anything that's not top-notch. She says, "I'll pick you up in the heap, lover boy. When are you going to get me my Buick?"

"That sounds awful," said Star.

"Well, it keeps Tom on his toes."

She was glad that Penny Haywood was putting the thumb screws (Larraine's expression) on Tom and that the house they'd just seen was outrageously expensive. She resisted the idea of moving out of the city. She didn't want to leave Larraine. She didn't want them to go so far into debt that her own plans would become impossible.

They had become McKay's most avid pupils, and he often stayed after class and kibitzed with them. He told them if they had the guts to bluff their way through, they could buy two houses and use one as collateral for the other without having enough money to really buy either one. It was the same principle as the trick of getting two VIP's to attend a party by telling each that the other was coming before either accepted. It was not really illegal. They wouldn't go to jail or anything, but they had to be very fast on their feet and have nerves of steel. "Right up my alley," said Larraine sarcastically.

"Maybe you'll find some sucker who will assume the mortgage himself for two women of childbearing age without jobs."

"Say that again."

"The owner, desperate to sell, or looking to invest in his own mortgage, will lend you the money himself. You pay him, just as you would a bank, with an interest rate that's preset."

"Why didn't you tell us this in the first place? Now we're getting someplace."

The call came from the chief administrator of the hospital at one in the morning. "Paul? John Beckwith here. This is important. Are you fully awake?"

"Yes." He was instantly awake and intrigued. John Beckwith was the head of the hospital.

"Can you come in ASAP? There's a young woman here with a slight problem. She's a VIP's daughter and her father has requested that you handle it."

"Be right over." He hung up puzzled but a little thrilled. Someone important had requested him. Beckwith, the haughty Brahmin who had never said much more to him than a cool 'morning,' had called him in the middle of the night. Beckwith needed him. Life was full of surprises.

The young woman didn't have a "slight" problem. She had a major one. She was in severe pain, vomiting repeatedly, and she was whiter than the sheet that covered her. The physical symptoms were suspiciously like appendicitis. Right lower-quadrant pain, rebound tenderness, nausea and vomiting, rapid pulse, and slightly elevated temperature. The white cell count was abnormal, but it was the red cell count that tipped him off to look elsewhere for trouble and that he confirmed by doing the mildest vaginal investigation: moving the cervix and waiting to see if she hit the ceiling. She did.

He guessed a possible ectopic pregnancy. Then he felt the mass and knew for sure. She murmured and moaned and he leaned over her to ask, "Do you suspect you might be pregnant?" He might as well have asked, Do you suspect you might be a whore?

"No," she screamed, terror in her eyes. "Don't you dare speak to me that way. *Daddy! Daddy!*"

Beckwith, who was in the hall, looked agitated and Paul went over to him. "She's hysterical. I asked if she might be pregnant and she went haywire. Who is she, anyway?"

"Paul,"—Beckwith looked wan and strangely emasculated without his white shirt and tie—"discretion is in order here. We can't afford to cause *Daddy* a moment's worry or unhappiness. If the young woman says she's not pregnant, she's not pregnant. Period. The end."

"Are you telling me to falsify records? From the examination, I suspect an ectopic. That could be a very tricky thing."

"I'm not telling you to falsify anything, as far as the records go. But as far as the girl's concerned and as far as the operating room staff is concerned, the girl is not pregnant. We're dealing with a highly sensitive culture here. You of all people should understand. Unwed pregnancy . . . well, I don't want to think of the consequences. Take care of the girl. Make her well and your future here will be infinitely smoother."

Paul shrugged. "I'll do my best."

"Of course you will. I'm glad he asked for you."

"Who asked for me?"

"The father. He asked if we had any Arab doctors on our staff. He specifically wanted someone with a background like his own."

"Son of a gun."

He had to be very careful. Any conceptus that implanted outside the uterus behaved like a malignancy and eventually led to hemorrhage because the muscles weren't built to adapt to such a large mass. A full vaginal examination could precipitate collapse and shock with massive hemorrhaging.

She was already showing some of the signs of shock. She was thirsty and perspiring and had difficulty getting enough air. There was also scant but persistent uterine bleeding, which, guessing from her paleness, had been going on for quite some time. He'd have to correct the shock symptoms before operating. He ordered the nurse to give her both morphine and oxygen and apply moderate tourniquets around the upper legs. Then he transfused six pints of blood and scrubbed up for the operation.

He ordered a stimulant anesthetic and cut her open. Fortunately for her (and for him) it was not a ruptured interstitial or cervical pregnancy, which would have required a hysterectomy. The mass was situated just where he'd guessed. In the right fallopian tube. He removed the products of conception and evacuated the gross blood and clots. He knew it was important to avoid adhesions if she were to avoid other ectopic pregnancies. For that reason he did not resection the tube. There were many things he could have done wrong, but he knew his job and he did it admirably.

She had been in the recovery room only twenty minutes when she began to come around. Her lips were stuck together in painful dryness. She had lost that sickening pallor, but she had a long way to go for rosy cheeks. Very young, too. Twenty, at most, he guessed. The pain had been excruciating and she had handled it well, so he knew she was tough. Spoiled maybe, but tough. He reached over and took her hand. He could see that her eyebrows had been tweezed in very stylized chunky arcs. For some reason it touched him that she had gone to all that trouble to improve her face.

He turned her wrist and read the plastic ID band: Rashid, Asha. "Asha," he crooned softly, "it's all over. You're safe and sound. You're all better. Can you hear me?"

Her eyes opened slowly. They were very large and very dark. "Yes."

"How are you feeling?"

"Like a truck ran over me. Who are you?"

He looked chagrined. "I don't like to admit it, but I'm the truck." She smiled. "Paul Halaby. I'm your doctor."

"You were holding my hand when I woke up." It was a gentle accusation coated with faint gratitude.

"Of course. I was very worried about you."

"Don't worry." Her voice became faint. "That awful pain is gone. Thanks."

"No thanks required," he answered gallantly.

"Oh, yes, they are."

* * *

If the girl's father had even been mildly aware of the care and expertise Paul Halaby used with his daughter, he would have showed his gratitude in an extravagant way. As it was, John Beckwith outlined in minute detail what could have gone wrong and how Paul's finesse had made it right. He made an elaborate diagram (the word "pregnancy" was never used) to show each delicate step and the consequences of mismanagement. When he was through, Rashid Ibn Rashid was burning with fervor to show Paul Halaby his gratitude. There was nothing too good for the doctor who had saved his Asha's life.

Rashid didn't like to give unimaginative rewards. Expensive jewelry, tickets to Europe, even cars didn't leave the recipients with any lasting benefits. He much preferred to give seed money that would create a new ongoing source of wealth.

He had been known to offer no-interest loans for down payments on property, for stock purchases, and for fledgling businesses. He was uncanny at discovering the needs of the recipient and creating the most imaginative financial-aid package. To help him, he had the services of a first-rate private investigator who was an FBI retiree.

For Dr. Paul, who saved his beloved firstborn, Asha, his plans were elaborate. Money was nothing compared to what the good doctor had done for him.

The first of many confusing calls came to Paul two weeks after Asha Rashid was sent home with prescriptions for an antibiotic and iron pills.

"Dr. Halaby, this is Linda Peters, Bethesda Realty. I showed you the house on Bradley."

"Yes."

"Are you still interested."

"Very much. It isn't sold, is it?"

"Well . . . yes and no. Someone has made a substantial down payment in your name. The papers are in order and ready for your signature. In the meantime, there's no reason why you shouldn't have the keys. Would you like to come and pick them up or shall I bring them to you?"

"Is this a joke?"

"Not at all. The house is being purchased through the Mara Management Company. I met only the lawyer. As I understand it, they're holding the mortgage, which you are to repay interest-free. Mr. Halaby,"—her voice became low and confidential—"somebody at Mara Management sure does like you."

"Could you bring the keys to Bedford Hospital? Just leave them at the desk. Oh, and thank you. Thank you very much." He felt odd. And there was a buzz in his head. He tried repeatedly to dredge up some connection that would make what had happened logical. He looked up the Mara Management Company in the phone book and asked for the president. "You mean Mr. Rashid?" asked the operator.

"Is that the president? Mr. Rashid?"

"Yes, sir. Shall I connect you?"

"No. Well, yes. I guess you'd better."

"Who shall I say is calling?"

"Paul Halaby."

"Thank you."

The voice on the line with its distinct accent brought back all his childhood. "Is this Paul Halaby who saved my daughter's life?"

"Yes. But I want you to understand that any good doctor would have done the same. I think you feel I did more than I did, and perhaps you're reacting from relief and emotion. I'm flabbergasted to hear that you've made a down payment on a house for me. How did you even know I wanted that house? That's an extraordinary thing to do. Maybe you'd like to reconsider."

"I don't want to reconsider. That house is only the beginning of what I'm going to do for you. Tell me, Paul, when can we meet?"

Their lives changed dramatically. It wasn't only the house. They received invitations to lavish dinners and mixed with the powerbrokers of the city. Rashid sat patiently with Paul explaining why it would be a good idea for him to get into the stock market. "There's money to be made, and why shouldn't you make it?"

"I don't know anything about the market." Paul, quite rightly, demurred.

"Don't worry. My broker will take care of you," said Rashid. "He won't let you—how you say it?—lose your shirt."

Paul's practice underwent a change in clientele. Before, his office was mostly filled with middle-class wives who were proudly wearing maternity tops by the fifth month and sometimes paid with crumpled bills. Now, his nurse often sent in fastidious women in linen shifts who paid with pastel checks. Their pregnancies never bloomed in the same gargantuan way. Their heavy gold bracelets, dangling from thin, tan arms, made a sound that pleased him. Sometimes, these women asked if they could have cesareans so they wouldn't stretch "down there." "No, my dear," he would say, enjoying their brashness and their expensive perfumes, "you certainly may not." The new women weren't afraid to question his advice or call him by his first name. When he thought they were being too familiar, he'd become firm and cranky and tell them some gruesome story of how dieting during pregnancy could result in an underweight baby for whom birth would become an unbearable stress.

Rashid insisted on the Halabys' appearance at his enclave at least once a week for dinner and spoke to Paul on the phone more often. Star caught Paul smiling the dazed, wondering smile of a man who felt blessed and lucky. She was less enchanted. She didn't quite believe that all this largesse came without a stiff price tag. What's more, she had the odd premonition that Rashid really wished that she were not part of the package.

Real estate agents called it "nervous money" and claimed they knew before anyone else where the next world trouble spot would be by the cash bundles that came to them across the oceans.

Rashid had not sent his money from across the ocean, only across town. He had arrived in Washington via London at age thirty with seven hundred dollars and a severe case of jaundice. He regained his health, gratis, at the National Institute of Health, which found him an interesting guinea pig. His roommate was a stock broker, dying of cancer, and in a breathtaking six months of reckless trading, was able to amass three hundred thousand dollars for himself and parlayed Rashid's seven hundred into just under eight thousand.

When Rashid left the Institute, weak but recovered, he scoured the District for a building that cost seven thousand dollars but was worth fifteen. Many days, rather than spend his capital, he dined on half-eaten fruit salads and fancy bread, T-bones, and filets rescued from restaurant garbage. After four months of daily preoccupation, he found the right property, paid cash, and then used the building as collateral for two others.

In 1940, before the war plunged Washington into a housing crisis, the letter streets of M through Q were lined with narrow, well-built residences and commercial buildings that were going begging. Rashid couldn't buy them up fast enough. They were streets of potential gold lying right on the edge of the creeping commercial heart of the city.

He was the first to recognize the commercial value of the land around the circle that connected Maryland to the District line. Soon after he bought the acreage, it was planned as the most luxurious shopping complex south of Fifth Avenue, attracting prestigious stores and the monied residents of both side of the District line. He had been the first to raze five one-family homes on Connecticut Avenue, above the Calvert Street Bridge, to make room for multi-story apartment complexes.

In ten years, Rashid Ibn Rashid was transformed from a cadaverously thin, unkempt, dangerous-looking foreigner, to a benefactor of the Mellon Gallery of Art and the National Symphony Orchestra.

When he was ready to buy his permanent residence, a unique mansion came on the market situated on a cul-de-sac off Connecticut Avenue, halfway between the Calvert Street Bridge and Chevy Chase Circle. In that rarified neighborhood, an acre of land was considered extravagant. The house had two.

The deal was surrounded in secrecy, not because Rashid was politically sensitive but because he had ingrained in him the taboo of broadcasting his moves. He was the consumate bedouin, moving his tent in the stealth of night to surprise his enemy. That his tent was now a quarter-million-dollar mansion made no difference. Connecticut Avenue was just another wadi across which lived hostile tribes waiting to rob him of his grazing grounds and herds. He had no desire to display his wealth for strangers. It was solely for use as a power base for his family and his entourage.

The house had been refurbished in authentic Biedermeier and Empire, but he ordered it gutted and redone in a Bauhaus style he had seen in a magazine. The decorating firm had a hoot over it, yet the Gropius style was a reasonable translation of the bedouin tent with its minimalist decor, where form also followed function. The bathrooms were the only departure from simplicity. They were marble with the faucets plated with gold, which the zealous maids rubbed away with harsh cleansers.

The first servant he hired was a chauffeur. He had never learned to drive and he liked to visit his properties every day. Next was a male secretary cum interpreter, who ironed out the finer points of the language. He added a wing for his servants, and another for his wife and two daughters. Rashid slept all over the house, sometimes on a divan in one of the large drawing rooms, sometimes on a small French daybed that barely accommodated his two hundred pounds. When the gravure section of *The Washington Times-Herald* ran a cover story on the new magnate, he confided to the interviewer, "I sleep all over the house because I don't like to go to bed. This way, I fool myself."

Rashid appeared soft-hearted and slightly foolish. In reality, he had twice wielded the saber that had separated a thief from his hand. Like all sons of the desert, he was inculcated with the belief that a thirst for blood was synonymous with manhood. In his new life, killing was not practical, so he learned to control through fear and money.

His decent, plain-faced wife and two daughters were sacrosanct and the joy of boutique owners along Wisconsin Avenue. One daughter was shy and obedient, determined to excel in science and become a doctor. The

other daughter was a nymphomaniac who had attended Foxcroft, a posh
girls' prep school, but had also been sleeping with boys since the age of
fifteen. She was attractive in a hard way from too many sessions at Elizabeth Arden. She had had her hairline resculpted, her eyebrows reposi-
tioned, her skin defoliated. By age twenty, her flippant attitude toward
birth control almost cost her her life. It was at this point that Rashid Ibn
Rashid's shadow spread like a malevolent moving canopy over the lives of
Paul and Star Halaby.

"Daddy, can I come in? It's dark in here. Are you praying or sleeping?"

"Thinking . . . maybe praying. Come in, come in. How do you feel
habibty?"

"Better. Better every day. The chauffeur checked me out of the hospital
but I don't know if he paid or not."

"Don't worry. They'll send the bill. Come. Come sit next to me. Maybe
you should be in bed. Have you seen your mother?"

"Mama went to cook some soup for me. I'll get in bed, but first I want
to tell you something."

"Are you all right?"

"I'm all right." She bent over to kiss him and he kissed her back several
times on her forehead and her eyes and the top of her head. She sat very
close to him and he held her hand. "Something happened when I came out
of the ether in the recovery room. Something I can't stop thinking about.
Dr. Paul was there holding my hand. He was tapping it and whispering,
'Asha, can you hear me? Are you awake? Tell me how you're feeling. Is
the pain better?' He was so sweet and gentle. He didn't even know I was
listening. I saw his face—just his eyes over the mask—and he was so
concerned. Daddy, the pain was so awful, so dreadful, and he was the one
who took it away. I can't help thinking about him. That's the kind of man
I want to marry. Someone strong but kind. So capable. So gentle." She
began to cry. "I've never had anyone . . ."—she gulped and sniffled—
"talk to me with such feeling. It was beautiful. I've never felt like that
before. So *emotional.*"

"But why are you crying *habibty?*"

"*Because. He's already married!*"

"Shush now. Don't cry. Here, take my handkerchief and blow your
nose. Nothing's so bad. Go to bed now and rest. I'll take you myself.
Forget about everything for today and just sleep. Tomorrow . . . who
knows? Everything will look different to you."

39

You marry Amercani? *I'm surprised.*

The first time he met the Halabys, he said, "How dee do?" And then, looking sheepish, added, "How do you say it? How do you do?" He knew perfectly well how to say it, but he pretended to be socially clumsy. He looked straight at Paul. "You marry *Amercani?* I'm surprised."

Paul looked alarmed. "She's not American. She's from one of the first families of my homeland. Her grandfather was Sheik Saleh. Her father began the wine industry on the West Bank. He has the best vineyards in Judea, the oldest olive groves."

"You're telling me that only Arab blood flows through those veins? Hah! No, no, no! *La!* This is an American face."

"She's all Arab," Paul insisted.

Rashid shrugged and did a little dance with his eyebrows as if to say, I can't account for all the strange things on this earth. "Well, Star, of the famous lineage, come and sit by me tonight. And your mother,"—he continued when they had begun to eat—"she's Arab, too?" His voice dwindled to make a point.

"Yes." There was something wrong. He was being sarcastic. Why?

"Hmmmm." He smiled. It was insulting. He might as well have called her a liar.

As if tuning in to her thoughts, he became solicitous, assessing each of her selections from the serving platters.

"Tell me, Star,"—he enjoyed using her name—"do you have brothers and sisters?"

"No."

"Strange. No son to carry on Sheik Saleh's name."

She shrugged. "I'll carry it on."

"Aha." He laughed as if she had said something hilarious. "That's the spirit. You're a strong woman, hah?"

"*Very* strong." Everything he said had several meanings, and she found herself emphasizing what she said, too.

"Good. You can bear Paul many sons."

"That's not what I meant."

"Shu?" It was the unique bedouin cry to signify emotional surprise. "What then?"

"I'm interested in having children, of course. But also, I'm drawn to business."

"Shu! Business? What business?"

She was sorry she had brought it up. He would hardly be sympathetic to the idea of a woman in business. "A friend and I are getting our real-estate license. Eventually—you understand we're still a long way from this but eventually—we'd like to buy and manage property. Small houses. Fix them up . . ." Her voice trailed off.

"But you just purchased a house. Paul tells me it's magnificent."

"I don't mean a house to live in. I mean property." She was saying too much. Was it the money that made him so charismatic? Or was it the innocent concern to feed her the most succulent morsels from his own plate? "You know,"—she tried to make a joke of it—"an empire."

He made his hands into fists, one inside the other. "You've been bitten also, is that it?" She had expected him to disapprove. "All right,"—he rose —"come with me. I have something to show you."

He led her into a paneled room with a massive desk behind which was a carved map of the metropolitan area with winking lights scattered at various locations. "The lights are my properties." He grunted with satisfaction.

"The brightest light is your latest? Or your largest?"

"My first and smallest. A row house on P Street. I love that house. It was the one that made me delirious with happiness. My valet lives in it now and sometimes I plead with him to let me sleep in it."

"I can understand that. Certain houses arouse a kind of delirium. Do you share your secrets of success?"

"There are no secrets. It's plain common sense. Very simple. But people are afraid of the obvious. You want advice?"

"Yes."

"All right. What is the most obvious thing? We would all like to buy cheap in a forgotten neighborhood and then see it become—how you say? —*hot.* Desirable. The other way is to find empty space—just a few years ago Chevy Chase Circle was a field of weeds. And now . . . And who would think Hyattsville would become a bedroom community? That was —how you say it?—the boondocks?"

"You bought into those places before they were built up?"

"Mmmmm." He touched his head. "I used this. When I was a hungry young man, I had all day to think about getting wealthy. I went to the Bureau of Records and watched to see who came to apply for building permits and where. There were two or three men who were *the* commercial builders in those years. There was Rosenberg, Roth, and Gilbert. I kept track of everything they did. I hung around where the blueprints were reproduced and paid the man a few dollars. He showed me everything."

He stared at her midsection. "But you can't do that. You're pregnant. A young mama can't go around bribing old men. But you can keep track of the building permits and read the public notices. They tell you who got a mortgage and how much. Read everything in the real estate section. If the prices in a certain area begin to go up suddenly, that's a clue. When you think a neighborhood is getting active, go there and walk the streets. You'll see For Sale signs. The poor aren't blessed with patience or foresight. If the next-door neighbor sells for twenty-one, they're thrilled with twenty-two. They don't think, Next year I'll make thirty. Don't be greedy. Offer a fair price and don't make enemies. Get yourself a subscription to *The Washington Construction News* and *Commercial Review.* The little trade papers print more valuable information than the *Herald* and *Star.*"

"You make it sound simple."

"It is simple. I told you so in the beginning. But you . . ." he added thoughtfully, "you must be careful."

"What do you mean?"

"You must deal only with a reputable bank—a bank can make or break you. My bank is First National. You must get yourself a lawyer who specializes in real estate. The right lawyer . . . very important. But the most important,"—he smiled and tapped her belly—"is right here. That comes first."

"Of course. We don't have any concrete plans. My partner and I have to find an owner willing to take back a mortgage. All the banks have turned us down. We have a down payment, but even if we had jobs women can't get loans."

"Do you have a property in mind?"

"Many. There is a row of frame houses on North Capitol Street . . . I'd buy them up one after the other if I could. The neighborhood has to change . . . that close to the Capitol building. Prices are reasonable because the houses need work. But you can see the potential."

"Have the bank call me," he said. "Perhaps I can help."

His big, slightly bulging eyes were, in turn, dreamy, zealous, intelligent, and childishly excited. His voice was comforting. He spoke with authority and her respect for him seesawed wildly. He made her want to please him, as if she were his favorite child. Yet she also had the feeling that he had it in for her. All that nonsense about her not being Arab. All those pointed questions about her family.

Larraine would swoon at the map in his office and swoon over Rashid, too. They shared the same directness of personality. They reduced everything to the simple truth.

He shut the overhead lights and led her back to the living room. Paul was still huddled with the same man he had been talking with all evening, a stock broker. If Rashid presented her ideas as acceptable, Paul would be accepting. He would take her seriously, or at least be neutral. It was so seductive to let Rashid do what he could for her. He could fix everything.

"I want you to look down there. It feels funny."

Asha fiddled with the chain on a thin alligator bag, wrapping it around her index finger over and over. (What could she possibly carry in such a thin bag? Paul wondered. Loose hundred-dollar bills?) He was wary of this one. Her eyes were odd. Combat eyes was the phrase that came to mind.

"I know for a fact that you attended a very fancy school and a good university." He tried to sound paternal. "You can be more articulate than that. What feels funny? Does it hurt when you urinate? Is it tender in any area? Any more bloody show? Is the discharge diminishing each day?"

"I'm weepy all the time. I'm depressed." She didn't look in the least depressed.

A white linen coat, the collar flipped up, was draped over her shoulders to create a tableau. The portrait of an indulged child. Her lips were outlined and it looked like a painted pout. The face had been worked on. It was poreless, hairless, and unmarred. She probably had had electrolysis— every little hair plucked away. The crease under her nose—had it been surgically shortened?—hiked up her pouty lips, making her look permanently petulant. Somebody hadn't given her what she wanted. Well, Dr. Paul wasn't going to give it to her either.

He got up and went around his desk. "Are you taking your iron pills? Let's see if you've got good color." He pulled down the lower lid of her right eye. "Looks pretty good." He leaned back against the desk and took one of her hands into his. It was an innocent gesture meant to reassure, but she jumped like a rabbit in heat. She had crossed and uncrossed her legs a dozen times. She had let her skirt ride up and scratched her thigh. Probably, if he sat back far enough in his chair and bothered to look, he'd see right up to her legs. Is that what she wanted? Even if he were so inclined— the idea of Rashid finding out could keep his prick limp for a century—it was medically unsound.

"Are you going to examine me today?"

"I don't think it's a good idea. The less we disturb the healing process, the better. Any fever?"

"No."

"You've had a remarkably quick recovery."

"I have a remarkable doctor."

"Asha, you've had a serious operation." He made himself sound grim. "We can't afford any more scares. What would be ideal now is for you to marry and start a family as soon as possible. Get everything operating properly."

"Do you have anyone in mind that I can marry?"

"Very funny." He raised an eyebrow and pursed his mouth. "You're teasing me." He went back to the other side of the desk. "You have to go very slowly. No douching or anything like that. And certainly *no penetration* for at least two months."

"Why would you tell me a thing like that?" She was daring him to spell it out.

"Are we going to play a game? Okay. Whatever you say. In case you're thinking of using tampons, don't."

She got up and he thought she was going to leave but she came around and knelt at his side of the desk, swung his chair around and wedged herself between his legs. "I'm here on a mission," she smiled.

"What mission?" He tried to twirl himself back, but she had a firm hold on his crotch and was tugging down his zipper. He could stay calm, couldn't he? He was afraid—and this was hard to admit—of offending her. The pressure of her hand was already making it difficult to think. He was getting hard, but he didn't want to give in. This was not only wrong—it was dangerous. Maybe if he did nothing he'd call her bluff.

"Now it's your turn to play games," she said sarcastically. "Okay. Whatever you say. My promise to play house. It's time for dinner." None too gently, she took out his penis, flicked her tongue over the tip—a tentative taste—looked up and smiled.

Her hair—black and shiny and plentiful—was twisted in a voluptuous upswept bun, and he wanted to tear it apart and grab it in his fingers. But she might not like that. *Oooooh.* He hadn't wanted this. Horny spoiled bitch. "I'm going to come right in your mouth . . ."—the words were being squeezed out of him by some diabolic need he couldn't control— "right into that big, spoiled, pouty mouth."

Right then, right at the point where he felt as if someone had a tourniquet on his scalp and his skin was too small for his body, she stopped dead. He wanted to slam her head back down, but he didn't dare. "That sounds mean," she smiled. "Is sweet Doctor Paul a mean lay?" she asked coyly. He couldn't believe how controlled she was. "Could you get up a minute, please?"

He complied. Everything she said was potentially a keg of TNT when he thought of her father. She snaked her slim skirt up her body until it was at her waist, then sat down, and straddled her legs over the arms of his chair. "Make me come with your tongue. If you can do it in one minute, I'll finish you off." It was incredible. From the waist up, she was the picture of propriety. Down below, her lips were parted from the stretch, and her three holes were exposed and presented to him. "That's blackmail," he said.

"Why? Don't you want to do it?" She was cool as a cucumber. No shame. No shyness. "It won't take long. I've been thinking about you for so long I'll probably come with the first little lick."

"Your father wouldn't like this," he said soberly, then felt utterly stupid for bringing her father into it. Could she really want it? Was it a trap?

"He'd like it less if you were unkind to me," she answered sweetly. He knew she had him and knelt down. "Okay," he said harshly, digging his hands under her buttocks, "I'll give daddy's little girl her money's worth." His last coherent thought was of the whopping bill he was going to send Rashid.

During the spring and early summer everyone who knew him noticed Paul's grayish look, but it wasn't the sort of thing you pointed out. You couldn't say, "God, you look awful." The telltale color first appeared as an unhealthy circle around his face but it was most obvious in fluorescent light, so Tom Heywood, who saw it daily, finally said something. "You feeling all right, buddy? Isn't it about time you linked up with somebody so you can get a full night's sleep?"

"Menden takes over for me when I need him."

"When's that, once a month? You need a regular partner. I've been with Gareth over a year and it makes all the difference in the world. What are you going to do with all that money, anyway, but give it to the government?"

Tom's patronizing attitude rankled. "I'll decide when I need a partner," Paul said sharply. He didn't want people to think he worked too hard. It made him appear money-grubbing and that wasn't an image he wanted to cultivate. Every obstetrics case was two hundred and fifty dollars in his pocket. Every cesarean was four hundred dollars. A hysterectomy was also four hundred. If Menden did the delivery because Paul was unavailable, he got one hundred dollars, two fifths of the money for catching the baby.

He didn't like giving up any of the money when he saw what it could do for his house. He'd had the front lawn completely torn out and resodded. Surrounding the evergreens—where the grass had never had enough sunlight—were new wide collars of pachysandra and impatiens. It was orderly and opulent and satisfying, and he found himself going out at odd hours to stare at it. Fixing the lawn had led to replacing the plain white entry door with two hand-rubbed oak ones with etched-glass panels and ornate brass hardware. It had taken the carpenter an entire day to hang them properly, but now the entrance—connected to the street by a new brick walk in a herringbone pattern—looked stately. The new lawn and door made the inside look shabby. The house was sumptuous, but it needed refurbishing. The large living-drawing rooms deserved oversized Oriental rugs, and that brought up another point. How could you furnish such graceful, exquisite rooms with ordinary manufactured furniture?

At every step of the refurbishing process he'd serendipitously discovered something crucial about the next step. Just about the time the house was painted, he went to an auction and, with the help of the doctor who took him, picked up a Biedermeier sofa upholstered in peach silk and a hand-painted black-lacquered Oriental coffee table. The same doctor took him to a private sale of Cissy Patterson's estate, and he left with two delicate pecan end tables with inlaid leather tops. They were expensive but his friend assured him they could only increase in value. The restorer who cleaned the new purchases was expensive, and the private trucker who moved them from place to place was expensive, too. Yet he became obsessed with finding ever more precious pieces to make his palace perfect. He was a habitué at the Wednesday and Saturday morning auctions held in the Mayflower Hotel ballroom, even though frequently he'd been up working the previous night. It was cheaper to buy things at auctions than to patronize the antique shops. He knew he was being selfish in always buying the things he liked, but Star didn't have strong feelings and she was caught up in her own renovation of the house she had bought with Larraine. He had come to realize that her friendship with Larraine had its advantages. He could work as much as he wanted without feeling guilty that his wife was sitting home resentful and lonely, which was the main complaint of all the other doctors' wives.

Like everyone else, he had bad moments. A few times, he got carried away and bid too much for something and afterward would become dejected. Momentarily, he felt out of control because he wasn't able to stop himself. He caught naps on the cot in the doctors' dormitory and lived on sandwiches and coffee. Three of his colleagues mentioned that he looked pooped, and Tom Haywood kept giving him pointed looks and shaking his head. "You're burning the candle at both ends, buddy. Who's keeping that pretty wife of yours company while you're here slaving away?"

"We make our time together count," Paul answered. He was glad to be reminded that Tom's wife had thick legs and a blunt androgenous face. "Actually, Star's busy, too. She's working in real estate."

"No kidding? And after this pregnancy, no more children?" The question was a rebuke from a father of four.

"There'll be more children. My wife's a determined woman. She'll handle it all." He *was* proud of Star, if a little surprised by her ambition. This desire to be "in business" was a wrinkle he hadn't expected, but it made her more interesting. She wasn't just an empty-headed beauty. Anyway, he liked playing the role of the expansive, modern-minded husband.

Tom walked away with a rueful look and although he had bested him, Paul felt depressed and alienated. He had no real friend at the hospital to confide in. And what was there to confide, anyway? How could a man confess to being confused and obsessed at the same time? There were many evenings, as he waited for a patient to dilate, that he would look out the window at the string of cars on the busy avenue below and yearn to return to his own hometown and be a simple country doctor. He thought longingly of the large family gatherings, the generous quantities of food, the simple eagerness to please any guest. At home, he would have prestige without qualification. He was astute enough to realize that without the demands of the clan, he had drifted into an amoral life. He had stopped seeing Rita but only because he lacked time, not for any moral reason. He was in debt to Rashid for a staggering amount. Not only the mortgage for the house but a twenty-thousand-dollar loan for stocks he had purchased over the last few months. What was worse, if anything happened to him, Rashid, not Star or the coming baby, would get everything.

What bugged him most of all was the fact that he was no longer invincible. He had begun experiencing debilitating headaches and was easily fatigued, which he thought could be cured by more sleep. What was the old saw? A doctor who diagnosed himself had a fool for a patient. If he admitted to feeling ill, he'd be told to slow down. He couldn't slow down. He was in over his head.

40

---◆◎◆---

We have the only wrought-iron garden gate. I know it won't keep anyone out, but it's a nice touch.

"Here," said Larraine, "I'm not going to let you help me unless you wear this." She handed her a paper filter mask that fit over the nose and mouth. "It says right here on the can that it's not good to inhale this stuff. And don't you dare climb the ladder. *I'll* do the top. You do the bottom. You shouldn't even be doing this, except I need your moral support."

"And I need yours. And I want to be here. Hand me that putty knife."

They arrived each morning at eight to let in the plumber and carpenter. They had—with great excitement and stomach-gripping anxiety—purchased a frame row house behind Capitol Hill in a neighborhood of lopsided sidewalks whose supposed "renewal" was still a deep secret.

The house had cost twenty-three thousand five hundred dollars. They had put ten percent down and were using the balance of their five thousand stake (after lawyer and bank fees, it had dwindled to twenty-four hundred dollars) to begin renovation. The only hopeful news was that the government was giving them a tax break because they were revitalizing a hopeless section of the city. The house had four floors and, by adding kitchens and baths, they could (according to McKay) create two floor-through apartments and a duplex (really a triplex if you included the basement, which was half out of the ground) to rent out at a possible monthly rent roll of three hundred ninety dollars, which was one hundred and forty dollars more than their expenses (not counting money they would owe to tradesmen). On paper, it sounded wonderful.

There had been two good surprises (three if you counted the fact that a fifty-year-old wood house had no termites) and two bad ones. The bad ones were the condition of the furnace (dangerous) and water in the basement. But the floors (nice broad pine) and the roof (slate) were sound and viable for the forseeable future.

Fortunately for them, Mr. Heath, the plumber, was a chivalrous man nearing retirement. He took it upon himself to save two hapless women who were in over their heads. The plumbing bill alone could have put them dangerously in the red. He sat down and worked out a budget. "You pay me in part. You pay the electrician in part. Get your basics in, so you can rent right away and get some income. This area's going to come up in time. You're within walking distance of the Capitol building, so your tenants can save carfare. That's a big plus." He advised them to do all the raw plumbing and install just one new bathroom. On the upper floors he offered to put in used fixtures left over from other jobs. "It's your good fortune that everyone wants colored bathrooms these days," he said. "I have a backyard full of white sinks, tubs, and johnnies." The used fixtures were in good condition and had many years of life in them. When Mr. Heath offered to wait for the balance of his money until they were "on their feet," Larraine was certain that he had a crush on Star.

Anything they could reasonably do themselves, they were doing, including the inside painting. America was in a do-it-yourself craze and decorating advice for the layman was plentiful. Each morning, they spackled and taped a room to be painted the following day. They had learned a bitter lesson: Preparation was the key to success and simple tricks—setting the cans upside down the night before—could save valuable time.

Once Larraine was settled on the ladder with her tray of paint and her lamb's-wool roller, she stopped fussing and relaxed. "This is the best part. Instant satisfaction. I love it. This is the best house on the block."

"That's because it's our house. You always love what's yours."

"That's not always true. I don't love my nose or my nearsighted eyes. But I *loooove* this house. It has those extra carved doodads across the top, which makes the building look more distinguished. The garden is by far the nicest."

"What garden?"

"The one we're going to plant when we finish painting. We have the only wrought-iron garden gate. I know it's not going to keep anyone out, but it's a nice touch. Can you believe we finally did it? I can't." Every day, she went through the same litany of satisfactions.

"Yes." Star's response was a notch less exuberant. "With Rashid's money."

"Look, when you're that rich, you have a direct line of credit to the money vaults of the world. The bank lent him the money and we're paying him more interest than he is paying the bank, so don't feel sorry for Ibn Rashid." She pronounced it *Eebeen Rasheed* and distinguished all four syllables. "He's nobody's fool, sugar."

"I wish it were some other way. He holds the mortgage on our house in Bethesda, too."

"That's got nothing to do with us. That's soul money for his daughter. Stop worrying. Your baby will come out with his forehead all creased. When this house is done and rented, it'll be fine collateral for another one. I have my eye on the corner one. Besides, you could have cashed in that fur throw he sent as a housewarming present and bought a nice sized lot." She reared back and inspected the room. "What do you think? Should we leave the floors light or stain them?"

"Let's leave them light. Some of these rooms are too dark."

"Mmm. I guess. Some tenant will probably cover them with carpeting."

Much of the time, they worked silently, each lost in thought. Larraine talked about her life in North Carolina and then would ask Star questions about her background. Their calm, contented voices echoed in the empty rooms. One hot afternoon, as she stopped sanding long enough to wipe the perspiration from under her hair and direct her face to the small fan they had brought, Star told Larraine about the day she had met James.

"I don't find it strange that you tended sheep. I used to feed the hogs, myself. You know, if you're a girl from the deep south, Washington is in your dreams. A place to escape and find an exciting man. I always dreamed I'd marry a senator or congressman. I wanted to start out as a secretary at the White House. I thought all you had to do was show up and they'd say, 'Miss Reardon, come right in. We've been waiting for you.' I was so dumb." She grunted and stepped down a rung. "So when the handsome horseman rode away from you in the desert, you didn't know who he was?"

Star related how James had gone from school to school with the meager information and finally found her. At this point, Larraine stopped working and sat back to appreciate such a romantic act. "He held his hand over your mouth so you wouldn't cry out and give him away?"

"Yes. Not that I would have. I was thrilled to see him. From the beginning, I felt we belonged together." She put down her sandpaper and rubbed her chin with the back of her hand. "Larraine, how could I have been so sure of him and then been so wrong? I still can't get over that part of it. I still feel as if something isn't resolved."

"You're not over that part or any other part," Larraine said quickly and then started to run the roller furiously, fearful she had said too much.

Star, too, got back to work. "I'm a married woman and about to be a mother," she said flatly.

"That doesn't mean you can stop your heart from longing."

"He was my first love. We were so natural together. Like two halves of a whole. He used to play practical jokes on me to make me laugh. I can't remember ever being so happy."

"And now?"

"This is just very sane. You know . . . being married is just being settled. I guess."

"It's not supposed to be *that* sane," said Larraine. "I was so much in love with Chuck, nothing else mattered. I wouldn't have traded places with the Queen of England. But look what happened. Life's unpredictable and there aren't any guarantees. If some fool drops one of those A-bombs they're testing at Yucca Flats, we're all gone. She came down from the ladder and refilled her pan with paint. " 'Course, at other times I feel damn grateful to be alive and doing something I like. I wouldn't mind a man in my life. If you're single too long . . . well . . . the single women I know are going to classes or taking up a sport so they can meet men. That's what I should be doing, too."

The next day when she had settled in with her roller, Larraine said, "Why didn't you go looking for James? Why didn't you shake the truth out of him? Even if you wouldn't have liked what he had to say, he owed you an explanation."

"My father wouldn't have allowed me to do it."

Larraine was dipping the roller into the paint pan and then rolling across the wall in wide swaths. As she talked, she pressed the roller harder to punctuate her words. "Sugar, you're not going to like what I'm going to say, but there's something basically wrong here. If the guy was nuts about you, why did he just sit around and let you get away? Why didn't he move heaven and earth to be with you? And, as for you, why did it never occur to you to stand up to your father?"

"I couldn't. He expected certain things from me."

"Like what? Your life? What kind of love is that? Would you expect that baby inside you to fulfill your needs? Why bring a slave into the world?"

"My father's word was law. It didn't matter to him how much I loved James."

"You may have loved James, but he wasn't the most important man in your life. Daddy was." Star was quiet. "Mad at me?"

"No."

"Still my friend?"

"Yes."

"Good, then I'll say one more thing that's on my mind. There are some women in this world—quite a few—who don't know who they are until some man tells them, and for this they are eternally grateful. You've let three men decide that for you and you're loyal to all three." Silence. "Now you're mad for sure."

"No comment." A few minutes later, she said, "How about this? No man told me I could buy a piece of property and fix it up and rent it out."

"Touché. And doesn't it feel good?"

"Mmmm." She didn't add that from the time she could talk and understand, she had been prepared to be in business. Her psyche had been methodically primed and if there was anything to all the theories going around, nothing on God's earth could have kept her from going into business.

"Suppose James walked in right now. Suppose there was some horrible misunderstanding that kept him away, and he suddenly found you and begged you to get a divorce and go with him. Would you go?"

"That's not going to happen, so it's silly for me to answer," she said stiffly.

"You never know, sugar. Life can double back on you. You just never know."

In the spring of 1956, the nation's children were being inoculated with the new Salk poliomyelitis vaccine and *Beat The Clock* made the top ten most popular TV shows.

The fortunate few who had summer homes along the Delaware shore began to air them out and bring them to life. The horsey set—including the Walker clan—had left their Tidewater mansions and migrated northwest to Bowie, Maryland, for the racing season.

During the spring that he was courting the Halabys, Rashid had bought a working horse farm southwest of Baltimore that included a large farmhouse right out of Kansas. The compound was a feast for city eyes—lushly green, neat, repaired and painted, and smelling of hay and horses. The main house, full of wicker and starched curtains, was both restful and gracious. Well away from the house, where it couldn't compete with the rural scene, there was an oversized natural pool that incorporated part of a lake. Rashid, too busy to make much use of it, offered it to Star during August. "Go and get away from this heat. It's not good for you or the baby."

She had gained thirty pounds and the baby was very high, so she couldn't walk twenty yards without sharp rib pains. She felt the urge to urinate every fifteen minutes. Besides, she and Larraine were ready to advertise their apartments and meet prospective tenants. The last thing she needed was an hour-and-a-half ride to a strange house, a strange bed, and a strange bathroom, but she went anyway because Paul looked awful and he had promised to come on the weekends.

Later, she would remember that summer as one when Paul would get up early and begin building something right away, sometimes still in his pajamas. She'd find him measuring shelving or planing a cabinet door. Tools would often break or malfunction just at a crucial moment when a project was going over the major hump. "Maybe I can go out and get it fixed," she would offer. She felt sorry for him.

"I don't think you can."

One day she took a malfunctioning drill to three fix-it shops, but none would agree to repair it in less than two weeks. It was a good idea to lure him away to a place where he had to relax.

She couldn't have predicted that she'd feel happier at Mara Farm than she had since coming to Washington. Ned Risley, who managed the farm, was pleasantly surprised with her knowledge of horses and invited her to share in any activity that suited her.

"Paul?" He was lying so still that she assumed he was asleep. He had lain by the pool most of the morning and she was afraid he'd get too much sun. "Sleeping?"

"No. It feels so good just to lie here."

"Mr. Risley—the manager—he wants to know if he can take us to the yearling auctions."

"Star, I don't want to move." He sounded worried, as if she would insist. "Why don't you go ahead? Do you mind?" He spoke without opening his eyes. He barely moved his lips or his head. She'd probably do him a favor by leaving him alone.

"All right. I'll go. I'll probably have lunch out. Is that okay?"

"Yes. I only hope I don't get a call to go back. Menden's wife has a slipped disk and he can't cover."

"I hope not, too. I'll call you later, okay?"

"Mmmmm. Is the baby kicking?"

"Constantly."

"Good. Have fun. Bye."

"Bye."

How her mother would enjoy this, she thought as the station wagon sped to the armory. There had been letters back and forth discussing a visit, but finally Nadia had decided against it. "I don't want to leave your father just now," she'd written in explanation. "There's been a drought and he's concerned for the grape crop."

"I'm going to sit with some of the trainers," said Mr. Risley apologetically after he helped her up one of the aisles. This was an event he looked forward to all year, and he wanted to enjoy it with his friends.

"Don't worry. I'll be fine right here."

The auction went quickly. Two horses were sold in the first twenty minutes for eleven thousand and eight thousand. She thought they were exorbitant sums, but the buyers had used very modest gestures and no one seemed overly excited.

She looked out across the large room and inspected the crowd, which was predominantly of one type—reserved, and dressed in expensive but casual clothes. Their faces were tan, but she would bet it wasn't from lying out in the sun. Most likely they were out riding early in the morning and gardening all afternoon. They reminded her of her mother, and she experienced a wave of homesickness that left her sad and desolate.

She leaned back and closed her eyes and, as always happened when she was quiet, felt the baby kick. Over the loudspeaker, the auctioneer read the biography—the sire and grandsire—of the next horse. She listened with closed eyes and even dozed off for several minutes, totally oblivious of the fact that her biological grandmother, Mary Walker, still a beauty at seventy-five, was seated not fifteen feet away.

By the end of September, she was comfortable only standing up or sitting on the stairs and letting her legs stretch down. She couldn't take the long ride to the farm, which was a real loss because she had come to love the peacefulness of the place.

The outside of the South Capitol Street house was still unpainted, but Larraine had managed to uproot all the scraggly bushes, beef up the soil with bags of fertilizer, and plant flowers and ground cover. The brick walks all around the house were sprouting weeds and needed repair. The outside trim paint was peeling. There was a bad water spot where a gutter had failed over the front windows and part of the frame had rotted away. They had splurged on one holly bush to cover part of the foundation and, after a month of advertising, managed to attract three tenants for the units. The rents they settled on were less than expected but still eighty-nine dollars over expenses. Each month, a time payment of thirty dollars went to Mr. Heath and another thirty to the electrician. The other twenty-nine dollars went into a repair fund. Larraine was making a small weekly salary plus commission working as an agent for Fred McKay and he was after Star, too.

"You think anyone's going to buy a house from a pregnant woman?" she had asked.

"Yes, I do. You'll get sympathy business."

"He's joking, of course," said Larraine firmly. "You cannot go traipsing around in the ninth month. Stay home."

"But you're doing everything. I feel I should help you."

"Honey, this is the last free time you're going to have. Babies get up in the middle of the night. They cry for no reason. They can't tell you what's wrong with them. *Please!* Enjoy these last few days."

"There must be something nice about it." Larraine adored babies and would stop carriage-pushing mothers in the street to ooh and aah over even the homeliest infant. Yet, true to her word, after that first time, she had never again mentioned her dead child.

"You get a lot of smiles and a lot of babbling that occasionally—accidentally, I'm sure—sounds like *mamamama.*"

"I wish it could have happened some other way. If I'd only known. I think sometimes . . . what an awful way to repay you for your friendship to me." Nadia still brought it up when Julia asked for news from America. She hadn't known that Paul Halaby was courting Delal before he married Nijmeh. Even now, she could feel Peter's bitterness, but Julia had never blamed them.

Julia hunched her shoulders, resigned. "It was Paul's decision. If he wasn't one hundred percent certain of Delal, it wasn't meant to be. Delal is very happy in Scotland. She's determined to be a broadcaster, whatever that is. To please Peter, she's also taking international politics. She wants to be a political commentator. Again, I'm only spouting words that she feeds me in her letters. I have no idea what she'll actually work at. I can't say that things worked out for the best because who knows what's in store for any of us, but Delal is all right. What about Nijmeh?"

"The baby should come within the next two weeks. She and Paul might come next summer."

Julia played with a string of pearls around her neck and stuck out her lower lip. She wanted to bring up *the* subject. Nadia had planned to bring it up herself. "I know what you're thinking."

"Even after all these years, it's on my mind."

"Right now it's on my mind, too, because Samir and I are going to Beirut for our anniversary and I want to leave something with you. It's the locket and ring I took from the parents. If someone comes in while I'm gone . . . I wouldn't want them found." She reached into her pocket and brought out a small velvet pouch. "Keep this for me until I come back."

"Of course." Julia opened the pouch. She took the ring in her hand and the locket, then put them back and drew the string. "What about your jewelry?"

"I'll take it with me."

"Where will you stay? At the Commodore?"

"No. There's a wine growers' convention at the Mediterranée. Did you think Samir would go for a simple vacation?"

"I suppose not." Julia sighed as if the vagaries of human personality made her spiritually weary. "Both our daughters are across the ocean," she said. "The way things turn out . . . it's out of our hands."

Nadia nodded. "Why don't you come with us? Samir would love to have Peter along."

"He can't go. I know he won't admit it, but he's got gout. It's almost impossible for him to walk some days. I won't mention it. I'd hate to embarrass him and make him admit that he can't walk comfortably."

"Julia, I'm sorry. You've been such a good friend to me over the years. The best."

"Oh . . . posh. I've done very little. Have a good time. Buy some expensive clothes and, if you're thinking of bringing me something, I could use a nice piece of lingerie."

"Oh . . . yes. Of course. Nightgowns? Slips?"

"Either would be fine." Julia rose, smoothed her skirt, and dropped the velvet pouch into her pocketbook. "Have a lovely trip."

Nadia went to her sister-in-law and embraced her. "I love you."

"And I love you," said Julia, somewhat surprised but with not the slightest premonition that it would be their last moment together.

She had never looked so beautiful to him. Lying there, with the welcome scalding warmth of the Mediterranean midday sun, he watched her test the blue-green water and felt a resurgence of his teenage longing. He had forgotten how appealing were her firm, long legs. Her shoulders were broad and her back gently muscled and tapered, with the hips flaring out just enough. He knew her skin would be sun-warmed and smooth, and he wanted to stand behind her and run his hand from her neck to the little hollow in her back and feel the thrill of a woman's well-made body. The years had slipped by and he hadn't really seen her.

There was another thought that he had pushed away for several weeks, the truth of which made him sad and uncomfortable. They were closer and happier since Nijmeh had left. Instead of watching each other warily over the child's head, they relaxed. They laughed together. Often, he held her hand or draped an arm over her shoulder. He was reconciled to the facts of his life and he still loved his wife. She had a permanent hold on his imagination just by being herself—the sum and substance of her existence. I love her, he admitted simply. If she were gone from me, I couldn't bear it. She hadn't given him the thing he had wanted most—a son and heir—but he couldn't imagine life without her.

Was it prescience? News stories of those who had sudden, tragic losses are fraught with agonized retelling of premonitions. "I dreamed of a giant fish swallowing up my little girl," said a grief-stricken mother whose child had drowned in a well. "I called him back this morning and gave him his umbrella. I don't know why," said a young widow. "The sun was shining but I felt he needed protection." The husband was struck by a falling brick from a building under construction. Samir had reason to remember his impromptu meditation on his wife as he watched her cavorting in the sea.

The second night of their stay in Beirut, they attended a dinner dance— the highlight of the grape growers' convention. The hall, meant to hold, at most, a hundred and fifty, was overcrowded. By ten o'clock, more than two hundred, sun-reddened people, their inhibitions dissolved by too much of their own wine, decided to dance to the bouncy Latin tunes played by the orchestra.

The man with graying temples was impressive in his tuxedo. The voluptuous bow tie and snow-white shirt dramatized his healthy, handsome face. His lovely wife wore a dress made of rose silk georgette, the back hem of which was short enough to display her legs. On her feet were silver T-strap sandals. Her hair, still a shining, burnished red-brown, was upswept with a soft fullness at the sides, giving her the dreamy look of adolescence.

"We could dance . . ."

"Oh, no. Samir . . . we need practice."

"Let's give it a try. Look!" He pointed to a grossly corpulent man leading his wife daintily as he angled for more space. "If he can do it, why can't we? We're athletic. Maybe it's not so difficult."

"All right."

He rose, took her hand, and spearheaded the walk to the center of the floor. She folded easily into his arms. With her high heels, they were precisely the same height and he brushed his lips against her cheek, pleased to be close to her. "You're a tall woman," he said.

"Didn't you know?"

"Yes. I suppose it's a hard thing to admit."

"My mother was slightly taller than my father but, in his own way, he managed her very well."

"But Nijmeh isn't as tall as Paul . . ." He was eager to be on another subject, but she pressed on.

"Are you trying to find similarities—some thread of continuity in three generations of women?"

"No. I'm not trying to find meaning in it." His special knowledge of her biological father and her ignorance of it, made her vulnerable. He pressed her closer and spread his hand against her back to include the hollow above her hips. She stopped talking.

They were in each other's arms, feeling all the emotions of rebirth—poignancy, longing, sweet ruefulness, a devastating concern for the beloved—while at the same time sharing the peculiar anticipation of lovers. It was a moment out of time. And then it happened.

At least two hundred dancers were shuffling and pounding their feet on the slick maple floor—unique in a land where wood was so scarce—to a dance called the mambo. They didn't hear the warning creaks and faint rumbles or pay attention to the progressive sponginess of what should have been solid support. Forward . . . step . . . back . . . back . . . step . . . turn . . . chase . . . turn . . . chase . . . forward—there was the sickening crack of wood tearing under unbearable weight. Whoosh . . . The floor dangled crazily. Men and women, screaming—*screaming!* —were slipping down, down . . . twenty-four feet to the floor below . . . *Eeeeeeeee!* Everyone screaming . . . *Oh, God, help me! . . . Mama! Holy Mother of God, pray for us sinners . . . Joseph? . . . Joseeeeeeeph! Jesus is my savior. Oh, no! Oh, no! Oh, nooooo* . . . They were thrown together in one dizzying pile . . . the top ones crushed the first with the deadly power of hurled weight.

The plaster dust rose like a giant cloud from an erupting volcano, making it impossible to see the fate of those who fell, but there was no mistaking the hellish screams and agonized yelps of pain and cries for help. *Help me . . . please help me. My chest . . . I can't breathe!*

It was difficult to breathe. They gasped and tasted dust. Samir was being pushed, crushed by throngs scrambling to reach the sides. His lungs were squeezed of air. He still held Nadia's hand, but he couldn't see her. A burly man with his elbows held high and using them as weapons to knock his way out of the crowd gouged Samir's eye and momentarily blinded him. In that second, she was wrenched away from him. *Nadia!* The plaster dust grew dense. He pushed with all his strength and grasped at a wisp of rose silk. At the same instant another part of the floor gave way under him. The weight of her as she tore away pulled his shoulder out of its socket before he went down . . . down . . . down. Oh . . . my God, *no!* A scrap of fabric was in his hand and the echo of her scream . . . . It was her scream. She had said his name.

He landed on another man and it saved his life. There was the sound of human flesh being pounded to death. A gagging noise equivalent to the most horrid vomiting. Please, God, he was already dead. I didn't kill him.

There was something wrong. He couldn't move without excruciating pain. Oh . . . my leg! A bone jutted out crazily. But nothing could keep him still. He had to find her. He began the gruesome crawl over the mounds of soft remains and debris. There was a persistent sound . . . the sound of . . . *murmuring*. Exactly like the nuns at the Russian Church calling out the attributes of Mother Mary. *Mother most pure. Mother most chaste. Ivory tower. House of gold. Refuge of sinners. Help of the sick. Fountain of love* . . . "Nadia . . ."—he was whimpering—"My wife . . . where is my wife?"

He crawled for two hours, looking for anything pink, closing his eyes to the worst sights. The dust had covered everything, and all night bodies were being pulled out from the rubble and moved to a makeshift morgue. It was merciful that he didn't find her. She had been crushed to death.

They didn't want to let him identify her. The government pressed for a mass burial because of the gruesomeness of the bodies . . . crushed skulls are not a pretty sight. He had a broken leg and a dislocated shoulder but he kept trying to escape the hospital and look for her, shrugging off restraining arms with uncanny force, hobbling around like a crazed, whimpering animal. Nothing had ever hit him so hard. Nothing ever would again. Finally, they saw it was best to lead him to her. He kissed her crushed face over and over, sobbing softly against her. "There, there. I'm here. I'm here." He cradled her in his one good arm until the attendant, weeping, too, led him away.

At seventy-four, Miriam was still slim, her hair black, her spine straight, but when Nadia died, her back bowed overnight and she went gray. Her behavior was so erratic that Zareefa feared for her sanity. She went to Nadeem's grave and clawed at the dirt as if to wrench him out to comfort her. No one could convince her to stop. Zareefa, in her wisdom, found Nadeem's wedding ring and the small broom he had carried frequently to sweep snow or debris from the path to their house and put the two objects in Miriam's hands. Only then could she lead her away from the grave.

"I need him," she said, looking back with such pathetic anguish that Zareefa had to walk away to keep from breaking down. "He was the love of my life. I didn't know it." Miriam continued talking, her husky voice still hauntingly beautiful. "I've lost everyone now. My baby boy, Esa . . . then Max . . . Nadeem . . ."—she bent over and squeezed the inner corner of her eyes with two fingers—"and now . . ."

They made their way home circuitously. She held on to Zareefa and the words spilled out. "Zareefa . . . so many times . . . I felt anger toward her. Horrid anger and resentment. It's a mystery . . . why should I have resented my own daughter? I couldn't stop myself. So many times I tried to hold my tongue . . . but *I couldn't.* I never really knew Nadia. I didn't. She never knew Nijmeh, either. I swear it. We couldn't deal with our daughters. My mother never accepted me. Do you think I did that to her?"

"I don't know," said Zareefa. "I think you remember only the bad times now, but you loved her. Nadeem loved her."

Miriam didn't hear her. "We were powerless to change anything, Nadia and I. It's a defect. The heart constricts. *Ya Allah.* We wanted those daughters so desperately."

41

*Your wife was admitted as
I came in.*

Rita was still trembling in the afterglow of an orgasmic shudder. She was so generously lubricated that he had slipped out and was eager to reenter before coming on her stomach. "Oh, by the way," she said, "your wife was admitted as I came in."

He grunted in dismay and, as his mind made a complete about face, his erection dissolved. "You bitch."

"Uh-uh-uh. Don't alienate your one operating cunt. You're not going to be getting any from Starry-eyes for God knows how long."

"Shut up." He felt like slapping her, but that would be stupid. Nobody had tied him down to this coarse, resentful woman. He had come of his own free will. "Don't talk about my wife."

She ignored him and patted his rump. "Better run along. You're probably a daddy by now."

The maternity ward was like a second home, but now that Star was there it was an alien place. They were wheeling her back to her room as he raced in. She looked so beautiful and pale that he felt his throat close up. Part of it was seeing her in a hospital gown, which, for him, meant the possibility of danger. "Darling, I'm so sorry. Nobody told me . . ."

She raised her hand and touched his cheek. "It's all right." Her eyes were uncertain. "Are you disappointed?"

"Disappointed? About what? Is something wrong with the baby?"

"No, no. She's fine. She came so quickly they didn't have a chance to give me anything. The nurse showed her to me and she's fine, but I know you must have wanted a son."

He hadn't even known the sex. "How could I be disappointed," he said magnanimously, "when she might turn out to look like you?"

When they brought the baby, her thoughts and feelings were nothing like what she had expected. The small round face was bright red and indignant, the tongue vibrating with the exertion of crying. She butted her face into Star's chest, hicupping, and rooting. Star was nervous and unsure over nursing and also a little frightened. The nurse had left a bottle of sugar water, but she considered that a dirty trick to play on the starving baby and finally undid her nursing bra.

"Here, here . . . shhh." The baby, smelling or sensing the object of her desire, raked her face against her mother until she found the nipple. She wasn't frail. She was wild and greedy. It was such a peculiar realization. It confirmed that the baby was a real person and not an extension of herself. "If Nurse Turner sees this," she whispered, triumphant at having stopped the crying, "she's going to have a fit. I don't care. I'd do anything for you," she said passionately and then looked around to see if anyone had heard. *Oh, Mama. If you could only be here to see this.*

She wouldn't have dared unwrap the baby, but then Paul came in and, to her surprise, casually undid the receiving blanket and began to pull and probe. There she was—mostly skin and bones—legs and arms flailing, belly protruding, totally helpless. Star's heart jumped out for her daughter and she wanted to snatch her back.

Paul raised the baby up and held her close to his face. "Hello, little angel. I'm your daddy. Yes."

"I think she's still hungry, but I don't have much milk to give her."

"That's okay. Let her suck just the same. It's good for both of you and she's getting something." He kissed his daughter. "I have to fill in the birth certificate." They had thought of three names, Margaret, Julia (for each of their favorite aunts), and—just because Paul liked the sound of it—Cassandra. "What shall it be? Dependable Margaret, sweet Julia . . . or Cassandra?"

She was relieved to find him so calm and agreeable. "Which would you like?"

"Cassandra. I like it because it's fancy. This is a very fancy little girl. Look at this mouth . . . ooh! I've never seen a little round mouth like this one."

"We could call her Cassie. Cassandra Halaby . . . it goes together. If you like it, it's fine with me."

When the baby left and Paul left, the nurse urged her to go to sleep, but she couldn't relax. Her mind kept darting from thought to thought. Instead of feeling relieved and elated she felt unsettled, as if something could still go wrong. If only the baby were next to her. Maybe Cassie was crying right now and there was no one who cared to console her. She lay in the dark, imagining people dying on other floors, sighing their last breath, with no one to notice. It made her anxious and afraid. She realized with a feeling of helplessness that she badly needed her mother and father.

They brought the baby to nurse every four hours, which was too long between feedings. Cassie always arrived screaming, stopping only for a desperate gnaw on her fist. The nurse disapproved. "The formulas are so much more convenient. You'd know exactly how much the baby drinks and she wouldn't cry so much."

Star didn't waver, although it hurt to hear that the baby cried a lot. Her breasts were engorged with milk and Cassie was passionate about nursing and expected it. She spread one hand over the breast while she ate to protect her territory. Paul became her ally and she was grateful to him.

In the afternoons, Ginny Hargrove and Dick Menden's wife visited, each bringing a sterling silver gift from Garfinkels. Ginny said, "We must get together when you're squared away." It was just something polite to say during a duty visit but, unexpectedly, their exclusion hurt. Larraine had warned her that her looks made the women wary. "If you looked like Ma or Pa Kettle," she wisecracked, "they'd want to be thick as thieves. But you're a threat." She had thought that motherhood would make her more acceptable.

A bushy schefflera was delivered with a card from Penny and Tom Heywood, and Tom himself stopped by and raised his eyebrows quizzically when he found her breastfeeding. "What's this? You're much too attractive to be doing that," he said bluntly, as if he were giving her sound social advice.

Larraine arrived with wine, cheese, crackers, and two goblets. "You'll have to excuse me," she wiped tears from her eyes and uncorked the wine. "That little girl has touched me. I'd forgotten that they look so . . . *finished*. The dimples on each knuckle were the final straw." She cleared her throat and held her glass in the air. "I would say Here's to happiness, but you look miserable. Anything I can help with?"

"I don't think so. Paul says I have the postpartum blues a little early."

"I won't tell you you have everything in the world to be grateful for. If you feel blue, you feel blue and that's it." She took a sip of her wine. "Anything specific?"

"I miss my mother," said Star. "It's silly because she was timid around babies. But it would mean so much to me to share the baby with her."

"Yeah. I guess these are the times when a girl needs her mother. Too bad." She looked stumped. "How's Paul taking to fatherhood? Is he being a pillar of strength?"

"Paul has to deal with the house. He's supervising all the work, and the rest of the time he's here or at the office. I've seen more of him here than I usually do."

"What do you mean, 'all the work'? I thought the house was perfect."

"There were a few things. The front walk and the lawn. Some flagstones in back around the lily pool. Things like that." She was embarrassed to tell Larraine all the things Paul was doing to the house because it sounded crazy. Paul couldn't seem to stop redecorating.

Larraine cleaned her glasses and put them back on her face. "By the way, I talked to the owner of the corner house on North Capitol. The brick one."

"You asked him to sell you his house?" Star looked alarmed.

"No. I asked him—now don't throw up—if he knew of any *desirable* houses on the market. Some as nice as his."

"Ooh. Did he throw you out?"

"No. He offered me a cup of coffee and said he'd get back to me if he heard anything. He also asked what we were willing to pay."

"What are we willing to pay?"

"If ours was twenty-three, five but smaller and not a corner lot, I thought around thirty, but I said twenty-eight. I figure if he's interested, he'll come back with a counter offer."

"Mmm."

"Star, I know you're a mama now, but I hope you won't lose interest in our plans. The second time around will be easier. We don't need Rashid's help anymore, I don't think."

"Don't worry. I won't lose interest." Three chimes sounded, the signal for visitors to leave. She felt the milk rushing inside her breasts. "They're going to feed us and then bring the babies out to eat. Come again, okay? I'll be here another three days."

"How soon can you take the baby out?"

"In a month, I guess. Something like that."

"Why that long? She has to go out to go home, doesn't she?"

"Yes."

"Think about taking her out sooner. Make believe you're taking her home, if that's the magic ticket. I want you to see that corner house."

"All right." She smiled for the first time. "I'll take her out sooner."

When Larraine left, Star felt exhausted and desolate. Paul stopped in to have dinner with her and then left to look over the work that had been done on the house during the day. She didn't know where all the money was coming from, but he said everything would be paid for if he worked a little harder, which seemed impossible. The darkness around his eyes was permanent, and no amount of sleep made him look less haggard.

She heard a happy squeal from the next room, which meant the Italian woman had her baby. She was nursing, too, and the previous day her mother had reprimanded the nurse for making a derogatory remark about breastfeeding. "Don't you dare speak to my daughter like that again. You made her so nervous her milk's drying up." Star had been thrilled to hear that speech.

The door opened. She heard an interloper in the hall being shooed away. "Babies are out. Babies are out. No one's allowed on the floor." She turned out the overhead light, smoothed the bed, unhooked her bra, and waited. She could hear Cassie's cry echoing in the hall. When she arrived, she was crying so hard her eyes were squeezed shut and her body was shaking. She began sucking without missing a beat. Every third or fourth swallow made her choke, but she kept on eating. She choked, gulped, and shivered until, exhausted and sated, she fell asleep.

Her forehead was slightly sloped from birth; otherwise, she was a near image of her mother but with different coloring. Her eyes and hair were dark brown and her skin was faintly tinted. Star prodded to loosen one of the little fists. The baby opened her eyes and grabbed her mother's finger tightly. "Hey," said Star, smiling down at her daughter, "you're a strong little girl. Do you know I'm your Mom?"

When Paul took them home from the hospital, he urged Star to put in a transatlantic call to her mother.

"It'll cost a fortune."

"Never mind. We can afford it. It'll make you feel better."

There was limited access over the water, and calls had to wait their turn. The operator said the best she could do would be six in the morning, Washington time. But then came the disappointing news that no one was home. According to Muffi, who answered, her parents were attending a wine growers' convention as a special treat for their anniversary.

The telephone rang at dusk with a warning shrillness. "Hello," she said. The operator asked her name, there was a series of clicks, and then, "Nijmeh? It's *Baba.*"

"I have a baby girl. I wanted to tell Mama," she blurted out.

"Stop. Don't say another word. *Please . . .*" His voice faded in and out. "I wanted you in my arms for this, *habibty . . .*"

The first two days, she wanted only to sit by herself, perfectly still. If she dared tell anyone what she was thinking, they would be shocked. She herself was shocked to be mesmerized—Oh God, why? It seemed so perverse—by gruesome, detailed pictures of her mother. She wanted to be able to grasp and understand the horror of the worst moments. Over and over, she ran the scenario in her head—the floor giving way; the panic; the screams; her father reaching for her mother's hand; heavy, ugly shoes mindlessly grinding her mother down, easily crushing her skull, her jaw, the sockets of her eyes—the crisp, cracking noise reverberated in her brain. She couldn't bear to look at any photographs of her mother sound and whole.

The first few nights were dreadful. She had to bring herself up, struggle up, through dark rings of *deadly weight*. She awoke rigid with terror—her temples throbbing, her throat emitting unintentional sounds—and thought No, no, no! It can't be. There are too many things still left unsaid. Mama! On the worst day, groggy from the sedative Menden had given her, she thought she was still in the hospital giving birth and something had gone wrong with the baby. She began to cry with deep, wrenching sobs, and when Paul came to comfort her she told him Cassie was dead. Her milk dried up and a nurse was brought in to care for both of them. It was two weeks before she could gather her thoughts enough to send any words of comfort to her father.

My dearest *Baba*,

When I wake up in the morning, there's a moment when I think: It didn't happen! Mama's alive and I'm going to take Cassie to see her. But then . . . the truth just falls in on me. I call out to her and say, "Mama, *please don't go.*" I worry that I'll go under and what will happen to my baby? Those few moments before she died . . . she must have thought about leaving us—leaving you—and it must have broken her heart. If we could only have taken that pain away from her.

I'm trying very hard to do what I think would make her happy. Not to despair and not to break down. *Baba,* I want to make mama proud of me, do you understand? I want to be like her. I want to be good. Mama was like no other person I've known. She never felt misunderstood, which is a gift. She did what made her happy without a fuss. What made her happy was to love you—that was easy to see. And to love me. I dream about her. She's atop a splendid horse and her face is backlit by the sun. It's so sad that she never saw the baby. She would have been able to let go with Cassie in a way that she couldn't with me.

This little girl I have will help me through this ordeal, but who will help you? I have such an urge to come home. I need to see the farm and walk around. If I were there, perhaps we could get her back . . . you know . . . in a special way. She wouldn't be totally gone from the farm. That was her *place* and if she had her choice, she would stay there for eternity. Don't worry, we'll go there together and find her.

Your daughter, now and always,
Nijmeh

Truth withheld, Ead Bolus had learned, almost wills itself to surface. That's why, when people were intrigued by his profession and amazed at his investigative success, he told them sincerely, "It's not as difficult as it might seem."

He picked up an amazing amount of information with very little effort by asking the right questions and listening carefully to the answers and filling in the emotional pauses with educated guesses. He had done many jobs for Rashid, who enjoyed stockpiling blackmail material "just in case." Ead had looked into many, many closets, including some belonging to government people, but this job was uniquely satisfying and creative. High class.

The very first day, from the girl's father, who was uncommunicative *and* unapproachable, he found out the most important thing of all.

They met at a large family affair. Ead had wangled an invitation by persuading Jameel Mishwe that he was related to his wife, Zareefa. How could they refuse when he promptly handed them a "small gift from the States"? "It's nothing, really. My wife wanted to be remembered to you." It wasn't "nothing." It was an electric blender. If you brought someone a present, claimed kinship, but asked nothing in return except acceptance, how could they refuse? And they did not. He gambled that Samir would attend any large family affair. Wasn't he the "patriarch"?

Both calculated gambles proved fruitful. It was easy from there on.

"I had the pleasure of meeting your lovely daughter," he told Samir when they were introduced. "We have mutual friends." He didn't miss the hopeful look in Samir's eyes before they became guarded.

"Was that recently?"

"Two weeks ago. She appears radiant. Like any new mother." There. He's never thought of her in those terms. "Your granddaughter is impressively precocious and looks very much like her mother. Paul is enraptured by his baby girl." He paused only an instant before adding, "You must have been much the same at your own daughter's birth."

Samir was reflective, mulling over this information. "No. I was out of the country when Nijmeh was born."

"Too bad. But I'm sure your wife had many others to marvel at the exquisite creature God had seen fit to send her."

"On the contrary." Samir was taking pleasure now in deflating this stranger who had access to his daughter and granddaughter. "My wife was quite alone when our daughter came. She had no one to even help her with the birth except for my sister. They did it together and managed very well, when you consider the result."

This was better than he'd hoped for. He could have probed further on the paucity of children. Why, if the result was so grand, had they had only one child? But that was information easily had elsewhere. No need to antagonize a man who already had had enough torment.

The following afternoon, he stopped for coffee at the Grand Hotel, where the local businessmen could be found in the evening, chatting as they smoked the narghilla. "What I miss most about living in Palestine," he mused to the local druggist sitting next to him, "is the gossip. I would never have predicted how comforting it is to discuss everybody's affairs and chew over people's misfortunes. I miss it dreadfully."

"Mmmm." The man clamped his lips over his pipe, wondering briefly if it would be to his advantage to admit that he, too, loved to hear gossip. He decided to admit only enough to allow this fool to rant some more.

"Who heads the gossip mill these days?"

". . . Ah, you mean who has the biggest mouth? Nothing,"—he held the pipe away from him and thrust his chin in the air to emphasize what he was saying—". . . but nothing is said or done that doesn't pass through Rose Muffrige's lips. She works in the post office. So she knows what is going on here *and* also in the far reaches of the globe."

"How many days for mail to reach the States?" He had chosen the earliest hour to go to the post office so she would have plenty of time to talk.

Rose Muffrige shrugged. "Who knows. Am I there when it arrives? I only know how many days from there to us." She sniffed, as if to imply that he had to earn her respect and had not done so yet.

"Of course. How stupid of me." His eyes narrowed and he leaned close to the grille. "I need your advice," he said conspiratorially. "I attended a social event with Samir Saleh and when I inquired after his wife, he walked away from me. What's wrong? I don't want to make a faux pas or cause anyone pain. Is she ill?"

"His wife is dead," she said and, when that shock sank in, added, "She was crushed to death in a hotel that collapsed. In Beirut."

"Poor man. No wonder he walked away from me. To lose his wife so early in life." He sighed. "I'm glad I cleared up the mystery." He made signs of being on his way but Rose leaned over, planting her arms and ample bosom on the counter. She wasn't about to lose her audience so quickly.

"The marriage was not an ordinary one. Samir could have had his pick, but he had to have Nadia Mishwe. No one could understand it. She was set to marry someone else, but Samir got his way. He tricked her into marriage. She was heavily veiled and thought she was marrying an Englishman." She shook her head in disapproval. "Samir had reason to regret what he did, time and time again."

"Why? He loved her . . ."

"Nadia couldn't carry a child. She got pregnant several times but always miscarried."

"But she did have a child." He stepped back, confused. "I've met her."

"Well, *that* was a miracle. The midwife made her stay in bed for the whole nine months. Even so, she didn't have much hope. She confided to me that Nadia probably wouldn't make it because of some internal problem. But . . . she did."

"That was Nijmeh?"

"Mmm. Sweetness itself . . . a little angel." She patted the back of her hair. "When the time came, I arranged her marriage myself. Samir came to me for help." Having said this, she removed herself from the counter and began to straighten two stacks of forms. She had said enough for one day.

"Strange," he mused. "When this eagerly awaited baby was finally born, no one was there to greet her."

"Who told you that?" asked Rose as if he had betrayed her.

"Samir. He said only his sister helped with the birth."

"I never could understand that at all," said Rose. "Mary Thomas, who had helped dozens of women give birth, was just down the road, but Julia never called her. I could never understand why she took such a chance when Nadia had had such difficulty. But,"—she hunched her shoulders and widened her eyes with puzzlement—"they did it all themselves. Everything. I thought that was very foolish. Very foolish."

From Rose he went to offices of *The Palestine Post*. A man as prominent as Samir must have provoked a story or two. He was hoping to see the birth announcement but something much more intriguing caught his eyes. A story of a bizarre and tragic plane crash with a large, ghoulish picture of the wreckage and the mangled bodies. He looked at the picture for a long time. Then spent equal time perusing the passport photos of the couple:

young, attractive . . . he had an eerie feeling. They looked vaguely *familiar,* especially the woman.

He read the account carefully, catching his breath when he came to the next to last paragraph: "The body of their infant daughter, also a passenger, was never recovered. Authorities, certain that the baby could not have survived such impact, decided that gruesome speculation over the whereabouts of the body served no purpose."

He found it almost equally provocative to learn that "a white, untanned circle on one of Kenneth Walker's fingers attested to the presence and mysterious disappearance of the dead man's ring."

When he went to see Julia, he had to be more inventive. He had to tell her that he was there on behalf of the Walkers. It was a stroke of luck that the Walkers lived within eighty miles of his own residence in Washington. Therefore, it was perfectly reasonable for him to tell her that they had asked him to find out anything they could about the circumstances of their son's death.

The moment the name was off his lips, fear transformed her face. He had known what to look for and he had found it. He really didn't need to ask anything else. He was that certain, but being that he was there and the room was so pleasant, and he always enjoyed a brandy in a well-decorated room with an easy chair and a fireplace, he stayed and let her dig a deeper and deeper hole. He was almost embarrassed for her and afraid she would say *too* much. She appeared almost hysterical enough to admit to what he now knew she and her sister-in-law had done.

When he returned to the States, he went to the archives of *The Times Herald, The Washington Post,* and *The Evening Star* to see what the society pages had on the Walker family. Two papers had the story of Jason Walker's suicide. There were the usual wedding announcements and a family portrait in the Sunday gravure magazine. He got a formal Bachrach engagement photograph of Carolyn Walker, née McCarren; Walker's mother and father, Mary and Jason; Walker's sister, Charlotte; Charlotte's daughter, Sally; Carolyn's mother and father. He laid them all out and convinced himself that his conclusions were accurate.

Next he visited a photographer and requested a composite made from all the photos, using Mary Walker's chin and spectacular Oriental setting of the eyes; the McCarren forehead and the straight, silken hair and elegant nose of Inga McCarren, née Lisle, Carolyn's mother. The result more than supported his hunch.

He wrote out a report in diary form, presenting his case, and stood looking out the window while Rashid Ibn Rashid read through it. When he saw the papers drop to the table, he said, "Star Halaby is the genetic beneficiary of the McCarren-Walker clan. She is not the natural daughter of Samir Saleh or Nadia Mishwe. As best I can piece it together, no one—certainly not the girl herself and certainly not her father—knows of this. The mother knew, but the mother is dead. There is one person left who was there. An aunt. I went to see her and when I mentioned the name *Walker,* it was as if I'd shot her mother before her eyes. I would bet my life that Kenneth Walker's missing ring is in her keep."

Rashid was silent and Ead prepared to leave. "What will you do with this information?"

"Nothing right now." He closed the folder. "But I like to keep my options open."

"Forgive me, but . . . who is there to manipulate with this information? Certainly not Nijmeh Halaby."

"It's complicated. If I wanted only to hurt the girl, I could tell her all this and confuse her. But it wouldn't mean much. The only way I can use this information is to threaten to tell her father. She'd never want that. She knows it would kill her father, and she would do anything not to have him know."

"And what is it that you want from this girl? What does she have that you want?"

"I want her husband."

"Her husband?" Ead Bolus was not often surprised, but this bit of news sent his eyebrows north. If Rashid was homosexual, he hid it well. *Her husband.*

"Yes. I want him for my Asha."

The little coffeehouse was overcrowded and steamy. The windows had triangles of frost at the corners and the diners were hunched over their food, glad to be indoors. The waitresses, tendrils of hair escaping their pleated caps, bustled from table to table.

Delal poked at the crust of a meat and vegetable pie and served herself a spoonful. She sighed, cut a piece of meat into tiny pieces, and then put her knife and fork neatly at the top of her plate. "Aren't you hungry?" asked James. "I wouldn't mind having some of yours if you're only going to mush it up."

"Huh? Oh . . . go right ahead." He took the serving spoon and helped himself. She buttered a large piece of bread and placed it on his plate.

"Thanks. What's the matter?"

"James. I've got something to tell you . . . you musn't get upset. It's not your fault. I took all the risks on my own. You never pressured me to have sex." He stopped chewing and looked around, which made her think she was talking too loud. She repeated the last sentence in a whisper. "You never pressured me to have sex. I take equal responsibility. I'm a big girl."

"What are you talking about? What do you take responsibility for?"

"For what's happened."

"What's happened?"

She imagined that he looked impatient, a bit annoyed. Just wait, she thought. Here's something worse. "I'm pregnant."

He looked so stunned and surprised she thought he might keel over. "God," he said making the word so dense that it hung in the air. "I'm sorry. I just never considered that something like that could happen to you."

"What'd you think?" Again his look made her return to whispering. "What'd you think? I've got all the same equipment as the next lass, and you've got all the equipment as the next laddie. And . . . look . . . it happened. We made a wee bairn." She was trying to sound gay and brave and cool and collected.

"Delal, it's not funny. How can you joke about it?" He was leaning way over the table to keep the conversation private.

"I think joking is preferable to crying, don't you?"

"You feel like crying?" he asked solicitously.

"Not right this minute, but I might a little later on . . . when I've got to face the music."

"What do you mean? What music?"

"Well, the way I see it, I have two courses open to me." She put out two fingers and counted her options. "One, I could have the baby. Go home for the summer while I'm still fairly flat and then come back here and give birth and give the baby up. Two, I could try to have an abortion, but I have difficulty with that because . . . well, because I'm a fool for babies and when I think about a baby that might look like you, I have a hard time thinking of killing it." She was going to make herself throw up just listening to her own drivel. Oh, God, James, please, don't look so bewildered.

"Delal you've been thinking about this a long time, but it's all new to me. Give me some time to think about it, too. I don't want you to do anything just yet. Good God, don't think of killing it, by any means. I have to adjust to the news." He pushed the dish away and signaled to the waitress and asked for the check. Delal reached for her purse but he put out his hand. "No, no. It's all right."

He didn't say a word until they were back at her house. Even then, he just sat next to her on the couch, tapping his knee, and looking straight ahead.

She stood up but then reached for the table to steady herself.

"What's the matter?"

"I feel a little lightheaded." He rose instantly and led her to the bed. She sat down and he picked up her legs and laid them on top of the spread.

"Are you sure you should be walking around? Are you taking care of yourself? You should go to a doctor."

"That's very sweet but, you know, it's not as if pregnancy kills you." Telling him was just about killing her. "Look at all those women in India who give birth in the fields. They squat right down and . . ."

"Just the same, I want you to be careful. I'll take you to a doctor. I want to be sure you're all right."

"If you insist, but I think you're making too much of the whole thing." Thank God, he wasn't angry. He wasn't blaming her.

She lay still and closed her eyes. "It does feel so good to lie down. Pregnancy makes you *soo* sleepy." She opened her mouth very wide and yawned. She felt as if she had crawled up a steep escarpment and was now safely on flat ground. "I'll just lie here for a bit." She closed her eyes, relieved beyond words that the ordeal was over. He knew.

He leaned over and kissed her forehead so tenderly that she had all she could do to keep from crying. She was frightened to death. Suppose her plan didn't work. Suppose she had misjudged him. The idea of having an abortion made her palms sweat and her knees tremble. She wanted to beg him to marry her. She wanted to weep and she *had* wept for hours the night before. She would rather have died than admit to her father that she was pregnant and not married. But he need never know. She had to be brave and independent and continue her act until it sunk into James's brain that there was only one solution.

42

·—●—·

I think he wants to do something hurtful to me.

Paul was yawning before they reached Chevy Chase Circle, which was only halfway to Rashid's house. She put her hand on his arm. "Would you rather turn back and go to bed? I wouldn't mind." She was hoping he'd jump at the suggestion. The baby had been cranky all day and she hadn't wanted to leave her.

"No. Not at all. I'm fine."

Poor Cassie. She had a right to look up and find a mother with a cheerful face, not bleary, swollen eyes and a mouth drooping from grief. Her mother's death was a daily, painful truth that showed no signs of diminishing. She felt alone and frightened and there was a new wrinkle to her torment. At night, she closed her eyes to the sight of her mother falling.

"It wasn't your mother who fell," Paul kept reminding her with exasperation. A letter had come from Peter (at Julia's request) with a detailed account of the accident. "It was your father. If she had fallen, too, she'd probably still be alive."

"I know." She couldn't understand why in her nightmares her mother was being hurled down. It was gruesome enough to think of her being trampled, but she couldn't shake the image of a body in midair.

"You have to snap out of it, Star. You're going to work yourself into a nervous breakdown."

"Oh, no, it's not that bad." That's precisely what she was thinking about him. He was so irritable lately and he looked so haggard. All his youthful vigor was masked by a paleness that had the tinge of illness.

They stopped for a light and she had the crazy hope that they could still turn back. "You were gone most of the night. Did you get any sleep at the hospital?"

"I took catnaps . . . ten minutes here and there." He rubbed his eyes.

"He probably wouldn't miss us if we didn't go. There are going to be so many people." She had to be careful what she said to him or he'd start shouting. Fatigue made him short-tempered.

"Star, that's ridiculous. Of course, he'd miss us. It would be rude not to go."

"Rude?"

"You don't think it would be rude?"

"That's not the word that occurs to me when I think about Rashid."

"Oh? And what word occurs to you?"

"Well, he's one of those people who makes you do things out of obligation." She was about to say "out of fear," but Paul would scream at that.

"He doesn't make *me* do things out of obligation. He's our friend." He made it sound as if she were being critical and also ungrateful.

"How is he our friend? I don't think of him as a friend."

"We couldn't be living in our house if it weren't for him. And there are a lot of other things . . . especially at the hospital. He's smoothed the way for me at the hospital."

She had a lot of crazy thoughts about Rashid that she couldn't share. She had the feeling that he thought about her even when she wasn't around. He was a busy man with a large management company to run, as well as other commitments, yet he thought obsessively about her. How could she convince anyone that Rashid didn't like her and that, right now, he was thinking of ways to make her feel inadequate and frightened? Maybe Paul was right. Maybe she was on the verge of a breakdown.

"Your way was smooth at the hospital before. I can't see that he helped you so much. And as far as the house goes, isn't that just a business deal? Don't we pay interest?" He didn't answer. "Don't we pay him interest?" she asked again. Her voice sounded ugly. She didn't want to harp and ask so many questions, but she couldn't stop herself. The accusations—that's what they were—flew out by themselves.

"You really have to change your attitude," he said angrily. "You like living in the house, don't you? A bank would never have given us such a large mortgage. You can't accept the man's generosity and stab him in the back at the same time. He's a kind, generous man. Do you think you and Larraine would have been able to get your house without him?"

"Possibly not. But as Larraine points out, we pay him more interest than he'd get from a bank. It isn't generosity. It's a business deal. So is our house, isn't it? We're going to pay the money back, aren't we?"

"Yes. But we still wouldn't have gotten such a large mortgage without his help."

"Paul . . . there was a call today from a broker. He couldn't reach you at the hospital so he called the house."

"Yeah?"

"He sold a block of stock. He said your stop loss had been triggered.

Does that sound right?" Her voice trailed off. He looked wearier than before, but now she had to finish the message. Maybe it was crucial. Too bad she hadn't thought of this before. Now it would be too late to call the broker back. "A thousand shares at thirty-one. He said there was a dip in the market."

He blinked several times and swallowed. "He shouldn't have called you."

"Why not?"

"I don't want you bothered with those things."

"Where did the money come from to buy the stocks?"

"I didn't have to put up all of it. Some of it was on margin."

"Who'd you borrow it from?"

"The brokerage house. If you have a certain amount of stock and you're employed, the house lends you half the money to buy more stock." She kept thinking that he would tell her to shut up, but he answered in a docile voice.

"Suppose the stock goes down?"

He shrugged. "Suppose it does? You don't need me to tell you what happens. But it has to go down pretty far to be a real risk. And you can always put up more money."

"Where did we get sixteen thousand dollars to buy the stock in the first place?"

"Now, wait a minute. Is this the Inquisition?"

"It came from Rashid." She had a look of desperation.

"I don't see you refusing his help."

"No. It's true. I have no right to say anything. How much of his money did we lose?"

"I bought the stock at thirty-eight. We lost seven points."

"That's seven thousand dollars."

"I've made money, too."

"More than you've lost?" He shifted away from her against the door. The gray light of dusk made his skin look dull and pitted. "Paul, please. Let's go home. You look awful. I feel awful. I'm still mourning my mother. We could sell the house tomorrow and pay everything back and start again on our own."

"Good God, you're hysterical. Pull yourself together before we go in."

"I don't want to pull myself together. I don't want to go. Are you afraid *not* to go?"

He pulled over to the side of the road and turned off the engine. His eyes were so hard that she was sure he was going to hit her. He gripped both her shoulders and gave them a hard shake. "Shape up, do you hear? I don't say anything while you and Larraine fart around down in that slum putting bandaids on a shack. So you shut up about Rashid."

He let go, turned on the motor and slipped into the line of traffic.

They passed a stretch of road lined with cheap restaurants and gasoline stations and suddenly she felt a stab of homesickness that made her eyes brim over with tears. She wanted to see the ripening fields of wheat falling away into the horizon and the men and women singing and working. She needed the dry brown hills—as familiar as her hands and feet—and the special hard blue of the arid sky. Anything . . . the flowers, the domes, the smell of newly pressed oil . . . one familiar thing from home. Oh, God, There's something wrong with my life.

They arrived just after dusk, but you could still see the beautifully ordered hedges and lawns. Paul let her out at the walk in front of the house and went to park the car. She waited for him at the door, ran her hand twice under her hair to cool off, licked her lips, and took a deep breath. The perspiration was soaking the upper portion of her dress, which was new and expensive. It was a princess style with a pellon lining that made the skirt stand away from her body. "Every gal a potential Venus on the half shell," Paul had read from the Garfinkel's ad and, later, he had come home with the dress.

"Aha . . . the guest I've been waiting for." Without her ring, Rashid had opened the door. He wore a beige double-breasted suit and a white head cloth with a brilliant green rope.

"That's hard to believe," she said, sounding more sarcastic than intended. "I saw a lot of important license plates out on your drive." Her mouth felt so dry; the skin on her lips was ripping away.

"Yes, but they come willingly to my parties. You have to be coaxed."

Had he put a microphone in their car? She managed a rueful giggle, for which she hated herself. "That's not true, Rashid. The food alone would tempt me." Why did he make her act like an idiot. She would have liked to put an end to his baiting by saying, I don't like large parties, yours or anyone else's. I feel suspicion pouring out of your eyes every time you look at me. You're manipulating my husband and the strain is making him ill.

"How are your . . . how you say it? . . . deals and wheels?"

"My wheeling and dealing is coming slowly. I'd like to keep buying on the same block, but we're cash poor at the moment." She had resolved not to talk about their plans, and now she had blurted out their status in the first minute. He put his hands together meekly. "You have a good eye and a good nose, Star. That area is attracting seasoned investors now. Maybe we should do business together. You be my scout, hah? Look, here he is." A look of delight transformed his face. "Here's Paul. *Ahlan wa sahlan.*"

He grabbed Paul by the shoulder, even though he had to reach up, and kissed him on both cheeks. It was an extravagant greeting, which did not include her. She wondered if he would have greeted a *Nusrani,* a Christian, like that back home.

"*Salamtak,*" said Paul, returning the embrace.

Rashid led the way through the foyer, with its vaulted rotunda, into the main room already filled with elegantly dressed men and women. She recognized a few faces—the ambassador from Saudi Arabia, a prominent newsman, and several congressmen. She didn't know anyone well enough to join their conversation, nor did she want to. What she wanted was a stiff drink. "I want Paul to meet some people . . . financial people," he said and winked—a warning that she wasn't meant to tag along. "And you . . . Star . . . you wait for me right here." He stopped a waiter and spoke to him in Arabic. "What you drink? Scotch?"

"Vodka and lime juice."

He spoke again in Arabic but included the words "Rose's Lime Juice" and then "gimlet." Again, she had underestimated him.

She sank into a tan leather sofa, grateful for the air-conditioning and waited for her drink, aware that some of the women were giving her stealthy looks and closing ranks. A small combo played dance music at one end of the room. Waiters were passing drinks and food on large carved trays. There were all the right noises of an elegant party. Conversational buzz. Sophisticated music. Tinkling ice cubes.

The waiter returned with her drink and a napkin. She took a sip and noticed the young man at the other end of the couch.

"What are you drinking?" he asked wistfully, as if he were sorry he hadn't asked for the same thing.

"A gimlet."

"Oh . . . it never occurred to me. I thought they might think it was a sissy drink."

She smiled. He had a strong British accent and a lovely timbre to his voice. "What wouldn't be a sissy drink in your view?"

"Bourbon or Scotch, but I have to admit I don't like the taste."

"Want mine? I'll order another."

"I'm afraid you can't make them understand. The help speaks only Arabic."

"I speak Arabic. I'll order it for you."

"You speak Arabic?" He looked sheepish. "Sorry. Didn't mean to sound so . . . astounded." He moved two feet along the couch.

She motioned to a passing waiter and ordered another drink, with exactly the same words Rashid had used. The young man offered to return her drink but she demurred. "Keep it. I can wait." He was clean cut—his eyes a little red and tired—with slicked-down brown hair. What she had come to think of as the snobby British look. It was James's look, although his face had had a lot more character than this smooth-chinned son of England. Since her mother had died, her mind had returned to James as the last place of succor. She had dreamed of him twice and afterward allowed herself to daydream. His face and voice were vivid and the muscularity of his arms holding her. "I don't do well at parties like this," she said to the young man.

"Why on earth not?" He looked surprised then thought it over. "If you mean because of the size and the superficial conversations, I agree."

"Not only the size," she said brazenly. "It's a duty party. My husband thinks it's our duty to show up." He was surprised and she was surprised to be so instantly personal as if they were on a sinking boat and it was too late for formalities. Was a man who looked like James enough to make her spirits lift?

"A duty for me, too. Of course, I don't feel that way now," he smiled shyly. "You haven't been superficial. You told me the truth right away."

Her drink arrived and she took a large swallow. Inexplicably, her eyes filled. "I'm sorry," he said. "I didn't mean to upset you. I was just about to ask you to dance." He peered discreetly to see if her sad moment was over. "I can't even get another drink—which I badly need—without your linguistic help." He was trying to cheer her up.

She smiled and motioned to a waiter to bring another round. Her eyes were still glistening. "I'm sorry. I've had a bad shock recently."

"No need to apologize. Anything I can do to help?"

Before she answered she looked around and saw her husband and Rashid staring in her direction. They watched as she took another large sip of her drink. Paul's grim expression made her feel rebellious. "Well . . . I'll take you up on that dance."

"Delighted."

The musicians had ended a medley of tunes from *South Pacific* and were playing "Stardust." "I don't even know your name."

"Thomas Reardon. At your service. Whatever else happens in your life, you can always think, Well, I can count on Thomas Reardon to help me."

She smiled. "How did you find your way into this fine party?"

"My banking firm does business—a great deal of business—with Rashid Ibn Rashid. Junior members are encouraged to attend his parties as *extra* men. Don't be offended, but I wish you were an *extra* woman."

"My husband and I are here on demand, too." They danced half a minute in silence. "Rashid doesn't like me." She felt a daring need to expose all her crazy ideas to this stranger as if it were her last chance. "You probably won't believe me, but I know I'm right. Rashid wants to do something hurtful to me."

"Oh, I believe you. He's a very strange individual, with a vindictive streak. I've seen it and there are stories by the truckload in the office. Once you cross him, watch out. Have you done anything to cross him?"

"Not that I know of. He just has something against me. My husband operated on his daughter, and he credits him with saving her life. He's very generous with my husband, but there are too many strings attached."

Before he could answer, Rashid cut in. "May I?"

"Of course," said Thomas Reardon, passing her over reluctantly. "I hope we see each other again."

"I hope so, too," said Star.

"Did I do the wrong thing, cutting in?" he asked with mock innocence.

"What do *you* think?"

"I don't know what to think," he said sweetly. "I don't pretend to understand any woman, especially not you."

"Why especially not me?" She became very serious. "I feel that you think"—she stopped and took a deep breath—". . . I'm more complicated than I really am."

"Could be." He shrugged. "In any case, I wanted to offer my personal condolences on the death of your mother. It must have been a terrible shock"—he waited for three seconds to tick by—". . . even though she wasn't your blood mother."

She let go of him and stopped dancing. "That's not true. Where did you get that idea? Of course, she was my mother."

"I'm sorry," he said. "Where *did* I get that idea? Forgive me. I must be mixed up."

She knew Paul was angry the minute they got in the car. He was also drunk and his driving was erratic, but she felt that pointing this out would provoke an outburst. The car kept drifting over the divider line but not far enough to cause real danger. Paul was silent except for an occasional sneering remark. "You were so cheerful tonight. And outgoing. I couldn't believe it was my subdued wife throwing out charm all over the place. What did that guy have that brought you out of your shell? I'd like to know his secret."

Please don't talk. Her first reaction was irrational. All she could think about was that she didn't have Thomas Reardon's phone number in case she needed help. Suppose it wasn't in the phone book? She'd lose touch with him.

"Answer me!" He had grabbed her arm, and she crowded against the door and said nothing. He returned to silence for the rest of the ride and she thought his outburst was over, but when they arrived home he went to her side of the car and pulled her out. "I'm not finished with you. Not by a long shot."

"I wasn't flirting. I was being pleasant. We were discussing how much we dislike large parties. The man meant nothing to me, Paul. I told him I was married." His face had never looked so grim. She could see he was struggling to stand upright and felt sorry for him. Was it the liquor or fatigue? Oh, God, I'm sorry you're so tired. He let go of her and clumped inside the house as if his feet were encased in lead. Fortunately, the sitter was a young girl who lived three houses away because he was in no condition to drive.

While Paul went to urinate, she searched the phone book frantically and almost cried with relief when she found Reardon's number. He lived on California Street, a street she knew. Armed with the number, she felt such a rush of energy that she couldn't sit still. Instead of running the dishwasher, she began to wash each dish until Paul asked her what she was doing. Then she scrubbed the sink and the refrigerator while Paul paced through the house. Each time he walked near the telephone directory, she expected him to feel some telltale heat escaping.

She was scrubbing around the blade of the can opener when she felt his arm around her waist and froze. Oh, no, please. Not now. "You've never laughed aloud the way you did tonight. I was watching you. Your face was so bright and delighted. You looked so beautiful. More beautiful than the first time I saw you." He had lifted her hair and was kissing the back of her neck. She shrunk. He was using her for support, leaning heavily on her shoulder. Why didn't he just go to bed?

"You look so tired. Can I help you to bed?"

He straightened up and mimicked her. "No, you can't help me to bed. I'm going to help *you* to bed. We're going together. You've never been that glad to talk to me, goddam it! But you know what? I get to fuck you, and your little English dandy doesn't. How do you like that?"

"It wasn't anything like that. Please go to bed, I'll be up soon."

"Oh, no, you don't. If you won't come up, I'll fuck you right here. On the kitchen floor." He unzipped the back of her dress. It was constructed not to need a bra so when he pulled it away from her, she was fully exposed on top. "You have the most beautiful breasts of any woman, and I've seen thousands." His eyes lit up maliciously and he took each nipple between his fingers. "I've never told you this, but some of my patients come on to me. When I'm examining them, their legs begin to shift and they move their asses around on the table. Sort of like a bump and grind. I get a lot of rich women now, and I've discovered they're very horny. I think of them as my long, cool numbers who never show they're pregnant until a week before the kid pops out. I don't understand it. They get pregnant, the kids are born, but their asses never get wide. They're not the least bit embarrassed to proposition me. One of them said to me the other day, 'A hundred dollars if you eat me right now.' "

"Don't tell me this," she pleaded. She wanted to close off her mind until he collapsed in bed and slept. Soon. He's got to collapse soon. "I want to look in at Cassie. I'll be up in a minute."

"Cassie's fine. You're coming with me right now." She followed him, thinking he'd calm down in bed, but he became more aggressive and pulled her on top of him, speaking in the same accusatory tone. "You were my beautiful, innocent princess, but now I see you can get as hot as anybody. Only not with me."

"Paul, please. Let me take off my dress. This is the first time I've worn it." She was trying to remain calm. Let him do whatever he wanted as long as it would soon be over.

"Fuck the dress." He hooked his hands at the bottom of the zipper and tore it open. Thrilled by his success, he ripped off her underpants. "What will it take to turn you on?" He moved his middle finger between her buttocks, but she fought hard to get away from him. "That's not it?" He was panting. "You want me to eat you like my long, cool ladies?" He spread her legs apart, but then he changed his mind and sat astride her. "Being in your cunt is like being in Antarctica. More than one woman has told me I've got a big cock, but when I'm inside the ice queen, it feels small and inadequate. You've never been a decent lay, but tonight I'm going to make you beg for it."

She was crying silently, waiting for it to be over. His actions didn't hurt her half as much as his words, which struck home with deadly accuracy. She was guilty of everything he said. She allowed him to do whatever he wanted without a struggle. When he demanded it—with his hand grabbing her hair—she took him in her mouth. She let him turn her back and forth to suit whatever vicious assault would help rid him of his anger.

When he was finally asleep, curled up like an angry child, she slipped out of the room and went to the extra bed in the baby's room. In the morning, she would think of a way to leave him.

43

·····◄●►·····

James Henry Sheridan Saad, wilt thou have this woman . . . ?

"Why are you marrying me?" Delal was sitting on the edge of the bed battling a wave of vertigo, looking worn out and pale.

"Delal, don't let's go through it again. Come on, we're going to be late."

"It sounds as if I'm looking for reassurance, but it's not that at all. When I feel so nauseated, it's hard to concentrate. Just tell me one more time." She was dressed in one of those serious suits made for business-women that, juxtaposed with soft wisps of hair and dewy features, make them appear more vulnerable than a frilly dress does. It was her wedding outfit.

He sat down next to her, making the bed sag, and they appeared to be huddled together over secret negotiations. He considered his words before answering. "I think . . . we can have a very decent life together." He stared at the wall as if the words—to his relief—were written there. "We're compatible mentally. You're smart. I'm smart. You have a certain managerial ability that will make life pleasant for me. I like the idea that you want to do something with your life—that's a bonus for you. Not many men would feel that way, so consider yourself lucky. As for me, I've been told I'm a good catch. I've presented myself to the bar and, if all goes well, soon I'll be a barrister."

"My father's going to cry when I tell him I eloped. All my life, he's wanted to make me a big wedding."

"Would you rather go back and get married at home?"

"No. It's better this way."

He was staring down at the carpet. She looked at his profile and rubbed a finger along the side of his neck. "Poor James. This was sprung on you. I'm sorry."

"It's my choice," he said crisply. "My baby. My responsibility."

His words made her feel desolate. No one who loved her knew this was her wedding day. She had gotten a call through to her mother the previous evening, but something Julia said preempted any news of the marriage. Her mother was going on a trip to the States during which she would visit

Nijmeh. When she hung up, Delal sat paralyzed for several minutes thinking that this was a terrible omen. Suppose she had blurted out everything? That would have been ghastly. She didn't want Nijmeh to know *anything* about her. Not until she felt more secure.

"Did you tell them?" James had asked.

"No. My mother is going on vacation and if I had told her, she would have canceled her plans. I know my mother. We can tell them when she's back."

They traveled to the Registry Office on foot. When he wanted her to cross one way instead of another, he'd nudge her and say, "This way." Otherwise he offered no conversation. She followed meekly—making excuses for his silence—making up a reasonable facsimile of his thoughts. I've already said the words that count—marry me—I'm not obliged to be chatty.

Sunshine was trickling through the buildings, creating random patches of light, but she was too distracted by her nausea to be cheered by it. Her high heels made a scraping sound as if he were walking too fast for her. He *was* walking too fast. He was picking up his pace, going faster and faster, aiming to lose her. At the point when she couldn't see him, he was going to break into a full run and go like blazes. Away from her to safety.

He turned. "You all right?"

"Fine."

"Just two more blocks."

By the time they arrived at the sooty gray and symmetrical courthouse building, she was very wet from perspiration. She had smoothed back her hair into a center-parted renaissance style, but it had crept out and stuck against her forehead. She could feel the dampness dissolving the little makeup she had managed to smear on her face. The silk beige blouse under her jacket stuck to her back. Her fingers inside beige cotton gloves, exuded water. Her mouth was so dry and sour that she feared to open it.

The registrar looked at them curiously and the obvious question hung in the air. "How'd you bag him?"

"Could we get on with it?" she asked curtly. "I'm not feeling well." Now he knows I'm pregnant, too. Bully for him. Pompous ass.

"Of course."

He checked their application and license and, seeing that it was in order, called to two clerks to act as witnesses and began: "James Henry Sheridan Saad, wilt thou have this woman to be your wife in all love and honor, in all duty and service, in all faith and tenderness, to live with her, and cherish her in the bond of marriage?"

"I will."

He had answered simply and without emotion. She hoped to do the same. "Delal Sara George, wilt thou have this man to be thy husband in all love and honor, in all duty and service, in all faith and tenderness, to live with him and cherish him in the bond of marriage?"

Oh, God. "I will."

There was an air of unreality to the whole scene. She felt utterly alone. She had engineered everything, but if she let go of the strings—even for a second—everyone would disappear. She should have felt triumph, but she only felt tired and unable to concentrate. At some point, James searched for her hand and placed a plain gold band on it. She had no idea when he had bought it or how he knew the size, but it seemed to fit. Well, she thought, he's well organized; that's one thing I know about him.

"By the authority committed to me by the State, I declare that James and Delal are now husband and wife."

She waited for his kiss, but it didn't come. He did shake hands with the official and, for a moment, she feared he would shake her hand as well. "Okay, that's it," he said with uncharacteristic weariness. "Let's get out of here."

The night of Rashid's party was never mentioned, but both knew the marriage was shifting and sinking to a hopeless place. The first few days, Paul was self-conscious and overly polite. He was eager to bolt out the door and go to work. It was amazing how little they saw each other. He stayed at the hospital most of the day and came home to sleep but made no attempt to touch her. He was barely interested in the baby.

Even without Paul there, Star felt uncomfortable in the house. Over and over, she imagined herself closing the pretentious, overly decorated door for the last time, Cassie in one arm and a suitcase in the other, and being out on the sidewalk, free at last. The idea lit a fire in her mind. She had never been free in her life. There had always been a debt to pay. But even in her imagination, the weight of the baby and the luggage was devastating, not to mention the emotional weight of taking Cassie from her father.

Sometimes, she could convince herself that he wouldn't care. All he wanted was peace and quiet, not a ten-month-old baby in diapers. But just when she'd think the escape might be easy—"Paul, I'm leaving with the baby." "Fine. Go."—he'd become the concerned father. "Has Cassie had her DPT booster? Her shots are very important. She's so alert. She can put all the shapes in the cut out ball."

Star had nodded dumbly, her spirits plummeting. He loved the baby. She had been a fool to think he would let them go. The *scene* of parting turned malevolent and her skin would prickle with the wrong kind of excitement.

Still, every morning she dressed fully, made the bed, and straightened each room as she went along. In the back of her mind, she played with the idea that this might be her last day in that room. What she wore would become a traveling outfit. It had to be comfortable and practical. Some of the fanatic neatness was just to get through the day. Doing one menial task after another was a way of keeping her mind from collapsing.

Ironically, it was Rashid who provided the means for her temporary liberation. "Would you like to take Cassie out to the horse farm for a couple of weeks?" Paul asked. "Rashid suggested it. I could come out on the weekends."

"Oh, yes . . ."

"He said the chauffeur could take you out."

In preparation for her departure, she spent the next two days helping Larraine with paperwork and waiting for the plumber to fix a leak in the North Capitol Street house. She assumed an almost religious patience, as if any wrong move would ruin her plans. She pulled out every weed in the flower beds, and polished the copper pots that hung from a rack in the kitchen. This is what made Paul happy and, after all, she was so grateful to be going that she could do something to make him happier, too.

The two weeks on the farm stretched into four. Larraine took the bus out and Mr. Risley lent them the station wagon to drive around to the antique shops. "I'm not being sarcastic," said Larraine, "but what do you find exciting about this place?"

Star had to laugh. "The air, the grass. The country roads. The smell."

"Mmmmm. Anything I missed?"

"There's the track, but that didn't excite you, either. I love being out-of-doors. I feel less confined and I can take Cassie for a walk without worrying about traffic. She loves the horses. *And* the chickens. *And* the goats."

"I've never enjoyed being the country mouse myself," said Larraine, "so I have to take your word for it."

Neither one mentioned Paul. The marriage was off bounds for conversation. What was there to say? Paul had visited twice, stayed overnight, and returned. He was thinner than when she left him and she asked if he were eating enough. Several times, she noticed a childlike uncertainty when he spoke, which made his mouth tremble and his eyes widen. "Is anything wrong?" she had asked. She felt sorry for him. "Are your stocks doing okay?"

"Everything's fine, but I've got to get back. I just came to see how you and the baby are getting along. Cassie looks wonderful. And you, too, of course." The three of them had gone out to dinner and no one would have guessed they were a family. Star and the baby were tan and casually dressed. Paul was pale and wore a suit and a tie. They avoided looking at each other and focused on the baby, feeding her bits from their plates and trying to coax her to talk.

"Say, 'Hi, Daddy.' "

She squealed and took a little jump in her seat.

"Hi, *Daddy.*"

"Dadadada."

"Atta girl. Hi, Cassie."

"Dadada."

Paul laughed aloud. "I'm your Daddy."

"Dadadada." She banged her hands on the top of the high chair and squealed. "I thought next year we'd rent a house in Rehoboth or Bethany," he said to Star. "Maybe during August. I'd take some time off."

He was trying to tell her things would be different. Maybe he was even trying to apologize, in his way.

She nodded and smiled, even though the idea made her shrivel in her seat. But she knew it was unlikely that he'd take time off. It was just something to say.

The last two weeks she stayed at Mara Farm, she began going to the track very early each morning to watch the horses being groomed and exercised. She dressed Cassie in overalls and herself in dungarees, a button-down shirt, and boots; and they were rolling down the road by seven. First they'd visit the horses in their stalls. Next they'd sit way up in the empty bleachers around the track, eating bananas and oranges and watching the trainers take the horses through their paces. Cassie, who had an open-mouthed, drooling passion for moving on all fours, would crawl along the stands, managing to pull herself upright and then, unable to let go, whimpering until she was rescued. Sometimes Star could coax her daughter to sit still and watch the beautiful thoroughbreds but, inevitably, Cassie, exhausted from climbing, would fall asleep with her head on her mother's lap. About ten o'clock, they were ready to go home.

The sight of a young, attractive mother playing with her baby daughter is probably one of the most appealing on earth. The sight of Star Halaby, chasing Cassie's bottom up the stands and then sitting like a sculpted goddess while her daughter slept against her would have charmed anyone who had seen them. The grooms and trainers liked to look up at her.

One man—against his nature and good judgment—found the sight of her so riveting, he returned to watch each morning. He was a man of utmost dignity and he worried that his daily appearance might be considered odd. To forestall comment, he became devoted to the horse he boarded there—an animal that had until now made him wince with disappointment.

He was a tall, rangy man of considerable wealth and wide experience not only with women but with the devastating lessons of war. It wasn't his style to moon over a woman. And now, at the least likely time of his life, he was chagrined to be caught like this, shy and slavishly intrigued by a woman who was not only married but a devoted mother.

For anyone who wanted the key to Andrew Larabee, there were several things that were important to know. He had loved an Italian woman during the war who had been married to someone else. It wasn't the typical wartime romance brought on by the possibility of imminent death. It was a deep and abiding friendship and a passionate love. They had seven months together and then, senselessly, Cecilia was killed. Ten years later he still thought of her and had no desire to marry. The last thing anyone would have suspected of him—after all, his Scottish forebears were among the first settlers of St. Mary's County—was that he would ignore the freckle-faced Tidewater beauties who attended his own clubs and his own schools and rode through his own hills, and fall for an Italian.

Today, with his pulse accelerating, he had made himself sit in the stands, too. There was a scattering of regulars, but he was the only one in her row. He sat in a way that allowed him to monitor their moves and—this was a bonus he hadn't expected—hear her voice. "Come back, Cassie. Don't go too far." The baby had raised herself and was managing to hold on to the upper tier of seats while her feet were planted on the lower ones. Suppose she started to fall? Should he get up and rescue her? Well, of course he should. Should he move toward her now? Maybe the baby was fine. No. The baby was half turned to give him a drooling appraisal. She was rocking back on her heels with a recklessness that frightened him. Only one stubby finger pressed to the bench gave her stability. If he didn't act this minute, she would fall over. "Here . . . perhaps . . . you'd like a little help," he said softly, but his stupid heart—it had been through combat without this much fuss—was coming through his chest.

The weight of the baby in his arms was so welcome. It took him by surprise. She sagged against him with an intimacy that was unquestioning. He had never held a baby. How pleasant it felt. It didn't hurt that Cassie was pinning him down with a wild, staring grin, her full pink lips glazed with saliva.

The mother was moving toward him hands outstretched for her child.

He didn't want to appear critical, as if she had been negligent. He wanted
. . . what was it he did want?

"Thank you." She smiled.

Oh! She was so much more than he had imagined. The beauty was only
a small part of it. Let me hold your baby a while longer, he wanted to ask.
Won't you sit down. Please, stay with me. What he said was, "You're
welcome."

He kept coming back for several days, but she wasn't around anymore.
Oh, well, he thought, that's all right because now I'll stop acting like an
idiot. But on his way out, he stopped one of the grooms, "That woman
with the baby, you know the one I mean? She came every morning."

"That was Mrs. Halaby. She was staying out at Mara Farm. Ned Risley
works there."

"But she's not staying there anymore?"

"Naw . . . they went back. If she was still around, she'd be right
here."

"I guess you're right." He walked away quickly, chagrined that he
should feel disappointed. What had he thought would happen? That he
could just persuade her to give up whatever life she had and follow him?

The Pan American morning flight arriving from London was half an
hour late. The pilot, in a curiously chatty moment, explained that strong
headwinds had worked against them. "A giant hand tugging to hold us
back," he mused to the surprise of passengers used to the dry recitation of
altitude readings.

Perhaps that's an omen, thought Julia. A giant hand was tugging at her
mind and heart to hold her back, too. I'm not going to start wavering, she
decided, eyeing the approaching ground below. I wish to God I weren't the
pivotal figure in all this, but I am. I'm the only one left to make the choice
and it has to be made. She clutched the small velvet sack that held a ring
and a locket that belonged to people long dead.

She had not slept well for a month, agonizing over the decision. I must
tell her. I can't tell her. That dreadful man who had come to question her
about the Walkers knew more than he was saying. Perhaps he knew everything. From the first sight of him she had felt menaced, as if his heart
could see straight into hers without any words spoken. The image was of a
huge black vulture pecking at her heart. Worse, exhuming and pecking at
poor Nadia's heart. If she felt this troubled, there must be something to it.

And if there were something to fear, wouldn't it be better if she told
Nijmeh herself? There was no one else who knew the truth or could explain the desperate situation that made them do what they did. It all rested

in her. If she could make any part of Nijmeh's life easier, how could she withhold that information? Nijmeh, you've lost not one but two mothers. Both died in the most violent situations. I don't know why you've been singled out for so much tragedy. Oh, God, I can't. I can't. But suppose that awful man tells her? He had mentioned the fact that there was a child. His lips had said, "Have you any idea what happened to the child?" but his eyes had said, "I know. I know everything."

"I'm going to visit Nijmeh in America," she told Peter. "I'll go alone," she added firmly. "I want to comfort her and talk about Nadia. She must need to let out her feelings." Peter was so unused to having his wife ask for anything that he not only urged her to go but to go first class.

Instead of descending immediately, the plane rose again. Julia closed her eyes and, at the suggestion of the stewardess who said they would probably be in the air at least another half hour, fell into a fitful sleep. She awoke to the rude, rumbling bump of wheels scraping the ground and a cry of fear escaped her lips. In just a few hours, it would all be over.

"You think of me as just your aunt, but I feel closer to you than that. More like another mother." You'll know why soon enough. They were side by side on a couch in the living room, awkwardly trying to face each other. Star was fidgety, knowing she had to hear all the heartbreaking details of her mother's death but also wanting to delay it. She could hear Cassie babbling in the nursery and thought, If she let her skip the nap and brought her back down, they could be distracted. But then she'd have to go through it at another time.

"*Amti,* let's go into the kitchen. It's chilly in here."

Julia rose and followed her through the house. Their shoes clattered on the various surfaces . . . wood, then tile in the foyer, then linoleum. "This is a lovely house," said Julia nervously. "Paul must be doing well." Paul looks dreadful, she was thinking. He had left early and held no promise for returning at all that day, mumbling that he had to cover for another doctor who was on vacation. Julia felt that perhaps he was embarrassed to see her because of Delal and she wanted to reassure him, but couldn't find the right words. She had too much on her mind already. She had left her suitcase packed as if she might be ordered to leave immediately.

"It's Paul's dream house," emphasized Star. "I would be content in something far less grand if it would mean he could work less. But I don't think that would happen." She was trying to exonerate herself as being the cause of Paul's haggardness. She wanted her aunt to think well of her and, for the length of her visit, keep up appearances.

"If you have money problems," began Julia awkwardly, "you have *sidi*'s inheritance; perhaps you've forgotten. It'll be yours in a few years."

"I've never thought of it and I don't think Paul would take it. I don't remember *sidi* very well. Was Delal upset because I received money and she didn't?"

"Delal has more money than she'll ever need. No. She's not upset." She fell silent and twisted restlessly in her chair. There was no easy way to begin. She wished they had remained in the larger room. The kitchen was too intimate and casual a stage for her to play the role of the cruel executioner. Star . . . Nijmeh, darling girl, you're not who you think you are. We stole you from your parents. We tricked you out of your rightful heritage and used you to console a woman who couldn't have children. We willfully gave you to a man who became obsessed with you. "I didn't know what else to do. She wanted a child so desperately. But we didn't have the right . . ." She was whimpering aloud.

"Amti! What's the matter? Are you all right?" She stretched out her hands to touch her aunt.

"I'm not all right. I'm eaten up with guilt and apprehension but I've got to tell you. There's no one else left who can do it." She yanked her hands away and curled them in against her heart. "Nijmeh, this is awful. It's news that will shatter you, and you don't deserve it. *Oh, my God, please forgive me."*

"Forgive you? For what?"

"I love you like my own child. Maybe it was because I nursed you myself. I still had milk from Delal and your mother . . . she couldn't do it. Not that she didn't want to. She did. But it wasn't possible because . . ." Those clear green eyes were waiting . . . waiting in a deathly stillness. "Nijmeh . . . darling . . ."—she turned her palms upward in a gesture of helplessness—"it would be worse if you found out another way . . . if someone used the information to hurt you. Your mother, Nadia, was not your mother. Oh, wait! I didn't mean to begin that way. Please . . ."—she turned away—"I'll tell you everything, but I don't have the courage to look at you." She stared steadily ahead. "We were at the farm . . . sitting outside at dusk. Delal was crawling at our feet. A plane roared overhead and we became upset. It was flying very erratically . . ."

44

I want Paul.

It was so easy not to believe it. In the morning, she would wake up and think, Well, it's not true so I don't have *that* to think about. She would get Cassie out of her crib and change her diaper, sponge her bottom, and put on dry clothes. She would hum as she took her down to the kitchen and placed her in her infant seat while she warmed the milk for the cereal. She would push her hair behind her ears and pour the pabulum into a bowl and then carefully add the milk so it wasn't too mushy or too dry. She would tie the terry bib around her daughter's neck—there was a duck on one side and quilted plastic on the other. She would smile down and say, "Okay, Cassie, here comes breakfast." With an unconscious smile—giddy with desire to please the baby—she would add a heaping spoon of apple sauce because Cassie loved it so.

It was then, at the moment when the sweet fulfillment of making Cassie happy was uppermost in her mind, that the truth would *electrify* her. I was the helpless trusting baby. They took me. They made decisions, and I was powerless to resist. It stunned her over and over, piercing through the past until all memory of her mother was crisscrossed with confusion and melancholy, anger and despair. And for herself? Shame. She felt ashamed for having been the victim of such a shocking crime. It was a crime of theft. Never for one instant did she consider telling anyone.

She realized with a sense of foreboding that by simply opening the phone book, she might find a Walker relative. Larraine told her the library had phone books for other states and far-off areas. She worked up the courage to look in the Leonardstown, Maryland book and, with her heart fairly beating out of her chest, she saw all the names: Charles Walker, Charlotte Walker, Edmund Walker, Mary Walker, Sis Walker. Walker and Abbot Insurance Brokers. Walker Feed and Seed . . .

At night, when all the other emotions had run their course, she became so fearful her body trembled as if she were out in the cold. She would leave the bed so as not to wake Paul and go down to the kitchen for a cup of tea. If Samir found out, it would kill him. But how would Samir find out? Aunt Julia would never tell him. No one else knew. So why was she afraid? It was a riddle. No one else knows. No one else knows . . . *one else knows.* Rashid had said it. "It must have been a terrible shock . . . even though she wasn't your blood mother." *Oh, dear God, please, no. Don't tell my father.* There was no choice. She had to go and see Rashid.

The office was huge and oddly cold on this muggy October day. He was seated at a massive desk made of thick bluish glass over two columns of stainless steel. He was on the phone and his back was to her. When he turned around his face was innocently quizzical. "Hello, *habibty. Ahlan wa sahlan?* How's the baby?"

She had come for a confrontation, but that seemingly kind welcome undid her and she collapsed into a chair and began to cry. He walked to her side and put his hand on her shoulder. *"Shu?* Is Paul sick? The baby? What's the matter?"

"Oh, God," she sighed and wiped her eyes. "Where do I begin? Rashid,"—she looked up at him like a hurt child—"Why are you doing this to me? I haven't hurt you. You took our lives—mine and Paul's—and turned them upside down. We're deeply in debt to you, with no hope of getting out, and you keep tempting him with more. It's taking a terrible toll on him. I worry that he's going to collapse from overwork. I know you've always hated me, but why . . . *why?* . . . did you send that man to frighten my aunt? It's all so *evil* and I can't make any sense of it. Why? What do you want?"

He went around and sat back at his desk, put his hands together in front of him, and fixed her with a deadly stare. He wasn't going to waste time refuting her accusations. He was going to get down to business and she had an ominous flutter of the heart, as if her sentence were about to be handed down for a crime she wasn't aware of having committed. "I want Paul."

Paul? She was so confused she couldn't react. Paul? She wanted to laugh, but she knew that wasn't the proper thing to do. She closed her eyes and waited. "I want Paul for Asha."

Tears squeezed through closed eyes. She couldn't look at him for fear he would see the relief. Paul is what he had wanted all along. He had no intention of telling her father anything. She was close to hysteria, but she would sit perfectly still until she had a hold of herself. Count to ten. Say a Hail Mary to calm down. Such soothing words. Holy Mary, Mother of God, pray for us . . . She opened her eyes. "And what do you propose to give me in return?"

He looked confused. He had expected something else and now he was at a disadvantage. He cleared his throat. "I'll forgive the mortgage on the

North Capitol Street property . . . twenty thousand dollars. You'll be able to use it to buy something else. I have faith in you. You'll be all right. Of course, he'll allow you to keep the baby. You can go to Mexico for the divorce. I'll leave it up to you to choose the time to tell him."

She opened her bag and put her handkerchief inside. Her voice was hoarse and it cracked as she spoke, "How do you know Paul will do what you want?"

"Because, my dear, it's—how you say it?—an unbeatable deal."

All at once, the room seemed to be out of air and she felt as if she were suffocating. She had to get out of there or pass out. "I'll wait for the transferred deed," she said coldly. "Then I'll decide when to tell him."

Paul was busier than usual that fall. He even joked to Menden that there must have been a lot of dull television during the winter to have made so many women reach term in September.

He had stayed at the house to oversee the installation of new flagstones around the lily pool and now, if he wanted to finish rounds before office hours, he had to hustle. The staff elevator was being held for a dolly with lunch trays, so he opted for the stairs to the third floor. After one flight, he was breathing so hard he had to stop. He felt a tightness like a heavy sandbag laid across his chest. The weight pressed against his lungs, making it impossible to take a full breath. He had to sit down. A janitor, swabbing his way from landing to landing, reached him. "Something the matter?"

The tightness began to ease. "No. Just ran up too fast. I'll be all right as soon as I catch my breath." His chest held the memory of the recent pain and he wondered if he had wrenched a muscle while lifting one of the flagstones.

Early in his second term, President Eisenhower had had a mild heart attack and each time he had a check-up the newspapers listed warning symptoms of a myocardial infarction. Every literate citizen was monitoring his chest and arms for telltale signs. Paul never suspected. He attributed his recent bouts of breathing difficulties to a combination of fatigue, worry, muscle strain, and allergy to the plaster dust produced by the alterations on the house.

He had a lot on his mind and he didn't want to think about his health. One of his patients had developed toxemia during the last trimester and he had to induce labor. There was a good likelihood that the baby would die, but he had no alternative. The mother was critical. The day she had walked into his office he had known her fate before she spoke—the upper torso was gruesomely bloated, the head so full of water that even her retinas were ready to hemorrhage. "Doctor, I'm dizzy and my head aches all the time."

He broke out in a sweat. "How long has this been going on?"

"I don't know . . . a few days. A week."

For this he didn't wait behind his desk. He got up quickly, tilted her head to inspect her eyes. "Any blurred vision?"

"Yes. Is it serious . . ."—tears began—"will it hurt the baby?"

"It's very serious," he shouted. "Why didn't you come immediately?"

"I didn't think it was anything. This is my first . . ." Whimpers and tears.

"I'm going to have to put you in the hospital."

Inducing labor prematurely always made him feel sad and clumsy. The image was of a senseless hand wreaking havoc on a courageous little soldier who was hard at work, racing against the clock, to make eyebrows and fingernails, to perfect lungs, to put some meat on the bones. The drive to flourish and survive could surmount many odds but seldom the insidious effect of toxemia. The slow poisoning tripled the heartbeat and exhausted the fetus until it literally died of fatigue.

All those feelings, the helplessness he felt, the knowledge that when he encountered it again, he would be equally powerless to stop it weighed on him. He felt the weight against his entire chest as an oppressive, crushing heaviness that came and went of its own volition. Throughout the next few days the episodes of pain and breathlessness came more frequently. He had only to walk briskly to bring on an attack, yet he still ignored the symptoms.

On the last Friday of October he was short of breath throughout the morning. His face was ashen, even after seven hours of restful sleep. Reluctantly, he made an appointment with Spenser Hodding, the cardiologist, for the following Monday so he wouldn't miss any of the weekend business.

About eight o'clock on Saturday evening he was waiting for Rachel Caldecott to dilate four additional centimeters and, anticipating the slowness of a first labor, went to rest in the doctors' room. He sat on the side of a cot but found himself unable to lift his legs onto the bed so he could lie down. Excruciating pain radiated across his chest and swept over his back, cutting deep into every muscle. The feeling was of a crushing heaviness pinning his entire chest against an unyielding surface. Breathing was impossible.

He fell to the floor and crawled to the heavy fireproof metal door to shout for help. He couldn't raise himself enough to reach the knob. Had he reached the knob, it's doubtful he would have had the strength to turn it. Had he opened the door, he would not have been able to even whisper his predicament. And if, by some miracle, help had arrived, it's doubtful they could have saved him from the massive coronary that brought his heart to a thundering halt.

It was unbelievable. The first word on everyone's lips was "No." It couldn't be. A thirty-five-year-old man doesn't just drop dead. Two of the wives hastily convened and, accompanied by Tom Heywood, came to tell the young widow. Star couldn't account for the entourage that appeared at her door at ten o'clock and momentarily she thought it might be some idiotic surprise party. But for what occasion? Then Penny Heywood said, "We didn't want you to be alone when you heard. Oh, dear, I'm sorry but Paul is dead."

The words didn't register. It was so ludicrous to have these strangers in her foyer at this time of night. For a moment she considered telling them to leave. What she said was, "If you're looking for Paul, he's at the hospital."

"Oh, God," said Penny, "she doesn't understand. Tom, you tell her."

There's none of the obsessive reenacting that came after Nadia's death. This is simple grief and a need to understand what it means to be dead. She has often thought that death must be like those moments in life when she is lost in thought and lost to self-awareness. Yes! That's it, she thinks triumphantly. Death is being unaware of yourself. It's just plain *being*. Maybe Paul is happy now. But then she must assume that her mother is happy, too, but that is too painful to contemplate. Good Lord! People should learn how to think of death before they need to. All those useless things she has learned in school. She tries to be very still so she can capture her true feeling. Is it despair? Or sadness? Fear or anger? Hysteria? She feels nothing. Her mind is as empty as space.

Two days after she buried Paul the bank called to say they had to foreclose on the Bradley Boulevard house. The mortgage payments were three months in arrears and, while this was just cause for foreclosure, they had been lenient because of Dr. Halaby's profession. They knew he was good for the money. Now, of course, since there was no working head of the household, they had no choice. They hoped she understood. Banks weren't in the real estate business. Foreclosure was the last possible choice, but what was there to do?

"What about Mr. Rashid? He's the co-signee. He told us it was all right if we didn't pay right away. He'll make the late payments until I catch up."

"I'm sorry, Mrs. Halaby, but it's Mr. Rashid who is foreclosing."

"I see." *I'm so stupid. I deserve no better than this. He must be furious that his plan didn't work out.*

"Who was that?" Larraine was sitting on the floor helping Cassie put plastic shapes into a plastic ball. "Now, sugar," she cooed, guiding the little hand, "you're holding a triangle; let's find the triangle hole . . . *there it is!* Star, look how she looks at me. Doesn't crack a smile. She's thinking I'm a raving idiot, and you know what? She's right. Who cares if the damn triangle goes in the triangle hole. Who was that on the phone?"

"The bank."

"The bank? About your accounts? Were they joint?"

She stared at the wall directly ahead and answered in a hollow voice. "They're going to foreclose. He hasn't been making the payments."

"But the payments were to go to Rashid, weren't they?"

"He's the one who's foreclosing."

"Holy God, what a son of a bitch!"

They were silent a moment and then Larraine got a queer look on her face. "Are you thinking what I'm thinking? Will he pull something with us, too? We should see a lawyer."

"How can he do anything to us? I have the deed." Her voice was unsteady. "You think there are hidden things we don't know about?"

"I know if a man like that wants to be vindictive, he has things up his sleeve we've never heard of. This is awful."

As unbelievable as his death were the aftershocks of Paul's financial affairs. He was in debt to Rashid to the tune of forty-eight thousand dollars over and above the house. He had been steadily losing money in the market and had received three margin calls in the preceding two weeks. Even with all the accounts receivable that were outstanding from the medical practice, she couldn't have satisfied his margin debt. The broker made a personal call, bringing records to her house. "Mrs. Halaby, at this point I would lend you the money myself, if I had it." He was a decent man with a crew cut and highly polished shoes. Cassie's wistful smile wasn't lost on him or her mother's youth. "Fortunately, everything was in his name so you won't be responsible. We'll just have to sell the stock we have on hand and eat the rest."

"Excuse me?"

"It's just an expression. We use it to describe funds that are irretrievable and we have to assume. We eat the losses." She nodded. He watched her warily, expecting some show of fear and anguish, but she only bit her lip and stretched a handkerchief between her fingers. "Things must look pretty dismal to you right now, but I bet you'll come out of it just fine. You'll marry again . . . a beautiful woman like you." He cleared his throat. "Call me if you have any more questions."

"I have no more questions," she said and led him to the door.

His clumsy attempt to console her had turned her mind in a new direction, and she was anxious to be alone and think it through. Until today, her head had been encased in gauze. She kept congratulating herself for doing simple things: putting on her nylons and buckling her shoes. When she bathed the baby and buttoned her up in her pajamas and made a supper of scrambled eggs, she felt triumphant. Any coherent action had been a miracle, but now this quiet, sympathetic stranger had cleared one pathway in her brain, and she saw what she was going to do. She was going to see her father again. And Aunt Julia and Uncle Peter. Her grandmother. Her great-aunt Zareefa and Uncle Jamal. Cousin Delal. She was going to take Cassie and go home.

"I don't want any more coffee, Delal. And I don't want you to heat the bread, either. Stop . . . *coddling me.*" He had been ready to use a more damaging word than "coddling." What? Stop smothering me. Bothering me. "We're married . . ." he added and then got up and left the table.

"What does that mean?"

"What does *what* mean?"

"What does 'we're married . . .' mean?"

"It doesn't mean anything. I don't know. It means I'm fine. I've got to go now, I'm late . . ." He kissed her cheek and hurried out the door.

She had all day to finish his thought. We're married now; you can stop trying to win me over. I can't leave you now. Stop trying so hard; you've already caught me. The language of marriage was the language of imprisonment. You landed or caught or hooked your man as if he were a fish. Still, when she thought about it—how it began and how it had ended—her marriage was a source of wonder.

They had been home four months, living in a rented cottage behind the King David Hotel. Her father had offered to build a home for the newlyweds, but James was appalled. "We don't need a home," he had said enigmatically, and no one had the nerve to ask what he meant. James kept the family at bay and set the tone for all encounters. They were somewhat afraid of him, although he was relentlessly polite and undemanding. They just weren't used to his reserve, or perhaps his physical difference—he was tall, rugged, silken-haired—made them timid.

Her father was unsettled around James and her mother became talkative and too cheerful. The gayer the George family became and the more they tried to please the cool, composed, inscrutable James, the less he wanted or needed from them.

Delal had envisioned James and herself at the dazzling core of a stylish life filled with lighthearted merriment. James would rely on her for everything—not out of weakness, but out of a passionate preference for her taste and resourcefulness. She had expected him to be greedy for sex. To wake up wanting her and to go to sleep with his arms and legs wound around her, his lips against her back or shoulder, his hands aggressively on her buttocks or her breasts, his constant demands a testimony to the ardor she provoked in him. He didn't demand anything. Not elaborate dinners or elaborate sex or even a button sewn on a shirt. It seemed to her that he didn't want to enlarge their relationship. Instead, he was minimizing it. Often he answered her with just one word.

Her appearance didn't help. There was a strange, dusky overlay to her skin—the mask of pregnancy, the doctor said. Her hair was limp.

He hadn't touched her in two weeks except for wispy kisses on the cheek to mark his arrivals and departures. He became the master of the unfinished sentence. "Sorry, I've got to dash . . . some work . . ." or ". . . some man" or ". . . some last-minute plans" kept him from lingering in bed or at meals. What had been sophisticated and provocative love play in Edinburgh for two unattached people without responsibilities was self-conscious and distasteful in Jerusalem. He was still gracious and attentive, but there was a longing in his eyes that tore her apart. Was it seeing the places where he and Nijmeh had been together that made him long for what might have been? Suppose he broke down and confessed, "I can't live without her, Delal. What am I going to do?"

There were few who missed the irony of Delal's marriage, and almost all experienced that moment of confused inquiry. Nijmeh had married the man Delal wanted, and now Delal had turned the tables. Everyone— including Julia and Peter—was slightly embarrassed. Even ignorant of the facts, James seemed to be ill-gotten goods. The first instinct was to protect Nijmeh, who already had had a terrible blow. What good would it do to mention it? Poor thing. She'd find out soon enough. Zareefa left the news out of her letter of condolence. Miriam, who had a mild case of pneumonia all summer, was still too grief-stricken to think or care about whom Delal had married. Samir, for the first time, was glad his daughter was far away and wouldn't be put through what had to be an awkward situation. That left Delal and Julia.

When the newlyweds came home, Julia had addressed and stamped two hundred silver-lined, cream-colored envelopes and stuffed them with an engraved announcement, a silken square of tissue, and the "at home" card.

Delal inspected the list and complained that James wanted as little done as possible. "He doesn't want anyone feeling they must send a gift."

"And if they do?" Julia challenged. She had been cheated out of making a wedding, and she wasn't inclined now to be cowered by second-hand pronouncements.

Delal shrugged and dug through the envelopes, which were alphabetized. "Is there one here for Nijmeh?" As she asked the question, she came to the envelope and pulled it out.

"Isn't it ironic?" said Julia. "Nijmeh married Paul and you ended up with James."

Delal's face went a shade paler. She was a girl who had never been afraid of anything, but she didn't want to hear those names. "Don't send this."

"Why not?"

She turned away from her mother's questioning eyes. "She was very much in love with James."

Julia sighed and rubbed the bridge of her nose where her glasses left a mark. "Delal, that was a long time ago. She's married and has a child. How can we not tell her?"

"Oh, send it if you want to. I just don't see what difference it's going to make. She's so far away. It doesn't matter one way or the other whether she knows right away or not. It's not going to make her feel great."

"She'll be happy for you," said Julia, but she felt less sure of herself.

"I doubt it. But do whatever you want."

Julia lost some confidence and when she realigned the stack of envelopes the one for Nijmeh and Paul was left out. "She'll have to know eventually."

"Mmm. But I'd give her more time . . . that's all."

Julia put the invitation in one of the cubbyholes of her beautiful pecan desk where she sat each day and did paper work. It was situated to overlook the narrow, private mews where the Sisters of the Holy Cross had an elementary school. She looked forward to being interrupted by the sounds of little girls at recess. But now her serenity was marred by the daily sight of that envelope. It was a reminder that Nijmeh's troubles had not ended. She saw something in her daughter's face that troubled her. Was it *too* coincidental that Delal suddenly *had* to go to school in Edinburgh? Oh, Lord, not another mystery. She had just rid herself of one burdensome secret and didn't want to discover another. Maybe Delal was right. Nijmeh didn't need any more disturbing news right now.

* * *

As her pregnancy progressed, Delal felt grotesque and less confident of her power to hold on to James. She became paranoid, looking at him for signs of unhappiness. She thanked God that Nijmeh—her mother said she called herself Star now—was in America, safely away, safely married, already a mother. But then, out of the blue, like a horrible, spidery hand coming out of the darkness to snatch her happiness, came the worst possible news. Paul was dead and Nijmeh was coming home.

45

Oh, Samir. She's not your little burden anymore.

He sat fidgeting for an hour before the plane landed. Several times he rose and walked rapidly as if going to a destination, then realized he had nothing to do but wait. Over and over he rubbed his palms on his trousers. He couldn't seem to get warm.

When he thought about greeting her, the only thing that came to mind was, I loved your mother very much. Would she blame him? He pictured her face flushed with resentment. You killed my mother. I hate you. After all, he *had* taken her to her place of doom. Uppermost in his mind was the thought that time had been rolled back. "I'm right back where I began with Nijmeh," he had said to Julia. "Except it will be harder."

"Oh, Samir," Julia had been exasperated and answered crossly. "She's coming home for some comfort. She's lost her mother and her husband. She's a grown woman with a child, and you can't think of her as your little burden anymore. Just be kind and accepting and play with your granddaughter. For heaven's sake, don't start planning what to do with the rest of her life. That's her business." Julia had hidden her fears behind impatience and a mission to charge her brother with a new attitude. She had no idea how the visit would end up. Suppose Nijmeh had a second, delayed, reaction to the news of her birth? If that were true, what Samir said or didn't say wouldn't mean a thing.

"She's coming home for protection and guidance," he had said.

"Don't be too sure. Why don't you let her tell you why she's home? What she needs is a sincere welcome."

The sound of the arriving plane brought him to his feet, and he paced restlessly until the first passengers straggled off. He saw her first. She was taking each stair carefully, hampered by the child in her arms and a bulky bag dangling from her shoulder. Only the top of her head was visible, but when she reached the ground, she raised her beautiful face and looked uncertainly toward the far side of the field, squinting and searching. There was a moment when their eyes met and both stood perfectly still. His heart shrank into a compact mass and fell away. All he could think of was how she had looked years ago, searching his eyes for approval with all the vulnerability of a little girl who wanted to please her father.

He went toward her, arms outstretched, his face in a grimace of happiness and pain. Was this all he could do . . . tighten himself around her? It didn't seem enough. The baby, her eyes dewy from sleep, stared soberly at the stranger. A replica of her mother. He could smell her sweetness. What tore at him in those few seconds was that Nadia would never see them like this. His throat closed up. He wanted to beg for her. Beg God to give her back to him for just the seconds it would take to welcome their daughter. Nadia, here they are. Look, darling, our girl is home. There was no answer. She was buried. Dead. Weighed down and hidden in the blackness of the ground. "Oh, my dear, my dear . . ."

"*Baba* . . ."—all pain was expressed in that name—"I was so afraid." She was whimpering and the words were squeezed out. "I needed you." She had not expected to say these things. She had expected to feel differently about him. Distant. But all she wanted was his love and his arms around her. "I needed you to help me." He bowed his head over her—an attitude of protection—but too late. The worst had happened. He hadn't been able to protect her at all. Cassie, caught between them, squirmed. Seeing her mother so distressed made her chin tremble, too. Her eyes were enormous and full of woe. "Mommy," she said and began to wail.

They turned to look at her. "Oh, I've scared you. I'm all right," said Star. "Don't cry. This is Grandpa. Your *sidi.*" Cassie glued her face against her mother and refused to look up. "Remember I told you we were going to see your *sidi?*" The tangled hair moved up and down, but her face stayed hidden. "Well, here he is. Don't you want to say hello?"

The head went sideways. "Oh, that's too bad. He'd like to say hello to you."

Samir put his hands by his side. "It's all right," he said. "I can wait. She needs time to get used to the idea."

This generous statement provoked Cassie to lift her head. She turned sideways to view the person who had such finesse. "*Oh,* what a lovely little girl." The look on his face—pleasure and a certain shyness—was not lost on Cassie. The handsome distinguished man caught her imagination and, with the unerring instinct for the right gesture that would serve her all her life, she turned away from her mother and stretched out her arms. Samir trembled as he reached for her. The last person he had held this way was Nadia, after she died. He felt ill prepared to resurrect those feelings, but what choice did he have? These are mine, he kept thinking. These are mine to care for. He pressed the travel-weary girl against his chest with one hand—a stuffed bear was still in the other—and was unable to wipe away the tears plodding slowly down.

The entire clan came to the sheik's village house where Samir still lived. It was just like dozens of other family gatherings—the smells of buttered pignola nuts and spiced lamb and briny olives perfumed the air. Outside it was very warm—a heat spell in February—but Samir had installed two air-conditioners. *"Shu hada?"* exclaimed a confused Umm Jameel, who was close to ninety. "How did he change the weather?" Everyone laughed but they, too, still considered the coolness remarkable.

Miriam had arrived early and after fighting back tears unsuccessfully, she put down the boxes of cookies she had brought and took Cassie in her arms. "She looks like you," she told her granddaughter. "Too bad Nadia couldn't . . ." She stopped. "Please, *habibty,* bring a dish for the cookies and put them out on the table. The butter will soak through and ruin the cloth." Nijmeh did as she asked, happy to deal with the cookies and not her grandmother's eyes.

"Your mother used to hate it when I brought food to the sheik's house," Miriam said, looking around. "She thought it made us look socially stupid because the sheik didn't need food. I couldn't convince her that it was important and necessary for other reasons. If I told her this was the way we'd always done it, that was like declaring war. Maybe you feel the same?"

"No. I understand."

"I had the rebellious daughter. If you told her to wave hello, she said good-bye. She couldn't embroider. She couldn't cook. She didn't like to sing. She hated to visit. Our pleasure—especially in those days after the war—was visiting and she hated to visit. She couldn't sit still. She hated being kissed by relatives. And then, after all that, look what happened."

"What happened?" asked Nijmeh.

"She married the sheik's son." Miriam looked triumphant. "She couldn't have done anything more *traditionally right.* It was the most wonderful thing and I was sure it saved her life and her happiness." Too late she realized what she had said. "Oh . . . my, it didn't save her life. *Oh, dear!* I didn't mean that."

"Don't worry, *siti.* I know what you meant. You meant she stayed in the clan instead of seeking her fortune in the outside world."

"Well . . ."—Miriam looked perturbed. She didn't like the way that sounded—". . . yes. And I also meant that it was the *right* choice. She loved your father. It was a match that I fought for, but she soon discovered she really loved your father." Cassie squirmed in her lap and turned to play with Miriam's earrings. "And you . . ." she asked timidly, "how do you feel about coming back?"

"Peaceful," said Nijmeh automatically. Questioning and in turmoil, is what she meant. She was thinking also that, unlike her mother, she had never learned to love Paul. That *hadn't* been the right choice. While her grandmother was talking, she thought of the Walkers. If she had grown up in that house and Mary Walker had been her grandmother, she would have felt just as comfortable sitting around a long, formal table, eating corn on the cob and codfish cakes and fried chicken and going to the First Presbyterian Church every Sunday at eleven. *That* was the crucial point. She wasn't rebellious as her mother had been. She had done everything her father asked, but it had all gone wrong. How could you explain that? By coming back, she was putting herself in their hands again. They must have rules for widows, just as with everything else. Something in her pushed that idea away. "*Siti,* this will make you happy. Remember you gave me three thousand dollars when I married Paul?"

"That money had a long history. From time to time your grandfather Nadeem would get the idea to start on an enterprise and, for one reason or another, he always needed financial help from me. Of course he paid me back. The money went back and forth several times, and it ended up with you."

"You'd be pleased. I bought a house that I rent out. And we—my partner and I—used that house to buy another house. Having that business meant a lot to me, and your money made it possible."

Miriam didn't respond. Did that mean she was going back to her business and her partner? Did that mean she wasn't listening to anything Miriam was telling her? Then she mused, "Your grandfather was always buying this little building or that one, too. He was crazy about owning a structure and caring for it. Perhaps you got that from him. It's in the blood."

Nijmeh winced. How could she admit that her sweet, patient grandfather was not her grandfather at all? There was pain and confusion around every corner. "I think you're right. He was always in my mind when I was looking for the right property."

Miriam looked down and began to smooth Cassie's hair. After all these years, she still couldn't think of Nadeem without feeling the full, searing jolt of fresh pain.

The rest of the guests had begun to arrive. Miriam rose and put Cassie in a little fenced-in play area that Samir had devised, but when she cried she carried her outside. "All right, I don't want to be the one who puts you in prison."

Zareefa and her husband came with their three daughters and their families. Aunt Diana, close to eighty and weighing more than two hundred pounds, her legs streaked with overburdened veins, was led to a chair by Janin and Deenie, where she sat meekly staring at Nijmeh. "Her mother dies, her husband dies . . . what is this?" she muttered.

"Hush, Mama," said Janin, "They'll hear you."

"So? It's not big news. *Haram.* Too beautiful. It was too much. Where's the baby? Did you see her? An orphan. A year old and an orphan already. How does she look? Like the mother? Another one with bad luck?"

"Mama, stop. *Amti* Miriam took her outside. She's like Nijmeh but with darker hair and brown eyes." She turned around to see who else was coming in. "Here's Aunt Julia and Uncle Peter and—she put a hand to her mouth—"oh, my God, here's Delal."

"Deenie, Janin, help me up, *yullah.* How does Delal have the nerve to show up here?"

She was in her ninth month and pregnancy had robbed her of clear skin, healthy hair, slender hips, and energy. She was breathless and cranky. And right now, also perspiring. She seldom felt cowered in her life, but this morning she had awakened with a feeling of dread that crowded out everything else. Suppose they figured out what she'd done? How could James ever love the child she was carrying? But she didn't feel repentant. She thought of the phrase in *Gone With The Wind* where Rhett tells Scarlett, who has cheated her sister out of her beau, "You're like the thief who's not in the least sorry he stole but is terribly sorry he's going to jail."

Her mother had insisted that she come to welcome her cousin home but had agreed that it was not a good idea to bring James. "Let him think it's a get-together for the women," Delal had urged. "I don't think Nijmeh's ready to meet up with her old love. Not yet, anyway."

She had arrived purposely late, and then wanted to leave immediately, but her mother had driven and she had no graceful way of getting back home. Besides, what would she say to James? No, I didn't stay. I couldn't stand seeing the woman you loved. Love? Yes, she's as beautiful as ever. More beautiful. Breathtaking, now that tragedy has given breadth and depth to her face. Sorry you didn't go? Sorry you couldn't get her alone and kiss her? Sorry I'm not dead? Maybe I'll die in childbirth and you'll be free to marry her, after all.

She went from room to room, and finally caught sight of her from a distance of twenty feet. Her face was in profile and then, as someone called to her, she turned and looked squarely at Delal. Holy God, this is what I took away from James. He'll hate me forever.

She was coming toward her quickly, a wide smile of anticipation on her face. "Delal . . ." Her arms were outstretched. If she hugs me, I'll die. "It's so good to see you. Look . . . you're pregnant . . . I didn't know. When did you get married?" Please! Please, shut up.

"Not long ago. We sent an announcement . . . Really, you didn't know?"

"No. Congratulations."

"You may want to take it back."

"Take what back . . . my congratulations?"

"I'm married to James."

Her mouth slackened. "James? James *who?*"

"James . . ." Delal couldn't get herself to say more. It was easily the worst moment of her life. Here's another blow for the little widow. I didn't plan this. I'll stand here perfectly still and wait for it to be over. What can she do to me? What can he do?

The look on Nijmeh's face was quizzical. Then understanding crept over her face. It was sickening to watch. "No . . . not my James! Why?" Her voice was a pitiful whisper.

"Look, I didn't do it on purpose. I mean, you *were* married. Who ever thought Paul would die?" She realized she was speaking too bluntly. "I'm terribly sorry about Paul. What can I say?"

"Is James here?"

"No. I didn't think you needed that kind of a shock on top of everything else. Look, I could lie and say he was sick or busy, but you deserve the truth. Tell me, did I do the right thing? Should I have brought him here?"

She shook her head. "No." She took a deep breath and looked around the crowded room. "Let's go get a drink. I need a good stiff drink."

"You bet."

Her father had bought her a stroller and had Muffi remove the skinny wheels and attach fat rubber tires so she could wheel the baby through the orchards. The unpredictable weather of late winter was over. The days would start out with a thin sun that soon became strong and direct. The tiny purple crocus had bloomed and wilted and the sweet narcissus and hardy cyclamen took their place, filling in both rocky cracks and fertile beds in their eagerness to multiply.

"Fahwah?" Cassie would ask, pointing down. "Flower," her mother would respond. The baby had never been so petted and fussed over as during these weeks, and she seemed relieved to be alone with her mother. Samir had driven them to the orchard cottage to stay overnight. "This is where Mama liked it best," Nijmeh said when he prepared to leave. "I want to be alone here a few days to think things out."

"Stay as long as you like. Julia and Miriam will fight over taking Cassie." He looked uncomfortable. Something was on the tip of his tongue, and he was looking for the right time to speak. He had on a business suit but no tie, and the sight of his bare pink neck made him look vulnerable.

"Tell me about Mother," she said, choking down the word.

His eyes darted around the room as if seeking to escape, but after a moment his shoulders sank and he gave in to his fate. They sat down opposite each other, and he held Cassie in the crook of his arm. "I knew her all my life," he said as if that were the most important thing and then, all different images flew out as they entered his mind. "She was a very private person and not out of shyness, either. Out of strength. She knew what she was and was content. She adored horses. From the beginning, when she was a very small girl, her father would lead her around on a horse they owned—an old dilapidated thing—and I remember *Ami* Nadeem saying that was the only time she smiled easily. She didn't want to marry me, you know. I was a catch, believe me,"—he widened his eyes and smiled shyly—"but, of all the girls, she was the one who didn't want me."

"Are you sure? Maybe she was just afraid."

"Perhaps. But she wasn't the type to be demure. For whatever reason, she gave me a hard time. But not afterward, of course."

"Was she always beautiful?"

He was surprised. "Did you think she was beautiful? Most people didn't. She had something . . . I don't know, it appealed to me immensely. She was the only woman for me up until the very last moment." He couldn't trust himself to say more and they sat silently for several minutes. Cassie had fallen asleep with her thumb in her mouth and Samir smoothed back her hair. "Don't worry," he said. "We'll work everything out."

"I may not settle here, you know." She hadn't planned to say that. "Are you expecting that I will?" Two powerful emotions were working in her. This was the man who had made her lose James. This man . . . he wasn't even her true father. He appeared far different to her than when she had left. Was it because she had grown up and was more on an equal footing? Was it because her mother's death had made him seem fragile?

"I thought you would need family to support you. Our family. Some of them appear silly. Your Aunt Diana—my God, I expect her to topple over any moment . . . But they're part of the fabric of our life. The past is important, just as much as the future."

She nodded. What he was saying meant nothing to her. Who was there

here who cared about her happiness? *Support,* she wanted to shout. What sort of support did you give me when my happiness was at stake? She couldn't shout at him. He needed her sympathy.

"I went into business," she said to change the subject. "You shouldn't be surprised; you were always preparing me to run things. I still remember how much we had to charge for crated raisins to make a profit. Thirteen cents a pound. If you received fifteen, you said it was time to open the champagne. We have a house with three apartments—I even did some of the refurbishing myself—and we rent it out. It's something I enjoy."

"Really?" The news made him melancholy, but then he remembered something. "Your grandfather left you a sum of money. He left bequests only to you and your mother. He loved you in a special way."

She sighed. "I could have used that money last year. My partner and I had a difficult time getting a mortgage."

"It's waiting for you any time you want it." He rose so as not to wake the baby. "Take your time before making any decisions. You may find you like it here."

"I'll take my time," she said and walked with him to the car. He placed Cassie in the back, with a cushion to brace her against the seat. Then he faced his daughter.

Sometimes the most naked moment sneaks in during a leavetaking, and that's how it was for them. Samir blurted out the thing that was on his mind. "Do you blame me for your mother's death? Do you think I could have done something to save her? Say it if you do. *Say it.*"

She was shocked by the outburst. She *had* been blaming him. Couldn't he have done *something?* But her doubts were a failure of the spirit. He had never done anything second-rate. Never. She put her arms around him and spoke with certainty. "I don't know why mother died, but you couldn't have stopped it. You loved her. She knew that so well. We all have our destinies to fulfill and she had hers."

She had no idea where these words came from or how she could say them so calmly. Several times, she had been on the verge of screaming at him that he had ruined her life by being so hard on James. He had been wrong to do it, but there was no good outcome to such a scene. None at all. It must have been her love for him that made her momentarily lucid. He didn't know the most important thing about his life. Poor, poor *Baba.* "Perfect love," he had once said to her, "is what parents feel for a child. "It's love that wants nothing back." She wanted to give him peace. And she wanted nothing back. "I don't blame you," she said and kissed his face twice. He did look better. Wan, but out of relief, not worry. "I'll call when I'm ready to come back." He nodded, got in the car and drove off.

* * *

For the next two days she walked over every part of the farm. Only when her legs were moving and there were no barriers could she cope with her feelings of hopelessness. Memory was cruel. At night she said aloud, "Mother, help me understand. Help me see what made you do it. I'm so confused. I want to make peace with you, but it's difficult." She made an effort to concentrate only on her mother, but Delal's words sprung out at her in infinite variations. "I'm married to James." It was so irrefutable. If she had said, I'm going to marry James, or I'm going to take James away from you, she could have fought against it. But now there was only a muddy hopelessness. They were married. She was carrying *his child.*

The third and fourth day, her mind opened up. She was disgusted by her own obtuseness. Larraine had seen it right away. "If he loved you, he should have moved heaven and earth until you were together again. He wasn't the most important man in your life. Your daddy was." She had been taught to be submissive and she had accepted whatever came. Thinking of the things she had accepted made her perspire and feel nauseated. She had been a docile, stupid child, playing at love.

By the fifth day, her mind opened up totally and she realized with a devastating humiliation that Delal *had* done what was necessary to get what she wanted. She saw it all clearly and felt deeply ashamed to have been so easy to cheat. Retroactively, she despised all her myopic goodness. How could James have loved her? She had been a vacant, silly fool. Delal deserved him.

She kept moving, going farther afield each day, even when the fair weather was momentarily interrupted by rain. If she stopped moving, she couldn't cope with her thoughts. The first day of the second week, she asked for a gentle horse, mounted it, and went for a slow ride into the wilderness. How tame and flat it all appeared, not the frightening open wilderness she remembered. She returned to the cottage calmer than she had felt in many months. That night and most of the next day she cried. She would begin with tears rolling down her cheeks over some remembered sweetness from Cassie and then it would escalate. There were heaving sobs for her mother, punctuated by frightened shouts. *"No. No. No."* There was steady keening over James. There were even silent tears for Paul.

Slowly her mind began to wind down and she felt detached. She thought about Larraine with affection. Larraine had the power of clear thinking and directness and friendship. She wasn't afraid of the truth. They'd accomplished something miraculous together.

Her daughter, Cassie, was a strong tie to life and reality. She was happy to have something positive with which to remember Paul. Poor Paul. How burdened he must have felt with all those debts. Perhaps he had hated Rashid, too, but couldn't afford to break the ties. She felt enormous sorrow for Paul and the life he had led. He never had the energy to enjoy any of his possessions. She couldn't remember a time when he had spent more than a few minutes with his daughter. At the end, there had been a sense of desperation about him. He had been afraid.

Every succeeding day, it was a game of peeling back layers of her own sensibilities. She had always been someone's daughter or someone's charge or someone's wife, and now there was no one left to define who she was. But then who am I? she asked. Where do my thoughts and feelings spring from? What makes me prefer one thing to another? Why do I welcome responsibility and feel comforted by it?

She was comforted by the hills that were seldom out of sight and she recognized her emotional tie to this familiar territory. She was rooted in these traditions just as those irrepressible flowers sprung through the cal- cined earth, with barely a drop of moisture to encourage them. Her con- sciousness was uniquely molded and there was no changing it now. She was her father's daughter. Through those loving days of association, they had exchanged ideas, feelings, hopes, and energy. He had nurtured her, fed her from his own store of knowledge and goodness. His love had sustained her when she was unable to rely on her own unformed will. He had infused her with courage and principle. Even her body—the discipline to be ath- letic—was from him. She was Samir's true daughter.

The binding ties her father had in mind still bound, but they no longer constricted. She still grieved for her mother and felt compassion for Paul. As for James, what was to be made of so much pain? An inexplicable but evil retribution that had run its course. Surely there was nothing worse in store for her?

She had been planning to call her father to come and get her. Having made her decision to return to the States, she was eager to put her plans out in the open. Just one last ride up and around the olive groves where her mother had carved out a scenic path. Mama, look at me. I'm using your road. I'm walking in your footsteps. She was fixing all of it in her mind.

The early morning mist, like trailing gauze, masks the mountains until the sun silently burns it away. She wants to catalogue the fine details. The limestone dust that powders the roads. The shocking contrast of green against blue, and blue against the infinite variations of brown. It's more than the eye can enjoy at one time. Over many years, it creates a thrill of possession that enlarges the heart. That's what her father has told her. The land—and everything on it—holds and nourishes, heals and comforts, melds one generation to the next. There is nothing more important on the earth than *the earth itself.* She stands perfectly still and opens herself to accept it. It is indelibly etched in the fabric of memory and is hers forever.

When she returned to the cottage it was past noon, and she was surprised and annoyed to see a small red car in the driveway. Now she would have to be sociable. She prepared her face before she entered, putting on a stiff smile. Who could it be?

Oh, no! Her heart seemed to harden inside her and became a weight dragging her down. She'd created him so often in mind, reached for him, and held him close, but now James was no more than a dozen feet away and her legs were sunk deep in the ground. Her arms hung uselessly at her side. The room was so quiet that her ears buzzed and she became aware of her own racing metabolism. Now her heart became a pendulum and it was rocking weightily inside her. Her blood rippled just under the surface of her skin as if her pores had dilated to supply her with extra oxygen. Her vocal chords didn't work at all. James was no better off. The two of them were locked in place, taking in and devouring the beloved.

"I hope I didn't scare you." James finally broke the spell. "Perhaps I should have waited outside."

"No. It's all right. I didn't realize that was your car." What a stupid thing to say. Her voice came from some deep and distant place.

This was not how she had imagined their meeting at all. She was supposed to run into his arms coming to rest against him. She had never thought beyond their embrace.

"You must be weary after that long ride. I'll make coffee." Thank God for banal conversation. It was created to save people in moments such as this. In the kitchen she rushed to the sink and ran cool water along her wrists. Then she became very busy with the pot, filling it and carefully measuring the coffee and putting it, with trembling hands, on the fire. She placed several oranges on a plate, rushed inside to make sure he was still there, and was surprised to find him in exactly the same spot where she'd left him. "I've got to watch the coffee or it will boil over," she said and he nodded. "Maybe you'd like to come with me." The truth was she was afraid to leave him.

"All right." He followed her and stood with arms crossed in front of him as she bounced the pot to keep it from boiling over.

She placed the brimming cups side by side, then, disappointed that her chores had ended, forced her eyes up and over to find his. "What are you thinking, James?"

"I'm thinking how the first thought you always have is to feed me. Is it so ingrained in you?"

Please don't talk to me as if we have a future. "And why not? People have to eat. And at the same time it implies friendship and love." She sucked in her breath, embarrassed to have said the word. "Besides,"—she tried to get hold of the moment—"it's polite."

"Does that mean you're still my friend?" His voice cracked in a sickening way.

"Your friend? Oh, James,"—all her feeling came thundering back, dissolving her will—"much, much more than that." She could tell him anything. What did it matter? "The thing that hurts most,"—her eyes were brimming over—"is . . . how simple it is to see you. At one time, for over a year, I had it in my mind that it was impossible to see you again. That it would be miraculous. Why does the thing we want to madness lose its simplicity? It's staggering to realize that in order to see me, all you had to do was get in the car and drive here. Why was I convinced that it was impossible?"

He put his hand out to touch her, but she shrank. "Don't . . . If you touch me I'm lost."

"You don't know what it does to me to see you again."

Her shoulders slumped. What were they going to do with all the sickening information? How could it help them now? She moved closer but not into his arms. How faithfully she'd remembered him. His dear large head, the deep-set eyes, the perfect slice of hair across his brow. He wore a nubby wool jacket and she wanted to slip her hand beneath it and touch the familiar firmness. This is where her face belonged, against his heart, against his warmth. He reached over and trailed three fingers down the left side of her face. "I never stopped loving you."

It was useless to respond. What she needed was not words but his arms around her. All those wasted years of longing and useless dreams. "I've given you too many years," she said angrily. "I want to feel your arms around me."

They stood there, pressed against each other, afraid to move. Desire, ignited by their closeness, blocked out sorrow and conscience. Again and again—a tortured soul—he placed and replaced his mouth over hers, driven by hunger and greed, anger and despondency. She whimpered in his arms and hung on him as if they were draped over a precipice. *"Don't let go. Please don't let me go."*

The bed was right there, in a nook behind a low screen. The door was unbolted—a tribute to the sheik's desire to let any traveler find respite—yet she unbuttoned and unfastened everything quickly as if she were used to readying herself for love on the spur-of-the-moment. Her eyes never left his face. There was no need to hold anything back. Look! This is what I am. This is what I've wanted to be to you. I became a woman under your hands. Please, please, touch me now!

The thick feather mattress billowed around them so that they sunk into it and into each other. He took her in every possible way, recovering an erection only minutes after ejaculating. They were constructing a building and had only a limited time to finish. She urged him on. "Make your tongue hard," she told him. "Go in and out." The fourth time, he sat on the edge of the bed and placed her on his lap, facing out. He made her drop forward and held onto her breasts as her legs went back. While she "swam" out in the air, he thrust himself so deep she let out a piercing shriek. "Am I hurting you? Does it hurt?"

"No, no! Do it! Just do it!" And afterward, she cried out, "Damn you. I waited and waited for you to write. I was ready to do anything. Why didn't you make it work? Why?" He had no answer.

They knew it was dusk because the light changed from greenish-yellow to rose and then to purple. They heard a decadent, high-pitched, prolonged whine. "What's that?" asked James.

She got up and walked to the small high window. "It sounds like a hyena. Usually they don't get going until midnight. You'd think they were wounded, but it's only that they're high-strung." She took a robe off a clothes tree and put it on. "I'm starved. You?" The commonplace—the idea that she could prepare a meal for him—was miraculous.

He nodded but called her back to the bed. "You never answered any of my letters. There was only one letter and that was to announce your marriage."

"I didn't write you any letter! I had no idea where you were because you never wrote to tell me! I was convinced *you* had dumped me."

He lay back on the pillow and closed his eyes. "Oh, God! It's so pitiful! We chose Delal to be our go-between. Each time I wrote to you, I thanked her. How she must have howled." He ran his hand through his hair over and over. "The truth is so pitiful!"

She felt more sorry for him than for herself. "I should have acted but I wasn't strong enough," she said dolefully.

"You're the strongest woman I know."

"No," she shouted, her eyes filling. "I should have gone with you right away, but I lacked the courage and the understanding." She let out a long, painful sob. "Why did you cave in so easily? James,"—she beat her fists into his chest—"how could you have just caved in after all we were to each other?"

His face crumpled and tears slid down his cheeks. "I was untried," he said softly. "Life had been too easy for me. Delal knew me too well." He held her and made soothing noises with his lips against her hair. "It seems so obvious now what we should have done, but it was hidden then."

Dusk turned to night and they became aware that too much time was passing. They rose and sponged themselves off and she brought out two bottles of Dutch beer that were in the refrigerator, a pot of cold stew, and some cheese. "Come on," she coaxed him, "we might as well eat." When he didn't move she went and sat beside him. "We've so little time, James. Don't speak about it anymore. These few hours are all we have left."

He couldn't shake his despair. "Delal is pregnant, did you know? How could I . . ."

"Shhh." She held a finger to his lips. "I know . . . I know."

46

I have more choices in America. I can make a fuller life for myself.

Delal lay very still, pressing her hands against her stomach. Each time the baby kicked, her hands gave the foot resistance. It was a little game she played, which made the baby kick harder. "Resistance is what you're going to get in life, so you might as well learn to fight back," she said aloud.

"What?" James raised his head off the pillow.

"I'm talking to our child," she said carefully and looked up at the ceiling. "He's kicking violently. Do you suppose today's the day?" She counted to ten, waiting for his attack.

"I don't know," he said and closed his eyes again.

His 'I don't know' had a neutral inflection which meant he wasn't in a murderous mood. Actually, the inflection was a notch better than neutral. It was reflective and . . . a bit philosophical, as if his 'not knowing' covered more than just the baby. She knew he had been to see Star. And afterward he had been silent as a ghost. She had to pry his mouth open for a word. And then, worse, he had left on a business trip. The oldest ploy in the world.

She had taken the car and driven like a madwoman up to the orchard to find Star and make sure she hadn't gone with him. As it turned out, she was staying with her grandmother. She found them sowing flower seeds, but a change had come over Star. She was *harder*. Delal had had some difficulty squeezing out of the car with her very pregnant belly, and Star had sat back and fixed her with a murderous stare.

"So," Delal had asked, intimidated by this new woman, "how long are you going to stay?"

"Not much longer." Her eyes remained on the ground and her voice was hollow. Miriam sized up the situation and excused herself. "Why so interested?" Star said icily. "Would you like me to stay?"

Delal began to perspire profusely. She felt bloated and coarse, irredeemably homely and unlovable. By comparison, the sight of her cousin, the embodiment of lightness and elegance, ignited a lifetime of resentment.

"I don't give a damn if you stay or go," she screamed. "James is my husband and I'm carrying his child, and all your cool, ladylike disgust with me won't change a thing. You hate me because you weren't woman enough to do what I did. You thought all you had to do was breathe and the world would come worship at your feet. The thing I hated most . . ." —Delal's eyes were protruding dangerously, as if an expanding core of anger were pushing everything out—". . . *hated most* was your sense of *entitlement!* You just assumed you were entitled to everything. But you weren't entitled to James, dammit. *Wanting* it to happen was not enough."

Instead of quelling her anger, the words fueled it. She didn't know where to turn and picked up a clump of earth and flung it at a pristine portion of the cobblestone path. She shook with high-pitched sucking sobs, limped back to the car, and sat at the wheel holding herself tightly.

When she got home, James had just pulled in and was changing his clothes in the bedroom. The thrill of shouting out truths too long held in gave her a daring high. "I just had a screaming match with your girlfriend." Clearly, he wasn't expecting that. His mouth dropped open and his complexion became wan. "That's right," her voice rose. She felt thrillingly in control. "I did most of the screaming because the golden princess chose not to respond. Shall we have our screaming match now, as well? Do you want to rant and rave at me and tell me how evil I am?"

He hadn't said a word. He had rebuttoned his shirt, put on his jacket, and gone out of the house. "Go ahead," she had shouted after him. "Go comfort her. Kiss her tears away. Isn't that what you want to do?" He was in the car and roared away, leaving her holding the door to steady herself.

She had spent the evening in a warm, soothing bath, even though the doctor had warned her against it. So what if it brought on labor? She hoped it did bring it on. She imagined James hearing that she was in the hospital and feeling instant remorse. At the very least he'd be curious to see the baby. She slumped in the water and wept again but, this time, they were tears of fatigue. She had been down a long, arduous road, holding too many things. Now it was out of her hands. There wasn't anything else up her sleeve.

He had returned very late that night and although she was aching to touch him she remained perfectly still. Sleep had a way of softening even the hardest hearts. She would see how things were in the morning. After all, he wouldn't lose sight of the fact that she was carrying what she was certain was his son.

James opened his eyes again and put his hand on his wife's stomach. "Let's feel that kick," he said and her heart leapt. She was going to cry again. She had cried two or three times in all of her adult life, and now she cried every few minutes. 'Let's feel that kick' was a conciliatory statement. It meant he wasn't totally hostile to the 'little stranger' as the maternity handbook called the baby. She had been prepared for the worst. Harsh words. You lying bitch. I hate you. Or worse than that, a soft reproach: you took everything from me. But somehow, miraculously, he was back without any visible hatred. He was subdued, but she'd take care of that as soon as the invader was out of her body. She'd make life so perfect for him. She knew how.

"Why are you crying?"

"If you had a world-cup soccer player making goals against your ribs, you'd cry, too."

"You think it's a boy?"

"Is that what you want?"

"I can't say that it matters."

"It matters to me. I want a little boy that's exactly like you."

He sat up. "That's the only sentimental thing I've ever heard you say."

"And?"

"And I'm surprised." He didn't seem surprised. He seemed emotionally weary.

"Oh, James." The tears flowed faster and instantly congested her sinuses so that she had to ask him to bring her tissues. "Is this all because of the kicking?" he asked.

"No. It's because I love you so much."

"That's very nice," he said softly. But it didn't make him say he loved her back.

She had said good-bye to everyone but saved Aunt Julia for last. Despite what Delal had done, her aunt had behaved courageously and deserved to have some peace. She had wheeled Cassie through the narrow streets of the Old City, trying to absorb and fix it in her mind. Already there were so many changes because of the Partition. "Your house is the most charming. I love to come here."

"Nijmeh,"—Julia's eyes were blurred with tears: her cheeks were flushed—"you're going back. When will you come again?"

"When I feel more sure of myself and what I'm doing. When I feel stronger."

"If you're not sure, why not stay?"

"I have more choices in America. I can make a fuller life for myself."

"I think that's true. But won't you be so alone?"

"I was alone when Paul was alive. You saw how little time he spent at home. I learned how to make a life for myself and now that's what appeals to me. I need to know that I can plan my own life and not make a mess of it. It would be so easy to stay. And I worry about straying so far from where I came from. Right now it seems the thing to do, but perhaps later I'll regret it. It's a big decision, especially if I ever marry again. What will Cassie know of her background? My father is the sheik's direct descendant. And I . . . I'm next in line."

"Oh, darling, you don't know how happy it makes me to hear you say that. I worried so that you would hate me. That you would want to turn your back on everything."

"I couldn't hate you. You did what you did out of love for my mother. I only wish I had known when she was still alive so I could have told her it was all right. It did trouble her, you know. There was a hesitancy. I always felt it and couldn't understand why. Now I know."

"But you brought her a lot of happiness." Julia waited to collect her thoughts. "If she hadn't had a child, it would have destroyed your mother. So in a very real sense, you saved her life." Star nodded but didn't respond. Her mother's life had been pitifully short, but she had been well loved. "Is your father very upset that you're going back? Has he said anything?"

"*Siti* said more than my father. She's certain that it's a mistake."

"Oh, dear. I'm not much help in that direction, but you have my blessing. Whatever you do, I'll support you. I would have done anything for your mother and I feel the same about you. As much as I'd love having you here, I think—as a young widow—you'll have a fuller life in America."

"Thank you, *Amti*. I know you love me and I know you'll always tell me the truth."

She and Cassie left the next morning. The plane stopped at Beirut, where they changed to a plane bound for Rome, where they stayed overnight. The next day, she and Cassie flew from Rome to New York and then on to Washington. By nightfall they were home. "Over here!" Larraine's voice carried across the length of the terminal. Cassie began to squeal and strain to get loose from her mother's arms.

"Look," said Larraine, taking the baby in her arms, "she remembers me. I missed you both. I thought maybe you'd decided to stay." She frowned and threw Star a questioning look. "How was it?"

"We all did a lot of crying. Except Cassie. She had a wonderful time. And I did, too, in a way. Larraine, I put away a lot of ghosts. A lot of ghosts."

In the cab on the way home, Larraine talked nonstop. "I'm going to be selfish and gloat that you decided not to stay there. I need your support and your advice. The furnace went and they want five hundred dollars to paint the outside of the house. There's a lot of sanding to do and the trim around the third floor windows has to be replaced. It's all rotted away. Chuck sold our house and I—thank God it was in both our names— received half the money, which was a nice surprise. Thirteen thousand dollars. Think what we can do with that! Except I moved into the top floor of the corner house. I hope you don't mind. We'll miss the rent, but I had to move somewhere. I'm still working for McKay parttime for the income. Maybe you'd like to do that, too."

"Maybe. My father told me that I had an inheritance left by my grandfather. So I went to the bank to sign the papers and sat there waiting for a check or a stack of money—I didn't know what to expect. The man handed me this beige sack. He said, 'Well, madam, here it is.' So I thought, Oh, boy, this is my big inheritance. I thanked him and waited until I was outside to look."

"What was it?"

"Gold coins. French gold coins. Dozens and dozens of them. They're beautiful, but I don't know if I can cash them in. It's the strangest thing. I don't know if I'm well off or if they're just keepsakes. And anyway, how could I sell them? They were *his* coins and they're in his money pouch. He probably wore it around his waist and had it all his life. It's something precious . . ."

"Well, God bless him. I like it. He probably had no faith in paper currency. Isn't that nice? I hope you told them about the mess Paul left you in."

"I couldn't. I want them to think well of Paul. They know his family. The whole town thought he was a wonderful man. How could I tell them otherwise?"

"I guess." Cassie had fallen asleep against her shoulder and Larraine looked over at Star and then pointed to the baby. "This one's out like a light." She searched across the seat in the dark and put her hand over Star's. "You did the right thing, coming back. There was no other way for you to find out who Star Halaby is. No other way. And that's the truth."

The next few months were busy ones for Star. She moved from the second floor of the North Capitol Street house to the first, which was larger and had access to a small backyard. She painted the walls white and put white curtains in the two bedrooms and white carpeting on the floors. She stored the huge Oriental rugs and sold most of the furniture from the big house to an antiques dealer.

Three days a week, she took Cassie to a playgroup run by the YMCA and worked for Fred McKay. She also took an evening course in accounting so they wouldn't have to pay someone to do the books. The happiest image of herself in those shaky first weeks went like this: She was walking down their own block, carefully avoiding the dips in the sidewalk, a grocery bag in one arm, Cassie's hand in hers, her mind free, her heart open. Going home.

Once in a while, she and Larraine would go to a movie or eat out at an Italian place, taking the baby with them. But then Larraine began to date one of her clients, a man named Sam Hollings, who was newly separated and in need of a house. She began to buy clothes and fixed up her hair. One afternoon she came into Star's kitchen completely made up—eyes outlined like Cleopatra's, rouge, eyebrows tweezed, cheekbones highlighted—the works. "I went into Garfinkel's to buy a lipstick and they made me up. No charge. What do you think?"

"You look lovely." She tried to look cheerful. After all, Larraine was walking around the linoleum as if an audience had paid to see her. She was rolling her hips and thrusting out her breasts and, all of a sudden to make a point, she gave a little kick backward as if she were the last girl in the chorus line and wanted the audience to remember her. Larraine was giddy with . . . was it relief? Happiness because there was a man in her life? The reality of being found desirable had transformed her from a frecklefaced ex-housewife into a credible beauty. It was a jolt to Star, who now felt a need to take inventory.

She was a twenty-four-year-old widow with a child and no immediate family. Not for a moment did she consider contacting the Walkers. The emotional repercussions—there might even be legal ones—would be so destructive, and what would she gain? *Cousins for Cassie.* If she waited until everyone who might be hurt were dead, she and Cassie would be too old to benefit from it. But that's it, she thought; I have to bury that information.

She realized with a sense of irony that she—who had no Arab blood—was deeply rooted in the Middle East, while her daughter—who had Paul's blood—was thoroughly Yankee in spirit. Cassie would never fight to remember the tantalizing sights and smells and the feel of that peculiar velvety air. Her heart wouldn't stumble at the sound of that unique accent shaped by twenty years of British occupation. It was a realization that made her wince because—with all she knew—America was now her best and only hope.

* * *

When he had seen the obituary in the evening paper, he thought he misread it, but instead of checking he got out of his chair and began to pace. Back and forth. Back and forth while his heart changed its beat. It was a long, graceful room with tall, arched windows looking out on rolling lawns and deep woods, but his eyes were on his feet. He wanted to concentrate and calm down. His mind had always worked on reason, but now he felt superstitiously tied to Paul Halaby. For the last three months, outside his control, he had been suffused with an exquisite longing for the dead man's wife. But he hadn't counted on fate opening the road for him so *decisively*.

He had invented a past for her and convinced himself that she was in great need of being saved. Was that foolish? Why would such a beautiful woman be in trouble? For one thing, her eyes weren't aloof—a woman like that could be spoiled and demanding, but this one was full of understanding and (surprisingly) sadness. When he had heard her voice, his reserve had cracked. Desire changed from a chaste gauzy dream to open—and unchaste—desire.

I want you. That phrase was meant for slushy songs and teenage love talk. He was a man of the world. Wasn't he? Those banal words had nothing to do with him. But they precisely fit what he felt. He *wanted* her. When he allowed his mind the freedom, it latched on to the idea of making love to her in every possible variation. He imagined a room, upholstered in silk, with huge, square divans and soft lights. He wanted to place her in the middle of such a room—position her like a queen—and give her everything he had. His manhood, his mind, and life experience, the sum of his saved-up love.

He stopped pacing and sat down to read the obituary from beginning to end. Like any premature corpse, Halaby was survied by a long list of relatives, including his wife, Star, and a daughter, Cassandra. Her name was *Star.* A condolence call was the very least he could offer. Would she remember him?

By the time he got around to calling, she was no longer living in the same place. At the forwarding telephone number, a woman said she was out of the country.

"Will she be back?"

"I certainly hope so."

He waited six months to call again and by that time, to his intense relief, she was listed in the telephone book.

* * *

"Hello, my name is Andrew Larabee. We met at the Bowie track." They hadn't met at all.

Silence. Would she pretend to remember? "I'm sorry, I don't recall."

"It doesn't matter. I'm calling to offer my condolences on the death of your husband." Her husband had been dead too long a time for condolences.

"That's very kind of you."

"Perhaps you'd like to spend some time up here around the horses. This is the prettiest time . . ."—his voice was coaxing—"I know you used to bring your little girl."

"That's very generous, but I can't accept."

"I have a vacant guest house. No one would bother you."

"It isn't that. I have a job and this our busiest season."

"Oh. Too bad. What do you do? Train with the Washington Senators?" Good God, Larabee, you've gone crazy.

She laughed. "I work for Fred McKay, the real estate firm."

"Well, that explains it. Perhaps another time."

"Perhaps. And thank you."

Damn. Why hadn't he just asked her out to dinner right there and then? Why had he made that insipid joke? He should have been more spontaneous. He couldn't call back now; she'd think he was an idiot or a crank.

Larraine was buffing her nails so vigorously she generated considerable heat. She doubled her hand over and admired the pink glow. It was a slow Monday, and Fred McKay had left her alone in the office. She had to type up three new listings on little white cards and do a little filing as long as the phones stayed quiet. The office was on the parlor floor of a brownstone off Connecticut and M. On the street floor, which was down three steps, there was an Italian restaurant, and the smells wafting up were making her stomach growl. She'd close up and let the service answer the phone while she went down for lunch. She put away her nail buffer and reached in the drawer for her bag, but then groaned with disappointment. There was a client at the door.

One look and she forgot her annoyance. Everything about this one was whispering *money, money, money.* McKay had told her how to spot a Dunhill suit, and here was the real article staring her in the face. "Look at the button holes on the sleeve," he had instructed, "If they *really* unbutton and if the buttons are bone—they'll look striated—it's the genuine thing or at least as expensive." She could see that the button hole on his sleeve—his arms were folded across his chest—was the right kind. Mister, I'm going to sell you an expensive house, so help me God. "Yes, may I help you?"

"I'm interested in a house."

"What kind of a house?"

He looked blank. "I hadn't thought about it."

"Uh-huh. Well, that's all right, I guess." She was stalling. Men were seldom vague about what they wanted. And he didn't look like a kook. He looked like an ambassador. An ambassador to the great outdoors. Lovely tan. "Neighborhood?"

"I hadn't thought about that, either."

"Size?"

"Small."

"Now we've really narrowed it down." She smiled and hoped he would, too, but he didn't. His mind was elsewhere. He kept looking around. "Just for yourself, then?" There was no Mrs. Ambassador?

"Yes."

"Well, how about this: A small but elegant townhouse either on Massachusetts or N or M, in back of St. Matthew's Cathedral. Or perhaps up around California Street or New Hampshire? Are you familiar with those streets?"

"Vaguely. Is Mrs. Halaby here?"

"Oh? Has she already taken you around?"

"No."

"Someone recommended her?"

"No. I simply know that she works here and I thought I should ask for her." Something was going on, but she wasn't sure what. "I met her up in the country."

"Do you know that she lost her husband?"

"Yes, I do."

"And you wanted her to take you around? She won't be here again until next week." The right hemisphere of Larraine's brain was searching doggedly for a vital connection which had to be deciphered. This man didn't want a house. He would buy one if he had to, but he was here for other reasons. The news that Star was not available seemed to stump him. His eyes—staring out of that rugged face—were beseeching and that tugged at her motherly heart. Out of the blue, she blurted out, "Did you want to see her very badly?"

That got his attention. "Yes, I did."

Oh. So that's it. He's interested in Star. "Well, Mr. . . ."

"Larabee. Andrew Larabee."

"Mr. Larabee, perhaps I can help you. That is, of course, if your intentions meet with my approval."

She had bought a new dress for herself. Slim and black. "Every woman needs a little black dress," the ad had said. "Let this be the one." It was *sexy*. Sort of sexy. "Well, look at you," said Larraine. "Getting ideas again?"

"Of course not. It's just a dress."

She had bought the dress because McKay was having a "shindig," as he called it, and she was invited. A sit-down formal dinner for sixteen associates and clients. She knew what that meant. He wanted to woo investors or repay those who had generated business and commissions for Fred McKay.

The night of the party she stood in the library of McKay's impressive mansion and peered at each new arrival with some nervousness. One of them would be her partner. Maybe he wouldn't show up, which would be a relief. She'd be able to eat without worrying about keeping up her end of the conversation. But then she'd be the floating guest. Whom would she talk with? Maybe her partner was already there, although there weren't any men who appeared at loose ends. The doorbell rang again and she jumped. I wonder if he knows I have a child? It shouldn't matter; after all, it's just for the evening. Maybe I don't have to mention Cassie at all. It's not as if I'm likely to see him again. Oh, God, this is so awkward.

He had to tie his bow tie three times before he got it right. He hated formal dress, even though women told him repeatedly that, on him, a tuxedo was dynamite. He looked distinguished and very handsome. At the last minute, he had serious doubts about Mrs. Halaby's reaction to him and began to think of excuses for cancelling. The barn might burn down or one of his horses might become ill or he'd sprain his ankle. Maybe the White House would call and ask him to come right over. Or an eighteen-wheeler could jackknife across the road, blocking all traffic. He put on his jacket. How foolish he felt. His heart was skittering around his chest. He knew that if his heart were really to skitter around his chest, he'd be dead on the floor and it wouldn't matter if Star Halaby liked him or not.

Star went and stood by the first bookcase because it was tucked in a little bend in the room. Here, at eye level, were the B's. Balzac, Browning, Byron . . . Had Mckay actually read these authors? They were probably for show, but he'd be the first to admit it. She could take out a book as a prop and read it. That way she'd be doing something when McKay brought him over. *Oh!* Was this the one? He was tall and vaguely familiar.

She'd seen that face before. But where? It was a strong face . . . already tan so early in the year . . . a shy smile . . . how handsome men were in tuxedos.

The moment he saw her, his muscular legs—they had been gripping horses' flanks for thirty years—felt less sturdy. He wanted to bolt across the room and tell her how much she meant to him. She was wearing a dress instead of the dungarees she had worn to the track, but the face was exactly as he had remembered it. God, why did he feel so weak? He should have felt strong. Elated. She was smiling at him.

Perhaps he looked familiar because he reminded her—vaguely, of course —of her father. "Hello," she said. "I'm Star Halaby, your dinner partner."

Across the room Larraine felt her eyes fill. She had seen Star's face look so anxious and now relieved. Wasn't she due for something good? Maybe this was it . . .

The letter from her grandmother came a few days after she met Andrew Larrabee. It was a valiant effort written in a spidery hand, the H formed with such care but still so wobbly it broke her heart.

"Promise me something," it began without any salutation. "Don't believe that you have bad luck or that bad things happen to you. I've been around a long time and this is how life continues. I've had many blows— one still cuts and breaks me. My baby boy died a terrible death. He had the kind of illness that made him lose all his fluids. I couldn't comfort him or even touch him. His skin would have cracked and burst. Right now, when I think about his face, I feel like weeping. He was a little boy and he looked like an old man. I can't account for such cruelty from God, but there it is.

"We must take things hard that are hard but also go forward and not ask too many questions. Your mother's gone, but I'm still here. Why? Perhaps for you. Perhaps to help you not lose hope. I can't remember a sweeter girl than you. I'm left to tell you what a strong, good girl you were to your parents and how happy you made your mother. I want to say that I love you all the way from here. How strange. I have never in my life told anyone I loved them, so you see, miracles happen. One will come to you. Your *siti* now and for always."